T0365696

"STRAWMAN COMETH!"

"STRAWMAN COMETH!"

A TALE OF ETERNAL
TRUE LOVE, OF
WAR, AND DEADLY
CONFLICT AGAINST
AN UNHOLY TERROR!

BOOK 1

LT. COLONEL (R) JEFFERSON AZGARD DAVIS

ARCHWAY PUBLISHING

Archway Publishing books may be ordered through booksellers or by contacting:

Archway Publishing
1663 Liberty Drive
Bloomington, IN 47403
www.archwaypublishing.com
1 (888) 242-5904

ISBN: 978-1-4808-7788-7 (sc)
ISBN: 978-1-4808-7789-4 (e)

Library of Congress Control Number: 2019906883

Print information available on the last page.

Archway Publishing rev. date: 11/7/2019

CONTENTS

PROLOGUE

"Evil will be challenged, wounded, and destroyed in the eyes of those who complete such gruesome dangerous tasks; but evil in its incredible resilience never sleeps for long; or forever! Always sleeping with one eye open, it waits in the shadows for its next opportunity!"

Quote from Ravi; The Ancient Sage of Hima to Lieutenant Cavendish in 1897

(Books 1 & 2)

In Book 1, this strange tale of Strawman begins on the eve of battle between the small British garrison at Malakand in 1897 and by twists of fate ends near St. Louis Missouri in 1975. In 1897 British imperialist control in India was about to face a major setback on July 26 as well over fifty thousand Islamic indoctrinated Pashtun tribesmen attacked both the outposts of Malakand and Chakadara in northern India. Just over three-thousand British empire troops faced this tsunami of hill tribesmen bent on their complete destruction!

The story of British Lieutenant James Ambrose Cavendish begins here, on the eve of battle, leading his scouts on reconnaissance outside the outpost. Cavendish will survive this epic battle as British cold steel miraculously rules the day. During this siege Lieutenant Cavendish will meet the beautiful Jenny Farnsworth who will become his future wife. Before this comes to pass, the aftermath of this battle signals the beginning of strange adventure for him and his men as they are forced by illegal orders into a strange unknown realm of death and supernatural terror in an uncharted valley in the southern Himalayan mountains.

In a series of events, James will become companion with an ancient race from a place called simply "The Village," and fight a serious war against an ancient evil enemy called "Kali" and his legions of green devils. In this conflict Cavendish will also fall in love with a beautiful ageless woman from this race. He now has two loves in his heart; one human and one from an ancient race of shape changers. A strong bond is formed between the British and shape changers against the threat of Kali and his undead hordes. In the ensuing trials and tribulations of war against what can be described as a powerful fallen shape changer, life will drastically change for Lieutenant Cavendish and his family.

Due to future circumstances, James is forced from his military life, marries Jenny, and they move to Jamaica to help run the booming family rum business. Paradise is incredible, but will soon be destroyed by the terrible encounter with Ayiti Deschamps, a strange refugee from Haiti who is actually a powerful voodoo king; the unholy terror and forced to flee Haiti under death sentence. In Jamaica this Ayiti will soon be smitten by his beautiful sister-in-law Annabelle! Ayiti, also known as Strawman when he changes into the form of his familiar to wreak havoc and death.

The lust fueled overtures of this old dangerous creature to capture Annabelle will bring it face to face with James Cavendish and his companions for "Strawman Cometh!" The ensuing conflict exposes this monster to be of the same ilk as Kali, another fallen shape changer. This clash is costly, bloody, and demands the help from the ancients of the village! Yet Strawman can only be trapped and not destroyed. Something must be found and destroyed first! The lust of Strawman for revenge is epic and ageless!

The tale of Strawman continues in Book 2 as life for the Cavendish family resumes after the terrible conflict and incarceration of Strawman. It remains at White Hall in the basement! The years pass where James is involved in World War I sustaining near fatal wounds in the Battle of the Somme. As the players in the game age and [pass on, the evil legacy of Strawman fades into antiquity as time ages circumstance into myth.

However, Strawman's legacy is not forgotten by everyone! The great grandson of James Cavendish; one James Ambrose Sullivan, will become the next family member to be privy to the real family secrets including the curse of Strawman in 1975. Before his mother dies of cancer, she gives him a letter for his eyes only. Upon her death he reads it and is guided to an old faded red steamer trunk hidden in the attic wall of her house in Webster Groves where James and his sister Katie reside now.

It is here that he learns the details of his family's past including the fantastic account and terrible secret of some character named "Strawman." He finally shares all these secrets in the trunk with his beloved sister Katie. The stories of India, Kali, the village shape changers, and of Strawman, seemed too fantastic for them to believe! However, to their angst Strawman, not considered real by James and Katie, will escape due to the chaos created by the Socialist Manley government in Jamaica in 1975.

Finally, aware of the new reality it now finds itself in, this ancient monster, becomes bent on savage vengeance against the Cavendish seed against those who trapped him long ago! The seed of James Ambrose Cavendish is top priority! The epic battle between the combined forces arrayed against this vile evil will erupt when "Strawman Cometh" comes to St. Louis for vengeance! Will the long-hidden personal item; the "Achille's Heel" of Strawman be discovered? If so, will the curse of Strawman and his kind finally end by the banks of the Mississippi River? Will it ever end?

ACKNOWLEDGEMENTS

<u>AUTHOR:</u> **Jefferson "AZGARD" Davis** was born in St. Louis, Missouri and grew up in Webster Groves graduating from the high school in 1967. He then attended Southwest Missouri State College in Springfield, Missouri (MSU) where he earned his B.A. History in 1971 and M.A. in History in 1978. He was a member of Sigma Tau Gamma Fraternity where he earned the nickname "AZGARD!" He spent his next two years on active duty during the Vietnam war. He retired in 2008 as a lieutenant colonel in the Military Intelligence Corps. LTC Davis completed many Military colleges including the U.S. Army Command & General Staff College in 1988. He is a lifelong student of Chinese Kenpo Karate with Tracy's Kenpo Karate since 1974. His accomplishments and honors are many. He was a personal student (and friend) of **Great Grand Master Al Tracy** as well as permanent student of **Grand Master "Doc" Roger Greene** (considered as my brother). In 2015 he was promoted to Grand Master (Judan 10th Dan) in both Kenpo Karate and Kenpo Ju Jitsu. In 2017, he was promoted to the Grand Master rank of Kudan (9th Dan) by Grand Master Roger Greene in his "Roger Greene's Martial Arts Association." Davis still teaches seminars and is one of five Grandmasters chosen by GGM Al Tracy to sit as a permanent member of the Tracy's International Kenpo Karate Senior Advisory Council before his death in 2017. Davis was also chosen to sit on the executive board of the Roger Greene Association after Roger passed on in 2018. Kenpo Karate is his life! OSS! NOW HE WRITES!

    <u>ARTWORK:</u> Cover and spine of Strawman Cometh were created by **Tony Vertburgt**; A friend, free-lance artist and Kudan (9th Dan) in Tracy's Kenpo Karate from Springfield, Missouri.

    <u>MASTER EDITOR:</u> **Richard Davis Grater**; A lifelong friend and Nidan (2nd Dan) and my student in Tracy's Kenpo Karate.

    <u>SUPPORT ELEMENTS:</u> My constant support in writing this tale was by my beloved **lady (now wife) Sylvia Fraley,** who constantly encouraged me to continue with this tedious work rife with problems. Other great support came from Copper (Our wonder dog), and attack cats: Oscar the Gray Walker, Esmerelda Boo Boo, Clown Face, Orca, Love Sponge, Cheetah, and Fireball.

    <u>GENERAL DISCLAIMER:</u> Having written numerous published sensitive "all source" intelligence documents and DAPAM drafts as a senior intelligence officer for high level intelligence agencies in service; I well understand plagiarism and copyright laws. I have the greatest respect for other writers, their works, and mine! In <u>**Strawman Cometh**</u>, I derived all of general historical information/details from public histories surrounding real historical events. This includes a host of public sources. The characters, their views and opinions expressed by my characters interacting in these events are from my mindset. The basis for this story came from the notes I took each morning after a bizarre series of dreams I had for six nights straight in 1979.

BOOK
ONE

CHAPTER ONE
THE BATTLE OF MALAKAND

It was July 26, 1897 and the popular semi-annual polo matches between the garrisons of Chakadara and Malakand in northern India were to be a great event this day. These matches were to be held outside of the Malakand fort outpost in the open field at the rustic dusty town of Kar to be a crowded and exciting today. The dry heat would reach over one-hundred degrees today in the shade. Back in his office in Malakand, British Major Harold Deane studied his latest intelligence report dated July 23, 1897 from Major Tiberius Nephew. Deane's real power came not from his military rank but as the powerful political officer assigned in charge of the Malakand District in northern India, which included the very disputed Khyber Pass region.

All these reports from Nephew belated the continuous massive buildup of Islamic led Pashtun tribesmen in this Malakand region of north India. Their winding columns were also moving towards his northern outpost of Chakadara. Afghan troops and Russian advisors had also been observed in this mix slipping in from the Khyber Pass. His scouts from the outpost had seen nothing like what the major had described! It was a fact that the scouts working for Major Nephew were out in the bush deep unlike his patrols. What disturbed him besides this information he viewed was the author of it.

Major Tiberius Nephew was considered as a top of the line Intelligence officer whose accuracy in his assessments were spot on! He indicated that over fifty-thousand could already be on hand for attacks on both the British outpost forts of Malakand and Chakadara! There were further indications that the total strength of this native army could be as high as two-hundred thousand! If all this was true, then the British were in for a whole series of disastrous problems. But words were words to Deane for now, and there was little else on the table. The popular semi-annual polo matches between the garrisons of these two forts would begin on time today! He would not bend this schedule to fit the concerns and fears of Tiberius Nephew regarding such a fantastic number of savages about! Deane fired up a cigarette and took a sip of warm whiskey as he leaned back in his office chair.

He had met Major Nephew once and knew his reputation as a respected professional soldier preceded him. Nephew was a handsome soldier and known as a very rough individual. Because of his expertise he had been assigned to the command of General Bindon Blood who was the supreme commander of all military operations in northern India. Nephew was considered his favorite in the inner circles of gossip. The major was viewed as a rogue man of mystery who kept to himself and small inner circle of comrades. However, Nephew was seen as a boy who seemed to "cry wolf" often lately as it related to this developing concern regarding the savages.

Deane was a rather large person with round head set with a stuffy tomato face set on top of his white summer suit. He fingered the report carefully as he puffed on his next cigarette. He thought about the polo game and his wagers. Then he also thought about the large gathering of British expatriates assembling for the games and festive party afterword. He mused at the images of the flamboyant English ladies dressed in their colorful summer dresses who seemed, like the early flowers of spring, to be blooming everywhere. These ladies along with many other expatiates had ventured to

Malakand from Calcutta for this event. His favorite bubbly lady was here, one Lady Vespa Mayfield! He smiled as he had planned to get her alone tonight in this office and bang her! Yes, bend her over his couch, pull up her dress, grab her huge boobs and mount and ride her just like the last time she visited. She loved his crudeness.

Deane finished his whiskey and refilled his glass as he fired up a new cigarette. He then considered doubling the guard to offset any possible attack but then decided not to as to not alarm the crowd or create concern amongst his troops. This was one event Deane loved because it reminded him of home in Britain, when he was young and played polo. He downed his whiskey and poured another. It was to be a day hotter than usual with over one-hundred degrees in the shade! He surmised that the Malakand Fort area would be a scene of sport and fun today, and not shut down for fear of an invasion from a bunch of frantic prehistoric hill people. The game would begin on time in the hot sun on a dry barren field in Khar.

However, in the world of those sworn to destroy British rule in India was quite different from the cavalier perceptions of Major Deane. The "Mad Fakir" as he was known to the British, was seen as a divine messenger to thousands of superstitious tribesmen. Unbeknownst to the arrogant complacent British authorities who ruled India, this alleged madman had stirred a huge hornet's nest of a violent Islamic jihad to exterminate the occupying infidels! He had drawn in a massive array of hill tribes, plus more on the fringes. This mad leader had told his followers that if the British garrisons were destroyed, then the British would be finished in India. Islamic rule would soon replace the evils of British imperialism!

His hateful venom had infected thousands of hill tribesmen. Throughout the previous six nights the very well led hill tribesmen had been slowly moving into the adjacent valleys and vales adjacent to the British outpost of Malakand as well as the northern small fort of Chakadara. The tribal Lashkar (army) had been very quiet, as they had been moving in small groups beginning after dusk camouflaged in extremely hilly inhospitable terrain. The Ghazis (Muslim religious warriors) kept tight control over the hoard they were moving and assembling. If any tribesmen got out of line or made continued noise, a sharp knife to the neck would end both life and the noise.

The plan of the attack was set to begin together at night on July 26th. The outposts of Malakand, and the smaller hilltop fort of Chakadara in the north would swallow up the small British defenses in short order! The attack on Chital, an established city and British outpost to the north would be attacked using a fringe group under a strange Islamic professed group led by a chief named Kali. British rule of India would cease to exist in a few days. The Pashtun scouts ringing the large outpost had reported that the activities at fort were normal and even the polo games were being held. The bazaar in the large south camp in the crater crowded as usual with merchants and shoppers.

The small group of British scouts of the 11th Bengal Lancers rested in the morning shade on the Old Buddhist road. They had been working the region for many nights. British Lieutenant James Ambrose Cavendish's patrol had been observing the massive movement of thousands of Pashtuns entering this area. He was stunned at the size of the enemy. They had alluded any contact with the enemy as they wore native garb over their khaki uniforms moving with extreme stealth. Cavendish ran a small outfit of experienced scouts and he was proud to be a member of it. His reports had already been passed directly to Major Nephew.

Cavendish puffed on a cupped cigarette as he surveyed the area. He was a rather tall man with a lanky robust medium build. He had a handsome face partially obscured by a huge moustache, popular in 1897. He was tough and confident, who excelled in boxing, Greco-Roman Wrestling, and saber fighting. He bore a great sense of dry humor, which often lit up his steel blue eyes. Cavendish had been involved in several successful forays, but never a major battle which he had little doubt was coming soon. Cavendish was just finishing his second year of duty in India.

His small party of British scouts and guides sat at dawn, on a morning tea break on the high crest of a huge hill that overlooked the Old Buddhist Road some four miles from the huge crater that made up the south camp of Malakand. The color of their khaki uniforms made them a good blend with the red and sand hues in the hilltop, strewn with huge boulders. They were very interested in the layout of the Old Buddhist road, which offered the second route directly into the vulnerable south camp of Malakand.

The geography on this route offered a great opportunity for some type of ambush. The left side of this road was christened with huge cliffs and boulder laden tall hills. The other side of this road was a steep drop into a huge deep chasm. In the last two nights, the scouts had observed many large groups moving from the very rough hill terrain towards what seemed to be three huge staging areas within only four to five miles around the huge outpost. These areas had been already earmarked by super scout "Mister Griggs" in his earlier observations.

"Old Hooky" as he was named, was the senior noncom in the party and a veteran of the famous Battle of Rorke's Drift. He never really talked at length about it and was prone to quiet reflective moods, quite out sorts with his jovial happy character. Hook wore the Victorian Cross on his tunic proudly as a survivor and hero of the famous battle at the British outpost and staging area against the Zulus under a hot African sun in 1879. Only one-hundred plus British troops pared off against an estimated five-thousand Zulus drunken with victory and bloodlust after their slaughter of the British 24th Field Division at Isandlwana. Color Sergeant Hook wore his VC as a protective good luck charm.

Hooky reflected on this upcoming battle of Malakand as another battle in the drift! The British survived the terrible violent onslaught under the incredible leadership of Lieutenant Chard who was the assigned engineer officer just given command of this small trading post and supply dump. What Hook had endured at the Battle Rorke's Drift some years ago, had left obvious deep emotional scars in him. He had once said that part of his soul was left on that battlefield with his dead comrades, torn away in the terror, violence, and constant death of the seemingly timeless titanic struggle.

The very powerfully built sergeant always kept two loaded revolvers on him, a "Gurkha" knife, a shortened double-barreled shotgun, and his extremely hard Ironwood Zulu Spear. The hard wood Zulu Spear he took off a Zulu chief he had slain in combat was his talisman. Sergeant Hook told the Lieutenant that this spear was all he had left to defend himself towards the end of the battle as he was locked in close hand-to-hand combat. It was his last remaining weapon taken from the body of a Zulu war chief he had killed with his bayonet which remained lodged in his ribs. "Such is life" he would say over and over. He also said in his emptiness…." Never stop fighting ever! Harness your terror and fear and use it as a weapon…. or terrible death awaits you lad!"

Hook had also long despised worthless officers after the massacre at Isandlwana. They seemed to make terrible mistakes in their complete underestimation of the Zulus and many a good soldier died! "Cavendish, like his commander Lieutenant Chard at "the Drift," were good officers. Both were very practical men who supported their men by word and example. Cavendish was an honor graduate of Sand Hurst Military Academy. He had fondness for Napoleon and the American Civil War. He lived by the strategy of "see, deceive, and violently attack" (or get the hell out)! Because of this mindset and his commanding from the front, none of his scouts had been killed in their response to several ambushes they had fallen into in their scouting.

Cavendish loved the civil War because of his Uncle Jake and Aunt Miriam, distant relatives from St. Louis, Missouri. His aunt was a direct descendant of the famous General "Stonewall" Jackson.

Jake and Ambrose had become close friends since they met in New York in 1889 when he was sixteen years old. Uncle Jake was a college professor in history at the new Washington University college in St. Louis. He had a fondness for the American civil War. Ambrose became an aficionado of this period and relished General "Stonewall "Jackson and others. He also liked the exploits of Union General Tecumseh Sherman, who Jake referred to as the best Roman general in the Union Army. This is where he learned the effectiveness of Sherman's use of the "scorched earth" policy later employed by the British against the Pashtuns called "Butcher and Bolt!"

They stayed in close touch over the years and wrote back and forth on a variety of subjects on a regular basis. His most treasured item was the six shooter Colt .45 "wild west" revolver Uncle "J" had given him when he graduated from Sand Hurst. He always kept it in a shoulder holster and carried two-hundred rounds in his kit. At the insistence of Color Sergeant Hook, he also had his British service revolver on his side along with his Gurkha knife at the middle of his left hip attached to his belt.

Hook showed him how it could be pulled quickly and deliver a nice clean slash across the front in any situation. Hell, it seemed he was turning into his mentor "Hooky." He then smiled as he had all his scouts keep three extra pistols attached to their saddles that proved effective when they were ambushed. This practice came not from Hook, or his studies at Sand Hurst, but from Confederate General Nathan Forest and his boys who always carried several pistols tied to the saddles on their mounts for the same reason. The armorers at the 11th Bengal Lancers wondered where all their revolvers had gone.

Besides the six British, there were four Gurkhas, and two Indian guides in the scout group. The Gurkhas were men small in statures that were excellent tough soldiers in all ways who were usually distinguished by their blue pillbox headgear. Sergeant Hook had fondly called them "his kids" and nicknamed them long ago as Lord Nelson, Cornwallis, Gladstone and King George. In the scouting party were three Lancers named Wentworth, Holmes, and Harper. They all had been in country for just over a year. Holmes, a corporal, had the acumen of a sniper who was excellent at long ranges as a former member of the British Army shooting team.

Griggs was the other companion to the party, who they waited to return from up north. His name was Horatio Griggs. According to the lore, had been busted from the officer corps on a set of bogus charges a few years before down to this enlisted rank. His calm gray eyes behind a full beard, and tall build gave off the impression that he was more of a preacher than a professional killer and guide. He was always referred to as "Mister." His constantly rumpled khaki uniform was usually covered in a local long outfit common to native dress and he preferred a pith helmet when he was not sneaking about. He was a veteran member of the elite "Guides" which could literally find anything or lead troops most expediently to requested locations.

Griggs was an expert in his field, spoke the language fluently, and had been in India for several years. He, like Corporal Holmes, was a dead shot with both rifle and pistol. Griggs seemed well connected from the top and was an excellent working asset to his boss and friend major Nephew. He had been gladly assigned to work with Cavendish and his old buddy Hook over three months ago. He had dragged Holmes along with him since he saw great possibilities in his uncanny abilities.

Mister Griggs, was the one who had figured out the Pashtun staging areas before they had actually begun to form in this vicinity around Malakand and to help focus the scouts on the dispositions of this growing enemy. He had ventured the day before to the outskirts of Chakadara, that night to see what the tribesmen were up to in that region. He had taken one of the Gurkhas in the scouting party nicknamed "King George" and one of the Indian guides named Rashid with him on the thirty-seven-mile trek to this small fort which overlooked the Swat river with an excellent view of the surrounding mountains. It was a small fort on the top of a mountain that held a garrison of two-hundred men.

A junior officer named Lieutenant Rattery who was to play in the polo matches commanded it. They had found several of the same empty areas that were guarded by what appeared to be Muslim ghazis. This was exactly like what he saw around Malakand. Then they witnessed hundreds of Pashtuns quietly filter from the hills into this empty area. The long lines of them never seemed to stop as Griggs and company pulled away from the area. They had sent a warning message regarding this buildup to the command at Chakadara before they departed.

Cavendish raised his hand and signaled a meeting. Griggs and company were probably on their way back from their reconnaissance duties north, but action was needed now. It seemed a consensus that something was going to happen soon. Malakand was the obvious target…but when? The unanimous consensus was that most of the Pashtuns were in the staging areas now so the attack was eminent soon! This meant tonight! Alfred Hook spoke as if he were betting at the horse races.

"Warning the outpost directly is immediately obvious now, since we have seen enough and all confirm this. Our first action is to warn the command and face to face sir!" Then Hook smiled as he battled several flies away from his face. "The second step we can take is start some shit with these savages on this road entry route! Say, like rearranging a few boulders across this road with a big bang and really drawing their wrath?" Ambrose Cavendish smiled at this thought. "Hooky old top, now that's a capital idea!

I was just thinking the same thing. This would be a warning to the garrison rather than a diversion! Let's kick over the rain barrel and see what drains out of it!" The color sergeant said "We have four Gurkha demolition experts and they have a usual supply of explosives with them as usual" Gladstone smiled at Hook and added. "Yes sir, we can make a big boom and send many boulders down and across the Old Buddhist Road. We can easily set our charges after dark!" This plan made sense to all the weary scouts.

Gentlemen," began the lieutenant, "I am going straight to the polo matches at Khar and warn them of our findings. Tell Griggs to join me as soon as he returns." Hook took a sip of water and chased it with a shot of whiskey as all eyes turned to him. He smiled so wide his long moustache rose up and passed the bottle around to the drinkers. "Go warn our fearless leaders sir, and me and my kids will prepare to blow the hell out of something!" The group laughed together with the Hook comment. Cavendish then took a sip of the whiskey with water and smiled.

"I'll drink to that sir!" exclaimed Hooky. Cavendish, with the two Brits, and Pulbah left to report directly to the commanders present at the polo matches. The Gurkhas down the Old Buddhist Road choosing places for their explosive charges. The left side of this rugged path had large hills and cliffs. The other side of the road dropped off into a series of deep rough ravines, like deep gouges in the earth. Sergeant Hook covered their exploration as the "kids" returned and began to assemble some powerful explosives.

Less than an hour after Cavendish left Griggs and company returned from the north. The two NCOs sat across from each other as Griggs made his report. They looked at each other as mortal equals. Cigars and bottle of whiskey was passed as he began. "Hooky, the shit is going to hit the fan probably tonight at Chakadara! The boys and me observed massive movement of Pashtuns and their Ghazi masters into holding areas surrounding Chakadara all night. There are thousands of them! We had to pull out of the area there were so many! The situation here is the same but even larger!

The commanders cannot ignore this one or we all die maybe tonight!" as Hooky gave a long serious stare with a usual half smile.

He then instructed Mister Griggs to take his fresh horse and go to Khar where Cavendish was expecting him. King George joined his fellow Gurkhas work on the explosives the rest conducted security from over watch positions on the Old Buddhist Road. Griggs and Holmes ventured across some steep hills and rugged ground for a few miles and were soon on a rise in the company of Lieutenant Cavendish and the others with him sitting in the shadows of some huge rocks and scrub trees taking a break before descending down to the festive crowds around the polo matches in the old ball field at Khar village.

The bright sun made them all sweat profusely in conjunction with the heat emanating from the ground and rocks around them. The constant attacks from waves of flies was non-stop. Cavendish had just arrived within the hour to rest the horses from the heat before they ventured down to the field. The polo game was still in progress as the players endured an extremely hot cloudless day in the barren landscape of the playing field. The lieutenant gave a smile and handshake to both Griggs and Holmes as the others watched the game in progress. He took off his olive-green side cap and wiped his face and head of sweat.

"About time you returned, and how was the trip?" Horatio Griggs wiped his face off, saluted, and sat with his leader. Cavendish already did not like the mood resonating from Griggs's face and eyes as he began. "Sir, in layman's terms we are all in deep dangerous shit!" In the next few minutes, accented with Holmes's comments, he gave a complete report on the situation at Chakadara. The scout leader took it all in with grave concern as he commented. "Yes Griggs, we know the same situation around Malakand."

Griggs spoke. "There is obviously no way these natives are going to sit around in the heat another day. I think they will attack tonight for certain! Rashid told me he had never seen the likes of so many Pashtuns moving about ever." Griggs looked hard at his friends. "The hell storm will unleash tonight at the latest and we need to not just inform the commanders but must convince them now and spoil all their fun!" The group then mounted their horses and cantered down a long barren and dry sun beaten slope into Khar.

It seemed from the approaching scouts, that a piece of Britain had been transplanted into the midst of this rough and tumble arid landscape at the small dusky Khar village, constructed of stones and mud bricks. The crowds around the polo field seemed alien to the landscape as they were a merry crowd of soldiers, ladies, and children protected from the sun's rays by several large white canopies that lined the east side of the field. The South Camp, from their earlier observations, a short distance from Khar was bustling with activity as usual with many people moving on the main south road.

The Bazaar was thriving at this time, crowded with hundreds of merchants, and visitors. An air of merriment accented by the polo games was aloof. The aura of the polo matches had spread throughout both camps. The teams of players from the two outposts were dressed in their polo uniforms and in the middle of the third game when the scouts arrived next to the playing field. So far, each team had won one, so this was the match game. It seemed that a decent number of expatriates were in attendance to watch the game in their Sunday best.

Cavendish and his group had dismounted, tended their horses to water, and were casually walking through the crowd headed for the tents where the commanders and staff were enjoying the event. They all could smell what seemed to be an excellent bill of fare mixed with the gay chatter of the spectators. The aroma of it incited his hunger. Several members of the 11th Bengal Lancers who had played in the first polo game greeted him since they had not seen him for a while. He was distracted in their company for some minutes over a large glass of cooled flavorful gin and lemonade. Griggs and the others went for some food.

They soon headed to the crowded command tents, which was actually a huge tarpaulin canopy. The lancers had directed Cavendish and Griggs in the direction where Major Deane and Colonel Meiklejohn, the commanding officer at Malakand were last seen. They first approached Deane who looked paunchy and drunk, dressed in a white summer suite rather than a khaki uniform. It seemed that Major Deane was the center of this carnival in the wilderness, surrounded by many people. The games had begun at two and had continued with regular heat breaks throughout the afternoon.

Major Deane was surrounded by all manner of onlookers, which included a couple of visiting English ladies in their European summer finest. A jovial spirit prevailed for all present. Cavendish was welcomed and handed another cool drink of gin as he tried to edge near the chief political officer. James Ambrose was, for brief moments captivated and caught up in a conversation with a rather beautiful dark-haired lady with the deepest blue eyes who bumped into him. She was very pretty and my so friendly as she eyed the rather handsome Lieutenant who appeared greatly disheveled in a rather rumpled khaki uniform. She smiled and looked at his uniform. "Do you dress formally like this all the time lieutenant?"

"Always this sharp my lady! I thought the Queen was going to be here today! He snapped as the gin tickled his throat." James smiled broadly at this extremely beautiful lady with the captivating blue eyes and smile. "My lady, my name is "Keeper of the Old Buddhist Road!" She smiled deeply, "My name is "Keeper of the Khyber Pass!" He smiled at her humor. "I have heard of you somewhere!" She smiled as the shallow flirting continued until Cavendish realized why he was here, to report to Deane, and to Colonel Meiklejohn. But she was such a diamond in the rough here he thought. It seemed another ten minutes before he could gain an audience with Major Deane as this pretty lady stayed next to him.

Deane needed to be informed of the critical threat surrounding Malakand so he could end this game and get back into the safety of the outpost. If they attacked now? Colonel Meiklejohn was the ace in the hole to get the garrison battle ready to prepare Malakand for war! Where was he? He had to be found fast! Cavendish was all smiles as he mildly bandied his flirtatious comments with the beautiful lady who stood beside him as he moved up to Mr. Deane. The flirtation between his lieutenant and the beautiful woman made Griggs smile. Seeing an opening in Deane's area, he moved up to him. "Major Deane" He began, "I am Lieutenant Cavendish in charge of the scouts who have been out scouring the region outside Malakand and Chakadara.

I am here to personally inform you of the impending dangerous situation that is currently developing around both the outposts as I speak sir!" Deane, who had had one or two drinks too many in the heat replied, "Why mess up such a good party Cavendish? I hear this nonsense all the time and cannot this wait? I am sure no little brown savages will attack us until Christmas!" He laughed at his own joke. "But Sir!" exclaimed the frustrated junior officer, "This outpost may be attacked very soon, as well as Chakadara tonight! There are thousands of Pashtuns, led by the Ghazis assembling in huge numbers and surrounding us to be preparing to ….!" Deane cut him short by raising his hand.

"Not to worry" shot back an inebriated Deane, slurring his speech, as he bodily nuzzled up to a rather plump woman that joined him, whose bosoms popped out of the top of her dress like watermelons. Deane continued. "Can't you see I am protected by the ferocious Lady Vespa Mayfield?" The lieutenant had to laugh. "Yes Sir! That is a huge relief to me…but we have been watching the movement of a huge army of…." The political officer cut in again. "Why in hell have none of my patrols discovered these huge staging areas you speak about Lieutenant?" James Ambrose Cavendish was upset and found it hard to control his next words.

"I am in charge of a group of professional scouts assigned under Major Nephew tasked to conduct deep area reconnaissance far beyond area sir if you are unaware of this! We have been combing the hills for days watching thousands of Pashtuns and their Ghazi handlers move quietly through the rough hilly terrain forming into massive attacking forces in several staging areas some miles from your walls and scouts. I know your patrols are lucky to go more than two miles out since I have observed them.

Three nights ago, Sergeant Griggs and one of my Indian scouts walked around in one of these camps down the Old Buddhist road some five miles from the east gate! They estimated a couple of thousand savages there with more coming in all the time! He saw the same thing going on the outskirts of Chakadara just last night! Malakand is being completely surrounded by thousands now sir!" Deane listened and in a more relaxed happy state of being and repeated his former loose order. "we can deal with these two-thousand savages' son."

Cavendish gave a candid fixed smile as if he was betting in a poker game. "Sir, can we deal with between twenty and maybe over fifty-thousands of these savages?" Deane went crispy. "Enough!" Toned up drunken Deane slugging down a whole glass of gin and hugging rotund large breasted Lady Mayfield whose giant breasts where moving as if twin volcanos about to explode beneath her low-cut dress. One huge nipple popped out and she laughed. Horatio Griggs, decked in a pith helmet now and his disheveled khaki uniform interjected a quick comment as he stared down the giant rosy red nipple of Lady Mayfield.

"Mr. Deane, if we do not prepare for the enemy now and inform the higher commands we will be overrun and slaughtered to a man tonight!" Deane thoughtfully replied finally as he nuzzled the fair plump Lady Mayfield who was coddling him now and trying to shove her nipple back into her dress. "Go see Colonel Meiklejohn, and LTC McRae, who is the officer in charge tonight and in charge of the defenses here." Toned up Sir Deane, guardian of North India and Lady Mayfield's monster bosoms. Before he continued the nameless pretty lady next to Cavendish pointed over to an adjacent large white canopy in the next area secured on poles making it another nice shelter from the sun.

"You will find him standing there my great scout!" He smiled at her as she followed them as they moved into the next tent. The two scouts found an excited happy crowd in this area like structure as they entered. Chakadara had just scored! Cavendish approached Colonel Meiklejohn who was standing next to LTC McRae sipping on some cool gins observing the game. The lieutenant stood in front of them and saluted. McRae returned it. Cavendish began his report after explaining who they were scouting under. Cool glasses of gin and juice were offered and accepted. Griggs again smiled as the petite pretty lady followed behind his lieutenant silently as if a puppy that found its owner.

Cavendish cut directly to the chase on his observations. "We firmly believe that this outpost as well as Chakadara will be attacked after dark tonight by an exceedingly huge force of thousands of tribesmen!" Over the next few minutes both scouts detailed their information as the two colonels listened quietly exchanging serious facial looks. The colonel spoke. "Why in hell have I not been informed of this McRae?" The light colonel looked at his boss. "I have heard the rumors like you sir, but never any hard intelligence on this either!"

Then McRae said. "Deane has control of all the message traffic sir!" Both of the commanders gravely looked at each other as they now knew the answer to their question! Major Deane had withheld this vital information as Nephew's intelligence reports would reveal! As if on cue in some play scene, a messenger rode up from Malakand with a telegraph message from 2LT Wheatly to 1LT Rattery from

Chakadara, who was playing in the game. Colonel William Meiklejohn opened and read it. He then looked at McRae. "This message from the Wheatly, second in command at Chakadara is informing Rattery that thousands of armed Pashtuns have been observed moving into his area now." Meiklejohn looked at Cavendish, then at McRae.

"Colonel, get back to the outpost immediately, but not at a gallop to tip off the savages, and muster the 45th Sikhs to their positions at the east gate, and the 31st Punjab's to the main gate area. For that matter, alert everybody now. Looks like we will be very busy soon." Finishing a healthy glass of gin, the colonel then ordered the game to stop and informed 1st Lieutenant Rattery of the impending threat to his command up north after he dismounted at the tent.

In short order, the whole contingent that had come to the polo matches from Chakadara was assembled on fresh horses and was soon moving north on the paved road leading back to Chakadara with many in their polo uniforms. They would arrive at dusk, two hours before the massive Pashtun attack began. The Colonel then issued the order for the whole assembly of polo spectators to return back to Malakand in an ordered haste and not a route. If they were attacked before they could return to the safety of Malakand, it would be a massacre.

LTC McRae instructed Cavendish to report to him as soon as he could check the status of his scouts in the Old Buddhist Road. He gave his location in an old stone tower complex amongst ancient red brick ramparts to find him in the north fort on the hill above what he referred to as the "Crater south camp." McRae had to observe the muster and deployment of his 45th Sikhs pronto and rode off with three of his lieutenants at a fair trot

The third and final polo game had been stopped and the final score gave Chakadara the win. All Deane's wagers had come to nil and his pockets would be empty of many shillings and Florins he expected to win this day. He waved to Cavendish for reasons unknown, and abruptly turned with his bosomed rotund lady and headed to his buggy. Cavendish and Griggs mused cynically as the drunken Lady Mayfield groped Deane's wide ass with a deep slap and grab.

Cavendish paused and eyed his pocket watch... It was nearly half past four now. He had seemed to have lost track of the beautiful lady that stood by his side now, but as luck or fate would have it, he had another brief interlude with the pretty spunky brunette who had been standing behind him while he had talked to Deane and the colonels. She was so beautiful, and her radiant enthralling smile mesmerized him again. He kissed her hand and apologized to her for not being able to spend time with her "the keeper of the Khyber Pass!" "I promise that I will find you at the Malakand fort when my business is done in the field!"

She smiled, as her deep blue eyes seemed to penetrate his very soul. "What is your business Lieutenant and I demand it now?" She smiled and put her arm in his and looked at him ruefully now face to face. "Oh, we warned the command about the eminent attack on this post tonight by thousands of screaming tribesmen and then I am going to go into the bush and with my boys, blow up a bunch of them and warn the post of the impending attack. That is all my dear." He smiled broadly at her. "Just in a day's work! But I have warned you oh beautiful guardian and keeper of the Khyber Pass! Forewarned is fair warned in my book!"

He smiled at her and temptation forced him to kiss her on her forehead. She played sad face. "Lieutenant? You missed my lips and kissed my head." She was pouting from pursed lips now. James kissed her on her lips and she then smiled. He added, "I will definitely find you so don't stray too far! Be safe!" I must go now. We have surprise plans for our unwanted guests this fine night!" "I promise I won't stray far!" She retorted with a new wide beautiful smile. He climbed on his mount and gave her a departing wink and rode off. There was something special about this lass he thought?

As the scouts rode back to their spot in the Old Buddhist road, Cavendish suddenly remembered that he had forgotten to get her name. As the horsemen wound through the terrain, they again observed several hundred Pashtuns quietly moving in their direction who offered no resistance to them. Mister Griggs bellowed out loud over his shoulder as he slowed his horse to a trot. "Looks like they seem to be waiting for the signal to land we, the bigger fish Sir!"

Lieutenant Cavendish's thoughts of the pretty lady now flashed back to an impending dark cloud of doom moving towards Malakand. Within the next hour, they were back in the little secluded over watch position with the rest of the group. The horses were fed and watered from an obscured shaded area near a formation of boulders. Cavendish listened as King George reported to Hook. He smiled at Sergeant Hook in the fading hot light of the waning day as the tentacles of early night shadows wound into the hills in mass. "Everything is ready Hooky!" snapped the King, who smiled and crossed his arms like a superman under his pill box style hat that adorned his khaki uniform like all his fellow Nepalese in the British army.

Hook musingly sneered at King George's power stance as he turned to Rashid who had been observing the Pashtun horde way down the road. "What do you think Rashid?" "They are forming now and will begin moving soon after dark!" He added, "This is an endless stream of thousands of Pashtuns moving in formations up towards both roads to the main intersection two miles down this road now." The Indian scout looked scared.

Hook whispered out loud. "Where in the infernal regions of Hades did all these savages come from? Is all of northern India rising up against us tonight? This heat and devilish armies of flies also makes these regions infernal, like Hades itself!" Lt. Cavendish spoke to the assembled group. "I must get back to see LTC McRae as soon as possible regarding the details of our explosive warning of their attack. Griggs and Rashid will join me. I know the commander wants to hear as much information as we have amongst us." Then he looked at Color Sergeant Hook.

"Your evening plans?" SGT Hook gave a gruff cough and stood up. My kids have planted four large explosive charges at the juncture of those two roads yonder and three more up the road with the last one about fifty yards for where we are now. We cut timed fuses to be lit when the Pashtun hordes begins to march. When the charges explode, the whole first wave of several thousand will be caught! Once this is done, we will hightail it to the east gate. When the post hears these explosions, the savages are moving in for the attack!" Cavendish nodded as he added that he would be at the east gate to welcome them so nobody would get shot. Hooky was grateful.

Cavendish and his group were soon off at a medium trot towards the east gate of the south camp at Malakand as the sun faded. They knew they were being observed by Pashtuns along the way back. The south camp of Malakand and huge bazaar were located in a huge crater formation. The south camp was a tent city for most of the Punjab's and Sikhs in the British army. The east and main south gates would be the obvious focus of the mass attacks used to invade and destroy the Malakand garrison. But then the warriors could literally attack from any point around the crater! The merry throng of visitors at the polo matches were dispersed throughout both areas of the south camp and the north fort now.

Cavendish ordered Holmes to wait at the east gate for the return of Hook and the Gurkhas sometime after the planned explosions. It was after seven in the evening and the night darkness continued to wind like giant snakes across Malakand. Members of the 11th Lancers, 45th Sikhs, 31st and 24th Punjab Infantry Regiments that were assigned to garrison duty at Malakand Outpost and were being moved into defensive positions at the gates and other choke points. The 45th Sikhs were already in their forward fighting positions facing the vulnerable east gate.

However, the 31ˢᵗ and 24ᵗʰ Punjab's tasked to defend the main south gate, bazaar, and camp area were disorganized and moving very slowly towards their defensive positions. Besides the bulk of regiments of Punjab's and Sikhs garrisoning the south camp, a force of two-hundred lancers, and one reserve company of the 45ᵗʰ Sikhs, were stationed in the north fort built on top of a huge steep boulder infested hill. It was an imposing structure; medieval in all respects, built of stone and wood with towers, ramparts, and houses.

The defense at this site included one light field artillery regiment, that if needed could fire down at all points around the south camp and in it if the need arose. Two of these batteries were being sent to the east gate defenses to support the Sikhs. The soldiers stationed at Malakand were very experienced and well-trained troops led by expert veteran British officers who had fought in many forays and battles against the Pashtun uprisings of 1895.

The north fort was situated on very high ground and was the best defense of the area controlling activities in the south camp from its heights. The south camp would be hard to defend without the artillery support from above. He told his other two lancers Harper and Wentworth, to stand fast at the north fort gate after drinking a refreshing cool bottle of ale with them. His throat was parched and lined with the huge groundswell of eternal dust. Then there were flies, nearly as many as the enemy they faced tonight. He wondered if he would survive this when the sun came up?

Lieutenant James Cavendish was sitting privately in a rather ramshackle dusty small office with LT. Colonel McRae, Griggs, and Rashid. The lieutenant colonel who sat before them was a medium built powerful soldier with a salty look of experience outlined in his stern creased face. He bore a serious composure under a mane of long brownish hair and huge moustache. Before he began, he offered his guests cigars and cognac. Rashid declined citing religion. He had learned to love good Cuban Cigars from his time in the British colony of Belize, and relished one on the Lieutenant and Sergeant Griggs. He had saved the French cognac for a special occasion as impending doom was a good enough excuse to crack the bottle today. It was a wonderful gesture.

There was silence as each man lit their cigars and sipped a good pull from the cognac, served not in crystal snifters, but in army issue tin drinking cups. Colonel McRae was a consummate gentleman and allowed Cavendish to relax and take a pull on his cigar before speaking. "Welcome to my utopia Lieutenant Cavendish?' the Colonel began with a cynic smile. "Why thank you sir, I simply love the carnival life of Malakand!" McRae laughed and then added… "And besides all the culture??" Cavendish took a gulp of the cognac and mused. "Of course, Sir! AHHHH this culture! Actually, my fellows and me have been enjoying the local culture all along this area of northern India for the past month. So, enthralling to say the least!

… and sir, you would not even imagine the interesting culture moving towards this outpost on all sides now! We are based south of here, attached to the Guides Cavalry from the 11ᵗʰ Bengal Lancers for a couple of months. My group of scouts was tasked to gather intelligence on the movement of the hill tribesmen and the Ghazis. We were doing intelligence gathering for General Blood via Major Nephew who had sent regular reports to this outpost. McRae gave an angry look. "Fucking Deane sat on all of them and we may all die because of his crap!"

This is why we have been invisible here and north around the Chakadara fort sir. We have not bothered with Chital since they seem secure form this current situation so far. Our reports went to Blood's command via our boss Major Nephew and not directly to you. The discovery of Pashtun tribesmen creeping into these areas has been our concern for nearly a month! This concern was reflected in Nephew's message traffic to Deane. Seems like we all knew this except you and the command up the road!" Cavendish was quiet now in disgust at Deane. "Fucking Deane!' shouted McRae. "The size of these armed groups is shocking. We will do what we can to stop them!"

Griggs broke the silence. "Many of these Pashtuns were leaving home before planting season ended. Their indoctrination to radical Islam with hate for all things British by the Mad fakir and his boys was the unifying element so it seems! It has born a bevy of fruit as I believe they are coming for our heads tonight!" LTC McRae sipped his cordial then added. "Major Tiberius Nephew, the master intelligence officer who is so accurate in putting the pieces together! He is one hell of a saber fighter if I remember!"

Cavendish adjusted himself in the leather chair and took a good plug on the cognac. It mellowed him. McRae let Cavendish, Griggs, and finally Rashid finish their verbal observations. Malakand and Chakadara were now in the dangerous crosshairs of the Mad Fakir. These revelations bore ominous news. McRae spoke. "I just received reports of a lot of movement in the hills above the main south road an hour ago. Forward elements of the Pashtuns are now in Khar. I have already issued a deployment order for Major Taylor, commander of the 45th Sikhs, and the 45th pickets are now deployed into their forward fighting positions around the east gate area.

The 24th Punjab's are tasked to hold the main south gate on the paved road coming in from the village of Khar. However there seem to be problems mustering them as the 24th Punjab's are moving very slow tonight towards the main gate. At least the 31st Punjabis have mustered in mass as they are the reserve behind them. They have already set up their firing lines." He took a pull from his Maduro and bumped the long ash off it. He asked. Are your scouts ready on the Old Buddhist road?" "Yes sir, they have prepared their dice throw as we speak and I am certain we will hear their dice roll soon." Ambrose Cavendish was smiling at his little joke.

Sergeant Hook is in charge and…" McRae broke in with a laugh. "Hooky? The hero of Rorke's Drift?" I thought he had retired. Hell, he has to be an old man by now…" "Yes, sir somewhere near forty I think." retorted Griggs "But his ability betrays his age." McRae laughed. "Very true, quite an interesting fellow when he was under one of my commands long ago, a real hero at the Rorke's Drift battle. He saved many lives in the hospital and single-handedly fought off and killed scores of Zulus in a Berserker rampage so the rumor tells us."

"Does he still have his spear he used to carry? That Zulu chief's spear?" Cavendish laughed! "He sleeps with it like it is his pet dog Sir!" The colonel laughed out loud and gave a low smile. "Hook is a good man and what will be his signal for this attack?" Cavendish took a sip of cognac and smiled. "I would assume that once his crew have lit their explosives, they will warn us of their impending attack. I do believe my boys will thin the forward ranks of the attackers as we rearrange the geography on the road!" He has four of the best Gurkha sappers preparing this surprise!"

"The devil be damned… and would "King George be among them?" "Front and center sir" Replied the lieutenant with a smile. McRae continued. "I worked with him building roads once. He knows how to blow stuff up for sure. We don't need to worry now; King George will be enough!" The colonel chuckled and they mused the situation as they finished up the cognac in the tins. McRae poured another stiff round. The cognac with shots of water was mellowing Cavendish, as complement to the heat of this day. Cavendish asked. "What are your defenses going to be against this sir if I may ask?"

The colonel pushed back his head of dark hair as he spoke. The room was stuffy and they were sweating in the extreme heat of the day. "In my extreme boredom, I completely reworked the useless silly defenses that were in place when I arrived here. This camp was not created by fortifications planners but was assembled in haste in the wake of the 1895 rebellion. This whole outpost was completely indefensible. I added lines of overlapping defensive trenches and firing pits in front of both gates. I needed to enable our highly effective firing lines to work in concert under attack! I have tactically positioned all my artillery assets to support these forward defenses"

Cavendish sipped his cognac and added. "But I fear we will be attacked at once from every direction." The light colonel gave a serious stare. "The key against this is that I constructed excellent secondary defense lines behind the first ones at the east gate area and further up the crater to the rear area facing the south gate. My boys will be able to pour constant fire across the area. The continuous British firing line tactics are the backbone of our defense! My light artillery pieces can be rolled and repositioned quickly to both support and protect my firing lines!" I have two artillery pieces on top at the north fort to lay down covering fire throughout the area." He smiled and resumed.

"I even have a couple of the new automatic Maxim squad weapons to cover the open spaces. I accidentally fell into possession of these guns after a machinegun battalion passed through, we have a decent but limited amount of ammo for them. I am deploying one of them with some light artillery to the secondary positions at the east gate. The other one is in an over watch position at the north fort. I feel that our infantry in the front can bottleneck the initial attackers into an excellent killing ground. As reinforcements of the rest of the 45th move into the secondary defenses, and my forward pickets pull back to this line we will have powerful firepower."

The LTC was wound up now as he concluded. "If all goes to hell our last stand will be up here in the north fort. But honestly, it would take thousands of savages to overrun us." Ambrose stared at him with a fear in his eyes. Sir, there are thousands!" McRae sipped his cognac then continued. "Well dear Cavendish, the beauty of the plan is Colonel Meiklejohn is my real boss here and is a true professional soldier! He has already bypassed "Puffy Deane" and wired for reinforcements from our outpost south at Madan. A strong group of Guides Cavalry with supporting infantry should be on the way soon! But this damn heat and dust will slow them down I am certain."

Cavendish replied, as he smiled and knocked a long ash from his cigar. "Your defenses and reinforcements may just save our day sir!" Griggs gave the colonel a stern look. "Sir, if we get hit like I expect we need to keep the troops loaded with plenty of ammo to keep heavy fire in the kill zones! Nephew seems to think over two-hundred thousand of these savages are lurking in this region ready to wipe "we" of Her Majesties forces off the planet!" McRae took a long sip in his cognac and looked back at the tall scout. "HOLY SHIT!" It was time to break up the meeting and get to work. Lieutenant Colonel McRae excused himself to continue overseeing preparations of the 45th Sikhs at the east gate.

Down below the east gate many spectators of the polo game were having an ad hoc party complete with music… It was a strange dichotomy of festival and war planning in the same breath it seemed to Corporal Holmes from his view at the east gate. Cavendish and his two scouts soon rode along the defenses inspecting the 45th Sikhs who were preparing for the fight. They then rode down the hill through the busy crowded bazaar to see how the 24th Punjabis were progressing at the main gate area. They were not set up yet. McRae then instilled them with a harsh "fire and brimstone" banter as the scouts watched.

The cognac buzz had reopened the lieutenant's interest in the beautiful nameless lady who seemed to like him. He wanted more of her and her name as well! However, Cavendish's thoughts wandered to the Old Buddhist Road and the current status of Hook and company. No explosions had occurred yet! Darkness had completely overtaken the barren dry rocky landscape as the normal night bonfires now illuminated the camp sentry posts. It was a very hot July 26th. It was very obvious to the cadre at Malakand that something was "in the air" so to speak and this muster of troops into well supplied fighting positions was not just another fruitless readiness training exercise?"

The color sergeant stared at the advancing tribesmen in the distance from his position on this ancient road. He was amazed at how quiet the multitudes of tribesmen were as they seemed to be moving methodically in loose but massed formations snaking along the old road in his direction. They were going to attack tonight! He was concerned that the advance parties of the Pashtuns were already on the outpost perimeter behind them. This meant that they would be trapped between them and this uncoiling giant snake moving on the Old Buddhist Road seeking to devour their British host. Hook and the others had been hearing the wailing call to battle at the distant assembly areas for the last two hours. He looked at his pocket watch and it was now half past nine.

Earlier, just after sunset, the Gurkhas had placed four huge well concealed explosive charges starting at two-hundred yards down the road from their precarious position and set the rest under huge loose boulder formations every fifty yards as to gain the maximum deadly effects. King George had personally cut the fuses so when lit, they would all go up nearly at the same time. Each Gurkha was tasked to light one of the four charges in order then return back to where Hook guarded the horses. The roads would be filled with attackers when the charges detonated. King George knew this business like a surgeon.

At nine fifty King George crept out to the side of the road and watched for his three men who had gone to light the fuses down the road. He saw literally thousands of warriors streaming towards them in the shadows of night now. Shortly his fellow Gurkhas appeared with smiles and sweat covering their faces. The fuses had been lit! Hooky looked at his kids, all winded and sweaty from the heat and run. He gave his order to move down the road another fifty yards to a safer position after King George lit the final shorter fuse. As the group climbed off their horses in this new position, the blaring of hundreds of bugles, horns, and cymbals calling the Pashtuns to battle began to rumble.

The eerie strange bleating of the horns made their skin crawl as the scouts made it to their final position. Something violent and evil was bearing down on them. Sergeant Hook looked fondly at his men. "We must wait for the explosions before we ride now, or all of us will be pitched from our mounts to the ground. Hold your horses tight by the bridles and try to hold an arm around their neck! When the explosions are over, we shall ride like banshees!" His "kids" understood and prepared accordingly with smiles on their faces. Hooky took a salutary toast of whiskey from his flask as the seconds to the explosions ticked away.

The lead elements of thousands of Pashtuns and Ghazis had passed all the charges with the lead element only hundred yards from where the scouts stood with their mounts. Then, suddenly bright flashes heralded an inferno of explosions that rocked the silence of night! Large boulders and hundreds of rocks violently cascaded airborne into the road packed with thousands of tribesmen in sudden terror. The ground shook as the scout's horses panicked and reared up in shocked surprise. A huge soup like cloudy pall of dust had risen up and inundated the area.

The huge sudden flash of the explosions had momentarily revealed the silhouettes of multitudes of huge boulders mixed with bodies clad in white garments, visibly pitching into the air like ghost rag dolls. The deep ravines would be filled with the dead, many crushed and buried forever. Many other tribesmen near the epicenters of the explosions were evaporated. Many large ancient boulders, unleashed by the explosions rolled across the road, crushing hundreds of Pashtuns as they bounced and rolled from their ancient elevated positions across the Old Buddhist Road into the deep ravine. Then the bugles, silenced for many minutes by the massive explosions began wailing once again from behind a huge cloud of dust. Now recovered, an angry screaming horde of tribesmen ushered forth through the carnage on the road dust headed straight for the east gate.

The explosions jostled the horses wildly and the scouts had trouble mounting them. Color sergeant Hook yelled "Let's get the Hell out of this place… follow me!" They all drove their nervous horses to a fast exit from this position at a gallop. As they came at a hard ride around a bend in the road, the group smashed into a band of tribesmen standing in the middle of the road. They had come down from a large hill to the right and had stopped in the road when the explosions occurred. These Pashtuns in this first group where knocked down and trampled as the scouts rode over them in haste.

Edged weapons were unsheathed quickly as they smashed into the next group. Hook speared the closest rebel under the chin and through the skull with his ever-handy Zulu spear as one tried to grab the reigns on his horse. Two blasts from his shotgun cleared three more away. King George and the other Gurkhas slashed down other tribesmen with their Scimitars. In short order, they broke free, leaving many wounded and dying rebels in their wake pushing their horses at full gallop towards the east gate of the south outpost It seemed that the hillsides now answered the explosions with hundreds of rifle shots aiming into the South Camp at Malakand.

They could now hear the sound of a bugle calling the fort to arms barely over the din of the rifle fire now. The scouts were only minutes in front of several thousand savages surging from behind them moving in a human wall towards the camp of the hot dry night. One of the guards, scared out of his wits yelled out. "Who is there!" as the riders came out of the shadows of the dark road. Hook wildly yelled back. "Queen Victoria for God sakes!" He could hear Corporal Holmes yelling at them to stand down as he waved his arms in silhouette in front of the guard post bonfire. Hook caught up, jumped from his mount, and bathed in sweat and blood on his dirty tan tunic.

He yelled loudly with wild scared eyes. "There are thousands of them…thousands!" as he looked at the two British guards, Cavendish, and Corporal Holmes, who had moved to the gate after they heard the explosions down the road. It seemed to Hook, to be a return to the nightmare of Rorke's Drift all over again! Lieutenant yelled as the bullets began zinging about this area. "Everybody abandons this gate and back to the first defensive line! Pull back now!" The groups deftly moved back together to the first defensive positions of the 45th Sikh who wore their unmistakable turbans.

The scouts handed their rather sweaty and scared horses to an orderly who took them to the rear. Color Sergeant Alfred Hook gave his short frantic report to the McRae, Taylor and Cavendish who stood together in front of him. "Gentlemen," explained Hooky," I hope this command is ready for the fight of their fucking lives!" Cavendish smiled at his sweaty winded sergeant. "So how did the explosions go?" Hook gave a great smile at his Gurkhas then to him. "Perfect sir and free flying lessons for several hundred of the savages from what the blast allowed us to see! But sir, blowing up hundreds of savages was like just a few drops in a bucket filled to the brim! It will take a miracle to stop this horde of many!"

The battle for Malakand had begun as thousands of Pashtuns led by their Ghazi handlers began massed rifle fire at everything in Malakand Camp. Then came the expected massive human wave charges focused on the east and south gates. Many inhabitants inside the crater were gunned down in the indiscriminate volleys from the hills before they had a chance to find cover. The massive human wave attacks from both roads were designed to surround and completely engulf the south camp of Malakand in one quick violent assault. The British fighting positions held their fire until the distinctive silhouettes of the first waves of savages now appeared as one screaming wall, accented by wild screaming, bugle calls and drums beating loudly in the ranks of the Pashtuns surging forward.

All at once, British firing lines at the east gate cracked in unison into the darkness obscured wave of the enemy, with an accompanying chorus of direct light artillery fire. The rat-tat-tat of the lone maxim machinegun laced into the first waves of attackers, and would soon be out of ammunition.

The coordinated fire from the first defensive line pickets of the 45th slaughtered hundreds as their broken bodies created rather large piles in front of the firing positions. The first waves of sword and spear waving tribesmen completely disintegrated in the massed volleys of the well-coordinated British firing lines. The savages were dying by the scores at the east gate defenses.

LTC McRae, leading from the first line, had assembled his pickets in positions that protected them from direct fire and channeled the savages into a large bottleneck. Their masses continued to edge forward. LTC McRae was awed at the numbers attacking and knew that if reinforcements did not come soon, this position would be overrun, and the whole defense of the crater would be destroyed. The echoes from the perfect firing lines was followed in the rising smoke of gunpowder smoke from all the bullets and artillery rounds being expended. The wall of tribesmen continued advancing. Hook and his Gurkhas had joined McRae in the front.

Meanwhile, the 24th Punjab's which had been tasked to defend the main gate area, had been disorganized moving sluggishly into their positions. This was to prove disastrous for them now. When all hell broke loose, their first line was overwhelmed into hand to hand combat quickly! Thousands of savages with blaring trumpets, were pouring in a mass human tsunami at this gate! The Malakand south camp was being overrun. The second defensive firing lines of the 24th Punjabis were able to temporarily stop the approaching waves of Pashtuns as the first line of the 24th had disappeared into the wall of attacking tribesmen. Artillery rounds from the north fort landed into the tightly packed throng crowding into the main south gate with terrifying consequences.

The second defense line of the 24th now reinforced by the reserve 31st Punjabis opened a concentrated deadly fire into the approaching horde. These expert firing lines stopped the Pashtun onslaught cold as the bodies of the attackers piled up in front of them. Many of the attackers hesitated and backed away. On command, the Punjab's moved their lines forward and used the piles of bodies of the many dead savages as cover. The sporadic shots from muskets, spears, and arrows had wounded and killed many Punjab's. The tribesmen attacked again in mass and the concentrated rifle fire destroyed the onslaught of the enemy a second time. More crates of rifle ammunition were delivered as it was running low. Over half of the south camp had fallen to the tribesmen at this point!

The savages had forced back the defending British defenders at the south gate and had completely overrun the bazaar and the British supply/ammo dump in the south camp. The fight over control of this row of buildings became a huge brawl with fists, bayonets, knives, swords, pistols, rifles, and a variety of strange Pashtun edged weapons. This was becoming a very serious situation. Colonel Meiklejohn was on the scene directing troops amid all the combat. Massed sporadic rifle fire was coming from the hills constantly wounding or killing friend and foe alike in the darkness. It was inaccurate but deadly for many and this problem would continue harassing the defenders for the length of this battle.

Second Lieutenant Climo, of the Punjab 24th, directed his troops assembled with the 31st, to wheel their formation into the middle, linking up with the east and west wall defenders forming a new fighting line. The two artillery Twelve pounders at hand plus the artillery being directed from the north fort; was delivering constant destructive fire on the enemy combatants, cutting huge furrows of torn bodies everywhere. Then the furrows would be filled again by the seemingly unlimited supply of frantic warriors. Several British sharpshooters, including Griggs and Holmes, were on one of the rooftops secured in the close fighting being waged by the 24th Punjab to their front. They were firing at muzzle flashes in the surrounding hills with some success.

A pall of smoke and the smell of cordite covered the battle zone like a thick fog at dawn on the Thames river! It seemed the whole outpost was completely engulfed in violent battle. The first of two counter attacks to liberate the ammo dump were textbook offensive British tactics. 2LT. Climo, organized two deadly firing lines that killed many attackers in this area, then, he led a violent bayonet charge finishing off the savages who had captured the stores. They failed twice, because of being heavily outnumbered. This attempt failed with the loss of several British troops, including two officers. Colonel Meiklejohn would be wounded the next day leading a charge liberating this area.

British rifle fire cracked into the darkness along with artillery fire as the continued answer to the thousands of screaming Pashtun tribesmen charging wildly towards the first lines of the pickets of the 45th. McRae, seeing that his pickets were now in grave jeopardy of being engulfed by this tide of attackers, ordered them back to the second defensive line. Reinforcements had arrived and were now manning the second defensive line. The Pashtuns now overran the first trench line of abandoned defenses. There was a rolling sea of thousands of them converging from everywhere. The abandoned first defensive line was now choked with hundreds of savages as they began pouring over it and charging at the second line of Sikhs. Lieutenant Taylor, at McRae's command, instructed his sappers to light the demolition fuses leading to the abandoned first line of trenches.

In a few moments, the forward defense line of trenches and wood parapets erupted in a huge set of explosions. The forward attacking echelons of the tribesmen in and around the exploding first line of defense disappeared in the smoke and all was silent for moments. After a muted silence, hundreds more wildly charging Pashtuns surged out of the wall of dust and smoke directly into the well-prepared second firing lines of the 45th Sikhs. In simple terms, it was a massive slaughter for the savages. The accurate rifle and direct cannon fire completely pulverized the wall of attackers. The enemy attack faltered and fell back in disarray leaving hundreds, if not thousands of bodies in gruesome piles in front of the 45th Sikhs positions.

The expert lethality of the British firing lines and especially the artillery had kept the rest of the south camp from being overrun at this point. The remains of the 24th Punjab Infantry severely bloodied, were helping the well-prepared Punjab 31st extend their firing lines to link the east and west wall defenders as one powerful fighting line. The artillery focused fire on the enemy masses converging to the walls and to the front of the firing lines had done as much physical as mental damage to the attackers. Empty wooden boxes of rifle and artillery ammo littered the firing positions next to many bodies now as fresh ammo was constantly replenished from the stores in the north fort.

The north camp, the final redoubt, accented by an old stone fort complete with towers, buildings and walls, had not been under any main attack as of yet. Most of the two-hundred plus soldiers from it were reinforcing the south camp defenses. The rising pall of smoke from the battle now obscured Malakand's entire south outpost from good artillery observation from the high position of the north fort. In the melee, Cavendish and his Gurkhas minus Griggs, Holmes, and Hook, had moved up the hill to the north camp. They were hearing women screaming as they hurriedly approached the scene. They saw a group of expatriates had been jumped by a roving band of Pashtuns as they had been approaching the main gate of the north fort Cavendish and his Gurkhas jumped into the fight like mad dogs. Cavendish, with his .45 Colt pistol drawn shot and killed three Pashtun warriors immediately, with the blast from his pistol knocking them to the ground. The Pashtuns turned on them like a pack of wolves. Cavendish emptied his .45 into other attackers directly to his front and went for his scimitar. He was taught to attack with his sword from the sheath, so his first slash from his sheath slashed through the head of the warrior in front of him.

He parried off sword thrusts from two more behind the warrior and in quick circular strokes killed both. In a short violent brawl, nineteen savages were dead. Cavendish had been cut across the face and speared across his ribs, but not seriously. Quickly they herded the expatriates up the well-worn hilly path to the fort. As they moved along, Cavendish found that a lady had taken his arm. It was the beautiful blue-eyed brunette once again. She looked frightened. He spoke as he stared into her worried face.

"Looks like there will be no more polo today or tomorrow my dear because the party has been crashed by some very bad boys!" She gave a half laugh as she wept. He looked her in the eyes. "My name is Cavendish and I must get you safe and move on. Duty calls darling only if you tell me your name!" She nervously answered. "My name is Jenny … Farnsworth!" He handed her one of his two loaded service revolvers and an extra box of pistol ammunition. "The way things seem to be going my fair lady, you will need this before the sun comes up, I am afraid!" When they got to the north gate it was open and Harper and Wentworth were there at the ready.

"Get inside this camp, probably the tower and lock it. He dispatched Pulbah, Wentworth and Harper to protect her and the rest of the civilians. More soldiers had come on the scene because of the gunshots down the path. He looked at her and kissed her forehead, "Do not come out here again, until this is over and I have returned!" She gave a nervous smile. "My name is Jenny, Jenny Farnsworth" she said again "and…and I will comply!" She then grabbed the sides of his face and gave him a warm deep kiss on the lips, then she gave him a sloppy salute mocking him with a warm smile. He gave her a sharp salute and walked away. What a crazy place and time to have a crush on a woman he thought!

With that, the women were placed with protection in one of the stone observation towers by the main gate at the front of north camp. With warm thoughts now disrupted, Cavendish and his group returned to the main south gate area to help in the plight of the 31st and 24th Punjab's. It seemed the defense of the Old Buddhist road at the east gate was holding well at this point. After twenty minutes in their descent from the north fort, dodging many sporadic poorly aimed rifle shots from the hills they found Griggs and Holmes with other sharpshooters on the roof of a small single-story building.

The dark night had engulfed the battle as hundreds of flashes from the multitude of cannon and rifle fire flashed in a continuous cacophony from everywhere. They picked up rifles from a stack and joined in the fight. Cavendish joined Holmes and Griggs in their hill sniping as the Gurkhas added fire to the incredible continuously attacking throngs of tribesmen below. In what seemed forever, the sun rose above the hills as the enemy pulled back. Even the toughest veteran of the British empire was appalled at the still sea of dead tribesmen lying everywhere in deep piles in front of the British firing positions. Nobody had ever imagined the size of this attack or this slaughter! At dawn, with the battle ended, LTC McRae located LT. Cavendish and his crew on the roof. The four Gurkhas were below in elevated firing positions behind the weary lines of Punjab's.

Sergeant Hook had accompanied the colonel throughout the fight. As Hook dispensed several full canteens to the combatants on the roof, McRae spoke. He was covered in soot and dust. "We have word that LT Rattery and his boys safely got back to Chakadara before all hell broke loose there. Also, the Chakadara garrison is putting up one hell of a fight against sizable throngs of attackers. It seems those boys were ready for them and the walls have yet to be breeched. Also, I heard confirmation that a large contingent of Guides reinforcements are moving towards us from Madan and should be here in the next few hours.

"Great Caesar's Ghost!" Stammered Sergeant Alfred Henry Hook, "Seems like Rorke's Drift has returned with a fucking vengeance this time!" McRae smiled at his salty sidekick. "It does seem this way, but like the Drift, we are holding all along our established lines for now as they are still thankfully concentrating their main attacks at the gates. Our firing lines and light artillery have reeked total havoc on them. We have been slowly moving over one-hundred and fifty troops from the north camp to reinforce our positions here in the south camp, so when these buggers return, they will be met with increased British venom!"

"Who will be guarding the north camp Sir?" Cavendish asked. McRae stared at him, the strain in his face was obvious. "We are leaving a complementary force of fifty troops and another thirty odd expatriates who have taken up arms. The north fort is much easier to defend and as we are moving more artillery from there down to the south camp, we left two light field artillery pieces for defense." Cavendish fixed his thoughts on that beautiful lady named Jenny Farnsworth in one of the towers now. In his growing fatigue, he worried for her and for that matter, the rest in the north camp. This titanic struggle was less than twenty-four hours old!

He thought about that large group of Pashtuns they had fought had been scarcely fifty yards of the front gate last night. Although a strong position, a massed attack at the size of what was being encountered below would overrun it! Then what? Colonel McRae smiled at them and pulled out a full bottle of whiskey. "My gift to the brave fighting scouts!" "I'll drink to we fighting men!" Chimed in Hook as he popped the cork on the bottle and took a healthy drink, then passed the bottle to Cavendish who followed suite. Everyone drank except for Rashid who cited his religion again.

The colonel continued after a healthy plug of whiskey. "We also brought you a case of rifle ammo and another four rifles. The blokes that owned these will never need them again. Tonight, will probably be another wild attack. These hills are infested with them still! Make the shots count and happy hunting." He passed the whiskey to the two British NCOs that had accompanied him with the ammo and rifles. He stood up with a smile. "I must be off, since I have planned to create large bonfires tonight to help our artillery and riflemen see the enemy at farther ranges in the night. God's Speed!" He and his two men slipped out and left. Cavendish looked at his pocket watch. It was now half past eight in the morning.

The rifle shots from the hills continued at their usual annoying pace. Besides this, some jerk in the hills was continuously playing British bugle calls and doing quite a good job of it. He had begun this morning with the call to arms. "There goes that asshole again!" stammered Holmes. We need to shut him up. He has been playing all our favorite Bugle calls since last night! Griggs looked at him. "Get on the wall next to me and be ready!' He then viewed up into the hills using a nice set of binoculars. "Look for any reflection of the bugle in the rising sunlight for me" smiled Holmes with his rifle at the ready. Without a word, Holmes was on the wall scouring the rough mountainous terrain to the left of the main road. Minutes seemed to pass in seconds as all eyes were on the sniper team. "Got him! Look on the ridge, below it next to a huge boulder formation at about ten O'clock, maybe thirty yards below it! I can clearly see the reflection and that damned bugle!" replied Griggs.

Holmes was using the elephant rifle offered by Griggs sparingly since he had a limited supply of fifty caliber ammunition for it. This was a special target as he positioned his elephant rifle and began to take a slow methodical aim in the direction of the bugle's sound and reflection. There was complete silence, then one loud shot echoed from the roof up into the valley. The bugle abruptly stopped playing. A careful view with the binoculars revealed no body. But a shiny object was noted on the ground below the boulder formation clearly in the sunlight. "We are going to miss you oh Jihadist musician!" mused Griggs as both men were congratulated. The bugler was never to blow his horn again in the battle, but the sniper dual continued.

That day, July 28th, more ammo, food, water, and additional troops from the north camp were re-supplied to the 31st and 24th who had both been battered in these attacks. The 45th was holding strong. The mounted reinforcements entered the fray with an irregular cavalry charge coming in to the outpost cutting down many Pashtuns with their sabers hiding near the perimeter. The Guides reinforcements from Madan had come under heavy inaccurate enemy fire with some losses as they attacked into the camp. The British defenses on the 28th were growing much stronger. Attempts to reinforce Chakadara had miserably failed, so Lieutenant Rattery and his command were alone, on their own to win or die now.

The constant sniping and counter-sniping between the Pashtuns and British sharpshooters lasted all day. The constant overwhelming magnitude of the initial attack had completely exhausted and worn down the defenders physically and mentally. No one had slept yet. The sight of a few reinforcements from the south was welcome but added little against the tide of the threat still facing Malakand. At ten at night on the 28th of July, the next massive attack by the Ghazi led Pashtuns yelling praise to Allah began on the dime. Colonel McRae ordered all the bonfires he had set up that morning to be lit as the throngs of warriors emerged, now struggling over the mounds of decomposing corpses in their advance.

They were again slaughtered in droves but still came on. The British firing line was the key to the defense. It was deadly! Although the tribesmen breached the defenses in the south camp, they were now repulsed with great losses due the added reinforcements from the north fort and dismounted Guides reinforcements. Once again, the battle lasted at a furious and bloody pace for several long hours to finally die out in the wee hours of dawn. The British defenders were now beyond exhaustion. Would this ever stop? The scout snipers had no idea of how many Pashtuns they had dispatched in the hills and other target areas by now. It seemed that this would never stop.

In spite of the tidal waves of attackers who had hit this place over the last three nights, Malakand defenses were holding. Lieutenant Cavendish set out in the morning on a long climb up the hill to the north fort to see what was happening there and see Jenny of course! He passed several groups of British soldiers moving from the north camp to the south down the long steep rocky hill. Other eyes had also been watching this evacuation with great interest. It seemed to the lieutenant that this day was hotter than the previous three. The combat and related heat was having terrible effects on the combatants from both sides in this struggle now.

Cavendish entered the well-guarded front gate of the north fort, which had been left open to accommodate the withdrawal of troops from the garrison. He took a short tour of the soldiers left to guard this fort as he hailed them in his survey of the defenses. He coldly felt that this smaller group of remaining soldiers would not be able to withstand any huge attacks regardless of the weapons and positions they enjoyed here. He then returned to the front gate and approached the large observation towers that were positioned on either side of it. There he found Jenny and some others standing outside in the cooler shade of the towers and adjoining ramparts. Cavendish walked over smiling, as she returned a deep penetrating smile. The lieutenant began the dialogue. "So, I hear that you are now the commander of this camp! Congratulations my dear!"

Jenny smiled back. "Lieutenant, would you serve under me?" What a loaded question he thought and laughed in his reply. "Under you? Over you? Beside you? Behind you? Your wish is my command!" She laughed and tucked his arm under hers and hugged him. Well, if you change your uniform and take a bath, and get a nice hotel room dear…. all things are possible!" Ambrose could not resist her lips as from before, as her face was so close. He kissed her, and then she kissed him back. "Jenny, I will call the Majestic Hotel in London when I return to my fighting position…say what about tomorrow night?" She was now all smiles. "Lieutenant Cavendish, what an excellent idea, and don't forget the champagne!"

He smiled at her. "I promise I won't dear…and cognac, and would you be hungry enough to have a nice dinner before we retire?" She beamed a wide smile back. "Oh, yes darling, what a nice plan for our first date!" Then he gave a laugh and continued with the merry banter. "Hey, if you can get dates for all my scouts, can they come as well?" For a moment, she looked at him serious until she realized, as before, that in this fantasy, he was pulling her leg once again. She smiled back. "Why yes dear Ambrose, I actually have arranged dates for the whole 45th Sikhs as well!" They were both laughing together now.

They took a stroll together around the camp. The two light artillery pieces were centered to give maximum fire across the whole area of the camp. The maxim machine gun was secured in an over watch position behind the artillery on the roof of a building to inflict maximum death and to protect the gunners if necessary. Some thirty odd riflemen were placed in three ten-man balanced firing lines covering the both sides of the fort. Several citizens were mixed into the defenses with them. Cavendish honestly did not like these weak defenses at all. The north camp would be a prize if captured and could turn the battle in favor of the Mad Fakir. It was time for Cavendish to leave. He bid kind farewell to his new tart Jenny and trekked back down to where his men were in the south camp.

Cavendish soon decided to move he and his men to the north fort. He informed the commander of the 24th Punjabis to extend their line into his position since he and his men were leaving soon. He and his men quietly prepared to move into the north camp when fresh hostilities began. Nothing seemed to happen by eleven this night. The whole command, breathing a sigh of relief, began to feel as if the Pashtuns had had enough. Thousands of their torn and rotting bodies littered the areas in and around the south camp. The smell was terrible. An army of vultures had now joined this army of the dead during the daylight. Bodies of the slain Pashtuns were visible everywhere in the camp areas and on the hills surrounding the British positions. The stench of the dead bloated bodies, blackened as they rot were infested with millions of flies, nauseated everybody in the heat.

The night wore on wrapped in an eerie silence. Malakand was covered in a cloak of Stygian darkness, save for a glowing half moon and stars. Many battle-weary troops slid off into well-needed slumber. Cavendish sat in the rear of his soon to be abandoned position against a wall, with his scouts smoking a cigar. All was quiet. His sixth sense told him the night would produce another attack, for it was not over. While he was thinking about the foreboding "quiet" Hook spoke up. "Sir, this was just like the Drift. We had killed hundreds of them, and then there was a period of inaction like this, when we thought it was over. Then Sir, came the worse coordinated assault on our positions! They nearly got us that last time lieutenant and would have had our commander had not set up excellent second line of well-fortified defensive firing positions behind a fresh wall of sandbags.

Our front walls were breeched but we were safely organized behind the second defense. Then we gave them hell! By the time, we went hand-to-hand, the battle was nearly over. That was when I faced off with the Zulu Chief after escaping the burning hospital!" Hook tapped his Zulu spear and smiled at Cavendish. "The chief fucked up, and I didn't!" He slid a new bottle of rum to Cavendish who looked at it in surprise. "I fell into these bottles in the unguarded fairly trashed officer's bar near the bazaar which was partially destroyed in the attack at south camp. Thank the stars the Muslims don't drink or we would be dry now my son!"

Cavendish had to give a laugh as Hook concluded. "Sharpen your wits, you will need it before this night has ended." It was just at two in the morning, when the exhausted defenders, many given to slumber in place were awoken to a huge roar accented with blaring trumps, horns, and drums. It was the roar of thousands of screaming hill tribesmen emerging from all across the line yelling "Allah Akbar." They were literally coming from every point in the defensive line with lit torches accenting their weaving lines emerging from behind the dark hills. The torches were set to help the fresh waves of attackers navigate past the piles of their dead. These torches provided excellent firing points for the

British artillery batteries as they and massed rifle fire of the British lines came alive on these winding snaking hordes. All hell was breaking loose at Malakand! Hook would not be wrong this night!

The bonfires arrayed in front of the British defenses lit up the darkness in a huge semi-circle mirroring the crater and exposing thousands of wildly charging hill tribesmen. The artillery was now firing non-stop from every battery! The defenders were shocked for a third time at the multitude of warriors they saw pressing forward from all sides! The first waves of attackers were cut down in mass or blown to pieces by near point-blank artillery fire! They continued to press forward.

Then he saw it! Cavendish saw many distant muzzle flashes in the distance from the north fort now as he looked at it. It was now under attack. Mister Griggs soon verified it as he jumped over the wall next to them. He had replaced his turban with a pith helmet, so he wouldn't be mistakenly shot. The attacking savages seemed to pour from a wellspring that never ended, like a flood. 'Sir, the north camp is under and it is time to go!" Without a word, Cavendish signaled to everybody in his small command to leave, and soon they were spread out and moving up the incline hill to the north camp.

The group looked back to the south camp observing the flashes produced by rifle and cannon fire, amidst the huge bonfires across the south perimeter that created quite a panoramic view of the battle for the camps. It was a surrealistic observance to them as they ventured up the steep path. The muzzle flashes of every weapon coming from above them seemed to denote the size of the attack in progress. As they trudged up the steep hill, they encountered a huge body of tribesmen obscured in the darkness cutting to their right up the hill towards the fort. The scouts had not been seen yet.

Suddenly a massed line of fire erupted off to their left into the pack of enemy warriors. It was a hasty ambush by the British. A wall of lead dropped a whole group of the attackers in the muzzle flashes. "Fire at will!" Came a loud command from Cavendish. It was a barely audible above the noise of gunfire. The firing seemed to intensify as the Pashtuns returned uncontrolled and un-aimed fire in the night towards the British firing line, which seemed to be behind some good-sized boulders leading up towards the large gate of the north camp some fifty yards distant. The tribesmen moved down towards them to flank the British.

They still had not detected Cavendish and his men yet. When the tribesmen rolled their line to the left, the Pashtuns were then caught in crossfire from the small group of defenders and those of Cavendish. These warriors turned out to be a large group of Ghazi warriors who possessed new rifles, so bullets were flying everywhere. King George and Gladstone threw grenades in short order. The explosions rocked the scene as the bodies of slain Ghazis fell or rolled down the steep rocky slopes leading up to the narrow road to the fort.

Cavendish hailed the British NCO as he and his boys approached them. More enemy were firing at them from below as Cavendish knew that sheer numbers would decide this fray now. Seeing the reality that this little skirmish could cost all of them their lives Cavendish yelled at the Noncom in charge of the ambush. "It was a good stand, but we got to move back inside the gates before more of them show up!" He pointed down the hill at the new group moving towards them. The Noncom, who had been hit in the shoulder and was bleeding, simply nodded then spoke. He stared at Cavendish. "The North fort must not fall Sir!"

Cavendish took charge of the group and ordered a hasty firing line and a few grenades to hit the large group climbing up behind them. Many fell before he ordered them to fall back up the hill past the cropping of boulders and into the gate. A couple well-thrown grenades bounced into the mob coming up the hill which caused death and confusion, scattering the Ghazi and Pashtun attackers. The mixed band of British soldiers, Gurkhas and Punjab's entered the north camp gate which was then closed behind them and secured. Marksmen from the walls were continuously delivering deadly fire into the growing number of attackers.

Artillery rounds from the British twelve pounder artillery soon begun landing outside the walls of the north camp in a steady roll. This continuous cannon fire ripped holes into the dark hillsides and the throngs of crazed tribesman growing on the outskirts of the north fort. Climbing upon a wall, Cavendish's scouts silently looked to the south camp area. The spectacle of the massive combat ensuing in the south camp crater stunned their senses. The huge bonfires illuminated the battle as thousands of tribesmen could clearly be seen, charging at the British firing lines.

It seemed as if the whole land was violently engulfed. The sheer weight of the thousands of attackers would overwhelm the British and the south camp in due time. The combat was furious as the incessant crack of British firing lines and artillery prevented it so far. The reality of the massive Pashtun attack on the north camp was now apparent to everybody standing on the parapet behind the wall. "We need to hold the buildings and clear the walls when they come over from the rooftops, the towers, and walls." Yelled SGT Hook. "If they can't break our elevated firing lines or overwhelm our artillery, we may have a chance.

"Organize it!" shouted Cavendish. "The rest of you fall in with Hook and help where you can! Do your best!" Before the Pashtuns could breech the walls, the defenders were pulled back to form firing lines in sandbagged positions preset in front of the three main buildings. The British filled these positions and soon covered them from rooftop firing positions. The light cannon was also pulled back into this defense. The towers overlooking the camp were reinforced with the riflemen retreating from the walls. The maxim machinegun was placed in the center roof in the complex covering the parade grounds of the fort.

As the defenders were settling into these positions a huge fiery explosion erupted that blew a huge part of the south wall of the camp apart. The Pashtuns began charging in mass though this gap. They were also chambering over the walls now. The machinegun began firing non-stop volleys at the invaders clearing them off as they emerged over the walls. The light artillery fire now aimed directly at the gap. The exploding shells blasted the attackers as more howling tribesmen crowded into the gap in the wall again As the machinegun continued effectively clearing away attackers climbing over the walls, the riflemen were also adding to his deadly toll. Enemy bodies were piling up on the parapets where they fell. The Maxim gun shifted to the main parade ground and began knocking the attackers down in heaps as they charged across it. Soon, the gun went silent for its ammo was finally depleted.

One of the towers on the corner of the south wall began burning like a huge torch, and as the flames grew, lit up the battleground brightly. Cavendish had been fighting in the defensive position where the light artillery was firing in front of the main building. Holmes and two Gurkhas' ran up to him panting and sweating. "Sir!" exclaimed the corporal. "The savages were all over that tower and I felt that by burning it would increase our accuracy in hitting these bastards!" "Holmes! Are you asking me permission to burn that burning tower?" intoned Cavendish with a grin. Corporal Holmes smiled back "Well yes sir, kind of?"

"Permission granted ten minutes ago, Good plan Corporal!" the LT slapped him on the shoulder. Cavendish had kept his eye on the tower to the right of his position where Jenny was in with many other women and soldiers. The enemy were surging into the fort from the walls and gap in the walls. The British guns continued killing them in droves as their mangled bodies piled up like in the battle below. Lord Nelson and Gladstone joined him as they made their way towards the tower amid rifle shots, explosions, and Pashtuns emerging along the wall leading to the tower. Both Gurkhas, hard veterans of war had never been engulfed in a huge violent sea of pure chaos as this!

The enemy had swarmed between them and the tower and it was too late to get there now. They backed up and joined the ranks of the British defending the front of the main building. One of the light artillery pieces was rolled into the open area inside the main building, but the second one was being overrun as its artillerymen were fighting with swords, bayonets, and rifle butts to gain a clear retreat into the building. James Cavendish became separated from everybody except Griggs in the tumultuous brawl. He joined the bloody fight over the artillery piece that remained in the open in front of the heavily defended building.

Putting him between the wounded artillerymen, the lieutenant emptied his .45 colt revolver point blank at the enemy warriors who were climbing on the light artillery screw gun. The lone remaining artillerymen at the gun next to him fired one round they had previously loaded point blank into the horde of attackers closing in. Pieces of bodies scattered in front of the gun for yards. The artillery blast immediately blew them back into the others behind them, giving Cavendish and Griggs time to help herd the wounded artillerymen into a large bay door.

The doors were shut and secured. In an overwhelming panic, he and Griggs ran to the roof. Pashtuns now wheeled the abandoned field piece around for direct fire on the large secured door. As they looked for a round to load it, a lit stick of dynamite cascaded down from the roof landing between the wheels of the artillery piece. A huge explosion ensued and, in a flash, the gun and attackers were blown to smithereens. Cavendish soon found King George crouched by the front of the roof. He was smiling at his boss, "I had one left sahib!" King George the sapper had struck again.

The constant rifle fire and sounds of battle filled the area as Cavendish yearned to go to the tower across the way where this Jenny was holed up. He now found himself in command of the soldiers and expatriates battling from the roof. After the huge explosion which destroyed the artillery piece, Griggs, and the two Gurkhas exited the large doors and ran through a confused and dazed mob of Pashtuns to the tower per previous orders. They had assumed Cavendish was already there since they had lost contact with him.

Mister Griggs and the two Gurkhas fought and killed a few Pashtuns in front of the tower with their knives, then entered it. They were let in by Wentworth who saw them coming. A new explosion at the artillery piece across the quad knocked all of them down. They quickly crawled to their feet in the dust, shut the door and secured it. Griggs, armed with his rifle climbed up into the tower and took up a position facing the south wall, or what was left of it. They joined the other soldiers and huddling expatriates in a cacophony of constant fire into the surging mob below.

Two of the soldiers, were dead, shot in their heads. Mister Griggs found Hook peering out one of the broken windows who informed him that there were a couple of expert snipers firing from the edge of the burning tower at the end of the quadrangle. He pointed to the lifeless bodies of Pulbah and Harper. The tower near the huge gap in the south wall at the end of the quadrangle was still burning brightly. Sergeant Hook had already located them through his binoculars, as the light cast by the fire offered up their images. Griggs extended a pith helmet on the end of his rifle so they could ascertain the methods of these snipers.

One would watch while the other quickly fired at the helmet, and then they would reverse roles. They were very shrewd shooters. Hook and Griggs played the reverse on them. After a few tense minutes, Griggs bagged the one waiting to fire. The other, after ricocheting his shot next to the window seemed to disappear in Grigg's next two rapid shots. As the sniper duel ended, the tower door was broken down. Private Wentworth fought like a caged animal along with a couple of Punjabis but were overwhelmed and killed by the frantic charge of tribesmen and Ghazis storming through the lower entrance door.

The British now held them at bay from the top floor. Alfred Hook took center and smiled as he saw a beautiful brunette methodically empty her pistol into the first three attackers ascending the stairs. They tumbled down the stairs forcing the followers to stumble and stop. They were, in turn shot dead when Hook emptied both barrels of his shotgun into them. He reloaded and fired again blasting the next attackers off the stairs. He continued to hold the high ground at the top of the stairs with Jenny, using shotgun and eventually his pistols to keep the crazed warriors out of the second floor.

Hook winked at Jenny as she reloaded her pistol again. He admired her calm poker face as she began shooting new targets emerging from the first floor up the stairs. They held their ground! The first floor and around the stairs was covered in slain bodies of the enemy warriors. More were packing into the area from the open door. Two grenades tossed by one of the Gurkhas blew the attackers into the walls. There was no room for new attackers to step which became a temporary halt in the attack. It seemed that one of the savages had set the tower on fire from below, with the smoke began to fill up the second floor as it now wafted in with the huge pall of smoke that already hung over the north fort.

LT. Cavendish had lost all perspective as his attention turned to the tower across the way. He had been awake for days now and heavily involved in terrible incessant combat. Fatigue was killing him, as was the thick smoke of cordite and burning buildings. The fight continued as he saw the tower began to burn like a huge torch in the darkness. He resigned himself off to the reality that his comrades and this woman Jenny were to die this night. "Where was the dawn?" he mumbled.

All the surviving combatants on the roof at the north fort viewed the sunrise as salvation from the horrors of the night. The light of the dawn struggled to shine through the wall of smoke surrounding what remained of the north fort as well as the south outpost camps. The sunlight had forced the Pashtun attackers to retreat, back into the shadows. Cavendish stood on the roof peering around and at the smoldering remains of the tower near the front gate. His thoughts for Jenny and the rest of his people went blank for now. He was sure extreme trauma would come soon.

He wondered if they on the roofs were the only survivors. How many more attacks could they take! His appearance spoke for all the survivors, for his uniform was torn, tattered and covered with dirt and blood. His olive side cap was long gone as his bearded dirty face had the thousand-yard stare resulting from extended violent combat. Cavendish felt completely lifeless now. He had used up all hundred rounds of his .45 pistol. The rest of his ammo was left with his kit in McRae's office in the tower next to the gate which was still standing and was battered but not destroyed. He had given his service revolver to Jenny but had acquired two more off the slain bodies of a couple of British officers somewhere in the battle outside. He had fired them from both hands until the ammo was gone. Both slain officers he had borrowed their pistols from had been beheaded in the frenzy. Mutilation seemed the fate of anybody who fell into the hands of these fired up savages!

In the post chaos of the night the lieutenant sat on a short dividing wall on the roof of the building he had been defending. In his daze he was staring at the two empty service revolvers at his feet thinking about more ammo. "Jenny? He thought of Jenny all of a sudden. He stood and stumbled awkwardly to the roof wall facing the tower, reeling from many small wounds, abrasions, and extreme numbed fatigue. Cavendish had no idea what time it was or how long he had been standing there in a fatigued daze. Every joint in his body ached. He began to notice a rather large contingent of fresh British soldiers and Punjabis moving about the ruins. They were reinforcements! "Allah Be Praised!" he mocked in a whisper.

The sporadic firing within the north fort by the newly arrived troops signaled the end of many Pashtuns and Ghazis who had been wounded and left behind. In a humanitarian sense, there was little reason to keep them alive for they were in great pain and would soon be dead from their wounds anyway. There was little medical help available to attend to the hundreds if not thousands of wounded tribesmen left behind. The same event seemed to be going on in the south camp. The spirits among the survivors were jovial shock and great relief. Bottles of whiskey appeared and were being passed about. Ambrose took a couple of long pulls from the whiskey and chased it with water from his canteen. The whiskey burned his mouth but calmed him.

He put a bottle in his blouse and began to walk down the roof stairs to go outside. Piles of slain tribesmen were everywhere and their blood trails seemed to cover the ground income macabre artwork. They were everywhere, mixed with the few British soldiers and Punjab's who suffered ghastly ends. The tower that housed Jenny and his scouts was a burnt smoldering blacked relic. All that was left was the blackened stone shell. As he neared the large tower, he saw that it had been burnt to the ground on the inside. He stood in muted silence just staring, totally devoid of all emotion. The wind seemed to pick up around him as he heard a faint voice in the distance.

Someone was calling his name. He turned and a feeble smile crossed his face. It was SGT Hook! He tried to yell back but his throat was parched dry. Soon he was engulfed in Hook's massive Bear hug. They just stood there without talking then let go of each other. Ambrose smiled with cracked dry lips and handed Hook the whiskey bottle. They both took long drinks and coughed from the dryness of their parched throats. Hooky interjected his usual funny comments as he passed his lieutenant his canteen.

"Sir if I can speak candidly? you look rather…like shit! What would your teachers at Sand Hurst say about your proper uniform today before you even inspect your troops? You can't inspect the troops looking like that my fine sir!" Cavendish stared at the huge burly Sergeant and studied him and his huge toothy smile across his face and under his large moustache. He was covered from head to foot in blood, grime and especially black soot. There seemed no more room for the dirt on him. He had a gash in his right cheek, a black eye, and had lost a sleeve on his tunic. The Zulu spear was in his belt, as were his two revolvers, and shotgun slung on his shoulder. Hook looked as exhausted as he now felt, and he reminded Cavendish of some gladiator of ancient times; wounded, unbeaten and very dangerous. He must have taken the Victoria Cross off his tunic during the battle because it was the only clean item now displayed on his chest.

The LT. retorted after his visual inspection of his color sergeant. "Hooky? Seems like you have been rolling with the pigs again!" Hook smiled as he stuck his Zulu Spear in the ground pulled out a bottle of rum from his kit bag hanging by a strap around his shoulder. "All's well that ends well my fearless leader!" Sergeant Horatio Griggs appeared next to Hooky with a mute smile. Without a word, they took several healthy plugs off the rum bottle chasing it with gulps of water in complete silence. "Want your report Sir?" Finally bellowed Hook. The drink of both the whiskey and rum in his condition made them nearly drunk. 'Yes, Sir Color Sergeant! Give me the report. They exchanged weak salutes as Hook spoke. Griggs laughed out loud at the sight of his two friends trying to have some aspect of military decorum.

After a pause, Color Sergeant Hook gave his report. "Wentworth, Pulbah, and Harper are dead Sir! They died defending the tower and were cremated in it. I account for their bodies. My kids are all right as well, but like you, Holmes and Rashid disappeared while fighting with the relief at the front gate last night. For a moment, Cavendish was silent in mourning the loss of his fellow soldiers and companions. The Color sergeant continued reporting. "We are all lucky to be alive, Blood's reinforcements have surrounded the rebels in the hills and reports tell they killed several hundred more as they moved to defend Malakand. God Save our Queen and the souls of our fallen comrades!"

Cavendish hoisted the bottle of rum then asked. "What happened to dear Jenny?" Hook gave a wide smile. "Sir, after we were separated, I joined most of the gang in the tower. Several of the expatriates were also huddled with us. The women were safe, helped us reload, as the savages broke into the bottom of the tower, and also used crude ladders to get in from the outside. On we fought forever it seemed! Miss Jenny was a real hellion and helped me defend the stairs. As the rebels overwhelmed the tower with ladders, we fought them off hand to hand. Wentworth, died fighting the horde as it invaded the first floor.

Harper and Pulbah were killed by effective sniper fire on the top floor. Gladstone expended the rest of his grenades that kept them at bay. We fired directly into the Pashtuns below until the ammo was low and the flames were high. The fire was raging by the time we lowered a rope from the second story window facing outside the walls. The smoke and fire filled this place and area which obscured our escape. All of us got out and crawled into a ravine where we hid. We were lucky that there were no tribesmen anywhere during our escape, they were busy inside.

This is where the battle ended for, we defenders of that tower! "Okay SARG … what of… where is Jenny?" Asked the lieutenant with great concern. Hooky gave a fatherly grin. "That beautiful girl accurately and coldly killed many of them as they were attacking up the stairs. She was good with the pistol and helped reload mine. She escaped and I handed her, along with all the civilians over to a crisp contingent of British reinforcements about an hour ago. She and the rest were taken into protective custody by that large contingent of reinforcements in the south camp. She is very safe!" He handed Ambrose an envelope. "Here is a note from that Jenny lass! She seems a keeper to me sir!" LT. James Ambrose Cavendish read Jenny's note carefully after picking up a photo that fell out to the ground.

My Dear Lt. Ambrose Cavendish.

SGT Hook told me your middle name is Ambrose and I like that name. Thanks to you, my life was saved in this terrible event and the pistol you gave me saved my life! Your Sergeant and his men defended the tower and protected us until this morning. I am very grateful. I am now safely moving away from this terrible place, one that I will never forget nor ever return too. I am returning to England. Life goes on LT. Ambrose Cavendish. When you come home to England please visit me? If I remember we made a date, dinner, at the Majestic Hotel? My address is The Farnsworth Estate, #8 Devonshire Road, London. Please take care of yourself. I have something that belongs to you and I will keep it safe. Also, send me your address and I will be glad to write! I do look forward to seeing you soon. Here is my picture in case you forget what I look like. Very Fondly Yours and with a special kiss!

Lady Jennifer Ruvane Farnsworth

Accompanying the letter and photo was a very pretty and well-perfumed handkerchief in the envelope. Ambrose tucked it with the note and photo into his blouse. The perfumed handkerchief would help mask the stench of so many rotting torn bodies; black with millions of flies in the hot sun. After several more gulps of water and rum, Cavendish and Hook surveyed the piles of bodies as they walked towards the burnt south tower where Griggs stood. Griggs was interested in the enemy snipers and was carefully examining a couple of bodies and holding a sniper rifle. Cavendish and Hook walked around some rubble and bodies and stood next to Griggs.

To everybody's amazement Corporal Holmes emerged through the huge hole in the rubble of the south wall destroyed in the attack. He walked slowly, using his rifle as a crutch. He walked up and gave a salute. All faces were smiling. Cavendish slapped him on the back and Hook plied him with rum. "Kind of late for our morning formation corporal?" said Sergeant Hook with a phony scowl across his battered face. The medium built Welshman looked a little better than the rest and retorted. "Sorry I was not here, I lined up with the wrong formation in this damn smoke SARG!"

He smiled. "But after I set the tower on fire, I was held up for most of the night shooting at Ghazis and their pet savages from outside. So, I spent my time sneaking about killing many armed with those Russian rifles." He held up one of them he used as a crutch. "Good Show son!" smiled Hooky. Holmes looked at Griggs who was holding one of the sniper rifles. Holmes kicked the corpse at Grigg's feet. "This one is your trophy savage, since bagged his buddy on the other side of this tower as he ducked your two shots into my bullet. They were a well-trained team of shooters."

"They killed Pulbah and Harper from this position." Added Hook. Griggs was intently studying the corpse of the dead man before him. He looked very different. He took a long plug of rum that seemed to come from nowhere. There was something very unique about his calm spirit. Griggs now wore the serene innocent look more of a preacher as he examined the corpse. His soft gray eyes, which obscured the tiger within, carefully and in contemplation led the group to find the shooter Holmes had bagged when he had missed. The second sniper was missing the top of his head as they stared at the body. Griggs then spoke to them.

"These snipers we killed are completely different in their looks." Griggs then found a huge satchel charge in a carrying bag around the neck of this second body. He looked at his friends. "These two also planted the charges that destroyed this rear wall as well!" He pointed to the differences as he continued. "These corpses have a bluish mainly green dye on their faces and bodies, weird tattoos, and look how they have filed their teeth into fangs." Griggs went on picking up the rifle next to the body. "Brand new Russian rifles they used with scopes." He passed one to Cavendish who inspected it and fished a load of rounds from the dead man's kit. They all marveled at the strange tattoos covering the bodies as Hooky now labelled as "green devils."

King George had also approached the group and now looked at the bodies as a visible fear crossed his face. He mumbled some inaudible phrase in a whisper not meant for any ears to hear. "What was that George?" Asked Griggs. King George gave an extremely rare look of fear as did Gladstone who was present now. "The demons of Kali, the spawn Asura Raktabija have arisen! This is the proof behind rumors I have heard through the grapevine for months!" "Glad to hear this Mr. King George?" Intoned Color Sergeant Hook with a grimace. The Gurkha composed his thoughts fearfully looking at his comrades. "These are not Islam and why they are with them surprises me!" They wear the blue-green colors of Kali and tattoos of the demon Raktabija! They are Green Demons from Hell!" He continued:

"This cult has not been seen in nearly two-thousand years according to myth. The ancient history of my people tells of the epic conflict between these demons of destruction all across India. It was a union of rajas under the great King Asoka that finally destroyed them during his reign around 229 B.C. The ancient stories and tales of myth relate how these green painted warriors become one with the evil demon spirit of the Kali and produced all manner of horrors." All could see the concern in his face. "Anything else about the nature of these devils George?" queried Griggs.

King George recounted. "Ancient Legends tell of their savagery and cannibalism. They attack in the night, using hideous weapons and methods. It is said that they always used to live off the defeated!" "Living off the stores of defeated enemies is normal Lord George …" as Cavendish tried to lend common sense to the conversation. "No sir, not live off captured stores…for these demons followed the blood drops that created Raktabija … believed that by eating the flesh of their victims, and their brains captures the souls of the slain; that it fuels power via Raktabija directly to Kali! These demons are the mindless walking dead; extensions of the vile will of those that lead this resurrected cult and answer directly to this demon god of ancient Hindu lore!"

King George was staring at the corpse on the ground. "If they are already dead George, we have to kill them twice?" Smiled Hooky as he added his humor. King George had to give a half-smile as Griggs began a closer inspection of the corpses. As he poked the tattoos with his Gurkha knife, Gladstone, who had been quietly watching spoke his words. "These tattoos and markings are evident on the very ancient surviving statues of Kali who was also seen as a female goddess. The rumor of this lore, of evil now have a face in reality, once again, I am afraid!" Everyone grew silent as Griggs looked at and inspected the razor sharp-filed teeth of the slain demon of devil.

Cold sweat ran down the back of Griggs's neck. His sensitivity was alive with a primeval fear he had never felt in all his experiences. He had heard tales these evil myths and fairy tales prevalent around late-night tribal campfires in Northern India over the years. He well remembered the vivid campfire ghost stories of how Kali's demons of Asoka's days prepared its victims for dinner made him grow cold, like a small child left outside in a winter wind without a coat. But this! He touched the sharpened fangs of the dead green devil with his knife. "Fucking Cannibals!" He muttered in half fear. He had heard stories, tales, but this glaring reality? He wondered where they were camped, how many of them existed, and when could the hunt to kill them begin?

Corporal Holmes now spoke up in the fatigued curious silence. "I found a few more blokes like this I killed in the boulders down the path outside near dawn." The group left the camp and walked into the formation of boulders. Bodies littered the ground were the previous night's skirmish had taken place. Holmes took them directly to where the bodies were located. This is where they had nearly been cut off in their retreat to the camp. It appeared these ugly green demons had good military skills? They located three corpses, two with headshots and the other with a shot through the chest. They spent some time analyzing these strangely robed corpses. They found another bag with a large satchel charge in one of the bodies. "Looks like Holmes stopped them from blowing up the main gate!" Added Cavendish.

Again, these bodies resembled the other two in all respects. The robes on these bodies denoted they were some form of leaders or priests. Gladstone produced a small bag with some brown opium cakes in it from one of the bodies. The others had the drug on them also. So, opium was part of the green demon preparation for battle? One question continued to race across the back of Griggs's mind. Why had there been little information of green devils in any intelligence reports or circles anywhere as his tired mind raced to the question that vexed him. "When will we meet again green hounds of hell…when?" The bottle of rum was passed around.

Early on the 30th of July a huge relief force under Major General Bindon Blood continued to reinforce the successful relief of the Malakand siege. By a set of skillful diversions, General Blood's army of sixty-eight hundred Infantry, seven-hundred Lancers, and twenty-four mobile artillery guns seized the high ground catching the remaining savages between two large assault forces. This skillful move resulted in the destruction of nearly all the rebels in the high slopes surrounding the main road into Malakand's south camp. The guns finally fell silent at Malakand by July 31st. The two-hundred-man garrison at Chakadara survived the terrible onslaught killing hundreds of attackers before the siege ended on August 2nd.

The Battles of Malakand and Chakadara rest in the official British military history as incredible Spartan victories. Over ten-thousand Pashtuns and Ghazis were killed in both battles. Over a thousand more tribesmen were killed by General Blood's relief forces. Losses to the British empire were considered very light in comparison. The tactics of effective British firing lines supported by mobile artillery defeated the huge enemy onslaught! The thousands of enemy bodies were unceremoniously cremated on several huge funeral pyres for many days after the battle ended. The fallen British subjects were sent home for burial in England or cremation in their village.

Estimates of total enemy strength in the joint attacks on Chakadara and Malakand were more than fifty thousand effectives. Colonel McRae, 2Lt. Climo both would later receive Victorian Crosses for Bravery... Meiklejohn was the true hero in running the defense of Malakand by all estimates and reports. The Mad Fakir was wounded in the last major attack on the south camp, and his radical Islamic heir apparent to the throne of India was killed. But has history would reveal, this madman and his twisted jihad was not yet finished.

Major General Blood, who understood exactly what the Mad Fakir's intentions were, was creating the Malakand Field Force to pursue and destroy what remained of this massive army. On August 7th, this bloody series of British campaigns commenced against the Islamic rebels in northern India. This included the defeat and destruction of all Afghans forces and Russians involved in supporting this jihad against the British.

The Malakand outpost was left in a shamble after the battle. It needed a complete overhaul and would have to be rebuilt as a professional defensive zone rather than a "Hoge Poge" staging area erected in the wake of the 1895 conflict. A huge ammunition, supply dump, and staging area were to be constructed between Chakadara and Malakand to supply the Malakand Field Force expedition. This expedition began on August 7th and hopefully would be finished by December 6th in 1897.

As the Malakand field force departed, on August 5th Colonel Hillary Wadsworth arrived in Malakand with his large cadre to assume the command, security, and reconstruction operations of Malakand and the huge British supply dumps. He came in on August 4th as the Malakand field Force departed the next day. Wadsworth was a large built man with a round balding head and a rich lambchop style beard on a face only a mother would kiss! He was truly despaired for many reasons by commanders and peers alike! Many wanted to kiss his puckered smart-ass face with a kick or punch! What made him despicable besides his unchecked arrogance was his noble blood that seemed as his mantel of protection from justice! He was reckless and had a scathing black mark on his military record. Under his rather mindless leadership, he had gotten several good soldiers killed as his courts martial read.

His family's noble connections had saved him from being drummed form the army and jail! Even worse was that the army could not get rid of him! His courts martial records were closed and the power of his father Sir Elroy Wadsworth kept his son in the ranks. Instead of being kicked out, he was permanently relegated to non-combat command operations until he could be kicked out! This seemed the safe place to stow this idiot. He was loathed by all the officers and noncoms who knew of this pompous clown who relished wearing the red dress tunic in the field rather than the drab khaki blouse. He also commanded his staff to wear as well.

However, his new position would set Colonel Wadsworth on the path to make his personal mark on British history. A mark that would hopefully fulfill his dream of being a modern Lord Wellington and proving to the general staff that he was the best! All he needed was a cause, an opportunity and a Napoleon to face and destroy in his conquests? Wadsworth had commanded a huge staff of fellow incompetents of his ilk he dredged along with him while jumping from one insignificant command assignment to the next. Besides his large group of lackeys, he also commanded two regiments fresh green auxiliary troops that were assigned to security operations with him.

"Sir Hillary", as he loved to be called by his minions was a determined spoiled glory hunting conniver. He seethed at any chance now to lock horns with the enemy for his greater glory and earn that VC he so cherished! He knew that his chance to fulfill this dream were becoming nearly impossible at this point in his military career. Hillary was dead set to win his place in the annals of British military history in India. Sir Hillary had been hopping mad at being assigned as the rear echelon relief commander at Malakand. This completely removed him from the war! The war was at the Khyber Pass! He envisioned himself, as walking out of India like Lord Wellington walked off the battle field at Waterloo. He would be knighted by that old stuffed bag Queen Victoria! He hated her!

Circumstances were soon to allow "Sir Hillary" to create an opening and enable his warped desire into reality! It all started with a telegram earmarked for General Blood. The northern British city of Chital was under attack now and reinforcements were needed! Confused manipulation of information was immediately on his mind. All was possible as a commander especially if nobody was supervising him! Justification to relieve Chital? But of course! "While the fat cat is away, Sir Hillary will play!" would be his mantra as he launched into his nightly whiskey drunk! Sir Wadsworth's rendezvous with destiny waited north, as determined by an emergency message. The record of his sterling exploits? His grand victory? … would forever be erased in official British military historical records surpassed as rumors to the tabloids and ghost stories to children! Terrible memories of those few who survived them.

CHAPTER TWO
WE MUST SAVE CHITAL!

The turgid black smoke produced by the many distant fires at Chital some kilometers away etched billowing dark silhouettes against the setting sunlight in the blue clear sky. It reminded the indomitable color sergeant of the wafting clouds of locusts he'd observed in the Sudan many years ago. The ominous dark clouds, like the Locusts seemed very out of place and ominous in a peaceful landscape of greenery that surrounded Wadsworth's relief force in this valley. However, was very hot, with an encroaching full complement of humidity to spike the heat into a terrible plight for man and animal. The Battle of Malakand and victory had kept him on a nervous edge of remembrance of his past exploits in Africa. But now his "nervous edge" had grown considerably because of the strange new circumstances he had now found himself in today! He was now part of some haphazard mission to relieve the attack at Chital. But it was his gut feeling, that told him all things were wrong!

There had been little rest since the new commander, of very questionable character, had been assigned to provide "robust" leadership in the reconstruction, clean up, and security at Malakand. This was in support of the gallant expedition and undertaking of the Malakand Field Force under a well-respected General named Bindon Blood. His objective was to capture the Khyber Pass, to cut off, and destroy estimated massive enemy forces still up for a fight. All was well until new orders that allegedly authorized this clown Wadsworth to drop everything and move north to save the besieged town and garrison at Chital under attack now in the wake of these previous two major battles.

Then Hook's mind drifted off to his information about Chital. The official British account of the siege of Chital 1895 would remain as a great victory. This story told of a heavily outnumbered British garrison and their successful defense that spared the city from the attacking rebel tribesmen. A victory against huge odds like the ones just fought in Malakand and Chakadara! However, circumstances went terribly different for Chital during the Sepoy Rebellion of 1857. It was called the Camaiore massacre of 1857, where this city, named Camaiore then, was overrun with most of the British Punjab garrison and townsfolk terribly slain. The city was renamed Chital to obscure this massacre into history.

The sergeant did not dispute the bid to foster relief to this besieged city, that was not what vexed him. It was the very nature of who was being dispatched! Why was Blood not sending forces to do this? He was in position to do this! Hooky puffed on his pipe as he wondered of the fate of Chital in 1897? It was defended by a crack regiment of the 14th Punjab infantry. Victory or a repeat of 1857? He could smell the wafting billowing smoke which permeated the valley. He clearly smelled burning wood but it also was laced with a slight tinge of burning flesh. It reminded him distantly of the smell from the hospital that burned to the ground at Rorke's Drift in the latter part of that famous battle. He could only save so many wounded soldiers from it! Leaving them to burn was the deepest of his dark memories!

One never forgot the smell of burning flesh! But in his heart, he sensed something big was amiss with everything here. He took a nice plug from one of the several bottles of rum he liberated by his absconding them from the detritus of Malakand. Hook wiped running sweat from his brow as he took another drink of rum. The rugged natural beauty of northern India with its tribes of unkempt natives stood on one hand, as compared to the impeccably dressed "poppycock" and downright arrogance of Colonel Hillary Wadsworth on the other. It was not just the impeccable dress of Colonel Wadsworth displayed in this untamed and uncaring environment. It was his strange protocol in abandoning a critical supply dump to galvanize a hasty relief quest at Chital?

Cavendish felt the same way with reason. He looked around and studied his current plight. If he had not hotly defended Cavendish in that spat with Wadsworth at Malakand he would be riding with his scouts now. Wadsworth wildly jumped on him for defending Cavendish's request to visit Blood since there seemed to be grave problems with the telegram communications. It was when he offered to personally ride to question General Blood on the obvious validity if this plan. His request was vehemently denied by this clown of a colonel who became unhinged. He coldly ordered him to join his personal staff as they moved on Chital as he yelled; "Never doubt my legal orders or I will have you shot you upstart!" Where Wadsworth's last kindly words to him!

The color sergeant objected to this threat and the conversation became ugly at best! Hooky has put under some sort of house arrest and was now nothing more than Wadsworth's prisoner, or more like a "tag along" house pet! However, Hook was appalled as he witnessed the idiot commander muster his relief force in extreme comic disorganization as they marched out of Malakand. Comedy would soon turn to tragedy was his estimate! Most of the veteran troops had been ordered to remain at Malakand at the angry insistence of LTC McRae who also had been kept under close observation by the colonel's minions or lackeys to give a better description. What was this Wadsworth hiding seemed to dominate Cavendish's thoughts?

It appeared to Lieutenant Cavendish that the preciseness of Wadsworth's pompous demeanor and absolute authority vested by new orders were masking something. He was, for all reasons, never to be trusted! He has not just hated by the troops and officers forced to serve under him, but would have been a convicted war criminal if his powerful noble father had not put pressure on the courts! Wadsworth was fifty-one years of age, and to great annoyance kept his lips usually pursed as he loved to answer with his eyes in conversation. He once had been a strong and stout man in his youth, but in his later years had let himself go. His stoutness was now sort of a roly-poly rounded look, which included a bulging stomach distressing the buttons on the red Army dress tunic he wore as a silent accent to his overt regal ego.

Poor Hooky cringed at his image when he again reviewed his past history. Like the commanders who underestimated the Zulus at Isandlwana, "Old Waddy or Wad" as coined by the large rough sergeant, could create a new Isandlwana for the British soldier in 1897 if a dire situation presented itself! The contrast of Wadsworth's poppycock image beneath the distant dark spiraling clouds emanating from the remains of Chital sniffed of foreboding dark doom. The veteran color sergeant also abhorred the gaggle of staff 'suck ups" who stuck close to him in some form of hero worship! These clowns even dressed in red like Old Wad and danced about surrounding him like dilly dolly little puppets or flies on the carcass of a dead animal…or more succinctly, on a pile of shit!

Hook noticed one tactical error he compared to the fate of the British 24th! Wadsworth had not posted any pickets to guard his camp! It was like a fucking Sunday picnic in Hyde Park in those plains in Africa as a well-honed Zulu army was creeping in for the slaughter! Then, suddenly and without any warning, thousands of screaming Zulus emerged from well concealed positions, that a good exterior security element would have revealed! The British 24th were slaughtered nearly to a man. The Zulus were greatly underestimated by the cocky British, for the 'Queen's Own" was the best of the best! Now he viewed another fine example of the "Queen's Own!"

What was the composition of Colonel Wadsworth's relief force? He had taken both is auxiliary units which were small battalion size consisting of about five hundred troops. They were trained and assigned for security operations and not combat! He had about a hundred lancers mixed with another forty odd mounted scouts. Except for one other veteran light regiment and the artillery people, the bulk of his regiment at hand were untested and poorly trained for field operations. This relief force totaled about eight hundred effectives. Hooky knew Blood well enough to know that he would never send a force like this into unknown combat!

According to LTC McRae, the initial message that fell into Wadsworth's hands was a distress telegram sent from Calcutta via Chital Instructing Blood to send reinforcements immediately to the besieged city. Chital, had strangely not been attacked during the uprising and was secure. This attack which came late was strange indeed since the Mad Fakir's army were fighting in the northwest region. Who was attacking them? The British expeditionary force fighting them was well northwest of this city outpost but could have wheeled around it's uncommitted units at the time and made it to Chital in short order according to Cavendish. The colonel however, collected this telegram and several more sent directly to Malakand. Wadsworth dawdled during this crucial time then sent a telegram back stating that in the absence of Blood, he would comply with the order. In effect, it could have sounded fairly plausible. But who would now secure Malakand? This was when the communication problems began.

Then Colonel Wadsworth announced that he had been instructed by higher headquarters to assemble a relief force to invest Chital. The question of who had actually approved Wadsworth's request of permission to mount a relief mission was shared by both Cavendish and McRae. Then all hell broke loose between these parties as the colonel began quickly stripping the outpost of security elements to be included in his relief force. What chain of command approved this questioned McRae? It could not be Blood or anybody in his chain of command!

However, unbeknownst to the lieutenant and McRae, Wadsworth had secretly secured validity of his request to relieve Chital completely outside Blood's official channels. He had referred his request outside of regular military channels to one of his buddies high up in a diplomatic post in an adjacent command section in New Delhi. This highborn butt buddy of "Old Waddy" was the originator and not General Blood! In simple terms, this approved request was bogus. Wadsworth was not concerned about this if exposed. He would just blame his buddy and play stupid! Besides, off the hook once meant he could get off twice! He wanted his VC!

Cavendish had been caught by Old Wad's boys who guarded the telegraph. He and his scouts were put under a sort of house arrest by the snooping muscle of the colonel's staff until the assembled command of Wadsworth's group could leave. LTC McRae and his support staff was also sequestered away during this time under constant watch. Lieutenant Cavendish was then sent north with his scouts and several of Sir Hillary Wadsworth's trusted staff lackeys to make sure the scouts did not drift from their mission into Blood's camp. General Blood was kept completely in the dark about Chital and Wadsworth until later.

The telegrams from Chital abruptly ceased on the third day as this relief moved out of Malakand. Wadsworth now had a free hand to pursue his glory as long as Blood did not catch up with him! When McRae finally got to the telegraph, it had been destroyed by fire the night before Wadsworth departed with his relief force. The lieutenant and his men were the forward scouting party well in front of the disorganized main body. Cavendish, angry as hell, had conveyed the whole story to his men in private just before they were ordered to scout north.

Colonel Wadsworth's attitude towards the enemy was that of a fox hunt with his troops being the dogs chasing the elusive foxes! However, he had not seen the real face of the fox. He had simply ignored the story of the size of the Pashtun attack on Malakand. But Old Wad, in his complete pompous stupidity had failed to understand the real nature of what he was hunting. This was a mysterious extremely large dangerous fox covered in blueish-green dye! Wadsworth had been driving his "dogs" ruthlessly for two days and nights up a mostly good road northwest towards beleaguered Chital to the north.

Lieutenant Cavendish had been sending back couriers with reports routinely. Sergeant Hook was missed on this ride. He was Wad's "special pet" which brought laughter among the scouts! They had encountered only visual contact with the tribesmen but no attacks. "There was nothing significant!" read the simple report. Towards the smoking caldron of Chital ambled the British expedition facing unknown odds to encamp several miles from it. Why wasn't Wadsworth pushing on wondered Hook? This seemed to remind him of the African world in chills of remembrance when the 24th marched through the huge open savannahs in Africa. The 24th was swallowed up nearly whole as this relief army would be swallowed up if they faced a good enemy! Hook took a larger plug of Rum, and toasted his dead comrades. He blessed the Muslims for being non-drinkers and the well-stocked rum supply in the ransacked officer's club at Malakand and smoked his pipe now.

He mused with a smile that he had been such a young upstart in 1879. He chose to be conscripted into the army rather than a long prison sentence from a variety of criminal convictions mustered from his violent and troubled youth in 1877. Young Hooky was full of life and fire then. "Join the army for six years and work off your twenty-year sentence of hard labor Mr. Hook?" Asked the old salty judge, looking more dead than alive in his powdered wig and black gown in the immaculate clean wood polished courtroom. He smiled in remembrance at that one. "See the world and serve the Queen Hook! Be a man!" He agreed with a wide smile on his clean-shaven baby face. The ghoulish judge smiled back from his severely wrinkled face revealing deeply yellowed rotting teeth.

Hook mused. Service to the "Queen" eventually placed him with Her Majesty's Royal Engineers with a British field army in some forlorn place called Rorke's Drift. He was just a young oversized brat conscript with an unruly attitude. "See the world son and serve the Queen!" in the middle of nowhere mused Hook! Then it was abject fear that transcended all fear after he learned of the slaughter of the 24th at Isandlwana! Many of his comrades were dead, all dead and several thousand Zulus were headed for the drift to kill him! It was the fear of being out in unknown terrain, alone, no reinforcements, and facing some enemy thousands stronger than you. This expedition of Poppycock Wadsworth was bearing the same deadly resemblance…if this relief was unsuccessful! After all, "1879 reversed is 1897!"

He could never forget that moment the Zulus appeared on the hills around Rorke's Drift. They now came for them, many wearing the red tunics of the deceased British soldiers, drunk with the slaughter and ready to destroy their small contingent of barely over one-hundred troops! Then came the Zulus, like the Pashtuns, thousands of them! Then it seemed everything became a blur. The battle at "The Drift' had never left him…would never! He surmised many times in a drunken stupor…. that he had left his soul at the drift! Tears ran down his face as he now saw the faces of his comrades who he could not save, burned alive in the hospital.

How he frantically dug escape holes through the walls with his bayonet so they could exit! The army chaplain told him in the aftermath, "Son, one never gets over the death of someone you love. You learn to live with it!" His comrades were his family. Hook had been awarded the Victorian Cross for bravery, for heroism, and saving many lives from the burning hospital and elsewhere in the battle. He was no hero, but was trying to save his buddies.

Digging through hospital walls with his bayonet, creating holes to pull sick and wounded patients out and killing Zulus mainly with his bayonet, and bare hands as he moved several wounded from room to room with the ferocious Zulus on his tail the whole way! In Hook's eyes, anyone who had fought in that near fatal disaster deserved the Victorian Cross. He wore this medal always and proudly for two reasons. First of all, he wore it to honor all his comrades who died at the drift. He also wore it as his personal good luck charm.

He rubbed his VC on his chest. He had hidden it in his tunic at Malakand so he would not lose it. But again, it adorned the chest of his new khaki uniform. This good luck charm was his magical bond with his deceased comrades and the past; of escaping death, … living proof! The dangerous unknown faced him again. Yet it was the terrible events at Rorke's drift and his decorated hero status that compelled him to stay in, to be a lifer of all things! It was this choice that later promoted and transformed him to the famous Color Sergeant Hook.

But the shadow over his current circumstance pulled him back, like an organism struggling to understand its existence, and especially it's needs to survive in the environment it had landed. His focus fell back into the present predicament. He entertained himself as he viewed "Poppycock" Wadsworth having a spot of early morning tea with his more important cronies… as if he was sitting in Trafalgar Square at teatime! He looked over to where Hook was slouched. "A spot of tea Sergeant?" He asked his pet hostage. This clown was exhibiting such cocky arrogance in his voice. Like he was a real soldier like MG Blood! Hook detested most officers; the bad ones seemed to use men's lives as fish bait! But there were a few good ones, not many in his estimate, but good ones like Lieutenant Chard his commander and VC winner at the Drift, LTC McRae, BG Blood, and especially LT Cavendish. They were true leaders, who inspired their men to fight and were never afraid to get their hands dirty. Their men came first, not medals or glory, or promotions!

He looked at Wadsworth with his salty grin. "No thanks sir, but I would rather take a long reflective shit!" Wadsworth winced. Hook smiled at his desired effect. Cavendish would be along soon with his report and would hopefully liberate the venerable color-sergeant from the fond clutches of this asshole, hopefully! Hook laughed as he thought. "If he were a Bull dog he would piss on Wad's leg, and as he shook off the piss, would then snaggle-bite him in the balls. He took a stroll away from the tent.

Cavendish sat at the ransacked office behind a disheveled desk in the remains of the Counsel-general's office. The view of the slain in the adjacent dining room had appalled him to the soul. He had closed the doors. What remained of Chital was terrible in all respects! This once peaceful thriving town had been turned into a smashed gruesome gallery of horrors! The city had been destroyed as fires continued burning in the town behind the administration building where he sat. Any civilized aspect had been erased in this violent orgy of destruction. The remains of dead soldiers and citizens found was horrible since they had been so mutilated that even the toughest combat vet was sickened to his soul. It seemed that most of the dead had been savagely devoured!

Griggs, Holmes, and Rashid sat in arm chairs on the other side of the cluttered desk across from Ambrose. King George and Gladstone stood by the entrance door, which had been smashed to pieces. The ransacked room professed dark pools of sticky blood across the floor. Nobody talked or looked around since they had seen what was left in the dining room. All three were lost in the terrible spectacle they had witnessed. Griggs walked over and looked in some cabinets. His search finally produced an unmolested bottle of whiskey. He opened it, took a plug, and simply passed it around…

There was more silence then Griggs spoke… "This is the thing nightmares are made of sir! It seems this nightmare was created by the green demons rather than Pashtuns this time!"

More silence…then Cavendish spoke… His hands were shaking, as he belted down the warm powerful drink from the bottle, gave it to Holmes, and back to Griggs who had located another bottle. Cavendish weakly smiled "I have never drunk so much in my life as I have in the last fortnight!" Griggs smiled "tis a mortal wound of combat my friend" and toasted the air as he finished his second drink from the bottle. Cavendish then began uttering weak questions to nobody in particular, almost like a child randomly asking his mother irrelevant questions. All the terrible combat of the recent past had scarred all of them, but this spectacle cast them all into a new ghastly reality.

The horror was enough, but the terror garnered from this whole scene produced a collective deep fear. Each man asked themselves introspectively "What creatures could do this? What savage monsters were waiting to do this to us?" According to current spot reports, the population had been brutally slaughtered along with the 14th Punjab Regiment that garrisoned this town outpost. Many of this population was also missing. Cavendish's brain was inundated with some basic questions regarding the missing people. Did they escape into the jungle, or down the river? Were they captured? What happened to them? Then his mind snapped to the next obvious question. What in Hades are these green devils? He had seen many of their bodies strewn around outside.

He broke the silence with his next thought. "This was not an attack by Pashtun forces or anything related to the Mad Fakir! This was the ritualistic torture and hideous slaughter of many innocents by something totally different indeed!" There was a continued muted silence, for all were concentrating on this point. Holmes added in weak tones. "It was a fucking feast… these buggers are cannibals!" They passed the whiskey until the bottle was gone then Griggs produced another.…Being drunk was a good remedy now so it seemed, but everybody knew they could not afford to be drunk now. These monsters were out there and rest assuredly could come back at any time

From his careful analysis of the city battlefield, the 14th Punjab's had superbly defended the city after the initial attacks. From the hundreds of bullet dings in the front of the concrete building it was obvious to him that the attackers possessed many rifles and as the garrison was slowly reduced by the massed rifle fire. Then they were overwhelmed in furious hand-to-hand combat. Indications were that most of the defenders never made it to their final defenses inside the buildings. They had been wiped out fighting in their primary fighting positions. Then the city was overwhelmed, sacked, set on fire…then, the unimaginable manifested!

Chital was the Battle of Malakand gone badly against demons; these green devils! Everybody present was lost for words until a rather nervous lancer entered the room and snapped to attention. He looked in horror at the spectacle at a partially opened door in the dining room. "Sir!" the veteran Lancer began, "What are your orders?" The Lancer was staring at Cavendish in primeval terror. Griggs muttered an "at ease!" and let the soldier take a plug from the whiskey…there was a pause. "Did you find anyone alive corporal?" Interjected the lieutenant. "No sir! From what we could find" … he wavered… "we checked up and down the river…nothing sir except the mangled corpses of less than twenty, all floating in the river. It seems that they had tried to escape by small boats.

Griggs asked. "You think there were twenty bodies corporal?" The lancer stared at him. "Many body parts sirs." Seeing the fear and fatigue in the Lancer's face Cavendish ordered him to sit and to join them. The lancer sat down next to Griggs who supplied him with more spirits…. he was thankful to this order. "These fucking demons!" yelled the lieutenant enraged. "Where in blazes did, they come from in such numbers? How did our intelligence miss them?" Griggs looked across at him. "Major Nephew had heard of this Kali but never a horde of green devils ever! Until we found those strange green dyed bodies at Malakand, we had proof they really existed." Cavendish then added after a minute of silence. "How many thousands of these green monsters are watching us now?"

Cavendish ordered Griggs and five other scouts to ride to Wadsworth's relief encampment and break the terrible news, and send reinforcements immediately. How could forty men hold off any mass attack? He ordered the remainder of his scouts to create a tight defense in the main building and guessed that this huge stone monolith had seemed unburnable to the devils. This concrete administration building was a solid structure and fields of fire could initiate from all four sides. He further instructed his men to create huge bonfires in front of their positions to foster a better view of the attackers by the fires. Griggs and company left in haste.

Rashid remained in this huge disheveled office and held his head in his hands. Lieutenant Cavendish looked his way and spoke; "What is with this cult, these green creature-people Rashid? Lord George had made comments about some ancient cult earlier." Rashid was slow to speak; "Sir, this seems as a horrible myth come true, and a terrible one! It is my belief that these seemingly invisible green devils are somehow using our opposition as a tool to gain their lasting prominence and superiority down the line. In ancient myth, it was this cult that effectively infiltrated factions seeking to overthrow the established rule under Asoka the "King of Kings!" long ago sahib! Their attack on Chital was probably their part of the bargain in this uprising. I think they have greatly infiltrated the ranks of the Mad Fakir. Like the tales of old, this cult was invisible until they attacked Asoka, but he was ready for them. The cult was destroyed! Look how invisible they have been to our intelligence people; to Nephew of all people?" He paused then looked at the lieutenant.

"These devils will use these groups to gain absolute power over the Jihadists, then cast them out, convert them, or destroy them. This cult is probably feeding the collective hate into all these groups who want to bring British occupation to an end. We now have witnessed in Chital, their power and terror...their spectacle of destruction, horror; madness completely beyond civilization! Until now!" He paused and took a drink of tepid water from his canteen then continued, "This primal cult is very ancient and according to myths cursed these lands in dark ages long before the Aryans came here. They have returned sir to eat our souls! This war against the British is a perfect set up for the reemergence of Kali my friend." Cavendish lit a cigarette then asked. "Eating souls Rashid? King George said the same thing."

The lieutenant's civilized mind was in a quandary. "Sahib, legend states, that they are devout cannibals...they horribly torture their victims as ritual to charge up their souls, before they eat them... they eat the brain first, to digest a victim's soul in ritual then devour the rest of the body as food! Look around you sir? Their hideous work seems to be everywhere here as I carefully checked a few remains!" Cavendish understood now.... the horrible specter of the remains with missing body parts, cracked open skulls, the burnt offerings. They would later find a massed grave of dead devils less than a mile from the front of the town.

He remembered the face of one of these green painted savages...ugly crazy stare, eyes wide open, and his teeth filed into sharp points...The rear part of this creature's head was blown off with a neat bullet hole through his forehead. I very sharp strangely twisted sword lay next to it. It had been a good shot! He was shaking again...filled with an eerie feeling. He looked over to Rashid. His guide had tears running down his face, as the foreboding of a combat veteran sensing terror rather than combat. His stare was focused on this deep horror, a stark reminder to Cavendish, which he would have to face... soon. Both men knew nothing about who led these monsters yet.

Mister Griggs and company rode at a fast pace in the dark hot and dusty night on the road that connected Chital to the world. Upon their arrival at the encampment, his group was shocked at the laxness as they were never challenged by any sentries on the outskirts! It seemed there were none. They rode into the center of the camp where nobody seemed concerned about the enemy. His ride back had taken them nearly an hour. Cavendish was left in a dangerous situation. They dismounted near the command tent where he ordered his men to water and feed their horses. The tall lanky veteran walked to the front of the command tent and announced to the sentry his presence. It had been the first one he had seen!

If these troops had seen what his eyes had witnessed, they would be running scared for mommy! Many of Wadsworth's staff lounged around inside the front of the tent like it was the end of some training exercise. A bottle of whiskey was being passed. He was hearing yelling at the far end of the tent in another section. The voice sounded very familiar and it was shouting at Wadsworth, who was vainly deflecting it retorting pompous remarks. He smiled at the exchange as his presence was announced to the colonel. The yelling ceased as he was told to wait outside of the large white canvass field tent. As Griggs was walking over to the shade towards his group the familiar face of Color Sergeant Hook seemed to pop into view by a large shade tree. It was amazing how cooler a simple shade tree was even at night.

"What's up Mr. Griggs? Does the lieutenant need me to save him yet?" Hook interjected as he was smiling and holding out a bottle of rum. Griggs took a sip then passed it to his troops. He then returned the smile. "Not yet boyo, but soon, I fear!" Hook smiled back and asked the obvious question. "What is going on in Chital Mister?" Griggs stared at him. "The things that nightmares are made of my darling friend. Chital is a prime example of what happens if a British controlled town falls to green savages of yore. It was a massacre worse than 1857, the most terrible one I have ever witnessed, I fear! Between you and me…we are in for it now! From what I saw, these green monsters could be ready to attack now from everywhere for we seem to be in grave danger as I speak!"

Griggs retorted before Hook could reply. "What in "Great Caesar's Ghost" is going on in the tent Hooky?" The color sergeant gave a fond deep smile across his rugged face. "That darling Major Tiberius Nephew just seemed to pop out of nowhere and is crawling up Old Wad's ass with a pitchfork now." Griggs laughed out loud." Since the very appearance of Nephew in this mood reminded Hook of the handsome villain in the live vaudeville-like shows back in England. He had dark greased hair with a widows-peak, and a long black moustache that adorned his stone face. Then there was the hypnotic gaze of the steel blue penetrating eyes of Tiberius. "The Major came alone." added Hook. "…and is climbing all over our fearless "poppycock" leader about abandoning Malakand with orders that appear to be dubious at best!"

"What in the stars Hooky; dubious orders?" replied Griggs. Sergeant Alfred Hook became serious. "From what I have been listening to so far, is Wadsworth had no official orders via General Blood to do "Jack Shit!" That the orders he received to relieve Chital came from somewhere else in another chain of command. The gist of this argument surrounds the point that this strange order is considered valid until the originator of it can be located!" Hook continued, "From what that darling Major Nephew was saying, or yelling out, is that BG Blood would have been able to send a relief force to relieve the siege on Chital several days ago while the town was still holding off the attack! He is wide-eyed pissed off!

Blood had been left in the dark by the obscured message traffic from Chital for reasons unknown at this point. It is rumored that Wadsworth was directly responsible for this! Evidently, after McRae sent a courier telling of this communication mess it was too late. General Blood's boys had become heavily engaged in combat as his columns had caught up with massed enemy. He is now involved in a huge series of skirmishes and battles in support and coordination with all his Brigades. So, guess what? Blood now cannot spare anybody at the critical time to come to the immediate rescue of Chital as he could have days ago. Until he learns of the exact size of the enemy he faces, he is stuck!"

Mister Griggs took a plug of rum and let Hook's words seep into his brain. "We also have a problem with the size of the enemy Hooky! Blood may not be able to save our asses now as well; if what destroyed Chital is moving on this jolly party now! At this point, we very well may already be in a huge trap surrounded by thousands of hungry green demons in a large trap old chap! We also cannot forget all the thousands of Pashtuns roaming about either! Chital may be the bait!" Hook took another plug of rum as it was passed back around to the lancers as they listened to the conversation. Hook commented "Wadsworth has contrived all of this reckless fanfare I am afraid." Griggs nodded his head and elaborated.

"Chital was destroyed by monsters in unspeakable fashion. I have never seen the likes of it ever in my life! Hooky…if we were simply fighting Russian and Afghan backed Pashtuns like Malakand, I would be overjoyed. Things are different now I am afraid. We seem to be facing extremely sinister, unknown, and dangerous forces; ones that nobody in the British high command or intelligence have even seen or known about … it seems to defy imagination at this point. You should have seen what we…" He abruptly stopped as his mind crossed over the remains of Chital.

Hook looked into Griggs strained face and got the picture clearly as the rum was passed again. At that moment, a yell came from the command tent for Griggs as Hook followed him into the command tent. Griggs presented himself in front of Colonel Wadsworth and Major Nephew and abruptly came to attention and saluted. "Sergeant Major Griggs Reporting from Chital Sir!" Major Nephew sat in a chair, across a table to the side of "Old Wad" as he had been nicknamed by many. It was clear to see that the major was extremely vexed and was drumming his fingers on a table. His deep blue eyes flickered with anger and his hair was tousled in contrast to his small well-cropped moustache. He was the master villain today. A slight breeze came through the flaps in the large white command tent.

Major Nephew, unnerved at the idiot Wadsworth's rancor, began noticing the rare extreme nervousness in Griggs's demeanor…something was not right in the eyes, fear he saw from a Noncom who was a legend for his bravery under fire; who literally lived amongst situations where fear was a constant companion. He and Griggs had worked together many times in the past and had formed a tight bond in the dangers they had faced. He was one of the only others he welcomed on his obscure independent operations.

"Old Wad" haughtily asked "I thought Cavendish was to give this report to me personally Griggs? I demanded it!" "Sir" replied the sweat soaked senior scout covered in a pasty dust. "Because of the extenuating and unusual terrible nature of what was found in Chital, Lieutenant Cavendish chose to stay and command the remaining forty odd lancers and scouts. There is a great concern of renewed attacks by the…the enemy sir!" Colonel Wadsworth yelled back. "I am sure the 14th Punjab's and their British officers can handle any renewed attacks! Well Griggs!"

The tall NCO stared hard at the colonel. "I think they would offer excellent defense if any of them were alive sir! Chital has been wiped off the map and now is the carnival of nightmares and death sir!" Griggs was angry and his voice raised several octaves. Lieutenant Cavendish told me to tell you he requests a large contingent of reinforcements to come immediately without delay. If they attack now, they could be …" "Be what! Wiped out by the natives?" interjected Old Wad not relinquishing to the terrible news. Griggs held his ground and retorted. "These were not Pashtuns who attacked, but a horde of green dyed warriors feared to be a long dead cult!" Old Wad exploded. "Green natives Griggs? Maybe they are moon men or Martians!"

Wadsworth pompously stood in front of Griggs with his hands on his waists as his unbuttoned red tunic opened. "What else besides green Martians can you tell me?" Griggs shuffled and became irritated as he began his report gazing through the eyes of Wadsworth. "After what appeared to be a short but brilliant defense at Chital, I sadly announce that the garrison was wiped out and the city overrun. The dead were brutally killed, mangled, and in many cases feasted upon sir! We suspect many civilians are missing, presumed captured as hostages. These attackers seemed well organized and a very effective military force to defeat the 14th! The bodies we found were dyed green and covered in tattoos. Their teeth were filed like fangs…and…"

He stopped talking. His eyes wandered and his face became flushed… He retorted again," LT. Cavendish requests immediate reinforcements to bolster his light defense in case of counter attack by these savages; green devil's sir! He requests a hundred lancers and two batteries of light artillery tonight! He fears an attack at any time and thinks this whole command may already be in a giant trap." Colonel Wadsworth snapped at him. "Who does this "whipper snapper" think he is in telling me what I should do!?" He gave an evil smile.

"We shall see about reinforcements tomorrow when my column arrives there! You go and tell Cavendish that I want reconnaissance performed to the north of Chital tonight!" "Sir!' butted in the irritated sergeant, "It was a huge enemy force of these devils you call "moon men" that defeated a veteran regiment of over five hundred Punjab's! There is evidence that they were armed with new Russian rifles! The scouts have few men to even think about stopping an attack like this one much less to scout tonight!"

Wadsworth ignored his comment and yelled, "I want reconnaissance north of Chital!" "Tonight? Griggs saw Wadsworth for what he was, a pompous idiot who was endangering the lives of several hundred soldiers of the British empire. He unloaded his frustration and anger at this man. "Reconnaissance operations conducted north of the city in the dark with a total force of forty-five lightly armed scouts on hand? with no tangible rear area support? This is insane! Sir… I…" "Yes Griggs, tonight, now and I hold you in contempt of a lawful order in combat! Get out of my sight!" Major Nephew had had enough of this idiot Wadsworth! He sharply interjected as he stood." I act in the name of General Blood colonel as I already told you! You will comply with Griggs's request now!

The only reason you have not been relieved is the general does not know if you were granted a lawful order or not at this point in time. McRae seems to think all of this is crap and a result of your bogus fabrication to get into combat! There is no time for your arrogant banter because we are facing a new enemy of unknown size and ability if you can figure this out yet! What is wrong with this picture Colonel Wadsworth? Chital has been wiped off the map, so there is no relief operation left! As I told you when I first arrived! Blood had sent me to inform you to get to Chital as your orders read and stay put. Blood obviously does not know of this massacre yet! So, this is where we are going and to stay put! And stay put until General Blood gets his hands on you and the bottom of this mess!"

Wadsworth began to stammer and mumble off confusing babble back at Nephew. Old Wad needed a stiff drink of the cheap whiskey to calm him now! Major exploded and kicked the table in front of him over. The lanterns within the tent swayed and flickered against the dark shadows. "Listen to me Colonel Hillary Wadsworth! I command you to send a relief force to Chital "ASAP" which means right fucking now! Griggs is right, we do not know what is out there watching or assembling against us!" Nephew looked at the sergeant-major. "Take what the lieutenant requested per General Blood and not this colonel!" Then he looked at Colonel Wadsworth. Get your fucking bugler sounding the colors and put this force on combat alert now! Your security here is shit!"

Nephew looked at the dozen or so staff lackeys of Wadsworth now standing now. "I order you to get out there and get this force ready for war now!" He then chased them out of the tent kicking a couple of slow ones hard in their asses. Then Major Nephew got in Wadsworth's face nose to nose now. "Sending good men to the slaughter again colonel?" Wadsworth winced at the verbal barb launched by the major as the memory of his near courts martial two years ago, resonated through his brain. The Major was seething...He and Wadsworth were hated rivals. The Major had been a key witness on the board that court martialed him until his noble father and friends saved his ass! This arrogant idiot had cost the lives of several good men in another fruitless unauthorized mission. Several had been personal friends of Tiberius. The major spoke icily now:

"You are now under serious inquiry colonel! I told you, that any relief force sent by MG Blood is not forthcoming now due to widespread military actions of the Malakand Field Force! The only thing that is saving your ass is that you are, for strange reasons, here in place of the relief force MG Blood could not send because of some magic communication problems between Blood from Chital. I am the "hand" of the general so be clear on this! My orders to you from General Blood are simple; that you will go no further north than Chital! NO further north! ...By orders of the Commander of all British-Indian Forces Sir Bindon Blood! You will wait until he catches up with you!" Major Nephew continued as the inflection in his voice rose like a volcano exploding. "I think you are responsible for this message fuck up and this massacre colonel! By Jove! Do you realize that even the city of Chital may be a huge trap right now as Griggs stated? This expedition of yours could be surrounded right now by thousands of these green killers! How would you even know this you fool...?

Your intelligence on enemy dispositions in this area does not exist since you ordered your security away to the doomed city! In my journey here I saw many hill tribesmen spread out in groups behind you on my path here. Do you know that I rode right up to your tent from a side trail with no one challenging me???? You lead a gaggle of sitting ducks Colonel! See the picture?" The sound of a bugle suddenly began to blare in the night. Major Nephew stared at a rather plump officer standing in the corner. He was a major as well. He looked at him hard. "Who are you, my kind equal?" The officer stammered nervously.

"I am Major Pillroy the operations officer." Nephew looked at Griggs.

"Tell Pillroy what you want for this reinforcement it now!" Griggs smiled at his old friend. "Yes sir!" Both soldiers walked out of the tent. Nephew stared at his quarry. "Get these troops in Chital immediately, break camp in the next couple of hours colonel and set up a defense! So, your force we will not be ambushed lollygagging and wiped out on this road! .... Now damnit, do something and do it now before we are all dead...NOW SIR!!!! Or else!"

A bullet between Old Wad's eyes made Nephew grimace a smile. Colonel Wadsworth exhibited an aghast look, and his pompous counter rant now erupted. "How dare you disrespect my rank and command in this manner? Who do you think you are Major? A major is going to relieve a colonel in combat with no written order to do so?" He laughed and looked at the three of his officers left sitting in the room. "Who is going to arrest me and relieve me little Major Nephew?" The taunt was obvious. Nephew gave and evil smirk and his eyes flashed; "Why Colonel Wadsworth, remember that I am the lapdog of MG Blood.... and when I give an order, I am speaking directly from him!"

He held up the letter Blood had given him authorizing his power. Do you want to read this? Sorry I forgot to show it to you when I arrived! Please read the document before this "lapdog" bites you in your sorry ass at your next and final courts martial ... if we get out of this alive!" The fiery Nephew the villain was at full tilt now. Major Nephew gave his favorite evil smile and meant it! "Old Wad" rightly had an internal fear of Nephew. His testimony at his last courts martial was so detailed, well delivered, and damming in all respects, that it was a key nail in the grave of his conviction. Then daddy Elroy saved his ass just like he would do again this time!

The colonel studied this medium built broad-shouldered Welshman whose dark blue eyes turned cold black when enraged…like a mongoose stalking a cobra. Nephew was only reinforcing his point, as he unbuttoned the top button on his khaki blouse…He knew this whole debacle the colonel had cursed on his troops and the command was far from over. It was only beginning. So, he stood facing Wadsworth fingering his service pistol. I bullet in the head of this pompous jerk would be a "feel good" moment! "Major Nephew glowered, refused to salute, turned and left storming from the large white canvas tent.

Griggs and Pillroy stood outside the tent as Hook joined them. All his requests to the rather rotund nervous major were finished as he wanted them assembled in minutes. He was requisitioning seventy-five lancers and two batteries of light artillery. Pillroy nodded and wandered or waddled away to tell his commander. Sergeant Hook smiled at Griggs, winked and walked away. Plump Pillroy, called by many, returned shortly from Wadsworth. The artillery was denied! As they walked away Major Nephew appeared and slapped Griggs on the back and gave him a warm smile as they walked to where the other scouts stood under a nearby tree.

"Looks like fate has really put us together in the fire on this one Mr. Griggs!" commented Nephew. Griggs smiled back and replied, "Can't think of anybody else I want with me now Sir and we have the "famous" Sergeant Hook in tow as well!" "I sense that we are in some very deep shit I am afraid!" Griggs knew Hooky was up to something good and without comment introduced the famous Color Sergeant Hook to Major Nephew, who replied. "My pleasure Sir, I shake the hand of a living legend and have heard many great stories about you!" Nephew smiled as he extended his hand. "Same to you, color sergeant, your actions at Rorke's Drift are legendary and classroom lore in all respects!" "I'll drink to that Sir!" added Hook as he pulled out a bottle of rum from his saddle, causing a few well-deserved laughs.

"Where did you find rum in this world of whiskey Hook?" He smiled at the major. "I liberated the destroyed officer's bar in the battle at south camp in Malakand sir and was awarded several bottles for my heroism!" Nephew laughed along with Griggs. The bottle was passed as Griggs asked his friend. "Major? I saw you fingering your sidearm in the tent." Nephew gave a grin. "I would love to put a bullet in his fucking head Mr. Griggs, but I want to save him for the wrath of Blood!" They all laughed.

Griggs was able to give them a detailed and depressing overview of the carnage at Chital. He added that no survivors had been found and many inhabitants were missing he feared. They watched as the lancers were mustered on the road. Even their horses were nervous as they sensed a foreboding terror down the road. In the quiet of his tent alone for now, Colonel Wadsworth nervously fingered the letter sent by General Blood via the Major. He prayed that the report on the massacre at Chital was overstated, since the manipulation of the message traffic was a direct result of him, and he was responsible for the delay of Blood's reinforcements. He gulped down whiskey from the bottle as he knew he was directly responsible for the carnage at Chital!

Instead of allowing this reality to stifle his plan, it reinforced it! Wadsworth was on a mission; his own mission and he would show all of them the outstanding military leader he was … especially that cursed General Blood! He would relieve Chital and destroy the green devils! If they are not there, he will search for them! Then he thought of an even better opportunity to justify this hunt for these green "moon men!" If many residents at Chital were kidnapped and hostages, then his plodding north to rescue them was enough justification? This ploy would forestall his being relieved and arrested by General Blood until? He was sweating nervously as all these possibilities piled up in his simple booze-soaked brain. He smiled to himself. If Nephew got in his way? He would deal with this bastard soon on his own terms. He took a swig of whiskey and read Blood's letter.

Date: August 18, 1897
TO: Colonel Hillary Wadsworth
Commander of Auxiliary Troops
Malakand

IMMEDIATE ATTENTION!

All communication with chital via Malakand was stymied for reasons unknown. The courier from LTC McRae shed a disturbing light on this problem which I will address with you in person. Your orders to relieve Chital are strange to me and this field command, regarding their exact origins. They were never issued by my command! The original orders for the relief of Chital were earmarked for my command via Malakand and seemed to have been lost? I will get to the bottom of this debacle with you. I am at present, heavily involved in a huge battle against incredible odds and will prevail soon. I understand that mistakes can happen but sense something troubling in this situation Wadsworth!

If you, in any way manipulated this message traffic for any reason, you will be held responsible for any negative outcome in the situation at Chital! I could have sent a relief force their days ago! Due to these strange circumstances the safety of Chital is your responsibility to relieve and protect now since you are on your way. This is my direct order! I further order you to stay there until I arrive after this current campaign is finished. Under no circumstances are you to move any forces north of Chital except for routine reconnaissance operations. Protect the inhabitants at all cost's colonel!

Major Nephew is my advisor and extension of my command to you until we meet in Chital. Obey my requests per Nephew to the letter or else he is authorized to relieve you and be placed under arrest!

Respectfully,
MG Bindon BLOOD
Commander
Malakand Field Force

Within thirty minutes a squadron of lancers trotted up the road to the remains of the once proud British garrison city and fort of Chital, with Major Nephew and Griggs in the lead. Colonel Wadsworth was not going to release the light artillery but before he could even pass down any order Hook had already gone into the bivouac where the artillerymen were and roused two artillery sections to move into a defensive position on the road north of the encampment. Sergeant Hook told them to follow him. When they got to the edge of the camp, he ordered them to continue down the road. The young artillery sergeant in charge of the two field pieces looked at the old grizzly NCO and asked. "where should we set up color sergeant?" A smiling Hooky answered, "Oh just a little farther to a place called Chital, and ride at a good pace for the green devils are all around."

The lancers rode off in a canter around the winding partially obstructed road also carrying supplies of food and water in a couple of wagons in the rear. Nephew was pissed off about being denied artillery until he rounded a bend and rode up behind the two artillery teams led by Sergeant Hook. He gave a hearty laugh and waved at him as the lancers took formation in front and behind the artillery. The relief force came into Chital at a steady pace in forty-five minutes and halted in front of the huge stone administration building which seemed to be the only major structure left standing in the area. They arrived to see huge bonfires lighting up and keeping the encroaching shadowy tentacles of the dark moonless night at bay. The fires were being fueled by about anything that would burn. The smell of burning wood emitting from the fires did little to stifle the smell of rotting death in the area. The town buildings behind the admin building still were smoldering with some still burning.

The lancers moved into a huge defensive staging area behind the main administration building observing the spectacle and smells of "Dante's Inferno." Orders for the defense were issued and the horses were lodged in large adjacent stables directly behind the administration building. The darkness of night had spared the new arrivals the horrible visual effects of what the greenies had performed on the inhabitants of Chital. The first group of scouts that had witnessed it all, was written on their facial expressions of revulsion and fear as they greeted the newcomers. The troops settled in to a cold dinner after setting up their defense. They encountered Cavendish and Rashid in the officer of the counsel-general peering over a huge map of the region they had recovered from the pile of trash and broken glass about the floor. They had affixed it on the wall with several silver dinner knives.

The lieutenant smiled briefly and jumped to attention, which gave a keen laugh from Major Nephew who replied. "As you were cadet!" Cavendish gave a sharp salute and met Nephew's extended hand in a firm friendly handshake. Major Tiberius Nephew had been a senior at Sand Hurst when a young plebe named James Ambrose Cavendish had been admitted to this prestigious military school. They had hit it off as cadets and Nephew had admired Cavendish's excellence in fighting with the saber. No senior cadet could beat him. Tiberius Nephew was the son of an ancient history professor who so named him "Tiberius" after a famous Roman general as James was the son of a wealthy farmer. The Major could see the stress and fatigue on the faces of both Cavendish and Rashid. He had been told the details already by Griggs.

Major Nephew was a foremost expert on the Pashtuns and allies in their strengths and weaknesses. In the epic collision of this conflict, Nephew had known of their huge size and the use of "mass" as their primary battle tactic! Selling this threat to subordinate commands had been a waste of time. They just did not see it! However, other than campfire stories, the major never placed green devils and their leader Kali or Rakitabija as he was called on the intelligence radar. They had been invisible until Chital.

After the pleasantries, the major was s brought up to speed on conditions at Chital. Cavendish began as he briefed the Major on how he had planned his defense of the area directly around this large government building and row of military stables behind the large stone building to house all the horses. The rest of the destroyed town was across a wide street that separated these remains from them. Ambrose looked at the major. "I had the boys set kerosene with explosives in those burned buildings so if they do attack, we will light up this whole area again illuminating our fields of fire in the rear. When we set off the rest of the bonfires around this building area, we will have, like at Malakand, visible fields of fire.

Lieutenant Cavendish *smiled* as he addressed Major Nephew. "I have no clue as to the size of the enemy we face sir and I sense we are in grave danger. I have picked one platoon to serve as a fire brigade to reinforce strongpoints under mass attack doubling our fire as needed. Hooky gave me this idea from his Zulu stories at the drift. Wherever the enemy masses in strength I we can double our fire at any point where they are attacking! I will be posting expert riflemen on the roof to counter fire on their sharpshooters and targets just outside the shadows."

Then he continued. "I think they will rush us in mass like they did this town if they come. Major Nephew looked at his crude diagram drawn on the wall and smiled. "looks good to me and the idea of a mobile British firing line is awesome!" Afterwards, Hook and Griggs left the two officers and Rashid alone. They had to get ready. Major Nephew could see the strain and fear in Cavendish's face and eyes as he began added different points in his long tale.

"Chital had been attacked and destroyed by a large number of these green devils that spared nobody. The inhuman mutilation, torture, and vile deaths of many subjects was a monstrous act!" When Ambrose got to the Green Devils, Rashid told his story about them and their origins. The major was amazed at how this leader named Kali and his devils or demons had stayed so well under the detection of British intelligence. After the briefing Cavendish eased himself out of his chair and poured himself and Tiberius each a large shot of cognac, liberated from the missing counsel-general's liquor cabinet. Tiberius enjoyed the rich sharp taste of it. After several moments of quiet contemplation observing the well-lit bonfires from the broken window Nephew spoke.

"Ambrose, I am afraid that this whole relief event is a bogus affair, contrived and manipulated completely by Wadsworth! He is in grave trouble but we are stuck with him now until General Blood can sink his fangs into him. The jig is up for Old Wad! It has become very evident that this bastard acted completely on some form of bogus orders to nearly abandon Malakand for this, or shall I say his folly?" Cavendish, almost in a forgotten after thought told him what had transpired at Malakand. Old Waddy's outrage after they questioned him on the orders. He they and McRae were all cloistered away for safe keeping. Cavendish fired up a cigarette as he paused before he continued.

"After this falling out, I was ordered with my scouts to forge ahead towards Chital under the watchful guard of his staff lackeys. Here I am! All of us in a huge unknown dangerous fucking mess right now!" Nephew relit his cigar and puffed on it quietly for a minute then spoke. "He hid all the messages to Malakand via Calcutta or directly from Chital! Blood initially believed if anything it was a communication error. That was all! Then somehow, unknow to us, someone in Calcutta issued orders out of the blue for Wadsworth to initiate a mission to relieve this place with seventy percent of the force tasked to guard the supply dump and Malakand?" Cavendish laughed and added. "I bet the orders from Calcutta authorizing this boondoggle included destroying the telegraph by fire at Malakand?"

"I hope Waddy gets a visit from the axe man which I volunteer to be when this is over!" He sipped the cognac and continued. "His powerful noble father, old asshole Sir Elroy will not be able to save him now!" He then paused in silence collecting his thoughts then continued "Anyway, I need to get a good read and estimate on the size and abilities of this newly discovered threat of Wadsworth's "moon men!" This will determine the mobilizing of an even larger expeditionary force from General Blood to deal with this problem. I wonder if it was Russian advisors and Afghans supervising this group of" Green Devils" as you call them?"

"Sir," replied Ambrose, "I just can't see Russians or Afghans being this bloodthirsty and allowing such horror at all! But as for supplying them? Yes." Cavendish produced a new Russian rifle leaning against his desk and slid it over the Major. He said, "They were very well armed, like the ones we found at Malakand on the dead bodies of the greenie sniper team and Ghazis. It seems after this battle, most of the rifles and unused ammunition were retrieved from the dead greenies. It seems that a few of them, like this one, were missed in this cleanup. The massive number of bullet holes in the façade of this building is testimony to how many rifles were being fired at it.

All the weapons and ammunition of the deceased 14th Punjab's were cleaned out. The darkness of this night obscures a terrible reality befallen this "jewel of a town" and what monsters we are facing sir." Major Nephew was deep in thought, puffing on his cigar. He looked at Cavendish who now fired up a fresh cigarette. Nephew asked. "Were there any bodies of Ghazis found here?" Cavendish looked at him. "No evidence of Ghazis, Russians, Pashtuns, or Afghans found here major, unless their remains were buried across the way in a mass grave which even the burial of their fallen is strange based on their vile atrocities here. We have only found the remains of filthy green painted savages." Nephew puffed on his cigar then added. "This cult does seem to add a completely new dimension to the problem of enemy combatants. We have a conglomeration of identified enemies and support, and now these strange devils? Seems like we are possibly embarking on a new religious war of sorts…. Perhaps a really bad one as most religious conflict always seems to be as we now face with Islam!"

The lancers were not interested in defending a destroyed city but defending themselves from possible annihilation. They waited behind their barricades not wanting to become the fate of this dead city. A couple of the bonfires were stoked to offer visual warning of an attack this night. The rest would be lit when attacked to illuminate targets for all to shoot. Both light artillery pieces had been effectively placed to the front and in the corners giving better fields of fire covering three directions. A line of skirmishers waited at ground level in front of a rock wall surrounding the administration complex. The main defense was the second line situated behind the low stonewalls surrounding the huge long monolithic building. The last line would cover for the first two lines if forced to move back into this last defense line in front of the building and reinforce it along with the sharpshooters already posted in it.

Fires continued to burn brightly as any items including furniture, lumber stripped from the destroyed buildings, and wagons not used in the defensive line. Each lancer and scout had been issued triple the amount of ammunition. The "fire brigade" waited inside the main hall at the ready if or when needed. If a mass attack came, then their only hope was in well-coordinated and effective British firing lines and accurate artillery fire. The Gurkhas, expert sappers, were now working in front of these positions preparing their own explosive defense as soldiers continued stacking wood and broken furniture on the six large bonfires. The sapper explosions would be set off under the latter waves of attackers after the bonfires were lit. After all, it was rumored throughout the ranks that they were fighting monsters tonight!

The eerie silence of the night continued into the early hours. In the darkness before dawn the sentries on the south side of the encampment began to see movement in the shadows just beyond where the light from the two bonfires met the turgid darkness…. they seemed to grow in the darkness as animated shadows to the pickets on duty. Movement was also seen among the remains of smoldering buildings to the north. The second battle line investing the four sides of the defense zone were nudged awake and were quietly ready in minutes to fire…. In the quiet of the night all eyes could now see movement flowing and zipping in the darkness. Something was out there … Seemingly everywhere!

In the stable area where the horses were tethered, the two guards there were sitting up talking… suddenly a flying object went directly over the head of one soldier and completely severed his head from the body of the man sitting across from him at the neck! Out of rote panic the other soldier grabbed his rifle, rolled to the ground and fired a shot into the direction the flying object came from. Several chilling screams returned as he fired several more rounds. The whole camp was alerted and the stable area became alive with lancers. At that moment, the first line of skirmishers just inside the ring of bonfires on the south side opened fire on the shadows as their numbers grew. These swelling shadows now charged.

After a couple of volleys, the first line of skirmishers retreated behind the wall of the second defense line. Once they were back inside the perimeter, they reinforced the concentrated firing line as the troops on the south wall opened up a deadly volley from their carbines. The artillery opened up on the masses. In moments, the firing lines on all four sides of the compound were engaging well-concentrated fire from their positions as onrushes of enemy sprang from everywhere. Many savages began firing back but the well-made fighting positions protected the British as they returned fire. The good fields of fire, the artillery, accented by all burning pyres now lit, permitted the lancers to pour deadly accurate deadly fire on the screaming throngs at hundred yards.

Like the opening effects of the 45th Sikhs at Malakand, the first waves of advancing screaming onrush of enemy were torn to pieces by the powerful volleys from the British. There seemed like hundreds of them! Grenades were thrown and began to explode into the surviving first ranks attackers as they neared the defensive firing lines behind the stone walls. However, the attacking force now began to increase their rifle fire at the compact British firing lines, killing several, wounding others, and forcing many to duck for cover. The fire brigade as it was called jumped into action at the main front wall. The green devils were stopped cold. The bonfires illuminated hundreds of screaming attackers as they a new mass of devils charged forward in waves.

Lieutenant Cavendish, Major Nephew, and others jumped from their chairs and ran down the stairs entering the midst of this pitched battle. The firing lines were loud and intense as the enemy continued charging British lines. As the weight of the frontal attack shifted to the left, the "fire brigade" platoon shifted to face it with the help of direct artillery fire. A wall of lead crashed into the attacking ranks in bloody chaos. The tight British firing lines were knocking down rows of attackers but on they kept coming. The artillery, set at corners of the government building was able to concentrate its fire exploding bloody holes in the attacking ranks to be filled up with more savages.

The eerie screams and wails of the savages was accented by strange horn blasts unlike the ones that haunted the battle at Malakand. The explosions and concussions from the grenades and non-stop firing from the artillery piece gave the lancers time to reorganize their second defensive position behind the rock wall. Many lancers were already moved within the admin building and continued firing from the many large open windows to support the second line heavily engaged behind the stone wall. As the remaining savages of the first and second attacking waves reached the defenses, extreme hand-to-hand combat raged with rifle butts, bayonets, shovels, fists, and anything available that could be used.

The third attacking wave of devils, which would have overrun the main second line of the British Lancers was stunned in their charge by several huge explosions amidst their ranks. The sappers had lit the fuses to intercept this third mass of screaming savages. Bodies of the attacking force were enveloped in the flying debris of the large mushroom clouds created in the fiery blasts detonated by the Gurkhas, well concealed in the rubble. These four huge consecutive blasts almost looked beautiful in the pre-dawn darkness. Fortunately, these blasts sucked the wind out of this third mass-attacking wave of greenies. The sharpshooters observed masses of attackers slowly beginning to pull back and kept firing into them.

The British firing lines and reinforcing fire brigade ended their deathly brawl with the attackers in the second defense line. They reformed and poured excellent aimed fire into the enemy pulling back into the shadows of the dawn. The intensity of this attack was appalling to the British defenders. These larger attacking forces, this third wave, if left unmolested would have in all probably, overrun the British defenders casting them to the same fate as the 14th Punjab's days before. Cavendish and company had charged into the fight with both service pistols drawn into the confusion of this mass attack.

He had joined with the British firing line in the front at the south wall where he emptied both revolvers at a group of green savages closing near the wall. He kept his trusty .45 unused as the last resort. When he heard and saw the huge explosions along the front between the bonfires, he smiled for King George and company had averted possible disaster! The third enemy charge faltered under the explosions. However, there were many "greenies" running insanely loose inside the perimeter now. The violent hand-to-hand frays were everywhere at this point. The savages had breached the wall. With no warning, suddenly a group of these crazy screaming devils came out of the shadows and began their attack at the main entrance to the admin building.

Nephew first noticed their rush at them. He calmly shot the first five attackers in the head and they fell to the ground from his cold well-aimed service revolvers in both his hands. Cavendish emptied his .45 pistol into another group emerging from another direction knocking them down. Major Nephew was still firing at movement in the shadows when one jumped out in front of Cavendish. His pistols were empty so he quickly parried off the first bayonet thrust as he drew his scimitar knocking it down to the right, then came back with a clean upward slash of his razor-sharp scimitar, severing the tattooed devil's head. The one directly behind him caught the downswing of Cavendish's arced sword and fell to the ground with his head hanging from a few flaps of skin not cut in the saber slash.

The scimitar adopted by Cavendish had proved its worth in agile sharpness with his speed. He then parried the attacks of two more and killed them. In the meantime, Rashid had taken a kneeling position back on the top step at front of the door and was calmly killing several more who were advancing at a shadowy distance with his carbine. All attackers were on the ground. Nephew's sharp eye caught three of the enemy he shot in the head were still strangely moving on the ground. They should have been still! The trio continued moving into the fray killing several more with bullet and blade helping the defenders clear them out. Then the attack and fight seemed over as quickly as it had begun. The British now knew of the immediate fate Chital experienced. The speed and violence of this massed attack told the story in a very unsettling way. The lancers had been ready for these devils and sadly, the 14th was not?

Nephew and Cavendish stood in the dawn as Griggs joined them. As the night gave into the dawn, the enemy had peeled off and disappeared as a canopy of thick smoke from the battle hung like a morning mist. The piles of dead attackers shocked the lancers as they stood peering at them. This fight was over, with several British lancers being wounded and killed. Their well-prepared strong defense had prevented more causalities. Quick estimates from the line officers and NCOs put the attackers at roughly a couple of thousand. The sentry who had fired his weapon from the ground in the horse rest area had accidentally shot through three attackers with his finest unaimed shot, who had formed a single file line creeping up on them.

The lucky shot had warned the camp and probably saved the horses from being killed. He was given a hero's status as the troops hailed their victory with gunshots and toasts of grog. The lancers and scouts had lost eight men killed and another thirty-seven wounded. The line had held and the mobile British firing line had produced deadly effects on the masses of devils they faced, as they moved from one hot spot to the next. The official body count of dead Green Devils was over five-hundred and twenty-eight on the ground with a small batch of wounded found.

The torching and explosives in the remains of the town buildings on the north side of the administration building as part of their defensive plan had worked wonders in exposing the rampaging green devils as they attacked across the wide street to invest the rear of the admin building and stables.

The wide street between the destroyed town and admin building was littered with bodies. The remains of the torched buildings still burned and smoldered against the backdrop of the morning sun creating huge black clouds forming in the sky above them. Hopefully, the clouds of smoke and distant firing would encourage Wadsworth to move at Godspeed now! It was sun up and that bastard was still not here!

Major Nephew was now in his intelligence collection mode as he quietly walked among the fallen enemy warriors. He had enlisted the help of Griggs to make notes from his verbal assessments. These dead were just like the ones found at Malakand according to mister Griggs. Nephew surmised correctly that many of the wounded had been dragged from the field. He pointed out that there were several more wounded that had had their throats slit. If they couldn't be removed, then they were killed he surmised. He noticed the drag marks on the ground. Although there were many Russian rifles in close proximity around the main defensive position at the wall, there were none left in areas away from it. So, most of the rifles and other discarded weapons had been removed. Several of the marksmen on the second floor and roofs had observed this as well.

"These seemed to be all "greenies" as Hooky had nicknamed them, which underscored what they already had sensed. They looked hideous even in death. He noticed the green dye on their bodies, many tattoos and disfigurations in their faces, and their teeth; sharpened into pointed fangs...like a dangerous pack of ghouls, but worse. The Major also noticed a smell coming from the bodies. He walked over to where He, Cavendish, and Rashid had been jumped by the devils. A careful analysis of the one's he had shot in the head, and continued moving, brought out the same smell. He had smelled this before and it was Rashid who looked at him and said "They smell of opium, some form of it!" He tossed what looked like a brownie to Nephew. I found many of these dead men had some of these cakes on them. Just like the ones at Malakand sahib!"

"Like grandmother's brownies" chirped Hooky standing nearby. Nephew nodded in agreement and examined the opium cake. It was sticky and had an unusual deep pungent odor to it. He then tasted some of the residue and found it to be exceedingly powerful. This opium in their bodies prevented them from feeling pain or actually dying on the spot from fatal wounds. He later heard of the same problem from other lancers who had stabbed and shot the greenies with fatal blows, only to have them continue attacking and having to be killed twice. Then several of the circular throwing weapons were delivered to this group. They had heard that several of the dead soldiers had their heads severed by them. The hero of the horse stable told him he never heard anything, just saw one hit his fellow guard and remove his head then lodging in a pole. Later examination revealed nearly seventy of these were stuck in the walls and barriers.

After two hours of collecting information and talking with survivors Nephew, Cavendish, and Lieutenant Wallace, commander of the lancers stood on conference. An orderly had delivered each officer a steaming cup of hot tea, the bedrock of the British army. Major Nephew looked at Wallace. The severity and size of the attack bothered them. Lieutenant Wallace reported had nearly fifty percent of his command were killed or wounded in the attack. He had been wounded in the shoulder and head as well. The effective bombs placed by the Gurkhas had literally prevented the third wave from closing in for the kill. The Gurkhas had saved the day it seemed. Wallace would personally see to medals for them and several others in this battle.

Major Nephew told the lieutenant to collect many of the opium cakes and give small doses to the wounded to ease their pain. The greenies had donated a powerful pain killer in their wake. He continued. "Wallace? you are in command of this force until Colonel Wadsworth decides to show up. It is nine now, and the main body should be here soon I pray. Repair your defenses and be ready for another attack. Brief the colonel what has been going on when he arrives and inform him that I am conducting a scouting party north while the trail is hot. I will return later today when I am done. He looked at Cavendish, "Gather the scouts!"

Lieutenant Wallace looked at Cavendish. "Did you notice anything unusual in the eyes of the dead green devils?" Ambrose thought only for a moment the answered. "They had no retinas, just the whites of their eyes." Tiberius lit a cigarette and offered one to James. Griggs looked at his boss. "Major, on the two that were alive; they seemed to be in some sort of trance, like they were commanded by something we can't see! They just stared off into nothingness and mumbled something in strange language. Gave me the creeps!" Major Nephew took a drag on his pungent Turkish cigarette and smiled at his men. "We are leaving shortly to follow our little green devils!" Hook smiled back. "Can I tell you how excited I am sir?"

Major Nephew was looking for specific things in this scouting mission. The size of this force was now confirmed as large, but how large was the complete force? They were fearless, violent, full of opium with the possibility of being in some sort of group trance. He wanted to capture stragglers for interrogation and information. Where did they come from? What was their place in this uprising? Who was actually supplying them and how? Where was their camp? Kali? He wanted to know about this evil leader. Six groups of two scouts each peeled off and spread out over the narrow flat plain housed between two long rising wooded hills north.

Nephew rode in the middle of the shallow valley floor crisscrossed with copses of trees and underbrush with Rashid next to a small river that cut down the middle of the long valley. Scout security was extended to cover the flanks from the ridges. The rule was not to engage, unless ambushed. The intelligence officer wanted prisoners, living ones. As the party moved north, they soon found items from Chital discarded among the bodies of a few chopped up civilians and savages that died from their wounds that were carried from the battle. Several of these grotesque savages had bled out. A few other wounded had been killed and discarded like rubbish. Sergeant Hook compared them to the Zulus. The only difference was the Zulus had attacked piecemeal and these green boys had attacked in mass. Also, the Zulus had eyes and not the whites!

They continued moving slowly north, the detritus of the slaughter was obvious covering the path many miles away from Chital. The tall long grass on the floor of this wide flat valley had been smashed flat by thousands of footsteps. The lower branches of nearly every tree were broken off or hanging. There were abandoned items from Chital lying throughout the wake of this trampled path, about anything that was dropped or fell from wagons loaded with loot. Griggs pointed out that It was not the latest retreat by the savages, but the initial one from the fall of the city. The bodies lying in this wake were badly decomposed to bones. There were wheel ruts running from a dozen places north as it seemed a whole army of green devils and their plunder went this way.

The discovery of remains of what appeared to be hostages along this path showed they had been eaten like snacks with their bones, stripped of flesh. The scouts were a tough breed of men. Every one of them were repulsed by these sights, especially the remains of the devoured children. They bore witness to the aftermath of the violent unimaginable slaughter of a whole civilized city. It must have been the same when the Vandals destroyed Rome of old, Cavendish thought. The small compliment of scouts were some thirty miles out in the late afternoon when they found old campfires by the dozens near an unnamed small stream that flowed from east to west.

These fires had been fueled by dead wood and some of the carts and wagons taken from the city. It was an old campsite with more discarded loot from Chital scattered about. They surveyed the dead campfires and found the gruesome remains of crushed human skulls, scattered bones, discarded clothes, shoes, hats, bonnets, and some uniforms scattered about the dead campfires. A terrible smell of burnt flesh lingered about the charred ground. Rashid showed one of the uniforms to Nephew. "Sahib, this is an Afghan uniform." The Major examined the torn bloody piece. This made little sense since the Afghans were allies to the opposition forces helping in supplying anti-British forces. Why would the green devils be any different?

To a man, the scouts were living in sickened revulsion, laced with a rising bone-chilling fear. Cavendish ordered them to search for clues in this area. In the search of this cursed place Holmes and Gladstone found a survivor hiding in a copse of trees. He was an Afghan soldier who told them he had been one of several advisors to these monsters. He was scared out of his wits and was very disheveled. After initial questions and mild first aid from Rashid and Gladstone, they gave him some water and food. The man was in shock. After the gruesome discoveries around the campfires and vicinity they stopped to let the horses' water and eat from the lush grass by a small spring. Taking complete caution, with security covering the flanks and rear, the group ate a small lunch.

Rashid finally got the Afghan to talk and gave his brief report to the scouts. "Sahib, he began, the Afghan was involved in the actual siege of Chital and was the party which delivered the rifles and ammunition to these devils with a platoon of men and two Russian advisors a month ago. The Russians were in the company of three very tall Savages wearing dark long robes and silver face masks. They left after the successful victory leaving him and a squad of Afghans to travel with these savages. They were tasked to protect the ammunition and secure rifles collected from the battlefield. He said he was near this camp relieving himself in the bush when his comrades were attacked and killed by these screaming devils.

He fled into the woods to save his life. He said something forced another wave of these green monsters to go south again as he watched hundreds return towards Chital three nights ago. It seemed to him that these madmen were instructed to turn on them. With the exception of this man, all the Afghans were murdered, and eaten; some alive. He watched the horrible ritual from the bush. His men and several village captives were tied to poles, some were cooked by spit alive and others not cooked, simply had body parts cut away in a mad feast." There was a pause. "Bring him to me." Ordered Major Nephew. The interrogation lasted about thirty minutes. The Afghan was shaking and scared.

Nephew kept it simple. His first question had to do with numbers of green devils. He was told thousands, perhaps as many as thirty-thousand all told. They were all green warriors with no Pashtuns or Ghazis in their ranks. It seemed to the Afghan that all the green warriors were in some way brainwashed in their actions like robots. They never spoke to him or the other Afghans. He added that the Ghazis and Pashtuns, other than being collaborators for war against the British under an independence movement had nothing to do with these green monsters. Their warpaths were separate. The Kali had presented himself as a devout Muslim to the fakir, but from what I have seen?

It was a ploy to join the ranks of the liberators! The attack on Chital was led by the Kali and his forces only!" The major let a cigarette. "Kali?" questioned Nephew. The Afghan replied. "Yes, Kali, the alleged supreme leader reincarnated to lead this movement to destroy the British! But Kali is not of Islam, Kali is an ancient god of destruction but from Hindu lore!" Nephew continued, "These Pashtuns, Islamic, and other British opposition groups have no formal bonding alliance with these green devils then?" The Afghan said "Absolutely not! From what I heard, there was only a secret unofficial military alliance between the leaders only to drive the British out which was a common reason we all knew! Kali conceded, used Islam to solidify the anti-British alliance only."

The prisoner further revealed that these "Sons of Kali" sprung from the blood drops of Raktabija, as they were called, have a massive camp located somewhere well beyond the reaches of this river and deep in a jungle inside the Himalayan Mountains. It was called the forbidden zone. The Afghan told them he had never been to this encampment because it was the sacred valley of these warriors and their insane religion. He did say that Russian advisors were the only outsiders who had any access to this place as far as he knew. Major Nephew was greatly surprised at these revelations. Since his intelligence and research had led him to believe that these anti-British alliances had all been identified. Cult of Shiva, of Kali had existed only in the belief system of British Intelligence as a campfire tale until now.

He surmised that this war of independence was obviously legit, and the Afghans wanted an Indian victory so they could claim the Khyber Pass! The Russians relished this conflict for concessions and especially influence since the British would be gone! These green devils of Kali or whoever were a completely separate entity all together. They were a new and dangerous wild card, but what did they want in return for their services? Nephew correctly saw how this Kali character was secretly manipulating and supporting the rebellion at the same time; to drive out Britain first, and then probably usurp power throughout India. There could be no other reason!

Nephew lit another Turkish cigarette and took a few drags from it. He wondered who this leader Kali of this vile army could be? He was obviously a human desiring to grab power and not a god! Kali symbolized the formal ethos "destruction and death! The "Age of Kali" was the "Age of Destruction." Chital was his example! Major Nephew accurately surmised that the British now would have to deal head on with basically two extremely powerful and dangerous forces, one currently in the crosshairs of General Blood's field force, and this other mystery. He asked the final question to the prisoner. "Tell me of this Kali?" The Afghan, still with a resonating fear on his dirty face looked at him then answered. "They call him "Kali the Cleansing Hand and Messenger of Allah!" It is told that Kali is a powerful god, who is ancient with many powers over men."

Nephew smiled for this Kali god was just as human as he was but with a good unique political spin in his estimate! After the interrogation the Major stood on the banks of the nameless small river, quietly smoking his pipe alone in deep thought as he listened to the ebb and flow of it. It was going to be night soon. "Kali?" He was viewing the huge mountainous base of the Himalayas which began some distance across this river. According to the Afghan POW, beyond the next larger river existed a plush jungle valley protected by the huge mountains that went back for miles and miles. It was another day's ride.

The view of the Himalayas at sunset was a breathtaking view as the purple shades of night slowly edged out the sunset. He wanted to see this mysterious land beyond since it was his nature to seek. He returned to the camp which was set in a defensive perimeter with the horses ready to be mounted for a quick exit if attacked. The scouts had built no fires and they ate cold rations. All eyes were on the surrounding river and terrain features visible in the light of the moon.

The next day's travels continued beyond the small river to reveal the broken paths forged upon the sparse undergrowth by the green devil horde as they continued north. They passed into short valleys filled with pristine clear lakes as the foliage and forests began to erase the barren dusty areas south of them. The mountains, part of the Himalayas, rose sharply up to their front with beautiful picturesque snow-covered peaks. Late in the day they finally came to a large river with clear deep emerald colors with many rapids crashing across and around ancient boulders that had tumbled into it from antiquity. Bluffs covered with large wild foliage rose up steeply on the opposite bank.

It was an awesome sight to behold. Rashid commented that "This river is not on the map and not part of the Swati River we crossed earlier!" The major ordered Cavendish to ready his scouts to find a possible crossing point at this new river. Soon a place was found by following the track the enemy had taken. The scouts were held in awe as the landscape between a huge crack in the bluffs gave way and entrance to a huge jungle beyond. It was evident that thousands of green devils had trekked this way. Griggs and Rashid went ahead of the rest to scout the area for enemy.

The group all sat on the bank of the river looking at the clear flowing pool between two sets of rapids. All-present felt the extreme humidity emanating from across the river which now soothed them from the dry heat behind them. They were going to gain access through this huge opening or crack in the bluff used by the devils. After a short rest, the scouts forded the river, which was little more than seven feet deep in the middle with its clear cool waters offering a steady but not dangerous current. The group floated some forty yards downstream before emerging on the opposite side in front of the large crack in the bluffs.

Climbing from their mounts the scouts followed the opposite bank back to a huge opening in the bluff. They entered it and to their surprise stood in front of an incredible massive triple canopy jungle some hundred yards from the huge rock formation they stood next to. The hundred yards before the jungle was a field of tall saw grass mixed with some enormous trees. It seemed to them that this jungle tropical zone in the valley was protected from the cold elements by the huge mountain ranges on either side. "Never in my life would I ever believe what we are seeing here. Oh, the stories of the magical wonders in the many stories about the Himalayas I have read." Rashid smiled at Major Nephew's comment and added. "We have travelled far from the Swarti River today, farther than I ever have."

They all admired the gigantic mountain ranges which seemed to grow in size as they came closer to them, emerging in the distance like waking titans. As they moved into this vast hot jungle with soon to be discovered myriads of clear fast streams crisscrossing throughout its lush thick vastness. The heat from this green monstrosity seemed to emanate a strange hot humidity on the gentle breezes. After venturing a couple of miles in they discovered the other source of warmth in this strange jungle; many hot springs pushed heat and humidity aloft.

Cavendish marveled at the stark difference of the barren landscape from where he began this expedition, the greenery around Chital then into more barren waste of hot by day and cold by night climate; to this? Evidence of the large movement of men was obvious on a central route of large well-trodden paths. The jungle was both beautiful and foreboding. The sounds of unseen birds and animals rang out as they warned of more people in their domain. Major Nephew swore that they were on the doorway of legendary Shangri-La.

Under tight security, the horses grazed on the lush foliage the scouts took turns submerging themselves in the hot pools and cleaned both body and uniform at the same time. After lighting up a cigarette Cavendish yelled the order for his scouts to mount up. They had come well over one-hundred to one-hundred and fifty miles to this place without maps, just guided by an enemy path of retreat, careless in their exit from Chital. Griggs had constructed a rough map using all the landmarks. This was in all respects, enemy territory, that probably began at Chital now. The scouts were apprehensive about being here because of this! It looked like they were going to ride back with a few rests on this one. They had information on where the green devils could be found.

As Nephew rode back, he felt that this whole affair was slowly moving off the charts of normalcy. His mild assumption would soon be blown completely to the winds! He contemplated that if the numbers of these savages were accurate according to the Afghan POW, Colonel Wadsworth's army could never withstand any violent attack! In the disorganized shape the relief force was under Old Wad the clown, they would be wiped off the map quickly! Even General Bindon Blood would have his hands full if the size of this green devil threat was true! Then he added a thought from Sergeant

Hook's observations. "These devils had to move fast like the Zulu impi in their retreat from the battle! They were never found as we rode after them on horseback! Hours after the fight!"

General Blood needed to know this new enemy equation in the mix as soon as possible since this was critical! This huge jungle paradise they had found? He smiled and could see the gray eyebrows of General Bindon Blood rise at his future comment of "We found Shangri-La sir!" For the first time in his exploits in India, the weary major felt overwhelmed, like he was slipping on wet rocks or falling through thin ice, all the while trying to escape some dangerous specter closing on him. He felt a deep fear emerging in all he had witnessed. The strange Kali, green devils, cannibalism, opium cakes, this jungle; the list went on! The scouts crossed the cool emerald river as they called it, the scouts' rode to Chital with one terrified Afghan POW in tow.

"Wadsworth's Folly" finally made it to Chital! It took the sterling leadership of Wadsworth and his disorganized command nearly eight hours to enter Chital the morning after the battle. As this relief moved into the outskirts of the doomed city, none in them could get the smell of rotting burnt flesh out of their nostrils. The once scenic city was a shamble, a burnt offering given by Kali. Wadsworth saw It had been destroyed with the remains of battle everywhere. Everything had been left exactly as it had been after the pitched battle at dawn except with the collection of the British dead. Their bodies had already been lined up in neat rows in the side courtyard wrapped in blankets for burial.

The overall cleanup had barely been performed since all minds were focused defense against the possible return of the enemy. The multitudes of dead greenies killed in the dawn were decomposing in the heat and sun, waiting patiently for their slow journey to the bonfires turned into funeral pyres for cremation. The horror show exhibited by the many dead mutilated civilians and soldiers had partially been cleaned up, but a few remained where they were savagely murdered. The Colonel and his army were now witness to this destruction and horror show. Barely hiding his revulsion, Wadsworth rode up to the administration building and noticed the many bullet holes and fighting positions amid the carnage of the previous night. Lieutenant Wallace hailed him with a sharp salute. "What the hell happened here last night?" Asked the colonel in his haughty voice, as he well remembered all the distant cannon and rifle fire just before dawn.

The lieutenant, with a bandage across his head and left arm, replied. "We were attacked early this morning before dawn by hundreds of these, these green devil's sir. It was one hell of a fight but we held!" Colonel Wadsworth surveyed the carnage from his horse. "Why has this mess not been cleaned up yet? You knew I was arriving today!" Lieutenant Wallace shot back. "Half of my command is either dead or wounded and the rest, per my orders are ready for any new assault sir!" Without further comment the colonel ordered his troops to help the few lancers finish cleaning up the area and tossing the bodies of the slain "greenies" into the cremation fires.

As the colonel viewed the carnage of the battlefield and peered down the ranks of those remaining on guard, he could not help but sense their pervading fear, like an odor permeating invisibly in the air. Something more than a battle had occurred to rattle veteran lancers. He dismounted and walked towards the administration building steps. He began confiding his arrogant thoughts of absolute victory to his band of loyal and faithful "suck-ups" who joined him. He talked as if he had personally commanded this battle! He knew there was no turning back now from whatever appeared on the murky horizon of his ambitions of glory. He knew in his actions to stoke his personal ambition in his "last chance" attempt to be a recognized commander in battle that he was responsible for this terrible massacre here. Blood was creeping up on him by the minute.

In a sudden thought the colonel turned and looked back a Lieutenant Wallace. "Where is Major Nephew and LT. Cavendish Lieutenant?" The junior officer squinted in the bright sun and replied;

"Sir, they left several hours ago to track the green devils north and gather intelligence on them and their whereabouts. I do not know when they will return sir." Old Waddy was silent as he turned and walked away. He was completely aghast at the slaughtered devils lying everywhere! He needed a large gulp of whiskey to quell this smell of rot. The lieutenant had suggested he take a tour of this place so he could get a complete picture of what happened. Wadsworth declined and asked him the last question. "Tell me how many civilians and soldiers survived the initial attack on Chital?"

The lieutenant had looked strangely at him and replied. "Sir, they were no survivors here when Cavendish came here or none found after we arrived. There were only mutilated bodies left and most were eaten sir!" Wallace then had added. "These green devils or demons are cannibal's sir!" We seem to think that many hostages were taken since many were not accounted for in the numbers of dead we counted. Several hundred could be in their hands and their fate is uncertain!" Only the slain are present sir!" Wadsworth cursed under his breath. But he mumbled the saving of grace word "hostages!" He gave a cruel smirk

Wadsworth was shown into the office of the dead governor and the temporary headquarters of Cavendish. He pulled out his flask of whiskey and drank a huge gulp of it. He had been drinking so much of it since before he left Malakand. The booze seemed to steady him and his plans. He was now toying with his newly evolving plan to escape this charnel house and the wrath of General Blood. the idea of a noble attempt to a hostage rescue up north was the next perfect piece of his plan developing in his mind now. It was his only piece left! If these green devils were not going to come to him? He would go find and destroy them and rescue the hostages! After all, Cavendish and Nephew would supply him with the necessary place to find this green devil threat and the hostages!

Victory over these savages and the rescue of the damned hostages would stave off Blood and the general staff! This success would allow his dear noble father Elroy to vindicate him like the last time! This new plan could give him time to show that ass wipe Blood "who" Colonel Hillary Wadsworth was made of as the VC was pinned on his chest by Queen Victoria that royal whore! If he could rescue civilians and destroy the green Devils, then he could get away with all the bullshit he had engineered. It was a "win win" if he succeeded! Failure was not an option here! In a dismissive attitude he looked at Lieutenant Wallace who was now standing behind him at the door. "Have the scout leaders report to me when they return lieutenant!" "Yes Sir!" and the lieutenant, with a bandage on his head saluted, turned and left.

The scouting party finally returned by after dusk two days later. They had learned the whereabouts of the invisible and dangerous green devils They all returned to Chital in decent spirits and returned to the huge admin office they had taken over earlier as the request of LT. Wallace. Their former trashed office had been cleaned up and was now Colonel Wadsworth's briefing room. It was after nine at night when "Old Wad" finally showed up smelling of whiskey. He had left the scouts and others waiting for over an hour. At least the returning scouts were able to eat a dinner and sport a couple of shots of a newly liberated bottle of the deceased governor-general's cognac and cigars.

The room soon began to fill up with the Wadsworth's staff decked in their red uniform jackets so ordered by Sir Wadsworth to blend with his fine red jacket. The others present wore the regulation tan uniforms. There were about forty of them that settled down where they could find room to sit or stand against the walls. There was no conversation against Wadsworth's staff and the scouts since they loathed each other at this point. The assembled group stood at attention as commander Wadsworth entered the room. He stood in the front and turned facing the crowd giving his broad theatrical smile began. "Good evening gentlemen!" Everyone stood to attention as Colonel Wadsworth saluted them and told them to be seated.

One officer tripped over his sword and fell over a chair to the floor creating laughter. "Old Wad and his close circle of officers took a front seat as they waited to hear the reports from the scouts. Major Nephew had offered to chair the briefing because he had also planned fireworks for the imbecile Wad as Cavendish was his second! The major stood poised like the composite officer-gentleman he was in a rumpled soiled uniform since he had not changed it upon return. He introduced Cavendish and began a composite introduction of the recent events. His first words were music to Old Wad's ears. "Gentlemen, we have located the place where these green devils inhabit! But first we estimate that Chital came under a fierce surprise attack probably over a week ago by several thousand devils well-armed with Russian rifles! It was a brutal surprise attack of great speed and audacity as we experienced here in the dawn hours a couple of days ago.

The garrison here put up a good fight but was simply overwhelmed by the speed, size, and firepower of these green devils. We experienced this deadly ferocity, were ready for them and nearly overrun by their numbers!" The information we gleaned from the only Afghan POW we found went like this. He stated that over ten-thousands of these savages launched a sudden surprise attack on Chital in the dawn from all sides. The regiment of the 14th Punjab's put up a decent fight but were finally overwhelmed. The town was plundered and burned. The victims were savagely mutilated with strong evidence that they were eaten since devils are devout cannibals! These savages we fought were dangerous." Nephew paused then continued.

"It appears that this attack was solely the work of what we have termed "green devils." This bunch, led by their mysterious leader named "Kali" have nothing in common with any Pashtun, Ghazi, or Islamic liberation forces! They are part of the opposition to British rule, but a completely different animal! We can only surmise this based on the interrogation of the Afghan POW who also told us that there is a possible thirty-thousands of these savages loose in the north living in a jungle valley inside the Himalayan Mountains we found about two days ride north from Chital. Besides some unusual edged circular throwing weapons, they seemed to have been armed in mass with new Russian rifles." The Russians serve as advisors to all these opposition groups including these monsters! He produced one and handed it to Colonel Wadsworth.

Nephew continued with the briefing. The room was now silent to a man. "Sir, from what I have learned about these Green demons is that they are not from any normal Islamic influenced Pashtun tribe, but from some dangerous cult of the old god Shiva the "destroyer" who have blended expertly in with the Islamic hopes, wishes, and goals of the Mad Fakir and the others. Existing at the fringes of this anti-British movement …and now amid in the chaos of this rebellion have come out in force against British interests in a terrible way here at Chital. Until now, this cult was born of ancient myth. I will be perfectly honest; this Kali has pulled a fast one on the whole British Intelligence community! Quite an embarrassing moment!" He lit a cigarette and resumed.

"It seems that many hostages and even some Afghan soldiers made it to the dinner plates of these demons as we evidenced by the terrible remains strewn around their dead cooking fires, we found up north. I can't imagine what this spectacle was like to witness…but it is black unimaginable horror, as verified by the Afghan who was not eaten and survived to watch his comrades devoured. He did tell us that many more of these unfortunate expatriates and some soldiers are still prisoners were captured and were taken to their huge base camp north into their jungle haven!" He tapered off, as the room was completely silent. He then made a serious statement.

"Gentlemen, from what I have also learned, this evil cult of Kali and Raktabija as they were called was once real, but was brutally destroyed over a thousand years ago is now resurrected, and become real! Also, the leader of this cult has a name now. He is called the Kali! This evildoer and his minions live in the "Shangri-li jungle!" As we call it. This part brought on a few laughs among the men present. Colonel Wadsworth sprang on the moment. "So, major, you suspect from the prisoner that there still are many British citizens and soldiers being held by these green devils?" Ambrose stood up and looked at Old Wad, dressed in his red tunic. "Yes sir, it was verified by the Afghan. We do not know how many survived on the trail or from the cooking fires, but many must still exist sir."

Major Nephew began adding in concluding points to the briefing. "Gentlemen, we sit in an extremely dangerous position now, since we have an estimated thirty-thousand green devils these greenies to our north or somewhere near, and elements of some estimated two-hundred thousand Pashtuns and Ghazis possibly surrounding and closing the door to the south! The Malakand Field Force has been engaged in much resistance in their campaign for many weeks now. The size and array alone of our enemies is disturbing as it has put all of us in a dangerous situation. I am sure the Green Devils are far from finished with us yet! General blood wants us to stay put here until he can arrive with reinforcements. Then we can deal with the green devils and hopefully rescue the civilians. He took a drag off his cigarette. He then added.

Thankfully, we have yet to see any use of Russian artillery estimated to be in their hands as reported to us by the Afghan POW; yet! These savages are fierce and fearless warriors as we experienced here; especially in the fact that they seem to be under the influence of some powerful form of opium and brainwashing. Many of them had to be killed twice" He dumped a box full of little black sticky cakes on the table. "We took these off many of the dead! I did instruct the medical doctor to collect and use it this on severely wounded soldiers in great pain, since we were low on morphine." Nephew sat down next to Cavendish.

The silence in the room settled into a growing murmur. Colonel Wadsworth, bedecked in his theatrical red tunic now stood in the center of the room like some proud peacock. One could see the emerging arrogance and pompous attitude before he spoke. It was the way his lips curled and pursed in the flickering candle light. Wadsworth, by his own estimate, was about to tell of the new mission. He had hit pay dirt on the word "hostages" and had added the other word "rescue" for his golden opportunity to enlist his whole command in this epic event! He would not only rescue the captured citizens, and soldiers, but would be credited for defeating this Kali and his horde of evil green monsters? Or was it devils? Moon men? Or whoever they were. Why he might even be "Knighted' by the Queen bitch after receipt of his Victorian Cross…. His contemptuous leering smile was now evident to those who sought to stop him.

"Yes, Old Wad! Opportunity knocks but once for you…and if ever opportunity knocked it was now!" Commander Wadsworth mumbled under his breath. Blood would not be close for days if not weeks! By then he would be in the north, possibly this jungle world kicking the pants off this Kali fellow! He had ample forces to destroy these savages and now seethed at this opportunity! Nephew would kiss his ass! My how his father Sir Elroy Wadsworth and his noble circle of friends be incredibly proud, if not terribly envious of his great impending achievement! His name would be a household word, his historical place in the annuals of British military history would be assured…and this event would get it for him…at all costs…every cost! So, his thoughts coalesced into quick orders…orders that would elevate him to hero status! Screw Bindon Blood and all those motherfuckers and buggers! They would be too late to catch him and stop his quest to glory! Action was necessary and to begin now.

He stood, elegant, poised and very self-assured facing the crowd of soldiers in conversation. He began his great speech as they listened. "Gentlemen. After carefully listening and assessing not just this victorious battle here, but the fate of so many British citizens and soldiers killed and taken hostage by these savages; I have reached my conclusion! I feel we have an obligation, a sacred duty to immediately rescue these kindred souls and, to destroy this very sinister force revealed tonight. This is our sacred duty to maintain British power in India! All Hail the Queen! And Hail Britannica!!!" With the exception of a completely shocked Major Nephew, Lieutenant Cavendish, and his scouts present, all rose and hailed the Queen. Wadsworth shot an evil glance directly at Nephew and laughed a laugh of "what the fuck are you going to do now!" As the banter died down the colonel was quick to speak. "Lieutenant Cavendish will immediately assemble a scouting party north and will leave before dawn to set our course and offer us a good reconnaissance in preparation of our victorious campaign ahead. "The colonel then stared across the room.

"All commanders will have marching orders within the hour! We leave at daybreak!" His word trailed off in the clamor of concentrated "Hip! Hip Hoorays!" from around the room. Major Nephew, enraged at this revelation climbed on top of the table. He quelled the noise with a shot fired into the ceiling with his pistol … "Silence!!" He raged loudly as the group turned their attention his way. "Colonel Wadsworth was ordered by General Blood to stand fast here in Chital and "NOT" move north for any reason!" Colonel Wadsworth laughed out loud. "We leave at dawn and I just issued combat orders! We are at war!" Nephew scowled. By command of General Blood, I relieve you of this command as of now! All forces under your in command will remain in Chital until reinforced by Blood's command!"

Old Wad sneered at him and laughed in his face. The villain in Nephew had reached a crescendo. He aimed his revolver at Wadsworth. "I hereby relieve you now Wadsworth and place you under house arrest by order of General Blood! I am now in command!" He looked at the room full of the colonel's lackeys laughing at him and pointing at him. Then a smart "fuck you" grin came across Sir Colonel Hillary Wadsworth's round face, greatly reddened by the circumstances and booze. "Thank you for your kind interaction Major Nephew! However, in case you need to be reminded I am in charge and we are in combat conditions! Who in hell are you to play such silly games?

Yes," conceded Old Wad," these are my new orders, and now this mission to stay here in Chital has changed drastically in purpose by your General Blood!" He waved a folded telegram high in the air so all could see it. Wadsworth completely ignored Nephew's pistol aimed at him as he cleared his throat and went on. "We must march to the enemy's cannon fire and liberate our citizens who are in great peril now…. Period! This is the order I just received from Blood!" His pronouncement was supported by more "Hip, Hip Hoorays!" from his staff which filled the room and the few who now surrounded Nephew who still stood on the table.

Led by Wadsworth, all of his staff filed out of the room to prepare to move north at dawn. Rashid, Nephew, Cavendish Hook, and Griggs stood motionless until the room was empty. Hook passed around a bottle to his comrades lost in a silent rage. He smiled at them and said. "Drink up ladies, for we who are about to die will not salute Wadsworth!" The stern-faced villain Nephew replaced his pistol in his holster and jumped from the table. He took the bottle and drank a long pull as he contemplated that telegram which he knew was bullshit! He was going to see this telegram! He passed the bottle to Cavendish and said. "My fucking day is not done here boys!"

CHAPTER THREE
DARKNESS RESIDES IN SHANGRI-LI

Colonel Wadsworth stood in front of Major Nephew and the scouts after returning to the room a few minutes later. He stared at Major Nephew with complete consternation bordering on hate. He had assembled three rather large armed guards from his escort who had followed him into the briefing room. Old Wad commenced speaking crisply. "Major Nephew, since you are so ingrained to disrupt my official orders in the face of this completely new urgent situation, you will either be arrested or will take charge of this city with the contingent of the lancers that fought here and were bloodied! Security here is still necessary until reinforcements arrive. This is your choice!"

A reaffirmed shock crossed both Nephew's and Cavendish's faces as they stared at each other instantly. This was insane by all rules! This situation was out of control and obviously hijacked into the hands of a pompous fool. Amid attempted further protests from both Nephew and Cavendish, "Old Wad' lashed out: "These are my orders…. irrevocable! If anybody, especially you two, tries to countermand them… you will face immediate execution by firing squad! These are orders in a combat situation so both of you know what any violation of them means! I march at dawn and Cavendish! You march in one hour!"

Wadsworth exchanged a stare of hate with Nephew…then a pompous half-smile …. a "screw you half smile" … for the colonel was technically correct about failure to follow the orders of superiors in combat. He could execute them both and seemed to be looking for an excuse. However, this asshole was countermanding a direct order from the high command! However, the general was not here and the power of this buffoon was in place. This insane mission was shaping into a grim reality. Colonel Wadsworth wanted to silence their mouths. Major Nephew repeated one last key question as he yelled back: "What is your new authority to authorize this mission or campaign now? You had better show me this order with Blood's signature on the bottom!"

Major Nephew was directly in Wadsworth's face now. "I made it abundantly clear yesterday that the senior command in India via MG Blood did not authorize you to even come here at all! So how can Blood suddenly change his mind to support your irresponsible actions? Your actions are directly responsible of this massacre you bastard and you know it!" Wadsworth gave a smartass laugh and pursed his lips to hear more of Nephew's wild banter continue. "Relief forces sent by Blood could have broken this siege in short order and prevented this massacre colonel!"

Nephew gave a laugh then went on. "Blood thinks you have rescued this city full of unmolested people! They are dead or hostages facing terrible circumstances and chital is destroyed if you haven't yet noticed! You speak madness colonel and are criminal! You have no clue how outgunned you are against this green enemy right now! We killed nearly six-hundred here just the other night! They were crazy ferocious savages! How many did I tell you were left you fool! Do you really think your disorganized mainly green force can fight against an estimated thirty-thousands of these crazies with no resupply or reserves on unfamiliar terrain? Did you ever study the fate of U.S. General George Custer in the American West Wadsworth? Did you? This whole command is in extreme danger right here and now and you will suffer the same fate as Custer at the Little Big Horn if you dare to move north! Like you, he was an arrogant glory hunting idiot ready to sacrifice his whole command!" Nephew took a fresh cigarette lit by Griggs. He added that

"You have no authority! I relieve you of your command until Blood's reinforcements arrive and you are put in chains! Now colonel, show me the written order you waved to the room; NOW!" Wadsworth was not going to let this get away from him for he had plans for this bastard lapdog of Blood's! He told a big lie, like most little men in power who want it their way. "Excuse Me," retorted the Colonel…sweating from everywhere and rife with anger…. with his round red face was popping out of his buttoned red tunic. "You think you know everything that goes on here? …You are the sweet little puppet that sits on General Blood's lap, maybe his bugger bitch? I would guess you are his beady-eyed little cock sucking fellow boy? What you don't know was that while you were scouting north, I received a messenger dispatch ordering me to secure this area and move forward to destroy enemy forces and rescue any and all hostages.

This was a direct order from the high command major! It came directly from MG Blood damnit!" Nephew was in complete disbelief. "Very Well commander…. Now let me see this signed written dispatch so I may somehow believe this poppycock and balder dash tale you now present! If you do not have one then I will relieve you at gunpoint, place you under guard, and send a message to Blood affirming this situation." Wadsworth's eyes bulged like some giant frog as he could barely contain his anger. "Very well Major, I will show you shortly and in private…. as for the rest of you and Cavendish? Go and prepare to leave soon as planned! Prepare to embark with your forces north within the hour tonight and I need that map Griggs created." … that is a direct order! Understood?" They looked at each other coldly, then Griggs handed his map to the colonel as they quickly marched from the room. Griggs had already created a second map if it was needed.

"Major Nephew stay here." This was old Wad's arrogant pompous finest hour. He was just warming up as the room cleared of the scouts except his three men and the major. He waited a few moments after the room was clear of all scouts then smiled at the major. The major did give a side glance that there two rather large NCOs and one of his junior officers that remained in the room. Colonel Wadsworth spoke in sort of an excited gibberish to the very silent major who gritted his teeth. "Major Nephew?" Came a condescending voice. "You have refused to obey or comply to my direct orders verified by your serious insulting outbreak in this meeting. You dare to question my authority in combat…in danger. You have tried to compromise my orders in front of my staff!" Wad paused briefly; he really needed a plug of whiskey. He rambled on after clearing his throat.

"I can have you shot for this for I am the commander and I am the power! You have no power here at all! Your just some twerp who came here to push me around… I am taking control of a desperate situation, a rescue operation!" Nephew sneered back "I was Blood's "Hand" and his authority here Sir! Let me see his orders you waved over your head!" "Wadsworth handed the major a folded message with a glaring impish twisted smile on his face. Nephew opened it up and was astonished to see that it was the original message he had delivered to Wadsworth days ago; it had a large red "X" crossed through it! On the nod of the colonel the two guards grabbed the Major and took his pistol. Major Tiberius Nephew shot up…" You fucking liar! You bastard! I knew you had no message! If you go through with this, and survive, you will not escape justice like the last time you fucked up! You are finished and finished for good! If you become responsible for the death of one more soldier, I will see you hang, hang you slowly myself!"

Old Wad retorted snidely: "Maybe so in your eyes…but after my defeat of these devils…and safe rescue of British citizens…all will be forgiven! My daddy will see to it!" …He winked at the major, "just like my father got me off the hook last time!" Wad chuckled. Nephew was fuming…. He watched as his NCOs bound his hands as another NCO dropped the Major's pistol on the table. The Colonel continued with a laugh. "By the way, I am writing you up for insubordination and failing to follow lawful orders in war. I plan on having you shot….so simple isn't it…shot at dawn! So romantic don't you think? There will be No More Major Nephew…no more problem from Bindon Blood's dead little lapdog!"

Tiberius Nephew had a reply. "Colonel Wadsworth? If General Blood were here, he would have this to say to you!" Wadsworth put his hands on his hips standing squarely in front of the major waiting for this answer. Nephew gave a large smile then kicked the colonel so hard in the balls his feet left the ground. "Old Waddy" came back to earth flopping to the floor holding his crouch moaning. Nephew gave a laugh. "Blood's lapdog little cocksucker has spoken asshole!" "Get him! Arrest him! He struck an officer!" shouted the colonel in great pain from the floor. The two burly NCOs grabbed the major and relieved him of his second pistol. They pitched his revolver on the table with the other one as they bound his hands behind his back. He was taken into a back room and tied to a chair. The guards then posted at the door outside as the duty officer helped Wadsworth off the floor and into a chair. He then consumed the contents of his flask as he threatened to kill Nephew.

Instead of leaving the building, Hook, Rashid, and Griggs had not exited the building after they left Wadsworth. They had crept into a side room next to the main one and heard everything that transpired. Rashid, who had tagged along at the last minute was sent to inform Cavendish of this plot. They were planning to spring the major from this execution detail and would catch up later when this scene settled down. Both were quietly laughing as two other staff officers arrived to help Wadsworth out of the area. Man had the major shellacked Old Wad's balls with that kick!

Within the hour Cavendish and his small group of handpicked scouts, which also included his Gurkhas, Rashid, Holmes, four reliable lancers, and five of Wadsworth's watchdogs headed out into the night north towards the mysterious jungle world inhabited by the green devils. When the assigned staff officer in charge questioned where Griggs and Hook were, Cavendish told them they had already left to the north right after the meeting. They were the lead security element of course!

As Cavendish and his group left the Chital encampment, they observed mass confusion and disarray as the mostly green British empire force of Punjab's struggled in their preparations for departure the next morning…. Lieutenant Wallace and his remaining lancers assigned as the rearguard stood out of the way manning the weak defenses, stripped down to over fifty men and no artillery. Their dead had been buried and the other thirty-seven wounded were of little use. They had been spared joining the column by a last-minute security concern of the colonel who had forgotten them by now. Besides, there was a second squadron of lancers to go north.

Griggs and Hook waited patiently for the next two hours to pass as Nephew's captors settled down. They later approached the lounging guards, in the near darkness of night only illuminated by the light of one kerosene lamp on a table. The guards were happy to see them as it had to be their relief for dinner. Hook, the imposing one came to formal attention in front of the guards who systematically jumped to attention after seeing light bouncing off the tan pith helmets and the stripes on Hook's arm. "Everything all right boys?" Asked the smiling color sergeant. "Yes Sergeant…all is well here!" "Jolly good!" continued Hook. "We have come to take the prisoner to prepare him for execution, for dawn will soon be upon us; release him!"

"Sorry sergeant …AAHHHHH…" Replied the guard squinting in the shadows trying to see Hook's face in the dark under his helmet. "We can't release him to you, we have specific orders." Griggs added. "You must release him to us now! This is an order directly from Colonel Wadsworth who is waiting below!" Hook bored into the guard. "Who are you to countermand this order!" The guard thought for a moment then answered. "Ah yes, Sergeant, but we still can't do that. We were told that only the colonel could fetch him personally." The guard never saw Hook's right punch hit his jaw as he fell to the ground...Griggs, standing next to the second guard, hit the other guard with a pistol butt. Both were out cold and tied up.

Swiftly, they breeched the door and entered to find the major tied uncomfortably to a chair. In short order, Nephew was freed and grabbed his pistols. Suddenly the watch officer entered the room as they were tying up the two unconscious guards. The duty officer was a brand new 2nd Lieutenant named Robert Allenby of His Majesty's Artillery. He pulled his revolver quickly aiming it at the two culprits. "So, what do we have here? Looks like an escape attempt?" Allenby looked extremely sharp in his red blouse uniform complete with white pith helmet, almost like a fashion model for a British uniform company. His lips were pursed tight like his boss under his thin piccolo mustache. His revolver was aimed right at the chest of Sergeant Hook. "Looks like three will be executed at dawn now my boys!" He snapped in manly form. "Look who you call "my boys!" entered Major Nephew's voice.

"Now put down your gun so we may report this madness to General Blood and stop this illegal affair before it commences and people get hurt! Let us go!" "How can I? "Stammered the growing nervousness in the young subaltern's voice. "Do you know what the colonel would do to me if he learned that I released you, aided in your escape so to say?" Nephew looked the villain as he stared and talked back. "I suppose having the meat on your bones sawed off by a green devil knife for dinner as you watch will be better? Yum Yum!"

Suddenly, from out of the shadows leapt Griggs, who knocked the gun out of the soldier's hand and stuck a sharp knife to his throat. 2LT Allenby froze as he was pushed into a wall. "What are you going to do with me?" He yelled. Major Tiberius Nephew looked deeply into his fearful eyes. "You my son are going for a nice moonlight ride with me towards the Khyber!" The Major sat silently on his horse viewing the chaos in the camp. He held the reins of 2LT Allenby's horse, who was tied and gagged to his saddle. He and his new charge were going to ride in haste to General Blood to warn him of the impending disaster about to unfold. Mister Griggs, and Sergeant Hook sat next to him and they had placed themselves well beyond the defensive perimeter.

Griggs and Hook both aimed their Russian rifles at a high angle then fired several shots from them over the camp. The sound of these Russian differed from the British ones that instantly received return fire from the nervous pickets. The camp fell into chaos as everybody went to the ground or began returning fire in every direction. "This will keep them busy for a few hours sir." Said Griggs with a grin. Nephew gave them a salute as the two scouts disappeared into the night going on their separate ways. The chaos and confusion created by the rifle shots in the wake of Nephew's escape was significant in a lengthy stall in the preparation to embark north by the relief. It was dawn before it was discovered that Major Nephew had escaped.

Colonel Wadsworth was insane with anger at this news. Wadsworth insanely banged his fists on the table yelling, and cursing. The smell of whiskey on his breath was obvious to Lieutenant Wallace who stood at attention and had discovered the escape. Old Wad knew exactly where Major Nephew was headed! He now realized that he needed to move a lot faster north to evade a quicker response from Blood after Nephew personally informed the general of his plans. Then there was the wrath of Major Nephew. His balls still ached from his kick!

His booze fueled insanity was evolving by the minute as drool seemed to form at the edges of his mouth when he blabbered out commands. The warnings of the dangerous threat to the north were ignored and blown to the wind for the obvious reason. Colonel Wadsworth was running from prosecution, prison, and maybe execution! His only saving grace now was victory over this Kali and rescue of hostages! All of his cards were on the table. Unlike Lord Nelson who was killed at the Battle of Trafalgar, he planned to live to relish this grand success. He fumed at Nephew's comparison of him the General George Armstrong Custer!

The able veteran lancers from their formation, saluted the departure of an expedition of over eight-hundreds of Her Majesties British led colonial conscripted soldiers north to fight the green devils and rescue all British captives. Wallace knew he and his men were lucky today. His gut feelings hinted that this expedition was doomed and he would never see these men again. After all, his troops fought a surprise attack of some two-thousand of these savage deadly devils and were nearly overrun. He could only imagine facing thirty-thousands of them in the jungle far away from any support! His top NCO then walked up and handed him a note along with another letter for LTC McRae, with a sad smile. "Sir, Nephew gave this to me before his escape last night." Wallace gave a half smile at the comment then looked at the cover of the folded note and it read "LT. Wallace; Open after Wadsworth is gone!" He read the short hasty hand written message.

"You have been ordered by me, to abandon Chital as soon as Wadsworth is gone and return to Malakand immediately. No reason for you and your men to guard a graveyard? You face obvious slaughter here. There are thousands of the devils about! Good luck Wallace!" Major Tiberius Nephew.

Lieutenant Wallace ordered his top sergeant to prepare his lancers to depart as soon as Wadsworth's columns were out of sight. After his safe arrival at Malakand, Wallace personally delivered the letter from Nephew to McRae. McRae was stunned at Nephew's chronology of events, intel on the devils, and the insane plans of Wadsworth. His angry attitude now turned into rage and a new enemy concern had come to light. Now we had thirty-thousand screaming savages who were fearless and dangerous! All he could do was prepare Malakand for possible attack with what he had left at his disposal.

After riding well into the afternoon, Major Nephew stopped and pulled 2LT Allenby from his saddle. He untied him and gave him water. Nephew took a big pull from a bottle of malt scotch he had found in the liquor cabinet of the deceased administrator's office. He had earned this treat as he did not like whiskey. Allenby had yelled up a storm after his gag had been removed then was silent. He spoke. "Sir, I have no knowledge of what is going on and I know I will pay for it when Colonel Wadsworth finds me." Major Nephew looked at the youngster and smiled.

"You will never ever have to worry about running into Colonel Wadsworth ever again, and you are already vindicated by me. You were following lawful orders and doing your duty before we got the jump on you." This assurance calmed the 2LT's restlessness somewhat as he took a small sip of scotch offered by the major. As they continued to ride Allenby questioned just what Nephew had meant regarding "never having to run into Wadsworth again." He did not understand it at this time, nor that his present circumstance had saved him from a horrible future circumstance. Finally, the major slowed his horse and was next to the lieutenant. He stared hard for his answer in his greatly troubled thoughts. "Wadsworth and company face complete annihilation in the most gruesome manner imaginable Allenby!" "All of them sir?" "Yes" was the solemn reply.

Young Allenby someday would learn that circumstances and the handmaiden fate, forever play a small but a significant game in war for each individual… life giver and life taker." It took two nights and nearly three days of weaving in and out hilly and mountainous terrain and dodging bands of Pashtuns to reach the British Forces General Blood. The distant sounds of rifle and artillery fire offered a continuous echo from the mountains as they drew closer to the battles in progress. Blood was using a "scorched earth" policy, against the Pashtuns who now feared the British destruction of their food supplies and villages before the coming winter. Hundreds had already surrendered, laid down their weapons and went home. However, many had not as separate battles for the Khyber Pass and surrounding area continued against massive numbers of armed enemy insurgents.

Major Nephew and 2LT Allenby finally arrived at the huge British encampment in the evening of the third day and reported directly to MG Blood with sharp salutes. At first Blood was agitated at his missing intelligence officer. His agitation was born out of concern for Nephew's welfare rather than any insubordination. He smiled and offered both men a chair. He poured each officer a long stiff shot of whiskey. Several kerosene lamps that flickered and struggled as they beat back the darkness of night lighted the tent. He listened as the major previewed his dilemma with Wadsworth. General Blood began.

"So, this idiot Wadsworth was going to have you shot at dawn? Please tell me this tale!" Then he looked at Allenby. "And who is this fine lad with you?" Allenby, jumped from his seat to a stiff position of attention. "This is 2LT Allenby of Artillery, on Wadsworth's staff, who was the duty officer in charge of me after my arrest. Blood looked at him. "Why do you wear the red uniform son, kind of outdated now?" Allenby replied. "Colonel Wadsworth expected all his staff to wear them sir!" The general gave a weary nod. Major Nephew then pulled a journal form his bag and laid it on the general's desk.

"This is my summary of all the events sir you can read later! I forgot to add to this that I gave Old Wad a stiff kick in the balls for you, Queen and country sir!" Blood gave a laugh. "Did it hurt son?" Nephew smiled back. "Yes sir, I left him flopping like a tuna on a hot deck!" He took a sip of whiskey and continued talking. "The reality is that Chital was overrun and except for suspected hostages, the garrison and population was slaughtered gruesomely. A cult or group we refer to as "Green Devils" fielded hundreds if not thousands against them and then attacked our relief forces soon after we entered Chital! We learned from a terrified Afghan POW that these hideous devils are led by some character called "Kali."

Wadsworth has countermanded your orders I delivered to him personally to hold at Chital! He has taken his very green disorganized relief force north to fight the devils and rescue hostages!" General Blood saw the obvious hate in Nephew's eyes, and exploded in anger. "Great Caesar's Ghost! That rotten good-for-nothing idiot!" He took a sip of whiskey and looked at the major. "We found the little bastard noble buddy of Wadsworth who issued the bogus order for Wadsworth to go north to Chital! This little high-born scumbag buddy of the colonel is on his way home in chains if he gets that far! Wadsworth will be held responsible for the massacre at Chital because of his actions! I could have sent my squadrons of lancers! Major Nephew smiled grimly and added, "Can I be the headsman sir!" Bindon Blood gave a wide smile.

The major paused then continued. "When you read my reports, I am afraid you see just how bad this adventure will end! Blood's mish mash of units will be wiped out!" The general passed Nephew a cigar and they fired them up in silence. Nephew now added. Sir, my deep reconnaissance to the north in the south Himalayan Mountains did find one gem? We found Shangri-La!" Blood rolled his eyes as he let out the expected laugh Nephew had desired. Musing at the comment, the general poured more whiskey into the tin cups. The general, lost in this information but finally cracked a long smile from the bottom of his huge gray moustache, changing the weathered lines on his face.

He looked at Allenby, left frozen at attention holding his cup of whiskey during the short conversation between he and Nephew. "Lieutenant Allenby, please sit down and how long have you been in India?" "Ye-s- Yes sir! I just arrived a little over two months ago and was assigned to the support command of Colonel Wadsworth before he was ordered to march to Malakand." A minute of silence followed as all but 2LT Allenby drank their whiskey. "You don't like my fine whiskey lieutenant?" Chided General Blood with a look of hurt crossing his weathered face. Nephew was laughing as his boss toyed with the junior officer. "I am authorized to drink all of this sir, in uniform on duty?" Both Nephew and the general laughed. "Son" began the General; "You are duly authorized to take a huge drink now! That is a lawful order"

Poor Allenby finished off the whole cup and began coughing… more laughs and smiles…. The general then refreshed all their drinks from a nice crystal decanter. The general was in a drinking mood now after the dire revelations. He knew he was helpless to do anything at this point. Wadsworth was now four days north. He wanted to hear Allenby tell his story. "So, what was your part in this plot son?" Allenby looked at Nephew with glassy eyes from the whiskey. "Be candid son, don't hold back!" Allenby gave a short smile. "I…I was the duty officer charged with the detention and holding of the Major by direct orders of Colonel Wadsworth. He was to be executed by firing squad at dawn for refusing to obey orders in combat!" "So, did you help Nephew escape!" asked Blood. Allenby looked at the major…. and continued "Well sir, in a round-about sort of way I suppose…." Nephew smiled. "Griggs helped him make his decision to help me escape with a Kurri knife at his throat!"

Major Nephew eased himself in the nice comfortable chair and looked around the tent. He loved the slight feeling of England the general always had in his command tent as he smiled at a portrait attached to the tent of Queen Victoria in her magnificence sitting on her throne. He remembered that this year marked her Diamond Jubilee. Blood settled back and took a sip of whiskey, Blood continued after puffing on his cigar. "You were going to face a firing squad Nephew? Does this story get any better?"

Major Nephew gave a serious smile. I am afraid so sir, now comes the part where, as Griggs said" the things nightmares of all shapes and forms are made of…." He trailed off for a moment to collect his thoughts and pull on his cigar. Blood interjected, "Why weren't Hook and Griggs with you here after the escape? "Sir, they were supposed to be with Cavendish and his scouts heading north under orders and the watchful eyes of a few of Wadsworth's boys. They held back and busted me out. 2LT Allenby could identify them, so, he came with me…" The General sat quietly for a few moments… then replied, "So where are they now?"

"They are probably deep in the north country at the base of the Himalayas eying this huge strange jungle inside the lower reaches of these magnificent mountains. They were ordered to scout the path for the main body following under the insane threats of death and duress by Wadsworth. Old Wad knows that his end is near, and this insane foolhardy expedition is all he has left." General Blood nodded his head in disgust. Over the next thirty minutes Major Nephew gave a complete report on the green devils, and surprise dawn attack they pulled against the relief compliment in the ruins of Chital. He described these monsters in detail and their hideous rituals under some leader of their cult named Kali.

"You know Major, by the time we get forces through to even Chital, it will be impossible to save Wadsworth if he is already deployed north by now and drawn into any sort of battle." "Odd Zogs!" His face reddened in the flickering lamp light as a breeze passed through the tent. The general was thinking. "However, I plan on sending a whole compliment of my Lancers with you back to Chital in the morning. I am fighting an infantry and artillery battle with these hill people and have made positive gains in the last two weeks. My lancers sit as part of my reserve and because of the nature of the terrain and battle have only been used in limited infantry roles. So, I will send my lancers and a spare battalion of light mobile artillery in the morning…. This is a tough bunch spoiling for a new fight anyhow."

Major Nephew nodded in agreement. "Seems like holding out in Chital with reinforcements is the only possible choice we have for now sir to help any retreating part of Wadsworth's army. I will keep you apprised of our situation as it evolves." BG Blood then summoned his orderlies. "Before we conclude your lengthy report, let us have a good dinner." The orderly ushered the two soldiers to the dinner table in the next room… Blood remained momentarily at his desk. As he sipped the last of his whiskey as his mind was rushing into time, backwards…his mind fluttered into ancient history …of what terrible snapshot would be compared to the possible fate of Wadsworth's command?

But what was itching his mind…then it was there; a picture, a panorama of thick forests in his mind…. He saw the 18th, 19th, and the 20th Roman Legions marching through the thick forests of Germanium in column formations led by an incompetent lawyer buddy of the Caesar. They were spread out for miles. They had no effective flank security, as they seemed so "cock sure" of their invincibility. Impossible forest terrain completely restricted them from the ability to organize into their deadly fighting formations, which were the key to the Roman army's ability to defeat nearly any form of attack, especially barbarians. These Roman Legions, poorly led, were completely destroyed by waves of savages charging from the bush! In one violent onslaught, all along the spread-out Roman columns, hordes of barbarians tore into the Romans from all sides unleashing a hell storm of violence and death upon them. The bones, broken shields and weapons of Rome littered these forests for years, and even became holy sites for the German barbarians.

This clown "Julius Caesar" Wadsworth, regardless if he were fighting these green devils or the women's temperance union, was in the midst of committing this same blunder of horrific proportions! He wisely surmised. Those who do not study and know the lessons of history are cursed to repeat it, especially in war. In modern terms, it was Islawanda all over and he grieved for all those fine soldiers soon to be lost if all calculations were correct! After a great refreshing dinner of Mutton roasted on a spit, Yorkshire pudding, and some refreshing white wine, the trio plus a stenographer came back to his well adorned office and recorded a summary of what Major Nephew had told thus far.

After his two visitors, had gone to sleep MG Blood sat in his office sipping one last whiskey from his tin cup. It was late into the night and he now had a disturbing impression on this whole affair. General Blood loved his troops and lamented over a foreseeable loss he had little power to prevent! Nothing in his power to stop this fool Wadsworth in his lawless madness; no way to save his soldiers! He cursed Wadsworth and all the fucking power-hungry nobles that seemed always to be a pain in the ass of the common soldier. He raised his glass in gallows humor" Ah Germania, we have returned to your forests!!!!"

The long ride through the hot unforgiving mostly barren lands of northern India took a couple of days of steady riding. The aides that Wadsworth had sent to watch Cavendish kept falling behind and slowing their forward progress. Lieutenant James Cavendish was amazed at the spectacle being revealed in front of him. After they crossed the Swarti river into a better climate of light forests, they stopped on the banks of what they believed to be a tributary of the Swarti. Griggs had not been able to locate it on any maps he found at Chital or anything on this jungle valley. They all again admired the huge snow-capped mountains which were the guardians of the long ancient jungle valley beyond the crack in the huge bluffs.

It seemed as if the deep jungles of Asia had been transported to this huge valley as they approached the emerald green waters of the river. They could feel relief again as the damp humid heat emanated towards them in an invisible wave at the river bank. Rashid rode up next to him. He wore his large turban as was common with the Sikhs of Hindu Faith. He was the best of scouts who also wielded a 6th sense. "Sahib! Sahib…over here!" Cavendish rode up and viewed the calmer waters between two sets of raging rapids that crashed hard on the huge boulders above and below this fast-moving stretch of calmer waters.

The Indian guide spoke. "I would wait a minute sir!" Rashid pointed at what appeared to be logs but were huge crocodiles in the water in the far bank fifty yards upstream which they had not encountered on their first foray here. "They must have ventured from the jungle streams to enjoy the river sir." Cavendish froze and stared at the behemoths floating about near the far bank. Lieutenant Cavendish commented. "All we need now are elephants and giraffes!" Rashid laughed, as did the others. Lieutenant Cavendish's blue eyes sparkled as he smiled...the eyes that attracted so many women along with his very well-founded dry humor which was his final selling point. He had completely sold one Jenny Farnsworth! The scouts sported their iconic large moustaches with several days' growth on their faces. It seemed to be their bond with the exception of Wad's boys who were clean shaven and stayed together. They looked very uncomfortable as they gazed with fear at the crocs in the river.

For a moment, Cavendish stroked his long handlebar moustache and studied the landscape around him. He realized for the first time just how hot and humid this area had become since they had descended a rather steep grade to get to the river. It's dark emerald waters, steadily moving along showcased a completely different scene across the other side. Once past the field of long green grass, it was a dense primal antediluvian jungle with massive trees and huge fauna undergrowth. It seemed a land untouched since creation except for the crude paths made by all the recent passing of two massive groups of Kali's green devils. He was amazed at the presence of crocs as well. A shiver of fear tingled up his spine as he thought of another danger ahead, cloaked in this green labyrinth.

He had little clue about how deep this green jungle they would go before they made contact with the enemy. What else would they encounter here? He looked at his scouts. "Before we cross, I want everybody to check and secure their weapons and ammo. Everybody was armed with at least two or more Webley six-shot cartridge loaded revolvers, a light carbine version of the 1894 Lee- Metford large caliber rifle, and saber. All these weapons could be used on horse or on foot. Cavendish had ensured that everyone had an extra load of ammunition for their weapons as well as extra rations. He figured that most of the ammo would be used in retreat if any ambush on them occurred. He had already given orders for every man to individually cut and run if ambushed.

They all had grave forebodings about this venture; illegal, undermanned and oblivious to the actual threat of these green devils in un-chartered lands. A cheerful Corporal Holmes smiled at the three staff officers and two strong arm enlisted men sent along by Old Wad to watch them. He was eying their red dust covered tunics. "Hey Lieutenant! Send these boys across first because those crocs love the color red and would make great bait!" The captain in charge of the little party replied. "I will hold you and your smartass remarks in contempt corporal! We were ordered to see you to this place and wait here until you are finished then return to the command!" He pulled out a small pad and a pen and began writing.

"Come on!" interjected the corporal who was enjoying this, just give us one, say that fat one yonder." As he pointed at a plump Lieutenant in the rear who shuddered. In the end, the three officers sent by Wadsworth wanted nothing to do with crossing this river, so they delegated their two enlisted men to go across with the scouts to keep an eye on them. The disrespectful remarks issued by Holmes was recorded for future punishment by the fat lieutenant. Like the rest of the scouts, Holmes detested them. The three staff officers would wait on this shore for them to return. Their decision was music to Cavendish because he really did not want to baby sit for these clowns, arrogant and cocky like their fearless leader Wad!

The two enlisted men they sent were in the khaki uniforms and not of the ilk of Old Wad. They could guard their horses and provide rear security when needed. As planned, they had a small cold lunch as they waited for Griggs and Hook to show up. After about two full hours of waiting in a camouflaged glen, the two riders appeared. Hook and Griggs were all smiles. They joyfully told the Lieutenant Cavendish in private of the escape of Major Nephew along with the kidnapping of one duty officer named Allenby. It was the Captain Stevens, in charge of Wadsworth's group who now grilled the returning scouts. "Where have you been? Why I thought you were supposed to be ahead of us? Why are you riding in from the south?" Mister Griggs gave a disarming smile. "Well sir, we have been scouting up and down this river to see if there are any better points to egress it if we have to retreat and cannot use this one. We were also monitoring the movement of a few bands of green devils as well, they are everywhere!" Captain Stevens brought the story as Hooky added; "Those cannibals looked famished!"

The scouts, unlike Wad's boys, had no illusions as to the outcome of this fiasco in the making. Cavendish explained how they were going to operate inside the jungle, and they moved to the river's edge. What to do about the crocs was the question? Rashid pulled out his trusty crossbow and aimed at a rather big croc. He carefully sent a silent arrow into its brain through its left eye. It thrashed around as if crazy drawing interest from several more hidden in the foliage on the other bank. As the croc settled into death, its huge carcass floated in the steady current down towards the end of the huge pool. Shortly, the other crocs attacked it and a feeding frenzy began. The crossing was now clear.

Griggs added. "The crocs, like the devils are also cannibals!" Rashid was smiling back at Cavendish like he had just won a jackpot. SGT Hook had taught him the game…the finer aspects of poker and how he used to cross crocodile infested rivers while he served in Nigeria using a crossbow. Rashid had become a rather good player at both endeavors and by professional luck always carried a crossbow, the silent killer of enemy sentries. Card games were a way in keeping good informal relations with enlisted men, a practice still shunned by most British officers of the day. Cavendish had been taught long ago by some old vets, that close bonds with your troops were the essence of survival in combat. However, dead, alive, victorious, defeated, or losing to NCOs in poker.

James Ambrose Cavendish would hold one distinctive honor; he was the first British officer to cross this strange unknown river into a mysterious world where the jungle blotted out the sunlight. In tight formation, they moved into the river in a column of twos in about five to six feet of moving water, pistols ready and keeping well away from the feeding crocs downstream. The humidity grew intense as they rode out of the river, along the cliff face to the huge crack in the bluffs. Rashid and Griggs then crossed the long grassy field laced with huge trees as the rest of the party spread out into a line formation. Into the thick jungle they rode as the blue sky was blotted out and the group was now riding in the dark shadows of the jungle floor.

Sweltering heat would be a mild statement! The two scouts soon gave the all-clear sign and the rest followed. They rode by several hot bubbling springs keeping on one of the large crude paths created by the travels of the green devils. More discarded personal effects were noticed. Rashid guided them off the beaten trail and led them to the far left up a steep rise where they could navigate on what appeared as a remote seldom used path. Stealth was the mindset of everybody. The party soon dismounted and walked their horses as they ambled along this rough trail for what seemed hours.

They finally stopped for the night. No one slept because of the constant fear of an ambush. There were no fires and they formed a circle with the horses tethered in the middle. During the night, each man felt they were being watched, if not by the greenies or curious animals, but by something else observing. The next morning the small group continued moving up a slow rise then stopped to let the horses drink water and rest. The humidity in this jungle was unbearable as they were all soaked in sweat. Everybody took turns submerging in a small pond fed stream to cool off wearing their clothes. Their uniforms were already soaked completely through with sweat anyhow.

They continued farther into the dense jungle to the left in the morning as the ground seemed to rise up leaving the jungle floor behind. The group noticed a wide variety of birds; monkeys, large insects and other creatures roaming at will and invisible in the underbrush. They were making all sorts of noises. This was good since their chatter betrayed little noise of their movement to a possible enemy waiting or moving ahead of them. They walked in the large shadows of triple canopy jungle. Hook made the observation that these devils seemed to have traveled on one set of paths down the center of the valley since no evidence of them was on these smaller paths off the beaten trails. These huge groups of devils were simply moving towards their final destination without any fear of attack. It was their obvious domain.

The interesting find was a rather large ancient road which headed east-west which they crossed. There were ancient relics of statues and monuments at the top of the large hill with carved glyphs that were strange to all. Jungle growth had obstructed most of what appeared to be a stone road of great antiquity. Cavendish told the scouts to make a mental note of this lost jungle road in case they needed to escape on it. The group trudged north along the jungle rough terrain as this path continued to elevate them above the bottom of the valley with a large stone bluff rising on their left. They were seeing small areas where sunlight shown through the canopy around this trail.

Griggs finally appeared from his trailblazing with Rashid. It was late in the second day and he put his finger to his lips for silence. He beckoned only Cavendish to follow. The party was hot and exhausted and ventured to a nearby mountain stream where man and horse slumped into its clear shallow moving waters. Griggs now led Ambrose by foot along a huge cliff face on a steep climb to the left for another hundred yards. "Sir, I think you need to see this," as a solemn faced Mr. Griggs signaled for him to follow. They walked for an additional half-mile continuing up a much steeper slope to the crest of a cliff overhang, forever hidden by the jungle. They crept up to where his Indian scout was positioned.

Rashid handed the field glasses to Cavendish. What the lieutenant saw was amazing. Cavendish stared out from the cliff over a thousand feet above a huge deep valley gorge that seemed to go quite a way…In the thick jungle's greenery, he was mesmerized by a huge waterfall with its green cascading waters that seemed to split the gorge to the far left in half. It fell, rained showers of water over two-thousand feet into a large pool which boiled with the falling water and exited into twin fast-moving rivers that seemed to split north and south. As he looked around his area, he mused that this entire fauna seemed very prehistoric. The huge valley below was mainly covered with very tall grass accented by huge outcroppings of huge trees spread all across this plain.

The view was breathtaking. In the far distance, he could see the snow-capped mountains of the southern Himalayan Mountains that were extended down to form the huge mountain ranges that protected this massive jungle valley. The contrast was awesome to behold. However, the admiration of beauty seemed to come to an end as Griggs pointed to the floor of the valley. In this long valley with large areas of tall grass broken up with small forests of trees, thousands of greenish dots could be clearly seen from their vantage point. They had found the green devils! They reminded Cavendish of the tide of attacking Pashtuns at Malakand: "army ants!"

This place became their encampment. Cavendish estimated that they were, as the crow flies, about three miles from this throng on the heights. He adjusted his field glasses and in awe was shocked at the size of this group. There were thousands of them…milling about typical of a huge camp with many fires burning in the centers of what looked like small villages. He had trouble viewing towards the end of the valley because there was too much haze from the fires below. Rashid beckoned him to follow him farther up the step rocky path which paralleled the cliff.

He went into his bulky equipment bag and pulled out a beautiful brass telescope complete with tripod. It was a well-made expensive brass medium sized scope. It was the scope that Cavendish had found unmolested next a window in the counsel's office at Chital. He had entrusted it to Rashid. Cavendish smiled; he had forgotten about it. This scope, he figured, was more valuable in the field than in the shambles of Chital. This telescope did invoke a grisly memory... The memory that had shocked them all when they had first arrived. The counsel had been taken, but what these demons had done to his wife and two maidservants! Cavendish remembered well why they had been muted by the scene before them when they first entered the counsel's office and residence the first day they arrived in Chital.

All three women had been tortured hideously and gang raped over a period of time. The wife had been flayed alive, burnt with a hot iron to her eyes and sensitive parts. Her heart, liver, and brains were gone...and her grisly remains had been hoisted up hanging from the chandelier. Only demons from the infernal regions could have done that, as she resembled some puppet returned from hell. The maids had suffered similar fates, with the remains of one decent looking maid being ritualistically tortured and prepared like dinner in the kitchen...the only way he could tell she was cute was that her head minus brains was impaled on the wooden end top of a large dining room chair... as if she was invited to her own dinner...the remains of her gnawed bones were evident on the table and floor.

As for the other maid servant? She seemed to have been sport or entertainment. Her burnt remains were still tied to a chair, which was crumbling into ashes.... All present had vomited at the sight and stench.... They were shocked into silence as they later removed these slain unfortunates for burial. The Lieutenant then remembered what Rashid had told him; "That these savages were the ancient enemies of civilization, and this, according to old tales was the way they operated long ago! Cavendish then reminded himself about the ritual torture and eating of brains to "steal the souls for Kali" Then they had sat back in the office chairs staring and mute at the gristly scene in the other room; shocked to their souls! Erasing this horrific spectacle with large gulps of whiskey and other spirits found unmolested in the governor's liquor cabinet.

He was lost in this trance of remembrances when Rashid grabbed his arm... it was the worst imaginable of finds seen at Chital. "Sahib? Are you all right?" Cavendish nodded with one after thought...that he would save the last bullet of his forty-five for himself; delivered right under his chin! This decision would be reinforced as he peered into the scope in silence for several minutes. He witnessed the large numbers silhouetted as the night cooking fires were burning. He was aghast at what was on the menu tonight! Hostages! What he saw at the end of the valley interested him.... It was a narrow opening in the end of the valley, where he could clearly see people moving into it... next to a very fast running river, another one created by the falls....

He saw part of a bridge that connected this side of the valley to something beyond obscured by a huge set of bluffs that cropped out from the massif. Day was now growing into night. He called for a meeting. He ordered Hook to lead everybody back and to collect the three Wadsworth clowns on the other side of the river. He was to return at great haste to warn this pompous jerk. He kept Rashid, Griggs, two Gurkhas, and Corporal Hoskins. It was useless to keep everybody in harm's way at this point.

Corporal Winston Hoskins, the young but salty lancer was chosen to accompany Cavendish on his scouting mission after he was observed fighting at Malakand. Like Griggs, and Holmes, Hoskins was a rough and tumble lad and a dead shot at long range. He loved to fight and smiled at an adversary before he hit him. He said that smiling before a fight took his opponent off guard. His skills would probably be needed if problems arose now since Holmes was needed to add security on the trip back. He had proven himself at the Battle of Malakand after killing scores of attackers from a high position in the north fort. He appeared to have gotten along very well with the others in his group. Cavendish handed his dispatch to Lord Nelson, for if anything serious occurred, Lord Nelson would make it. The dispatch read:

Colonel Wadsworth,

After our long trek of three days across this unnamed river north of the Swarti, where we followed the trails of the green devils deep into a huge jungle. After many miles in this jungle we climbed very high into an overwatch position where we observed their encampment in a huge valley below. Sir, there are literally thousands of them below! The jungle terrain is very rugged and would be impossible for effective British military formations or maneuver operations. Ambush in this area would be easy and impossible to detect and due to the size of the devils, a massacre for our forces! You are extremely outnumbered by a foe I deem very dangerous! Any attempt by you to engage this army would spell complete disaster. I strongly urge you to stop all of your perceived operations against them now!

I am sending you this as a dire warning. I doubt if many hostages will be alive soon. From my vantage point I clearly saw many of them roasting on spits for dinner last night! Your only hope is to stay in Chital and prepare an excellent defense. These green devils are far from finished and are probably preparing to return to destroy you at Chital! Let these masses come to you sir! General blood is on the way I am certain. This is your only chance for your command to survive the storm coming at you. Me and my remaining scouts will reconnoiter out into this strange area to further assess the enemy and try to locate any surviving captives if there are any. I beg you to stay in Chital at all cost's sir! Death and destruction await you if you come here. I hope my point is clear!

LT. James Ambrose Cavendish
Scout Section, 11th Bengal Lancers

Cavendish gave instructions to the departing scouts; "I need to know what Wadsworth is actually doing?" He silently cursed, because if that idiot was in route by now, then it would be too late for General Blood to stop him! The scouts left, walking their horses in a slow column into the small jungle path down the side of the mountain towards Wadsworth, hopefully still at Chital. The remaining scouts settled into the night. Rashid and Griggs had found a nice deep shelf fifty yards to the south. It was big enough to shelter the horses and men. They even lit a small cooking fire, obscured under the cliff shelf as sleep was a tough commodity now.

They had witnessed via the telescope earlier, the ritualistic torture, murder, or cooking many hostages alive. These cooked humans were rabidly devoured. The worst repulsive display of this horror among these horrors was a large English white woman. She looked like she had already been raped, and tortured. Her clothes were in bloody shreds. To his horror the cooks forced a long wooden pole into her ass and forced it out of the side of her neck after a struggle! Her shrieks and screams of pain and terror were bone-chilling, echoing far below from the deep valley floor. They watched as saw several holy men in some green full-length black robes presiding over this gruesome spectacle. Cavendish was sickened to his soul.

As her body was basted, she let out a final spat of terrible inhuman wails and screams as she was roasted in the rising cooking fire. After she was done, the spit with her on it was placed on a crude table and her remains were savagely torn apart first by the visitors in cloaks, then finished to the bones by the other green devils waiting their turn to feast! "Dinner was served!" In his now appalled and shocked state of mind, Cavendish made a mental note to kill all of these green-cloaked demon leaders if he got a chance. "Kill them all!" he whispered. It was very hard to sleep after watching that horrific spectacle below.

It was not just the night creatures and their noises, which kept the party awake, and on its toes in the night. Their senses told them something else was watching them from above, but what? In the pre-dawn hours, they prepared their long reconnaissance by trekking up and across the huge massif adorned by the huge waterfall. Any other way down below would be too risky. They all commented over morning tea that they felt they were being watched again by some unknown force, of what sounded like huge night birds of some sort above them. They were all thankful that they were under a huge overhang that jutted out from the cliff. What else lay in this mysterious jungle, lost from the civilized world thought Griggs? Like the actions of Wadsworth, this mission seemed to grow stranger by the minute.

The lieutenant hoped that Major Nephew could return in time to warn General Blood and be able to stop Wadsworth's folly even before he got on the road north. He looked at Corporal Hoskins who gave him a happy smile. Cavendish smiled back. He was a happy seeming Welshman who loved his ale, women, and a good fight. Rumor had it that he had a girlfriend in every city. He was a ruggedly handsome man with dark hair and Brown eyes. He possessed a powerful build and was extremely fast for his size. He had a very disarming sense of humor, which seemed to cover up the fact that he had honed the art of a very cold professional killer.

He spent his first overseas assignment attached to British advisors in Nepal; first teaching the Gurkhas the British way of soldiering and then learning the complete warrior culture of these extremely effective warriors. He alone, literally became one, learned the language, and was accepted as an equal amongst the Gurkhas. Hoskins was sharp and an excellent find at Malakand for this group. Hoskins later spent a lot of time "problem solving" on tours in a few English possessions in Africa. He was busted as an NCO for disobeying orders in which he managed to save many lives in a native attack in an African colony. Then he was awarded a medal for bravery. This never made sense to him but the commander who had busted him was relieved of his command, so Hoskins continued to serve in the enlisted ranks.

He was then transferred to India less than a year ago at his own request He was offered the job as a courier for the command in Madan and took it. As fate would decree, he was trapped in Malakand when the Pashtun hordes attacked and proved his deadly skills in the struggle. He was discovered by Griggs and now attached to a great bunch of guys as a scout. He had become a very independent soldier from his African experiences and was very much in his element now. He carried the standard issue weapons and a pump 12-gauge shotgun which had been very effective in close combat in the jungles of Africa. Like Holmes, he also carried a nice high caliber hunting rifle with scope tied to his saddle on his horse. He had mysteriously supplied a few shotguns to the scouts when he heard of this jungle in the Himalayas.

On the high ridge vantage point overlooking the huge valley, Lieutenant Cavendish studied the situation and his options. He had Griggs, Hoskins, Rashid, and two Gurkhas Gladstone and Cornwallis. This made for five effectives plus corporal Holmes, who returned from the group after it had left. Holmes wanted to stay and play. The lieutenant observed that very few of the green devils seemed to be moving this early and they had not posted any guards at the myriads of small camps. Then, as they were preparing to leave, Holmes, viewing the green devils below summoned Cavendish and Griggs before they began their assent to the massif.

"You will not believe this shit" as Holmes ushered them to the brass telescope. Ambrose was astounded as he viewed the scene far below. The thousands of green devil warriors were lined up in rows; neat organized rows standing silently and motionless in the dawn. Several black-cloaked leaders stood in the same manner to their front. It was both an awesome and chilling sight to behold. The myth of wild green devils was just shattered! They all wondered who commanded them at this point! The rest of the scouts took turns viewing the huge non-moving silent formations below as if they were thousands of statues. Griggs commented. "Old Wad will never have a chance against this Ambrose!"

Regardless of this truth, Cavendish needed to get a complete heads up on what lay beyond the valley at the end of the gorge. The Afghan POW talked about these savages having large caliber Russian Artillery and he needed to confirm this! He was now thinking about General Blood and not the asshole Wadsworth! He estimated it could take a few hours to traverse the rugged ridge above and beyond the gorge. The faster they could get a complete assessment of what lay beyond this valley, the faster they could leave with the complete picture! Rashid was the last one to view the massive formation. He looked at it for a while then looked at the lieutenant.

"Remember the eyes on the slain devils at Chital sir?" Cavendish nodded. "They had only whites for eyes and no pupils." Cavendish listened silently. "Sahib?" he retorted. "Those men had no souls; they were walking dead." He pointed to the view below. "These men are the walking dead as well; commanded by who knows or how they got this way. But we face dead men!" Ambrose looked at his nervous friend then focused through the telescope. It was then he saw the whites in the eyes in every row he viewed below. He had thought the whites of the eyes appeared after they had been killed! He had never imagined anything like this in his life and was mortified. This game now had changed! Then Rashid concluded. "We need to find and kill one person to stop this army of the dead! His name is Kali!"

Within the hour, the reconnaissance party set out slowly, using ropes, climbing up the side of the gorge at the ridgeline, staying completely away from the tall massif and out of sight. They were impressed at the continued spectacle below them. The expansive formations of green devils had remained unmoving now for four hours. The climb up to the huge massif was steep and hard. The return rappelling would be easy. Once on top and away from the huge cliffs, it became a flat boulder and forest ridden ground. The good thing was, that there was no sign of any human activity as this area.

It took them nearly two hours to prepare a safe way to cross the raging fast river that emptied over the gorge. Anticipating this obstacle, they used rope to make a slide for life from their side, then constructed one for the way back across upon their return. The scouting party finally rounded the huge forest and rock formations obscuring the mystery at the end of the valley by midday. It had taken them several hours. Night would come soon and would fit nicely into their planned night reconnaissance.

They moved closer to the gorge now so they could see what was on this side of the huge extended bluff formation that reached from the massif like a huge "L" shaped formation which obscured this side. They finally got clear of the foliage that had obscured their view. They all sat in awe at the sight that now had unfolded before them. They now observed a huge ancient castle with huge walls and ancient spires that seemed to touch the sky. Although an obvious sinister place, the extreme ancient fairytale beauty of it was not hard to behold. This structure was carved as it seemed into the jungle that surrounded it against the tall massif behind.

A beautiful sunset was visible and enjoyed above the thick greenness of this ancient jungle. The new bonfires and myriads of green warriors were now to their collective right, beyond this little hidden valley. Griggs and Rashid had moved down the front to the edge of the massif to get a good view of what was in a huge open space between this monolith castle and the solid wall of the bluff which reached to the river before the castle grounds. They returned after nightfall to make their report. Griggs gave off a low whistle, which indicated that he had hit pay dirt. "There are what seems to be civilized devils down there and our friends of the Russian army sir!"

Cavendish and Hoskins, along with his two Gurkhas, carefully moved towards the ancient castle along a path next to the cliff but stopped as they saw lights ahead. Corporal Hoskins handed him the field glasses and he immediately located a long bridge located at the rear of the castle which connected it to the massif. It connected to a road in all probability they had not discovered yet. It was lit with huge torches and guarded. From his position he now had a great view of the grounds below to the south of the castle as he bounced his view off the areas lit by many torches and a few campfires. He was amazed as he looked at a huge well-fortified castle and the bridge attached to the wall of the cliff.

It seemed like some fairy tale castle with spires, minarets, domes, huge ramparts and walls. This place added to the growing mystique of everything they had encountered as of late. They noticed that there was some sort of temple built on the roof of this massive structure lit up by huge fires. Rashid later pointed out the many strange statues of great antiquity. Huge torches lit up portions of the castle. The jungle growth seemed to swallow up the huge walls to the south side of the fortress with huge vines that were hundreds if not thousands of years old. The front of the castle had a huge sally port that faced the river and offered cobblestone roads which led to a couple of bridges that crossed the fast-moving river between the bluffs which hid all of this to the right. The huge plain and green devils resided on the other side. This was civilization?

As Cavendish scanned the complete area, he rested his view at a place below in this south part of the castle area. The torches below had reflected on something of great interest! "Where in the hell did these come from?" His eyes fully adjusted to the shadows that crisscrossed a row of heavy caliber artillery pieces. Some of them were shielded partially under huge tents along the adjacent cliff wall. The torchlight was just enough to give off the silhouettes of the large caliber Russian artillery pieces lined up in a row. Cavendish knew these artillery pieces were much larger than anything Wadsworth had at his disposal. Rather than being small mobile field guns packed on mules, these pieces needed horse teams to move them. The rumors of enemy artillery given to him by the Afghan POW now rang in great truth!

Cavendish was looking for a way in the castle and felt he had found it.

He slowly dozed off in a short nap thinking, is "Wadsworth's Folly" going to be a combination of the "Charge of the Light Brigade" at Balaclava and "Custer's Last Stand" in the American West? He thought of Custer's Last of barely twenty-one years before. He was an arrogant glory minded leader, who barged into Indian country with poor intelligence on both terrain and the Indians. This underestimation of their abilities and possession of modern repeating rifles led to the masterful slaughter of the 7th Cavalry and without one artillery piece! Several military historians later compared the cavalry expertise of Chief Crazy Horse to those of Napoleon's great Field Marshall of his cavalry Marshall Ney. History had spoken!

Cavendish saw the same dangerous underestimation of the enemy by Wadsworth among other negatives. But unlike the Sioux at the Little Big Horn, these devils had artillery! Then there was some incredible mind control over these devils! He now saw the shocking dichomy between lockstep green devil discipline and ferocity they unleashed in combat! Although terrain knowledge was a huge factor, the green devils seemed not to have to rely on it after seeing them from both sides of the coin! Even General Blood would have his hands full with this threat! The "village clown" Wadsworth? Yes, he would find his combat and all his glory probably spit roasted special for the Kali! Ambrose had to smile at that possibility as he now wondered what other surprises awaited this night?

At two in the night they were all awake and ready to conduct a recon of the castle and area. They needed to know as much as they could about this "enchanted" evil place as possible. The approach to the huge fort via the rear bridge was a no go since it and the other gates seemed well guarded and patrolled. These devils in this area seemed to be more regular type humans and not the tattooed monsters on the other side of the valley. They were not the hunched over creeping wild devil types that slavered and drooled from their sharpened teeth over their human feasts. The green devils in this area all wore black hooded robes and seemed to carry themselves in more civilized manners, mingling with some Russians they observed. They needed to get inside the stronghold. Perhaps a few hostages still remained alive and uneaten! They would split up to conduct two reconnaissance missions of this place. Cavendish had a great plan to get inside the castle.

The ride through the jungle on the return to the relief force was a living hazard. Hook, in the lead, had already been knocked off his mount twice to the laughs of his Gurkha companions. It took them a less time-consuming way to return since they now had a trail route already blazed. Instead of two days, to traverse the jungle, it was still a full day to get back to the sound of the river towards the end of the day. They did not see any crocs close in their crossing point and forded the large flowing pool of emerald colored water without problems. They called out for Captain Stevens and the others but to no avail. Other than a burned-out campfire there was no sign of them. Hook suddenly realized that these idiots had built a campfire, which was an excellent beacon to any green devils in the area.

They gave a brief search of the area where they had been seen last but found that the lackeys from Wadsworth's staff were missing without a trace. Hook assumed that they must have left and run home to mommy "Wad." The group headed south at a fast trot in the closing rays of sunlight. Some five miles down the road they found a rider less horse eating some leaves from a scrub tree off to the side. They stopped and recovered the lone horse. King George discovered a good amount of blood on the saddle. The group now conducted a cautious search and located one of Wadsworth's men leaning against a rock close by his grazing mount. He was barely conscious and appeared in bad shape and his red blouse masked the blood that had flowed from his chest wound."

Water, Water!" He bellowed as he saw them approach. The two enlisted men of Wad's group who were also present went to his side and poured water from a canteen through his parched bloody lips. Hook dismounted and walked over after telling the rest to spread out and be vigilant. He knelt down next to the gravely wounded staff officer and relieved him of his empty service revolver. The officer was all slashed up and was missing his left ear and part of his nose. Hook asked in a loud tone.

"Sir, what happened to you and the others?" The man, in short pained gasps looked at Sergeant Hook. The deep gash in his forehead had exposed his skull. "We got jumped last night at mealtime by a pack of…of these green devils and lots of them! I was collecting more firewood a distance away when they attacked. I was able to shoot three of them before others jumped me. I was speared through the middle but slashed his head off with my saber! I fought off two more who kept slashing me killing them. I left my saber stuck in the last one's chest. Then I climbed on my horse and escaped."

Hook then asked. "What happened to the others?" The dying officer continued. "I do not know," as he gasped from his sucking chest wound. "All I saw was a huge brawl going on by the light of the campfire." He leaned back against the wall with his life ebbing. Cornwallis had come over and was checking his wounds. He slipped a piece of an opium cake in the man's mouth. The most serious one was a spear wound through his chest and lung from the rear. The pie faced son of Nepal looked at Hook and gave a negative nod. In just a few more moments the officer of Wadsworth's personal staff was dead, bleeding to death. The two enlisted men with them from Wadsworth's staff were quiet as Hook spoke.

"We will cover him with rocks and leave him, there is no use moving a body back now, it will slow us down." The NCO objected and Old Hooky unloaded. "If we do not warn your commander to stop his insane plan to invade green devil land, then you will be seeing, from heaven I am certain, another seven-hundred plus men looking like this one and before dinnertime! That is dead! Dead hopefully before they are eaten by these monsters!" He pulled the dog tag from the body and handed it to the mute NCO. The group piled rocks on the body and departed. This body would never be recovered, that would remain forever in the landscape and mystery haunting the minds of the scouts moving due south across the hilly wastelands of north India.

However, to their surprise and to the consternation of Hook and his party, they ran headlong into the advance guard of the relief column encampment the next morning! Colonel Wadsworth was not in Chital! His columns had pushed at a breakneck pace two days north of the city ready to fulfill Wadsworth's illegal rescue mission. Colonel Wadsworth was on an obvious roll. Running from justice into certain doom! "Where is Colonel Wadsworth?" Hook bellowed as he rode up to the sentries in the north of the encampment in exasperation. They pointed to the headquarters tent in the distance. The burley color sergeant and companions rode off without further comment. When he arrived in front of the command tent, he saw it crowded with many staff officers.

Must be a briefing he thought. Hook and King George walked directly up to the front of the tent, came to attention and saluted the officer at the front. "Sir, I have your intelligence report from Cavendish!" He waited to the limit of his patience and taste for some rum until an orderly approached. Colonel Wadsworth is busy, what is it you have to say?" Alfred Hook became visibly angry and retorted. "Tell the Colonel that I hold the message that can give life or death to every man in this command! Tell him now!" Shaken, the orderly disappeared back into the tent. Within a few minutes SGT Hook was ushered in alone.

He walked up to where Colonel Wadsworth was sitting and came to attention. "Color Sergeant Hook reporting SIR!" Seemingly amused and puffing on his pipe Wadsworth spoke. "Well, well, wouldn't you agree that you are quite out of uniform?" Hook looked down at his weathered tan uniform; full of sweat, dirt, and the rough native cloak he wore. In his hand was a rather beaten up tan pith helmet. The sergeant looked him right in the eye, "Not out of uniform for the duties I have been assigned Sir!" Wadsworth smirked in belittlement and continued; "So sergeant, what fairy tales does your Lieutenant have to spin here tonight?" There was laughter from all Wad's cronies in the room.

Hook was quietly aggravated and spoke. "If it pleases the Colonel, I will now spin you a fairy tale!" More laughter arose as he handed the colonel the message. Wadsworth was silent as he read it then told Hook to speak. The sergeant spoke with intense sarcasm as he gave his verbal report. "Well sir, it is like this, once upon a time in a magical land called Shangri-La; where the Good fairy Cavendish and his elves discovered this huge encampment filled with thousands of screaming green devil nomes, moon men as you call them, who were under the central control of the evil witch named Kali! We enjoyed the spectacle of these moon men savagely torturing and eating a few of your beloved hostages every night for dinner! It is estimated by the good fairy Cavendish that you and your white knights are outnumbered upwards to twenty to one at least!

Next, good fairy Cavendish flew over the area and concluded it will be next to impossible to fight in British battle formations in this enchanted land. There simply is no room to maneuver or fight using British tactics for miles of rough jungle! Your army will be forced to fight face-to-face engagements in the thick jungle only yards from attackers hidden in the beautiful enchanted jungle. If you somehow make it to a rather open field after your jungle episode, then you will probably face the bulk of these screaming savages in tall grass! So, the good fairy told me to tell you that if you continue with this campaign, your relief force will more than likely be wiped out, whose survivors will make a good crispy dinner for the greenies! SIR! Seems like they love white meat! I know you do not want the Kali biting you in the ass! Why I heard them in the valley just yesterday chanting "YUM YUM EATEM UP!"

A few present laughed at Hook's obvious sarcastic smart assed statements. Then a studied silence followed as the remote possibilities of truth sunk in. "Where are my staff officer's I sent with you?" demanded the colonel. Hook gave his sarcastic leer. Then Hooky dropped the bloody identification tag with the rank epaulets of the dead staff officer on the camp table Wadsworth sat behind. "Your staff officers refused to follow us into the jungle and built a campfire against our concerns of they being discovered by the green demons. These idiots built a frigging campfire anyhow! Your two NCOs came with us and are here safe. Two of your three officers are missing and presumed captured. We found the third one mortally wounded some miles away from the river." Hook pointed at the bloody tags.

There was a registered silence as the color sergeant continued. "Before your wounded officer died, he told us they were jumped by a pack of these "moon men" last night at teatime. Unlike the other officers who were probably captured, he was spared being served up like a roast pig last night!" Wadsworth pursed his lips in thought, then spoke a different note…irritated at this smartass. He ordered the two enlisted men who went with the scouts across the river to enter the tent. Both men supported Hook's story about the jungle and events they had witnessed. Wadsworth listened as if he was contemplating the story, then completely changed the conversation with his next question.

"Sergeant Hook, what do you know about the escape of Major Nephew from my command post at Chital?" "Escaped Sir?" innocently retorted Hook, "Why I thought you put him in command at Chital? Why would he escape from his own command?" Little laughs. The colonel summoned one of the guards who had a swollen jaw and nice black eye that now pointed at Hook. "He's the one sir, the bastard who hit me!" "Why you little liar!!!!" Stormed Hook with his best agitated lying voice. I was not even in Chital at the time!" "Don't act so innocent Sergeant," came an angry retort for the colonel! "You were in on it like the rest of you infernal scouts!" Added the colonel with his twisted smile.

Hook was now smiling back, "May I inquire what an escape has to do with the impending disaster and probable slaughter of every soldier in this command including you…SIR!" Wadsworth was grimacing in a red-faced anger now. He was trying to get away from this damned report. He yelled back slamming his fist on the wooden table. "Major Nephew tried to stymie my important rescue mission in combat sergeant! British citizens are at stake here, as well as countless citizens of that city also taken captive! I have my orders!"

He stared directly at all present. Hook interjected. "You do have legitimate orders colonel? Only the ones you have that were fabricated by you! Haw Haw…Old General Blood is going to get you if the Kali don't SIR!" Wadsworth was now hopping mad and began throwing items close to him at Hook. Then he pulled out his gold-plated personalized pistol his father had given him and aimed it at Hook in his rage. "You bastard Hook! I ought to kill you right here! You do not understand that we have too much at stake now! You are a traitor like Nephew! You will take his place in front of my firing squad!"

The color sergeant smiled a "screw you" smile at the pistol pointed at him. "At stake my dear leader? No, I would say you will be impaled on the courts martial stake by Blood, or as in steak dinner for the Kali in fairy land!" Wadsworth, sensing that he was losing control of this argument under the gallows humor of this bastard suddenly jumped on his feet like a red clothed puppet whose strings were just pulled sharply up by its puppet master. His composure was gone as he now drooled as he yelled. "Your report is inaccurate and deplorable! It was written with silly information by the traitor Nephew to disrupt my serious legitimate mission!" He then turned to his staff officers who had remained silent. "We will destroy these savages with British steel! Just like at Malakand! Just like Chital!"

Sergeant Hook was now laughing at this miserable screaming toad. He had gotten Old Wad's goat in spades now and was relishing it completely! The screaming red-faced toad continued ranting. "I will see that you and the rest of your little gang involved in this campaign of disinformation and in this escape regarding the traitor Nephew are stripped of your rank and drummed out of Her Majesties Army forever!" Then he gave his ugly face. "Or executed for treason like you will be before we break camp! Cavendish and the others will suffer the same fate as you, you bastard! You are now under formal arrest!" Hook looked around and saw that all eyes were upon him, a few had concerned looks, but most cocky. Hook smiled as he concluded. "Yes Sir, my report is filed; for the "fairy god mother Cavendish" has spoken! SIR!" Then he added his spin on the famous lines from Sir Tennyson with a slight change in the lyrics:

"Half a league, half a league, half a league onward,
All into the valley of death rode the six-hundred! Or is it eight-hundred this time Wadsworth?"

There was muted silence as an armed guard entered the tent. A very green junior officer named Bertram Collins stood at rapt attention and saluted Colonel Wadsworth. "Arrest this scum, now and keep him under careful guard until his execution before dawn!" Hook thought as he looked at Sir Hillary Wadsworth with a wide smile. "Old Wad's" red puffed up face was about to blow off. "Dear sir?" added Hooky, "You are so adorable when you are hopping mad." Wadsworth began screaming at him after this comment. "Color Sergeant Hook?" crisply beckoned 2LT Collins, of her majesties royal engineers, "I have been assigned to take control of you so would you follow me to my tent."

The color sergeant looked at the short and very proper 2nd Lieutenant still smiling. "I know sir, for I was standing right here when you were so ordered!" This lad appeared more as a boy scout than soldier. Hook thought of the other junior officer that Nephew shanghaied and mused; would there be another one perhaps? If not, then Hooky would see his last dawn. "Why yes sir 2nd Lieutenant, lead the way." He replied, then followed Collins out of the tent, where two more Punjab guards joined behind them.

King George and Lord Nelson who had returned to the tent had heard everything between their boss and the colonel from inside. They both stood close and watched as he appeared from the tent under guard. "Finding what Cavendish requested boys?" Inquired a smiling Hook. Lord George and Lord Nelson both smiled and nodded. They had already been busy with pre-procurement operations in the unguarded engineer supply tents. "Great my lads, I am supposed to be detained by this officer and not able to go back…Colonel Wadsworth is going to execute me by firing squad before dawn. Please drop by my prison tent and wish me farewell?" He winked at his men as they smiled back with a thumbs up.

"Tell the boys I will miss them and tell Griggs I love him and he can have my Zulu spear." King George smiled as he looked at the sharp dressed junior officer. "Is it all right if we visit Old Hooky to say farewell before we depart sir?" The short boy-officer gave a curt look. "I see nothing wrong with this as long as you conduct yourself properly." "Thank you, sir, I promise we will be on our best conduct! We want to see him before the possible green devil attack later. They are out there watching us now; thousands of them evil cannibals!" The 2nd Lieutenant gulped nervously. Hook winked again and moved forward under guard.

Later, Hook was reclining on a cot in his tent fully clothed in all his gear piled next to him. 2LT Collins came in and sat on his cot across from him. Two Punjab guards sat outside in front of the tent. Bertram inquired after looking at the sergeant's gear. "Color sergeant Hook, please give me your two service revolvers and that long knife?" He retorted to the young officer. "No, I won't give you my pistols, or my Kurri knife until after I am executed! I want to be armed until after I am executed SIR!" The lieutenant gave a short laugh as Hook finished. "I sense those green devils are everywhere now creeping up on us for the sun has set! Son, I...." Collins cut him off sharply... "SGT HOOK! I am 2LT Bertram Collins of the Royal Engineers, and will be addressed as such and not as "son!" Do I make myself perfectly clear?"

"OK "As SUCH!" I get it!" NO SGT! Not "son" or "As Such" but LT COLLINS OR SIR!" "DAMNIT SON! SUCH! SIR! Make up your mind!" Hook was smiling with his eyes closed. Frustrated, Collins continued "Well sergeant, give me your weapons, you are not going anywhere except to a firing squad." "Sir Collins! They are in my holsters and my shotgun is with my kit, not in my hands but at the ready in case! How long have you been in India?" Hook then opened his eyes and stared at the officer. He noticed again this "sir" looked more like a frigging boy scout, not a hair on his face, in a well-creased uniform. Sweat was on his brow for it was a warm night. The green lieutenant, crisply said "I just arrived in country about one month ago with a new rotation of officers and was assigned to Colonel Wadsworth's Auxiliary force at Malakand as my first assignment to build up the defenses at Malakand!"

"Well son such Sir! Seems strange to you that your mission at Malakand was aborted for this clown parade? If you had seen what I have seen you would be ready to fight to the death at the drop of a hat like I am now...SIR!" and I will never use my pistols against you! You are safe! I do think death by firing squad is better than being slowly spit roasted by Kali anyhow. It is time for me to die!" Collins was flabbergasted at what Hook had said and let the guns go for now. 'What is "spit roasted" sergeant?"

Hooky looked very serious. "They stick a sharp pole up your ass through your guts and push it either out your mouth or neck. Then they tie your arms and legs to your body. The devils use the neck because they love to hear their meals scream during the roast!" Collins face ashened at this terrible thought! He looked at the sergeant and said. "But the colonel calls this field report nonsense, fairytales of sorts and propaganda from a traitorous officer to weaken this rescue order!"

Hook sighed. "You obviously were not in the attack against the lancers at Chital several nights' past or saw what we did in the jungle to the north." said the burly NCO, as he rolled up into a sitting position. The handcuffs were tight on his wrists. "Old Waddyboy" says this because he is a washed-out old bastard seeking a last chance at glory to save his compromised ass from General Blood! No orders were given under the hand of General Blood for any movement from Wadsworth to leave Malakand! Major Nephew came to relieve Old Wad and that is why he was arrested to be shot! Wadsworth's orders were concocted from dubious sources outside the command! Blood is on his trail hunting him as I speak to stop this madness sir son!" Hooky leaned forward and continued. "Colonel Wadsworth is a supreme asshole who will get all of this command killed in the next few days! Mark my words Boyo! I will be waiting at the Pearly Gates for you with a shot of *Irish whiskey!*"

Collins was aghast at the insult. "How dare you insult our commander like this? I will have you reported!" intoned a red-faced subaltern. Sergeant Hook gave a smile. "Go ahead...report me, and he can have the firing squad shoot me twice! All of you will be dead soon...for I have seen the enemy and they are thousands of opium high brainwashed killers waiting to defeat you and put each and every one of you in a cooking pot! Fresh pork for the green cannibals!" Collins unbuttoned the top button on his red tunic and stared at the huge veteran seated across from him with several deep scars on his face who sported a VC on his chest. He was silent and finally inquired about what Hook had seen.

"I need a shot of whiskey or rum to tell my story Sir and take the pain and fear of my execution away. Please consider this my final request in this world? I admit only to you that I have done bad things in my life, and no Pearly Gates for me! Hell, I can't even get to my liquor supply now!" He raised his handcuffed wrists. "Well I have my rations... I don't drink." Answered Collins. "Good, now I will be a nice Sergeant Hook the story teller if you give me some?" The young Collins grabbed a bottle of whiskey from his kit and handed it over to a smiling gracious Hooky who popped the cork with his teeth. Collins added, "Whiskey is all I have and I trade this for other things, can't stand the taste of it!" implied the Boy Scout lieutenant. Hook took a long plug from the bottle...then took another.

2LT Collins was aghast at the amount he had drank. "How can you drink that stuff like that?" Inquired Collins. "AAAARRRRRRRR!" replied Hooky. "It does take time to learn this trade and combat experience is a good teacher!" He continued and spent the next hour educating the young officer who became all ears. At seeing the VC on Hook's chest, he was first told the tale of "The Drift!" Finally, after the green devils were discussed, the young officer spoke. "But I never could believe this about what we possibly face on this mission sergeant, it is too fantastic to comprehend! I have never heard anything about these green devils ever! If what you say is all true, then we will never have a chance!"

SGT Hook continued with a happy smile after half the bottle of whiskey was gone. "What really makes this mission worse is that it is completely illegal. Old Wad" then countermanded official orders with this bogus rescue mission and a "maybe" we will destroy the bad guys as well" line. Then he had Major Nephew arrested and was going to have him executed. I Now you know why we sprung the Major and why Old Wad had me arrested?" "This could make sense." The new 2LT was having a hard time believing this and nodded his head in some abject motion. Hook took another plug from the whiskey bottle. "Tell me lieutenant, are you good with explosives?" The junior officer gave a confident smile. "Yes, I am one of the best at it and was the top cadet in my class!"

Hook smiled. "This is good!" Suddenly, in the darkness, there was an explosion to the south of the encampment. The familiar sound of Russian rifle fire cracked. The guards, which were posted in front of Hook's tent prison, ran off to see the commotion. Almost immediately the camp exploded in a rash of return rifle fire into the darkness. Soon after there was a slight rustle outside the tent... Collins looked scared. "Uncuff me Sir! Do you want me to die like this at the hands of those savages? Spit roasted into a tasty dinner?" 2LT Collins complied with shaking hands and the cuffs came off. Lord George quickly entered the tent and winked at Hook.

"Better turn the light down...the green devils have poison dart guns you know and are moving between the tents now!" As 2LT Collins carefully reached over to turn down the kerosene lamp King George was upon him now joined by Sergeant Hook. They gagged and tied the squirming 2LT up in moments...Collins choked in terror... "Got the goods George?" "Yes sahib, already outside the camp with our sniper!" as King George gave his perpetual smile. Gladstone will meet us on the trail after he is finished disturbing the camp." More rifle shots and another explosion rocked near the camp. The camp guards were continuing returning fire into the darkness in the chaos consuming the camp. Hook looked at Collins as serenely as possible and said "YUM YUM EATUM UP BOY! AARRRRR! ...Or live?" He then grabbed Collins kit sitting unpacked on the cot. SGT Hook looked at King George and laughed, "Our group is going to have to quit kidnapping junior officers! ... and we have this explosives expert under our cuff tonight!"

Within minutes to the engineer officer, he and his kidnappers rode swiftly past the crouching sentries north on the barren path. Seeing the red tunic Collins wore and not the gag or rope restraints, the sentries crouched in a gully quietly waived them to pass in a fast trot. Old Hooky pulled his horse in the dark by its reigns. His gagged yells were muffled by the sound of hundreds of rifles being fired at a non-existent enemy to the south of the bivouac. The noise of the hooves coming up in the dark a couple of miles away from the encampment signaled the approach of Lord Nelson and three pack horses; the author of the explosion and diversion. 2LT Collins, of her majesties Royal Engineers, in his first assignment after graduation now was embarked on quite a new twist in his assignment career. Decreed by fate, like Allenby, he now had the possibility to survive the ordeal to come.

The ruckus in the night around the camp created by the explosions and rifle fire subsided after a couple of nervous hours. It was discovered at dawn of the disappearance of Hook and his Gurkhas. The boyish lieutenant Collins also could not be located. When the officer assigned to execute Hook reported this to Colonel Wadsworth, he was given to renewed drooling rampage and drank nearly a full bottle of Whiskey. Old Wad had been duped twice now in ridding the world of these antagonists whom he hated more than the non-existent green devils and the Kali! He smiled to himself as booze and drool drained from his chin. He would deal with Hook and the rest when the next opportunity knocked, and it would "knock" soon! He would make this whole band of jerks all disappear forever.

Continuing with his booze fueled rage, the next day was terrible on his troops. Hillary Wadsworth relentlessly drove his force north and on the fast march in the stifling heat. Many soldiers were dropping from heat exhaustion in the dust. He needed to find and finish the job on these green devils as soon as possible. His sixth sense told him that somewhere behind him was the approaching wrath of General Bindon Blood.

Hillary Wadsworth force-marched his army at a backbreaking pace into the next night to the moans of so many exhausted hungry troops. The encampment was a disorganized mess since the troops were too tired to put up tents. Most men slept on the open ground with meager rations. Security was minimal and haphazard like the camp. Wadsworth's bloodhounds would continue ferreting out these devils the next day, every day! By the end of the two days of forced marching, the exasperated conditions of his troops were near disaster. The troops were beyond exhaustion, by lack of rest, and all-consuming heat was beginning to take a fatal toll on men and horses. Both were collapsing from heat exhaustion with several deaths reported.

The sun beat the dusty columns of men and horses into a bedraggled thirsty near mob as they trudged along under the yells of most of the colonel's red-coated staff. Over one hundred men slipped out of he ranks and deserted, including the two enlisted men who had accompanied the scouts into the jungle. They knew the deadly reality this relief force would face in this inhospitable terrain. The long dusty broken columns came to the first river course of the Swarti. Mobs of hot thirsty troops plunged into the shallow waters at the crossing point. This mess held up the column for three hours. Discipline seemed to be ebbing in the ranks.

The relief army slowly crossed the river and later came upon the second tributary in the more exotic environment of trees and undergrowth on the approach. The wet heat was welcome. They had finally made it to the beautiful picturesque emerald green river. The columns again broke ranks and surged as a mob into the cool waters of the river. This river was different than the other one. It was deeper and the green waters moved faster. Several large crocs attacked and devoured several of the exhausted troops before they even noticed them skimming slowly towards them as they frolicked in the water. After a barrage of rifle shots, the dead bodies of the slaughtered amphibians floated away into the rapids below along with several mangled bodies of the unfortunates who first jumped into the river to cool off.

Order in the remaining ranks was finally restored and the detachment of engineers minus their commander 2LT Collins began building a wooden bridge across the emerald river between two huge sets of rapids used by the scouts in their earlier trip. Night soon fell over the land as work on the bridge continued by torchlight. Many huge bonfires lit up the riverbank as setting up an ordered camp remained a problem. Most of the soldiers were sound asleep from the forced march in the heat. Sentries were doubled for the night as Colonel Wadsworth was on edge. This jungle did exist after all! So, the possibility of thirty-thousand green devils could be real as well? He had thought that all this fanfare created by Cavendish had been a ruse to keep him from continuing on his crazy mission! But his crazy mission had concrete purpose to save his ass!

The group of scouts Wadsworth had sent across all returned before dusk with the remarkable story of a huge prehistoric jungle which seemed to run for miles between the ridges of two huge mountain ranges. They also told of huge well-defined paths in the jungle that revealed many people had trudged on them! The night passed without incident and there were no attacks or contact with any of the estimated thousands of green devils! This came as relief to all the officers that had heard the report of the absent renegade Sergeant Hook who had skipped his firing squad appointment! The rank and file troops had no knowledge of the danger they faced and were oblivious to the concerns of the officers. To them, it was a rescue mission of hostages kidnapped from Chital against a few bands of dangerous poorly armed natives; so, they were told.

The jungle had eyes everywhere that night as hundreds of devils monitored this body of troops. Back at the castle of the Kali, captured Captain Stevens, was forced to watch the fate of one of his men. Stevens was a small wiry man and the chosen meal was much larger and more to eat! He was ritually tortured before he was roasted alive on a spit in front of the Kali and his high priests for a tasty repast. Captain Stevens, to hopefully save his ass as he watched this horrible spectacle, gave a complete rundown on the plans and size of Colonel Wadsworth's army to what appeared as a Russian officer disguised in a long black hooded robe.

There were plans for Stevens forced to join in the feast of his fellow officer. He stood in the temple room at the top of the castle facing the Kali and shaking in abject fear of this monster before them. He thought this kali was just some large guy dressed up in a scary costume at first. Kali was over seven feet tall and his mask looked like a silver metallic one. This mask sported very large insect like eyes and a large mouth of teeth accented on a pointed chin. The body of this freak was long with huge dangling arms that ended in strange looking claw hands. This image was terrifying as he now observed this nightmare shapeshift into an exotic dark-skinned Indian woman sitting on the throne before them.

She said "We have decided to spare you like many of the captive soldiers we took from Chital. We want you to join us rather than have you on our menu!" This bigger than life size women dressed in a dark gown with long black hair mused with an exposed wide fanged smile. She left the throne and approached Stevens. Her perfume was intoxicating as she was nose to nose with him now. Stevens now noticed that her nose was moving like a small snake. Then she grabbed the side of his head with superhuman strength as she plunged its proboscis of her moving nose into his ear. Captain Stevens jerked as his brain was frozen, frozen to the will of the Kali! He had now been conscripted as thousands of others had forever. The whites of his eyes bulged in their eye sockets as Stevens was led away to be prepared with tattoos and green dye. They would look great against the backdrop of his red jacket!

Stevens would never know that he had been privy to both the Kali's personas: transformed from the violent god Kali into its other façade which was the evil goddess Raktabija! Kali had used many other shapes and names in his long past on this planet, but now he used the shapes of these two deities to evoke ancient legends of godlike terror and his will on the world. The fear of the return of Kali was well entrenched in the ancient lore of India! This was why he chose this persona to do his bidding. The chaotic "Age of Kali" would be his gift to the masses when conditions were right! Kali had appeared simply as a noble Islamic holy man when positioning his horde with the Islamic forces aligned against the British. He had used his shape changing abilities for centuries with good results.

But the destruction of the British was not the only group he held plans to destroy! He had an old vendetta. The survivors of this approaching British army would soon join his ranks to kill a bigger fish. Kali needed thousands more conscripts to replace his destroyed minions and prepare for his rule first in India then ... Onward across the planet! Many of the hostages had been doled out to his minions to be devoured as rewards for their victory over Chital. He also had kept a few for his own personal pleasure and feast. It laughed a loud, a whole army of new recruits was headed his way! Kali later sat on his dais in the open temple on the roof of his castle after the nightly feast picking a piece of staff officer lodged between his teeth with a dagger. The British officer had been a tasty meal for him and his top subordinates. He viewed the pile of bones left scattered on the table as he thought how spit roasted Europeans tasted like swine.

But now he began contemplating his distant past as it sipped a golden goblet of red wine. He reflected on his life before his return to this region of the planet. It was his quite enjoyable life as a conquistador under the Spanish empire, plundering civilizations and enslaving thousands in terror, fear to his will. Their meat was so tantalizing and rich in taste, like the women he loved to rape. It seemed better than the Europeans. He had been Cortes then and the plunder of the "New World" had been his game. He mused at how he had assumed the persona of this conquistador as he had met him on a ship as member of the crew. As this new Cortes he learned of his aspirations from the queen of Spain. Like a parasite, he was looking for something new to attach too! He had to escape his previous life or be killed by them! He found it in the Americas!

Over the course of his existence he had discovered the many powers it had possessed. Shapeshifting and mind control over humans were paramount to his many abilities! His father had been destroyed and like his father before him he learned that humankind was his toy to play with and manipulate always. Just like when he played the noble Catholic liberator of the Spanish queen in the new world, he now played the role of the long-feared deities of both Kali and the goddess demon created from his blood Raktabija. However, he had first played the role of the humble deeply religious Islamic leader to join the firm opposition for the war of destruction against the British invaders! The use of religion to further his ends was a powerful tool in his arsenal!

His morphed persona as Cortes came to Spain at a perfect time! Though his loyalty and success in helping win several religious wars haunting Europe, the Queen of Spain offered him a chance to go spread her empire and the power of the Church in this new world. Kali "Cortes" was hypnotically convincing in his several private sessions with the queen and addicted her appetite to his unusual sexual abilities, since parts of his body could shape change at his will! He crossed the ocean for the new world. It was a perfect place to spread his chaos and destructive energies in wiping out well-established civilizations. He relished these times as both savior and destroyer of them, just like he was planning for India now. But his concerned thoughts now rested on the eyes that had been watching him since he had returned to this subcontinent. The ancient eyes that had killed his father were the ones hunting him! His pursuers were also like him, cut from the same tree! "them?" He had returned to this subcontinent to "them" to destroy once and for all!

His agenda to hunt and destroy "them" had originally been planned from necessity with his father since the Ninth century. He could barely remember his real name buried under so many others he had used and chuckled. How the temporal humans live behind their personal temporal mantels of self-being, position, power and religion for the few years they live? These vestiges were his tools to manipulate them constantly! His only religion was the worship of himself as god! Kali and the handmaiden Raktabija were perfect? If humans only lived long like him, they would learn this truth. Unbeknownst to Wadsworth, Kali had his army under constant surveillance since they left Chital! They would be allowed to venture deep into the jungle to the threshold of his plains by the water falls; to be sacrificed, or in more military terminology, destroyed, captured, and conditioned! Yes, he laughed, he was Kali of the Islamic jihad!

Griggs, Gladstone and Cornwallis were assigned the task of recon of the area surrounding the huge monolith of a castle that extended from the massif to the river covered in dense jungle. Rashid, Corporal Hoskins, and Lieutenant Cavendish were going to search inside the castle. No contact was to be made period. At this time of night, the castle guards were few, and the devils had settled down throughout the encampment below. The only movement in the area was the flickering of the waning torches and butter lamps. The two groups slipped off into the night to collect as much information as possible. They were to meet back at this location, and if all hell broke loose, to beat it back to the camp and horses then 'beat feet" out of the jungle.

Hoskins and Cavendish had surveyed this huge ancient castle at length before the sunset. There were too many sentries at the huge rear gate. They decided to climb down the massif on the huge ancient vines hidden by the jungle fauna. These huge vines had overgrown on the southern wall and would make an easy undetected climb possible. In about forty minutes, the three scouts had edged down the sloping massif clinging silently to the vines masked by the vegetation. They worked across the vines until they could climb into the parapet walkway of the castle. In the shadows of the ebbing torches they moved towards a huge wooden door across the parapet.

Previously, before their descent, they witnessed some strange rituals near a row of statues on the roof temple. This cloaked priest in charge was huge in size and was chanting out loud with a crowd of at least fifty odd black-cloaked hooded green devils. Their droll rhymed chants continued as Rashid had wanted to get a closer view of this group in the open temple where they heard horrible inhuman screams. As the Indian scout moved away Cavendish felt it was an opportune time to venture into the castle proper. They observed no guards or movement in this area. Inside the huge door they discovered the rooms in the first corridor seemed to be empty.

As they descended to the second level of old damp stone walls as they soon discovered crates of Russian rifles and large rooms filled with rifle ammunition, gunpowder, and stores of artillery ammunition. The shells were huge ones, probably forty-four calibers. Russian writing covered the crates. Hoskins opened one to find an assortment of new fused hand grenades. He smiled at Cavendish in the dim light as he handed six to the lieutenant and took six for himself. "You never know Sir!" He was smiling as they stuffed them into their haversacks. They moved on taking mental notes on what they found on each floor; then suddenly a shadow leaped out tripping Cavendish. Hoskins jumped the shadow with his regulation bayonet unsheathed. The shadow squeaked in fear. Hoskins put his hand over the mouth of this shadow, which turned out to be a small British boy of about ten years of age. 'Shush" ordered Hoskins. "Be quiet!" The boy was silent as the Corporal had spoken in English.

The corporal removed his hand. The boy was speechless as another form emerged near him from the shadows. It turned out to be a little English lass in a tattered blue dress, its luster long gone. Both Cavendish and Hoskins looked at them in silence. The little girl spoke in a very scared voice. "Please help us, we need to escape from here! These goblins have been searching for us!" By this time another form emerged, and with this Cavendish pulled out his Kurri knife. "Relax darling" came a soothing female voice catching both soldiers completely caught off guard.

"What gives with you?" Asked the corporal staring at the little girl. The little girl told them her name. She was Robin and the boy Robert was her brother. Then she looked at the figure, taller in the shadows. "This is my mother Andréa." In short succession, the group moved into a dark side room. "We are British scouts. I am Cavendish, and this is Hoskins." We are scouting out this place which may be under attack soon by the British Army." This announcement left Andrea and the kids unmoved. Both men saw beyond her extreme disheveled appearance noticing she was a very buxom blonde beauty. She answered them. "We escaped from the guards last night and have been trying to get out of here but seem lost in this evil place!"

"How many captives are left?' inquired Cavendish. "Not very many, and I think they...." Her voice trailed off..." They will all be gone soon to terrible deaths or transformed soon. They have been savagely torturing, murdering, ..." Her voice went silent momentarily...." And devouring them every night on the roof!" she went mute then continued. "Two more British officers were delivered a couple of days ago and they told me they were captured at the river. Then they were dragged away to the roof. This is when we had to escape! We were the only ones left I believe." Cavendish gave a disgusted look. He pulled out his gold pocket watch and viewed the time. It was nearly five. The sun would be up soon.

"How did you get out of that room?" Asked the lieutenant. Andrea stared at him. "We found a small crawl space of sorts inside the room behind a loose grate where we were held. Robert discovered it was some old shaft of sorts. We climbed down and ended up here last night. We have been hiding ever since. We were next I am sure. This leader, the Kali is a real monster!" She was shaking. Cavendish replied. "Very good, but if we are going to survive, we need to get out of here now." So quietly, sneaking outside and to the wall they went. Just after all were safe on the other side of the wall, they could all hear the many footsteps filtering down from the passageways from the top of the castle.

So far, luck was on their side. It took at least an hour for all of them to work their way up the massif on the vines back to the rendezvous spot on the massif. The children were tied to the backs of the men. The sun was just emerging from the ancient jungle as Griggs and his two Gurkha companions returned to their rally point. LT. Cavendish, Hoskins, and Rashid with the three freed captives had already eaten some rations and drank their fill of water. Her kids were actually eight-year-old twins. They remained silent as the two groups traded information. Cavendish and Hoskins explained what they found, in the form of munitions and weapons stores. The three rescued hostages were all that was left!

Rashid gave his confused impression of his observations on the roof temple. This Kali was a huge person and seemed to control all present. He was appalled at what they did to the hostages before they ate them. It was the same fate as the other hostages they had observed. He was physically sickened. Griggs and the Gurkhas relayed their report. They counted fifteen heavy Russian artillery pieces, with caissons, and horse teams to pull them. There was a huge stockpile of munitions in a temporary structure next to the cannons under the huge tent they had seen earlier. They had also found other military stores. This was huge. They reported that it was Russian advisors they had watched, who were guarding this artillery and munitions storage. No Ghazis, Afghans, or Pashtuns were seen anywhere, just more civilized acting green devils. They also estimated the small bridges leading from the huge encampment into this redoubt only stretched across the river some seventy yards. It was a tight passage, mostly filled by a fast-moving deep river.

Two reinforced wooden bridges were the only crossings from the castle to the other dry side of this little pass. The large one was for wheeled traffic and the smaller one was for troop movement. Gladstone mused "We can blow both of these bridges easy Sahib! Maybe blow up the whole pass if we had the right number of explosives in the right place!" Cavendish mused about what he had told Hook to borrow from Wadsworth's engineers. Just maybe? The others, with the exception of the new arrivals smiled and nodded yes. But it was time to get back, find out if Hook had returned which was doubtful at this time. What was their plan? It all depended on if that folly Wadsworth had even left Chital. Otherwise, he was going for General Blood.

The group moved out back into the flat terrain of the forest jungle and soon encountered the rough rocky forest terrain as they neared the mountain river. It was morning when they crossed the fast-flowing river that fed the huge waterfall. Both children and mother were beyond exhaustion, malnourishment, and a forever fear had etched a dark scar on each of their souls. However, Hoskins seemed to take control of them and wherever they were, so was his strong presence of encouragement. The good news was there had been no direct encounters with the greenies or their Russian allies at the castle or along this huge massif, so for now they were safe.

The group returned to the camp not to find Color Sergeant Alfred Hook. They settled down into a dinner mode, helping the ex-hostages to relax and eat some food. After dinner, they all stripped down and enjoyed the warm cleansing in a set of small hot springs adjacent to the place where their camp was located. Andrea and her kids washed separately. Cavendish estimated that his sergeant had been gone for a good four days now. He would wait one more day before leaving this paradise. That night Hoskins and Cornwallis were on guard duty. They both felt that someone or thing was staring at them from above as they felt the unmistakable presence. Rashid joined them in the late night because he could not sleep. He was bothered as well.

Hoskins commented to Rashid. "I feel like I am being closely watched, almost like something is right next to me I swear! Do you?" Yes, corporal I sense the same thing but from above and cannot figure out who or what is observing us! If they were devils, we already would have been attacked. I have felt this like you every night to be honest. Whatever it is it is not showing any malice as of yet. Perhaps it might be another mythological specter watching us, perhaps a good one?" Hoskins looked at the wise old guide. "What other spawn of myth could it be then?" Rashid smiled. "Corporal, it could be the ancient shape changers, another product of ancient lore like the destroyer."

Hoskins was grinning at him. 'So, what are these shape changers then?" Rashid grinned back at the handsome rough looking Welshman. "They can be anything they want to be my dear man according to the lore! Many who saw them said they appeared as gods or angels to them." Hoskins nodded his head with a low smile and patted the Indian guide on the shoulder. "Many thanks for this important revelation. Maybe Andrea is one of them?" Rashid saw his smile and it broke the seriousness of his thoughts. "Yes, maybe she is an angel for you."

Late the next morning Sergeant Hook, Lord George, Lord Nelson, and what Hooky called his newest recruit walked their horses into the camp. They had to avoid several groups of devils moving towards the river since they were now on alert for what was coming from the south. Hook made his report that he encountered Wadsworth's columns two days out of Chital encamped. It seemed this relief force was moving at a very fast pace and seemed in disarray; real mess and ill-prepared to fight anything!

He explained how Wadsworth ignored his report and had him arrested for helping Major Nephew escape. He was identified by the guard he had cold-cocked in front of Old Waddy! So, he was remanded to a tent under guard for a firing squad at dawn. He surmised that if the greenies did not attack Wadsworth, then the whole caboodle would soon be at the river before the jungle valley. There was a silence as this bad news permeated across the minds of all present. When Cavendish inquired if he had borrowed anything from the engineers the salty old NCO gave a big smile and a wink of his eye.

"Yes, my two lords did a grand job absconding, or I shall say "borrowing" some great stuff from the engineers sir! I thoughtfully borrowed one of Her Majesties finest royal engineers to gladly help us! Oh, yes sir, those three staff officers that stayed at the river? Two were missing and we found the other one mortally cut up a few miles down the road from the river. He told me that a large group of devils attacked them that night. He died." Cavendish replied, "They were probably sitting about a campfire drinking tea thinking this is a joke. I am certain they spilled the beans since Andrea, a captive we saved saw two of them in custody before she and her kids were able to escape."

He then said. "This is the worst news regarding Wadsworth! Major general Blood will never be able to catch up now, but Kali will!" He grew silent then pointed at the boyish looking British second lieutenant that had stripped off his Pashtun robe which covered his red blouse. "Your guest is this fine engineer Hooky?" asked Cavendish in abandoned askance smiling. Hooky smiled. "Sir, I apologize, but we have done it again! We have kidnapped another junior officer. May I introduce 2nd Lieutenant Bertram Collins of Her Majesty's Royal Engineers! He was guarding me until my summary execution just like Major was going to buy it in Chital!

Well, those green devils attacked and we saved Collins from the cooking pot! Besides, he was on this boring rescue mission with "Sir ASSWIPE" and I felt he was ready for some real action in-country. I didn't want to disappoint him!" Hook patted his prisoner on the back. Bertram winced and looked long at Hook, then Cavendish smiled beyond the flames generated by the small fire and sighed "Reporting for duty again I guess!" The scouts all seemed to laugh, for this recent escapade was about as crazy as everything else going on.

Hook interjected as he cleared his mouth. "Our new engineer officer told me he is an expert in explosives and may be of use as this scenario from hell evolves!" Cavendish looked Collins directly in the eyes and said "We will have good use for you now I fear!" The prisoner replied. "But Sir, I am not under your command and have been brought here under extreme duress!" Snarled the youthful bedraggled officer staring angrily at Hook and his Gurkha handlers. Cavendish was silent and smiled again as he took a measured pause then resumed. "Because of fate and action by one Sergeant Hook, "Hero of the Drift," you may have a chance to get out of this with your skin! So, listen and learn me boy!

All of "we official outcasts" know the reality of Wadsworth's insane and very illegal mission which is headed straight to complete disaster and death!" When the sun comes up, I will let you preview for yourself what Sir Wadsworth and company will be facing when they walk into the valley below, if they ever get that far! If you want to return after you see what lies below in the valley, I will send you back when they enter the jungle. If not, then consider yourself under my command. You are very needed. We may be planning a huge surprise to blunt the dangerous attack these devils are planning for certain, which will be our next subject! So, 2LT Bertram Collins of "His Majesties Royal Engineers???? What is your decision?"

The young boyish officer looked at Cavendish and around the small fire. "I will think about it and let you know at dawn after I see the threat you speak about!" He was later shown the hundreds of campfires in the valley that night. Later, in the dawn, he viewed the thousands of green devils lined up mutely and motionless in their formations. He needed little convincing after seeing this, for he was completely unnerved by this strange spectacle. He was now in the game. Finally, he spoke to the group. "Under these circumstances I will throw my lot in with you, Sir!" Hook pulled out a bottle of rum and took a plug, then handed it to Collins. "Go ahead Sir, you are part of our elite team and have earned this one!" The new member of the group took a hearty plug from the bottle, coughed, adjusted himself and took another plug. The rum was good. "That's the spirit boyo, welcome to hell!"

They finished their repast around the small fire the next night amused with the complete story of Hook's arrest and imprisonment under the watchful eye of 2LT Collins. The conversation now moved into planning their attack on Kali and his boys. After a couple of hours, the complete picture of their war plan was set. The main targets were the castle, bridges, and cannon and ammunition storage dumps. Then came the possibility of blowing the end of the precipice up and blocking the whole end to the valley? The Gurkhas had acquired liquid nitro. They planned to spring their attack before the greenies could spring their huge ambush on Wadsworth's relief forces. This warning could buy some time for the condemned British to organize for a good fight or to possibly escape. Proper timing and coordination were of the essence!

Cavendish sent a small team led by Griggs, to locate the position of Wadsworth's columns. This was critical now. They would have to figure out how much time they had before the British force was near the huge open grassy plain beyond the jungle. The rest of the group stayed behind, joined by the new recruit Collins, after checking on how much explosives were on hand, he and King George worked out the details of their mission to destroy the key enemy positions vital to their ability to fight. These targets included both bridges, the artillery park, the castle ammo stores, and if possible, the huge rock bluff formation that blocked the castle view at the end of the huge valley.

Thanks to Hook and his Gurkhas, they had three horses loaded with dynamite, blasting caps, liquid nitroglycerin, and ammunition for their small arms. Mister Griggs saw this collection and laughed. He told them that there were enough Russian munitions stored in the castle to destroy most of it when ignited. Only a small charge was needed. He would take care of it. Most of the explosives could be used on other targets. The group was weary and settled into a fatigued rest after another dip in the bubbly hot springs below, but restful sleep was robbed from them again. Something or things seemed to dominate the night above and near them on the ground now. These shadows seemed so close.... seemed to glide around in the air.... Hoskins, sensed this strongly and shielded the twins and mother with his body and a blanket armed with his pistol so they could sleep.

Cavendish seemed to drift off finally. He found himself standing in this beautiful jungle, in a peaceful light. Then she appeared, a most beautiful woman, the epitome of Indian beauty he had ever witnessed standing in front of him. Her scantily covered breasts tugged at her jasmine silk gown, her hips full, and her libido breathtaking. Her hair was a rich deep black that flowed to her supple waist. Her olive skin was scented in a rich perfume. A huge diamond was in her belly button, as a smaller one piercing her aquiline nose. Her eyes and smile were captivating and hypnotic. Cavendish was completely mesmerized and stared at her.

She walked up to him and held his hands facing him, looking deep into his soul with her deep purple retinas. Then, this strange beauty of his dreams kissed him gently on the lips and said "I want to welcome you to my village Ambrose! Then she pointed to the image of the old broken and overgrown road back a few miles leading east to west. "West" he heard her say. He stared at her beauty until he felt a hard jerk on his arm. He awoke. It was Griggs bearded face and not the beauty! "The dawn is upon us sir!" LT Cavendish rubbed his eyes and soon over a cup of hot tea listened to the verbal report delivered by Scout Griggs.

The look in Griggs face betrayed bad news. He reported that the main body of Colonel Wadsworth's army was presently at the river across from the jungle now. "They are constructing a bridge so the army can cross. There were so many green devil scouts watching them that not even Cornwallis could get close enough to deliver your report. It will have to be delivered to them after they have crossed the river, and into the jungle." Cavendish looked around the campfire at the others. He knew his final intelligence summary to Wadsworth was useless anyhow but would send it! He gathered his scouts around the small campfire. "Men, we put our plan into action against the Kali tonight; before dawn! The pace of Wadsworth will put him there at or near that time so it seems!"

INTELLIGENCE SUMMARY (08/97) REVISED

Colonel Hillary Wadsworth
Commander
British Relief Forces

URGENT!!!

Sir! This is the revised final report of what else we have found. It is critical that you regroup your army and pull back to Chital immediately. If you do not heed this report and take immediate actions to pull back, your force will be completely destroyed if you engage the Kali in battle!

Enemy strengths: They are now confirmed near 25,000 effectives (Green Devils). Be reminded they are very aggressive, dangerous, who seem to be very high on opium (as evidenced on their attack on Chital against my advance relief guard). Shockingly sir, we have observed thousands of them; lined up in perfect silent formations for several hours each morning! Whatever disciplines them is a moot point now, they do it!

Leadership: Kali was hard to observe, but his staff includes many Russian advisors. Direct line leadership comes from powerful black-hooded priests in this enemy force.

Armament: NEW! 15 44-caliber cannons, with horse drawn mobility; hundreds of new Russian rifles, grenades, and vast amounts of munitions have been located to support the devils.

Terrain: Heavy jungle, DANGEROUS! Estimated between 17 to 20 miles of it and a main detractor in any effective British deployment of forces in the necessary fighting lines.

Other: (1) Enemy has huge stronghold beyond valley, which harbors the artillery and munitions. There are two bridges crossing a fast-deep river separating the stronghold from the pass (2) Status of Captives: Three escaped hostages were found in my recon inside castle. They stated that all other captives have been ritualistically killed (Devoured) or have been somehow conditioned/converted into the ranks of the green devils in some sort of brainwashing. There are no hostages left alive to rescue so the main reason for your campaign is null and void now! Your two officers were captured at the river. One was eaten for dinner and the whereabouts of the other remains a mystery.

Summary: Your British forces are severely outnumbered, outgunned, and in very indefensible terrain once they enter this jungle. If your army reaches the plains you will face an enemy with up to 20 times the size of your force! The Russian artillery will sit out of the range of your artillery and blow you to pieces! There can be no organized retreat once you are attacked. The jungle you have put behind you will now be the lid on the coffin of your whole army! As of your whole army is in extreme danger of being attacked! Leave now or die!

Lieutenant James Ambrose Cavendish
Scout Leader
11th Bengal Lancers
Scouts

CHAPTER FOUR
THEIR FATE IS NOW MANIFEST!

It was extremely hot and humid as the scouts made their preparations in the remote mountain jungle encampment. Cavendish was stirred by the relentless specter of the beautiful woman captivating his mind and body from his previous night's dream. She was incredibly stunning and beautiful who fired up his passion. He was sitting against his saddle, with a fresh cup of tea provided by Griggs grasping the situation as he viewed the prehistoric jungle. 2LT Collins had finished helping the Gurkhas prepare their explosives from the material absconded from Wadsworth's engineers. He had a fresh steaming tin cup tea in hand the young junior officer joined Griggs, Cavendish, and the rest of the group. They would be leaving soon.

The woman Andrea and her kids, the sole survivors of the horrible experiences had joined the group still exhausted mentally, physically, and spiritually from their ordeal. They were now under the protective wing of Corporal Hoskins. Corporal Holmes, who had been conducting a solo late-night reconnaissance, back at the river walked into camp leading his horse. He smiled as Lord George handed him a fresh tin cup of hot tea. He was wearing his tan uniform which was completely soaked in sweat. He sat down next to Sergeant Hook and looked across at the Lieutenant.

"Ready for my report Sir?" The lieutenant waved his open hand in a silent "yes." "Well, Old Wads engineers and many more helpers have erected a bridge across that last portion of the river. Quite a nice bridge actually!" As he gave a sarcastic smile before he went on. "I watched them assemble it as did droves of green devil scouts in the area. I noticed that a large advance party had crossed the river earlier and was blazing and widening that rather large central path we initially found when we crossed. It seems our boy is in some huge hurry and once the bridge is completed, he may be in easy reach of the valley perhaps the morning after tomorrow. His troops looked beyond exhaustion."

Cavendish questioned. "The green devils are not trying to ambush them?" Griggs looked at him. "Sir, the devils are steering clear of them and are only observing. I followed the rather huge party clearing the jungle path and they were some six miles into this jungle when I left them. Greenies were just out of eye shot watching them. Let's assume this party is left unmolested, can clear another five miles today. This would mean they would be staying about ten miles from the valley by nightfall tonight. So, I think that they could be in the valley by sunrise the morning after tomorrow unless our little green friends attack them. But I doubt that will happen based on my theory!

"By Jove on Olympus! They will be in that cursed valley of death soon?" Exclaimed Lieutenant Cavendish as he stood. Griggs twirled the ends of his long moustache, rubbed his beard and commented, "This conforms to my estimate that the green devils want the British on the plain below, not in the jungle. There will be little chance for any retreat, and the jungle behind them will be the trap! Makes me sick! They really all look completely exhausted to a man." Cavendish pulled his handwritten report from his tan tunic and looked across to Cornwallis who by all standards was the best tracker scout. He looked at the small Nepalese soldier who bore deep dark eyes and was known for his stealth and speed. He was also expert with his Kurri knife.

"Looks like you get the award!" comment Ambrose with a smile as he handed the retort to him. "Give it to the head of the advance guard in the jungle clearing party. Let him read it before they pass it on back. We can only pray for a mutiny at this point to save the whole lot! Then return here to guard the camp and our freed hostages. Cornwallis nodded his understanding. He left and would wait for the first opportunity to hand off the intel summary. Once he returned to the camp, by using the telescope, Cornwallis would have a bird's eye view of the whole spectacle below in the valley; as the ominous events unfolded.

Holmes gave a grim smile and commented. "Sir, why don't you let me assassinate the old bastard? One nice shot from the jungle? Then we can hijack this relief force and order it to get the hell out!" Cavendish smiled back at him. "That would be a good idea, and I have considered this. But it is too late at this point I am afraid! If we did kill Old Wad, then there would be a power struggle between us and his gang of staff clowns! Also, I feel that we would generate mass chaos and confusion throughout the ranks. Obviously, the greenies would see this mess and attack and overwhelm them in short order. I just do not have any authority to kill a senior British officer! This plan is a day late and a silver crown short!"

The next cup of hot tea had warmed up Cavendish as he thought out the timing of their plan. Their plan of attack was centered around the well-placed explosions set to disrupt the supply, command, and control of this enemy. If the green army was left leaderless by their efforts, fate would favor the relief force. However, after seeing thousands of these devils lined up mutely in formations in the plain below, he doubted it. Then he spoke to Collins: "Got the targets and charges figured out?" Bertram Collins straightened up. "Yes sir, I have created a huge explosive to take down as much of the bluff formation between the castle and plain as possible. We will blow both bridges and the ammunition dump and that Russian artillery. Griggs said he will handle the destruction of the castle." "I have made a special explosive for him for this task!"

"Good job!" Commented Lieutenant Cavendish. He continued with the plan. "We need to be in position up yonder by the castle by tonight for a final reconnaissance and preparation of our attack plan. We will plant the main charges tomorrow night. Our attack is contingent on Wadsworth being at the valley the morning after tomorrow. We must destroy that artillery from being used at all costs! Our lines of retreat will be from the rear castle bridge for we who are inside, and the vines on the massif for our sappers at the bridge. I have assumed that there will be return fire on us, so Hoskins and Holmes will set up a series of sniper nests to cover the area from the castle across the main staging area to the precipice.

If all goes well, we will all leave this infernal place in one piece! With all of that done, the other explosions on the bridges, Artillery Park, and the big bang on the bluff done in a timely manner, will warn the British columns of the imminent threat, if it really matters at this point." He paused to sip his tea then continued. "Lieutenant Collins, you will supervise the planting of these charges on the bluff with King George. He will scout the bluff for the best place to plant it before you place it. My crew of Griggs, and Hook will set the explosives inside the castle ammunition stores and be ready to set them after the big one goes on the bluff."

"Yes Sir, "came a weak nervous reply from Bertram Collin; who pondered the moment. "So, if I help plant them, who will light them sir?" All fingers pointed at him. He gulped. "Lord Nelson and Gladstone will do the honors on the bridges and Artillery Park as we call it. King George and you get the bluff. The bridge team will set off the blast in the artillery park on the way to the south wall, to mask their retreat protected by our snipers. With all that in motion, the last big bang will be in attempting to drop as much of the bluff on the pass as possible. 2LT Collins, Rashid, and King

George will be on the bluff as you do the honors on that blast. Rashid will be your security there, as Holmes and Hoskins will cover all of you and the boys down below from the massif to the south wall of the castle."

Then the lieutenant looked at Collins. "Did you create a bomb for the bridge between the massif and castle?" King George smiled at him. "Yes boss, we made a great big one, just like the one we made for Mister Griggs!" Cavendish finished his tea and poured himself and the others a fresh hot cup from the pot on the small fire." He looked at the party. "Between the battle on the plain and our timely detonation of explosives at the castle, the chaos created should give us enough cover to get out. The Lieutenant reviewed the plan one more time. Cavendish quietly sipped his tea and added one last item. "If we get separated in this attack, or things go wrong, then it is up to each of you to separately return to our camp, collect the lady and kids, and get the hell out of here and report to General Blood. The "fog and friction" of war can change any good plan in a second as all of you know!"

Cornwallis was in route to deliver what Hook called the "Last message to the doomed!". He rode his horse carefully along the old trail next to the tall set of prehistoric cliffs that they had previously used and slowly wound his way some miles back to a position observing Wadsworth's army. He saw that the engineers had completed the wooden bridge across the river. They had effectively brought lumber along just in case an obstacle of this nature confronted them. Cornwallis was impressed at their foresight. The army had already crossed and were foraging their way to the valley along the large cleared pathway. The wily Gurkha also noticed the eyes of several green devils in the area below him shielded by the thick jungle growth making the same observations as well.

The focused Gurkha began to shadow the long slowly moving columns winding on the path deep through the massive jungle. It was near dusk he was able to finally slip by the green devil scouts and reach the advance guard of infantry, which was providing protection for the many troops tasked to clear and widen the uneven root crossed pathway. They seemed to be right on schedule. The Gurkha was appalled at the complete lack of flank security and how the whole column of Wadsworth's army, like a lazy snake, was vulnerable to ambush. The relief force was literally strung out for miles with many units losing view of the ones in front or behind them. The troops carelessly moved along the rough cleared widened path, as many green savages hid in the thick jungle growth an arm's length away in many cases.

Cornwallis quickly entered the columns slogging forward in the extreme humidity under triple level canopy jungle. Soon he contacted the officer in charge of the advance guard as he made his way to the front. The forward troops continued widening the crude jungle path forward at a backbreaking pace. He walked his horse up to the officer and identified himself as a messenger sent by the scout commander with a report for Wadsworth. The British lieutenant was very apprehensive and nervous as were the others sitting around eating their rations. Cornwallis saluted and gave the dispatch to him. The officer then opened it and read it twice. Two other British officers read it. He then sent one of his men back with the report to be given to Colonel Wadsworth.

He then looked at Cornwallis. "Have you actually seen this twenty-thousand or so army of green savages?" He looked into the Gurkha's eyes in grave concern as sweat ran in rivulets down his face. "Yes sir, maybe more than that, we have been observing them from a high place on the massif to the left of the valley for several days now." The officer was glum and fear echoed from his face. He asked. "If there are so many of them then why haven't they attacked us in this indefensible jungle trail yet? Wouldn't this be the right place since we are so spread out" Cornwallis thought on it then remembered what Griggs had said. "Sir, they want this army to fight them on a huge grassy plain

some miles ahead. This jungle will be your trap! Any organized retreat under fire will be futile sir."
"Futile?" questioned the British officer.

The scout sighed and continued. "They want to completely destroy you in one deadly strike I would think! You are already being watched very closely by them since the river crossing." Cornwallis then climbed on his horse, "Sir, be ready for the big fight when you leave the jungle. My boss, or lieutenant told me to tell you to get your artillery forward with your lancers! We are preparing a big surprise for them, which will signal you to go on line quickly! Listen for many explosions down the valley sir! They will be waiting in the tall grass! Listen for the explosions and come out of the jungle ready to fight! Good luck!" He saluted the lieutenant, now mute in his anxiety, and rode off before he was trapped to join them by an order he would never obey.

As he rode away from the columns and deeper into the jungle, he literally ran into three green devils that suddenly emerged from the side of the small clearing next to a deep ravine. His horse literally slammed into the trio catapulting the first one off the path into the adjacent ravine. Cornwallis was thrown off his mount in the impact. He had his Kurri knife drawn before he hit the ground. The first attacker, a squat green devil with sharpened teeth and beady eyes, was on him immediately as he jumped to his feet, He quickly ducked a flying circular throwing saw from the second foe. The closest attacker ran at him aiming some jagged looking long knife at his stomach. Cornwallis swiftly dodged to his left deflecting his opponent's knife wielding arm down with his Kurri blade and open left hand. He then reversed the flow of his knife hand and cut deeply up the inside of the devil's arm driving the blade up his flayed inner arm into the green devil's throat slashing it through.

The second attacker who had thrown the saw charged him slashing a curved sword at him. Cornwallis caught the devil's back swinging arm from the outside blocking it with his left hand and Kurri knife in his right hand. The block delivered with his Kurri knife severed the green devil's wrist off. He then reversed his body and delivered a counterclockwise slash with his knife into the devil's throat cutting his head completely off. He looked for the other one he had first hit with the horse and found that he had knocked this greenie into the deep ravine next to the pathway. Cornwallis grimaced as he watched a rather large Python like snake with the devil's head in its mouth. The devil was squirming as the huge snake was crushing his body to pulp in its coils. Cornwallis winced as he noticed a bunch of baby snakes moving about near this fatal death struggle in this deep ravine. It looked like the uninvited green devil had fallen into her nest and mother was not happy.

He retrieved his horse and the circular saw weapon stuck in a tree. He carefully walked it for a couple of miles with his sword drawn since a pistol shot would draw in multitudes of devils. Cornwallis finally stepped off the path and waited to see if he was being followed. There was nothing behind him in the encroaching nightfall of the triple canopy jungle as he ventured back to the camp. He had orientated himself on the huge massif rising to his front and continued riding towards the large towering cliffs now lit up by the new moonlight. He was back on the small path to his camp where it oversaw the vast green valley below. He knew he had visited the company of doomed men. Their fate was sealed by a madman! What phase did his grandfather use in such dire cases? He remembered; "Their fate is manifest!"

Colonel Hillary Wadsworth sat smoldering both in the green oven of the jungle in his camp chair and from the message he had just received. Like every living soul in his army, sweat covered his face, body and soaked his uniform. His personal tent and headquarters wagons were set up to the side as the columns passed. He and his staff were nearly at the end of the huge column as it stumbled forth. Colonel Wadsworth was not setting any positive example of leadership in this race to accomplish his mission. If he was preparing to lead in the impending battle from the front like a good leader, he was missing this opportunity completely. He had forced his units ahead of his headquarters company throughout this insane march north. Many soldiers had died from heat exhaustion as many more had deserted. His ranks had thinned. He eyed the dispatch sent by Cavendish and yelled out when he found that the messenger delivering this had not been detained. "Where were these despicable bastards anyhow?"

In his anger and whiskey stupor he yelled to his many staff suck ups that doted around the area. He loved to make his little pussies jump! Concern now crossed his whiskey-soaked brow. At last he thought, is this really the truth? It was too late now for the lieutenant's scary tales of millions of moon men to compel him to slow down or quit! The wrath of Bindon Blood was behind him ready to sink his teeth into his face! He took another drink of whiskey and was finding himself fairly drunk again by now. Thank the queen that he had a liberal store of it in his wagons.

Only sure victory over these green devils and their complete destruction was his saving grace now. There was to be no grand rescue of captives according to Cavendish since they had met their fate on cooking spits! He took a swig of whiskey and savored that thought that he would be elevated to Sir Hillary Wadsworth of North India for his bravery and foresight. General Blood would never be able to touch him then! Queen Victoria, the old whore would knight him in the presence of all the nobles who favored the house of Wadsworth! He was definitely forced by all circumstances to see this expedition through, whatever the cost! In his encroaching drunkenness today, he knew one way or the other, a coffin waited at each end of his path.

One path would perhaps kill him miserably and the other he could survive in victory or complete disgrace. One symbolized the death of his career, if he failed without engaging and the defeat of this menace now. This was his only good card left to recover from all his serious illegal activities of late. The obvious other was possible defeat and death at the hands of this green devil enemy and Kali; a rather permanent career stopper. He knew his troops were worn out, but his bloodhounds had to find these devils and kill them all! His arrogant spiteful ego, now laced with great fear could never allow restful clemency for his men now! They were his saving grace; they were his blood hounds on the hunt!

Wadsworth drunkenly sensed the intrinsic dangers he faced at this moment with his command strung out in columns, in this terrible suffocating hot jungle and with night coming. Clearing the jungle trail would be halted at nightfall. His engineer officer told him that they would probably arrive at the plain sometime between tomorrow night and early the next morning if they continued clearing the trail at this pace. Wadsworth slugged down a mouthful of whiskey and tried to remember some historical parallel to the position of his expeditionary force? He simply could not find it in his booze-soaked brainpan. But it had to do with a professional army attacked in a forest and destroyed? Was it the Romans, French, or...? His worse subject in school was, of all thing's military history!

He read Cavendish's report again then took a match and lit it on fire! Fuck him, Nephew, and that Blood! If these green devils were so plentiful and aggressive, then why had they not attacked him yet? Why in hell, according to Cavendish, would they allow him to go to a good area and set up properly for battle? They were easy pickings here in the jungle! It made little sense to his befuddled mind. It made little sense, yet it did make great sense to the Great Kali, who was receiving very good advice from his Russian advisors. Draw them in deep, close the door behind them, and then capture them, the ones not killed! Kali always needed more devils since his plan for his usurpation of India needed many more minions!

As the scouts' broke camp for their journey across the massif, Hook added "Today begins the Swan Song of Kali and his beautiful ancient castle!" The scouts were laden with their weapons, ammunition, and several large well-constructed explosives attached as backpacks. They exited the small secluded camp where Cornwallis would return later that evening. The employment of nitro to be mixed in with the dynamite would increase the magnitude of the explosion and decrease the need for more cumbersome amounts of dynamite. Weapons had been cleaned and readied as edged weapons were sharpened. It seemed that Hoskins and Andrea had a mutual affection growing between them. She and her children were to stay in the camp under the guard of Cornwallis. They all would have a front row seat to the impending battle in the huge valley plain below.

The first group of Cavendish, Griggs, and Hoskins left an hour before the second group. They were to conduct reconnaissance and security for the second group laden with their explosive creations, weapons, and extra ammo. This group included 2nd Lieutenant Collins, Rashid, Corporal Holmes, Lord Nelson, Gladstone, and King George. The rope climbs up the face of the massif from the camp took most of the time in the trip. Rappelling down it on the return would be easy. Collins's red blouse had since been traded for a tan one as his red Wadsworth blouse had been bequeathed to Andréa along with an extra shotgun.

Although the scouts already had an accurate lay of the terrain and castle, they needed daylight to correctly assess their plans with any changes. Then they would plant the explosives at night and wait to ignite them. Destruction of the castle ammo stores was the prime target. Perhaps they could kill Kali? The long fingerlike precipice which obscured the castle from the adjacent plain was a key target since the destruction of it could cut off reinforcements from the plain or vice versa and aid them in their escape. The explosives were all laced with small bottles of liquid nitro glycerin which was a real explosive multiplier! The big bomb planned for the bluff weighed nearly two-hundred pounds and had to be carried on a makeshift stretcher. All the small bottles of nitro were carefully packed and safely carried in the backpacks of the scouts.

As the second group took their first break by the gushing mountain stream before crossing, Holmes pulled out his favorite rifle for sniping. It was a bolt action .50 caliber Elephant gun he had acquired on one of his exploits in Africa. The ammo was heavy, especially with the fifty rounds he carried to the castle in his knapsack. He also carried a modified 8MM Mauser rifle, a German one, a newly developed rifle he had acquired from the Germans in Africa after winning a match. This was for closer targets, with plenty of ammo. The scopes were modern optics and immaculately cleaned safe under their covers. His Elephant gun was simply amazing in accuracy and in exploding humans he had killed with it. He had often used them both back and forth in hot spots. He felt he was about to enter the "hotspot" of his life soon, very soon. He had given his second extra Mauser rifle to Hoskins with one hundred rounds. Both men also had sawed off shotguns for close protection.

Holmes ran details of his fire mission checklist through his mind beginning with creating several different firing positions; deadly fields of fire long and short range in the huge semi-circle to his front. He had great concern for possible snipers in the jungle above the bluffs across the river to his front. Look for smoke and muzzle flashes when they fire like at Malakand. Observe, observe, observe! Fire and move back and forth from four selected firing positions on the bluff and keep Hoskins moving as well. A fixed sniper was a dead target! The fifth and last firing position would be to clean up anything left.

He was to be one of two angels of death. In the back of his mind there arose another specter; enemy snipers from the castle, the massif outcrop and from across the way in the jungle bluffs from across the river? It would be a perfect enemy sniper semi-circle if this possibility was coordinated properly! He pondered this for most of the rocky, tedious jungle passage. They secured a sturdy line across the dark blue turbulent river a mile above the huge falls and transferred everything painstakingly to the other side by lifelines.

They left it intact for the happy escape and moved off to the castle; drenched in sweat, and drinking the cold water in their replenished canteens from the river. Corporal Hoskins, climbing up the steep rise far ahead of the second group, switched his thoughts on the sniping mission to beautiful Andrea and her kids. They seemed to be the only survivors they had saved in the nick of time. He thought of the instant chemistry initiated between the both during and after their escape. Her beautiful golden locks, large blue eyes, to compliment her voluptuous breasts, and the warmth of her kind soul He prayed for salvation from this current dilemma. Hoskins, at the worst of times, was falling in love. He didn't know it, since he had never fallen in love before. Lust and love were now two distinctive things to him now. He refocused on his mission to kick ass in the castle and get home alive for Andrea. He laughed at the thought.

The scouts combined their respective groups after nightfall. Everything was checked and secured as the hunkered down for the night. The next morning, they observed the dispositions of the enemy and assigned targets as they watched the intensity of the camp grow. The green devils were preparing for war. The crazy scene in the valley seemed to intensify during the day, as the smell of burning tar wafted into their positions. It was the smell of thousands of opium pipes burning. the activity in the area in and around the castle had been busy but subsided by late afternoon. All the nitro was carefully unpacked and now attached to the huge stretcher laden bomb and other explosives. Fuses cut and timed as they would detonate the explosives in a correct sequence.

The next night was soon upon them. 2LT Collins, Lord George and Rashid prepared to plant the big explosive on the precipice bluff. But first, King George was to set the explosive under the bridge between the massif at the rear of the castle. This was carefully done just after dark with a four-minute fuse cut for it. Gladstone and Lord Nelson were to plant charges both on the bridges and in the munitions dump inside the huge tent next to the row of artillery as their last blast. It already seemed to the scouts that Wadsworth's British Expedition winding up the trails was creating quite a diversion for their activities. Now it was time for the scouts to observe and wait to plant the explosives.

There was still much activity by the castle, and to the dismay of the scouts, the green devils, under the guidance of what appeared to be Russian Advisers, limbered up four of the large cannons to horse teams and pulled them across the main bridge off to the other side of the pass. They watched this in the descending light. Holmes followed them intently from his far-right firing position through the sight of his elephant gun. Lt. James Ambrose Cavendish looked at his scouts intently. "It looks like they are preparing for Wadsworth who must be on schedule. Everybody knows what to do? stealth until that moment!" He smiled as he completely reviewed the plan again.

A bottle of Hook's rum was poured into each scout's tin drinking cup. Cavendish made a toast. "God Bless the Queen! God Bless we scouts who are about to enter hell; and may we all return safely after we destroy this evil enemy!" Griggs then added. "May God Bless all those poor bastards being pushed by Wadsworth to their deaths!" The rum was gone, it was late at night and time to move out. Lord George had slipped out soon after dark to check out the huge rock formation and jutted from the massif to the river. It ran in a horizontal path from where they were on the massif.

He returned with his usual smile. George had located the best place to position the explosives but had also located a guard shack on top of the jungle covered formation. There were three nicer versions of green devils guarding it. Rashid nodded in confirmation. Cavendish looked at his gold pocket watch and gave the order. "We have perhaps four hours before they arrive." He looked into the faces of each of his men and continued. "Everybody off to the races now and remember this is our rendezvous place after, unless all hell has broken loose. If you are separated, our small camp will be the next rally point; after that? Every man for himself! God Speed and good luck boys, to you all" King George and 2LT Collins ambled off with the stretcher bomb in tow, led by Rashid, with crossbow ready.

Cavendish, Griggs, and SGT Hook prepared for their venture into the castle from the massif to the vines, to climb them up the huge south wall and inside. They were joined by Gladstone and Lord Nelson who were loaded down with the explosives for the bridges and artillery area. Planting the bomb on the rear castle bridge that connected the massif to the castle had already skillfully done by King George as the first contribution to their surprise party. He had become literally an invisible monkey, as he scaled up and across the massif to plant the explosive device housed in a backpack under the massif side of the bridge.

Corporals Holmes and Hoskins had an excellent view of the whole panorama from their middle position between the bluff and castle. They had set up five different firing positions running some thirty odd yards on a stretch of the massif overlooking the castle area to their left and huge valley and encampment to the right. From his right firing positions, he observed the orgy of thousands of crazed warriors dancing, and screaming around myriads of bright campfires across the huge valley. The shadows these warriors cast were an eerie sight. The artillery had moved up a large hill with the guns aiming towards where the British would enter this area. Holmes had a clear aim but it was a long shot; nearly a mile. To his immediate left where Hoskins was resting, they had a great field of vision down into the shadowy torch-lit areas around the ancient gloomy castle.

There was movement, but it seemed no more artillery pieces were being moved. Wagons of shells now crossed the bridge for the field pieces; as expected. There were small irregular groups of men moving about the area and both snipers wondered if the Gurkhas would be able to plant their charges. Then their gaze rested on the castle itself. There was little to no activity on the wall Cavendish was going to ascend, but something on the top of the castle made him freeze. He adjusted his binoculars and caught torches lit on the top of the castle. Holmes, the elected angel of death, went to his far-right pre-selected firing position overlooking the vast valley beyond again. In the back of his mind he realized that he would have to deal with the Russian artillerymen.

He now returned to his far-left firing position with Hoskins and observed some huge ritual with a large group of black-cloaked greenies and standing before them were three huge leaders. He stared transfixed through the scope of his elephant rifle. They were dressed in mostly the same but wore some very elegant bejeweled turban like headpieces. He stared at the tall figure in the center. Holmes was filled in a sort of awe and with extreme fear now. If this guy was not wearing a mask, then his large face was the embodiment of pure evil. He evidenced a long-pointed jaw, matched by an elongated nose or protrusion and cheekbones. When he spoke, his teeth were long pointed spears, like a shark. His or "its" eyes were huge, and the impact he had on the crowd was absolute.

Holmes hoped that he was just wearing a mask. The two other men standing next to him looked the same, but not so pronounced. Then he had to rub his eyes since he swore this large leader had somehow transformed into a tall, woman in dark, with long dark hair. She turned her head to the right and stared in his direction as if it sensed it was being watched from several hundred yards away. Holmes ducked in reaction and pulled Hoskins with him. After a few moments, the burley corporal sat back against a rock wall, swearing in the heat of a dark moonless night, but sweating out of some terror now manifested in his soul. He had seen the devil king, now a devil queen and he sensed that whatever it was sensed him observing it! He would save a .50 caliber round just for it.

To quell his fear, he moved over to check on the distant artillery positions. The artillery was easy to see in the near moon light, since large campfires near them also gave clear view of the four-gun positions. He plotted his firing from his Elephant gun. It seemed as if these positions were maybe longer than a mile away. He had rarely fired this gun more than a mile before, so he began to calculate the range and wind age. One thing caught his attention in the middle of the night. The noise and wild party of the green devils had suddenly subsided. He now observed thousands of them standing in neat rows, hundreds of rows, silent and motionless like they were waiting; waiting for the British. He felt a long chill rise up his spine and tingle his brain.

He showed this spectacle to Hoskins who was shocked. A couple of swigs of whiskey settled them down. Holmes looked at his companion and questioned his nervous disposition. Holmes looked at him and said. "I saw this monster turn into a tall woman in but a few moments!" Hoskins smiled. "Was she a hot babe?" Holmes had to laugh at this notion. "Yes, my son she was very hot; say hotter than Hell?" They were both continued to be held in awe as they waited for the great shitstorm to begin! One thing did catch their attention later in the night. They could see fires, nearly completely obscured by the jungle, burning high on the bluffs from across the river that ran by the castle directly across from them. Snipers? Why not?

Rashid moved fifty yards ahead of the explosive laden stretcher team as they began to climb up the steep path towards the top of this huge lengthy rock outcropping. They followed the illumination from the sentry campfire towards the middle of this elevated part of this ridge formation. Rashid identified a couple of guards standing up in the small guard post. King George saw three now. The shack had a small roof on it and a fire burned near it. They wore long black cloaks, and like the rest of these cloaked devils, seemed more normal than the valley devils. They were talking out loud. This was an observation post, and in a careful check, Rashid saw evidence of some type of crude early warning system. It consisted of a huge oil pot sitting next to the fire on a three-foot crude wall, set to be poured into the fire if needed. If the British arrived too soon, this oil pyre would warn the castle.

Rashid made a brief rustling noise in the foliage and drew their attention. They both asked who it was loudly. No one answered so two devils near the fire pulled out a rather large swords and began walking towards him holding torches. The third guard grabbed a rifle and backed into the door of the small guard shack to cover his companions. Rashid had moved off to the right and gained a good aim on the guard who was standing in the door of the guard shack. King George had circled around to the left to locate the other guard. Suddenly, a crossbow bolt struck the guard in the shack in the throat. The sudden powerful impact knocked him staggering back into the shack. The bolt impaled him to the wall where his limp body stood upright pinned to the wall as his rifle clattered to the floor. The other guards wheeled around and looked at the shack.

The guard closest to Rashid lurched forward and flopped onto the ground with a crossbow bolt entering his spine just below his cranium. Rashid deftly reloaded his crossbow and approached the area after George gave him a thumbs up to his left in the tall foliage. King George then appeared on the other side of the shack and tossed the severed head of the third guard next to the fire. Collins was aghast at the sudden killing of three men in front of him. He had never seen a dead person in his life! King George then smiled at Collins and Rashid. "A bad night to be on guard duty!" He then walked back down the path with Collins to move the stretcher next to the now vacant guardhouse carrying their explosive package on the stretcher. While Rashid donned a long black cloak and played sentry, the others prepped the stretcher born explosive in the fire light now disguised wearing the black cloaks of the deceased guards.

While Rashid maintained his vigil at the guard post, the huge explosive was transported towards the place King George had located to set the monster charge. They moved methodically in crouched silence. They left the explosive tied on the stretcher as they located the position King George had found. He had brought a couple of long ropes to get the explosive down in position. King George, after tying off a long rope went first over the precipice and disappeared. He returned in ten minutes smiling. "We are ready to place our bomb sahib!" He had previously located this deep cave-like indenture; some fifty feet down the bluff side which went under the cliff some forty to fifty yards. Collins was amazed and asked how he could find it again in the dark? King George told him he had memorized terrain and distance from the guard house and the tree features here.

In a short time, Collins was lowering the explosive device by rope to King George on the rough outcrop ledge below. Collins rappelled down and they dragged stretcher bearing the explosive as far as possible into the deep cave like indenture. Collins then carefully set the final explosive charge attached to four bottles of nitro securely into the dynamite. He mentally thanked Hooky's boys for having absconded all of this from the supply tent. He looked at his comrade. "My dear King George, this will be a grand explosion since this cave-like opening will massively exacerbate it!" King George gave his usual smile and patted him on the back. Collins looked at his pocket watch. There was time left before they lit this bomb.

Lord Nelson and Gladstone, loaded each with three haversacks of explosives strapped to their bodies, deftly climbed down the massif like hungry monkeys and landed into a small ravine. They were parallel to the huge tent, which housed the munitions storage next to the row of remaining Russian artillery pieces. Collins had already created the explosive charges with dynamite wrapped tight around a tall bottle of nitro. This would protect it from breaking. The fuses were already attached. They waited quietly for thirty minutes until most of the people had moved out of the area and across the second smaller foot bridge.

These bridges were about one-hundred yards apart with their intersecting roads across the river. They first approached the munitions tent and placed the first explosive just inside the end of the munitions tent close to the end of the row of artillery pieces. They camouflaged the fuse in the dirt floor protruding outside the tent for a quick light. Holmes was observing them through his scope and knew the proximity of the explosive from the torches burning in the area. He could set it off if the Gurkhas somehow failed to do so. Nitro was Nitro! The two sappers next went for the bridges. They crept across a long flat space in the shadows behind the row of artillery and the length of the huge looming precipice.

They crossed the last fifty yards in open ground and slid from the bank into the fast current of the river. The river's current quickly pushed them in the river current under the larger of the two bridges where they held fast to the uprights. Working in tandem, they carefully planted the large explosive on the castle side of the larger bridge, then floated and set the next one on the smaller footbridge. Both bridges were expertly built and reinforced. No guards were present on these structures. There seemed that no formal security had been found for that matter. Who would attack this place with over thirty thousand savages at the front door anyhow?

After the second explosive was placed Gladstone worked his way back under the next bridge by crawling next to the riverbank, which was depressed from the main area. The cool river current was cool and refreshing as they both waited in wet dark silence for the signal flare from Rashid on the huge ridge projection. This would signal them to light up the explosives and unleash Hell! The plan was simple, light both explosives, run and light the third one in the munitions tent, throw a short fused fourth bomb into the row of artillery; then skedaddle for the south wall and up the vines. Until they saw the signal flare, they both would stay put under the bridges and wait. The bridge traffic seemed to pick up towards dawn. There also seemed to be movement around the artillery park as well. This was accented by the random waning torches in the area.

Regardless of the situation with the relief force, the flare would go off at 5AM. This would be an hour before dawn and even if Wadsworth's columns were not at the plain, they would definitely hear all the explosions. Like the group waiting on the precipice, the two Gurkhas under the bridges could hear the distant strange haunting hum from the army of green devils on the other side of the pass issuing forth from their unmoving formations. It was never ending.

At the same time the Gurkhas were planting their first charge in the munitions tent, and just after Rashid and company had dispatched three guards, Cavendish, Hook, and Griggs breeched the hundred-foot south wall by climbing up the huge vines, ancient as the castle. Slowly and methodically they climbed over the wall and moved across the flat exposed parapet into the adjacent doorway as they had before. There were no guards present which seemed understandable. Who was going to attack this place anyhow seemed to echo again? The shadows beyond the torchlight masked their movements.

Color Sergeant Hook hid behind the large wooden side entrance door inside the castle as Griggs, and Cavendish ventured beyond and down a row of steps to the huge storage rooms they had previously located. Griggs went for the storage area as Cavendish began to track out any survivors by climbing up the crawlspace route given to him by Andrea. The sound of drums and music flowed from the huge open space above permeating them with strange ancient music. He reckoned that "The destroyer Kali" was preparing for the big event.

As he waited inside the huge oak doorway, Hook summed up the order for the surprise party. The explosions would go in the order of bridges first, munitions and artillery close second, the long precipice ridge between the valley and castle third, the ammo and weapons storage in the castle next, and finally the bridge connecting the castle to the massif to protect their escape! It was nearly now after four in the morning and hell was on the way as he gave a cryptic smile.

Cavendish slowly peered out of the crawlspace vent into the rooms where the prisoners had been held and found the place was empty. He ventured into the rooms and up and down the shadowy gloomy hall outside. There were no guards, and he knew that all hostages were dead or converted in whatever that meant? He returned to Griggs as his depressed eye contact told Mister Griggs the story. The explosive for the ammo storage had been placed.

Both Corporal Holmes and Hoskins were wide-awake and watching developments below as they sat in their chosen initial firing positions. They had been intently viewing the bluffs directly across the river facing their position on the jungle covered bluff. They were also constantly overlooking the high position on the soon-to-be destroyed long rough finger of rock bluff that separated the green devils from the castle complex. Rashid had already given them a thumb's up in the silhouette of the campfire at the guard's shack. All was on the mark.

What now vexed both snipers were how the wild noises and rollicking of the savages seemed to trail off a couple of hours ago into complete eerie silence of motionless green devils standing in rows. Then came a low unanimous humming from these devils which was unnerving for both men. Holmes was already in a state of fear after what he witnessed the evil transformation in the temple hours ago. If there were snipers across the way, then both Gurkhas were in grave danger! Also, regarding the huge precipice, the darkness combined with the jungle foliage seemed fairly dense at the end of the bluff; yet gave way to lighter scrub brush existed for about forty feet where the long finger of bluff met with the massif to their right. This would allow Collins and company to be exposed in the early light if they were slow in their exit! They could be food for sniper crosshairs if there were snipers across the way!

Movement was beginning to occur on a more routine basis inside the huge area around the castle by half past four. Holmes also saw some movement from the battlements where Cavendish and his group had gone over an hour ago, The group on the roof…. the "Easter Sunday" service of the supreme devil was over. The three-tall ominous evil leaders had disappeared, yet about half of the cloaked goons stayed, milling around on top as if awaiting orders. The corporal checked his weapons and ammo.... He had loaded and placed both his rifles in two adjacent firing positions with the elephant gun ready first. He felt that he should have removed the head of that monster turned large woman in charge of this evil affair with a fifty-caliber bullet!

A short time after Lieutenant Cavendish returned to the storage area, he heard steps approaching from the dimly lit gloomy passage. He and Griggs were soon trapped in a huge storage room filled with artillery shells and other war material. They ran back to the end of it and hid. The fuses for the explosives in all the areas were lit to go off shortly after the flare fired at five. He observed several greenies entering the room he looked at his watch. It was exactly quarter to five! Hook was also looking at his pocket watch upstairs and it was time to light the fuses and run! Hook had noticed more movement around him. A second group of greenies passed him and went down the long row of stone stairs. He edged out the door, peered around to see no one close from across the way. The flare was fired and he knew they should have been gone by now. What was the holdup?

It was a beautiful shot as the red flare went straight up for all to see in both valleys. The advance guard of Wadsworth's columns who were standing just inside the jungle facing the grassy valley plain saw it clearly. The officer in charge of the column had prepared his lancers and artillery with the infantry. At the sight of the red flare he issued the order for his bugler to call assembly. At this point the troops began boiling out of the jungle into the chest high grass. The light of a new sunrise had yet to even give scant light to the east, for the sun would be up in a little over an hour. The shadows in the valley would then dissipate fast.

Lord Nelson and Gladstone had lit their respective fuses and swiftly climbed from under the bridges and ran anticipating the flare which soon burst into the sky above them. However, other eyes were also watching them running towards the safety of the artillery pieces. As the Gurkhas ran to light the third explosive and toss the fourth, the distinctive crack of a rifle broke the silence of the dawn. Then two more rang out in studied progression as both British snipers vectored in on the muzzle flashes from the bluff across the way. The first round passed harmlessly over both Gurkha's heads, but the second shot caught Lord Nelson in the back of the neck, blowing him into a mad tumbling motion forward, killed instantly.

Gladstone mimicked this movement and avoided two more shots. He began to zigzag into the munitions dump behind the artillery pieces ducking six more shots. Holmes meanwhile had observed the muzzle flash and smoke from the shooters and centered his riflescope to a small position, across the river on the opposite bluff. It looked like a well-camouflaged tree house, which had been where the fires had burned in the night. He had targets now. Using his Elephant gun, he carefully aimed and fired. He saw the snipers shadow explode from his shell in very obscure light of a fire illuminating his body behind him. What a fool Holmes thought.

In quick succession, he reloaded and aimed where he saw another individual, a moving shadow lurking in another firing port of this tree house to the left of his dead comrade. The small lamps from the inside of this tree house made his shot possible and effective. He took a deep breath, fired, and saw a floundering motion in the shadows after the wall disintegrated from the shot. He had scored his second kill, both lucky shots in his estimate. Hoskins fired several random shots into the area Holmes was engaged in. Something exploded in this hidden enemy structure as fire and smoke billowed in the jungle. Holmes moved to a better firing position to watch as Hoskins was now firing at muzzle flashes from across the river. Bullets aimed at them all seemed to hit well below their position. They both moved to a new firing point and continued. Holmes observed the still body of one of the Gurkhas on the ground some about fifty yards from the fast-moving river as the light of the dawn hinted in the east. He cursed and continued firing at new muzzle flashes coming from across the way. He had switched to his Mauser.

Meanwhile, Gladstone had made it to the munitions tent. As he entered it was jumped by a couple of guards. They had been watching him running and dodging the sniper shots. In seconds, Gladstone made quick work of them with his Kurri, slashing their throats in rapid succession. Sheathing it, he pulled his service revolver and shot down three more who began firing at him. No stealth now! He was wounded and staggered into the huge munitions tent where he had planted his explosive. He then lit the fuse after he pulled it in from the outside. He had just lit a match, when he was shot several times in the back by an advancing Russian advisor, who entered the large tent followed by several more guards.

They moved swiftly in his direction as he aimed his service revolver at the large strapped bag holding the bomb and fired point blank into the bottle of nitro. Nothing happened, his pistol was empty, and he was again hit. Gladstone knew he had fatal wounds. Knowing that when the Russians got to the bomb, they would render it inactive, in his last noble act, he pulled the pin of one of his grenades, and fell across the bomb. He was also carrying the extra bomb for the artillery. Hands grabbed him but it was too late!

Nearly simultaneously, Hoskins and Holmes saw a monstrous explosion at the huge ammo dump and artillery park! It was so powerful that the huge tents evaporated in the explosive flames. Then soon after came the explosions that destroyed both bridges! These huge blast waves shook throughout the shadowed valley. The corporal, from his high position whistled as he saw two bridges, in the pre-dawns light, one loaded with a formation of greenies rip apart throwing them along with the wooden bridge fragments hundreds of feet into the fast-moving river and all directions.

The explosion in the munitions tent was much greater than both explosions on the bridges. After the initial shock of the dual first explosions, the third one ignited and engulfed everything in the artillery holding area. The tents were blasted to pieces as huge fragments of debris and the destroyed artillery pieces fell like rain throughout the compound and front of the castle. The blast wave was deafening and the force of it blew like an angry typhoon snuffing out every torch in the area. Sergeant Hook and the approaching greenies were all knocked to the ground as a huge mushroom like cloud rose in the dawn's first light. Holmes had already moved to his second firing position when several rounds struck his first one. The angel of death was now hard at work. It was soon after the explosions that Holmes heard distant rifle fire open up at the end of the deep valley. Wadsworth's doomed army had arrived.

Hoskins patiently waited for new movement from the other side of the bluff, which came in two more dark forms, partially hidden in the jungle growth were moving across the bluff sideways towards where the first snipers had been. He carefully aimed his rifle, and in rapid succession, dropped both of them as their bodies rolled off the bluff and splattered into the fast-moving river below. They both were then engaged by more snipers from the roof of the castle and still coming from across the way from the jungle bluffs. Enemy fire seemed to be everywhere at this point but at least it was not coordinated as Holmes had feared. The sniper duel continued with enemy bullets ripping all around them as they moved to their next firing positions.

If Collins, Rashid, and King George were to survive, these pesky snipers had to be reduced in numbers. Holmes continuing with his deadly game, exploding the bodies of more snipers with the might of his .50 caliber Elephant rifle. Like Hoskins, he literally had to move from position to position each time he fired now. Holmes then opened up first on the shooters from the castle who were less accurate, exploding castle masonry with his bullets killing the devil shooters as his high-powered rounds penetrated through the ancient walls. It seemed to Cavendish in the castle, that all hell had broken loose around him; the Russian led greenies in the storage where they hid, quickly grabbed boxes and some rifles, but stopped. They smelled the lit explosive fuse which Griggs had snuffed out.

Sensing this, both Brits opened up with their shotguns gunning them down where they stood. Griggs looked at Cavendish, "Go on sir, get a head start, I will wait a couple of minutes and relight this this charge!" With no prodding, Cavendish took off in great haste to catch up with Hook and he yelled a loud "Hurry Up!" at Griggs. The crafty man who went by "mister" instead of his rank had anticipated two or three minutes and lit the shortened fuse. He had but a few minutes to escape! With his shotgun, ready, he exited the large dark and dusky room. Twenty paces down the dimly lit hallway Cavendish ran into another group of greenies. He cleared them out with several close-range blasts from his shotgun. On he ran, reloading.

Hook, who had been resting behind the shadows of a huge door that led to the outside of the south wall, heard the shots ring out from down below the staircase. He readied his double-barreled shotgun, with reduced stock. He called it his "pirate gun," nearly as favored as the Zulu Spear attached to his belt. He heard footsteps coming from the keep and yelled out. Then he heard wild screams as several greenies emerged from the stairs. His first double blast blew four of them back onto their colleagues behind them. They all seemed to fall backwards down the stairs. Quickly reloading, Hooky caught the second wave in exactly the same way, blasting more greenies from the stairs, back onto more of their colleagues charging up the stairs behind them.

He leaned back into the shadows he reloaded his shotgun for the third time. As he readied for the next bunch, he heard shots from the bottom of the stairs, and the unmistakable noise of another shotgun blasting away. His boys were coming. He swung around and peered out the entrance to the large stone escarpment as more greenies approached. This time he pulled a grenade from his bag and tossed one in their direction. The blast rocked the flat area as several additional green devils were brought down. He added shotgun blasts to those that lingered unaffected by the grenade. The devil bodies were piling up.

Hook wheeled into the opening and caught several more with two more devastating blasts from his shotgun. He let his shotgun, slung to his side drop, and pulled out his spear. By the time, Cavendish arrived, Hook had savagely slashed and speared two more who had been wielding long knives. The bodies scattered around the sergeant revealed his handiwork. He looked at Cavendish briefly and in a saddened voice added. "Both Lord Nelson and Gladstone brought the bank sir! I saw it all. Snipers got Lord Nelson and Gladstone never made it out of the tent before the explosion!" Cavendish grimly nodded, "We need to move over to the wall and wait but a couple of minutes for Griggs. He set the fuse again after we were attacked. Then he thought about the possibility of the massive explosion so close to them. They had to move away. Griggs would follow after all, if anybody could get out, it was Griggs!

The lieutenant gave the order, "Let's go, be ready, we are headed to the bridge. We are too close to this ammunition!" They began to run full- speed, heading up the left side of the castle's parapets on the south wall. Corporal Holmes saw both men finally appear and followed their movement along the parapet in his rifle scope sights. He was moving along in front of them looking for targets of opportunity where he found several. The snipers from across the river had been reduced, but still fired at them. Hoskins was now tasked to deal with them as Holmes concentrated his fire on the castle. The ammo storage room now exploded and the whole interior of the castle shook like an earthquake. It seemed like a slow-motion movie with another deafening effect.

The center of castle seemed to drop as the lower floors disintegrated and collapsed the center of the castle. The blast of the explosion seemed to implode inside the castle as balustrades and age-old masonry blew out in every direction which was falling everywhere like deadly huge snowflakes. The rocking of the explosion, which seemed like minutes after they left, tossed Hook and Cavendish to the ground. A wall of dust seemed to blot out the morning sunlight covering both them and the devils in a fine white dust. This unexpected dust cover helped them to get up and run past many of them since they all seemed to look the same in the haze. They were headed to the bridge. They both quietly wondered what had happened to Griggs? Holmes was now blinded by the dust clouds emerging from the destruction.

After Griggs, had relit the charge, he had borrowed one of the hooded cloaks from a rather large dead greenie they had killed by shotgun blasts. He grabbed a Russian rifle from the storeroom wall and a tin of ammo from a stack next to the door. Instead of trying to move and fight his way to where Cavendish had gone, he turned abruptly to the left and ran in the shadowed corridor in the opposite direction, which offered least resistance. He estimated three to five minutes before the explosion. Off he went with his instincts telling him to climb to the right at the end of the corridor. Greenies seemed to fill the hall going in the opposite direction past him as he moved. The distant sounds of gunfire seemed to echo from everywhere. He hoped his comrades had made it out to safety, away from this impending blast.

Bathed in sweat, Griggs was just climbing a long staircase out of the floor when the interior explosion rocked the castle in a massive shockwave. He fell on the steps and covered his head as the sound of the explosion rocked around him like a freight train. It seemed that time had vanished with the blast, as a wave of dust seemed to rise high in the air. He finally renewed his erratic climb towards the north wall parapet. He arrived at the side of the wall and looked down. There were no huge vines, just a sheer wall which dropped one-hundred feet onto rocks in a dry moat. He then ran up the stairs towards a tower structure which faced the huge green river below which emanated from the huge falls and where the bridges had once crossed. It was a fast cascading current of dark green waters that flowed into a huge jungle off to his left.

He seemed to still be alone at this point as he stood at the top of this northwest tower. He had loaded both rifles as he had crept up the last flight of stairs to the open tower. When he entered the tower, he met out a quick death to the two-posted guards with his shotgun. He flipped their bodies over the tower wall where they fell far down splashing into the river. He surveyed his situation. First, he saw that he would have a clean, but very high jump from this tower into the river, his only escape. Next, he began to look around from his position. He immediately found that he had a clear line of fire up the length of the bridge connecting the castle to the massif. The debris and thick dust had not risen high, but seemed to have moved outward, sideways in the blast.

He was able to discern that the blast had dropped the central portion of the castle, and the temple two stories perhaps. He viewed a pile of broken stone with the large flat temple floor sitting on top. Griggs had no way of knowing whether Cavendish, or Hook had made it to safety. Just in case they did get out, he was going to help them. So, he carefully set the sights on his rifle and aimed at a cluster of guards some three-hundred yards at the end of the bridge connected to the massif. They seemed to be guarding a large iron gate affixed between two small stone guard towers, which made up part of the bridge construction. They were standing in the open on the bridge all holding rifles.

He took careful aim and began to fire at the guards. He hit three of them as they fell on the bridge. Several more just stood there looking at the fallen without moving away. Evidently, the extreme noise of the battle had dimmed the guards' ability to hear his shots. He continued firing at the guards and more fell. In this confusion, a few moved back behind stonewall and into the twin guard towers. Then Sergeant Griggs observed the huge explosion at the end of the adjacent bluff in a massive orange flame that initiated what now seemed like a larger earthquake engulfing the whole area. He hit the floor of the tower covering his head. When he looked up, he saw a distinctive wave of dust from this explosion carpet the area as it approached his position in the tower.

Corporal Holmes and Hoskins were blinded by the clouds of dust created by the massive interior explosion in the castle. Holmes only had fifteen rounds left for his elephant gun to use against the very distant Russian artillery, so he converted over to this German rifle. The huge cloud emanating from the castle was beginning to obscure the whole area around the castle and the targeting of enemy snipers across the river was impossible to perform at this point. The enemy shooters faced the same dilemma now. Just as the British snipers spotted their three sappers moving out of the huge precipice, then came a monstrous explosion behind them from the long-outcropped bluff that ended at the river. The ground shook wildly as both snipers saw a huge white mushroom cloud rising from the blast area. Huge dust clouds now blanketed the whole area.

The whole world had gone completely quiet after this last mega blast! The morning winds seemed to take charge of the smoke and dust clouds as they began to flow away past the castle now. The focus of the snipers turned to their three escaping comrades from the extended bluff if they had survived such an explosion! Corporal Hoskins was first to see three shapes moving through the tall grass and short trees coming towards them. Then they both saw a sight that concerned them. A group of at least twenty more cloaked greenies led by what appeared to be Russians, had moved out of the smoke-filled staging area below up a steep rocky path towards the area where their trio was before the explosion. They would now be cut off!

They both moved to firing position number four, which gave them better focus in this immediate area. Hoskins spotted the trio stopped just behind a shallow tree line as the dust clouds were thinning out by the winds coming across the summit. They were oblivious to the new threat off to their right as the enemy movement was coming up the steep incline at a fast pace. They would be caught out in the open! Both Hoskins and Holmes now aimed at the party coming up the hill and opened fire.

Holmes got a clean shot on the first Russian in front of the column as Hoskins began picking off unsuspecting targets in the rear of the line. They hit several but the enemy combatants went to the ground behind some rocks and small scrub brush returning fire in their direction. Bullets began to pound their positions again from the castle wall. "My, oh my, we are very popular today Hoskins!" Added Holmes with a big smile." The line of enemy devils fired as they continued moving up the steep ravine.

As the lead element broke from the trail, the trio trying to exit the destroyed bluff had sighted the enemy first and began concentrating fire on them with crossbow and pistol fire. Lord George lobbed a grenade which bounced on the steep path that exploded killing several devils. More greenies fell, as the two groups closed within yards of each other. Since the trio was each armed with two pistols, they were more effective at close range than the rifles used by the devils. It resembled a western shootout as everybody was firing their pistols at near point-blank range. Both snipers killed more of the green devils as they popped out of the ravine trail behind the gunfight.

King George now heaved a lit stick of dynamite down the trail at the unmolested greenies crawling up the trail in the rear. The explosion and screams were deafening and destroyed the enemy focus on this escaping trio for valuable seconds. Holmes and Hoskins continued picking off targets as fast as they appeared. The wild west gunfight was over in moments. 2nd Lieutenant Collins had hit the ground to reload and checked the Russian advisor near him, who had one of Rashid's crossbow bolts planted deep into his forehead. Collin's service revolvers were empty so he holstered them. Fearing more green devils and no time to reload his eyes rested on a German Broom handle automatic pistol lying next to the dead Russian. He grabbed it and prepared for more attackers. He killed two more closing on him.

Lord George had tossed another of his short-fused sticks of dynamite down the trail and ended the enemy attack. This explosion found its mark creating a rockslide crushing the remaining devils hiding on the steep trail. Interested in this pistol, Collins undid the Imperial crested belt buckle of the dead Russian taking his belt, and large wooden holster and ammo pouch attached to it. He was now rearmed with the new state of the art German Mauser pistol complete with the wooden stock that served as a holster. As the two snipers gave them covering fire the three ran into the jungle foliage below their positions.

Corporal Hoskins killed two more firing from the castle wall as the dust clouds began to subside. 2LT Collins and company were soon reunited with the snipers in their firing positions. Lord George grabbed Collins and they quickly left to be in position to light the last explosive under the bridge between the massif and castle. Holmes, armed now with his elephant gun, assumed his fifth firing position that over looked the huge valley and Russian artillery. He was waiting for more of the dust cloud to settle. Cavendish and Hook were still heading towards the bridge on the upper level of the south wall. The huge dust cloud was still settling in their area. They could hear rifle and artillery fire in the distance now. Wadsworth's boys were in battle now!

Cavendish and Hook had made excellent progress towards the massif bridge disguised in the dust that covered both friend and foe alike. Because of the mass confusion and dust, they were encountering small resistance at this point as they moved along. Then came the big explosion full force. Cavendish and Hooky saw huge yellow and orange flames lighten up the receding darkness left in the slight glimmer of dawn as they glanced in the direction of the precipice. The force of the explosion sent a massive energy wave suddenly knocked down everybody along the parapet. The noise was deafening, and the blast magnificently huge.

They were able to watch a huge chunk, of what was the complete top and end of the bluff, disintegrate into large pieces and plunge into the river and on part of the castle staging area after the flash of the explosion. Hook and Cavendish moved faster towards the bridge in the chaos around them. King George would be on time. Rashid stayed with the British shooters after the other two left to blow the last bridge. He had also taken a bullet in his upper arm in the gunfight and with all the bullets flying in the gunfight; felt he was blessed.

Holmes continued to peer through the scope of his elephant gun to see that this blast had literally floored thousands of greenies in the adjoining valley who had been standing silently or moving into position awaiting their time to attack Wadsworth. They were getting back on their feet and moving back into their rows waiting for their orders to attack. The battle erupting at the end of the valley was obvious to them because the crescendo of the rifle and artillery fire that was growing in volume. Both the sharpshooters also noticed that several thousand of the green Devils who had been waiting motionless were gone. Holmes squinted through the large scope on his elephant gun. It seemed like only a handful of minutes had transpired, but it was more like nearly an hour. Holmes viewed British artillery rounds exploding in the middle of what appeared to be a living moving jungle at the end of the valley. Wadsworth's fighting [positions were completely hidden by large groups of trees.

A cloud of white smoke was rising over the huge trees in the plain at the juncture of the jungle and plain where Wadsworth's relief force had entered. Hoskins watched the distant battle unfolding in great sadness and knew his time up in the bluff was almost over. Escape was the next item on their agenda! He now focused on his last set of targets from his last firing position far to the right on the castle walls. He had to wait for a pall of brown dust to settle. Holmes now centered all attention on those Russian guns way distant across the valley as he waited for the haze to clear.

Meanwhile, Cavendish and Hook, minus Griggs, raced for the bridge. There seemed to be a lot of movement from the remains of temple stairs as they moved by it. A large group of cloaked greenies were moving towards them. The bottom rear massive staircase of the temple intersected with both parapets on the north and south sides of the ancient castle. On they raced, hearing the screams increasing in volume from behind them. They were some distance beyond the high staircase when out of nowhere jumped a giant greenie, which with perfect grace thrust his long knife at Cavendish, sticking it in his chest below his shoulder. It had a silver looking face or mask with bulging eyes and an ugly mouth filled with huge teeth like a wild boar.

Before this monster incarnate could pull his dagger free Sergeant Hook, a veteran of close violent combat was quick in his response. He had replaced his shotgun and carried his Zulu spear where he angerly and forcefully plunged it straight up under the throat and into the skull of this tall very ugly greenie. As the green devil died it clawed Hook across his face as it fell issuing grotesque spasms from its contorted face. Its blood was black! Hook yanked his spear out of the dying giant, as he speared him a couple of more times, then liberated Cavendish who was struggling to get to his feet. Both men then turned to see a huge horde of cloaked greenies near the bottom of the huge staircase, moving towards them with daggers and swords drawn.

Hook got between this greenie mob and his lieutenant rolling his last two grenades at their feet. The dual explosions destroyed the front of this mob. The devils behind these fallen comrades fell on the bodies which piled up preventing them from immediately chasing them. Their shotgun ammo was expended, so they continued moving towards the end of the bridge firing their pistols at anything in front of them. They made it finally to the gate in this confusion and settling dust cloud. Soon, the hoard was moving again in fiery vengeance! The three surviving guards at the gate were confused at what was taking place in the chaos and stood up to meet Hook and Cavendish. They fell prey to Cavendish's .45 revolver. It was the only loaded weapon he had left.

Hell had broken loose everywhere! Lieutenant Collins never believed that so few men could cause so much chaos and outright damage! He had proudly performed his part in creating this mess! He smiled as he followed King George towards the bridge, the last item to be destroyed. Both had retrieved their carbines from their stash left with Holmes. They moved to the side of the bridge to witness the huge melee brewing in the rear of the castle and towards the rear gate on the narrow bridge. King George finally saw Cavendish and Hook fight their way off the bridge. Collins went to collect them as King George slid down quickly shortening fuse, then he lit it. No time! He quickly climbed up from under the bridge and ran towards where his comrades were now located across the bridge at the sally port side on the massif.

2LT Collins secured Hook and the wounded Cavendish outside the entrance of the rear massif bridge after killing several more devils with his broom handle who were closing on them. He reloaded his new Mauser Pistol and emptied another full magazine into the continued mob of green devils closing on the bridge sally port. Completely exasperated, Cavendish, and Hook cleared the bridge as the observant 2Lt Collins slammed the huge iron shut with a huge clank! The gate had to be opened from the inside out and with this huge iron gate closed, the greenies pressed up against it in their ferocious zeal, cementing it closed with their body weight. The escape party did not wait for the explosion, but ran as if chased by the devil, since they were being chased by devils!

Rashid was watching the situation at this rear bridge with a pair of binoculars. He saw the safe exit of Cavendish being helped by Hook but no Griggs. He then witnessed with a smile at the massed screaming throng trapped behind the gate blocked the exit. Then a final explosion evaporated the massif side of the bridge. The orange flash erupted just below the narrow bridge giving an eerie light in the dust cloud. The bridge along with its occupants, rose up then shattered into a ball of flying debris, as the bulk of it, along with the mass of bodies bounced along the massif wall, dropping over three hundred feet, cascading below into the rocky swampy terrain between massif and castle. Rashid observed, at least half the bridge had completely disappeared. He looked at Holmes and Hoskins. "They are all safely across the bridge, and we need to go!"

Sergeant or "Mister" Griggs had emptied many rounds at the squad of bridge guards dropping several as the pall of smoke finally blinded his visibility now completely shrouded due to the new dust cloud generated by the blast on the bluff overlooking the river. Griggs then turned his hot-barreled rifle on any moving target remaining on the walls within view. He liked the Russian rifles. Greenies were falling after every shot. He suddenly realized that there were more greenies in his presence, but also realized he still wore the long black greenie hooded cloak and was camouflaged. They were lining up next to him firing at anything which meant that these idiots in a blind panic were killing their own people. "What a fine leader I am now?" He smirked to himself.

Before he began his sniper escapade, Griggs had secured everything he intended to keep after he hit the water below. He had an extra Russian rifle slung around his body and had filled his cartridge belts with more rounds. He had his haversack bag strap secured around his body. Using a Russian bayonet, he deftly stabbed the greenie next to him, then turned and slashed the greenie's throat behind him in one swipe of the bayonet. Before others could react, he had stabbed one more. He then pulled his Russian rifle from the wall and shot two more bad guys on the end. His leadership training of green devils was over.

In the midst of this carnage, one "Mister." Horatio Griggs of His Majesties Guides dropped his rifle and ran full throttle off the tower wall flinging his body as far as humanly possible out into the now turbulent explosion shocked waters below. The long fall into the river was terrifying, but the water was a cool relief when he hit it and bounced off the bottom. He bobbed up some fifty yards downstream as the fast current carried him away into the dense jungle. He kept his head above the surface of the dark greenish waters of the river floating into the safety of the jungle as he could hear the distant din of artillery. Griggs wondered if anybody had survived besides him?

Holmes looked forward to his last challenging firing assignment. The absence of his mentor and friend Mister Griggs vexed his mind. He peered in to his rifle scope with the thought "If anybody can make it, Griggs can!" After the final explosion on the bridge, a nervous Rashid informed him to be ready to leave. They both knew they had little time to remain in this position. The enemy was scattered everywhere and knew these deadly sniper positions well by now. But the chaos at the castle and the arrival of Wadsworth's columns on the plain had spared any concentrated counter attacks on them so far.

Holmes wanted to prevent the Russians from firing those big guns if possible. So many lives depended on this. Holmes had been hearing the development of a battle below in the distance but could not see it at all. The haze that had drifted into the valley and many copses of huge trees prevented this. He heard the incessant firing of rifles, and continuous fire from the British light artillery erupting. He had studied the Russian artillery positions from the scope of his Elephant rifle and could only really get good shots on two of the four artillery batteries. The two were depressed on the other side of the hill.

He figured that if he could get some accurate fire on those two artillery positions, he might disrupt them from firing for some time. His first two shots were low with one pinging off the wheel of the forward artillery gun. The gunners never noticed these shots. He raised his sight, set, and fired again, making a Russian gun captain, his first target. His bullet silenced by distance, erupted into him blowing him from view. He systematically poured in eight more shots, killing at least five more men who appeared, and a second gun commander who was definitely Russian. He saw no more targets. The remining members of the gun crews had obviously hit the dirt by now witnessing the torn bodies in their midst. The guns were still silent as Rashid nearly dragged him away from his position.

With their gear slung, and with a shot of whiskey and water, Holmes beat a quick haste behind Rashid. Hoskins was already gone. Their part in this wild escapade was over. Nothing more could be achieved. Holmes felt a deep sense of helplessness as he began his trek away from the massif, but held deep concern for Griggs. When the group regrouped at their assigned rally point, Rashid helped pull the stiletto-like dagger from below Cavendish's left shoulder and stop the bleeding. He then put a first aid creme on both sides of the wound and bandaged it. The lieutenant still had mobility and use of his left arm but it was painful. He would pop a piece of the opium cake later. Rashid handed James the bejeweled dagger. "Looks like you were stabbed with great wealth sir, these jewels are real!" The lieutenant smiled grimly and put it in his haversack as a souvenir.

Cornwallis would bear witness to the battle which was erupting in the valley below his vantage point in the mountain camp. He was appalled at the size of the attacking green devil army and how it was forcing back the British firing lines. He was soon joined by Andrea and her twins. The sun was just ebbing up in the east as the hint daylight approached the advance guard as it appeared on the edge of what seemed a huge valley plain with the backdrop of a huge line of cliffs with a huge waterfall in the center. They were awe struck at the vast magnificent view. They were all extremely exhausted from being driven all night by Wadsworth's lapdogs! Then came the red flare from the end of the valley arching brightly into the pre-dawn sky. Soon after huge explosions from down the valley out of eye shot were heard!

The lieutenant in the advance regiment, fearful of Cavendish's dispatch, had already positioned an infantry regiment forward as it crept slowly into the tall grass in a tight semicircle with the first echelon three deep to concentrate fire when it was necessary. The artillery had also been moved up front behind this formation to facilitate quick deployment. The gun commander viewed the grassy landscape and chose the nest of tall grass covered hills off to his right to deploy his artillery. As the initial formation of Punjab infantry moved to cover the ground between the plain and hills, the artillery was quickly dispatched to set up firing positions. The movement had been oppressively slow in the jungle, but now the bedraggled column was moving at a better speed into the plain; "Into the valley of death!"

The massive waterfall in the distance, could be heard in the quiet of the dawn as it poured millions of gallons of fresh water into the valley splitting into two rivers going north and south. It was an awesome site to the exhausted troops of Wadsworth's command fanning out into the open grassy areas of this ancient plain. Every other man that held a lit torch to provide light in the jungle now extinguished them as they entered the plain. The terrain was composed of many rolling grassy hills descending at the base of the rather large valley walls. Copses of large jungle canopy and chest high green grass covered most of the rolling hills on this landscape. The regiment of mounted lancers deployed inside the jungle to the left and waited for orders. Colonel Wadsworth was nowhere to be seen since he had passed out cold in his camp chair at the end of this long column a couple of hours ago.

The huge distant explosions galvanized the exhausted troops. There were shouts from the lead elements who had deployed in firing lines, followed by a huge concentration of rifle fire into the tall grass. The grassy fields in front of them were alive and moving towards them issuing many circular flying saw bladed weapons. Many riflemen fell as these circular blades ripped into their faces, throats, and bodies. The first wave of green devils launched a frontal assault from the high grass had been stopped cold by a well-organized veteran regiment of Punjab infantry. This lead regiment had formed in a defensive blocking line to the front between the enemy and the artillery batteries being hastily deployed for action.

As the artillerymen unlimbered their cannon and soon opened fire into massive waves of green devils charging the British line, which was slowly moving as a screen in front of the artillery. The green Punjab axillary regiments exited the jungle and moved around behind the artillery over to the north side of the hills to set up their defensive firing lines. Their movement was poorly led and executed and only offered disorganized broken firing lines. The wave of green devils moving towards them and it was first noted that they were grabbing several of the British riflemen and dragging them away. The fear of this battle was slowly turning into one of terror as the hideous face of the green devils presented itself.

It seemed to Wadsworth's force, that this jungle was now moving from three sides of the valley. The first regiment had completely beaten off the first and closest assault. Any veteran who had fought against native forces would know that these devils were testing their firepower with the lives of these first waves. Soon, British artillery was firing salvos into the massive green yelling ranks, concentrating their fire to cover their right flank until it was in place. With seemingly terrible losses, the masses of devils continued moving forward and many were mingling with the disorganized right flank. It seemed that all was going well for the British until a well concentrated wall of devil rifle fire issued from the tall grass into the veteran regiment.

British soldiers began to fall by both rifle fire and the circular airborne saw weapons. Then came another huge visible explosion as the British gunners and infantry observed the top of a distant bluff turn orange and fall. The explosive noise soon followed with a rather strong impact airwave. For brief minutes, the battle stalled as the green devils paused to look at the huge bluff as the whole end of the precipice collapsed into the opening to the valley under a growing cloud of dust.

Then they renewed their violent onslaught at the British. The smoke from the artillery and rifle fire was now mixed with the fires ignited in the tall grass. Many wounded green devils and a growing number of British troops were burning alive as the grass flames consumed them in the field in front of the artillery positions. The smoke now obscured the fields of fire for both forces as they fired blindly into a smokey fog!

Colonel Wadsworth was shocked out of his drunken stupor as the noise of battle began far to the front of his command tent. The noise created by his artillery fire had done the trick! He was still in the rear of the column and stumbled into his staff tent trying to get his bearings. He took a large belt of whiskey to clean off his foggy brain as he then began yelling commands at his staff, growing nervous by the sounds of battle. His forces were now heavily engaged in a fight that he knew little about at this point!

Colonel Wadsworth finally climbed on his horse and rode to the edge of the jungle where it met the grassy fields. The confusion and turmoil existed all around him. The battle had been in progress for nearly forty minutes now and the smoke was terrible. He was shocked when he was able to view the sea of green devils moving across the valley at his forces. His troops were running everywhere being loosely directed to the battle beyond the jungle. He was able to locate his light regiment of lancers off to the left inside the jungle waiting on their mounts for orders.

What to do now surmised Wadsworth? He took a deep swig on his bottle of whiskey as remedy to continue clearing his emerging hangover stupor. What would Napoleon do? He then remembered Napoleon's brilliant left hook at the Battle of Austerlitz! He faked a right punch at the center with his artillery and delivered a fatal left hook slamming into the Austrian and Russian reserve formations. Then he waited until they were retreating across those frozen lakes and let loose on the ice with his artillery drowning hundreds if not thousands of men and horses! Brilliant he thought! In his stupor he was looking for frozen lakes but saw none!

Old Wad was now going to show his brilliance as a combat commander! They would see! Fucking Blood would see! In complete violation of dividing forces against an unknown enemy in unknown terrain, he ordered his whole regiment of lancers to arc to the left and envelope the rear of the green devil army which seemed endless. He further ordered his remaining full regiment of Punjab's to attack behind the lancers in their attack to obviously destroy the green devil reserves! He was offered to lead the attack by the commander of the lancers but declined. He cackled and took another hit of whiskey. "Austerlitz in the jungle and my victory!" he babbled as drool ran down his mouth to his chin.

The British artillery continued to roar, as both cannon and rifle pounded the waves of fearless savages that now pressed close to their formations from three sides. Their concentrated British style rifle fire was taking an obvious toll on British empire troops obscured in the smoke and tall grass. The green devils were closing in. Many front-line troops watched as the devils were dragging off British wounded and many not wounded. What appeared to be the decisive flanking counter-attack from the British as envisioned by "Old Drunk Wad," was soon to disappear in the valley forever. The lancers and Punjab's were charging towards their reserves all right, thousands of them waiting for them hidden in the tall grass, hills and behind the copses of trees. The motionless devils waited for their command.

The Russian artillery gunners, were first stunned by four large blasts in the castle area behind the tall buff extension that completely obscured the castle from the rest of the valley. They saw both bridges blown to pieces. Then came the third huge blast that seemed to rock the whole area. This mega blast created a large dust cloud that temporarily overshadowed everything in that area. As it cleared the Russian commander saw that this last explosion had torn a large portion of the huge rock formation off and sent the end of the precipice crashing down into the river. The Russian artillery crews slowly crawled off the ground and prepared or their fire missions. Their grid fire on the British position had been already set.

The Russian Commander wondered who was attacking the castle? It seemed to him that the British had some trick up their sleeves. He had little doubt that the castle was under great attack. He sent back a couple of his men to scout the area. As the dust was still clearing, they returned to report that the bluff on the left side of the pass had been blown into the river below, thus forcing the river to bank across what was the dry ground on the opposite bank. This river had become partially blocked by huge chunks of rock and debris from the falling bluff, forcing the river to grow into a small lake, which emptied into its new river bed. In other words, the pass was now engulfed in a new and larger river course which consumed any dry passage.

A pall of smoke and dust completely covered the area and castle which had suffered heavy attack. They were completely cut off from the castle and had no knowledge that the rest of their artillery and ammo stockpiles had been destroyed. As the dust haze, which impaired the Russian gun commander dissipated and cleared, he was pleased he would now be able to see his artillery spotters and adjust accurate fire on the British. Valuable time had been lost! He ordered his crews to be ready to fire!

He waited then raised his hand as he stood to the side of his guns. Suddenly and silently the Russian gun commander seemed to leap into the air as his uniform was torn from his exploding body. Then came the report of a large caliber rifle in the distance! More of these silent rounds hit more crewmen seeming to blown them into the air like jackrabbits, to pieces. Seeing this horror, all the crews dove to the ground fearing they were the next target of this silent killer! The employment of the Russian guns was stalled again.

The regiment of Punjab lancers quickly cut into the expanse of valley in three waves, soon crashing into a sizable group of green devils positioned to their front. The lancers, intermixing lances, carbine fire and sabers, crashed full force into the devil infantry trampling and cutting down many as they moved. Their swords and lances were dripping red as they left the many bodies of devils scattered in the grass. They cleared the path of death and ran into the next large group in their path. These green devils set up a perfect British firing line and destroyed the first line of lancers and many mounts. The second line of lancers overwhelmed the devil firing line before they could fire a second volley.

The squadron of lancers continued moving forward encountering more and more formations of devils coming at them from every direction. Rifle fire seemed to increase as devils began jumping on the riders and pulling them from their horses. Lancers and mounts began to fall and disappear in the high grass. The lancers had outpaced the infantry because they were never told a Punjab infantry regiment was moving behind them. The combat effectiveness of the lancers had now been tactically reduced to a few survivors as they cleared the devils at the end of the valley.

In their élan and ignorance about the infantry support, the lancers had moved far in front of the Punjab infantry. The infantry marched in battle formation on the same route of the lancers but would never join them. They were beginning to meet more enemy resistance as groups of devils charged them or threw the circular saw blades at them. The Punjab's cleared them away with expert firing lines. Although they seemed to be holding their own, they were completely isolated and large numbers of devils were closing in on them from four sides! The communication links between Wadsworth's gallant left hook and commanders of the other regiments on line was nonexistent!

Effectively, Wadsworth had lost contact and control of two of his five regiments, which included his cavalry squadron of lancers and the Punjab infantry regiment that had been tasked as the reserve! Sun Tzu would comment that Old Wad had violated his cardinal rules: "of dividing forces against an unknown enemy in unknown terrain." He had infantry regiments left, one of veterans taking a beating to the front, and another larger one composed of his service troops on the right and a mishmash of engineers and others lined up in front of the jungle forming a "L" with the line facing the direct assault from the south of the hills. They were all falling apart under the massive pressure of the devils less than an hour into this battle.

The force of the massed devils soon compressed into the front ranks of the British firing lines everywhere as viscous hand-to-hand combat was occurring. It seemed the threat was everywhere at once at this point. The air was hot, as the Sun rose farther on the sky. The smoke-filled battle zone smelled of gunpowder, fear, and death. Colonel Wadsworth had finally ridden up to the artillery positions and watched in horror at the size of the enemy, moving forward, like a wall of moving grass firing rifles and throwing strange circular objects into the ranks of his troops. He turned and quickly left since it appeared that his regiments and artillery were becoming surrounded.

The six field pieces continued to plow death into the sprawling ranks of greenies, slowing pressing forward from west, north, and now from the south. They were surrounded. The vet regiment had pulled back in positions in front of the artillery and reformed their depleted firing lines. Many were missing. The smoke from all the firing continued to rise and obscure the battle lines as the dried grass continued to burn high in huge plumes. Many of the wounded on both sides were being burned alive as the blaze grew. It was observed that the greenies were pulling both their own people and any British wounded they could grab out and carry them away.

All the British regulars had to do was to keep firing straight ahead and they scored hits on the compressed mobs closing on them. Fear and terror began to rise in Old Wad as his eyebrows rose and his lips pursed. His army was surrounded! He then remembered his brilliant left enveloping attack. "It would succeed! These bastards where going down!" He weakly mumbled. His saw from his position on the jungle trail that his group of engineers and others were now heavily engaged in hand to hand combat! He yelled at two of his red bloused staff to prepare his camp to evacuate!

In a second thought he now also headed down the jagged crooked jungle trail to where his headquarters staff of clowns were smacking down pints of whiskey and some staggering with pistols drawn. He rode up and dismounted, stumbling from his mount after finishing a bottle of whiskey he had been drinking before the battle began. He walked over to his rather rotund chubby adjutant who gave him a nervous glance.

"Major Pillroy, we cannot hold, since we are being overwhelmed by large numbers of savages! Please turn these wagons around, see that they are loaded and prepare for a speedy evacuation!" "Retreat sir? Where will we retreat to Sir?" Asked the dumbfounded Pillroy in a nervous voice. Wadsworth fired back "No retreat never dear Pillroy, why we are going to regroup!" He was thinking hard about where to run now, then he remembered that old road about five miles back that crossed this path. Ancient it looked but it was a road. Besides, the way back to the bridge was too far to reach in time before his troops failed. This jungle was their final tomb!

"Fuck them all!" he mumbled. They had failed him and must pay the piper! The green swarm would overtake him and his staff on this crude rough trail preventing them from crossing the bridge in time. This old road did run east – west and could provide an escape. "Pillroy? We shall go to that old road and head due west!" The rotund shaken officer stared at his now crazy commander. "Yes Sir!" Major Pillroy then gave the order…And Wadsworth then noticed that his little handpicked staff of hanger-on, and suck-ups, stood motionless, staring at him.

"Secure the wagons damnit!" He commanded in a fearful yell. Their fear was bordering on terror as the din of the battle seemed to get closer down the jungle path now. Just as he turned to ride back to the artillery positions, he heard loud explosions coming from way off to the left. The spotters for the large Russian guns had just opened up on the Punjab regiment following the lancers into the left flanking attack. The air had cleared in that area. Nobody in Wadsworth's command had a clue what the explosions were now.

But no one could see, just hear large explosions. The Russian artillery spotters had more of an idea as to the location of this isolated Punjab regiment than Colonel Wadsworth! The lancers had suffered so many causalities that they were not even considered a viable target anymore. But it was the sound of distant artillery explosions, big ones at that as perked the interest of Wadsworth. He was back on his horse and chubby Pillroy had finally joined him in a wrestling match to get on his distraught horse. Artillery? Wadsworth had no clue as who was firing what at him. The worst battlefield intelligence a commander can have is the complete lack of it! Old Wad and plenty of nothing today!

The first rounds from the large bore Russian guns walked up into the ranks of the isolated Punjab infantry The Russian artillery flagmen in the trees had done their job well even though Holmes had bagged two of them from the massif who were waving their colored flags as he was leaving. The explosion blew large holes in their tight ranks scattering the doomed formation. Bodies were thrown far into the air, as the screams of the soldiers were buried in the second explosion. They had held their lines fairly well against the wave's invisible attackers in the grass, which only showed themselves when rushing in groups from it at close range to strike down any Punjab close to them with their jagged bladed swords, fire a rifle, or throw a circular flying saw. The Punjab's broke ranks in smaller panicked groups after the two salvos blasted their ranks and began to scatter in back towards the direction of the British artillery.

Kali wanted live prisoners! New recruits he had warned his commanders! Once the artillery ceased firing on the Punjab regiment, nearly two thousand devils, adorned in their green, tattoos, waving their weapons, and completely blown on opium attacked the Punjab's broken ranks from all sides. They then charged in complete wild rampage into the surviving Punjab's flailing their sharp swords and spears. However, it was not violent deaths that were expected by the surviving Punjab's; but capture! The broken shot-up ranks of a small number of little over a hundred Punjab's made a bold attempt to fire at the green waves and were quickly swallowed up by the tsunami of green death.

A wild scene of victory heralded the end of the Punjab regiment. At this point, the second most skilled infantry regiment under Wadsworth was wiped off the map with many captured to refill the depleted ranks to serve the Kali after their conditioning! The wounded and captured British empire soldiers were carted off as an orgy of mutilations, looting, and stripping the dead ensued. There would be a lot of fresh meat for the victory dinner!

The massive explosion on the bluff and resulting lust cloud had offered timely protection of Wadsworth's surviving lancers from enemy observation as it rolled into the northmost portion of the valley. By the time the remaining lancers had cut their way clear, at least seventy percent of them had been put out of action, some killed or pulled alive from their mounts. They disappeared struggling in the tall grassy fields which opened up wide between the forests of trees which dotted this valley. Several of the rider less horses not grabbed by the devils roamed in the tall grass or followed the remaining mounted lancers.

Commander Burrows had herded his survivors into a small forest to protect them from observation. He viewed the Russian artillery positions as it fired a fourth volley. These were huge guns and like the overwhelming size of the enemy, these guns were also mystery! Where is your promised cakewalk now Wadsworth? Grimaced the commander. He looked at his surviving lancers, scared and wore out as they all caught their last breath. They all knew the game was up. What would the last order be wondered Burrows?

As Wadsworth and his confident second in command, Major Albert Pillroy rode back up the uneven jungle trail towards the intense battle in the area around the hills. A sea of green devils was obviously forcing the remains of the regiments back on the hills from their previous fighting lines in front of the hills. The devil noose around the British was closing tight now. The regiment to the front which had taken severe losses was still holding and keeping the wash of devils at bay. However, they had been forced back to the artillery line. It would only be a short time before the advancing wall of enemy overwhelmed the artillery gunners in ferocious hand-to-hand combat.

The green British regiment on the right was now a shamble and overrun. A section of the veteran regiment to the front had moved over there to protect the artillery. Many of the green auxiliary troops in panic, had turned and run with nowhere to go except down the jungle trail and these unfortunates would soon be rounded up alive to meet new fates. The last stand of the British expeditionary force on the hills without names was in full tilt now!

Then there was a huge explosion in the middle of the artillery position number three which to a trained ear was an impacting artillery round. Wadsworth could not understand if it was enemy artillery or an ammo explosion." Where was this artillery!" he raged as his and Pillroy's horses began to rear up in sudden panic from the explosion. The gun and crew hit by the Russian artillery shell disintegrated into a dirty blast of flying debris, leaving a huge crater where the gun crew used to be. This explosion knocked everybody in the vicinity down as a second round hit nearly in the same place as the first! The second blast impacted Wadsworth and Major Pillroy, who were both literally thrown to the earth with their horses.

There was a temporary silence as smoke covered the hills, then rifle and sporadic artillery fire picked up again. Several British troops, weaponless, were running Pell- Mell past Colonel Wadsworth, who was on his knees holding on the reins of his horse. He arose and tried to settle his horse down and remount. Then four more artillery blasts rocked the British artillery hill with huge explosions. This second series of blasts completely removed another two light artillery pieces, the crews, and a group of soldiers positioned around them. Huge smoking craters and the wreckage of cannon and body parts remained. The sea of green devils charged into the gun positions from three sides.

The rotund Pillroy screamed from the ground for his boss to help him but to no avail. He and horse had fallen into a ravine next to the trail, and the chubby major, bedecked in his muddy red blouse, was having one hell of a time crawling up the muddy slippery side of it. His horse had jumped up in a panic and had run off. Wadsworth, barely controlling his horse again was thrown off his mount into the muck of the trail by the next salvo. All Wadsworth could do as the next salvos landed in the hills was hold on to his horse for dear life! The Russian guns continued to pour six more shells into the area, blasting into the ranks and artillery of the doomed British and killing many green devils mixed into the fray.

Then the powerful artillery salvos stopped. Without any thought of leading any last stand or orderly retreat, Old Waddy, ignoring the screams from Pillroy, and covered in muck, remounted his horse and headed towards the rear. He was happy to see that his four HQ wagons had been turned around for a quick exit. He issued his last orders to the two platoon leaders who had set up a tight semi-circular firing formation in front of his HQ wagons. Colonel Wadsworth's last order had been clear. "Boys, hold the line here and wait for the rest to fall back! I will reposition farther back to the rear and bring up the reserve." "Yes sir", replied one of the Platoon leaders. As Wadsworth left the platoon leader was confused. Hadn't the reserve Punjab regiment already been committed to support the lancers to the left?

Major Pillroy, covered in mud, had finally extricated himself from the muddy ravine minus his horse and staggered down the broken jungle trail towards the rear. He had drawn his sword from his dented scabbard as he barreled down the jungle trail waving it as if he was fighting an invisible enemy. After what would be his only military achievement of the battle, he shrieked as he ran past greenies emerging near him from the jungle to his rear. Pillroy ran helter-skelter into the front line of the remaining security platoons now ready for battle. "where is Wadsworth?" The fat muddy HQ commander yelled from winded breath.

"The colonel is gone sir!" Answered the NCO in charge. He is setting up a defense behind us!" The fat major seemed to fill up with air like a string less balloon. Pillroy's face turned crimson red then he shrieked and jumped up in the air yelling curses aloud in a high-pitched rant, which usually followed by his pissing in his pants. This was a problem he had had since he was six years old. His old Aunt Clara had tried everything to stop this "pants pissing when excited," but to naught. Swarms of Green Devils busted from the jungle growth firing rifles and throwing circular saw blades into the security element. The concentrated fire of the British felled the first ranks of greenies, but soon it turned into a brawl. Blood flowed on the ground.

Many soldiers who had run from the battle were caught in a large dragnet by green devils blocking their exit. In the midst of the battle, several groups of greenies had entered the jungle to prevent any retreat! The trap was closing on the fleeing refugees of Wadsworth's relief force of doomed souls. The main body of British troops that stayed and fought it out and locked in heavy combat around the hills without names were cut off and finished! Colonel Wadsworth made it back to his headquarters group who stood with rifles at the ready around the wagons as if waiting for the queen to pass in review. He yelled in a broken voice "Mount up! They are right behind us men!" In a fast pace the wagons and mounted cadres began a swift exit down the cleared jungle trail to a fate unknown in this strange land.

There were green devils, part of the dragnet, waiting for them down the trail. "Old Wad" was fleeing from the fight and abandoning hundreds of British Empire troops to terrible fate! He was surrounded with his staff of professional lackeys and several enlisted ranks riding horses in the lead! Wadsworth's group moved at a reckless pace down the rough trail, running over a couple of Punjab's who had escaped the battle. A group of devils stood in the trail ahead attempting to block their retreat. The reckless movement of their departure was so frantic and careless, that the lead riders and wagon crashed into the group of devils, killing and wounding many as the small group rolled over them.

It was not a clean escape for some however. Several of Wadsworth's gallant clown staff succumbed to wounds, and capture as they were pulled from their horses. As the gauntlet of green devils continued attacking this group, two of the five wagons along with several riders were lost. Finally, after what seemed ages, Wadsworth and the survivors made it to the ancient road, the broken aged stone monuments to some lost civilization! Like Cavendish, Wadsworth's staff had also noted it on their journey into what now had become the "valley of death!"

The group turned right and headed south by huge ageless time worn stone monuments. The party moved up a slow rising steep hill with horsemen in the lead. They pushed up this old road surrounded by thick jungle for several miles until the horses were completely exhausted. They consumed cool water from a nearby mountain stream. The distant echoes of battle seemed to die out after another huge explosion. Silence now dominated all of Wadsworth's surviving staff as the terror they had just faced sunk into their minds.

The Russian artillery ceased firing to allow the green devils to finish their gruesome tasks in victory. The artillery salvos fired into the British positions were devastating and tore open what defenses remained. The sea of green devils, amid the smoke and flames of the burning tall grass overwhelmed the remaining British resistance in terrible bloody hand-to-hand combat! They fought on until being wounded and captured. The effective British artillery and veteran firing lines facing the valley had left piles of dead greenies in front of around their positions in the tall grass. Whole swaths of it was burning now and the smoke had become a terrible choking fog below throughout the battle field.

The multitude of green devils converged in mass on the hills now covered in a fog-like midst from the grass fires and weapons. An old British sergeant of the artillery, overlooked in the post battle chaos, carried out the last act of defiance. He had previously wired a dynamite charge to an artillery ammo wagon, loaded with powder and shells. The artilleryman had already received a rifle shot wound in his left shoulder and was bleeding out. His tan blouse was crimson red. He crawled to the edge of this wagon he was hiding under and lit the fuse. He pulled out his revolver, and then emptied it at a group of greenies approaching, who were giving out their eerie high-pitched war cries and waving some unusual edged weapons, that had haunted all the British facing them since the start of the battle. He did not save the last bullet for himself, for it was not needed.

The lighted fuse set off the munitions and the ammo wagon engulfed the whole area behind the gun positions in a tremendous blast. Most of the greenies surging into the area were killed along with any remaining artillerymen mixed in with the infantry. All that remained was smoldering burning tall grass, military wreckage, and many bodies lying in the destruction around a crater larger than the ones created by the Russian guns, where the wagon had once been. The area was suddenly quiet, then the wails of the green devils emerged in a huge wail as they again overran the hill.

However, there was one event left in this tragedy of tragedies, authored by the infamous Colonel Wadsworth. The surviving lancers had fought clear of the greenies and had moved out of the huge copse of trees into a position in direct view of the Russian Artillery batteries. Those bastards had arrogantly raised the Russian colors over their position! They all watched helplessly as the guns began to fire rounds into the valley. This artillery was well situated on a hill, and the guns were aimed at their forces south. The commander of the lancers, Captain Burrows looked disparagingly at his remaining troops and yelled:

"We will take those fucking Russian guns for Queen and Country! men! Hail Britannica!" One of his last remaining British NCOs yelled "Remember Balaclava!" Since the lancers were all Sikhs, they did not understand the reference to the failed British "Charge of The Light Brigade "against the Russian artillery in the Crimean War years before this day. Captain Burrows gave a smile to him. The survivors moved silently in a line formation from the copse of trees in a fast trot. As they neared the base of the long hill the bugler sounded charge! Up the hill the remaining lancers charged in a broken line formation with revenge on their minds!

Several lancers where shot off their horses by marksmen near the cannons, but it was too late for the Russian gun crews. In quick succession, the surviving lancers who made it over the top begin their killing spree! They moved on their mounts around the artillery pieces, spearing with their lances, swords, and shooting down every soldier they could find. Most of the Russians and their auxiliaries were killed, including the third gun commander. Only a few of the gun crews ran into the jungle tree line and escaped. There was little time to blow the cannons if they wanted to escape. Captain Jonathan Burrows, ordered his few survivors to roll the artillery pieces off the side of a steep hill on the leeward side of the position, along with the two ammo wagons. The Russian flag joined them.

The artillery and wagons crashed down over a hundred rocky yards into a steep gulch. A sea of green devils was observed approaching from the deep grass below the Russian artillery position where the lancers had charged. Looking out, Burrows returned his gaze to the new white capped river course of rapids intermixed with huge boulders, newly created by the explosion. He estimated half of the rock bluff formation had dropped into the river by the explosion. He looked at his weakened and beaten remains of men, out of the original compliment of two-hundred lancers scarcely twenty were still mounted. Burrows was the only one of four British officers left. His last British NCO was killed attacking the guns.

Captain Burrows looked hard at his men. "Men, we are headed for that river which may offer our only escape. We will go sharply to the right in a "V" formation I will lead! Be ready!" They climbed up on their tired mounts, with several horseless riders using the large Russian dray horses from the now destroyed caissons. They trotted down the large hill, unsheathing sabers and pulling our carbines since their lances were gone, broken in the bodies of Russians and green devils found on the hill.

Once down the hill the lancers broke into a wild gallop across waist high grass beyond the canopy of dense jungle in a quasi-V formation. The horsemen soon ran into devils in the tall grass and began trampling, slashing, and shooting those who now crossed into their paths. The survivors were being speared or knocked off their horses, as greenies jumped on them pulling them and their mounts down into the tall grass. After some three hundred yards, only three lancers made it to the frothing river waters and plunged into it. The three survivors plunged into the water on their mounts, dodging rifle fire, as their tired horses kept afloat in the new white rapids that formed just inside the pass.

Huge boulders from the bluff explosion created quite a spectacle, as they bounced around and off of them on their escape down the widened emerald colored jungle river. Accurate rifle fire now seemed to come from the jungle bluffs above to their right. One more lancer caught a bullet in his back and keeled off his mount into the rapids never to be seen again, Captain Burrows, experienced in war, slipped off his mount just before two bullets hit the back of his horse killing it. Burrows floated next to its body as if he were dead. The other lancer was soon taking three bullets in his back slid off his dying horse into the newly formed white foaming rapids. The few surviving Russian snipers on the bluff had finally extracted some revenge for the many deaths Holmes and Hoskins had inflicted among them.

Captain Burrows drifted in the fast current with only his face above the water and holding the reigns of his dead horse under water. He glanced at the remains of two destroyed bridges, and a seemingly ancient smoldering castle as he floated by them. He was floating in some unknown river, into some unknown mysterious jungle. The colors of the lancer regiment had been left at the Russian gun positions, and flew proudly there, until they were pulled down by the victorious screaming green devils and the few returning Russian artillerymen.

Wadsworth called a halt to his group as it had moved a way down the ancient broken overgrown road of yore. No devils had pursued them since they climbed up the hill by the old monuments out of the valley. Wadsworth looked at only twenty-three survivors out of his staff of over thirty. There were another four enlisted British soldiers handling the wagons that had made it. He preferred white men near him and not the brown smelly natives. All of these little "poppycock" survivors never engaged in the combat of the day, nor ever saw the battle! Yet now they began to act cocky as if they had fought and perhaps won? Wadsworth wondered of the fate of Major Pillroy who he had shamefully abandoned in the fight.

He now observed his staff suckups strutting around the old road like some gaggle of gamecocks. Bottles of Whiskey were passed around to quell the fears that had engulfed his lads. He took a huge swig of whiskey as he pondered his relief mission. Colonel Wadsworth's great crusade to destroy the devils and rescue mission was a disaster well beyond description now. Two of the surviving three wagons were loaded with the food, whiskey, and water supply for the HQ and a regiment. In the other wagon was the personal baggage of HQ personnel both missing and present, with some extra rifles and ammo. All the tents, camp equipment and the regimental colors were gone with the two wagons that fell to the enemy along with several of his staff personal! He did feel blessed about this fact!

Kali, in his godlike hooded male form and his staff of dark hooded minions walked on the twisted wreckage of the battlefield. He was hailed by the multitude of his green devil children who stood on the hills surrounding him! Kali had taken many losses of his manpower today and would begin the conditioning process to replace his losses on all the British conscripts he had ordered captured for such a purpose. The age of gunpowder had made losses in battle costly! He was still confused at the action of the British carelessly sending this huge force of hundreds to obvious slaughter? Why? The British did not fight like this ever! It seemed that the greatest asset Kali had was this gross stupidity of the leaders of this British army! Kali was an old hand in conducting warfare and it seemed every principle of war and been broken! The destruction of the British forces was never in question. Kali was confused.

But the question of great concern to him was who had done incredible damage to his castle, and weapons stores? The immeasurable damage done to his staging areas and munitions was terrible! He had complete focus on the development of the battle against the British army and had never anticipated an attack on his castle even though at one point he felt that foreign eyes had been watching him. Who did this! He patted the barrel of one of the three British artillery pieces captured intact as he viewed the dead being stripped of uniforms, weapons, and personal effects. He entertained the thought of animating the dead but it was just too messy and time consuming. The dead, would be served up tonight as a victory feast for his devils! Besides, he had captured over three hundred prisoners which were easier to convert when he felt like it. The Kali had watched the battles at Malakand and fall of Chital with great interest and a grudging respect for how well the British held off the massive attacks by the Ghazi led Pashtuns at Malakand. This is why this recent blunder by the British made little sense to him?

He saw how his concentration of mass in the attack had quickly overwhelmed the British here and at Chital. Mass, when available, was a very effective tool! Kali was still amazed at how this British force boldly ventured all the way into his vast lair to be destroyed. They had violated so many protocols in conducting battle. In all his time in war on the planet he had never seen such stupidity in war by any professional army ever! He laughed as he felt this effort was completely unlike the British! He laughed out loud as his minions stood and watched him. Kali surmised that "A complete idiot must have led them!"

Besides losing many of his devils, many Russians guarding the artillery and munitions and manning the artillery had been killed. They could be replaced soon. The loss of the artillery pieces and all the ammunition in that staging area and within the castle were catastrophic! It would take time to replace this loss in a land now falling under the control of the British! He did have a supply of artillery ammunition left in another area and could salvage the four Russian guns rolled into the ravine from the hill by the horse men called lancers. There were also three intact British cannons and all their weapons to be used later. The bridges would be replaced, then the castle! In his final analysis it was a grand day of victory.

The night seemed to come very soon in the wake of the huge battle. The funeral pyres cremating over two thousand odd deceased green devils would burn large, and all night. The wood cooking fires would also burn long into the night roasting the many slain invaders now on the menu. The chaotic wild dancing around these burning funeral pyres by many devils wearing parts of the British uniforms, women's clothes taken at Chital, and firing captured weapons into the air, all stripped from the dead marked the victory celebrations. The smell of opium mixed with roasting flesh wafted through the long valley in the new moonlight. A couple of the captured soldiers were sacrificed in the ritual of stealing the souls of the enemy and consumed. There was enough food for all. There would be no hungry devils at dawn!

Kali, the tall one with the horrid grimace, was pleased as he now stood on a dais constructed in the middle of the devil's camps. Twenty-one of the surviving British officers and NCOs knelt before him in front of the huge stage he had constructed for the victory celebration. They had been spared ritual sacrifice and being on the dinner plate this night. Kali needed them in his army! Soon they would, like all their captured subordinate Punjab counterparts, be transformed into mindless flesh-eating green devils. He also had plans to force recruitment of the thousands of Pashtun tribesmen to vastly bolster his ranks! He would build his huge army, and would move on domination of India after he destroyed the British occupiers and Islam!

He stood on a platform, in front of his minions, giving praise in a strange language, hypnotizing them to humming as strange music and drumbeats echoed in the night. Kali was adept in numbing men's souls for his absolute control over them. He commanded thousands before! All in this ancient cult not conditioned feared his powers. He allowed rumors to guide opinions on him and his abilities. It was rumored that he could hear all that was said, that he could change shapes from Kali into the hideous she-devil goddess that loved to feast on the living humans. No one, including his very close advisors ever knew how old he was or where he came from. So, it was universally believed that he was actually what he had told them; two gods named Kali and she-devil Raktabija sent as the divine words of Shiva the Destroyer and was a proclaimed "god goddess!" He had power; proven godlike powers! He mused at his resurrection of these gods, crafted from ancient myth. If he had so desired, he could have been the Pope if it served him!

He had long ago learned the power that religion held as the most powerful motivator for humans. He had first learned this as his life as the conquistador Cortez, so blessed and protected by the might of the Catholic Church in the Americas! He thought about those days with his usual evil grimace. Now he was "Kali" the god and Raktabija the goddess here to spread the word of Shiva and age-old Kali; destruction of the world! He loved to imitate these tools of his trade in his manipulations of humankind! His father had taught him well before his end!

The tattered British regimental flags fluttered in the early evening breezes behind him accented by the many torches that brightly adorned his stage. He peered down on all the prisoners that had been collected, forced to kneel bound. These prisoners would all make excellent devils he thought as they were moved away to be secured for him to personally condition later. He did take a fancy to one very handsome British officer with a gash on his face. It looked like the man hungry she-devil goddess Raktabija would pay him a long visit tonight.

Another exception was one white British officer who was ushered to his dais. He was a plump one with fat cheeks who was unusually dressed in a red topped uniform with gold braid. He was covered with dried mud. One of the cloaked devils handed Kali the officer's sword as a symbol of surrender. It was a very well-made peace with a gold-plated handle and inlaid with rubies as the eyes of the lion headed hilt. The supreme master liked it. It eyed the fat officer and slavered at the meaty parts the rotund British officer had to offer. This officer announced: "I am Major Albert Pillroy, the commander of the staff under Colonel Wadsworth and I demand to see who was in charge to discuss the conditions of the prisoners and a proper surrender! There are rules in war you know!"

He gazed fearfully at the mob carrying the captured British away to an unknown fate. When he looked back into the sinister Green Devil leader's hypnotic stare he shuddered in terror. It spoke in perfect English. "I am Kali, the leader whom you seek!" The gaze of this monster of pure evil then reached deep into his soul! Pillroy saw a distinctive image of himself being basted while roasting alive on a spit like a pig over a huge cooking fire as the thoughts of the evil Kali continued to press into his feeble mind.

Kali laughed at Pillroy's inner question of what was being brushed on him while he cooked. "We like to use mango and pineapple juice and a hint of white wine! It sweetens the meat! Your meat!" The vision came to pass for Pillroy. After the long painful ritualistic torture and stealing of his soul before dinner, a well basted "Roast Pillroy" on the spit "was served as the main course to those at the table of the Great Kali. The plump Major was tender and succulent to the bite as Kali picked tasty bites of Pillroy speared on the nice sword his father had given him at graduation!

CHAPTER FIVE
THE VILLAGE

Corporals Holmes, Hoskins, and King George wasted little time force-marching tediously back across the rough terrain and crossing the fast-moving river on top of the huge massif. They would wait for the rest of the scouts there. The sun was high in the sky now as they set up an ambush on the other side of the river waiting for their comrades to show. Griggs was missing and both Gladstone and Lord Nelson were dead. Lieutenant Cavendish was wounded as he, Collins, Rashid and Hook were slowly following to the rear and would catch up with them at the river. They skillfully crossed the rope slide and kept up the pace with much lighter loads of equipment. When the trio showed up, they were helped in their efforts across the narrow fast-moving jungle river that emptied into the huge waterfalls.

In their escape from the castle area, they continued hearing the sounds of battle from far below that could not be observed by the huge smokey haze rising from the battle and grass fires at the end of the valley. The artillery fire seemed to wane as the Russian artillery scored what must have been direct hits on the British positions. After a huge final explosion from the vicinity of this bloody conflict an eerie silence prevailed. The echoes of artillery and rifle fire throughout the valley now had extinguished completely. It was over! The group, reunited rappelled down the steep bluff into the camp. They silently approached their little base camp with revolvers drawn. There was concern that something had gone wrong since there was nobody in what seemed an abandoned camp.

They found a smiling Cornwallis, Andrea, the kids hiding. Cornwallis, with the help of Andrea and her kids, had carefully camouflaged their hiding place under the cliff and had removed any sign of being there. They were all safe. She looked at Hoskins. "I hope you are all right?" She reached out and held his hand. Cornwallis and his charges had watched the whole battle until the clouds of smoke blotted out the action. Under the extreme circumstances the group miraculously had avoided serious if not fatal wounds! Rashid had a shallow bullet wounds in his shoulder and upper leg, Hook had several less serious wounds except for the slash across his face to his shoulder. Lieutenant Cavendish had suffered the worst injury.

The dagger wound had gone completely through his chest below his left shoulder. Rashid administered a second round of first aid as Cavendish stared at Hooky with a smile. "I hope that you are not my reflection in some mirror I am looking at!" Alfred Hook smiled." Now LT, I was just thinking the same thing!" They both gave out mutual exhausted laughs. Their khaki uniforms were bloodstained, filthy and torn; their faces were smeared with remaining residue of black grease used for camouflage. They were a mess, felt it and knew it! Rum was now produced from Hook's saddlebags.

Andrea and Hoskins walked over to the huge boulder above the cliff facing the valley. She grabbed him by the collars of his uniform. "I never want you out of my sight again Corporal Hoskins!" She then cried in his arms. She had seen more than enough in her terrible ordeal from Chital. Hoskins gave a silent sob in agreement as he hugged her. Her lush full voluptuous body and soothing lips reminded the ageless bachelor that he was now officially in love. In short order his tan blouse was removed to reveal quite a nasty slash across this back to his right shoulder. It must have been created by a grazing Russian sniper's bullet. Holmes supervised the cleaning of his wounds.

Cavendish knew they would have to exit this place in short order. He was certain that the Kali had figured out the fact that some other force in his neighborhood had attacked the castle. The scouts stripped naked and washed themselves and uniforms in the close by bubbling hot spring. Hook passed Hoskins the bottle of rum as they lounged in the warm spring waters. King George related the sad news of the heroic deaths of Lord Nelson and Gladstone as he summed up the fight at the castle.

Griggs was missing in action! Cornwallis, was quiet. He had lost two of his close brothers to these savages and would get his revenge. Gurkhas never forgive or ever forget! He refilled the canteens and watered the horses in a fresh clear nearby stream as his thoughts of revenge grew deep. After the brief respite in the hot springs they group packed up what they needed for their journey. The pack horses bore no loads anymore and would leave with the group. They sat around a dead campfire eating cold rations after the sun had set. Rashid then broke the silence. He had been viewing the activity at the north end of the valley since before sunset with the telescope.

"We may be lucky in our escape sir! This victory in battle had thrown the green devils into an expected wild celebration, and this can help ensure our safe extrication if we get moving soon." Ambrose Cavendish then added. "This makes sense; we do not want to encounter any of them now. We shall leave after we eat on our retreat to nowhere! We have to get word of this disaster to General Blood immediately!" Cavendish had stifled his growing pain with a piece of the opium cake which was a powerful remedy. He then walked to the cliff and joined Rashid at the ornate brass telescope on tripod. He gazed into the valley and many huge bonfires burning in the night below noting the thousands of forms dancing around them. Cavendish was sickened by the images of so many naked human bodies roasting on the spits, being basted like swine!

If only Wadsworth could see how his troops were being treated by these savages now! Was Wadsworth even alive he wondered? He told his Indian scout to pack up the telescope for they were leaving. Hook sat next to the young lieutenant Collins and smiled at him. "Not a bad job on the bluff Collins! You, Rashid, and King George kicked some real ass this morning and probably saved the day for all of us!" He patted the lad on the shoulder and passed the bottle of rum. Collins gave him a thousand-yard stare with a low smile and took a long plug on it and handed it to Cavendish who had returned. He took a plug of rum. Collins looked at Cavendish. "Do you think we will get out of here sir?" he asked in a distant voice. Cavendish looked fondly at the officer.

"Yes, we will definitely get home. We got in here twice and will get out again. We have a clear path and devil celebration below and night will be our friend. Cavendish called them all together for a short meeting to quickly discuss the situation and options. He said "Men, you have done an excellent job and we probably did more damage to Kali's war machine than we know!" Hook smiled. "But sir, it was your superb leadership and planning!" Retorted Cavendish. "We all did the best we could boys, a great team effort I would say! My Plans? They don't mean shit unless they are executed correctly gentlemen!" The Lieutenant praised everybody personally and toasted the loss of Gladstone, Lord Nelson, and whereabouts of Griggs last seen heading to the powder magazine. Cavendish added. "If Griggs survived the blast?" Hook added, "He will have found a way to escape! We know Griggs!"

They spent a few moments discussing the complete utter massacre of the British forces under Wadsworth. Cornwallis gave his disturbing observations. They all wondered if anybody escaped. It was decided that Cornwallis, Hoskins, Andrea and her kids would move out first and head towards the river. Perhaps the bridge was still intact. They would head to General Blood directly. The rest, in the second group would follow an hour later. Small groups had a better chance of going undetected.

They took what they considered valuable and discarded everything else. They watched as the first group left silently south along the huge cliff wall. One hour to the mark Cavendish and the remaining scouts abandoned the camp and followed the same obscure path south illuminated by the light of a three-quarters moon.

Six cautious hours later, the first group led by Cornwallis silently approached what seemed to be an intact bridge. It was nightfall and torches were burning brightly on it. He quietly dismounted and crept up to the north end suspecting green devils now owned it. He was amazed; it was still guarded by a platoon of Sikh Lancer sentries commanded by an old British NCO. The Gurkha signaled the rest. They rode up to the completely unmolested bridge and were greeted by the familiar command. "Halt! Who goes there!" The sentries closest were now approaching him with rifles aimed with their turbans reflecting in the torchlight.

Hoskins replied. "We are survivors from the scout section of Wadsworth's command!" The British sergeant in charge of the bridge detail, obviously reeling with anxiety asked. "Survivors? How did the battle go? We heard it and the noise of cannons and distant explosions echoing down the valley walls then silence." Corporal Hoskins unloaded the bad tidings. "Wadsworth's command was slaughtered, destroyed!" The bewildered British NCO looked at his equally dazed subordinates. Hoskins continued. "All of you are in mortal danger and I am amazed that you are still alive and this bridge intact! The hordes of green devils are everywhere! Please trust me! Follow us out of here or you will soon be fresh victims of these ungodly savages! I am certain the green devils will invest or destroy this bridge after they unwind from their huge victory celebration! A terrible fate has spared all of you for now! Please join us and get out now!"

The NCO was visibly stunned by the news as Hoskins saw fear run across all their faces as they gathered around listening. The NCO looked at them with grief. "You mean to tell me hundreds of British Empire troops; the whole relief force was wiped out?" Hoskins gravely nodded his head in the affirmative. "I believe your platoon of lancers are left!" The NCO asked. "What should we do with this bridge?" Hoskins looked across at it then looked back at the sergeant of the guard. "Leave it! You have no time to do anything I would suspect; the green devils are probably coming your way soon. We heard them in the jungle as we came out of the jungle. Join us now or you will die here!"

In the next few minutes the bridge guard, all lancers, the only combat platoon out of the whole relief force to survive the massacre, packed up what few possessions they had, saddled their horses and were moving at a trot behind the small party. They were headed straight for Chital. In less than twenty minutes after they departed the bridge, a large band of Green Devils riding captured horses, charged across the bridge firing their rifles indiscreetly to find it and the cooking fire abandoned. The green devils secured it as they now conducted heavy patrols from the length of the jungle to the river. The gate was not closed. Kali needed more conscripts!

Holmes and Rashid came to a sudden halt as they now stood on the ancient stone road that crisscrossed their escape path. They observed the ancient statues leading to a steep hill to their right. They all could hear the muffled din of a large group of hooves digging through the large expanded trail Wadsworth's engineers had widened days before off to their left some hundred yards. They were coming up to their left and fast. What to do was the question. In an afterthought 2LT Collins said. "I bet they are going for that bridge!" The greenies were now to their front in force now. The bridge area would fall under the green control if it already had. Cavendish hoped that Cornwallis and company had escaped ahead of their pursuit by now. Rashid was looking at the ancient rough trail to their rear right. He looked at his boss.

"This trail runs southwest and it would be wise to take it now. I fear we are surrounded and blocked Sir! At least we will be riding in relative safety away from this valley of doom until we can figure a good place to cross the river and escape." Cavendish agreed and the party ambled onto the trail and began to climb up a large rise passing the remains of ancient walls and monuments. After a couple of miles Rashid and King George both spotted something on the ancient road. After dismounting and surveying the old beaten roadway Rashid looked at the lieutenant. "There are recent wagon tracks on this path as well as hoofs! it looks like someone else came this way as well. … and recently!"

The exhausted listless group continued to let their horses navigate forward with King George in the lead. They were nearly sleeping in their saddles. Cavendish was in growing pain from his deep wound as he was wondering who might the wagon tracks belong too? The lieutenant decided to find a place to stop and spend the night on this old trail. They had moved far enough down the road where the noises of the night birds replaced the yelling and gunshots of the greenies far back and below their position. A moon glow above the vast jungle trees was the only light in the complete darkness of the jungle road. Lord George and lieutenant Collins pulled the first guard many yards down the road from the rest facing the jungle valley. The titanic ordeal had taken a heavy mental and physical toll on everybody. Better to be safe in the night than sorry. The real dangers were very manifest and seemed to surround them now.

In the deep jungle north of the castle sat Captain Burrows. He had finally climbed out of the river on a mossy bank with an overgrown dense jungle environment around him. He retrieved what little remained from the saddle of his dead mount which he quietly lamented in his grave sadness at the events of the day. He had seen that a couple of monstrous Crocodiles had been silently following him in the river current as he floated with his dead horse. Both amphibians jumped the body of the horse and in a frenzy of death rolls and fighting, tore the deceased animal to pieces and ate it in minutes. The same fate awaited the bodies of the horses and lancers who died in the river behind him. Burrows shivered. This horrible end for him had floated only twenty-five yards behind him. His loyal horse had saved him twice this day!

The sun was nearly blotted out by the tall jungle canopy and was low in the western sky now. The long terrible day was nearing its end! Night was coming and he was armed with his revolver and had maybe a dozen rounds left. He was able to pull his sword and knit bag from his saddle but little else. His khaki uniform was soaked from the river and his sweat. His pith helmet was gone, lost among the Russian cannons. He had been sitting for what seemed hours on the river bank, in shock and encroaching fatigue. He had nothing to smoke as an aura of doom had settled deeply into his soul. Why did he survive when all his men either died or were captured? He led his men in the attacks into the savages and Russians and was never killed or wounded? Fate was strange he thought as he just listened to the river flow as he viewed the massively thick jungle that seemed his prison; which seemed at least two-hundred feet high.

The emerald green river cascaded deeper into the jungle where Burrows sat facing an isolated doom. It seemed only the crocodiles floating nearby cared now. Then, to his astonishment he heard a strange voice in perfect English. "Sir, can you tell me where The Tower of London can be found? I seem to have lost my map!" The forlorn captain, confused, looked quickly to his right and their stood Mister Griggs holding a Russian rifle at port. Stupefied at the question and the sight, Burrows let out a laugh. Griggs, was dressed in his rumpled khaki uniform, torn and tattered like Burrows. His cloak and hat were but memories given to the river where he had plunged from the castle tower. He introduced himself, as did the captain.

Then there was a brief silence. "Anybody else with you Sir?" "No" lamented Captain Burrows, "They are either all dead or captured! But we got those damned Russian cannons before our end!" Griggs gave him "thumbs up", then commented "If anybody was captured then they are as good as dead! You smoke Sir?" Inquired the tall newcomer. "Yes, I would love one!" Griggs sat next to the Captain on the moss-covered riverbank and lit a couple of dry cigarettes protected from the water in his kit. Both of them smoked in silence, lost in exhaustion and their own thoughts pervading their minds for several minutes. Griggs passed him a bottle of whiskey he also had in his kit. They both took a couple of plugs as silence ruled their thoughts. After the silence, Griggs spoke; 'Sir, are you injured?" "No, I am fine but my soul is broken."

Griggs gave a reassuring look. "You did your best under the terrible circumstances Wadsworth put you and your lancers into Sir! Later I will tell you the whole story of "arch criminal" Wadsworth and his bogus orders!" Burrows nodded his head slowly. Griggs continued. "We have a long walk back and can begin when you are ready." After another cigarette and plug of whiskey each, both soldiers slowly began to trek out due west using the compass Griggs had pulled out. They both felt a sense of peaceful awe wandering in the beauty of the massive ancient primal jungle surrounding them with no end. Many days would pass in this paradise before they saw life as they knew it again.

The scouts resting on the ancient broken stone road heard sporadic rifle shots echo from the rise across the jungle valley all night. Cavendish, wincing from his festering wound as he prayed that his other group had gotten free of this place safely. The question was what to do now? Go back down into the jungle and move towards the river with probable ambushes everywhere, or continue on this ancient road? He put the question to his men in the dawn and they voted to continue west on this road. The farther away from the devils the better! After the horses were watered, they ambled up the continuing steep road they had been on for the next three hours. Rashid, leading the group stopped, turned and put his index finger to his lips, the universal code for silence! Soon, they could clearly hear voices; British voices around a steep bend.

They continued to ride until they could see three wagons and British soldiers milling about or sitting. Some wore the distinctive red blouse of Wadsworth's staff. As they entered this area, both groups just stared at each other in a muted silence. The scouts also smelled food cooking. As if on cue, Colonel Wadsworth, the architect of this disaster appeared. Before a word was spoken Cavendish could see the complete derangement emanating from his eyes. He had an air of drunkenness about him as well. Several of his staff drew carbines and revolvers in the silence. "Well Cavendish!" Began the Colonel slurring his words, "I am so glad you could make it here to join us!"

"The pleasure is mine colonel!" retorted the lieutenant sarcastically. "Please join us for tea and dinner!" intoned "Old Wad." Without any further words and in what seemed a civil meeting, the scouts dismounted and were all soon feasting on a well needed plentiful meal. Two of the surviving wagons were filled with the food and supplies for the large headquarters staff and company, many of which were gone; causalities of the battle. They sat quietly among Wadsworth's HQ staff unconcerned as they ate a much-needed meal. Cavendish's wound was beginning to hurt more as Rashid cleaned and dressed his wound.

Under the silent direction of SGT Hook, King George slid away to check the contents of the wagons. The scouts were soon quietly replenished with much-needed pistol ammunition and a couple of bottles of Whiskey scrounged from the baggage wagon picked through by Lord George. Without even the slightest mention of the battle James Cavendish soon addressed the colonel. "Sir, we need to keep moving, the green devils could close on us at any minute! They were all over the jungle below the rise in this road last night" "Oh Lieutenant!" He listlessly said. They are miles behind us now.… They!" He stammered and stopped as if some mental block had just hit him in the head.

Old Wad just stared into nothingness, fully aware of what had just happened in that terrible valley the day before. He then looked at the sun which was growing low in the west now. "No!", he continued mild mannerly, "The sun will be gone soon; we shall make camp and stay here tonight then continue at dawn!" "But Sir!" continued the lieutenant now seething under his collar, "They could be coming for us now! We need to move." "But Sir Nothing!" mildly commented the colonel, "we shall stay here!" "Sir!" came the angry words of Cavendish, "I will be leaving in twenty minutes whether you come or not!" "Oh, no Cavendish" came back a stronger slurring drooling command voice from Wadsworth matter-of- fact reply.

"You and your scouts will stay here, right back down that road as my security detail; and that is a direct order under combat conditions! I do have enough HQ staff to make a nice firing squad!" The insane anger of the colonel was overwhelming his senses as more slobber appeared on the side of his mouth. He smelled of urine, booze and was dangerously inebriated as well. "Yes Sir!" Replied Cavendish with murder in his eyes as he realized this. He saluted and returned to his men. Sergeant Hook was surprised that "Old Waddy" had not said anything to him or his adopted 2LT Collins about their strange disappearance from his encampment firing squad days earlier north of Chital.

LT. Cavendish was very clear on their position when he returned. "Old Wad is in a dangerous threatening drunken trance, and shock I would think. We need to play along until we can cut and run." He added. "Gentlemen, we have been ordered to pull security on the rear tonight under threats of immediate execution if we refuse. Personally, he has gone fucking crazy boys! We will deploy just out of sight down that road. If the greenies come, we will be able to warn the camp as we ride past them getting the hell out of here!" Hooky gave a laugh. "You mean Colonel Wadsworth is completely off his rocker, why when did this happen? When he was a child?" Ambrose gave him a concerned look with a broken smile. "Yes Hooky, dangerously off his rocker I fear!"

King George, and Lieutenant Collins volunteered again to keep first watch while the banged-up Hook, Rashid, and Cavendish could get some rest. It seemed that Cavendish's wound was worse. With the sun now gone from the sky, both surviving groups of the battle settled down for a quiet uneventful night in separate locations on the ancient overgrown road. However, all the scouts awake seemed to feel the same presence, a curious presence it seemed, that was watching them every night in this forbidden jungle landscape. It was not threatening or malicious, but passive as if a herd of grazing deer were taking an interest in them.

The dawn light seemed to come fast and manifested the high jungle trees, kissing the tops of them first. The sounds of birds, monkeys, and other morning chatter added to this primal element. Cavendish's scouts were invited to breakfast by a couple of British enlisted men sent to tell them. The colonel was not present and the mood seemed normal. The hearty breakfast was appreciated as the scouts ate and returned to their position down the road. It took over three hours for Wadsworth's HQ staff break camp. Hook viewed this effort as some sort of haphazard circus. They would have never survived the drift he thought and he knew how they had survived this disaster!

This clown circus of idiots had run away in the face of the battle. There were no injured in the company of these wannabe little gamecocks! The small column finally pulled out as Cavendish's group had been relegated to the rear of the group as security. They rode for a couple hours in the heat, taking short breaks along the ancient unkempt road masked in the shadows of the huge jungle fauna. Cavendish had made it clear to his men. Keep away from Wadsworth's boys and be vigilant! These staff lackeys were puppets of Wadsworth the puppet master! They were not to be trusted! He sensed that Wadsworth was a doomed man with no way out. He and his little circle of pets would be swallowed up by this jungle sooner or later. He had no plans to save them or join them.

The column continued on and Cavendish slumped in this mount from his wounds. As the scouts moved in silence two people appeared from the jungle growth walking next to the lieutenant. It was a very old man in robes and a little girl who was holding his hand. Cavendish then slipped from his saddle to the ground as his horse stopped next to the two strangers who caught his fall. The infection and weakened him greatly and he now moaned in pain from the ground. Very quickly the two figures sat him up as the scouts joined them. The beautiful little girl said "Sorry Sahib Cavendish!" From his daze, Cavendish saw an old man and a pretty little girl, obviously local natives. He wondered from his delirium how the girl knew his name.

They two visitors looked thirsty, and hungry. Hook, Rashid, King George, and Collins surrounded him and the strangers. The dagger wound inflicted on Cavendish had now become badly infected at this point and had sapped his strength. He had a fever. Rashid began an immediate conversation with the old man who was looking at his wound. The ancient man looked at the scouts standing around and spoke in perfect English. "If you allow, I can help this man." Rashid then removed the bandages now soaked in blood and pus. The lieutenant was dying. The old man cleaned the entrance and exit wounds with a cloth that smelled like it had medicine on it. Then he took out a bottle with a brown substance in it. He gently covered both wounds with it using the cloth. He helped Rashid bandage the wound. The ancient man smiled at Rashid and said. "Give it some time and he will be fine!"

Rashid saw the condition of the man and girl. "They need water and food" Came his request to the scouts. Lieutenant Collins handed them some hardtack and a canteen. Both seemed to inhale it and nodded their heads gratefully. After continuing speaking in an understandable Pashtun dialect with the old man, Rashid gave his report to the rest. 'Sahib, this old man is named Ravi and the girl's is named Pyra. They live in a village many miles down the road and said we are welcome. Ravi is the head man of the village and will give us safe haven from those who follow us. He said he will also give us guidance on how to escape this jungle. He also told Rashid that their village was facing famine and if we have any extra food it will help save lives in return.

Lord George remembered the two wagons laden with food he remembered in the two wagons he scrounged for more pistol ammo. He announced this find to Ravi and the scouts about the food stores that had survived the battle; enough to feed over a hundred soldiers for weeks. He did tell Hook about the store of whiskey in the third wagon to his delight! Meanwhile the scouts noticed that all of their horses had ambled over to the little girl and were nudging her as she laughed and patted them. How strange Rashid thought. They seem to love her. In a few minutes Lieutenant Cavendish was awake. Ravi and Pyra smiled at him as Collins and Hook helped him off the ground. It seemed that the lieutenant was already feeling better. Ravi then applied ointment to all the wounds presented to him by the other scouts. The positive bond between scouts and the strangers was now established.

As the small Colum of Wadsworth's staff moved along the road, one of Wadsworth's staff noticed that Cavendish's group was no longer behind them as he yelled for them. He reported this and was ordered by the colonel to find them. Down the road, a small group galloped onto the scene of the dismounted scouts and two strangers standing in the road. The red-bloused HQ staff officer named Billings curtly asked what was going on. He was informed that lieutenant Cavendish had taken a fall from his horse due to an infected wound and had fever from it. Hook also added the story of the village ahead and their offer of help. The green devils were following them as related by the old man named Ravi. Billings sent one of the staff officers back to the staff down the road.

Soon, he returned with a message. "Colonel says we will go to the village and to get moving. Oh, you can leave these people here. We don't need them!" He and the other two staff turned and left. "Bullshit!" yelled Cavendish weakly before the staff rode out of earshot, "He is the headman of this village!" Cavendish was feeling better now. He ordered his scouts to put Ravi and the Pyra on two of the three spare horses they had brought with them. They had been used to carry all the explosives taken from Wadsworth's engineers and had been spared.

Cavendish looked into the gentle hypnotic stare of Ravi and said "I will be glad to help you and your village, but I am not in command here, so" …. he smiled at Ravi, "We will probably have to do it discretely." Ravi understood completely what Cavendish had said in perfect "Queen's English" to the surprise of all that could hear him, thanked him. Before Cavendish could ask where he learned his proper English or how the little girl knew his name, they were all moving down the road once again. Protection, guidance, and survival to feed a village seemed proper and continued floating through his mind as they rode. Wadsworth and his band of cowards didn't need an eighth of the food stores in the wagons since the proposed time in the jungle would be limited as they were going to escape very soon.

In another hour, the small column stopped for rest. Rashid took off Cavendish's blouse and was looking at his once festering wounds. They seemed to be clearing up fast from the ointment the old man had put on them. It was obvious that the lieutenant felt better. He was about to put another bandage on it as Ravi stepped up and pulled a strange herb from his shoulder bag. He spoke in Rashid's native tongue again. "Rub this again into his wounds and the rest of the wounds of your men sir, it is a great herb for completing the healing process." Rashid looked at the deep kind gaze of the old man, baffled at his command of three languages so far, and complied with his directions.

After a short time, Cavendish, feeling much better, summoned Ravi and Rashid to follow him up the road where Colonel Wadsworth and his staff were carelessly sprawled around as if at Malakand. It was now lunch and teatime at Wadsworth's camp. This whole spectacle made Cavendish sick. This whole scene seemed to be a complete mindless mental abandonment of the horrible destruction of his army. They all acted like nothing had even happened! He solemnly approached Colonel Wadsworth, who, sat in the shade with his surviving higher-ranking lackeys, minus the spit-roasted Major Pillroy; looking chipper and engaged in mindless conversation over a bottle of whiskey.

"Sir" began Cavendish as he stopped and saluted, receiving none in return. "This is Ravi, who is the head man from the village we are going to and he told me he can help us to get out of here safely." Old Wad took a belt on the whiskey. "Oh!" minded Old Wad, "I thought I told my adjutant to dump this little beggar by the side of the road where you found him!" Cavendish came back full force "Sir, haven't you lost enough men already in your arrogant disastrous mission? Do you want to get the rest of these men killed as well? Ravi tells me that we are being followed, and he can save us if we" He paused…. "All Ravi wants in return is enough food to feed his small village that is experiencing famine. That is all Sir!!"

The sudden unnatural outburst by the lieutenant floored Wadsworth and a foreboding silence rippled through all his Staff present. A dark pall of reality permeated the frolic. A cold silence followed until the colonel spoke. "All right Lieutenant of the scouts! We will do this your way for now…. but I better have a plan, a good one from this beggar! Food for a good plan… or else!" Ravi, Rashid and Cavendish walked away against the backdrop of absolute silence. Back where Cavendish's group rested, Lieutenant Collins had followed them into the camp and had ventured to the hot chow line. He piled food on a couple of trays and brought them back to where the scouts were resting. Pyra's eyes lit up at the sight as lunch was now served. They all shared a pot of warm tea soon delivered by Holmes.

Collins commented that nobody including Wadsworth had even mentioned his or Hook's disappearance from the camp before the battle. Perhaps the trauma of the disaster in the valley was obviously dominating all minds now. It seemed to them as if Wadsworth and his merry men were caught in some sort of strange mind warp or collective delusional trance of denial. Nobody was even mentioning it. Ambrose Cavendish settled into his thoughts after a shot of whiskey for medicinal purposes. The opium cakes were just too powerful so he had stopped using them earlier.

Lieutenant Cavendish sat motionless under a large tree reviewing the terrible tragedy meted out to Wadsworth's relief force and their pyrrhic triumph at the castle keep. But none of their actions had come close to saving the lives of those doomed soldiers under Wadsworth. He hung his head, still recovering with slight fever. Then the old village headman sat across from him. Ravi spoke in a cryptic voice using perfect English. "Lieutenant James Ambrose Cavendish! You must never blame yourself for the terrible decisions of others that led to the terrible deaths of so many of your comrades. That water has now forever fallen from the dam. You did not fail. You did huge damage to the ability of the Kali to wage war. We of the village are grateful for the sacrifice."

James looked at him. 'Were you the ones observing my party in the jungle since we arrived?" Ravi then lit his long pipe and looked at the Englishman. "Yes, we were observing you and were protecting you in your mission! Kali is our enemy as well son." The lieutenant was momentarily dumbfounded as he then thought of the beautiful women in his dreams. Ravi continued with his gaze and smile. "You will survive what is to pass soon and I see a good life ahead for you, my young man…. a bright future, and success in your life! Be at peace now"

Cavendish was moved to tears by Ravi's kind words, and wept in the great sadness that had encroached on his heart since the disaster in the true valley of death! All those good soldiers slain; murdered! He then felt a strong kind presence surround him and comfort his anguish. Little Pyra put her arms around him from the back and hugged him very tight and kissed him on the cheek. How strong she was Cavendish thought, how vibrant, and such a sweet soul! How different and strange these two so-called simple beggars really were! Maybe he wanted children, a wife, and a life different than this predicament he found himself in some day and someday very soon! His thoughts rested on the beautiful face of lovely Jenny.

This hell that he had been subjected to had burned much of his idealistic zeal for the military life away. It was not the combat that did this, but the unnecessary slaughter of so many British empire troops by a crazy fool! The sickness he felt overwhelmed his brain. But James Ambrose Cavendish was a professional soldier and a realist; the sadness would be controlled and pass. Hooky had told him this based on his experience at the "drift." "Thanks Ravi." He said with a smile he turned and hugged little Pyra back. She stood next to him with her little arm around his neck. He continued; "This sounds almost crazy, but your language abilities, what you say and …"

Then he remembered how Pyra, a complete stranger, had said his name after he fell off his horse… "and you sweet Pyra knowing my name. All of this." She smiled at him. "James Ambrose Cavendish!" and gave him a new hug. Ravi gave a warm smile. "Sahib Cavendish, in good time you will know many things about us, our tribe, for your character is pure and intentions are noble. We have chosen you for a serious reason which will be revealed soon. We could never have anything to do with that false leader down the road!" James smiled at Pyra as Ravi added. "You and your men are under our protection so fear not! Besides, all the children from the village will protect you as well!" Cavendish looked at Pyra, such a beautiful girl with huge purplish-blue almond eyes. She was the most beautiful little street urchin.

He kissed her on the nose and said, "With you as my protector I will never worry again!" She gave a wide smile and hugged him. If Cavendish ever wanted a daughter, she would be like Pyra. Ravi chuckled out loud for the first time since he had read the lieutenant's thoughts. Then, as to switch gears Ravi stopped, closed his eyes then spoke. "We must now leave, danger is growing on the road behind us, some miles back, the wheels of the wagons have been found on this road by others…but these devils do not want to come our way cautiously for reason." Ravi looked at little Pyra with a smile. "the Kali's devils are forced to be brave once more." Pyra looked at Ravi and giggled.

Ambrose pushed the question of "why" back into his mind as he pulled himself to his feet. He was feeling better, alive and his fever had vanished. In what seemed moments, the scouts were preparing to leave as Corporal Holmes had already ridden forward to give a falsely generated warning to Colonel Wadsworth of the closing enemy pursuit. It was Hook's wonderful idea. Soon, in a faster pace than usual, the column was on the move towards the village where safety was promised to all. About thirty minutes into the ride, Cavendish realized that he had no pain from his wounds at all. Hook, who had liberal amounts of this greasy mix of herbs rubbed in his wounds felt better as well, since it just wasn't the whiskey to his estimate! Ravi's mixture had worked. His deep slash wounds were closed now.

It was early evening when the small British column came to what appeared as a rustic sprawling pastoral farming village of thatched huts and dirt streets. At first glance the place seemed like a dirty ramshackle impoverished Neolithic affair. The group dismounted and milled about. Soon they saw many villagers appear of all ages, with many children running around. The heat of the late humid day, and the journey on the broken ancient road had worn out everybody. They were all very tired. The whole staff group wandered in quiet and sat resting near the wagons. Ravi had the scouts follow him deeper into the village to rest. There horses followed Pyra to the stream to play joined with other children. The four enlisted men unlimbering the horses were amazed as they followed the group of children into the wide chest high stream as both species enjoyed play in the water. They soon stripped down to their underclothes and joined the frolic in the cool water.

As the sun left the sky a beautiful quarter moon appeared low in the night sky ascending above this Neolithic affair village lost to civilization. Some ten miles in the distance a large war party of green devils had emerged from their jungle resting place in a large group walking in full view down the road following the wagon tracks. The tall menacing black-cloaked leader had been on the British trail since the battle ended. It was his group that pounced on Wadsworth's retreating wagons and bore the honor of hunting the rest of them down. He and his hundred devils had stopped at the base of the large hill at the ancient road. The unconditioned cloaked leader was nervous and feared this excursion down the ancient road.

He knew that Kali had sent a large war party up the road to destroy a small farming village several miles down the road two years ago. Rumor control stated that not one devil ever returned from this event! Kali knew what had happened in this failed attempt and the reason why he did not go into this area for now! His motive for venturing into this area was in combing the jungle for British soldiers, not executing his other plan yet! The evidence of wagon wheel treads and horse's hoof prints in the dirt and mud betrayed this as the escape route to the green devil leader. The Kali ordered this group up the ancient road since the commander of this British disaster was still unaccounted for among the dead or captured. He wanted him! The green devil leader knew to defy this order meant either a painful death or being conditioned at the least punishment!

Except for the green devil leader, the rest of his warriors were conditioned, mindless robot warriors commanded by Kali. They were fearlessly conditioned to do the grisly bidding of the Kali at his request! They were brain dead! They were on this ancient road now with one mission to accomplish?

Capture British escapees! This was the eve of the second night for these devils as over a hundred walked in formation on the road. Their many torches lit up the night bouncing off the huge jungle on both sides of this unkempt old road. The leader finally ordered his devils to stand in their motionless rest columns on the sides of the road until dawn. Torches were extinguished leaving the area pitch black.

During the night the leader saw the shadows alive in the dark and thought he saw images in the moonlight as he cowered. He had already heard strange sounds from the groups of devils in the dark. By morning, he discovered that many of the party had just disappeared without a trace in the night. They were gone as if they had walked off, and no blood trails or signs of violence. The only thing that remained of these green devils were their weapons lying next to where they had stood in the night.

What had happened to them wondered the leader? It would have been impossible for any of them to run away, since they were all mindless, brain dead of any personal concerns or thoughts. The sun was now setting again after another day of carefully moving down the ancient road. The devil leader found the abandoned campsite left by the escaping British. Evidence that the retreating British had been here was revealed by several empty cans of Bully Beef, trash, and a couple empty bottles of whiskey lying about an extinguished campfire. Instinctively they moved forward another mile following the wheel ruts in the soft dirt where the road stones had vanished.

There was renewed hope that soon they would be capturing British soldiers! The group of under seventy left now, forged deeper down the road as their torch lights cut a path into the darkness. The band of devils, after another couple of hours, were ordered to stop and again rest by the side of the road. More seemed to be missing. The leader panicked and ordered his remaining devils to be ready to fight anything as he positioned them all on one side of the road surrounded by torches. The long black cloaked leader fell asleep next to a tree. Later, in a hot sweat he awoke, then shrieked in the moving darkness. The dream was too real and the shadow had almost gotten him! He was now awake shivering in fear. Safe he thought as he clutched a saber taken from a dead lancer.

His nightmare was a cat face like monster complete with huge claws that had been staring at him as he slept. It was so real that the hair on his neck rose up. His ears now discerned thrashing noises in the vicinity of his devils as if some muted battle was occurring. The torches were extinguished for some reason and it was very dark. He saw forms darting all around him silently plucking some of his men off the ground like huge birds of prey now. He aimed his sword to his front and yelled for his men to fight. Those where his last words and thoughts as he turned facing the shadow standing next to him. It had been standing next to him the whole time. Death was very unkind to him this night.

The party of Wadsworth and his subordinates continued around a huge bonfire after dinner was finished. Colonel Wadsworth was obviously drunk, along with most of his close-knit group offered up from the large store of whiskey. They were clumsy in their swaggering steps, laughing at nearly anything. Lieutenant Cavendish approached the head drunk. "Sir, I want permission to feed these people as agreed, they need to supplement their meager rations, as we promised! This is my third request sir!" "Old Wad" gave a leering laugh "Fuck these simpletons!" They don't need our food; they need our bullets!!!" And he then began waving his revolver around his head to the chorus of laughs from his little band of suck ups now mocking Cavendish around the campfire.

"No food now, and probably no food at all!" stormed the drunk leader, with slobber drooling down his chin. "and that is my final order!" So, the little party continued unabated well into the dark night. Without any comment, Cavendish walked away a distance to where his men sat, relaxing in the early night. They could see from his gaze; their leader was severely agitated. "Old Wad is not going to give any food out to these villagers!" SGT Hook retorted, looking at a silent Ravi standing close.

"Maybe Old Wad won't, but we will!" Cavendish smiled "You are correct old Hooky, and we need a plan to get those two guards away from the wagons for a while until we can unload enough food for Ravi and the villagers to eat!

Before anyone else commented, Ravi spoke. "I have a good plan to take their attention away for the time needed Sahib Cavendish!" They looked at this ancient man, who was smiling. Later, as the two guards sat by the wagons, sipping whiskey absconded from the supply wagon, occasionally humored by the antics going on up the long hill with the very drunken officers perched around the campfire. Then there appeared two of the prettiest native girls, dressed in sheer silk outfits and moving as if in an enticing dance. "Holy Smokes" exclaimed one of the guards passing the bottle to his comrade, both young British conscripts.

The other buzzed soldier took notice. On the girls came, rubbing their bodies close to them, caressing them in their privates as they laughed and caressed them. In a broken native like English both men were soon spirited off for the promise of sex. Just as they disappeared behind some low ramshackle buildings, the scouts set to work, systematically completely emptying the food supplies out of the leeward wagon and handing them off to a line of villagers. When they were finished, the scouts replaced the food containers with logs and re-covered them with a tarp, this whole affair lasted less than thirty minutes. The many readied cooking pots above the fires soon had real food in them and more for future meals. The village was being fed well now to the complete ignorance of Wadsworth.

Ravi looked Ambrose in the eyes and smiled. "We thank you for this and the risks you have taken. I honor you and your men for your efforts! Oh yes, I would not worry about the green devils following you here anymore. My observers told me they encountered serious health problems. All is safe now!" He winked with a smile. "We also have a safe plan for you to return south we will discuss tomorrow." Lieutenant Cavendish patted Ravi on the shoulder. "Thanks Ravi, hopefully we will be out of your hair tomorrow." Ravi bowed to him in respect and left as quietly as he had come. That night, the villagers all ate an excellent meal. Once again, at peace, the group of scouts settled down for a much-needed rest. Hooky nudged his boss. "Sir? Be ready for repercussions when Old Wad discovers one of his food wagons is empty?"

Ambrose retorted. "Yes, I have considered all of this Hooky, Wadsworth is drunk and insane now! What is he going to do execute me?" Somewhere in the dark, behind the buildings, each guard was engaged with his chosen prize. When the desired sex ended the beautiful girls slipped from their caresses and vanished into the night. The guards were left holding empty perfumed silk garments as a reminder of the intimate discourse. Bewildered but excited, both guards returned to their guard post at the wagons, noticed nothing and resumed sipping on the bottle of whiskey. The staff party continued on around the campfire unabated. Providence had alone saved the wagon loaded with the stock of whiskey from the devils! The frivolous drunk around a huge bonfire continued until the dawn.

The noises of the morning jungle woke all the scouts early. They had slept fitfully with no indications or nightmares of things moving around in the dark watching them, since they were now under their protection. They ate a short breakfast and were sipping their morning tea when Pyra and a couple of little friends approached. In flawless English, she spoke for the first time. "We want to take you on a tour of the other village if you would like to come." Cavendish smiled and said he would love to go, as both Hook and Rashid, intrigued Pyra's command of English, accepted the tour.

Lieutenant Collins and King George were working on preparations for the group to leave, as Holmes went swimming in the magnificent clear pond created by the stream behind a short rock dam. The little group led by Pyra walked through the small quaint village and just as they thought the tour was over, Pyra grabbed Ambrose by the hand and pulled him along. They walked in a long trail and crossed another small wooden bridge over a clear bubbly brook etched in the middle of the green jungle.

They soon enter a walkway which seemed cut neatly from the huge rock formations on both sides. Soon, the party came into an open area out of the tall jungle and were amazed at what they saw. Their gazes met a strange ancient city. It seemed built, or carved out of solid gray, jade green, and darker tectonic rock. Many of the intact buildings were tall monoliths and the streets were built with long flat marble plates. It seemed like some forgotten metropolis eons old. Several of the structures were cracked and some lay in complete ruin. Others were intact and reached into the sky. The city was neat and very clean.

The jungle had been neatly trimmed around the ruins, and huge gardens of flowers seemed to grow everywhere. Strange pillars, pyramids, and obelisk structures all stood magnificently in this place. It was obvious that this was a well-designed and organized city obviously built centuries before. It seemed very out of place in this environment as the symmetry was to be admired. The whole city seemed inhabited, but empty now. Cavendish approached a huge statue of a large cat with the head of a man. There were other magnificent statures of huge winged cats and other creatures along the ancient main avenue. As if she had read his thoughts, Pyra looked at Cavendish and spoke. "Many of our people dwell here Ambrose. Ravi wanted you to see this place. This city dates back far into the past, well before the dawn of your civilization and others before!" The writings carved into the walls that you see as strange were those of that ancient race of giants."

Even when he studied ancient languages in college, then "cadet" Cavendish had never seen this type of script before, or anything like the statues for the matter. He rubbed his finger on the etchings. Pyra continued. "It is said that this city was a coastal city once on a huge civilization that rested in an ocean now called the Pacific. However, a huge cataclysm put his city and most of the island here, forming these Mountains." Ambrose thought on this. "You don't mean the island we called Atlantis in our ancient world history and geography class days?" Pyra smiled and gave a happy childish "Lemuria or MU!" Ambrose silently admired this little street urchin turned historical archaeologist. Her poise and excellent command of English impressed him as he remembered. "Lemuria? We are really going back far my dear child!"

He mentally reviewed what he remembered of this Lemuria from his crazy but interesting physical science professor at college. It had existed over a million years ago supposedly and was a huge island that allegedly filled up most of the south Pacific Ocean. It was destroyed in Mother Nature's fury which sank it, pushed part of it to form the Himalayas and the rest frozen under mountains of ice as Antarctica! The obvious huge entrances to the surviving buildings were very large, which gave credence to the race described as giants. As they toured this city of the ancients, Cavendish and Hook played with the group of children who hung with them. More seemed to show up. It was becoming obvious to them that the inhabitants of the outward Neolithic village were more than simple peasant farmers. Yet, nobody could put a finger on it yet. Rashid walked around simply staring completely mesmerized at the images carved into the walls, the statues, and the magnificent structures.

Ravi soon greeted them and showed them some of the marvels, such as running water and plumbing. Ravi looked at Hook, Cavendish, and Rashid with his mesmerizing deep smile and sparkling eyes. "Your gesture of giving the village food under the peril from your commander has been noted son. This gesture was extremely important for more reasons than you know at this point. My village wants to sincerely thank you for the food you gave us last night, it went a long way in helping save lives in the village since we have many mouths to feed. Although the crops look good now, we experienced famine from the last two harvests. Lieutenant Cavendish smiled. "Your gratitude is humbly accepted Mr. Ravi; I wish we could do more! Too bad you cannot divine a technology to insure constant crop production."

Ravi gave his now common inquisitive smile. "Actually, we have used our technology the first time on this harvest since there had been no problems before. We suffered three bad harvests from a blight we know was caused by the Kali. He wants to destroy us forever my son. His devils came in and caught us off guard two years ago. We had been so careless in his threat; this ancient threat! When they attacked, we were able to destroy them, but not before they poisoned our crops. The damage was done. Kali was preparing his large army to come after us again but shifted his plans to aid in destroying the British in India first! He saw the value in joining with Islam to do this. Then he was to raise a huge army and then deal with us.

His part in this war was his attack on Chital which was a great and terrible success! Then came your strangely fielded British relief force to destroy the Kali. All his plans now became focused on the British and not us; for the moment! The aftermath of this is a sad chapter in history now." A confused Cavendish asked "Why does Kali want to destroy a simple farm village resting near an old harmless ancient city Ravi?" He wondered how Ravi knew of the events he just mentioned. Ravi then added. "The reasons for the Kali wanting to destroy us are as ancient as our race my son. As you will learn, we are not as simple and primitive as we appear for reason." The lieutenant then commented. "I never dreamed that I would experience what I have so far Ravi, in this strange valley and threat of the Kali. None of us could ever imagine it! How his whole army stood in perfect silent rows then went into battle expertly reverting from ordered ranks to vicious bloodthirsty savages!"

Ravi gave a deep look. "The army of the Kali, with but a few, is an army of dead men. Their souls have been stolen from them by the power of the Kali. You fight an army of robots!" Cavendish looked at the ground and asked. "I wonder how we can kill it; this Kali creature?" Ravi smiled. "Oh Mr. Ambrose, there are ways to kill the Kali I am certain; we have killed others of his ilk before. but Kali is old and dangerous; crafty in his ways. He is one who has learned his innate powers well over the centuries!" Ambrose stared at the ancient sage of a man and spoke. "Centuries?" He laughed. "This timeline at least, is good to know I am sure. However, so much has happened and we need to get back to our civilization and relate this disaster and this new threat to our real boss General Bindon Blood." They walked in quiet contemplation from the beautiful preserved dead city back to the farm village.

On the way, back, as Cavendish was playing with little Pyra, he lifted her up with both arms and smiled at her. "Pyra, I have decided that you need a special name since you are a very special girl and my guardian! From now on I will address you as "Angel Pyra" …or just "My Angel!" Pyra kissed him on the cheek and hugged him around the neck. They all walked back down the long jungle trail and across the bridge into the other world of this village. Little "Angel" Pyra walked along holding his hand. She so liked him as he did her. He thought if he and Jennifer would marry, he wanted a child just like her. Cavendish and his two companions crossed the bridge that crossed the clear stream of the second bridge.

Corporal Holmes now slept in the sun on the opposite bank catching rays on his naked prostrate body. Pyra and her small group of village children peeled away from the scouts at the stream and went swimming. Cavendish, Hook, and Rashid returned to their small camp a way back through the farm village where he had left Bertram Collins and King George who had been preparing for their departure. They were absent. Although their horses were gone, all their saddles and equipment were still stacked neatly on the ground. Hook then noticed the untethered horses were playing with the others in the large pond with the children in frolic. The trio sat down to rest and wait for the two scouts to return.

Suddenly, several of Wadsworth's lackey officers busted on the scene in their red blouses with their pistols drawn. Both parties stood still as Major Toddy "Longshank" Billings, a tall lanky former third in command of Wadsworth's folly, now appeared from behind some trees. Billings, who had an ugly face with a long-hooked nose, began kicking Cavendish, who had dozed next to a tree. "Put your hands up or else! Under the explicit orders of Colonel Hillary Wadsworth, I am placing all of you under arrest for the theft of Crown property and other specified crimes!" The officers accompanying "Longshank" were boisterous, rude, with many exhibiting hangovers and signs of renewed drinking.

They roughly undid the pistol belts of the scouts, as their side arms fell to the ground. With hands held high, they were marched off under guard, being prodded by pistol barrels. Little Pyra and a couple of her friends had witnessed this arrest from the side of the stream and quickly disappeared into the jungle. The group was marched up to where Colonel Wadsworth sat, with his red jacket unbuttoned, obviously suffering from a bad hangover and drinking once again. In a muddled tone, he began: "Well, well Lieutenant Cavendish, of His Majesty's Royal scouts! To begin with, do you mind telling me where a decent quantity of our food stores went last night? We are missing a whole wagon full!" The prisoners looked out to see King George and 2LT Collins with their hands bound behind them leaning in front of a walled hut. They both looked like they had been roughed up.

Cavendish did not mince his words, "The people in this village were promised food for our protection and a safe exit home sir. The green devil threat was destroyed, is now gone and Ravi has presented us with a safe plan to exit this place! We got their part of the bargain, when we are ready to travel! So, I took the liberty of fulfilling our part of the bargain since you refused and were also drunk sir! From where I come from a deal made is a deal delivered" The Scotch-Irish in him was beginning to explode. The colonel leered his mumbled words as he saw Cavendish's evil gaze.

"You disobeyed my direct orders in combat you bastard!" He looked at Color-Sergeant Hook. "He aided in the escape of Nephew and from me at Chital with the help of that Gurkha and then you escaped from me with the help of that treasonous Lieutenant Collins! I also accuse all of you for aiding and abetting the green devils with knowledge of our advance as well!" Wadsworth was completely delusional and out of his mind now. "HA! Your fucking orders Sir! "Yelled Cavendish, red with anger! "Your orders were responsible for the massacre, or shall I say murder of hundreds of good men!

I said MURDER YOU SONOFABITCH! Fuck you and your fucking orders! We aided the enemy? Who in hell do you think blew the fuck out of the green devil's artillery, their bridges, and that castle you never ever saw because you were hiding in the jungle behind your troops instead of leading them! Who blew up the large bluff and sealed off the castle from any more supply? I lost two and maybe three of my best men aiding and abetting the enemy you fucking jerk! I will see you hang for this, this lie, and the deaths of so many good soldiers! Right from the Tower of London, I will pull the rope myself you bastard and I pray I can use a headsman's axe instead of a rope!!!!" The lieutenant had completely lost his usual cool composure.

With no retort from Old Wad, Captain Billings, another grand suck up of Old Wads, kicked Cavendish in the groin knocking him to the ground on his knees. As one of the villagers standing near tried to help him up, the colonel, resting on a log, shot him point blank in the face, killing him instantly. The pain of this murder resonated through the village as many people were suddenly on the scene. Hook tried to speak but Major "Longshank" Billings, true to his nickname smacked Hook in the back of the head with a pistol butt, dropping him also to his knees. He then kicked the grounded color sergeant in the back knocking him on his face. Both scouts slowly crawled back to their feet. Wadsworth was laughing, but his laugh was that of a man insane. The scouts were in grave danger, as were the villagers, and they all felt it.

Cavendish stumbled over and stood in front of the small crowd of weeping villagers who now surrounded their dead man. He then turned facing the colonel and his men. "Go ahead you bastard, kill me and leave them alone for God's sakes! I take full blame since my men were following my orders … in combat" The village people understood the immediate danger, and in a quite sad procession carried away their dead member. The colonel continued trying to aim his gun at more of the villagers, but Cavendish, seeing Pyra and Ravi in the front of the group jumped in front of them as two more shots rang out.

Lieutenant Cavendish had been hit both in the chest and right side. He stared at the colonel and slumped back on the ground. Hook, and Rashid ran to Cavendish further blocking the villagers from the wrath of Wadsworth who now exhibited a deranged smile. Rashid was yelling for the people to run and they did now. "Maybe we need to kill them all!" yelled Longshank Billings. "Fuck them all for Queen and Crown!" Wadsworth gave an evil laugh, more of a cackle. He swigged a huge blast of whiskey looking at Cavendish's body on the ground he yelled, "Get this piece of garbage out of my sight!" As the scouts began to grab him the colonel yelled again…" Oh no not you!" He aimed his gun at them. Very quickly, Ravi and a few other villagers still close by, grabbed the lieutenant's body and hustled it out of sight. Wadsworth ignored this as he now centered his wrath on the remaining scouts.

"Like your great scout leader, you will all die soon enough!" Once again, he launched a tirade of insults and charges of treason, dereliction of duty, and disobedience to orders in combat. His muted and nervous staff members securely bound the scout's wrists in front of them with rope as the colonel continued bellowing his insults. Old Wad, paying little difference to the altercation and murders in front of him rambled on. "Tomorrow, before we leave, or shall I say my command leaves this terrible place, all of you will be shot for the following crimes I have levered against you. Treason! Executions start at first light!" Collins, seeing the lost gravity of the moment exploded "So that's it! Colonel Wadsworth! Kill more soldiers, to cover your ass, like all those dead back there in that valley, or maybe kill off witnesses against you at your trial!"

Colonel Wadsworth winced at the sudden comment. "My dear boy!" shot back Old Wad as he downed another plug of whiskey, "you may have something in that!" Then he laughed and pistol-whipped the outspoken 2LT to the ground. Many of his staff began to laugh and shove the prisoners. He then ordered them secured in a nearby old windowless walled hut under guard. As they were walking Major Longshank appeared in front of Hook. He was staring at his VC pinned to his chest. He whistled a strange laugh "I am stripping you of your VC you traitor, you won't be needing it anymore! I will keep it as a memento! Maybe I will piss on it each time I think of you?"

Hook was well beyond "had enough" after his lieutenant was probably killed. When Longshank placed his hands on the VC old Hooky gave him a violent deep head butt full in his face. The major screamed in pain as his nose and left ocular were crushed under the fury of the color sergeant's violent forehead strike! He went to the ground yelping in agony holding his bleeding face. "A hearty fuck you shit for brains! You earn these not from running from the battle like you did in the valley my dear coward and pissant!" Yelled a raging bull Hook. As Longshank whimpered on the ground with his sight blurred, Wadsworth's staff officers and now jailors shoved him and the others and gunpoint into a dingy hut without windows or ventilation near the scene. It was probably a storage building of some kind, surmised engineer Collins in his grief and anger.

They all sat on the dirt in the dark sweltering heat. Rashid took out his hidden knife after the door had been shut and cut the rope bonds off everybody. They sat in a place with no water, windows or ventilation, except for wisps of air blowing in from the crudely blocked door. The temperatures were soon horrendous to them. Later, the two privates who had botched their guard duty on the food wagons to chase and mate with the maidens joined them. They were trussed up and roughly pitched into the hut floor. They were scared and shaken up. "Why are you in here?" Inquired Color Sergeant Hook in his command voice.

A private identified as Benjamin Werth nervously spoke up "We were both accused of aiding you in the theft of the food last night, so we are to be executed along with you in the morning!" Silence pervaded the dark room. Then a voice spoke from the shadows in an empty corner at the end of it. "A lot can happen before dawn gentlemen!" All eyes followed the voice to the corner of the room. It was a new face from the village. He was a very tall younger looking man, handsome in stature." My name in Ronjin." He then passed around some jugs of cool water. The compassion radiating from his eyes was overpowering.

He spoke in a reassuring voice. "Lieutenant Cavendish is in good hands now so worry not about him. Be still, and do not leave this place, for it will be your safe haven this night!" Then he was gone. He simply disappeared in the shadows in the corner of the hut. Hooky looked at 2LT Collins and smiled. "Looks like you are in command now son, sir!" Collins smiled back at the swarthy NCO from his very youthful face. "Son?" That title will do just fine!" Hooky was all smiles and patted him on the back. But the old sergeant was beside himself with worry for his beloved commander. Cavendish had taken at least one bullet through the heart and that was usually fatal!

Rashid, who had been silent the whole time looked at 2LT Collins. "Sir, there is something very strange about Ravi and many of the people in this village. "What do you mean?" retorted Collins as he wiped rivulets of sweat from his face. "First of all, for simple farmers they have excellent command of several languages. They seem very intelligent and knowledgeable, leaps ahead of average people. There is this strange aura about them which I can't help but sense that they are very old souls and have many secrets deeper than that ancient city we saw today. Nothing adds up yet sir." He paused and took a sip of the cool water Ronjin had given them. He continued speaking.

"In the ancient lore of my culture, there exist very old legends about a people, or beings who have been alive forever, so the story goes; who can change or shift their shapes at will." Hook replied back, "Well, whatever they are, they seem to like us and I like them!" Rashid was nearly whispering now, "Be thankful, very thankful my friend that they do like us if they are the ones!" The water given them by Ronjin had literally saved them from complete dehydration and possible death. It had somehow restored their energy. There had to be something in the water. A new jug of water and some food later appeared in the place where the mysterious kind Ronjin had first appeared.

The time of the day seemed the Doldrums for the prisoners. The sound of gunfire awoke their senses all at once. It was now dusk and they could hear the noise of another drunken party going on in the area used the night before. Careful observation from cracks in the thatched secured door revealed that the HQ staff was drunk again and shooting up the place. Through a crack in the crude door both Hook and Collins hoped the villagers had left the area and were not target practice. The remaining pair of young British enlisted men guarding them from the outside saw Hook looking out the crude door. They were both nervous as the nearest one spoke. "Sir, they are very drunk again and most of the shots are in the air and aimed randomly at the huts."

Relieved at this the sergeant joined the group sitting back against the wall in the now dark room. They all now sat listening to the noises outside and giving to idle chatter. Everybody was very concerned about lieutenant Cavendish and sensed he was probably dead by now. The noise outside around the campfire seemed alive but slowly dimmed as late night approached. "Sir, Sir!" The words echoed in the back of Hook's mind, temporarily trapped in combat with Zulus, but green ones in his dreams now: the terrible acts committed on captives, the explosions! The burley sergeant jumped up with a start covered in his own sweat! "Wha...What...is it!" as he talked from a heavy sleep. He was looking in the shadows, peering at the forms of one of the guards. The other guard was standing behind him. They had both unsealed the door and entered the prison shack and their rifles were slung on their shoulders.

Hook looked at them and asked. "Is it execution time boys?" The guard nervously added. "No sir! Seems that strange things are going on out here." His voice exhibited fear. "Pull yourself together trooper and tell us!" Barked Hook in perfect drill demeanor now. The guard continued. "We have been seeing flashes of light, green light, shadows seem to be moving everywhere, living shadows and we have been hearing distant chants and drums, far away, but clear in our minds. Most of all is the deep fear we are feeling, like some monstrous unknown thing awaits us, entering our minds with the worst images." The other soldier added. 'Sir, if I may speak candidly, we are scared shitless and want to stay in here with you!" Never missing a note, SGT Hook commented, "So you want us prisoners to guard the guards? AAAARRRR!" He laughed, and it broke up the depressed state felt around the room by the others.

"Put your rifles against the wall then and join us until this so-called terror is gone," ordered 2LT Collins, adjusting to the scenario. Both soldiers quickly complied and sat together in a corner. Rashid and Lord George resealed the thatched door. At least they had two rifles to go down fighting Wadsworth's boys now thought Collins. It was then that it occurred to all of them that Corporal Holmes had been missing the whole time and was never arrested. He was last seen swimming in the blue crystal-clear pool to near the bridge. "Why don't we escape this place for the jungle?" Inquired Collins. Rashid took the floor, "According to what Ravi said, we are in here for our own safety this night."

As the night grew late several of the very drunk staff officers moved away from the huge bonfire on the hill. A few left to pass out but most left in the company of very beautiful local ladies from the village. They were dressed in very revealing silk outfits and spirited them away like sirens of old. Only a handful of drunks remained around the bonfire singing and drinking. They continued passing around a bottle of whiskey. They were singing way out of cord and musing at their loud and lousy efforts. It was late in the night. They even laughed at the few muffled screams they heard coming from the huts and even from a wagon. One drunk yelled "Must be a terrifying native fucking machine at work!" They all laughed as they completely missed the living shadows waiting in the area behind them.

It was in the dead of night and the loud banging of metal on a small gong seemed to absorb Wadsworth's pickled brain for what seemed an hour. He pulled himself off a floor bed of the hut he had fallen into in what seemed minutes before. He was pickled drunk and slovenly in appearance, with his red blouse unbuttoned. He staggered to the entrance of the door as he knocked over a chair. "All right! All right!" He bellowed as he pushed open the fragile wooden thatched door. "This had better be good damnit!" As he trumpeted his sloppy speech from his drooling mouth. He clumsily pushed open the door and stared. It was a young woman of crystal beauty, with flawless chiseled features. She was naked except for an open silk sari. He suddenly felt a new intoxication, from her erotic allure.

She smiled and spoke in perfect English slowly. "Colonel Wadsworth, I am here as a gift to you from our village, to do with me anything you want tonight. I am tribute for all of the food you so graciously bestowed our village." He stammered, "Food? Oh well, very good then!" He walked to a small weathered dining table in the room as she followed him. Old Wad took a huge slug on his half empty third bottle of whiskey on it. In a wisp of a moment she, sprawled on her back in the floor bed, with her legs spread out. He approached her and she leaned up and pulled down his uniform pants, which gathered around his polished boots. She then rubbed his member and began to give him oral sex.

My, he thought, it has been such a long time since this has happened. Those "proper" ladies of nobility around him back in England seldom sucked cock! He laughed, but Pillroy was the best cocksucker as needed on the journey north he mused. But here tonight? He wanted more of her and she now responded to his smelly, clumsy groping and kissing as he forced himself on her. He was entering her with his booze infested near limp cock and was completely mesmerized on whiskey and intoxicated with sexual allure. Finally, she rolled "Old Wad" onto his back and was straddling him. He could clearly see her ravenous beauty, large moving breasts, and charms by the candlelight. His cock took a hard jolt at the view. He wanted to bugger her like his missing bitch Pillroy!

"What is your worst nightmare Colonel Wadsworth?" She suddenly asked him in the midst of his erotic adventure. In the colonel's mind sprang the hideous specter of a horrible Banshee, with a huge mouth filled with crooked gaping fangs from ear to ear and bulging eyeballs. This fearful childhood specter had huge, talons, and withered dead white face with long twisted white hair. It talked to him in an evil high-pitched cackle. It was his worst childhood nightmare created by his overbearing aunt Cloris and the way she kept him in bed at night. She told him that the evil Banshee lived under his bed and would eat him alive if he ever got out of bed before the sun came up!

Needless to say, after she showed him some eerie drawings and would dress the part on occasion and creep into his room terrorizing him when he was naughty; made him a believer. It also made him a champion bed wetter, like "R.I.P" Pillory! After all, the banshee could get him in the bathroom for even taking an honest piss! Wadsworth drunkenly pondered the strange question. What a stupid question to ask while fucking he thought. He was ready to bugger her! He looked up and felt that she was off of him and back between his legs drawn out taught because of his pants around his ankles. He stared down his body, hoping to get a glimpse of her giving him more blow job! Then he saw her head, or a head rise up between his out-spread legs.

Instead of a beautiful hot little village girl, he was suddenly confronted with the terror of his childhood, horrible Aunt Cloris the Banshee! He reeled in terror as "it" plunged its venomous fanged mouth into his balls! In extreme pain and terror "Old Wad" stared as this fearful specter raised its head with his balls and cock hanging from its bloody mouth! Then as he lay screaming terrorized to hell in mortal pain, the banshee literally shredded his groin and inner thighs in moments as the milk white face and long tousled hair on her head thrashed like a buzz saw. Wadsworth's blood and pieces of his flesh and now his entrails flew into his face and across the room and sticking to the walls and ceiling.

The hideous blood covered face of the banshee rose up and plunged its long sharp talons into his stomach ripping out his intestines and gave a leering laugh as it lassoed a nearby chair with his guts. He had been frozen in immense pain screaming uncontrollably in pure terror! Then the voice of the beautiful girl emanated from its fanged ear to ear grimace. "Are you enjoying yourself colonel? You are mine now, for the rest of the night, maybe forever!" and laughed a high-pitched whine as it tormented, mangled, and ripped his ears, nose, lips, and other parts of his body away chewing on some of them. He saw his blood splattered again on the walls and ceiling. Yet he seemed not to die from these horrendous wounds, only to continue this painful terror filled prolonged attack.

His terror and mortal pain had reached one eternal terrible peak after another as the banshee continued with its gruesome craft. He was trapped in not orgasms of sex, but spasms of pure mortal pain mixed with a deep crawling consuming terror throughout the night. He screamed in agony as it chewed off his face spit it back into his skinless skull. Again, he screamed in pain as it ripped his beating heart from his chest, holding it up for his eyes to see. He felt every part of the mortal pain now inflicted upon him. Unknown to Colonel Wadsworth, he had already been physically dead of a heart attack for well over three hours. Yet the power of the specter of the banshee continued to arouse and torment his conscious soul to live this terrible torment until even his soul was whimpering dead.

Later, he would be found physically intact, lying across the bed on his back, Red tunic unbuttoned, with his trousers still down to his boots. His once dark wavy slightly balding hair was now bleached white, and in his face? His face behind his white lambchops appeared like a dried aged husk. His open-mouthed and eyes death grimace would clearly show that he had been literally terrorized to madness and death, over and over again. Old Wad's body was devoid of all hydration like a mummy with all his lifeforce sucked from his body and soul. Old Wad had now become and "Old Wad!" The village had rules that Wadsworth had broken. They also had punishments!

Similar terrible fates waited for all the others who had felt lucky to have picked up a hot village girl. Those who consorted with these women experienced an assortment of vile terror filled ends. Some of their screams and death shrieks continued to be audible to the drunks sitting around the fire. When the drunk British officers heard the screams, they laughed and screamed back until they sensed them as real. Led by a heavily bandaged Major "Longshank" Billings, all but two staggered away with their guns drawn, guided by torchlight. They were drawn to where they thought they heard Colonel Wadsworth screaming for help somewhere down the main row of huts. Each of the drunks became remotely aware in their drunken fog that something strange was adrift.

As the four walked by torchlight, they passed the whiskey bottle around to bolster their courage. They continued down the unlighted crude main street of the quaint primitive village. But as they staggered on, they also continued making humorous sport of their screaming comrades. Finally, they came to a door of a hut where Longshank Billings had remembered the colonel had gone. Billings looked into it. Major Billings saw Colonel Wadsworth sitting at a crude wooden table in the candlelight alone sipping from a quart of whiskey. "Are you all right sir, we heard screams." Inquired an inebriated new second in command after the unfortunate disappearance of Pillroy. "I am very fine and thanks for your concern major. Please come in and join me and we shall talk about our journey home. Ravi gave me the plan and it is a good one and I want you to review it.

Please send the others to round up the boys since we will be leaving at sunrise." The staff officer holstered his pistol and waved for the other officers to leave. He staggered to the table and sat across from the colonel. His long nose, or "beak" as it was called from behind his back was bent to the right and his left eye socket had sagged somewhat under his bandage. Longshank's face was all black and blue and painfully swollen from the massive head butt administered by one Sergeant Hook. He was going to kill Hook personally in the morning! The other three staff officers drunkenly left and moved down the street.

Alone now, back in Wadsworth's company seated at a crude table in the candlelight, Longshank Billings took a swig of whisky as it was offered. The major was drunk, sweaty, and wanting to pass out. His injured face still throbbed in spite of all the booze he had consumed. "Let us talk!" crooned Old Wad. "Yes Sir!' The major adjusted himself on the crude stool taking another belt of whiskey. The look in Wadsworth's eyes seemed foreign to the major from the dimly lighted room in the hut. He inquired. "Sir, are you, all right?" Wadsworth smiled. "But are you all right major? Let me see your injury."

The major quietly undid the loose gauze from around his head as this commander observantly looked at a huge bent and swollen nose, and saw his left ocular was pushed in, and that his eye socket had drooped. The black and blueness of his swollen injury was clearly evident on his pale ugly white face. "Oh my, let me look closer major!" As Wadsworth moved closer Longshank for some reason suddenly had a great fear of spiders, which he hated. He blinked from his good eye then realized he was looking directly into the smacking mandibles of a giant white spider! It grabbed him by the head as its hands turned into furry claws

Longshank screamed in agonizing fear and absolute mortal pain as this spider began savagely chewing his face into gooey pulp. Longshank screamed in sudden pain but nothing came from his mouth as he struggled helplessly against the powerful man-size insect. His jaw was then ripped and broken open and gaping open as he stumbled, in the tow of the spider and was tossed next to a body on the floor bed in the corner. He now stared in complete horror at Colonel Wadsworth's body, whose face was frozen in a lasting husk of shriveled terror. Longshank screamed from his throat in a ghastly wail, since his torn jaw gapped wide open freakishly down to his chest. The monster spider was not done yet!

It held him with its furry white legs now plunged its long sharp spear like stinger into his wounded eye as many fur lined eyes stared at him from the bulbous spider's head. He shrieked, wailed and moaned in his painful terror. He felt he was now fading into the control of the spider as it shot a stream of liquid through his eye socket into his brain. Longshank Billings then sat mute and still as the giant white spider began to weave and spin a huge web like pillow covering his head to his neck as it quickly moved its front legs around it. Longshank Billings was now frozen where he sat, now suffocating and blinded by the web wrapped thickly around his head. Then the venom from the nasty stinger took effect. The huge white spider looked at its victim and in a quirk of gallows humor added something to the white pillow shaped web that completely covered Longshank's head to his shoulders.

As the officers ambled and stumbled along the dusty dirt street, the sound of flute music seemed to come from the area of the pond and bridge. It was extremely soft and beautiful as the notes seemed to drift on the light wind. They walked down to the bridge that crossed the beautiful stream and peered across it to the other side. They were amazed at what they saw on the other side beyond the bridge. Sitting on the other bank illuminated by scant torchlight sat none other than Corporal Holmes and around him sat several beautiful women with a couple playing the flutes.

Holmes and the ladies seemed to be drinking something in tall goblets having a great time it seemed. The corporal waved at them as both bare breasted gorgeous women next to him, giggled and hugged him. One of the drunken staff officers pulled out his pistol and yelled, "Looks like you are under arrest like the rest of your infernal buddies and will be shot in the dawn with them. Come along now or be shot!" The other two staff officers leered and laughed. Holmes eloquently retorted. "Sir? Why don't you and your suck up clowns go into the woods and fuck yourselves!" He laughed and flipped them off. This enraged the drunks and pulling out their side arms they began to cross the bridge.

As they crossed it the women suddenly appeared in front of them in the middle of the bridge. Their pretty looks had sharply changed to the forms of erect humanoid croc like reptiles which were grinning at them. Before the drunk officers could react to this sudden affront, they were grabbed and pitched over the rail into the water. They began screaming and thrashing as the reptile creatures attacked them. The pond waters were now boiling crimson with the brief struggle ended. Holmes observed no sign of them bobbing in the once calm waters. Then from the waters emerged several strange beings. They were neither hot village girls or reptiles but seemed greenish, tall and slender. They completely re-assumed the forms of the pretty maidens as they approached.

The corporal was in awe, but the important thing to Holmes was they were naked, wet, and gorgeous! The pretty maidens were smiling at Holmes when they returned to him. One of the maidens walked up and dropped a torn red blouse on the ground in front of an amused Holmes who was thankfully feeling the effects of the excellent wine he had been drinking with them. Inside the rolled-up tunic he found the three service pistols of the now deceased soldiers. She smiled at him and added. "I would not want anybody to find one of these and accidentally hurt another, so I relinquish them to our kind guest sir!"

Corporal Holmes smiled as he took silent possession of them rolled back up in the uniform amid new sweet hugs and replied "I understand your concern, and will protect all of you my beautiful reptile girls?" They were all laughing at his statement. Sensing a new presence near him, Holmes stopped and looked to see a tall handsome greenish man in the shadows. He asked with a smile sensing no danger, "who may you be?" The corporal was very apprehensive as he noticed a tall very noble greenish looking being standing near him assume complete human form. Holmes rubbed his eyes in the confusion. He was just like the girls! The tall man who had very defined handsome chiseled features was smiling at him. "I see you have made some nice friends' corporal!" Holmes smiled and retorted. "I am in love with them all kind sir!"

The tall handsome man gave a smile, dressed in white robes now added in perfect English. "I am an elder of the old village named Ronjin. You may refer to me as "Ron" if you like names akin to your race." He extended his hand and the two men shook. Holmes then inquired. "What just happened, I mean pretty girls turn into reptiles and gobble up this group of Wadsworth's idiots? I do admit that watching this rather fatal swim party was enjoyable!" Ronjin continued speaking. "Colonel Wadsworth and his men will not be a problem or of any concern now. Like the three who met their fate here, so has Wadsworth and all the others in his party!" Ronjin smiled briefly to let that information soak in then continued.

"My friend, you have just witnessed our secret, for we are the old shape changers instilled in the myth of many civilizations." Holmes had first heard of these myths from the natives in Africa years ago, but not here until now, and from the source! Then Holmes noticed several other beings, just like Ronjin standing behind him at the water's edge. The two beautiful ladies hugged the corporal, as he seemed more confused. Ronjin spoke. "Fear us not for you are under our protection and have our gracious respect. Your commander, severely wounded will live and the rest of your party are safe from harm now. "Come with us to our next village down the trail for safety and for a good rest."

The group now travelled the jungle trail by torchlight into the ancient gray city of huge buildings that mankind would call "skyscrapers." Arm in arm with two beautiful giggling women, Corporal Holmes entered into such a magnificent huge gray stoned city twenty minutes later. He carried the unloaded pistols wrapped tight in the red torn blouse of a deceased officer of Wadsworth's staff. By now the stream current in the large pond had washed the shredded British corpses downstream in a fast spillway into the jungle never to be recovered. With but one exception, all of Wadsworth's staff of suck ups would disappear forever.

Once in the strange empty city, the two beautiful women ushered him into a large candlelit bedroom. They stripped him naked and all three enjoyed a refreshing bath in a pool near the end of the room. One of the women filled up their goblets with a sweet cold wine and they played in the pool for a while. It was intoxicating! The playing soon turned sensuous in nature and the passion in the pool soon led them to a large comfortable bed. Holmes had experienced the love of Indian women before and many women from all over the world from his many travels. Here tonight, he had met his match.

The lovemaking was incredible and ceased at dawn when the corporal expired in pure delightful exhaustion. They were so pretty and not once had these beautiful babes turned into reptiles to his relief! He awoke later in the day with a clean uniform and great meal served by none other than his two beautiful sensual ladies as a guest of the village. He never questioned how they had changed shapes, just begged them to keep the ones they had for him. They both laughed at him. His humor was on full tilt in this strange world.

As Holmes and his group headed for the ancient gray city, the two drunk staff officers left at the fire were completely inebriated, and fired off a few rounds from their revolvers. Then they saw someone hailing them and walking up the rise towards them at the bonfire. It sounded like Major Billings talking from behind a huge white pillow that covered his head and face completely. This rather huge bandage that seemed to make his head look three times its size covering his whole head. The two extremely drunk staff suck ups rubbed their eyes at the spectacle in front of him and started laughing at this spectacle. In their gay drunken abandon, the two officers had been completely engaged in booze fueled humorous banter in complete ignorance of the running shadows around them.

They did not give one care in the world, never quite understanding in their whiskey fueled mirth that all their fellow staff comrades had suffered terrible deaths. These drunks, completely oblivious to this, were singing drunkenly as Longshank finally approached the fire, which they had re-stoked. "Sir, is that really you?" asked one as he and the other staff officer stared at what appeared to be the major, whose face and head where completely hidden in a huge bandage of sorts. As Longshank Billings came to the fire both men clearly saw this giant pillow had some sort of face on it.

It was a doll face, complete with large button eyes and red sewn on smile. The drunks were now laughing again. It now talked from inside the large white silk like pillow head. "Yes, tis me!" stammered the unusually happy voice of the major. "The colonel fixed me up! How do you like it?" The drunken usually sloppy captain stared at Longshank's new pillow head look. Both of the drunks were now laughing uncontrollably holding their sides at Longshank. "My oh My" was Major Longshank Billings, the cocky asshole with the unusual beaked nose; way out of character to them!

In his laughter the captain replied "Oh sir, it is the most wonderful thing I have seen on you! Your smile, the smile on your face is wonderful Sir "Sir Pillow face?" Both of the drunks now began laughing hysterically again and slapping their sides. Sir "Pillow face" Longshank picked up a half-empty bottle of whiskey left by another staff officer. The two drunks just laughed as "Pillow face" Longshank poured the contents of the bottle into its pillow like face where his mouth seemed to be. Longshank then took a burning faggot from the fire and held it up. He announced. "Let there be light! I am now a "major burning pillow head!"

Before the two stunned soldiers could even move, the pillow exploded into flames with "Sir Pillow head Longshank" spewing a stream of flaming liquor into the faces and uniforms of the two stunned officers. They both immediately were enveloped in flames as burning pillow head began singing an old favorite British marching song. The two flaming drunks fled screaming into the nearby jungle. Their flaming bodies, now completely engulfed, illuminated the jungle darkness where they ran and soon fell.

The major, whose upper body and pillow were now a raging fireball, turned facing the bonfire and fell like a falling tree straight into the middle of its burning embers face down. His body ignited the flames, cooking off the ammo in his pistol and in his ammo pouch, burning his body to smoking charred ashes in the dawn. The night was finally basked in an unnatural silence. The village had spoken. Soon the songs and yells of the night creatures replaced the uncanny event.

Lieutenant James Ambrose Cavendish awoke peacefully to find himself immersed in a shallow pool of very clear refreshing water and noticed his head lay in the lap of what he saw as a very beautiful young woman. Her face was partially hidden by her luscious breasts. She was that women in his dreams in the jungle. She caressed him and was gently rubbing his head. He slowly remembered that he had been shot but his mind floated like his head partly submerged in the water in the candlelight glow around the huge room.

He was in a complete state of peace and had little clue if he was actually dead or alive. He watched an older man, different from Ravi, appear above him in the shallow pool checking his wounds and giving directions to others, in a very alien language. The room was of pure white and he sensed daylight activity from outside the huge doors and windows. Ambrose drifted off in peaceful slumber without any pain from his wounds. Pyra held him tight in her arms, for she would not leave him.

The prisoners of Wadsworth were aroused in the dawn by noise in the hut door opening. They discovered that whatever heavy stone had blocked the door in the night was gone. The hut doorway was now wide open. Sunlight and a cool breeze bathed their prison hut. Slowly, each man got up and walked from the hut into the sunlight giving the dawn a morning stretch. Ravi and many villagers were standing nearby next to a large table laden with all sorts of food and refreshments. "Good morning my friends please have a seat and enjoy a well-deserved meal we have prepared for you." Nearly in a daze, they all sat at the well provided table. They were thirsty and ravaged by hunger. Without saying a word, the group begin to consume a very pleasant meal of chicken, rice, fruit, wine, and other delicacies.

The food and sunlight began to restore them all. SGT Hook looked at Ravi, standing nearby, and asked. "Is, is Cavendish still with us?" Ravi smiled back with his deeply kind hypnotic stare and replied. "Lieutenant Cavendish was severely wounded and will make a full recovery; but it may take a few days." "Only a few days? Ravi? He received a fatal shot to the heart. How did he survive?" Ravi smiled at the large rough and tumble man. "Ah my kind-hearted color sergeant! The miracles of our medicine are truly wonderful in the village!" Then 2nd Lieutenant Collins asked a question. "Ravi, where are the rest? I mean Colonel Wadsworth and his staff? We heard all sorts of screams, gunshots and stuff going on last night and I just wondered."

"Wonder not Mr. Collins, for they violated our rules and will never bother you again. They are gone…forever." "You mean they are dead?" Ventured Hook with a mouth full of roasted pork. Ravi became serious "Yes Mr. Hook, they are all dead, for violating the rules of our village and well, to put it correctly, of our civilization!" He mentally perceived Hook's next question. "If you want to see the body of Colonel Wadsworth for proof, I can show you for we saved him just to answer your curiosity and soon the curiosity of others!" "For the record, Ravi, we all would need to see it, and well, I don't give a flying fuck about the rest…oh maybe Longshank Billings of course!" Ravi smiled "Oh Hook, like "Old Wad" as you call him, Longshank Billings was given wonderful attention but, alas, met with a sudden end!"

Ravi pointed over to the nearly extinguished campfire and pointed at some crisp charred remains in it. Hook and the others ventured over to the ebbing coals of the firepit after they finished their repast. He could make out the remains of a human skeleton face down in the coals, and part of a pistol that remained after the rounds exploded in it from the fire. Only the feet and soles of his boots remained. Hooky smiled and said "A fitting end for you! Major asshole!" Then Ravi shot the images of the last moments of 'Sir Pillow Head" into Hook's mind. Hooky broke out in a huge laugh to the amusement of Ravi.

The group of scouts accompanied Ravi down the main street of the village. The four surviving enlisted soldiers of Wadsworth's little party seemed very bewildered and wandered over to check their area around the wagons. Several very happy villagers accompanied them. The torn bodies of several staff officers were found piled like trash behind the wagons where they had obviously met horrible ends. All four enlisted men nervously sensed that they were lucky to be alive in this strange place. The villagers with them kindly reassured them they were safe.

Ravi ushered the scouts into a door of a crude shack in the middle of a dusty dirt street as several villagers looked at them with kindness in their faces. Ravi walked up to the floor bed and pulled off a cover that hid Wadsworth's body. Hooky saw a husk of a man whose shrunken face had been frozen in terror…like a mummy of sorts. Old Wad still wore his open red blouse and had his pants still down around his boots. 'Wow," Hook replied as he laughed, "Looks like Old Wad had one hell of a bad night or one hell of a roll in the hay with a lady!" Ravi smiled then laughed at him…. "Yes, Mr. Hook, I would say both! And his last!"

King George collected Old Wad's nice gold-plated engraved pistol along with his leather belt lying on the crude wooden table and smiled. "A fine present for our leader!" Rashid was viewing the remains of Wadsworth with concern as his mind raced with thoughts. He also sensed the concern from the others. Ravi addressed Rashid and the rest in his usual gaze to answer their mental concerns. He looked at the Indian scout. "You are correct Rashid; you are very correct about us and how we related to your ancient legends my friend. We are the shape-changers. There is much to our story and relation to this evil Kali! We have existed on this planet for many ages. Shape changing actually became a survival mode as my ancestors developed it so long ago!" Rashid gave a nervous smile. "Ravi, how on earth do you shape change?" The venerable ancient gave his usual kind hypnotic smile as he ushered the group to the pond area. Ravi asked them all to sit and relax as he continued speaking.

"My race has survived for hundreds of thousands of years on this planet my friends. Our survival was due in the fact that our ancestors culled the immense power of the universe into their souls and adapted our race to survive in the many tempests of mankind. We were able to transfer the thoughts of transforming into shapes in the spirit realm into this plane or dimension to change our physical appearances as needed. We already had mastered the lessons of advanced out of body soul transforming at will into any form it desires. Our ancestors learned to transform their living flesh into any shape desired to make this understanding simple. We learned how to transform our physical bodies at will and assume many shapes to protect us. This has to do with the altering of vibrations from one plane to another." Ravi smiled at the bewildered faces in front of him before explaining more.

"After all, everything from the smallest molecule to the largest elephant is made up of vibrations. Your history is full of myths of gods transforming into all sorts of things from human form. Myth and reality are mixed now in this power and we are a few of the last ones!" Collins asked. "Ravi, what is a molecule?" Ravi remembered that the current science of mankind had not discovered molecules or the atom yet. He smiled at the lieutenant. "A molecule is the tiniest part of what makes up everything around you, including you. If you had a tiny microscope and could see, say your arm for example. You would see billions of molecules in the order of making your arm. We are all constructed by them as is everything else in this universe! What our powerful ancient ancestors did is learn how to transform a thought form into a real image to cover their identity and protect it!"

The scouts were all silent like good school children as the ancient sage added. "You have nothing to fear from us, since you are all held in great esteem and honor, especially James Ambrose Cavendish who nearly gave his life to save us. Through your kindness of offering food to this village at the expense of your lives, proved to us your goodness of heart…something most of mankind does not possess! The act of shielding us from Wadsworth's bullets to save Pyra and me has earned Ambrose very special praise and place among us. We had to test you, to see this goodness in you because of a task which lies ahead for your world and ours together!"

Ravi smiled at Collins and Hook. "I will be honest. You were brought here for purpose! The village via our technology had enormous food supplies and the ability to create more easily. Your offering of food to us was a test that we set to learn about your nature. The crops of the village were destroyed three years ago by a blight imposed on us by our mutual friend down the road!" Hook looked confused. "You mean Kali?" Ravi smiled and nodded his head. "you will learn all of this soon!" Hook still looked confused. "You gave us a test that would have got us all killed by Wadsworth Ravi?" Ravi replied. "You were never in danger of being killed sergeant. Sadly, the shooting of Cavendish was an unpremeditated event we were not in place to stop. For this we are sorry! We had no interest in Wadsworth and his disastrous folly and were surprised that he survived."

There is a huge reason why we could not tell you the plan which will be revealed to you in the near term. It has everything to do with this plan remaining hidden from the Kali!" If anybody in Wadsworth's command knew our plan and was captured?" They all listened as the old sage continued. "We have been watching over you scouts throughout your ordeal at Chital and in this jungle against the green ones in grand secrecy. We have also kept close observation on the disastrous actions of Wadsworth. He was a fool and we could do nothing to save him or his army. They were in the Kali's grip when they left Malakand! In your case however, we made many of his devils quietly disappear that were stalking you when you came into the jungle. We gave a constant watch over you and your actions. We later destroyed over a hundred of them following you towards our village.

The Kali wants to destroy us for reason, let's say we are the eternal thorn in his side and a painful one! He returned to India for two reasons. The first one is to destroy us forever and the second is to create his base to conquer the world. He tried to destroy us with an ill planned invasion when he destroyed our crops. We destroyed this attack. But Kali is growing stronger and we are very concerned about this! We need to destroy his army to get to him, to kill him! This is where we need General Blood and his Malakand Field force to help us. We help him kill the green army and in doing this we kill Kali!"

He paused then added. "The shooting of Lieutenant Cavendish was a surprise and accident and our protection was not in place. Because of our very advanced medicine he will fully recover soon! Wadsworth's evil band fell prey to our darker side we offered in the night! The Kali and his minions also face this same collective dark side as necessary! We do what we have to do to take care of business my friends." Collins, acting his role as the officer in charge spoke. "We are all accounted for except Corporal Holmes. Is he safe? Ravi gave a smile. "Yes, Mr. Holmes had a ringside seat to the mayhem we extended to Wadsworth's loyal minions by this pond last night. He was made a special guest at Ronjin's house in the ancient city where you were the other day."

Ravi smiled and laughed. "Holmes is in the good hands of two special bodyguards especially handpicked!" Rashid mused. "I thought that you were simply the headman at this small farming village in the jungle and now all this revelation?" Ravi replied." This is true for I am seen as the father of this village and all the actual natives come under the explicit protection from us. We serve each other in many ways." "Please come with me to see Cavendish and I will explain more. He looked serious for a moment. What you will learn must be kept as a secret. We see you all as men of honor. As I mentioned, you were brought here to serve the future. It is important we trust each other for the road ahead will be a dangerous one.

As I mentioned, there are some grave issues that will be addressed soon which include Kali and General Blood. Much is at stake my friends. Your invitation here was planned and very necessary. Now, to the real village." Off they walked across the footbridge over the bubbling brook and large swimming pond where the horses played. As they walked between the narrow street with towering cliffs of solid rock on both sides, the grey city opened up in front of them. Engineer Collins was amazed at the layout and structures in this ancient place with tall buildings of dark granite, beautiful streets and gardens that they had never seen the likes of before.

Several of these monolithic structures seemed to have been destroyed long ago in the same upheaval that partially destroyed the street between the rock cliffs. Collins, who had been to New York city gave his impression from the perspective of an engineer and mused. "Some of these structures dwarf the ones in New York and this city is well laid out!" Ravi turned out to be an excellent tour guide as they walked among the ancient tall gray buildings down the main thoroughfare admiring the ruins of this once great metropolis of a long bygone race. All present were mesmerized by the unique statues along the way.

"So where are all the people Ravi" commented Collins, new here. "This city is inhabited by anyone who wants to live here as most of the village does live here. However, for security purposes it appears as a dead city and cover for our city farther on. "So, your people do not live here at all?" Ravi smiled; you shall see where we live in a short time. After walking beyond the ancient city, with strange writings etched in the walls and more interesting statues of a long dead civilization they came to a waterway with crystal clear fast-moving water. Ravi instructed them to climb in to a wide long boat, be seated and put safety belts on. He looked at his guests with a smile. "Prepare for the most invigorating boat ride my friends. With that he sat behind a wheel and pulled a lever. The boat seemed to float effortlessly into the rapidly moving large stream. The boat picked up an incredible speed as it went through a very long dark tunnel.

When it emerged, they were caught in a crescendo of fast rapids and decent drops as the boat seemed to careen around from side to side. The group viewed a landscape of huge pointed mountains accented in the most exquisite natural jungles. At this point the boat seemed to drop down in the rapids and continued so for what seemed several miles. After the initial shock of the first fall, the ride was exhilarating and fun for all. Finally, they emerged from the rapids into the most beautiful azul blue slow-moving waters and drifted up to a huge dock covered in ancient frescos and statues.

Hook was having a ball and yelled at Ravi. "Hey can we do that again!" the ancient man laughed. "As many times, as you want my son!" The group exited he boat then left the dock area. They admired the incredible architecture and scenery as they exited a long ornate naturally lighted tunnel to emerge see such breathtaking sights. They were standing high above the most beautiful enchanted city they had ever seen. It was a pure paradise of gold domed buildings, temples intermixed with the most wonderful gardens of huge flowers and trees. Many varieties of animals and birds seemed to be everywhere. Long bridges crisscrossed in, around, and even above the intricate structures.

It was like every building was a work of art with many inlaid with incredible patterns of precious jewels and gold. Ravi finally spoke as the group continued staring in awe at the strange breathtaking surroundings. "Welcome to Hima friends, this is home!" Rashid added. "Are we in what my father called the land of Shangri-li Ravi?" The wizened ancient man smiled at him. "No, the place you call Shangri-li is in another place, in a warm jungle valley and deep in the snow-covered mountains farther north. It too is a sight to behold as are the inhabitants. That is where the only group of giant Lemurines that survived the great world catastrophe live." Then Ravi thought for a moment. "There are other survivors from those days that have evolved differently, so to speak.

They are highly intelligent beings and very shy to mankind. Over the ages their bodies have, through necessity, become conditioned in evolution to protect them from the elements. They are referred to by your civilization as the "abominable snowmen or Yetis." He laughed. "Your theory of evolution has mankind evolving from the apes. In reality, it was the fall of civilization and the rigors of isolation in primitive jungles that turned humans into monkeys over the course of a million years." Collins, full of questions asked. "So, if we did not evolve from the apes, then where did mankind evolve from?" Ravi gave his usual smile. "Son, all the races of mankind, all the animal and other species were planted here by those who guard and rule this universe. Earth, like millions of other planets, earth can be seen as a garden. Some crops of mankind survive, others do not! The same is true for all other species of life!

Ravi brought them to the front of a huge temple-like structure. They were amazed at the extremely friendly and attractive people they met. He directed them into a huge building and they followed him into a room with a huge pool in it. The sunlight that entered this room completely lighted it throughout in some structural manner Collins could not figure out. Soon after they entered this great hall, Ravi bid them a temporary farewell and left. They were met by Ronjin and his staff. He instructed them to take off their dirty uniforms and to wash in the pool. They stripped off their uniforms and went swimming and washing in the warm waters of the pool. They were all amazed at how the soapy dirty water soon drained away and was replenished with clean water. Then a warm clean water replaced it and seemed to touch every pore in their bodies. The waters seemed to invigorate each of them.

When they finished washing, they soon discovered that all their soiled uniforms were gone and that each had a clean white robe and sandals waiting for them as they left the pool. Very pretty village women entered the long pristine room and handed them goblets of a sweet fruity beverage. After some time lounging about the room by the pool Ronijn guided them down the hall to another huge room. Soon they were sitting with Ravi next to a pool where Cavendish seemed to float in a shallow pool of water. He was asleep. An incredibly beautiful woman, oozing with libido approached them dressed in a very short robe.

She took off her robe to reveal the most gorgeous body and walked into the pool. She sat in the waters and placed James's head in her lap. She rubbed his head caressed against her full breasts and his eyes soon opened. From the other side of the room came Corporal Holmes through a large doorway with two extremely pretty ladies on his arms. He hailed them with a grand smile. "Hello, welcome to the Hima resort boys!" He and his ladies joined the group on the comfortable low couches as they all sat near the pool. Collins looked at Holmes. "We were worried that you may have been killed by Wadsworth's men."

Holmes smiled at the lieutenant then at the two lovely ladies clad in shimmering silk. "yes sir, the bad guys were just about to get me and these two lovely ladies and their friends gobbled up the bad guys and saved me from a painful end. I owe them my life and whatever else they want from me." He winked and they laughed. The woman caring for Cavendish was the most beautiful woman old Sergeant Hook had ever seen. He was staring at her beauty when she looked at him with a smile and a wink. "Hello Mr. Sergeant Hook!" and she nodded at Rashid. Hook had heard that childlike voice somewhere and looked at her in complete askance. "Pyra? Is that you?" She laughed back at him. "My" he stammered, "But you have grown so much since we last met!"

The satire in his voice made her laugh. She sat Cavendish up in her arms resting his head on her lap in the water. "Look Ambrose, you have guests today!" He gave a weak smile and waved his hand. "welcome to my world boys. The water feels great" Hook looked close at the scaring of the bullet wound in his chest at his heart. He was amazed at this. He looked at Ravi. "How did our boss heal so fast and from a fatal wound sir?" Ravi answered. "We were able to adopt many of the medical secrets of the ancients and others from say, their advanced technology. They left all their technology hidden in what you call time capsules.

This water, for example is specially medically prepared with many healing elixirs, medicine in the water and powerful ones. We were able to get the bullet out of Cavendish's heart and mend the damage soon after he was shot. We actually replaced half of his heart with what your future science will call "plastic. We also know that food can also be administered from the water to very sick people as well. "So, who are these ancients Ravi?" Inquired young Collins, completely mesmerized by all that he had seen and heard thus far. Ravi addressed the young boyish looking man who had helped blow nearly half of a huge precipice into a river in the attack on the castle. "Our ancestors learned many sciences long ago in union with an ancient race whose civilization was completely destroyed in a cataclysm over a million years ago."

Collins gave a whistle. The idea of civilizations being millions of years old was astounding to him. Ravi, reading his thoughts continued. "Son, the universe, all universes in the realm of Great God are and have been a continuum forever. "Forever" is the correct term here. There is nothing new under the sun anywhere in the universe for it already has been discovered, developed, and copied millions of times in millions of civilizations! Many different forms of life on millions if not billions of planets have learned to evolve over time. Naturally, many others were destroyed by …?" Ravi was searching for a parable; "from eating the fruit from the tree of good and evil in the Garden of Eden!" Then he had another one Greek in origin. "From opening Pandora's Box!" The sage smiled for he was proud that he remembered that one. Collins knew the significance of this and smiled. Ravi continued with his lesson.

Earth, like all others, come under the directives and guidance of an ordered council of space civilizations. Once a planet civilization has been planted, it was normal for those assigned to it to visit and walk among mankind to study the effects of their evolution." "You mean spacemen? Work?" The ancient man smiled at him. "Yes, my son." Rather than mankind evolving from a small microorganism, races and many other diverse species began their existence planted here fully developed biologically by the gardeners over a billion years ago. These planets like earth were designed as schools, universities in space for all types of life to exist and learn at this level of existence.

To enhance learning and spiritual growth, mankind was given free will to assess, learn, grow, decide, based from numerous life experience, and the information passed to them by guided learning processes. It is said that God gave mankind his love, laws, and the gift of free will! What the dominate race or species does with it is their choice for better or worse son." The lieutenant was confused and asked. So, mankind has the free will to destroy itself?" Ravi nodded his head. "Yes lieutenant, if a civilization eats from the fruit of the tree of good and evil, symbolically it has developed the means of its grand development in the universe or complete self-destruction!

Over time, advanced civilizations discover this crossroad by finding one thing that will enhance them into a new technological world or destroy it! We call it, this apple from the tree the "splitting of the atom!" The ancient sage relaxed and leaned back in his seat. "My race came to this planet so long ago when the civilization of Lemuria was developing so long ago that we of the new generations have no record of it or even where our race came from. We came as teachers as part of the plan to help this evolving world." Collins asked. "Your race was "space men" then?" Ravi gave a serious laugh and looked at his new student.

"Son, all of us, all of our origins came from outer space. Didn't I say we colonized this planet with races of mankind?" Mankind and their many handlers were together with both good and bad results over the ages. There were once tight bonds of friendship between us and humankind; unlike all the fear and mystery that now exists." Collins had to smile at this statement as Ravi added; "Didn't your Bible say that "God created man?" The story of Adam and Eve in the Garden of Eden is very symbolic!" We helped mankind to learn civilized ways and to grow together in peace, union, and make good choices. As the civilizations of earth expanded throughout this planet, our race completely integrated into them. As the ages continued forth, mankind then began to shift their desires and to make greed their god and resorted to war to grab power and gold!

Hate and strife developed among certain powerful groups and sub-civilizations vying for world domination. Alliances formed, weapons were created, egos replaced common sense, and then the usurpations of others began. Rebellions and revolutions led to wars against the motherland of MU or Lemuria. The problems now became of great concern to those who watched over the planet. Free will in choices could not be changed as the civilization now teetered of what we call nuclear war. The life of the whole planet was at stake. Not just life, but the life of the planet itself!"

Ravi took a sip of his tea and leaned forward in his chair to resume his lesson. "There had already been two catastrophes previous to the Age of Lemuria. The first was a huge war eons before between the first race of mankind on the planet. This nuclear war destroyed the life and ecosystem of the planet for a million years. This had to be fixed and corrected so it could sustain life and be re-colonized. The second age was a true golden age for thousands of years. Then came a planet that crashed into earth and completely erased this second huge civilization overnight. After this rogue planet struck earth, it began to orbit and became our moon. I could not begin to tell you how many hundreds of thousands of years it took for earth to begin a new life cycle after that massive catastrophe."

Collins was now completely mesmerized by the words of the ancient sage. MU or Lemuria was the next civilization or third "root race" upon this planet and is when my ancestors came to teach. MU was worldwide and its home island was gigantic and rested in most of what is the south Pacific Ocean. It was another grand civilization until the same problems surrounding the root problem of material greed began to flourish. Wars erupted and like the first root race war, nuclear weapons were being created to destroy earth again! Those who watched and supervised earth were not going to allow this to happen! Then came a huge world catastrophe to end the many dangerous choices on the table!

The whole planet earth violently shook as MU broke apart with much of it sinking into the ocean. The whole western part of this island was forced here to create what you call the Himalayas. The huge southern part of this grand massive island, pushed away by the tectonic shifts, formed the frozen landmass of Antarctica at the south pole. Many continents sank under the waves as new landforms rose from the ocean depths. The loss of life is still unfathomable to me but was huge. Millions died and the earth went dark for a long time. That was over a million years ago. However, the earth was now safe from another fatal nuclear destruction by the poor choices rendered by mankind. I will later explain what "nuclear" means.

The survivors of our race, like the remains of the vast Lemurian empire of nations were spread out across the destroyed planet and communication or contact was lost entirely." As the group continued to be enlightened by Ravi, a pair of large very ferocious looking dog like creatures entered the room playing. Their heads, mouths, and teeth were huge, ferocious, and multi-colored. They approached the group who became very apprehensive. They reminded Hooky of the huge Bow or Foo dog statues that protected many ancient temples in China when he was there. Now he was seeing living ones, dancing statures and barking at that.

He was amazed as the rest were terrified. Ravi laughed. It seemed that the strange dogs centered their attention on Color Sergeant Alfred Hook and playfully bounced in his direction. They head nudged his leg and one jumped in his lap. It was very heavy and licked his face. Ravi laughed at Hook. "Mr. Hook, you have nothing to fear from them, they serve as both our guards and pets. They existed among humans long ago. The breed survives here with us." The near one-hundred-pound huge fanged monster sniffed Hook's face, then licked it again followed by a huge head nuzzle. It reminded him of his beloved English Bulldogs long ago as a young lad.

Ravi laughed. "Go play with them, looks like the puppies like you!" "Puppies?" Inquired the Color Sergeant. King George and Collins were accosted by three more friendly giant puppies and could not believe how large and unusual they looked. Then Hooky looked down from his jest with his two large puppy buddies and saw their mother standing near with a wide fanged smile on her face from ear to ear. She had to weigh four-hundred-pounds. Their fear of them gone, Hook, Collins and Lord George were soon spirited outside to play with them. Holmes was spirited away by his two hostesses for another roll in the hay. Ravi and Rashid were alone by the pool, with the exception of Pyra and the sleeping Cavendish. Pyra was living proof of the ability of the shape changers. Ravi could sense the internal concern in Rashid. He looked at Rashid and spoke.

"The terrible myths that surround the shape changers or shifters are very understandable and bear truth Rashid. This is the problem we all face now. The Kali exists and is what I term the "dark side" of my race! The historical myths surrounding the shape-changers have offered both tales of good and evil. The cultural myths recount many stories of good and bad beings in the forms of gods and monsters. There are two sides to this coin, one of good and the other evil. Sadly, it is my race that has representation on both sides of this ancient coin Rashid.

As I said, my race was invited to earth by the powers that rule as the Age of MU was in infancy. My ancestors were known in the higher order as the best teachers. It was our time to contribute our efforts here. My race possessed extreme mind powers. After a thousand years of a golden age, growing problems arose between factions prevalent in the Lemurian Empire. The day for MU ended not by war, but with world cataclysm as I said! After a great earth cataclysm, all contact between our respective colonies on this planet were erased.

However, we were able, over many ages after this, using our focused telepathic energies, locate and bring back many survivors of our kind to form a new society. We inhabited this city of Hima which was oddly, one of the few Lermurian cities to survive the cataclysm. Our race was able to flourish and reclaim our purpose since the next and "fourth" root race was coming into existence on a series of huge islands in what you call the Atlantic Ocean. As you realize, we of Hima are the good side of this coin. There was a very evil other side of this coin created by those of our race we completely lost contact with in the cataclysms.

Many of these lost ones were children who survived and were orphaned in the violent post apocalypse world. This bunch possessed all the powers of our race and were alone and unguided. They became ensconced in the world of greed and of violent ways to gain power. They went far from our teachings and laws to exercise their own evil will on this planet. They became, in time what your religion calls "fallen angels." Many became a force of pure evil. They became the devil! They became like Kali! They took advantage of humankind in using their powerful intellects to manipulate human will and circumstances to gain power and riches! They became the authors of hate, terror and savagery who sat on their gold thrones washed in blood!"

Both men took Ravi's pause to sip their tea. Ravi continued after. "The dark side, which lies in all living things became their dwelling and the master of their life force! In the next age, these dark ones fine-tuned and masked their savage abilities to infiltrate and rule civilization in the next cycle. The conflict between this two sides of the coin became an obvious pursuit by us. In essence, our mission in life has been hunt them down and destroy them; all of them! Our ancient laws were to teach mankind to love, service, and to protect. As the Lord Jesus said in his Golden Rule; "Do unto others as you would be done by!"

He concluded. "Evil can grow in leaps and bounds if not checked because evil is never completely destroyed by those brave souls tasked to perform such gruesome tasks! Evil always sleeps with one eye open ready to create chaos and death!" Rashid now inquired the sage "I can accept this so far Ravi, for the Vedas speak about many things such as visitors from outer space and incredible technologies of old. But if you are the good forces, then who are the evil ones?" Ravi stared at the Indian. Over the ages we thought we had eradicated all of them but were wrong. In simple terms, we failed to destroy one who later rose up as the great Khan who nearly invaded the world. We killed him but his son escaped us. We later caught up with him in what is termed "The New World."

We missed him as he masqueraded as a conquistador leader destroying civilizations there in a reign of terror. We later found his next evil endeavor and empire as a powerful dealer in African slaves off the coast of the Americas. We thought we had killed him! Now he has come back as "Kali!" to destroy we the hunters! After the cataclysms that destroyed two civilizations on this planet and nearly extinguished my race, survivors of our race intermarried and interbred with the human race for tribal protection.

These were terrible desperate times and to survive we had to join and lend our intelligence to stronger tribal groups that survived. Our spreading gene pool produced very powerful leaders of both good and evil intentions in many epochs of history since these times. When we could supervise, and teach these mixed offspring's, there was little problem as they were guided to the light so to speak; to live in accordance of our rules and laws. Problems arose when we lost control of the orientation and educational processes of these hybrid children as the large tribes warred, split up, or wandered to new places sometimes at a moment's notice. We again lost contact with many of these children.

A few mixed offspring, realizing their powers were influenced and drifted to the dark side. As time passed these dark powerful souls basked in their hideous nature. We hunted them by being drawn to chaotic developments on the planet. We found and killed many in the last epoch of the Atlantean empire before it was destroyed. These dark ones had usurped complete control of this massive island civilization and had developed crude nuclear weapons in complete secret! The assured destruction of the planet was in their hands and in a costly struggle we stopped them! This was long before my time.

We did not get them all as a few escaped the destruction of Atlantis! A few of the worst ones survived this ordeal and we hunted them! Such is the sad truth Rashid. Your current epoch of world history is full of examples. Asoka the greatest leader and king of India was one of our good examples, as was Octavius, emperor of Rome. They brought civilization, order, and peace to millions around them in this troubled world. The sinister examples exist large and small as well. Genghis Klan was a prime example. He possessed all the powers of our kind. Although he brought a strange peace to most of the known world after he slaughtered most of it, his methods in achieving this were savage, brutal, and bloody.

We could never get physically close to him until later in his invasions into Europe. He was powerful enough to divine our presence and was well protected by his own select conditioned bodyguard. He ran his course and was actually killed by a human in our band; a human he failed to detect! We had banded with good humans in other quests rarely. Attila the great Hun in earlier centuries was another example we killed. After his great defeat at Chalon's Sur Mar in Gaul we were able to poison him while he was drunk." Lieutenant Collins, who had returned and was listening to Ravi had a question. "Ravi, you said "we" so were you there?" Ravi smiled at the young officer who sat across from him in his white robe as an innocent child. "Yes Bertram, I was there and was one of the few selected to end Attila's life, for the safety of so many others." Collins asked another question.

"Did you actually see that battle? We studied it at the military academy. Did the Frankish infantry really stand against the hordes of Hunnish cavalry in an open plain?" Ravi gave a short laugh; he had found a historian in the lad. "Yes son, I was there with others observing the whole battle fighting in the very ranks of the Frankish warriors, and they created an indestructible wedge in the front of the Roman battle formations that was never broken by the relentless cavalry attacks of the Huns." The awed British officer added. "I well remember my teacher telling us how the franks were pulling the Huns from their horses with these huge hooks, or "hangars" attached to long ropes." The old sage laughed, "we gave them the idea. The Franks would then pull them off their horses then drag them into their battle ranks and kill them. It reminded me of catching fish with a fly on a hook."

Ravi took a sip of red wine. "The brilliance in this victory was in the chosen field of the battle. After three days and nights of constant combat, the Franks stood like a rock, unmovable on the plain slaughtering hundreds of Huns. The best infantry beat the best cavalry on their ground! Even the Frankish women who guarded their baggage trains fought them off with bloody results! Remember that Aetius, the Roman commander at this battle spent years in an exchange between Rome and the Huns as a boy. Aetius went to the Huns and Attila went to Rome.

Aetius learned the power and how the Huns conducted and won battles. He knew their tactics. At the outset of this battle he shortened the width of the battlefield that canalized the Huns into a trap between two forests which bordered the battlefield. I greatly respected him! Later, I will take you to our little museum where I think you will have a grand time reviewing all the many artifacts from such battles and other things we have collected from our exploits over the many centuries of mankind." Collins was now all smiles. "Thanks Ravi, I would love to hear more, but how could you have been at that battle if it was in the Fourth century? I mean you would have to be over fifteen-hundred years old now!"

Ravi gave his new student a deep kind smile. "I will hold no secrets from you. My race lives a lot longer than the humans. I am considered an old man by our standards, which puts me at just over five-thousand years now." Lieutenant Collins gave a low whistle and for sake of nothing really to say he added. "With no disrespect, but holy shit!" Both Rashid, who was also amazed, and Ravi both laughed at the very bewildered young officer." Ravi now switched back to the subject of good and evil. "The dark side dwells within all of us and the key is to learn to control it. This one of the best outcomes of reincarnation. You "live" and "Learn!" The dark side is an integral part of all living things in the universe. The forces of good and evil are manifested in the philosophy of the "Yin" and "Yang" as opposites. Controlling the dark force is the goal of any good soul, so when a soul fails in this, evil dominates.

Colonel Hillary Wadsworth was a good example of a soul that drifted into the dark side early in life and failed in achieving higher goals of life! I see him as a corruptible soul, falling into this pattern in his well-padded youth as the son of a powerful noble. Fueled by his arrogance and self-serving quests for power and prestige his final act was in engineering the wanton slaughter of exactly seven-hundred and ten souls to be exact! The unchained ego and assured arrogance are a dangerous combination. This is why learning and abiding by the sacred tenants of humility is the master counter to it. Wadsworth was just a human engrained in evil by his corrupted greedy ego, but if he possessed our genes, as a powerful dangerous monster his destruction would have been huge indeed."

"Speaking of evil ones, tell us about this Kali?" Asked Rashid. "The Kali is my next topic." Ravi took a sip for fresh hot tea. "He is a fallen angel we have been seeking for several centuries now. Kali is a very crafty, old, and dangerous one who knows all the powers we as a race possess. We lost track of him after we destroyed his father the great Khan as his invasions were winding down in 1221. However, our hunters discovered Kali in the guise of the Conquistador Herman Cortes when he surfaced in his invasion of the Aztec capitol in 1520. We had been observing the bloodthirsty violent destruction of civilizations in the Americas and investigated. Cortes/Kali had skillfully formed an alliance with the other tribe's sick of the rule of the Aztec ruler Montezuma.

We were able to launch quite a large ambush against him and his conquistadores and killed many. We nearly got him but he escaped and soon returned with an army he manufactured from his allies in the state of Tlaxcala. The Aztec civilization was destroyed and we just could not get close to him. He was ready for us and several of my hunters perished at his hand. It. Under many different faces he alluded us and destroyed the Incan and Mayan empires. He then disappeared again. It was not long after this terrible usurpation and control of the Mesoamericans that we again found him. This time he was no longer a Spaniard but was a huge black slave trader that processed slaves into the western hemisphere from an island in the Caribbean. This destroyer of three civilizations in Mesoamerica now guided the brutal importation of African slaves into the early colonies to stay out of the limelight and harvest more material wealth. He became the foremost importer of slaves from Africa and again drew us to him.

He set up this unholy business in a small island in the Caribbean. He was responsible for the enslavement and sale of hundreds of thousands of poor souls. Many died in this unholy exchange from famine, murder, and especially from all the diseases passed to them from his controlled minions. We caught up with him as he had become careless in his protection as he prepared a new large group of harvested slaves for delivery to the sugar cane plantations in the American colonies, South America, and in the Caribbean islands. We attacked his headquarters and large holding area in an island whose name evades me.

We launched a huge attack and were positive we killed him with all of his key followers. It was a terrible fight and several of my hunters were killed in the struggle. We posed as slaves to get close. He had been able to read our presence in the Americas before. We fooled him this day by blending into the large group of slaves to be shipped out. Our sudden violent attack was a complete surprise and I saw him die by a sword I plunged directly into him during the large fight. But! Shape-changers can fool other shape-changers I am afraid. We killed him but somehow, he escaped. We killed one he had fabricated to look and act like his current form." Collins interjected. "Like a body double?" "Exactly but sketchy!" replied Ravi.

Ronjin had also joined the discussion now and added his word. "This now brings us to the point of the Kali!" The Kali was this Cortes and the slave master who was called "Big Ben" my friends! It must be remembered that evil loves chaos, war, and the ability to take control in these situations. They do this to produce even bigger chaos and death! Look at its bloody trail in the destruction and enslavement of the civilizations in Central and South America. It was well within its element. The great and powerful Kali is him, the conquistador of old. Unlike the fallen souls we destroyed of old, Kali is seasoned and extremely powerful now.

He has come back to this part of the world for the two reasons I have already mentioned before. Kali came back to destroy us. If he can destroy our civilization, then he will have no threat against him to eventually rule this planet which is his second ultimate goal. We first heard of this Kali and his growing army of green devils a few years ago. We saw him as a strange mix of the god Kali and Islam. We became aware of his danger three years ago when he sent a huge army and many of his conditioned demons to destroy us. We had anticipated this attack and were ready.

His main success was destroying an empty farm village and our crops to starve us. In this battle, we destroyed most of his invaders. We were just too strong for him at this time. He did learn the secret of the ancient gray city but not Hima! There are many reasons for this. However, he is growing strong and developing a huge army to return. We fear he will soon be able to overwhelm us and destroy our civilization. The brief distracting conflict between the forces of the Kali and Wadsworth put only a dent in his forces. The effects of your scouts in the destruction of his military stores has greatly set him back and weakened him for now. In time he will be resupplied and ready to finish us off. Then, the world will be his oyster!"

Ronjin now sat back as Ravi continued to finish. "Like Genghis Khan was, Kali is very protected by an array of strong physical forces he had fabricated and possible dark forces of energy he has also created. We know that on one day he may appear as Kali, then the next appear as the goddess Raktabija. If we could just strip him of his physical mantel of protection, then our job would be feasible." Lieutenant Bertram Collins had been a student in Ravi's classroom for over two hours now and had a vexing question. "Ravi sir, what do you mean by the use of the phrase "He fabricated and created?" Ravi paused as Ronjin now spoke again. "The power of the mind over matter is one law we have learned over the last million years as a race to survive.

We all possess many powers son and only learn about them as we fall into using them. Kali has mastered most of them as we have. When we say fabricating armies and others to do bidding? This means that the Kali can control others by forcing his will power upon them by some form of physical contact. When he, as the conquistador Cortes fell out of sight after we nearly got him in 1522, he went and converted nearly fifty thousand warriors into his new army by this method. It took months but he was able to trick them and get to them, all of them. They were a deadly and destructive force of what I can describe as robots, robots like the green devils!"

"But what do you mean about created dark forces kind sir?" Ronjin and Ravi both smiled at their new apt pupil. Ronjin continued. "As a shape-changer can alter their own appearance to satisfy their ambitions or goals in a given situation, they can alter others who are susceptible and, in their game, alter their abilities genetically." 'Genetically?" inquired the apt pupil? Ravi plugged in. "It is a term for physically altering a human, changing their physical abilities and looks by what future scientists will call genetic codes." Then Rashid remembered viewing the tall silver-faced monsters on the roof of the castle with the hideous faces from the sniper pits through the binoculars.

Ravi caught his thoughts and further explained. "Exactly my friend. You saw some of his creations; dangerous freaks designed of Kali with telepathic properties!" Ravi continued to ponder his next reply to the question, and then answered. "The great Kali, as he is named is a continued manifestation of his existence in all its extremes for many ages, as you have witnessed. He and all of his ilk have lived as the master parasites of mankind. Our genes have generated and enhanced the powerful evil monster within him. This Kali is the puppet master behind the scenes in manipulating this opposition against you British, by carefully infiltrating the secular and religious groups opposing British rule. We have seen him change shapes as a kind and concerned messenger to the Mad fakir and others. He has never shown his face so we could kill him. We have tried but the Kali is a wise creature. He well remembers how close we came to destroying him in the Caribbean.

One thing is for sure, the menace of the Kali is both a threat to us and to British civilization down the road! This is why we of the village and General Blood's army will play an important part together in future events! Together we have a real opportunity to jointly eradicate this evil parasitic force if we combine our energies and resources. This possible union is the first time we requested help from humans in many ages, actually since the days of Attila!" Ravi concluded. "If we combine our talent and resources with the British army under Bindon Blood, we will destroy Kali!" "General Blood?" inquired a weak Cavendish listening intently from the pool.

"How can Blood's forces help? They are tied down and heavily engaged to the northwest?" Ravi smiled, "Blood's forces cut off the main retreat of the Pashtuns and Afghans a few days ago. Also, his scorched earth policy is gleaning excellent results in thinning the Pashtun ranks. Many natives have gone home to protect their villages now from the British torch. Most of the tribesmen have returned to their villages and have surrendered their weapons. The campaign is drawing down to a victorious conclusion, and soon. General Blood has already pulled reserves from this campaign and has ordered elements of his huge northern force to advance north. He is personally on his way to Chital at this time where many of his forces and support have already arrived.

We also saw more British forces being sent from the south of Malakand and they will be there soon. General Blood is fully aware of the details of massacre at Chital. Your scout Hoskins and his party have safely reached Chital and have briefed the general on the details of Wadsworth's doomed expedition. This is why all of you are very important in our plan to enlist the support of the general and British government in this expedition! We have a plan to ensure a British victory by using our capabilities. The use of terror and fear can work both ways my friends." Concluded Ravi.

"Ask poor Wadsworth what we unleashed upon him and his men?" Smiled Ronjin. "Mind over matter can work on all enemies!" Cavendish had been listening intently from his repose in the shallow healing pool. "What fear do these savage monsters have Ravi?" Ravi pointed to the statues of a cat with a human head and to two winged cats on each side. The Kali is a chameleon who has been adopting various guises and religions to further its ends for a long time. He was the devout Catholic as Cortes as his previous example. Playing religions in the many aspirations of the human civilizations is a game to him.

However, He and all of his unconditioned minions believe that it is the winged cat with the human body that is the ancient bane and a real danger to them. It was an army of winged catlike avengers that tore his forces to pieces when they were coming after you on the old ancient road recently. Kali was terrified of it more because of the racial memory and when they appeared against his army. Fear of the cat does not apply to his thousands of brain-dead warriors in his army. They need to be destroyed and British steel will perform this task! After this, the terror of the cat messengers will destroy his Pretorian guard, and then we will have a free reign to kill Kali once and for all. Then, perhaps we will be finished hunting and fighting these fallen children for good." There was a moment of silence as the information soaked in.

"Messengers of what?" asked Rashid "In simple terms, the winged cats symbolized the messengers of the good, of light, of knowledge and TRUTH or simply, the force of God! The man with the cat body symbolizes wisdom of civilizations long dead, long before Lemuria or Atlantis. It symbolized the many Truths in real knowledge, learning, and universal harmony. We are talking of a civilization that ruled this planet millions of years ago; The Sphinx of Egypt remains as a vestige to this tradition, constructed by the survivors of the Atlantis race. Like all living things, civilizations have a life cycle. They have a birth, a life, old age, then death. Death of any civilization can come by the hand of mankind or be erased by Mother Nature. Then it all starts over once again.

However, the great truth of wisdom and knowledge; remains forever constant in the universe; all universes! These laws of God apply to all races in all worlds!" Ronjin added with a smile. "When the head of the cat replaces the one of the humans, it becomes the messenger of death and preserver of good!" Then came a new question from Collins. "How did you know this about Blood and his army?" Ravi pointed to the winged cats. "We are them, the eyes and ears of the planet my friend. We have kept a close eye on your commander since he left Malakand with his field force to fight towards the Khyber Pass. We are the observers of all human interactions, especially when they become questionable. We always look for evil that remains from our spawn." Collins asked. "Were you the ones keeping us awake at night in the jungle?" Ravi smiled, "Yes, but we didn't mean to…we were actually protecting you by blocking the more sinister powerful and conscious minions Kali had scouring the area.

We wiped out three bands of his devils that were getting close to your trail along the bluff. We wanted your actions against the Kali's fortress to proceed! You did a splendid job by the way!" Then Cavendish thought how light the sentries were in the castle when they entered it. Ravi added. "Yes Ambrose, a few of those guards had serious problems before you arrived. But the Kali was well protected and completely focused in other things at the time!" It was then that a villager entered the room and whispered something in Ravi's ear. He smiled and the messenger left. Ravi then commented with a beaming smile to his guests. "We have located a couple survivors from your group, one named Griggs, and another named Burrows who rode with the lancers. We are in the process of guiding them here."

The scouts all gave a sigh of relief on hearing this as Hooky muttered the immortal phrase:" if anybody could get out alive, it would be Griggs!" Then Rashid asked a question off the subject. "If your race has been around for so long, and you are over five-thousand years old; then how old are most of your people?" Ravi smiled, "Good question, and if we are to work together, then honesty is the best policy. I am just over five -thousand years of age as are a few others, and most of the villagers are between one-thousand and four thousand years of age. We do have a nice bunch of new children who range from a few years to over five hundred now."

Rashid was stunned, "What is your true shape Ravi, may I ask what you all really look like?" "Yes, you may. Understand first that when we assume shapes, they are biologically real for as long as we need them, like you seeing me as a very old man; I was an old man. Understand the power of our minds over the manipulation of matter. All things are vibrating molecules set by their composure in all dimensions. We change the status of these vibrations to create new forms we inhabit." With that said, Ravi stood up and in a muddled whirl of greenish light exhibited his true form.

Rashid and the rest were now looking at a very tall wiry being, with a clear immaculately shaped greenish body, with a large oblong shaped head, and very large deep penetrating violet eyes. It wore a very broad sincere disarming smile from his deep penetrating eyes. It was Ravi all right! Then Ravi pointed at Pyra. "She is a young soul and is one-thousand and ninety-five years old this year!" He beamed a smile. "She is also my youngest daughter!" Pyra, watching the awe in all their faces began laughing, "and I am still pretty in my natural form as well!" It was a good moment for Cavendish to have drifted back off into sleep.

The group now looked over to Hook who had made such a positive impact on these large fanged multicolored beasts as they would not let him free. There was love in the air between Hooky and beasts. Smiles at this new relationship beamed around the healing temple room. It was time for the group, less Cavendish to return to their camp in the farming village to get things in order. The group walked together casually admiring the beauty of the ancient city as a group of children played around and followed them. The boat ride back was as much exciting fun as when they came to Hima and all were amazed to learn that the boat ride was nearly fifty miles from their point of origin.

They returned to their camp, still wearing their comfortable white robes and in great spirits. The carnage that had befallen Wadsworth's staff had been cleaned up. They were all amused at some of the villagers wearing the red blouses so arrogantly worn by the pack of dead staff clowns. They were very fitting! They stood by and witnessed the last of the two mangled husks of Wadsworth's once pompous group, being tossed by the villagers into a large burning pyre.

Unlike the new owners wearing the red blouse uniforms of the dead, they found all their uniforms cleaned and folded next to their revolvers, pistol belts and other personal accruements laid out on a long wooden table. Even their boots had been cleaned and polished! Such was the way the coin had turned for them! Nobody changed into their uniforms yet. All of them preferred to wear the comfortable robes as they shared a few shots of whiskey from Wadsworth's large stash that had survived Colonel Wadsworth's final circus the night before. They all seemed to ease into a state of peacefulness, calm, and acting like a group of young men devoid of the terrible conditions they had thus experienced since Chital. They were free of the world's entanglements completely today.

The jungle trek had been very trying on both Burrows and Griggs. They were out of food, but at least replenished their water routinely from clear flowing streams that seemed to cross regularly and found trees filled with strange tasty fruit. It was dawn on the third day of their attempt to get back to civilization. Griggs wondered if anybody else in his group had survived the attack on the castle. It was hard to think if anybody made it as he reviewed the terrible situation surrounding him before his jump from the tower into the fast waters of the river to escape. The two soldiers had traveled to the west over very mountainous jungle terrain. Both men were physically and mentally exhausted in their tedious unending trek in the thick jungle in the aftermath of the terrible battle.

Captain Burrows knew he was essentially the only survivor of his ill-fated combat operation of lancers vs. the green devils and Russian artillery. Griggs had done his part in relieving Burrows of any personal guilt as being the lone survivor. He confided, that Captain Burrows had done his best under the catastrophic circumstances he was forced into. His lancers had executed an excellent attack that destroyed the Russian artillery and killed several hundred green devils in their path. Fate alone had saved him. Fate alone! As they sat in the early hot jungle resting the forms of two young boys and an older girl appeared. They were dressed in traditional village clothes. Both British soldiers simply looked at them in dull tired gazes.

The girl smiled and addressed them in perfect English. "We are here to guide you to our village where Lieutenant Cavendish and his group are now resting. They told us to tell you they miss you." Griggs and Burrows stood facing them. Mister Griggs immediately smiled as the girl named off all the people who were with Cavendish. In his fatigue, he was overjoyed and felt his strength returning. He wanted to be with his boys. Captain Burrows smiled and asked, "Did Colonel Wadsworth or anybody else make it?" The girl returned a pleasant smile, "No, they are all dead!" With that said, both soldiers, with renewed hope and consuming ravenously a nice lunch of prepared food and some special drink offered from the children. The two men silently followed the three children into the jungle.

Two days earlier, Corporal Hoskins now led his tired group up to the large forward defensive positions north of General Blood's encampment in Chital. The city was now filled with thousands of troops and their materials for war. He approached a sharp looking officer dressed in a well pressed Khaki uniform. He saluted the officer. "Corporal Hoskins and party reporting from the north Sir!" The young officer returned the salute and spoke in uncertain concerned words. "Where are the rest of, of Wadsworth's army?" Hoskins gave him a now natural thousand-yard gaze. We are it!" Then his voice became urgent.

"I need to report to General Blood the details first as requested by my commander. But I will say that Wadsworth's Army was in very dire straits the last time I saw them sir." The officer then ordered two mounted soldiers forward. "Take these people into Chital at once to General Blood immediately!" The officer saluted as he looked at the shabby group and the pretty blonde woman with her kids. "Get them some food and refreshments before you take them s over to Blood." The higher-ranking lancer saluted his superior, "Yes Sir, and will do!"

Back at Hima, Alfred Hook had become the pride of the Bow Dogs. He had fallen in love with all of them, like a little boy who gets his first puppy. However, Old Hooky had five seventy-five-pound new Bow puppies, as well as two wonderful Bow dog parents to contend with now. There were many more of these multi-colored ferocious looking creatures running about Hima. He was finally pulled from his new world by Pyra and returned to the main hall with the pools. The group at the pool laughed as they saw the old soldier return, covered in jumping crooning baby bow dogs as he rested his back against a wall.

He had decided to hang out with Cavendish while the others had left. He had asked one of the medical doctors about his boss. The attendant replied. "Mr. LT. Cavendish is fit and recovered. He heart is at one-hundred percent now!" Pyra joined the old sergeant with a happy smile. She was the most beautiful woman he had ever seen. Ronjin then joined them as they viewed Cavendish asleep floating in the healing pool. He spoke. We have briefed him and implanted our intentions telepathically in dealing with Kali while he was asleep. He will know what to tell the general before we arrive.

Ronjin smiled at the salty old soldier as he gave broad details. "You will like our plans for those green devils and Kali! We will completely obscure British movements by replacing their scouts and guards with our stand-ins." "Stand-ins?" Questioned Hooky. "Yes, we will began killing green devil observers and infiltrating or replacing them with our imitation lookalikes to generate a complete chain of false intelligence back to the Kali. He will be led to believe the British are in Chital when in reality they will be ready to attack Kali in the jungles. We must be very careful with this ruse!" Hook smiled at Ronjin and asked. "Shape-changers I assume? And I do want a second shot at these green weenies!" Ronjin was amused.

When Hook returned to their camp, they found everybody present and preparing for a standard hot military dinner meal prepared by the surviving British enlisted soldiers of Wadsworth's command. Collins had supervised them. "So, you are all dressed like beachgoers are you!" Bellowed Sergeant Hook at his men still in their comfortable bathrobes and flip flops as they laughed at his approach in his robe. "We shall mess in uniforms my ladies!" The soldiers were soon dressed back into their field khaki uniforms and all seemed at peace as Hook sipped on some whiskey with a proud happy fatherly smile as he gave his brief inspection and dinner was served.

Hook had noticed the change in his boy Collins. He seemed looser and exhibited a recently discovered self-confidence as an officer baptized in combat. Hook smiled, for nothing can ever prepare any soldier for the harsh reality of deadly combat except combat and surviving it! The lieutenant was turning into a fine junior officer by the day, and even shared an occasional shot of whiskey with him as requested. Many good men had been lost and Hook toasted their memory. The evening was spent in a good old poker game under excellent torch lights near a large campfire. The night birds sang, all was safe and peaceful in the village.

Back in the ancient city in the healing temple Ambrose Cavendish had been awake for a while, talking with Pyra, who had just shown up to greet him after he was helped out of the pool. An old sage like doctor examined his healed wounds and chest with a smile and pointed to a table full of food. Cavendish was so hungry, and was soon served the best stew, with a very tasty broth. He ate three bowls of it and consumed nearly a half-loaf of bread. He refreshed himself on a sweet tasting red wine. Ravi and Ronjin had joined him and Pyra for dinner.

The talk centered on the events surrounding his near fatal wounds and the grisly aftermath of Wadsworth and his men. Ravi began to tell him more facts about the village, the Kali, and the plans for the future. Cavendish took it all in quietly with constant amazement at the knowledge presented to him. He felt something had changed in him. His senses seemed much sharper now, more than ever before. It was like he already knew as truth what Ravi had told him seemed to have had all the lore of Ravi's people embedded into his mind. He was still processing the information as if pages of this knowledge kept turning in his mind. He had seen Wadsworth's terrified husk frozen on the floor bed from his mind's eye clearly.

Many images entered his mind as he ate. He thought of Pyra and her great beauty as again looked over at her, who now wore the image of that very sweet little girl then changed back to the older version of Pyra. Cavendish was stunned at her change. She spoke warmly with a smile. "Am I still your little Angel?" Cavendish laughed for the first time since this ordeal in the village began. "Yes, …AAAAA… Miss Pyra, you will always be my Angel, indeed!" She hugged him again and kissed him on the cheek, as he felt the fullness of her bosoms and warmth of body press against him. He was moved in more ways than one!

Ravi continued to speak. "We imprinted our whole plan with you while asleep so not to worry about details. You have them." He smiled then continued. "As I have said, we are a very ancient race, the last of our kind, whittled down after millenniums of adverse interaction on this planet. Our knowledge of mankind and the other knowledge runs deep. Our powers are strong. You nearly gave up your life protecting us, and we owe you and your family the same debt of protection… Do not protest this my friend, for it is the Dao; or our way and law! You are one human who has earned this distinction my son!"

Cavendish smiled, "Ravi, with great honor I accept both your great friendship, and protection!" He then smiled at Pyra. Ravi grew serious; "This protection goes beyond your life, and to future members in it, since our lifespan runs for several thousand years as I previously stated. We will watch over your future, your children yet to be born kind sir." Pyra put an old stone carved box on her lap, opened it and removed a beautiful intricately engraved gold ring with a large carved ruby in the center. It appeared to be the largest ruby he had ever imagined. "Yes, smiled Ravi, answering his thoughts. "it is a ruby, a very ancient one that can transmit messages from anywhere from you to us. These are what we use for communication when we travel this planet.

All you do to communicate, if in grave danger, is hold this stone against your pituitary gland in your forehead, Call on us by name. Soon, either another or myself will be there, wherever you are located. "Pyra took his left hand and slid on the beautiful ornate ring. The deep red stone was mounted on a very ancient gold mount and sparkled both in the dark and light. "This ring is yours Ambrose not just to communicate, but it is a locator beacon, and to be used so we may be attracted to where you are on the planet. Keep it close dear Ambrose." Pyra kissed him as she finished. The ring automatically sized on his finger.

Ambrose Cavendish was very humbled and gave a half-smile. "Thank you, Ravi, and all of you! What if I want you and Pyra to visit, to vacation?" Ravi's ancient eyes squinted as he laughed, "Oh my Cavendish, Of course we will visit when you want us to come! You are part of our family! You just have to mentally focus your message into the ruby on me, or Pyra Angel, and we will receive your message. I must also tell you that in order to save your life, we had to use extraordinary measures only used for our people. Essentially your vibrations were raised close to our level. This is why you see, hear, and feel things differently now. I apologize for this if it is an inconvenience."

In a flash, Cavendish understood why he had seen all the things he had while in his sleep state and now awake! All of his perceptions had meaning now. Ravi divined his thoughts. "You are correct in your assumptions my friend. Much more will be naturally revealed to you as time goes on. Always be calm to access your perceptions, never be angry for they will become masked. You and your men have become family to us, and it has been such a long time since this has occurred between our race and yours. However, as in the centuries past, we need to bond once again now for a serious purpose at hand! Now we must review the plan for the upcoming destruction of the Kali and his evil minions."

They talked long into the night, both conversing about how this planned strategy could effectively work. General Blood, once brought into this arena with the shape-changers, would have his whole world rocked! He would like this plan if it was made feasible to him, if he could believe it. The long interesting conversation at the sunken dinner table finally ended, accented by the snoring of several of the Bow dogs who were sleeping near the table where they sat. In his usual way, Ravi smiled and walked away in silence as did Ronjin. Pyra locked arms with him and they took a late-night stroll under a brilliant star cast night. Ambrose felt such intense warm feelings from her, as he sensed her feelings for him. She said. "You will be leaving here the day after tomorrow after the farewell party for you and your men. The dye must be cast to destroy Kali!

Taking Ambrose's hand, she walked him into a building and down a long hall with strange circular lights suspended from the ceiling. He was curious about them. "These lights are a thing called depleted fuel. We came across them centuries ago on one of our many journeys into the Himalayas. They never go out. They were located in a hidden cave, full of things including the medical technology that saved your life." He stared at the lights and asked. "Where was this cave with all the stuff in it?" She smiled. Ravi told me it was a huge "time capsule" left by an ancient race several million years ago. This race was sadly destroyed by orange balls of flames in a huge war.

We have used many things from this place such as the device that completely cloaks Hima from the external view of outsiders. Even Kali can't penetrate our invisibility here in Hima. Oh Ambrose… the secrets within the Himalayas are fantastic and many!" She led him into a room laughing at his childhood thoughts of space creatures. "Yes, dear Ambrose, there are as many space creatures as there are stars!" They entered a huge immaculate room illuminated by a few candles and smelled like orchids. The furniture was very ancient antiqued, truly magnificent. The aura here was calming and erotic. She undressed him and neatly lay his robe over a large chair.

He noticed his clean uniform and gear lying across a nearby chair. Even the bullet holes had been mended. She then put him in bed and slowly removed her long robe revealing the most exquisite body he had ever imagined, outlined in a shimmering two-piece outfit that resembled that of a belly dancer. She then crawled up next to him in bed and they embraced. "I have a confession to make Ambrose. I have fallen completely in love with you and can't help it!" The kissing was magic and the gentle lovemaking was electric. Cavendish's heart seemed mended, but it was now throbbed for this strange beauty.

It was a night Cavendish would never forget, nor Pyra. She had never been with a human before in all her centuries, nor he with a one thousand-year-old beauty as he was yet to learn!" After what seemed blissful hours lovemaking, they slumbered deeply, wrapped in each other's bodies. They awoke in the dawn for a last erotic lovemaking session. When done, they both lay together in soft embrace. "Ambrose Cavendish, I loved you the day I first saw you, and will love you forever!" He looked into her deep violet eyes and kissed her again. "Pyra, I love you as well, very much, and this makes me very happy! What are we to do?"

She smiled at him and kissed his forehead. "It is forbidden by our law to ever have children with humans because of what happened long ago with the gene mixing and failure to keep track of the offspring. Bad things came from it! But there is no law we have to say we can't love a human. Besides, you are a very special one to us, and especially to me! So, let's be in love and be happy!" James Ambrose Cavendish stared into her eyes again. "Pyra, I promise, whatever happens, I will love you for the rest of my life!" But he had a dilemma that burned in the back of his mind. What about Jenny Farnsworth? He was in love with her as well.

Just before Ambrose and Pyra had climbed into bed, the camp poker game near the village in the small camp was intense with Rashid winning a huge pot. A small group approached them out of the dark jungle appearing in the torchlight where the scouts were all seated playing cards. Griggs appeared behind Hooky and said, 'How in hell can you have five aces in your hand! I thought a deck only had four!" Hook turned around and jumped out of his seat. "GRIGGS! GRIGGS! You live!!!!" A round of hugs was awarded as Captain Burrows was introduced, who was hugged in turn. The game ended for now and the whiskey came out. The relief from both groups was obvious. Griggs and Burrows chowed down a pan of dinner left overs as the conversation as the events of the two parties were swapped. Into the night they told their stories of the battle as Wadsworth's whiskey was passed around. A spell of relief had descended on this little party around the campfire, the only light in the absolute darkness of the rustic farm village in the jungle.

Lieutenant Cavendish walked into camp in the late morning to find his group eating a nice hot breakfast expertly prepared by a group of happy villagers who joined the scouts in the repast. All present jumped to attention. "As you were scouts!" He ordered. But they all stood, amazed at the fact Cavendish was alive, and acting as if he had never been wounded gravely several days before. He smiled at them, reading their thoughts, then looked over to Mr. Griggs. He stated. "If anybody can escape from Hell; Griggs will!" Both men embraced in a long tight hug. "Good to have you back! We were very worried about you in spite of your reputation!"

Griggs smiled from his rugged handsome bearded face, below his usually unkempt sandy colored hair. "It was not a cakewalk sir, for sure, but we gave them hell!" The men settled back down to eat as Cavendish joined them. Griggs introduced Captain Burrows. Cavendish saluted his superior and they shook hands before they sat down. "Good to see you survived the ordeal Sir, and I see you have now become a member of our scouts and adopted by the village!"

"Thanks ", retorted the captain, believe me, all of you were a sight for sore eyes, and it was Mr. Griggs who saved me from an unknown fate. Thanks for sending the natives to find us." Cavendish smiled and covered his absence from this occurrence with "No problem." The shape-changers divined his thoughts regarding the absence of Mr. Griggs. Their search for him soon began. The village had dispatched many scouts to assess the conditions surrounding Kali and his devils in the aftermath of the battle.

As they ate, Captain Burrows gave his account of the battle and loss of his squadron of lancers in interesting detail. His anxiety and depression were obvious. He cursed Wadsworth and added. "Several of us had grave doubts about this whole mission from the beginning! But we believed that we were under authentic orders. Everything seemed wrong as we were force marched in columns in unknown terrain against an unknown enemy in complete disarray and exhaustion! Then all hell broke loose and time seemed to stand still." The captain grew silent as he re-collected his thoughts against his growing emotions and continued.

"Fucking Wadsworth divided our forces at a critical point in this battle! My lancers charged in three waves on line and were slaughtering one group of these devils after the next. There seemed to be thousands of them like the blades of that tall grass. We pretty well knew we were finished anyhow. So, for Queen and Country we charged up the hill where the Russian guns were located." Burrows paused to drink his cup of tea as he tossed an ornate star-burst medal on the table. "I took this "Order of The Tsar" decoration from the Russian commander I killed as my only memento from this mess." By the time we hit the river only a few of my men were left. Snipers killed all of them and nearly got me!"

When Cavendish explained his side of the story, Burrows now saw the whole repulsive picture. "So how did the colonel die Cavendish?" With a little thought, Cavendish looked the Captain deeply in the eyes. "Colonel Wadsworth died a terrible death Sir!" And somehow the horrible image of Old Wads terrified husk of a body resonated into his mind from the eyes of the Lieutenant. The shriveled husk of Old Wad was now wrapped in a blanket and rested in the former prison storage shed to be delivered to Bindon Blood via Ravi. Griggs then spun his story of his fight, escape and evasion in true style. Then Lieutenant James Ambrose Cavendish of Her Majesties Guides moved to the subject at hand. "Gentlemen, according to future calculations we will be going back to finish the job soon. We have an excellent joint operation planned between Blood's army and the village! We will avenge our fallen comrades and destroy Kali and his devils forever!

Tonight, we will enjoy a great farewell feast in the main city tonight and will move out tomorrow. Make all necessary preparations and enjoy your day gentlemen." Cavendish settled down to a much-needed nap in the warm climate under the shadows of a large tree since he had slept little in the embraces of Pyra. The rest went about their duties and soon were sporting their white robes and swimming in the clear peaceful stream pond. They were joined by many of the village kids, and very playful horses. It was a clear beautiful day with a nice constant breeze.

The huge feast was set in the ancient city square, festooned with large decorations. The newcomers to this ancient place were still enthralled by the incredible boat ride into this hidden city. The citizens appeared as a kind handsome breed and were dressed in their finest! The feast was the best. Many toasts were made, and the local wine and spirits were outstanding and strong. It was a great celebration and lasted well into the night. It finally ended, with the company of scouts all spending a wonderful night in the city as guests of the kind residents.

Many of the scouts seemed to disappear in the company of beautiful village women as the night progressed. Cavendish lay in bed next to Pyra, whom he had shared a great evening with laughing, and clowning about. They constantly laughed at Hook and his collection of Bow Dogs mulling about him all night. Even when he scored a pretty lady, his two favorite puppies had to sleep with them. What a bond they thought. Hooky was obviously the new village Bow Dog Master!

As he lay with his beauty after making love Pyra spoke. "Ambrose? I know you must leave tomorrow and I see your life before you, this is all ordained in your chosen incarnation in this ancient schoolhouse called earth. I will always love you, and," she smiled, "I will be around when you need me, to visit, to talk, to love!" He sensed her melancholy feelings and looked deeply into her beauty and her large soothing eyes, "I will always love you darling, and hope we can be together as well. Love does not separate but it will always keep us together!" Pyra would need to learn of Jenny; but Ambrose sensed she was well aware of her. They gave each other a long embrace in a room which smelled of rich lavender.

The light flickering from large candles illuminated the ancient granite walls, which Cavendish found extremely interesting. Future archeologists, if permitted to ever research this place, would find them to be in excess of one million years old. The etchings of animals, people, spaceships, and scriptures etched on the walls would tell them the true story of life on earth long ago. This truth etched on these walls would be hidden to humankind well into the next century, until the multitudes of aliens would pay earth many visits and appearances. They would raise the question of the real existence of alien life once again to the human race! The cataclysmic death of a whole world civilization had donated this ancient city to the race of nameless ancient shape-changers, keepers of good and of truth!

With everyone finally collected from the long night of celebration, the group left at mid-afternoon rather than dawn. The dawn muster was impossible since there was nobody at the morning formation. Finally, everybody returned relinquishing their robes for proper British military dress. They left down the ancient road continuing away from the valley of death guided by several villagers including Ronjin.

The wagons, all the extra food, horses, rifles, swords, side arms, ammo, and unnecessary supplies were left behind for the villagers. It was the final gift to the village that had saved them.

The scouts were going to ride fast anyhow and needed to keep their loads light to expedite a fast trek back. The villagers guided them from the road into a well-made trail to the river where they safely crossed. Ravi waved at them as they passed him and he said "I will see you soon my friends, fear not!" They were about a tedious three-day ride to Chital. General Bindon Blood would be expecting them since word of their return had already been implanted with the general by the very active Ravi. The lieutenant focused on what was to become his next mission as he rode back south in the heat and dust of the northern part of India. He sensed that It would be the biggest one in his life in this strange world he found himself! My how his life had changed since the Battle of Malakand!

CHAPTER SIX
REVENGE SERVED COLD

Guided in the safety of the villagers. the long venture out of the huge foreboding jungle was pleasant and thankfully uneventful for the group returning to Chital. They did backtrack after they crossed the emerald tinted river to check if the bridge constructed by Wadsworth's forces still existed. It was intact, as they momentarily sat viewing this last remaining vestige of Wadsworth's folly. It had been built by hands that would never build again. There were no signs of life, or green devils guarding the bridge. It seemed as an invitation for the next army to come in and die. The only life forms were a new batch of large crocodiles skimming in the slow currents south of it.

On rode this party for the couple of days across the quite different barren wastes of north India to the south which changed into more habitable forests as they neared Chital. In the late afternoon on the third day the group saw a very welcome sight as they approached the new massive defensive fortifications built north on the outskirts of Chital. Well-fortified breastworks ran in a semi-circle away from the main road to the north, so any frontal attack would fall prey to deadly artillery crossfire from the ends of the circle. Hook laughed when he saw it. "Hey, LT! Looks like the British have employed their artillery like the horns of the buffalo used by my old friends the Zulus!" Cavendish and Griggs, who were in earshot smiled back at Hooky.

After hailing the pickets, they rode in a column through the opening in the center of the breastworks and came upon an artillery lieutenant who saluted Captain Burrows, placed at the front of the group. He returned the salute crisply. The artillery lieutenant was looking up at them squinting from the sun's final glare of the day and asked "Are you from Wadsworth?" Captain Burrows looked at him "Once; in a manner of speaking! We need to see General Blood as soon as possible; he is waiting for our reports. Tell him that this is Lieutenant Cavendish's party of scouts returning."

The name Cavendish moved the watch officer as if he had been hit by lightning bolt. The name was now connected to many rumors spread from the command tent, generated by the report from Corporal Hoskins had well permeated the camp. The rumors of green monsters, of hideous cannibals abounded throughout the command, as did the complete slaughter of a whole relief force rebounded from this name. The artillery officer summoned a horse and mounted it. "I will personally take you to him in all haste, follow me!" They rode for over twenty minutes through stockpiles of military equipment, tent cities, and large groups of soldiers. They rode into a city once destroyed, that was being rebuilt back to normalcy in a great pace by swarms of engineers.

They observed a large encampment of all sorts of British regiments on both sides of the road with their regimental banners gently flowing in the breeze as they passed. It seemed that their tent city ran for miles. It appeared that the General had something big in the works. Soon they were in front of a well-guarded large white command tent next to the old administration building formally occupied by Cavendish, which now seemed an indiscrete reminder to the horrors it had held when they first came upon it. These events seemed like years ago, now.

The artillery lieutenant jumped from his mount and entered the tent ignoring the two guards who had snapped to attention. In short order, General Bindon Blood appeared in the entrance of the tent smoking his pipe. He appeared as a refined well-cut gentleman; with predominate white hair and well-trimmed white moustache. His khaki uniform was immaculate in all respects as he studied his guests for several moments with his head slightly cocked to the right. Then he smiled as both Captain Burrows and Lieutenant Cavendish, who cleared their mounts and saluted him. He gently, but firmly returned his salute.

"Please enter my humble abode my fond guests," he began, "I have been waiting for your arrival!" The general then turned crisply and reentered the huge command tent. Within a short time, the scouts had been led to a large mess table and for the next thirty minutes were served the best meal. Finally, as they finished, they were ushered into a huge partitioned portion of the tent, which served as Blood's sentimental office and war room. Sergeant Hoskins, newly promoted along with Sergeant Cornwallis, met them at the entrance. As Cavendish entered, he saw Major, now Lieutenant-colonel Tiberius Nephew who gave him a big hug.

The next thirty minutes were reserved for handshakes, backslapping, hugs, and jovial banter. General Blood greatly enjoyed this reunion and ordered a bottle of cognac and box of cigars. The stories of Nephew and Hook's escapes from the grasp of Wadsworth resonated just below the laughter. An orderly placed a box of cigars and a bottle of cognac on the table next to several tin mess cups. General Blood tapped his tin mess cup on the table to get their attention. "Before we begin, let us drink a toast for all our sacred fallen comrades with retribution in it! The tin cups were filled and passed around to commemorate the fallen with a healthy shot of cognac. Cigars were passed out and fired up.

Promotions are in Order by order of the Queen!" All present stood in quiet at attention. "Lieutenant Ambrose Cavendish you are now promoted to the rank of Captain!" Everyone clapped their hands, as now Captain Cavendish saluted the general, and waited as his new rank was pinned on each shoulder. Sergeants Hoskins, and Cornwallis helped the general. Next came the promotion of one-color sergeant Hook to the rank of Sergeant Major, who then had his rank handed to him by the general via the new Captain Cavendish. Hooky smiled and replied. "I plan to hold on to this rank this time sir!" The general, very aware of the legendary soldier to his front patted him on the shoulder.

Then came the promotions of both Rashid to lieutenant and King George to sergeant major of scouts. There was a round of applause. Finally, BG Blood looked at Sergeant Griggs. "You are to be promoted as well! My authority is promoting and restoring you to the rank of First Lieutenant as a chief of the Guides scouts. Once again, my son, you are an officer, and the negative aspects on your record will be expunged." He then smiled at the group. "You are now all directly under my command as my special scout section boys! It is my understanding that we have work to do!" corporal Holmes became the next to be promoted to sergeant. The immaculately dressed general then looked at the young 2nd Lieutenant Collins. You are now promoted to the youngest lieutenant in the history of the British Army!

The general ordered everybody to be seated. "Sergeant Hoskins gave me Cavendish's after-action reports of your part and the others in the attack on the Kali's castle." He looked at Captain Burrows and patted him on the back. I was unaware that any British officer under Wadsworth's direct command survived the battle. I will personally take care of you son. You are now directly under my command for the duration of this campaign. I will get your promotion to Major in order." Captain Burrows thanked him. Blood smiled, "strange promotions and awards in strange times my boys!"

There was a round of applause as the general's orderly poured each member, minus Rashid, a new large shot of very expensive cognac in army issue tin cups. It was a heartfelt moment, as Bindon Blood verbally reviewed not just the accolades of Cavendish, and the others present, but of the tragedy which befell so many under Wadsworth. All could see that the general was sickened by this terrible event! He raised his cup. "I make this renewed solemn toast to all the brave soldiers who fell in battle many days ago. It was one of those moments when the bonding of brotherhood was at its best.

Newly minted Sergeant-major Alfred Hook asked general Blood if they could make one more toast. Everyone laughed since they knew that it was a way Hooky could get another good shot as a new round of Cognac was poured. The salty scared old veteran raised his tin cup. "I now make a special toast to the memory and ultimate sacrifice of my Gurkhas Lord Nelson, and Gladstone! May our revenge be served extremely cold and deadly! God Save the Queen! Hip Hip Hooray!" They all, including the General repeated the chant, and finished their cognac. More cognac was poured as Havana's finest cigars were fired up. Blood stoically looked at each person present in deep silence. Minutes passed as he formed his thoughts. The kerosene lamps had been lit and the reflections of candlelight cast an eerie set of shadows on the tent walls as night manifested.

Ambrose sensed Ravi and his group of villagers standing outside the front of the tent. Ambrose looked in their direction and smiled since his vibrations were in concert with them. Ravi smiled back and entered the tent with his men all cloaked invisible to the group within. The general paced in front of the scouts taking a puff from his Maduro. "Before we continue with our next campaign plan, I must let each of you survivors of this terrible ordeal in on a little secret. If you notice how fast the engineers and certain contractors are rebuilding Chital? According to the official Crown policy, Chital was never attacked. Nor was there ever any misguided campaign by Wadsworth that claimed the lives of hundreds of empire troops and British personal. This order comes directly from Queen Victoria! This never happened for reason. What else will happen is now under tight security wraps.

Many of the dead soldiers will be listed as killed in action in the battles towards the Khyber Pass. Others, including residents here will be listed as dying of an outbreak of the plague. This includes Wadsworth. History is being remanufactured sadly." He took a serious drag on his cigar and gave is stoic business look. As I said, this is by direct order from the Queen, her top advisors and the heads of Parliament. I do not know all the reasons gentlemen, but they are related to an incredible breech of command leading to the massacre of a whole army by one terrible upstart. What a huge embarrassment for King, Army, and country! The culprit who issued the bogus orders has confessed and was dispatched by a headsman's axe aboard the ship carrying him back to England. It seems the poor bugger jumped ship in the ocean to grab his head!"

The silence turned into laughter at Blood's sudden humor. He continued. "Also, regardless of the rumors, we do not want to give official credence to our Pashtun and Muslim enemies of any confirmation that a British army was wiped out. They may entertain new ideas of attacking us. We are still fighting and defeating them in areas around the Khyber Pass. Your reports of this Kali and tragedy have revealed this new dangerous threat to us. All these units around you are not here according to official reports. According to the news, they are either in their respective garrisons or deployed to the northeast frontier in combat. They think I am negotiating a peace treaty at the Khyber Pass now which I left up to my generals in private. The truth of this horrible reality will probably stay sealed long after we are gone from the planet."

He took a puff off his cigar and continued. "This "secrecy" was passed on to me via crown dispatch signed by Queen Victoria personally at the Khyber Pass with instructions. How she knew about the general details of this mess is a mystery to me but she is adamant on her word. No outsiders have been allowed in Chital or this region for that matter. Now that you know of the official blackout, we can continue. "MUM" is the word gentlemen." Cavendish moved up close to where the general sat, and respectfully took another shot of cognac and lit a fresh Havana cigar. Cavendish had a strong impression of how the Queen knew about the situation because of his new enlightened perceptions. He smiled and knew it was time to introduce the general to his unknown very special guests standing invisible on the side of the group.

"Sir," began Ambrose, "You are about to learn that there is more to this story! We have some unusual allies to help us destroy Kali." The kerosene lamps cast strange shadows as they moved in the breeze that passed through the area. General Blood looked at Cavendish, "I am sure there is more to this strange story son, but I still wonder how the hell I will be able to meet and defeat these bastards in a jungle environment who will be waiting for me! They have to know we are here in mass by now." "AHHHHH Germania?" Came from behind the general, picking up his thoughts and fears. "Germania will not occur here kind sir!" Ravi had spoken.

General Blood was surprised at how his immediate thoughts were spoken as much as the sudden appearance of the natives next to him. He turned and noticed several individuals who had appeared from nowhere, standing next to Cavendish. He stared at what appeared to be two very ancient and exalted men wearing turbans and long robes who bore long smiles. Four warriors stood behind them. Blood wondered how they had divined his thoughts so clearly and how they got past his tight security cordon. The Destruction of three Roman Legions seemed to vex him at this point as it had already happened! He feared that this would happen again!

Cavendish interjected. "Sir, may I introduce Ravi, the headman of the village and Ronjin, his second. It was the efforts of these men that saved all of us from certain death after the ill fated battle and the ones we had to protect from Wadsworth's insane drunken madness before he was killed. They can help solve the question that perplexes you now." Bindon stepped up and shook hands with both Ronjin and Ravi as they mutually bowed in respect, "My pleasure gentlemen!" Ravi smiled then bowed. A third villager produced a body wrapped in a blanket and laid it on the floor. Ravi took the center. "Before we have our meeting, we felt it correct in returning the remains of this Colonel Wadsworth to you for disposition sir."

Cavendish looked at the general and added. "Colonel Wadsworth and most of his staff escaped as his forces were being overrun. We ran into him on the same road to this village. He was going to slaughter the village and met with a very unpleasant death along with his men sir." Bindon Blood walked over and yanked the blanket off Wadsworth's body. He stared at it in detail for a minute. He saw a horrifying terror filled waxen death mask. Its sunken eyes protruded from a shriveled husk still in a red blouse and with his pants around his boots. It definitely was Wadsworth, beset with an unmistakable terrified death mask; with all life sucked from him.

"What happened to him?" Asked the general as all present viewed the body. Hook and Griggs were standing close and the burley new sergeant major snickered. Blood looked at him with a crisp smile. "Well speak candidly Hook!" Hook now began laughing since he had been told about the whole escapade of Old Wad's demise. With a straight face, he spoke "If I may truly speak candidly sir, I heard that he received a really terrific demonic blow job…a real heart stopper!"

Blood smiled and looked as everybody stared at Old Wad with his pants down. The whole crowd then burst into a bout of resounding laughter. Sergeant Major Hook had scored again. Blood looked a hard stare at them. "Hooky and Griggs; take this disgusting thing out to that bonfire and pitch it in. Let the flames help us forget the memory of this fool, but never his fatal blowjob!" More laughter resounded as the NCOs whisked Wadsworth's light waxen corpse outside and pitched it into a nearby bonfire. The mummy husk of "Old Wad" went in a puff of flame, like a dried branch from a dead tree.

After a short break, the group was joined by the general's top staff officers. All were seated around a long set of camp tables. Security was tight which included several shape-changers working security beyond the tent area. A round of hot tea was poured for each since it was closing on midnight. Captain Cavendish began, keeping the help offered by Ravi as close to the accepted bounds traditional scouts could play in helping General Blood's forces move on the Kali's Green Devils undetected. To explain what the shape changers were really up to would make little sense at this point to rational people. He offered the plan in conventional terms rather than in those of the shape changers. He felt it wasn't enough to convince Blood.

Ravi sensed this as he laid out all the new dispositions collected by his people. The bridge, which linked the massif to the castle, had already been rebuilt and another large bridge had been constructed to connect the huge plain with the castle keep over the new river course. He told the general that the main dispositions of the devils in the valley since their camps had remained unchanged. The dispositions of the remaining Russian guns had changed. The two guns that had their wheels intact had been hauled to the top of the part of the small ridgeline between the castle and valley that did not fall into the river valley. It was very high ground that viewed the expanse of the valley. They were controlled and manned by Russians. They over watched down the valley to the jungle and were a great danger to any army at the end of the valley. They had to be destroyed before the British army appeared at the end of the valley.

The other two guns with wheels broken in the fall into the deep crevice were situated under heavy Russian guard in the castle area. They had been elevated and from the description were to serve as long range mortars. A new group of Russians had arrived and seemed to have brought a small amount of artillery ammunition with other military supplies. The approximate remaining size of the greenies numbered in the area of twenty-five thousand effectives with more entering the ranks daily. Ravi did not want to waste his time trying to explain the ways of how Kali recruited new soldiers. That was food for a later conversation.

Ravi was reading the general's mind which was swarming with so many conventional questions and doubts at this point. So, he walked up to the general with a smile. "Come with me alone for a minute sir." The two men left the room just behind a tent flap separating the rooms while the assemblage of soldiers began to swap tales and stories. "Let me give you a good picture of what has occurred and what we will be able to do in helping you." Ravi then looked into the general's eyes and grasped his right hand firmly in his hands. In what seemed as hours, the complete panorama of events flashed into Blood's mind like some future motion picture. He saw the Kali for what it was, it's threat, and all events surrounding Wadsworth, the battle and aftermath.

He then saw the monstrous flying creatures in the dark with huge fanged heads that resembled the faces of wild cats. The general took a seat at the table as this whole testament was absorbed. His first words were. "This Kali was Cortes the conquistador?" Then he continued as the panorama raced through his mind. "My god, they have turned all the captured Punjab's, Sikhs, and British personnel into devils in some sort of zombie ritual!" Then his vision focused of Major Pillroy spit roasted for the pleasure of Kali's dinner. He then saw the cruel cannibalistic disposition of all the slain men of Wadsworth's command and he was sickened to his heart. What concerned him most was the thousands of green devils standing motionless in long perfect rows guided by one mind.

General Blood's interest in Ravi's comments was total now. The panorama Ravi had given him continued to produce images now focused on the lay of the land and the plan. He was completely mesmerized for a trance that crossed his mind in less than five minutes. The general could actually see in his mind's eye how the battle would develop and cumulate in broad actions. He was versed on the unusual stealth and deadly abilities of the Shape changers. Bindon Blood, giving a rest to the Implanted vision looked at Ravi, who smiled at him. "I think I need a cognac kind sir! Join me?" Ravi smiled his smile for he loved cognac. Bindon added, "I am fascinated by your insight and grasp of military operations. Sounds like we will be able to pull it off in good order with your incredible abilities Ravi!"

He elaborated. "In the Battle of Chancellorsville in 1862, General Stonewall Jackson won a great victory against superior Union forces in the American Civil War. He placed only a small force against the main Union army as a very dangerous ruse. He moved the main bulk of his army secretly behind the vast union army and attacked them there. He used the tactics of being obvious to the enemy in a ruse defense posture and held the Union to defend on a prescribed front, all the while moving the main force in secret to deliver the surprise victorious attack on the unsuspecting union rear! Deceive, surprise, and violently attack! This was Stonewalls winning philosophy!"

General Blood was amazed at the images still passing through his mind like one of those viewers that showed photographs which were very popular now. They then returned to the room full of people. Blood now looked serious and grave as he continued. "Deception will be our guide in this campaign gentlemen! I intend to destroy all of them for Queen, Country, and for vengeance!" Ravi and Ronjin smiled in silent agreement as they both were thinking about an old Asian friend in their past who wrote the book, Art of War, who called these deceptive maneuvers as using the "Zheng and the Qi!" to win in battle. Ah the past, Ravi thought, Sun Tzu was a good man and true master of warfare.

General Blood then finished the meeting. The vision Ravi had given him had completely informed him of what needed to be done and the unusual support he would be provided by the village warriors in snuffing out the "eyes and ears" of those devils observing him. If his army could get inside the domain of Kali and be in position of the ruse before the battle started, it would be a Turkey shoot. The battle plan had been mentally etched in his mind to be manifested in detail in the morning. General Blood knew that Kali was the main target of Ravi as the green devils were the target of his army. He then gave his final address for the evening.

"Gentlemen, it is very late and we all have work to do in our preparations to defeat these savages. We will plan the execution phase of this plan of attack tomorrow!" All present exited the tent. The visions Ravi placed in the general's mind would visit him even after he fell asleep. Ravi and Ronjin were pleased. Implanting the whole mental picture in Blood's mind had saved a lot of time and cleared up obvious skepticism. He knew now that as the British army destroyed the Kali's army and breached their defenses, Ravi would, with other chosen warriors from the village, be hunting this abomination in the castle keep. Kali was going to die this time! The curse and threat to Hima and mankind would end and would be over.

As Ravi bid goodnight to Cavendish, another form ascended from the night shadows. It was Pyra in all her beauty. They held hands and walked to a place Pyra had prepared. They sat together in a sweet embrace, and exhaustion soon succumbed Captain Cavendish into a deep slumber in her arms. She watched him as he slept and gently stroked his head. She had never been so taken by a human before, never in the thousand years of her life. He was very special to her, for he had exhibited the best qualities, and had risked his life. She gently kissed him

She knew, in great sadness, that when all of this was over, he would be leaving India forever. Pyra also saw a woman in his life named Jennifer, a human, unlike her. A woman that loved him as she loved him. Pyra was not jealous but the opposite. She loved this woman since she loved Ambrose! Pyra knew that because of her great love for him, that she would never really leave his side; for her love for him was pure, and in pureness was the one word. He would be loved completely by two women from two different worlds forever. Everlasting! She then whispered her favorite quote from the book Les Miserable: "Such is life!"

Bindon Blood awoke and reviewed all that faced him and sucked it up as a professional under great duress! So much was on the platter now. He had a job to do, just like rolling up the Pashtuns! Planning for the military campaign began after breakfast at 0700 hours the next morning. All commanders present were in high spirits, ready to get on with the plans and begin the execution phase. Soon after they gathered, Ravi and six of his men appeared to join the meeting. Both Hook and Cavendish eyed the six men, all dressed and armed resembling tough swarthy fighters.

They gave off very mutual smiles as they looked into their eyes, for they were all friends from the village, in quite a different appearance. Cavendish nodded his head in jest as Rashid also nodded his head in respect. Old Hooky was the only other besides Cavendish and Rashid who knew. It would be a rather scary experience for all the humans if these warriors showed up in their true appearance for hunting green devils! Blood first allowed Captain Cavendish and Ravi to give an in-depth rundown on the enemy they faced and the terrain layout they would fight in Tiberius Nephew, in the mix since last night, was becoming a fast friend of Ravi and Ronjin's.

The plan called for the village scouts to be in front many leagues dealing death to devil scouts! They would be followed by Cavendish and his scouts who would interface with the regiments of Gurkhas and Highlanders behind them. Then would come the two main attacking groups comprised of what Blood called the ruse and the other called the ambush! These elements would move in one cohesive three-tiered formation spread out many miles to the front and flanks of the army as its advance north. General Blood was far from forgetting Ravi's mental enlightenment the night before either. He thought that "British cold steel" would be plentiful in destroying the green devils on the battlefield. The door would be wide open for Ravi to finish his very ancient mission.

The officers and NCOs charged in leading the main attack formations were brought up to speed in this meeting as all assignments were given. Ravi then gave details about the line of routes for the three British attack elements. He explained the obvious one from the river to the plain used by Wadsworth to be used by General Blood's group which was the ruse element or the bait. He then explained the route of the second huge ambush force and the cave complex. It would leave the main trail after crossing the river and head into the jungle towards the secret entrances of the caves.

Unknown to Kali, there was a little-known system of large ancient caves that went from the jungle many miles west of the river crossing under and through the huge massif to the plain below the large series of cliffs. The village knew all about these underground cave networks, filled with more remains of a long-vanished civilization. This cave system was huge and Blood's flanking force would literally come out of the massif well behind the army and encampments of green devils. The cave entrance facing the valley was sealed and camouflaged. The green devils would be forced to engage in attacking the bait led by Blood exactly where Wadsworth had made his fruitless last stand. Once the flanking ambush force, complete with screw gun light artillery emerged from the caves and positioned, the devils would be caught in a dangerous crossfire from both elements.

The attacking force at the castle would go a completely different way and cross the river some ten miles west of where the main army was to cross. This route would take them across the mountainous high ground, past the village and into the massif facing the rear of the castle. They would conduct the opening salvos in the battle like Cavendish's scouts had done before. That night, Ravi implanted the complete scenario and terrain features in the minds of the commanders as they slept. There would be no confusion in this plan! Ideally, the main force of green devils would be caught between the main force at the opening of the valley, with a dozen batteries five-inch howitzers, two squadrons of mounted lancers, and six regiments of infantry.

The force moving from the cave system would bring a dozen mule laden screw guns and another three regiments of infantry waiting in a huge ambush once the fireworks began at the opening of the valley. This three-pronged attack was now the plan. Stealth in the attack would be of paramount importance because the Kali was very obviously aware of the huge buildup of British forces in Chital and was on his guard for any movement north by them. However, proper deception created by the village warriors in their slaughter and replacement of the many devil scouts arrayed from Chital to the grassy plains in the valley. These shapes changed villagers now devils would tell Kali's commanders the British Army remained in Chital and was not on the move.

Captain Cavendish laid out who would be in the various attacking formations. He had included all his people in the attacking force on the castle to support Ravi's people. Colonel Nephew was on board with him. Captain Burrows and Lieutenant Collins, with three village guides would escort the flanking regiments of the ambush element through the caves. 2LT Allenby, not forgotten, was assigned as one of the commanders of a howitzer company at the end of the valley with the bait or ruse. General Blood never forgot who was connected to this strange affair. Tonight, the shape changers would begin negating enemy eyes within the Chital area and beyond before the army even mustered to move. The main base at Chital was guarded by two Punjabi regiments with the task of creating the atmosphere that this camp was fully populated just in case.

This meant that the last real message the Kali would receive before the British sprang their attack was, they were still encamped in Chital. General Blood wanted his army to travel light as to make a fast deployment to battle. Except for extra rations, ammo, water, and a blanket, all unnecessary equipment such as tents were left behind. If any eyes continued to watch Chital, they would see all this equipment in the camp, complete with hundreds of tents spread out in neat order. All regimental guides were left fluttering above their respective areas and dummy artillery pieces had been constructed using logs and wagon wheels.

All the support troops left behind were instructed to man them and mingle routinely among the long rows of empty camp tents as if they lived in it. After the devil observers were killed in the vicinity, a couple of villagers would remain near the Chital encampment to intercept and destroy any new venturing eyes from the Kali. Ravi was also aware of the abilities of the Kali's closest minions who had been manufactured with many of the qualities he possessed. If Kali was aroused and suspicious, his minions could be airborne to view the area a lot faster. This was one dangerous variable to this blanket of security.

The shape changers and those close to the Kali shared deadly abilities and included telepathy. Several of Kali's minions had been conditioned to fly when they observed Wadsworth's approach. The Kali's fabricated assistants were dangerous amateurs in comparison to the warriors of the Village but the problem was that there were so many of these altered demons! Ravi sighed at the obstacles facing him from this multitude. But he had good backup now to not just destroy the army of Green Devils, but to deplete the ranks of his bodyguard. The opportunity to kill the Kali would be hard endeavor to say the least! He would not fail this time!

Ravi and the elder shape changers longed for the moment when chaos created by the British army in the attack could work in their favor against Kali rather than aid him in his evil past! They would get a clear target on this elusive old fallen one; this destroyer of civilizations! It was obvious the British army would create ripe conditions. Ravi knew how to kill it, but wondered what method would finally kill it. The specially created forged long daggers was one method they knew from old. However, the daggers offered a slow terrible death. Kali needed to die quickly! The elusive Kali was given time in the 16th Century and he shaped changed into a dog, escaping them in a pack of them. There would be no dogs this time or anything left alive near it. They would be hovering above the castle waiting for their moment to end the evil reign of Kali!

The eyes of many savages had indeed been watching the huge buildup of General Blood's forces since they began arriving for nearly a month in Chital. They expertly used their communication net to convey the information back to the Kali routinely. Ravi knew this since his people had already been observing the green devils in the Chital area. They had all been identified along with their routes to the next tier of messengers who, in turn, related the information back to the next party of observers and so on. A whole network of these devils was positioned at various points from Chital back to the jungle and then from the jungle back to the castle. The evil one and his chief minions were constantly apprised of the situation from the castle lair. Using his devils was much easier for Kali than dispatching his winged bodyguards. He had other interests at hand as he relished the great victory over the British!

The replacement of green devil observers began at midnight the next night. The first green devil observation post to be altered sat just north of the huge defensive perimeter. The three devils were eating some cold rations when they looked up to see three more of their men walk into where they sat. The first of the new devils told them they had a message for Kali, an important one they had learned. As the attention of the devils focused on a phony dispatch, the messenger dispatched two in front of him with one deep talon slash across their throats. The third devil bolted from the position, but something winged landed talons in the scampering green devil's back. He was torn to pieces in seconds. It was the ancient rule of the village; if you had to use violence, then use it correctly!

After observing the faces of the slain the three assumed their looks and now moved to the next collection point when more devil messengers unsuspectedly waited. Then, the shape-changers would destroy and imitate the messengers as they moved back to kill and imitate more of them in this chain of spies. In this manner, by sunrise, the eyes of the green devils observing the British would cease to exist and be absent for miles in front of the army as it now marched north. The next important target of the village was clearing devils along the banks of the emerald green river into the jungle. The information passed to the last real devils by the river was the same as verified by the familiar faces of green devils reporting it. The British were still in Chital.

The forward scouts under Griggs had been moving at a steady pace for over two days north screening the front and keeping in close communication with the village warriors who were the vanguard. Captain Cavendish, Colonel Nephew and his scouts were close behind them and Griggs. Keeping the communication between the forward elements and the main force was wide open. After two days of forced march, secrecy was maintained. The green devils had been systematically wiped out along the way to the second river. Cavendish, because of his operation and altercation of his vibrations, kept a strange mental communication with the shape changers working to his front and was thankful.

He had observed these silent guardians sitting or perched on the high hill rock formations in the barren land guarding the forward elements at night. They seemed invisible in the daylight. He saw some of them as magnificent birds of prey that seemed to be having a good time hunting. They were hawks and the devils were the rabbits, or more like rats! With his new mindset in tune, he was able to see what their eyes saw and the deceptive kills they were racking up along the way. As he followed them, they acknowledged his presence. Telepathy was incredible!

Only in the end of the third night of the rapid march did it stop a few miles before the river. The village sentinels were conducting a thorough cleaning of greenies in the jungle facing the river and beyond. A patrol party of greenies had approached from the river to get within a couple of hundred yards of them. All these green devils were programed to relate information to their unconditioned superiors who were prime targets. The only conscious feeling the brain-dead devils possessed was physical danger as a self-protection element. Cavendish and Nephew had joined Ravi and some of his warriors in their small resting place near the river. It was late at night and these greenies had been hidden from detection inside a cave near the river.

Ambrose bore mental witness to the dark shapes alerted and now gliding in the night. The terrifying silent violent deaths these crazy green devils endured lasted brief moments. He saw them scatter in terror along the hilly trails like rats when attacked. Then one by one they fell prey to the huge unforgiving talons and fangs of the shape-changers that flew, hovered and dove into their ranks killing them all. The unconditioned leader of the devil patrol was tossed between two of the winged night stalkers in the air ripping him to pieces. Most of the other devils fell prey to the warriors in human form who needed to borrow the identities of the slain to keep moving forward in the jungle with phony information to the next group. No quarter was asked or given. The war of complete annihilation had begun at Chital was moving into the valley of death!

Ravi had told him the golden rule of war. "If one must wage war, then it must be a just war in self-defense only; never for aggression! The purpose then is to completely destroy the enemy where they can never oppose you again! The handmaidens of violence and terror must apply in total to the combatants and to the terror driven fears of any survivors. The green devils, because of their unique character as brain dead robots were all doomed! The power these shape changers possessed was disturbing to Cavendish as he settled into sleep. He could not imagine them as his enemies! But in his afterthought, he remembered that he was facing one; the Kali! Griggs stood guard along with Rashid after this violent event took place.

They could not see the end of the green devil patrol to their front as Cavendish did, but sensed something grim because of their honed instincts. Everything was strangely silent to them now. They did not have the visual insight Cavendish had. It was during this uneventful guard duty that the trusted Indian friend told Griggs the story and activity of these unusual beings and the ones they faced. Griggs listened in quiet amazement as he smoked his pipe. In all his days, he never expected to find this reality only born of myths. Old soldiers like him always hear all the strange superstitious tales. but he was now living in it in pure amazement.

After the devils were eradicated some distance into the jungle, the army began marching across Wadsworth's bridge with zero opposition. Two pontoon bridges were also constructed to aid in the speed of the British into the jungle towards the field and caves. Ravi was proving to be a man of his word to the extreme amazement of General Blood. Kali had been left in the dark. Everything was pitch black in the jungle this night. Tiberius Nephew, sitting on his horse next to Cavendish offered him a shot of cognac from his flask as he spoke. "I can't imagine that Ravi can find all the enemy spies captain. Is it wise to just stop here?" Then he looked at the renowned new Lieutenant Colonel Nephew and took a plug off the flask. "Sir" he began with jest, "you have no idea how safe and secure we are now!"

There was a great fear of Ravi's that Kali could offer a dangerous disclosure of this plan if he chose to observe or even send out his special minions if alerted in any way. Kali had the trait of being very lazy and loved to binge on opium and wine as he performed his evil hobby on his human captives. These vices were a helpful distraction now. Kali had thus far been given to the reliable message traffic in a network he had designed. According to this elaborate source, no British were coming and were still encamped in Chital. How could so many spies fail in this? The devil messengers reported to his field commanders, then disappeared into the jungle heading back towards another line of messengers waiting a short distance back for any new changes in British dispositions. It was a solid chain of messengers and spies. If the chain was broken in anyway, then he would know immediately. All was well at the castle as it seemed.

But the Kali had completely underestimated everything. His chain of spies was not broken, but annihilated methodically! He never ever estimated that the shape changers he hated would form an alliance with the British! Besides, they were still in Chital! Meanwhile, winged death stalkers continued to destroy hundreds of devils assigned to security and scouting as the whole British force continued moving towards the valley of the Kali. As the green devils were silently torn to shreds on the dark trails, their replacements continued spinning the false information to the castle. The British army moved forth. It was known to the shape changers that the bulk of the Kali's army was resting in a very disorganized fashion within their myriads of small camps in the valley beyond the forest.

In a sad note, the bodies of several conditioned British empire troops were recovered after they were killed in the advance. They were still wearing their tattered uniforms covered in green dye, tattoos, with filed teeth. The body of one deceased conditioned British officer was delivered to General blood. He was shocked at the condition of this body. If the Kali would have been aroused to the British invasion, with his call, the thousands of green devils in the valley would form up into their silent long rows waiting for orders. This had not occurred. The shape changers left them alone for now. However, using the shapes of green devil commanders, they would create havoc within the Green Devil ranks later during the battle. The masked approach of the British army was an incredible success as the British began to move into their assault positions.

The phony reports on the British continued to pour in from the shape-changers long after the forces under MG Bindon Blood had marched his main "bait" force in the jungle next to their battle positions. The regiments headed for the labyrinth of hidden caves had already moved into them to be in position before the main attack began. The combined force of scouts, Gurkhas, and a regiment of Highlanders had already arrived in their assault positions along the massif behind the castle. The force of Gurkhas led by Griggs and several village warriors disguised as hooded green devils were in their assigned positions ready to attack the Russian artillery positions on the bluffs facing the valley. They were the alpha of this attack meaning they would be the first into combat!

Everything seemed well in Kali's kingdom. He had continued his opium and wine filled evil binge for three days now. His close unconditioned advisors stayed clear. There was no alarm anywhere in the land of the green devils, as the continuous false messages seemed to kill any suspicion. The usual astute awareness of the Kali was now completely fogged by his vices and complete lack of divining anything amiss from his tower in the castle. He was completely occupied with torturing, raping, and killing the few prisoners he had chosen for his sport left. He would attack one victim as Kali, then the next as Raktabija! The Kali loved this power over these doomed people. The extreme terror and pain he inflicted sexually excited him as always.

His high opiated drunken state and focus on his doomed prey dulled his exterior perceptions completely over the last couple of days now. His minions always stayed away from him when he was like this. A few had been consumed by him before when they interrupted him. Therefore, no one in authority had issued plans to his army as they remained in a disorganized status across the valley. Even the usually skeptical Russians were drinking vodka and singing songs at their encampment near the front of the main castle entrance. They always stayed clear of the Kali except when formalities necessitated their appearance. They all lived in terror of him, her, or it?

Earlier in the day Captain Burrows and Lieutenant Collins entered the hidden cave complex with the guides from the village along with the commanders of the two regiments and village guides. It had been late in the afternoon when they came to the very well camouflaged entrance to the complex of caves. Once inside the cave opening, the caverns grew in size as the column, with horses laden with artillery and shells moved forth. As noted in the briefings, these caves were huge and regiments, taking the right path, could walk through them with little strenuous effort.

The engineers began lighting the torches as the troops began to pass into the cave opening. Extra-unlit torches were handed out as well. The regiments of infantry and artillery were mixed with a dozen very light howitzers in the tow of blindfolded horses began their interesting journey deep within the cool cave's recesses. It would take another three hours for lieutenant Collins to gain position at the end of the huge cave complex. They would be ready in the dawn for war.

He was amazed at the size of these adjoining caverns as the regiments moved in loose formations, often marveling at all the secluded remains of some lost civilization invisible in the darkness as they moved on through this labyrinth. The torchlight revealed many interesting artifacts hidden in complete darkness amidst many small flowing waterfalls and pools of mirrored dark water. The ancient architecture and glyphs were consistent to the ones inhabited on the surface by the shape changers. Long dead was this civilization, another bonus for future archaeological hunters perhaps!

Captain Cavendish was very surprised at how safely his force had proceeded as they made their journey to the massif behind the castle. There had been any sign of green devils. They had set out nearly due west in the dawn hours with many village guides and made an easy sojourn across an easy river crossing. The initial climb from the river to the top of the ridge was handled quite easily by his small but very agile force. The ground ahead, as he remembered it from before became rough and hilly forest terrain. They were in their final positions and preparing for their concentration of attacks on the castle and area below.

Each regiment in the "bait" prepared itself for a sudden huge thrust onto the plain from the jungle in the dawn. They all fixed bayonets in anticipation of the violent struggle that awaited them. The coordination of the movement of all three elements into attack positions was related by the telepathic communication of the shape changers. In this manner, General Blood knew constantly the progress of his three groups. General Blood wondered how this was possible and thought how great it would be if his army had this ability. The status of the green devil army in the valley was verified as unchanged.

This attack would not be the disorganized piecemeal lurch of disorientated British troops as the green devils and Kali had seen the last time. The advance scouts leading the huge "bait" force of Blood's on the widened jungle trail earlier had found the scattered remains of Wadsworth's dead army as they ventured along it. Pith helmets, parts of uniforms, broken sabers, wrecked wagons, looted content containers, and broken rifles littered it as they moved to the edge of the triple canopy jungle. No human remains were observed. The forward elements of the British advance guard watched in silent awe as they viewed hundreds of campfires burning among the hodgepodge of villages created by thousands of enemy combatants in the distance.

General Blood was further pleased when he heard all his other elements were moving into their assigned attack positions on schedule. He was in position and ready for the fight to begin! The shape changers, with precision communications between his elements had confirmed readiness for battle. He also had in his arms inventory a newly formed Gatling gun company with eight of these new quasi automatic weapons that arrived as special delivery to him just before they left Chital. He had five guns with his command to support his infantry, two with Burrows and the last with Cavendish. The hostilities were coming soon, like the sunrise, where life and death would embrace together this day. Such was war and coming soon!

Blood's powerful "bait" holding force would open up the fight at the end of the valley after the Russian artillery of the bluff was destroyed. The bait would be dangled in front of the green Devil army below. After the massed green devils had all moved to engage Blood, the "Zheng" force would exit the caves and set up their huge ambush trapping the enemy between two regiments of artillery and two full regiments of infantry.

The lancers, to the far left of the main force in the valley would then close in on the devil's right flank from the jungle if needed. They objective was to drive the retreating devils into the ambush between the two British forces and make sure none escaped the battlefield later! No prisoners were to be taken! Unlike Wadsworth's smaller ill-prepared force, Blood's force numbered several thousand professional troops with five times the artillery. The mysterious but highly effective warriors from the village had comprised deadly force multiplier and an incredible battlefield deception to this mix.

The Kali leered from his opium and wine high at his close advisors around the fire pit in the middle of the castle tower. The messenger reports were the same. The British were still at Chital! The temple roof had dropped one whole story in the explosion and sat nearly level on the remains of it. The grand central tower next to his open roof temple had remained unscathed in the explosion. Kali was now withdrawing from his drug induced high and sitting on his dais in a half trance. His focus was no longer on the victims he had raped, slain, and eaten. His fogged mind offered him the suggestion of attacking Chital and wiping the British off the face of the earth! He was amused at this thought! Why not? Let his conquest of India and the destruction of his enemies begin!

Dawn was coming soon and a couple of shapeless flayed victims of his evil wrath were strung to the side of his throne missing their tasty body parts cut from their bodies and devoured by the Kali as he hungered during his rampage. The seven-foot giant with the face of a chiseled demon licked his lips as his fogged dark soul now panned the area. The opium had made him thirsty. He requested more wine as his advisors nervously made their reports. Everything seemed to be well, too good it seemed to the Kali. However, the super aware sixth sense of the Kali was kicking in and seemed to indicate something was amiss; out of balance somewhere. His observers would never lie. This remote uneasiness had been itching the back of his drugged mind for hours. What was it he wondered?

All his manufactured guard and commanders were soon dismissed with the exception of his two special conditioned confidents, who had been blessed by the Kali with special and similar powers as he. Loyalty had its rewards even in evil world. His other confident had been killed in the previous battle against a still unidentified force that severely damaged the castle, destroyed his guns, destroyed his river bridges reeking deadly havoc. Yes, what was strange was that his deceased confident had been killed with a spear or something similar stabbed under its jaw up into its skull. Bullets? It could have survived bullets as Kali would.

Kali wondered if the village had been responsible for killing his third confident? They had been lurking nearby since his attack on them long ago. So many British potential recruits awaited his touch at Chital! Thousands of them as he had been told. When he defeated them, he would have an army to condition all the Pashtuns! There were so many of them! Kali knew the village had no part in the British attack because they kept away from humans as a rule. Only one body of a Gurkha had been recovered in the wake of the attack on the castle. Were they working with the main British column or were independent? Kali took a long drink of the sweet red wine and it soothed his throat. The remains of this lone attacker decorated a wall on the staircase to the tower since the attack. This war prize was in the last stages of massive fly infested decomposition.

It telepathically imparted orders into the minds of his special confidents. "Give me an accurate picture of what is going on from Chital to the plain! I have serious concerns for some reason!

Something is not right! Go in great haste!" Kali gave a long fang-infested smile to his close associates, which gracefully bowed, transformed into dark-winged creatures and were gone, flying into the night from the tower. Kali was in the process of transforming more of his confidents into these special winged demons. They were to be very important in his planed destruction of his rivals in the village in the near future! He knew that sooner or later he would have to deal face to face with that accursed Ravi.

The two minions of the Kali flew high in the sky and glided first at a quickened pace far above the jungle, then barren wastelands heading for Chital to view this first objective. This was the card that Ravi feared would be played by the Kali! It was too late! Kali was also late in realizing that his unsettled feeling had nothing to do with the British at his door, but with the close proximity of the shape changers now closing in which he had sensed! Within an hour, the dark ugly rat like creatures soared above the area of the massive encampment north of Chital. At first all seemed to be in place. Piles of equipment seemed everywhere, horses tethered, and sentries moving about in gun positions in the camp. The British artillery pieces in the camp seemed professionally fixed in their many defensive positions. Torches from many points lit up the area in the pre-dawn. Groups of troops idly walked around.

Seeing no one around the forward artillery positions, one landed on the long barrel of a large artillery piece in the forward defensive semi-circle. It noticed no metal ring when its talons abruptly landed on it. It scratched the barrel and a groove of shaved wood appeared. After further inspection the dark creature discovered the barrel was a large wooden pole. It found that the rest of the artillery on the line were dummies constructed to look like functional cannon made of wagon wheels and thick rounded poles. The other one had flown close to the hundreds of tents bivouacked in neat rows along the road. It began peering into many tents finally realizing over and over that the bedrolls were stuffed with blankets.

With the exception of groups of guards moving into the tent areas suggesting the presence of a sleeping army, the army was gone; but where? Kali soon picked up their mental notes as his winged scouts headed north towards the river and jungle in great haste. Their search for the British army was on as other airborne eyes now followed their flight. As both minions closed on the river, they saw to their shock two huge pontoon bridges with the original one in the middle! They were guarded by many British troops with an area loaded with supplies! This seemed impossible since all their messengers who claimed that the British army was still in Chital! Then Kali saw it; there were no green devil scouts or spies anywhere!

The British army was deep in the jungle! The minions were just beginning to see concentrations of many British troops moving on the trail below through brief openings in the jungle canopy, when the one to the rear felt a terrific pain as powerful talons slammed into its spine and head, driving it hard down a hundred feet into the jungle floor. The nearby British troops jumped in amazement as they witnessed two powerful flying creatures smash through the obstructing triple-level fauna of the jungle into its floor. There was a brief thrashing and terrible screeching noises…then it was as quiet as it began.

They witnessed a huge flying creature stand and stare at them. It's face and head resembled that of a huge Tiger, vicious behind huge yellow glowing eyes. In an instant it flew off in great haste crashing out of the jungle above. Fearfully, a few soldiers lit torches and began search of the area with guns drawn. They soon discovered the ravaged remains of another huge winged night flyer who was different than the cat. It resembled a large fury flying rat like insect with a horrible face and had a long stinger projected from its backside. The soldiers all wished the sun were coming up soon and the battle would start!

The Kali sensed the final moments of his confidant and winced at its brutal end. The shape changers in league with humans! Kali was riveted in shock now. In an instant, he next picked up the observations of his second confident sending distraught babble. It landed near a group of green devils barely escaping another winged pursuer which left. Kali's confident folded its huge dark wings in its tall menacing form and approached what it thought were devils.

It had been completely fooled. In an instant, imitation shape changed devils attacked it and hacked it to pieces with their spears and razor-sharp scimitars. The Kali had ordered it back at great haste and before it died sent one last message. "They are here with the British!" "They" automatically meant the shape changers, his nemesis now confirmed, as he saw the brutal end of his second close confident and bodyguard! Kali now realized why all the information was wrong.... the shape-changers were here and had worked their magic replacing his green devil scouts and spies; eliminating them as they left Chital! Kali screamed in anger for he had been completely duped, fooled like an idiot!

The Kali knew his close proximity of these enemies of old was what had disrupted his subconscious! He had picked up their vibrations! How in hell did they have an alliance with the British? This was impossible! He flew into a blind rage for several minutes. Kali instantly recalled all of his commanders and sent them to lead the devils he had just mentally mobilized for war. He guessed that the British were in the same area as the last bunch because of the trail. He began to focus his will down to his mind-controlled army. The thousands of green devils soon formed up into their silent still ranks to the concern of the British who were waiting for them.

Kali then aroused his special bodyguard to protect him from any surprise attacks. He sensed Ravi was coming for him again and he had no dog to escape in this time! They had near mortally killed him in the Caribbean, but he had fooled them with his body double and made a good escape! He laughed and imitated a dog's bark! His mind's eye now saw hundreds of British lined up inside the jungle. They were more of them and had immense artillery. The stupor of Kali was now given over to anxious panic.

Since the winged minions of Kali had focused on the British army in the jungle, they had not discovered all the British forces in place on the massif behind the castle. They obviously never saw the ambush force inside the cave system either. The three-pronged attack would indeed be a grave surprise for the evil one! Sergeant Holmes joined by Hoskins found their old firing positions in the massif still filled with expended cartridges from the last time they fought there. They both were armed with their best sniper rifles now and plenty of ammunition. A brand-new USA made Gatling gun was positioned behind them that could hit targets below, on the castle walls, and especially across the way to the bluffs if snipers were there again!

Several platoons of Gurkhas had descended down the steep vines on the massif under the guidance of King George and were going to wreak havoc below as the main force of Highlanders were positioned in to attack and take the newly replaced high massif bridge to begin their invasion on the castle. Behind several shape changed devils, Griggs was leading combined force of Scots and Gurkhas to destroy the Russian cannon on the summit of the precipice. This was the first objective with the attack now in motion.

Cavendish sat alone checking his weapons as Ravi approached. Cavendish could see something malevolent; unsettling, dark deep in his eyes when he said his words. "Today is the last day of this Kali! He will be destroyed!" Then Ravi adjusted himself and smiled at his adopted human son. They were part of the attacking force invading he castle; Ravi by air and the lieutenant on foot. Ravi looked at the British officer with a twisted grin. "I bet the Kali knows we are at the gate by now! Good luck!" Ambrose gave the old sage a thumbs up and he observed Ravi change into a tall winged black cat-like creature complete with wings. He could see the smile in its large yellow eyes; it was Ravi all right.

Off he went flying at great haste into the pre-dawn light, low to the top of the jungle towards the castle. Cavendish noticed other dark-winged specters joining Ravi with their awesome broad-winged forms etched in the ball of the rising sun. The imitation green devils killed the guards in their trenches near the guns. Griggs and his Gurkhas stormed into the gun positions as a violent but quick brawl insured. In short order the guns had fallen into their hands and several flares were shot over the valley to inform Blood. The "bait" force now moved quickly in order from the jungle to their preset fighting positions.

The "ambush" force viewing the thousands of silent green devils lined in their formations was waiting for them to move into their attack until they could move out of the caves and set up shop. As Griggs and his group seized the Russian guns, the shape changers imitating green devils made quick work of the cloaked devil guards the end of the rebuilt rear massif bridge. The Scottish Highlanders followed close behind them charging down the massif with fixed bayonets busting into a charging wave of black cloaked screaming greenies!

As the regiment of Gurkhas stormed into the area below the castle sniper fire from across the river from the bluffs began to take a toll. Holmes and Hoskins began pouring fire at them but realized there were just too many enemy snipers returning fire this time. The sniper duel had begun poorly but Holmes added a nice twist now. He crawled up next to the Gatling gun crew and under his direction, he directed the Gatling gun to fire heavy bursts at suspected targets on the bluffs with the rapid fire of this weapon at seven hundred rounds per minute. As the bursts moved back and forth across the bluff, the effect was immediate! Many tree branches and bodies cascaded from aloft into the river. The sniper fire from across the way was silenced.

Holmes having a ball now ordered the Gatling gunners to turn their fire down into the area below and around the castle. Meanwhile the fight on the bridge was now a giant brawl. The "Ladies from Hell" had wiped the first wave off the map to a devil! Then came another sizable counter attack from the devils which was welcomed by the Scots with cheers, yells, bayonets and fists. The devils had met their match and soon lost complete control of the bridge. The Scots brawled into the castle.

Hell, was in store for the sons of the Kali! The sun was shedding light into the peaks of the valley now as the attack on the castle grew. The swiftness of the attack had overwhelmed the guns on the remaining bluff in minutes. No quarter was given nor asked. Sergeants Hoskins and Holmes were now sniping targets on the castle walls with occasional sniper fire still from the bluffs across the river. The Gatling gun now directed to paste the walls of the castle manned by a large compliment of devils. Masonry exploded and many devils were killed, but their fire still came at them.

Hoskins now had a brilliant idea. He had been watching the activity down below with concern as the Gurkhas were having trouble reaching the walls or entering the sally port of the castle. The large number of defenders were holding them at bay. He grabbed his German sniper rifle, leaving Holmes to continue with his deadly work and ran at full speed towards the recently captured Russian guns up on the summit to his front.

The Scots, killing the devils to their front, now charged down the long bridge ramp into the castle and became further engulfed in a death struggle with a wall of determined and unusually powerful tall green devils. They were forced back into a quick defense, dropping many enemies with concentrated close-range line volley fire. The bloody stalemate was broken as the shape changers descended into the rear ranks of greenies and began to wreak death and havoc upon them. But most of the village warriors had one purpose today; kill Kali! The reduction of the force protecting Kali was ebbing by the moment.

The Gurkhas and Scots fought forward as violent hand-to-hand combat continued on the top levels throughout the fortress at this point. The battle was moving slowly towards the redoubt where Kali and his deadly minions were now engaging powerful violent attacks from their winged adversaries. Cavendish, Nephew, and Hook from the front of the huge Scottish brawl broke free of the fight and headed towards the temple and tower. The smoke and dust from the explosions and rifle cast a foggy pall across the castle area as the sound of distant artillery and rifle volley fire was evident to the British in the killing fields in front of General Blood's "bait" at the end to the valley.

Meanwhile, Hoskins, who left Holmes with his new toy directing fire with his new friends with the Gatling gun, searched for Griggs in the post combat debris around the captured Russian gun positions. The slain bodies of both greenies and Russians littered the ground as he walked up. He knew Griggs had orders to destroy them. He reached his buddy yelling. "Griggs! Oh, Griggs!" He yelled over the din catching the attention of the top Gurkha NCO in charge who was crouched near lieutenant Griggs beside the large wheel of one of the guns. The sniper fire from the walls of the castle had been pinning his men down since their attack. "Let's turn these guns around and help our boys attacking the castle Griggs!"

The Gatling gun is doing a splendid job but can't seem to get many snipers hiding in the castle parapets, firing on our boys below and here!" Griggs and the Gurkha looked at each other as a cruel smile crossed the newly promoted lieutenant's bearded face. He looked at Hoskins amid the dust and smoke. "Capitol idea sergeant!" He then snapped orders to his Nepalese cohort with a cruel smile of the new plan. Sniper activity was forcing the attackers down as they turned the huge cannons around facing the castle. Hoskins set up at the end of the bluff and immediately began supporting the attacking force below with effective sniping. It seemed that when he dropped one, another would appear.

He watched the Gatling gun firing cutting furrows in the castle wall protecting many enemy snipers obscured by the battlements. Soon the two huge Russian guns had been wheeled around and began firing. The Russian guns below had been captured and already destroyed with satchel charges by the Gurkhas led by King George. The first four artillery rounds fired into the front of the castle keep blew the huge gate and one of the towers to pieces. The next several salvos finally hit their marks on the walls infested by snipers that protected them from the Gatling gun. The rounds blew huge holes into the walls destroying them. Large chunks of wall and bodies fell into the area below.

Griggs now ordered a new fire mission. It was a shame to waste good artillery ammunition! He had his Gurkhas aim the artillery pieces at the huge bridge spanning the new powerful river course between the narrow openings at end of the valley. The bridge was filled with hundreds of green devils coming to relieve the beleaguered castle. There had been no plan to destroy this bridge but with a grand smile Griggs ordered the artillery to take it out.

The large caliber rounds began blowing large sections from the causeway style bridge which connected the castle across the newly cut river to a long bridge running along the adjacent bluff then out to the large valley. The last several rounds hit the bluff close above the bridge and caused a large landslide onto it. The hundreds of green devils on the bridge and causeway disappeared into the river to feed the giant crocs among the wreckage of the bridge and landslide. The multitude who did cross were now mowed down by the Gatling gun which had a perfect field of fire from the bluff.

The bridge was now completely destroyed. Griggs, now loving his new post as an artillery commander saw the next target pointed out by his Gurkha NCO. The next target was to blow a clean hole into the south castle wall that would allow the Gurkhas on that side a new access into the castle. After several well aimed shots the wall shook and crumbled leaving a gaping hole. The several rounds that pulverized the south wall of the castle created a huge screen of dust.

The resilient Gurkha and infantry now poured into the large hole and lower part of the castle with bayonets fixed, Kurri knives flashing and screaming battle cries. The happy Gurkha NCO, manning the guns, with kind advice from Griggs, soon turned these guns around on the valley to wait for any targets of opportunity. The Gurkhas fighting below were moving towards their Scottish companions fighting above. The remaining devils were soon being sandwiched between the attackers from above and below. No quarter was given; all green devils were to die today!

His much-reinforced advance guard, armed with five Gatling guns, had moved quietly into the valley just before the attack. In less than twenty minutes the British "bait" army commanded by General Bindon Blood spilled out in perfect order organized for the impending attack of thousands of Green Devils. The formations of silent motionless green devils were signaled to attack. They moved in massed formations double timing towards the bait.

The green devils came in a massed organized line of attack spreading throughout the tall grass in a huge semi-circle towards the hills now filled with British troops. This rolling sea of violent green now let out a huge collective scream as it went into attack mode. The British firing lines and artillery waited silently. Then the order was given to open fire. The direct fire artillery, Gatling guns, and firing lines opened up in mass. These first three waves of green devils were slaughtered as their bodies piled high in the tall grass.

The battle seemed to accelerate as the mindless devils drooled for a fresh kill on a British army devoid of fear. Like Lemmings running off a cliff, they kept committing their army into the British slaughterhouse! The savage charging ranks of devils, led by their cloaked battle leaders moved in mass with no knowledge of what was forming behind them from the obscure cave system completely unknown to them.

The Gatling guns, firing lines, and artillery firepower continued pulverizing the attackers as they attempted to engage the British at close quarters. General Blood was amazed at the size of this huge violent relentless enemy he faced! The tall grass was purposely set on fire by sappers a hundred yards in front of the British positions by pouring a stream of oil in a shallow trench across the forward battle area.

The rising flames soon trapped hundreds of greenies between the flames and the British steel. Multitudes of wounded green devils roasted to death in the encroaching fires. Fire scared the devils as many tried to run from it. Blood held his regiments of lancers in the jungle behind his flanking firing lines. They would be unleased soon after the trap had reaped its bounty of devils. As the main body of savages had evacuated their camps by the river in front of the massif and moved to attack Blood, the British regiments fresh from the cool caverns, briskly moved into firing lines along the bank of the swift river formed by the massif water falls.

The ambush force had the smooth chest high fast-moving waters of this river in front of them as a natural defensive barrier. They set up within eyeshot of the green devil camps as they heard the explosive battle shaping up some three miles to their front now. It was obscured from direct observation by clouds of distant smoke, the tall grass and patches of trees. The howitzers disbursed among the infantry in elevated positions were ready for action. The two Gatling guns were set on the line of infantry. The ambush was ready.

In a little over an hour of hard fighting, the slaughter of the green devils attacking Blood's force was a massacre, as the savages withered under the huge firepower and fires. The horde of devils not trapped in the fires soon ordered back to regroup. Blood's artillery pounded them relentlessly as the green sea moved back out of the killing zone. Thousands of the devils were dead or dying in front of the British guns. Part two of General Blood's offensive was now beginning. Thousands of green devils began to regroup in the crosshairs of the ambush force!

These devils began to form firing ranks imitating the British firing lines aimed away from the ambush force behind them. They were waiting for the charge of the lancers like the last time. They waited in vain as the complete line of ambushers opened up behind them with artillery, Gatling gun, and long firing lines. The impact of the first volleys completely destroyed the firing lines aiming away from them and many green devils waiting near the river.

The green devils were under a deadly surprise attack from behind! In the mass confusion, a giant shoving match ensued between retreating devils and the ones trying to defend this area from the perceived attack by the lancers. The artillery guns from both British positions found their deadly mark on the tightly packed confused throngs of greenies. The telepathic messages conveyed from the Kali to his few surviving battle leaders were disheartening to the monster now trapped in his own dangerous predicament His ancient enemies were closing in for the kill and many of his protectors were dead. Escape was his final plan since he knew all was to be lost today!

The forward observers and village guides continued to pin point the assembly points for the artillery on masses of green devils hidden in the tall grass or clusters of trees. The crack of the screw guns heralded the incoming rounds and end of many devils. The British ambushing rifle regiments became the dying focus of the remaining horde of greenies as the massive crowd under some command turned and charged directly at the ambush force positioned behind a berm across the fast-moving narrow river. Both the Gatling guns opened up joining the cacophony of rifle firing lines.

The giant mob, shaken by the direct fire moved as one towards and into the river like a wounded animal wanting revenge on its tormentor. Hundreds seemed to fall at the water's edge and in the fast-moving river as they charged. The screw guns now lowered their barrels commencing direct fire as the greenies were struggling before them in the river. It was then the British began to suffer obvious losses under sporadic rifle fire and a wave of flying circular saws released from the savages. Hundreds of green devils now jumped into the fast-moving waters of the river to cross and kill the British.

The barrels of the Gatling guns were white hot as rows of devils were mowed down! Many devils struggled with wounds slipped under the waters of the fast-moving river. The smell of cordite laced smoke added a thick haze along the river. The bodies of hundreds of slain greenies covered the riverbank and beyond. The fast-moving semi-deep river turned red with their blood as their torn bodies floated away into the jungle as a bounty of fresh meat for the residents of the jungle.

Then came two complete squadrons of lancers busting from the jungle to finish the job of harvesting green devils. The huge organized mass of green devils was broken, floundering like a headless chicken in the chaotic mess of battle. Blood's artillery went silent as the squadrons of lancers eager to have their day, swung a huge "L" formation out of their hidden positions inside the jungle. The hundreds of mounted lancers busted into the reeling mob of mindless green devils very aware now of the danger facing them, as lances and sabers introduced the reality of violent death. The mindless greenies crashed through the many small encampments as they ran not from their conditioned non-existent fear, but were blindly floundering to be reformed by their leaders and attack! Most of the black-cloaked leaders had been killed or were dying in the tall grass.

Kali was focused on his own situation developing in the castle and had lost his focus and control of his green devil army now being destroyed below in the valley. The rifle regiments extended their lines down to the huge magnificent two-thousand-foot falls and continued killing green devils at close range. The lancers had begun the grim task of killing anything green that moved to the front. The follow-on Punjab infantry units finished off the wounded and killed small groups that had evaded the cavalry charge. In every case the brain-dead green devils, having no emotional emotion to survive, fought to the bloody end. Kali's army of the dead had not failed him as they were destroyed.

Dealing absolute death would continue to the sound of distant bagpipes on the massif behind the castle now under fatal attack. What the bullet or artillery shell didn't kill, the bayonet, fist, or saber did. The British controlled Russian guns on the heights fired random shots into the large groups of savages below. The Gurkhas under the command of lieutenant Griggs were having a field day. He ordered the guns to stop when they saw the regiments of lancers, in a perfect "V" formation, move from the smoke-filled end to the valley past the ranks of infantry regiments and swing in a wide arc towards the masses of devils moving in confused groups towards the bridge that was no more.

No savages were to be captured or spared per direct orders from General Bindon Blood, as requested by Ravi. Revenge for the slaughter of hundreds of Wadsworth's British Empire troops was violently served cold today! The only prisoners that would be taken in the whole battle were eight Russians with three wounded who surrendered. They would later be handed over to LTC Nephew for interrogation. Then would disappear into Great Britain.

As the Battle in the valley was reaching its zenith, the Gurkhas and Scots continued their violent life and death struggle against strange forces inside the castle. Hoskins had returned to the sniper position with Holmes. They took refreshing plugs on a bottle of whiskey to calm their nerves. Both snipers watched the huge fight visible to them from their position. Holmes and Hoskins were running low on ammunition and the Gatling gun crew was completely out. Holmes invited the crew behind the fast firing gun to join them. There was nothing at this point they could do. The main action was in the castle and the time of the Kali was growing short!

Any mortal human who watched the horrendous battle between the village and the forces of Kali were scared out of their wits. The Kali had moved back up into his central tower with many of his fabricated warriors as a shield. Many of his special minions had already been killed by the winged cats, but mainly by the ground forces pressing their violent attacks. In sadness, several shape changers had also been killed or wounded. Kali and his minions were dangerous in all respects! The savage minions were dying, succumbing to the horrible wounds of the Scots, Gurkhas, and especially the shape-changers. The violent "fog and friction" of direct hand to hand combat existed throughout the castle as it slowly faded into the favor of Blood's army.

It was apparent to the Kali that all was lost, and that it was time to escape. Hadn't he done this in the Americas twice now? He would rise again elsewhere before Ravi got him! The stairs leading into the temple were now filled with ferocious Highlanders mixed with Gurkhas that had fought their way up from below. The combat was vicious! King George and Rashid were with them in this fight now. Cavendish and Hook in front of the charging Scots, fought their way into the ante room of his tower. The ferocious defense of the black-cloaked devils was remarkable and desperate. Even the village warriors were having a rough time dealing with these dangerous holdouts, but were prevailing slowly.

With the shotgun ammo gone, Hook and Cavendish had emptied their pistols at point blank range and were down to sword, Zulu spear, and Kurri knifes. The violent life and death brawl continued. The Kali was now isolated in his large stone tower grabbing the bags filled with things he wanted to take with him in this new exile. He was mentally figuring the best path to fly away on. He did not want to meet the warriors from the village now. The brawl between the savages and British just moved into the room below the tower stairs. Sensing the Kali with his new mental perception, Cavendish sprang up the stone stairs leading to the tower chamber. He sensed Ravi very close.

The Kali's group of conditioned familiars were all dead but one. This last familiar appeared between the stairs and his leader to give Kali time to exit. Like a drifting ghostly specter, it blocked the stairs facing Cavendish with a long twohanded sword. The captain pulled out his unused Colt .45, forgotten in the close quarters fight and carefully emptied four shots point blank into this demon. It moved backwards from the impact as the captain emptied the last two shots into his very ugly demon face. This rather large ominous green devil seemed different than the others since his bullets did not seem to hurt it.

As the specter was about to swipe Cavendish's head off with its scimitar, SMG Hook busted in between them spearing it in the throat with the bayonet attached to an empty rifle. His Zulu spear was lodged in the chest of another greenie on the stairs. As his bayonet struck home, the sword strike, intended for Captain Cavendish, missed its mark and cut deep into the sergeant major's left arm, decapitating it just above the elbow. He and his severed arm fell back down the stairs cursing aloud, into the melee below.

Cavendish now looked at the evil fanged smile of this black-eyed devil, as it cleared the rifled bayonet from its chest. Cavendish stumbled back against the wall, as it came for him displaying a cruel evil smile of triumph. Cavendish then heard the pitter-pater of an object bouncing next to him. It was the ironwood Zulu spear recovered by severely wounded Hooky and tossed it to him. He yelled at his leader.

"It worked before use it now!" Just as the rat-insect faced monster raised its sword high to strike him; the lieutenant plunged the spear hard into the demon's throat up into its skull just like Hook had killed the other one. The forward motion of this demon was only temporarily halted by the fatal wound inflicted by Cavendish. It staggered past him and fell down the stairs taking the battered Sergeant Major Hook with him to the bottom.

It was dead and a very battered and bleeding Hook rolled off to the floor clutching the Zulu spear in his remaining hand, covered in the dark greenish blood of the evil minion. Hook was bleeding profusely from the stump of his left arm. Captain Cavendish, ignoring Kali had jumped down the stairs to save his beloved NCO. He barged through the brawl and quickly grabbed a nearby-lit torch attached to the castle wall. He stumbled to him, who was awake, still cursing, and bleeding everywhere. "Hooky! Hooky!" Yelled the captain in the loud din of the fighting, "This is going to hurt, but I have to stop the bleeding!" Hook nodded from his position next to the wall and held out the stump of his left arm, cut clean above his elbow.

With that nod, Cavendish carefully pulled up his stumped arm and carefully pressed the hot flaming torch against the gaping wound. Hook grimaced, then let out a loud scream as his wound was cauterized. He leaned back against the wall, sweating profusely from the heat and the pain. "Captain, can you reach into the left top pocket of my blouse and fetch my flask? I seemed to have lost my left-hand sir! I need one now!" Cavendish crouched low dodging the continued scuffle, pulled the flask of whiskey out, unscrewed it and put it in Hook's right hand. He took nearly half of it in one gulp. Captain Cavendish obliged him then quickly reloaded his forty-five revolver as he ducked against the wall. He handed his .45 to his sergeant. "This will keep them off you SARG!" Hook gave a cryptic smile and handed him the spear. He forced his words painfully.

"Get that evil motherfucker my son!" Thanks Hooky, got to go for now, hang in there!" Hook smiled as Rashid and Lord George shadowed him with Kurri knives and pistols drawn. Nobody would get close to their favorite burly wounded sergeant. Cavendish now stumbled back up the staircase through more smoke towards the top of the tower, Zulu spear in his right hand, and reloaded service pistol in his left. He felt like he had been fighting the whole week today, and his torn, soiled, and bloodied uniform seemed to confirm it. He was terribly beat up and this was not over yet.

The Kali with his two large bags strapped to his body, was moving to the huge open window in the tower to make good his escape. Certain doom awaited him here. He was enraged at how well he had been duped by the strange combined forces of shape changers and humans that had attacked him and completely destroyed his empire and plans to pieces! Kali morphed into an image of a flying cat to fool his pursuers. This was better than a dog he mused. He wondered where Ravi was, for he had not seen him yet in this battle!

He sensed a presence at the top of the stairs. Ambrose had busted from the door way and was confused as he saw a winged cat. In an instant, he sensed that another powerful being had arrived. It was Ravi, dressed in his preferred form as the old wise man. He spoke with a twisted smile at his arch rival in its disguise! "Finally, we meet again! It has been a long time Oktoo, if you remember your original name! You came back to destroy us and conquer the world? Looks like this day will end you!"

Oktoo shape changed into the large seductive and sinister goddess Raktabija. She gave a gruesome evil smile and a leer followed by a high-pitched ear shattering wailing laugh. "Why Ravi, after I destroy you and your village, all I was doing next was preparing to bring the best out in mankind!" He laughed. Now I must..." "Go?" retorted Ravi. "Go somewhere else and use your powers to create another dark age?" "No Ravi, I call it civilizing…HAHAHA!" It continued to laugh then continued "mankind is weak and has never learned anything in this age or all the others, nothing! Play on their greed for power, material wealth, and religious superstition, and use all their evolving war technology…and I have an eventual winner every time!

I will win Ravi and win until you are gone forever and your race of benevolent ancient watchers is erased! I will be back!" Then, with its pompous declaration concluded, Kali? Raktabija? Cortes? Or just Oktoo now dove from the large open window into the daylight as Ambrose watched. He looked at Ravi who was smiling now. Then, in a sudden twist, the dark winged Oktoo bounced back through the open temple space to the floor. Ravi yelled. "Otkoo!! Ha… you have no wild dog to hide and run from me today?"

Otkoo launched a hard-slashing motion at Ravi's head, his descending talon smashing it full force. But the Ravi he hit was a well disguised likeness and Ravi's head burst into feathers and scattered like confetti into the air. Where was Ravi? It assumed the shape of a flying reptile like insect, then flew out of the tower again being thrown back by the invisible barrier blocking its chosen exit with great force. Kali or Oktoo smashed hard back on the floor of the tower as his bags were torn from him by the force. Then it felt great pain in its face.

A claw had come from nowhere slashing deep grooves through its evil mask of face now encased in a silver mask. The buzz saw attacks by the old sage continued unabated as Oktoo screamed in mortal pain and fell to its knees. Unknown to Ambrose, wounds delivered between shape changers were real. When Cavendish looked, he saw the image of a broken and bloody woman calling him. She was begging Ravi to spare her? Then he saw Ravi, in the image of the huge winged cat move to finish it saying! "Both Kali, and Raktabija die with you today Oktoo!" But in the last second, Kali bolted to the door and careened down the winding stairs into the room below. Then it saw Captain Cavendish, who it knocked out of the way off the stairs as it jumped into the chamber below full of Gurkhas finishing the brawling with greenies.

Ravi quickly jumped down beside the captain into his form as sage. He helped him recover from the ground and peered at the forms of several men frozen in place, stopped in their fight by what they sensed was among them. Ravi sent him a telepathic message; "He has changed!" Ambrose was looking around the room and saw Hooky sitting next to the wall where he had left him. Something was wrong with Hook. Ambrose mentally tapped into Ravi. "Hook lost his left arm and now he has it attached back sir!" Ravi immediately sensed that it was not Hooky as did Ronjin who was entering the room now.

Ravi threw an ancient bejeweled dagger at the form of Sergeant Hook like a flash of lightening. It stuck clear through his chest and it wailed inhumanly aloud. The seated form of Hooky was no longer, for it was the Kali once again struggling with a long dagger stuck to the hilt in its chest. Kali could not pull the dagger from his chest as he wailed. The Gurkhas scattered down the stairs terrified sensing a much different fight now. Ronjin speared Kali in the throat as it leapt back against the wall in fearful pain.

Other shape changers disguised as Gurkhas came for the kill now shedding their images. Then there was a short powerful explosion of something that filled the room with an eerie light. A huge hole in the tower wall was now evident as Kali was gone, fallen over one hundred feet to the rampart below. Ravi and Ronjin were hot on his trail now and followed the Kali off the tower. Ambrose noticed pools of a greenish-black liquid, which he sensed as blood from the Kali. He then turned and ran down the stairs. As he jumped to the first landing, he saw the real Sergeant Hook feeling the effects of whiskey and morphine, still under the protection of the Gurkhas.

They were moving Hook to the stairs just as the mind's eye of the Kali must have seen him and imitated him without getting a visual on his missing left arm was the thought that possessed Cavendish as he ran past him. The captain, clutching Hooky's Zulu spear, ran out of the tower at the bottom as many British troops viciously scoured the area mopping up the remains of the devils. Ravi and Ronjin were standing above the rampart on a stone wall peering across them viewing everybody including Cavendish. Their faces resembled those of wide-eyed Owls now as they scoured the area for their ancient target.

The captain nervously began to walk among the many soldiers on the rampart gripping the Zulu spear tight in his right hand. He was following the strange blood trail as Ravi measured his thoughts back on the wall. He then stopped and casually looked up to see a British officer giving crisp orders to several troops near him in perfect English. What was wrong with this picture thought Ambrose? This officer, this officer dressed in a red blouse? He knew this guy and had heard his voice and even talked several times with him but where? His stressed mind was racing to find the answer.

Then, the reality of who it was struck him like artillery explosion. It was Pillroy? Major Pillroy, Wadsworth's missing headquarters commander from the battle who was not among the surviving staff officers at the village! He shielded the spear by his side and now yelled as he approached the paunchy rotund officer who was ignoring him and still giving orders. "Major Pillroy! Hey Pillroy! So, glad you could make it today!" The major looked into his eyes that revealed the dark evil grimacing demon to Cavendish's altered mindset. Cavendish then noticed the greenish blood trail at Pillroy's feet and the dagger in his chest partially obscured by the red blouse!

Telepathically sensing Cavendish's thoughts, Ravi and Ronjin came charging at the Pillroy image from their perch on an adjacent wall. The Kali, mortally wounded by the dagger Ravi had thrown slashed at Cavendish who ducked his sword slashes. However, as the part Kali, part Pillroy with the metallic grimace backed to the wall. Cavendish saw his opening as Kali, focused on these two dangerous shape changers coming towards him now. Captain Cavendish was close and low and like the thrust of a bayonet rifle, plunged the Zulu spear up deep into the Kali's throat driving it hard into its ugly terrifying misshapen head! Kali's head moved around in a wild rapid circle as it wailed like a thousand banshees! Captain James Ambrose Cavendish continued pressure on the Zulu spear up into its skull just like the other one he had killed in the tower. All those present in the area froze in abject terror at the piercing wails and inhuman screams.

Cavendish stumbled back falling hard against the rampart holding the Zulu spear, covered with blackish blood dripping from it. Kali settled to the ground on his knees with dark blood gushing from his throat. Then old images Kali disguises had imitated through the ages of his evil tenure with mankind reflected briefly on his dead face like a strange panorama. Ravi swiftly beheaded Kali with a lightning strike from his scimitar. Its severed head bounced upon the rampart. The end of this evil fairytale was concluded! The lifeless headless huge twisted body of Kali sprawled in a pool of dark blood on the parapet. Then in an instant the huge corpse exploded into flames.

Both sages looked at the captain, who just started into nothingness, holding the bloodied Zulu spear in hands. He was in shock as to what he had just witnessed. Ravi brought him out of it with a kind pat on his forehead and stared into his confused eyes. Finally, Cavendish's mind cleared and he sat down against a wall. He looked into Ravi's smiling eyes and said "Odd Zogs Ravi, What the fuck was that?" Ravi and Ronjin both let out great laughs "It was a; "What the Fuck!" Added Ravi back to his human son. They all laughed together at the comment. Ronjin held up the twisted severed head of Kali and the beautiful dagger recovered from the ash pile left by the burnt body of Kali. He spoke with a grin. "We got him before he could change into a stray dog and escape us like he did on that island long ago." Both he and Ravi gave a laugh of relief. This long quest through many ages was over; ended now this day!

Ravi patted the Zulu spear held by the captain. He held up the magnificently beautiful jeweled dagger in the sunlight after Ronjin handed it to him. "This ancient dagger was specifically designed by them in their reign in Atlantis to kill us long ago. However, this lethality of this blade worked against them as well! This weapon, its manufacture a mystery to us, was unmovable once stuck into any shape changer and offered a slow painful death once stuck into the unfortunate! It prevented Kali from flying away as we had feared. We never made these, but absconded many of them from these fallen ones long ago.

Cavendish held up Hook's Zulu spear. "Why did this weapon kill the Kali and his familiar and not all the bullets I fired into it?" Ravi spoke. "The Kali is very old and in his superstitious mind from his past experiences must have feared this natural weapon made from nature by the hand of a man. He was probably seriously wounded by a wooden spear before he learned of his powers to protect against other types of manmade weapons. The "Achilles Heel" of Greek legend is true in many respects for such a powerful being my son. Even the most powerful possess deep seated fears of their destruction by simple means such as these. Fear can turn a simple object into a weapon and kill the most powerful!

He then held up the beautiful ancient jeweled dagger. The metal has special powers! Ha Ha… it was not meant for him, but for me! If it did not fear this spear then it would not have delivered the fatal blow. If it had escaped with a serious wound like in the Caribbean? Then it would have repaired itself as mind over matter!" Ambrose had another question. Ravi gave a venerable smile at James with the answer. "Remember mind over matter my son. It is extremely enhanced in the powerful minds of these fallen ones who by their world of upbringing are privy to this kind of mindset. They were never taught of how fear can be controlled and not create death by simple items like this spear.

"The Zulu spear did not kill Kali; his fear of it did? The ancient dagger would have eventually killed Kali because of its special properties. It was unmovable once in the victim and would soon consume the lifeforce and turn this unfortunate into a shriveled mummy of sorts." Cavendish added a rhetorical question. "Their own power can undo them in creating false pretenses for their destruction?" Ronjin chimed in. "The more powerful the mind is the more dangerous a simple belief in matter can be to the whole. Kali never divined this difference. Great power leads to great danger! Oktoo never learned these truths because we never taught him. Mind over matter continued to cross the captain's mind. James then asked his question. "What burned the Kali's body?"

Ronjin looked at Ravi and then at him. "We just cremated it from our minds eyes. This is our way of erasing all possibility that his powerful genes or DNA will never be exhumed or ever used. "What is DNA?" Asked James Ambrose. Ravi smiled. "It is the matrix of substance that makes up the physical composition of any and all things that exists at this level." Ambrose gave a silly look. "I always was a poor science student kind sir!" Then Ambrose looked at the bloody tip of the Zulu spear. A strange colored fire now burned off the Kali's dark blood to cleanse it!

Ravi winked at him. "Your science will discover this DNA in the next fifty years I am certain." Ronjin held up the Kali's head. "We will ritually cremate this at Hima as well!" Cavendish now thought of Sergeant Hook and sensing the question in his friend's mind, Ravi spoke. "Mr. Hook is safe now and is on his way back to the village, as a matter of fact he is being flown at this time and our advanced medical staff will be waiting for him. I am afraid he has lost his arm in the battle; but we saved his life. We have many other of our villagers on site here tending to the many wounds inflicted on your brave army. I wish we could save all of these brave soldiers, but I am afraid that is life in war son, or shall I say death and perhaps both!"

Later on, as the battlefield was in the early stages of being cleaned up and sanitized, Cavendish and Nephew joined the two ancients on the remains of an old stone wall near the river as it flowed rapidly in its new course around huge boulders that rested in it partly submerged. Tiberius passed his flask to Cavendish as Ravi spoke." Here are some details that you two should know. This evil Kali was the worst offspring that was born to the fallen ones long separated from our fold during the devastation caused by Mother Nature eons ago. To our knowledge, he was the oldest and worst of what was left of the evil infested ancient seed. Although we caught up with many of these hybrids, he was the hard one to catch. However, as I said; "The worst we know of." "Cavendish inquired.

"How long have you been searching for him?" Ravi looked a Ronjin who replied. "Probably somewhere in the 11th Century. Oktoo was the offspring of a very old fallen one who was a pure shape changer. His line goes back to the many of our offspring children left as orphans in the wilds of the global destruction of Atlantis. Well let's say until the rise of what the Greek philosopher Solon called Atlantis in the Ocean by the same name between Africa and the Americas two hundred thousand years later. This remarkable civilization spanned from their huge island kingdom across Africa and Europe to the Western Hemisphere. The wonders of ancient Egypt are but a small testament to their engineering and grandeur. It was an incredible golden age for a thousand of years.

Then came serious natural disasters which destroyed much of the island continent. In this time of troubles my ancestors first noticed the others like us who had a very powerful grip in Atlantis. We divined that these very bad ones had our powers and over the centuries had maintained the shadows of the dark side. There meddling with the elements of creation would eventually destroy them and Atlantis. A serious conflict between we, the bearers of light, and these dark ones became a manifested struggle for so long. This was where the theme of "good versus evil" took root in humankind.

Our conflict grew in violent intensity for the next few centuries as natural disasters plagued this civilization of many islands. It was once said that when mankind goes bad and hurts the planet, mother nature steps in to cleans the wounds and restore her health. After all we all see earth as a living organism in the universe! This seemed to be the case with the other civilizations. Anyway, some of these islands sank over time due to natural disaster like what befell Lemuria. However, a new cataclysm befell and destroyed Atlantis, spawned by the crazy scientific experiments controlled by those evil ones who now had absolute power.

Millions of citizens fled before the end. To our recorded knowledge, all of this old evil brood was destroyed along with their offspring. A huge war had erupted between them in control of Atlantis and the opposition empire living in what is now the Sahara Desert of north Africa across to Egypt. The aliens, disagreeing with the evil powers control and under new mandates to stay out of the problem, backed away from this mess, abandoning general humanity before the end. They, according to the powers that oversee millions of habitable planets in this universe became observers, watchers of mankind.

All of North Africa was what your Bible calls "The Garden of Eden" because from the Atlantic across to the Red sea it was an incredible paradise for millions of people who wanted to be free of the evil rule in Atlantis. In those days, the whole of what is now the Mediterranean Sea was one giant valley sealed from the Atlantic Ocean by a land bridge that was strongly naturally reinforced to protect this massive part of the Atlantis civilization. A huge statue stood at the Atlantic side of this protective land bridge what your legend calls the "Colossus of Rhodes." It stood magnificently several hundred feet tall as the symbolic guardian." He smiled. "Your island of England today was landlocked to the European continent in those days as well.

This conflict between our rival groups continued to increase over the ages before they were destroyed. The dagger that killed Kali today was one of these ancient weapons designed by them who had power in Atlantis. My ancestors were able to get some of these in combat and were able to kill or assassinate those in power using their own weapons. There were no cooler minds to prevail in this war. This conflict then went orange. This conflict did not last long and the destruction was horrific.

Not only did the remains of Atlantis sink but the land of paradise throughout north Africa was obliterated and turned into a wasteland desert as you see today. The land bridge protecting the incredible part of Atlantis civilization in what was the huge valley was destroyed. The Mediterranean Sea rests over it today. In minutes the huge waves washed over and destroyed everyone in minutes. The "flood" mentioned in your Bible is but a distant racial memory of this terrible event."

"What is "went orange" Ravi?" asked Colonel Nephew. "Orange is the term we attach to the huge mushroom orange clouds that were unleased after these massive bombs exploded. Your civilization of the future will call them "nuclear" when they learn of the technology. Essentially, they are huge destructive bombs that can destroy whole cities and countries in one blast. It has to do with splitting atoms." Nephew laughed "What in hell is an atom? I got the splitting part?" Ravi smiled at Nephew. Atoms are little particles that compose all things as a simple answer.

In the aftermath of their terrible explosion, they produce a deadly waste we call radiation that is fatal to humans and all life for that matter. Anyway, the remains of this once fantastic civilization can be found well beneath the sands and deep ocean. The only part of the civilization that survived was along the Nile river. It was the water source of the Nile that helped sustain the survivors." Ambrose looked at Ravi.

"So, all these pyramids and structures were the remains of this once proud Atlantis civilization?" Ravi smiled at him. "The pyramids were built all over the planet to help in controlling weather and for other means to control this planet. They had other functions in communicating with other planets once. Your archeologists will soon discover many of these, even larger than the ones in Egypt someday in the jungles of Central America, the south pole, and under the oceans." Then he changed the subject. "What is our sacred symbol of ancient knowledge and truth passed to us son?" Although Cavendish was tired, he was enthralled by this conversation. "Okay Ravi, it is the head of a man on the body of a cat." Ravi smiled. "What guards the pyramids in Egypt?" After some confusion, Nephew looked directly at him and Ronjin. "It is the Sphinx! The head of man with the body of a cat!" He was amazed at his personal revelation.

"The Sphinx was the ancient symbol of good, knowledge, truth, and protection! It was an ageless symbol just like then many found in Hima. Ronjin broke in after sensing his thoughts. "The Sphinx guards so much more than mankind knows and will not be revealed until a kinder mankind is ready to handle it." Ravi continued in his classroom lecture. "Most of my ancestors involved in the generations of strife in Atlantis escaped the fate of death and returned to Hima, which remained completely intact and hidden from the forces of the Atlanteans. Eventually, after centuries of darkness and chaos died away, there came new civilizations born of pastoral nomads brought in by what humanity calls the Neolithic Revolution of some ten thousand years ago.

We both were yet to be born when this began. It was then that the hunters in our small robust civilization began searching these new civilizations for any signs of the surviving evil seed. We never wanted this destructive war with them! So, it became our main objective to hunt them down and rid the planet of them! We all pray that the destruction of Kali is the last of this terrible blight on mankind! At least this parasite is gone forever!

To destroy us would have assured his global prominence he was being denied in our pursuit to destroy him. In this new life as Kali and Raktabija, he had carefully crafted an undercurrent of alliances with the Muslims, the Russians, the Afghans and others opposed to British rule of law and imperialism in India beginning in the 1840s. In ancient Atlantis, the same manipulation was used to slowly usurp complete power from the ruling castes over the centuries. Oktoo's skillful manipulation was completely invisible to us until he generated skillful opposition to the British by the Sepoys which exploded in 1857.

We had already infiltrated their ranks to glean what was motivating this opposition and basis for the Sepoy rebellion of 1857. We began to fear something under the surface for years after but only had rumors. Then came the Kali surrounded by powerful forces. It was then that he moved into this valley and took control of this ancient castle. He then planted a massive army he had built in secret around him. It was then our conflicts and his motives became clear!

Then he launched a huge attack on us in 1895 but we had prior knowledge of this plan. Then came his ill-fated invasion on us. We hit him hard. So now we were in a standoff. We realized that we had to enlist the British army in our war to defeat Kali. Their terrible grisly part in the destruction of Chital opened the door to this possibility. We never understood Wadsworth, but placed our resolve in General Blood. The rest this story is now history boys!"

Ravi smiled and winked at his new students. "We shall talk on this later, before you leave for England." "England?" Cavendish was perplexed. "Yes Mr. Ambrose, you will be privately honored along with many others for your great courage and bravery in dealing with the Kali and his army in private and publicly for your alleged heroic actions at the Khyber Pass battles." Ravi then put the bejeweled dagger into the captain's hands. "A gift of ancient Atlantean technology designed by them to kill our kind!" Ravi gave the biggest smile as he continued. "And my boys, wounding him with his own weapon felt so good and just!" He looked at the dagger he had given to Ambrose. "Keep this for ending the life of Kali, it is special my son! We have a few more at Hima. Go now!"

Ravi helped Cavendish to his feet since the captain bore several new bruises and wounds. Colonel Nephew was in better shape as he hopped to his feet. Ravi and Ronjin shook their hands as they all bowed in ancient respect to each other. "We will see you soon, as there is another who wants to see you as well." Nephew took a shot of cognac off his flask and passed it to Ambrose who indulged. He smiled at his friend. "I wonder what secrets the Sphinx holds?" Ravi ran it past Cavendish's conditioned mind and he was flabbergasted at the view. Ravi and Ronjin walked with the limping officer back to one of the village medics on hand who cheered him. Ravi told the village medic to see to the captain's injuries. Many of the attacking force of Gurkhas approached him. The top NCO walked over to Cavendish and saluted him with Lord George by his side.

They all knew that this British captain had destroyed something huge as their gut feelings revealed. Lord George who had protected Hook stepped up. "Sir, Sgt Hook wanted me to give this to you." The Gurkha handed him back his .45 caliber revolver and Cavendish thanked him. He asked where Hook was, and the Gurkha told him a couple of British medics took him away. Cavendish laughed to himself…British medics with wings he bet.

After this final day of the conflict, it took over two strenuous weeks to clean up the remains on the battlefield and cremate the thousands of dead green devils sprawled throughout the valley and castle area where they had fallen. The valley was to be cleaned up! What green devil survivors the vengeful British forces could not kill, the shape-changers hunted and plucked them up at their leisure. No green devils were to survive period!

On the morning of the seventh day General Bindon Blood called a meeting of Cavendish's scouts and all commanders involved in the battle. As everyone enjoyed their noon tea and after-action banter General Blood entered with his small group of three key staff officers. Among his group was a new face of a high-ranking admiral named Jerome Blackwood. He was decked out in his full-dress uniform bedecked with many medals and badges. The salty long faced admiral was introduced as the Viceroy of all operations in India and special liaison to the Queen.

In essence, he was General Blood's boss and direct pipeline to Queen Victoria. The admiral then took the floor began his comments after clearing his throat. "This was quite a show gentleman; the sun will never set on our glorious empire with the likes of fighting men as you. As General Blood, had instructed you days ago, the nature of this operation beginning with the massacre at Chital is now under the strictest wraps by the government. British military historians and tabloids will never be privy to these happenings, ever! If you love Queen Victoria and country, then you will be respectfully silent. He paused to take a sip of tea offered by his orderly.

A nice humid breeze flowed through the huge large white command tent as silence continued to prevail in the gathering. The admiral went on. "There are many decorations that will be awarded to you and to many enlisted soldiers for their incredible courageous contributions in this terrible fray! They will be awarded for actions preformed in the Khyber Pass battles rather than in these jungle "paradise" battles." He said with a grin. There were a few laughs from the crowd as the men understood the joke. A sumptuous lunch was served for all present as General Blood had already delivered the same fare for his regiments in the field. They had earned it! The lunch turned into a huge celebration as the grand admiral had cases of champagne carted out cooled in the mystic river nearby.

The British regiments completed their task of erasing the footprints of the Kali and his hideous green devil army. It took nearly ten lazy slow days after the cleanup for all British forces to vacate the jungle and return to Chital. Supply wagons had arrived continuously to provide the best meals and care for the troops on site and on their journey back. After the last British regiments crossed the pontoon bridge it was completely destroyed by fire and explosives at both ends, with its debris floating away in the green waters of the ancient river tributary.

The return trip was one of belated joy rather than the apprehension of battle. To the surprise of the returning soldiers, Chital was in the process of being nearly completely rebuilt. All the scouts and those British officers close to the planning and execution of this campaign knew one thing in its aftermath: Queen Victoria had made one decree on this whole affair; "MUM" Is the Word Forever Boys!" History of this epic would remain under tight wraps.

The next day, the first morning back in the restored city of Chital, MG Bindon Blood had a special late breakfast set up for his staff including newly promoted Major Burrows. This late brunch had given time for everybody to get much needed rest. Captain Cavendish and lieutenant Griggs wore clean uniforms and were fresh from hot water field showers. The mood was great. As Cavendish entered the restored former chief administrator's huge room as he admired Blood's rather cozy "taste of England" atmosphere.

He saw there were several other high-ranking British officers present. He sat down as usual next to Colonel Nephew. His other scouts followed. "Come in and get yourselves a spot of hot tea before breakfast is served" uttered a smiling cheery MG Blood. With salutes traded, all were soon seated at a very large table. After a few moments of frivolous conversation, Viceroy Blackwater stood up and spoke.

"Good morning gentlemen." He looked over to the other officers in his group. "I first want to thank you for your excellent after-action reports. They are now on their way to being delivered to the Queen. Blood continued with a smile ebbing across his face. "We needed all actions of this affair recorded for posterity, to be logged into our data of this campaign. As I warned you, this whole record is top secret for several key reasons by order of the Queen and her council. Record of this will be sealed for an undetermined period of time as in forever for what I have been told.

As you look around this city, it is being completely restored to cover up what really occurred here. Chital was never attacked nor did it fall under the terror and death of the green devils! The official events of this event have been expunged. All of your actions of gallantry are recorded in the battles in the campaigns towards the Khyber Pass as well. As for all of you present, please rise and line up at attention. Later, you will award the appropriate decorations to your men." He called out all their names as they formed a stiff line at attention.

General Blood confronted each soldier and presented them with a Victoria Cross for 'Gallantry and Bravery," then pinned The Order of India next to their VC. He saluted each and shaking their hands as he moved in high spirits down the line. Once all the decorations had been handed out, the Viceroy continued. "All participants in this battle will be awarded the Order of India medal for bravery. Captain Cavendish smiled at the list of Gurkhas dead and alive who would receive honors. Both Gladstone and Lord Nelson had been posthumously awarded the VC as well.

As the commanders and others mingled the newly promoted Lieutenant-General Blood approached Ambrose. He asked Cavendish, "How is SMG Hook? He gets a second VC today!" Cavendish smiled at his commander. "He is still recovering in the village sir." This reminds me Sir; Ravi and the village await your presence for their own ceremony to honor us, and then you can award Hooky his second VC." Sir, he was critically wounded and is recovering, and if I may, it would be an honor if you personally awarded it." General Blood looked at his notes. "I would love to go and when?" Cavendish replied. "We can go when you are ready sir!" "Very well Captain, and thanks!"

It was already known that General Blood was to be awarded the Victoria Cross by none other than the Queen and was to possibly be knighted as well. The case against Colonel Wadsworth and his whole folly had been recorded in secret archives but expunged from any historical records. It would be written that he was sent with a small contingent to protect Chital at the request of General Blood. The rest of his army were lost in combat in the Malakand Field Force campaigns to the Khyber Pass. It was the outbreak of the plague that killed many residents of Chital and Wadsworth's small relief force. However, there was another powerful person in England who had a deep interest in the death of Colonel Hillary Wadsworth! It was his father Sir Elroy Wadsworth.

Cavendish and Nephew sat by a stream sharing some cognac and cigars. Cavendish spoke. "There is the lonely wounded Sergeant major Hook we need to attend to. I have three bottles of good rum just for him." Nephew winked. "count me in!" Nephew further added. "Not to worry Ambrose, remember I travel alone? Ravi knew my soul was good, and I bonded with him before the battle. I was able to travel out with them the night they attacked the green devil scouts in the jungle and observed their gruesome handiwork! … and; Ravi invited me to the village!" Cavendish smiled…" By foot or by air?" "By air!" replied Tiberius with a smile.

It was time for the grand celebration. The grand boat ride to Hima in the wild river was a spectacular event for all. The guests were guided to a huge building where they were ushered to seats of honor as many residents filed in and found their seats. The crowd was joyous and the mood one of great happiness. Before they went to their seats, they encountered Sergeant Hook, fresh in a clean khaki uniform and beaming a great smile.

Cavendish laughed out loud when he saw that he was in the company of two bow dogs that sat next to him like temple guards. Hook was missing his left arm as both Nephew and Cavendish had been informed by Ravi. It had been too damaged and the time factor had prevented any re-attachment by their advanced medicine. He saluted the officers and Bindon Blood shook his hand. "those are some fierce dogs' sergeant." He added. Hooky smiled at the general. "they have adopted me and protect me like the palace jewels sir!"

The festive dinner and celebration lasted for a good long time. After the dinner, everybody mingled until the ceremony started. It began with the award of Sergeant Major Hook's second Victorian Cross and Order of India Medal. He saluted general Blood. After that, the general, with the help of Cavendish and Nephew, awarded over one-hundred Order of India medals to all the shape changers involved in the action; alive and deceased. Then he came back and awarded both Ravi and Ronjin Victorian crosses by direct order of the Queen. One of the bottles of rum given to Hooky was now passed down the line.

General Blood honored the Shape changers. "This Order of India medal is the highest decoration given for service and bravery in all of India. These medals are lasting tribute to all of you who helped us and sacrificed in this very dangerous time. And of course, Bindon Blood still doesn't quite know how you did it?" He paused with a smile and soon everyone was laughing, "But he is grateful and thank you from Queen Victoria herself of our great nation!" There was great applause as Cavendish soon made the rounds shaking hands with all the decorated villagers.

It was now time for Ravi and Hima to honor these heroes. The band of scouts and General Blood all lined up facing the crowd as Ravi and Ronjin handed each soldier an ancient Greek sword in a sheath and with a leather shoulder suspension. He then handed General Blood his. It was very ornate with gold carvings in its handle and hilt. He spoke. "All of you have shown incredible bravery against a terrible enemy. Because of your sacrifices and courage in defeating this evil in the name Kali, we cannot think of any better award to give than swords that stood for the same bravery and sacrifice long ago at a pass called Thermopylae.

We collected many artifacts, and many Spartan swords scattered at this pass after the battle. It was a battle I well remember and was astounded at the incredible actions and force the Spartans wielded in holding off one million Persians. If we had not destroyed the Kali, we would have faced a modern-day Genghis Khan and millions of his minions in the future I am certain! The scouts and General Blood were amazed at the historical artifacts and significance bestowed on them.

The festival party now continued. Ronjin asked the general if he or the others wanted to return to Chital. He looked around at the fun and bliss of the atmosphere. "No, my friend, I think I will hold here like my men until after breakfast." It was a night that all the guests would never forget. Sometime in the night, Pyra took James by the hand and led him to her luxurious room, full of nice memories the captain thought. They talked and kissed. He loved her in all things mind, body, and spirit!

She finally undressed him and put him in bed, laughing at his mild wine buzz antics. She held him in her arms as they made love. They both then drifted off to sleep. Pyra loved him so very much and knew that after this night, their relationship would change but never end. He would go back to England, and she would remain unless summoned, as was the law. But, in her world, love was long lasting and very eternal. When you loved, you loved completely no matter what? Separation by death was but a temporary veil for those who understood the way of reincarnation and the afterlife.

The body was only the clothes of the soul and its vehicle for living in this dimension; nothing more. Incarnation was usually a chosen endeavor to further learning and enjoy living! No soul ever died at death. The fear of death was a religious propaganda tool to keep the masses in check and to continue paying tithes! Reincarnations at this level continued until the soul had achieved its goals of this level and moved to the next one! Life was a living chapter in each life for each soul. This was the way all living things returned to this level. Some beings lived longer than others depending on their goals and from what specifies they inhabited. The love of the Creator was the glue that held the universe and relationships together in harmony.

There would be time for great lovemaking early in the morning, but she held on to him throughout the night, never letting go of her beloved human. Cavendish finally got free of the sweet embraces of Pyra in the late morning. He walked into the large central room to find both Hook and Nephew sitting together in the large pool. Hook was sitting next to the deck and had the direct company of five puppies sitting by his side. Old Hooky looked like some king of sorts as he yelled "attention" which all the puppies stood up in straight sitting positions. "At ease!" … and they all began to frolic about as everybody laughed. Another Bow dog puppy nuzzled Cavendish's leg as he approached the pool.

These monstrous looking beasts were filled with such love he thought. Puppies? The group all wore long comfortable white robes as food and tea were delivered buffet style to a large table. Tiberius spoke. "Get in here Cavendish, this water does great things for hangovers!" Ambrose smiled; he must have sweated out all his cognac and wine being quite busy love romping with Pyra. He kicked off his robe and entered the pool. An attendant offered him a large glass of some orange fluid. He settled in to water up to his neck. He realized that after thirty minutes all of his abrasions and wounds seemed fine and his latent hangover was gone.

He looked at Alfred Hook of double VC fame now and smiled. "How are you doing old friend?" Hook raised the stump of his left arm. "Top of the morn to you captain I feel great!" After Hooky refreshed his drink Pyra appeared with a couple of very beautiful village women that had kidnapped colonel Nephew after the celebration. In his estimate, there were no ugly ladies in this town!

Later in the morning as it was turning to afternoon James, Griggs, King George, Tiberius and Hooky sat outside in a beautiful garden at a table. They had just had their pitcher of sweet red wine replenished. General Blood. Rashid, and Sergeant Hoskins had already left earlier. The rest stayed and enjoyed the wonderful kind ambiance of Hima. They were all still laughing at the Wadsworth "Death Blowjob". Such a hilarious joke it was a permanent historical point among them. As the conversations settled down Old Hooky took center stage, as Bow dogs around him gave him loving head bumps.

He spoke as all fell silent. "My whole life has been rough, and if it had not been for a few loyal comrades like you, I would have perished long ago. My British comrades offered me sanctuary, real friendship! I fought always to save my comrades, with success and failures, but that was how I fought from in the army, from Rorke's Drift, and in this valley of death! "He was silent as he patted his Bow dogs then continued. Ravi had approached and sat as James poured him a goblet of red wine. They all exchanged pleasantries and Ravi sensed something from Hook as he spoke.

"Once I was given a couple of Bulldog pups and raised them like they were my children. They gave me so much comfort and friendship in my uncaring rough world! I loved them, and gave them to my aunt to watch when I went to prison and was conscripted to the Army. My aunt died and I never could find them again! My life became empty and my cup of sadness overflowed at their memory!" He began to choke up but continued. "It seems that my prayers were answered when I met these wonderful creatures among you great people Ravi!" Hook wiped tears from his cheeks and added.

"It was in one battle where I was decorated; where I lost my soul! Now I am awarded a second VC in a battle that may have taken my arm but restored my soul." Ravi looked with great depth into Hook's mind and answered. "This is your home for the rest of your life if you choose to stay Hooky. We love and appreciate you, and well the Bow dogs now have a real playmate and keeper. We will bring light into your troubled soul Mr. Hooky. This is our promise." Hooky smiled deep with tears in his eyes and gave the incredible old man a long hug. This world of goodness and love was so overwhelming to him in this place.

Hook's military career due to the grievous injury was over. He was done with it as well. He never had anyone truly close to him in England except a now deceased aunt and two missing bulldogs. Did he did not want to live in a dour cold old soldier's home rehashing the memory of events he wanted to put behind him? There was nothing to return to actually. The mother Bow dog, now named Martha gently balanced her three-hundred pound plus body on his back and shoulders with her huge paws and crooned him with her huge fluffy fanged head. She felt his pain, as did Ravi.

Old Hooky looked at Ravi and smiled. "Looks like you have a new Bow Dog keeper Ravi. I will take your offer!" Ravi smiled as did the very telepathic Bow dogs…little dragons in colored fur with huge gaping jaws infested with large fangs and teeth that danced in circles. He hugged several of them and turned to Nephew and Cavendish. Looks like I had a relapse right here and maybe it was the wine?" He gave a big Hooky smile. Gentlemen I am proud to announce that I am now deceased! This damn Kali killed Hook! Poor Ravi and his medicine could not save me! So, let's continue now with my wake fair gentlemen!"

At first both officers were confused and looked in askance at each other. Then, as the Hooky statement hit home, both began to laugh out loud. Nephew who was mesmerized by Old Wad's supposed death commented. "Looks like you died in the fight without the "death blowjob" sergeant! Congrats!" Cavendish raised his glass. "I make a toast to the gallant fallen Sergeant Major Alfred Hook of her majesties 11th Lancers!" Hooky's humor had struck again with a note of reality. The party continued as Nephew requested Hook to give his farewell death speech! Hook stood up, took a full belt of wine, refilled his glass and said. "It gives me great pleasure to be dead and able to celebrate it with the best of the best in officers and friends! In death we do not part!" They then put on a nice farewell to death drunk for the next two hours.

Later, before Ambrose left, he rejoined Pyra in her room for a farewell of sorts. He musingly told her of the great death of Hook, and his opulent death farewell speech, and plans after his death! She laughed and then looked him in the eyes with a deep and kind smile. "Perhaps the end of this part of us is now, but not the end of our love Ambrose. True love never dies or goes away, but can transform and evolve in good ways, never bad ones. We will, in one-way or another always be connected. I will always be at your fingertips… forever." "And you by mine Pyra! I truly love you!" They kissed deeply as he spoke. "Ravi tells me that soon I will be headed back to merry old England." She rubbed his head with her hand gently. "Yes, my darling, and you will have a complete life in store for you."

Their words abruptly ceased and they embraced. Their lovemaking was serious, passionate, honestly great! Late in the day she walked him to where the rest of the scouts were meeting at the dockside. He stopped to say farewell to Sergeant Hook. Nephew was also there. Hook reaffirmed his new existence as deceased. This announcement brought grand smiles from both officers. Sergeant Major Hook lamented. "Cry not for Old Hook me gentlemen, for he is dead! You are talking with my ghost now! Tis better to die a hero, then to languish and die in some godforsaken old soldier's home?" He was surrounded by the whole clan of his new Bow Dog children.

His comments drew the usual laughs from all present. Both officers completely understood. Old Hook respectfully handed his Zulu spear to Captain Cavendish "I give this to you my son, for you to carry into your next adventure, and may God be with both of you always!" Hook took off the VC he had earned at Rorke's drift and also handed it to the Captain. He tapped the new VC and said. "I will keep the VC that restored my soul and give you the one that took my soul along with my Zulu spear as a memento of our friendship!" He laughed. Mount these with my story on bronze and put it behind a bar and a good pub my boys!" Cavendish laughed. I know just the pub Hooky!"

This would be the last time they ever saw their favorite color Sergeant again. He would go on to live many happy years in Hima as keeper of the Bow dogs, and popular friend and companion to many villagers. Later, Hook would accompany his new-found family into their long treks of exploration into the wilds of the Himalayan Mountains. So many incredible things he would be privy to view and enjoy unknown to mankind. He would fall in love with the kind lady shape-changer slightly over two-thousand years old, who stayed by his side and would help him manage the Bow dogs. He would be loved by all and would finally really die on a September day in 1991. He would outlive both officers and all the others at the age of one-hundred and eighteen.

Sergeant Hook would be cremated by strict customs of the villagers in their special tomb, with his ashes resting next to his uniform, pistol, and this "lucky" 2nd VC pinned to the chest. Ravi and Hook stood near as Nephew, Cavendish and the others pulled away from the pier and headed for the wild ride in the rapids back to the gray city of tall buildings. Rather than be flown back to Chital like General Blood and others, they chose to ride back. Ravi looked at Ambrose with a broad deep smile before the long boat left. "Remember the ring …if you ever need us, we are always here for you. Otherwise, we will be in touch."

"I will Ravi….and take care!" Colonel Nephew showed Cavendish his red ring and smiled. "Looks like my friend Ravi was also concerned about my whereabouts as well." Ravi smiled at Nephew, "I adopted you along with Ambrose, so I do need to know what my children are doing from time to time!" Tiberius saluted Ravi and smiled…. "It is my pleasure to be your son, and Cavendish's twin brother!" Ravi smiled and gave an open hand farewell as Pyra, waved with heavy eyes. They waved at Pyra, Ravi, Ronjin, and the other villagers present, and Old Hooky for the last time. Later they rode their fresh horses from the dead granite city and through the rustic farm village of so many memories. They waved at all the villagers whom they had come so close to in the war against Kali. Down the jungle trail they went, engulfed by the heavy jungle foliage on the sides. They decided to have one last look at the valley of death before they returned back to the river from the jungle, and their world.

The defeat and slaughter of the green devil cult and the ancient monster Kali was complete. His death would be the basis of an annual celebration in Hima for many years after. Between the British and their unknown allies, the shape-changers; not one green devil or foreign advisor escaped to tell their story. It would be after WWI before the captured Russian Advisors were ever allowed to return to their native lands, if they wanted to return to the totalitarianism of the brutal new Soviet Union.

Nephew and Cavendish sat on the remaining summit of the precipice sipping cognac from their tin mess cups admiring how the jungle was quickly reclaiming its prominence over anything manmade!

Both men made occasional comments as their minds were lost in the previous deadly tempest that shattered the tranquility in this now peaceful valley. They leaned against the two huge Russian Artillery pieces across from each other that sat on what remained of the huge precipice. These sentinels were the only reminder of the terrible conflict that raged here. They faced the valley where so many had died. The noise of huge majestic falls was restored as the official sound in this valley. The footprint of Kali's green devil humming noise was gone, a memory like the ashes of their cremation. They viewed the destroyed castle in remembrance.

Finally, the officers finished a last shot of cognac and took a slow ride across the plain below to the hills outside of the huge jungle expertly defended by Blood's artillery and tragically not by Wadsworth's! There were no monuments to the fallen or to what regiments fought here because this whole series of events had never happened. The evil of the Kali left a huge terrifying imprint on both men's souls! The depth of this ancient evil was still beyond their comprehension. Both men prayed silently that they would never have to deal again with this evil vile darkness. Cavendish was quietly vexed by Ravi's statement regarding it. *"Evil may be challenged, wounded, and even destroyed in the eyes of those who complete such gruesome tasks; but evil in its incredible resilience, never sleeps for long, never sleeps forever! Always sleeping with one eye open. It waits in the shadows for the next opportunity!"*

CHAPTER SEVEN
JUBLIATION AND TREPIDATION

Captain Cavendish stood at the bow of the large Clipper ship "H.M.S. Shannon" as it careened up and down in the deep wakes produced by the channel winds of a huge storm approaching from behind them. The ship bounced in the wake of dark cloud covered seas as the frigid winter storm chased them. He enjoyed the roller-coaster turbulence as he viewed the cloud-swept outline of his beloved England. The vague outline of the Thames River estuary now appeared in the mist created by the waves before him.

It was the first day of December 1897. Cold and wet it was, but it was England! The relentless heat of India eluded him completely at this point. He was dressed in a large overcoat, resembling a giant penguin, for the cold gales bespoke that the fierce winter storm was upon his island nation. The wash from the sea had created a covering of ice on the deck and his beard where he stood in the foredeck. He had been carefully reviewing his exceptional recent past and found himself still amazed and confused at it. He had witnessed the extremes of tragedy and triumph in the extremes! He had made a close bond with a great race of beings and had personally killed a supernatural monster that defied all common reason of civilization. He knew one thing for sure as he smiled; he had two loves from two completely different worlds and loved them both!

Cavendish was thankful that he had accepted the invitation of General Bindon Blood to accompany him on a fast-moving elegant clipper ship instead of a slower mode of transportation. He urgently wanted to get home and he wanted to see Jenny. General Blood's leadership had been relegated to his field commanders in combat against the remaining opposition at the Khyber. It had been dimishing at a rapid pace since the British had threatened a scorched earth policy on the Pashtuns if they did not quit the fight. The threat of destroying their villages in the onslaught of winter was too much for most. Besides, a peace treaty was rumored in the offing and would officially end the hostilities soon. It was time for the diplomats!

He thought of all the soldiers who had fought the huge deathmatch against the very dangerous Kali! "Mum" was the word and these combatants had to be kept from falling into the eager hands of the press, tabloids, and public scrutiny. Many of the British officers, and NCOs involved in this conflict either remained in India or were being dispersed to other colonies to evade exposure. The actual record of this conflict was sealed by orders from Queen Victoria as verified personally by Viceroy Blackwood. Strange stories of this conflict abounded and had already found their way into a few tabloids.

In time, completely devoid of authentic documentation, these stories would slowly be given over to myth, and bountiful late-night ghost stories to scare children. These tabloid stories via leaks, bore a lot of truth in fact and were so fantastic to be believed by the public at large. The British government "rumor control" denied and scoffed at these stories as silly "balderdash." Besides, passing time was the element that would make all these stories tales of the future!

As the cold winds dashed waves against the frozen ice-covered bow, Captain James Cavendish smiled as he reviewed his farewell party at Malakand. He had raised Hook's Zulu Spear to his comrades pronouncing that he was "hoping that dearly departed Hooky would do well with his new issued wings and harp in the afterlife." He was roundly toasted with laughs and smiling winks of all present; since they all had been informed of his real fate as Hima's new Master of Bow Dogs. Great portrait photos in full bemedaled uniforms with weapons were taken of the group for remembrance early that day. Besides Cavendish, everybody would stay in India with the exception of Nephew, Griggs, and Hoskins.

The rest were all to remain in duty in India, to continue with the concluding British conflict in the Khyber and enforcement of a pending peace policy for now. Sergeant Hoskins, due for promotion to a second lieutenant, was to return to England to wed Andrea and to attend Sand Hurst Military Academy at the personal bequest of MG Blood. Hoskins had so impressed the general with his sharp mind for details, his strong military bearing, and especially his efficiency and courage under extremely dangerous conditions. Hoskins had asked Cavendish to stand in for him as best man.

All of the recipients of the VC were amazed at the fabricated circumstances leading to their VC awards. It was testament to heroic actions honestly described at the Battle of Malakand, then fabricated to include actions in the battles waged in the Khyber Pass region. It seemed that most of the British officers and noncoms who were killed under Wadsworth had died in the Khyber Pass campaigns. The rest of his men, including "Old Wad died in a plague epidemic which allegedly ravaged Chital. Nothing about the Chital debacle or anything after that was ever mentioned in the evolving historical records other than one Pashtun attack on their supply convoys. Cavendish had expediously penned every real detail of this conflict into his vastly expanded personal diary, a concise history of the war and all events beginning in the Battle of Malakand then the rest.

He had also made clear reflections on the village and events there. Ravi, Ronjin, Pyra, and the life in Hima was of paramount interest. Colonel Nephew, and excellent sketch artist included many of them into his diary which covered all aspects of his record. Someone in the future would learn the complete truth of it. He had folded his award certificate and included it into his pack of documents and letters in a pocket he created in the back of his diary. He had felt the sweet loving presence of Pyra several times while traveling home on the fast-moving clipper ship. My how the love from Jenny and Pyra were both wonderful but so different!

The Clipper cascaded to and fro in the choppy waters of the English Channel now, plunging deep in the sea froth, and then climbing high towards the overcast sky. But there she was, Pyra, his angel, so filled with sincere love for him, as he was for her. Her presence seemed so close. He also realized that it was a "fairy tale love" of sorts, like his whole surreal experience with the shape-changers. It was painfully real in all aspects, but distant as in an earlier chapter in some storybook. He smiled at the new life of Old Hooky, keeper of the Bow or "Foo" Dogs as they were also named. Ravi had a real case on his hands.

He touched the ring on his right hand. The ancient ring and large ruby stone with the directions for its use recorded in his diary. This ring was his link to that fairytale world. He kissed the ring and told Pyra he loved her. Then his mind slowly drifted to another woman, one who was in his real world beyond the stormy coast lines to his front. It was Jenny "Natalie" Farnsworth. He had her address and a couple of very warm letters including a photo, tucked in with his important papers. He had a longing desire to see her. There was chemistry between them; very human in nature. She existed in the real world, not in the now untouchable world of Pyra in Hima. He would love both of them since he surmised that there was no law against it! He had "Two true loves from two distinctly different worlds!"

"I thought I would find you up here old hat!" Cavendish turned to see Nephew, dressed in his huge penguin winter garb, and a huge furry hat. He was smiling at him in a hard wind that lashed the frothy seas onto the decks of the clipper ship. "Have a hot tea, milk with a spot of rum old mate!" Tiberius handed him a large mug, warm to his frozen lips as he drank it. Nephew continued. "We are sailing into Queen Victoria's Diamond Jubilee, which has been going on for a while so I have been so informed." Cavendish surmised, "I thought that the Diamond Jubilee was last year?" "No, she had it delayed until this year because of circumstances I was unaware of. General Blood informed me of this change over some good cognac and cigars that night before we engaged the Kali in the hell storm.

Oh yes, he also told me a few minutes ago, that we were invited to accompany him to a private audience with Queen Victoria in a couple of days." "Lunch with the Queen!" replied Cavendish. He then smiled back after he took a gulp of tea, as the ship seemed to reduce rocking in smaller waves in front of the violent storm chasing them. They were entering the estuary of the Thames River. "I wonder what the subject will be mused the light colonel?" Both men laughed and agreed never to expound on the truth about Ravi and his kind. Ravi and his people needed their protection forever, for the new enemy would be the curious danger of those who would attempt to exploit them, and the true secrets of the village.

Over the next hour, the H.M.S. Shannon docked on the Thames River after carefully navigating through the choppy waters now engulfing London, with sails down and the side-wheel steam engine moving it carefully to shore. London always seemed very drab and archaic to Cavendish. The streets were narrow and twisted throughout the patchwork of tall dark gray buildings for the most part, that would have been dwarfed by the ones in the ancient gray city between the farm village and Hima. The cold and snow blasted in by the huge storm only complemented this drab feeling. But then what existed on the inside of most of these buildings was quite different.

However, regardless of the winter and his opinion of the drab appearance of London; he was home, sweet home! The whole party was picked up and delivered to the very posh Majestic Hotel in downtown London via the small caravan of black royal coaches that had awaited their arrival on the snow blown docks on the Thames. The snowstorm was blinding on the brief journey through the cobbled streets to the hotel. As their luggage was being unloaded and delivered to their respective rooms, the newly arrived group of British officers and senior noncoms shook off their winter coats and hats, then entered the posh hotel bar.

A multitude of rounds were soon poured to warm their heart, souls and cold bodies. Bindon Blood informed the group that they were requested and invited to a large royal party at the Viceroy's estate mansion at eight tonight! They were to meet back in the hotel bar at seven! Later, after useless attempts to nap, both Cavendish and Nephew dressed in their finest uniforms, protected in winter military long coats, and visited a pub across from the hotel called the "Horned Owl's Bite." They still had nearly two hours until they were to be picked up in the hotel lobby.

The storm was now dropping a lot of snow as the winds howled down the streets of Victorian London. The winter storm was inundating the region in a fine deep while blanket. Lieutenant-Colonel Nephew and Captain Cavendish bellied up to the long-polished oak bar with the walls bedecked with many stuffed owls and paintings of them about. They engaged in jovial conversation as the cool pub ale and shots of brandy took effect. They reflected on their meeting with the Queen and what they would be asked by England's most famous lady. They finally returned to the front reception area of the Majestic after leaving the "Horned Owl's Bite Pub" and joined the assembled group in the hotel bar for more drinks.

The snowstorm and winds continued as the weather gods reminded all of the winter season at hand, and the heat of India was a memory. The long coach ride was a cold one, as fog and snow continued to obscure the road and tree lines. Nephew passed his flask of cognac to Cavendish to fight the numbing cold. Both men were feeling little pain at this point as were the others. A huge castle-like mansion eventually loomed ahead, partially masked in the snow clouds of cold misty fog. They approached the huge balustrade of stairs as the horses pulling the coaches were moved to warm stables.

The stone castle-mansion was huge, immaculate, and dominated the landscape as outlined by the huge torches illuminating the massive front staircase and light shining from huge windows into the white winter darkness. It was posh in all respects. They both climbed the wide marble stairs and were ushered into a huge well-lighted long hallway crowded with many well-dressed people. Cavendish marveled at the huge lights hanging from the elegant ceiling, which briefly reminded him of the ones in the temples in Hima. "Electricity my friend, an infant invention!" suggested Tiberius Nephew. It seemed as if all the royalty of the British Empire was present. This Christmas Party was also a celebration the Queen's Diamond Jubilee.

The elegance of this affair was exhibited in the beautiful gowns of the ladies and pristine uniforms of the many military officers gathered in groups celebrating the event. The interior of this castle was dazzling; with huge paintings of navy battles and ships. Suites of armor and all sorts of medieval weapons were arrayed in the vast lighted regal beauty within this huge hall and ballroom. It could have been a royal museum to the uninformed tourist. Attendants relieved them of their hats and coats as they and the rest of their comrades now approached the receiving line. Both the captain and colonel looked dashing in the dress uniforms and decorations upon their chests.

The welcome line was long, slow, and customary. Both soldiers began moving down the line shaking hands and making slight respectful bows to the many nobles, government and military personages, and their ladies in the line. A couple of high-ranking officers, seeing their medals, asked particular commenting questions regarding the war north of India, and even commented on the rumor of some secret expedition! However, both Nephew and Cavendish were able to deflect the questions with bold cognac fueled meaningless retorts as they moved down the line. Plausible denial was a good tool in these circumstances!

As they continued down the receiving line, a beautiful brunette, with deep blue eyes extended her hand. In rote action Cavendish grasped it and kissed it. He then looked at her, dressed in an exquisite white long flowing gown. She spoke. "I am Lady Jenny Farnsworth Protector of the Khyber Pass! "Ambrose stood motionless staring into this beauty attempting to retrieve that moment. "Hello, "He stammered as he smiled at Jenny. "I am Captain Ambrose Cavendish the protector of Malakand!" He was smiling, as was Jenny. She continued. "I even got a letter from a Lieutenant Cavendish, is Captain Cavendish the same person; the one who saved me from those bad savages?" He smiled, "Why I imagine that I am the same person and what is strange, I received two letters and even a picture from a person just like you!"

Still smiling, she turned to her father, Sir Roger Farnsworth, who was a retired admiral and a very successful powerful international businessman with connections. She introduced them and her mother Lady Penelope next. Colonel Nephew was also brought into the introductions process. The duke then remarked that he had heard a lot about them both! As the crowd in the line moved them on, she looked at Cavendish. "Captain Cavendish, I will meet you soon after the receiving line dies out; if it is all right? I still have something of yours! Oh yes, I think we have already set up a formal date if you remember James Ambrose?" "I do!" He replied. Then she gave a heartwarming smile as they moved down to the end of the huge receiving line.

Tiberius commented as they walked to one of the many bars set up in the hall. "You seem to captivate only the most beautiful ladies my friend!" "Yes Tiberius, a great gift indeed!" Nephew received a full bottle of champagne from one of the small bars down the hall as Ambrose grabbed a couple of glasses. They chose to sit out of the limelight sipping it from a couch under the full armored statue of a knight on a horse. They looked in continued amazement of all the attendees and the overwhelming ornate medieval beauty of the castle. Cavendish looked at Nephew after a couple of glasses smiling. "Sir, this castle is a lot nicer than the last one we were in!" Nephew laughed out loud.

"Good observation dear James, and the inhabitants seem a much kinder lot! I do not see any green devils, who were such rude hosts!" James laughed. "That Kali? So inhospitable and downright mean I would add!" They were amusing themselves as Nephew added. "I think our only enemy here tonight will not be those "YUM YUM EATEM UP" Green Devils!" It is going to be curious questions launched by the rumor mills regarding that conflict. That I may add, Lady Jenny is a real beauty!" James smiled back. "The best defense tonight is to be loaded and vague!"

Nephew agreed as they laughed some more in comparing this castle and people present to the one, they destroyed in the jungle. It was time for the huge sit-down dinner, so Nephew grabbed a fresh bottle of champagne as all guests were ushered towards a huge great hall room. As the two officers moved into this large hallway, Cavendish felt an arm slide under his left arm embracing it. He peered over to see the beautiful Jenny Farnsworth at his side. "I am so hungry Captain Cavendish, and I would love to have dinner with you and your friend!" "The pleasure is mine Lady Jenny!" She smiled at him and tightened her grip on his arm. The large crowd was moving to the tables.

They were soon seated at one of the huge round tables like the rest of the guests, which accommodated sixteen guests each. More champagne flowed as the guests ordered from a nice menu. Cavendish opted for the Roast Beef and Yorkshire pudding, while Nephew went straight for the rack of Lamb and potatoes. Lady Farnsworth settled for a sizeable piece of codfish. The conversation at the table was, like all the champagne being poured, light "bubbly" holiday chatter as plates of excellent appetizers were delivered to the hungry guests. It seemed to Ambrose that everybody was starving, as the plates of appetizers were emptied quickly.

The copious amounts of champagne and wine exacerbated the hunger for the main fare. The mood was one of frivolous gaiety and laughter, with the tinkle of many glasses as countless toasts were made to Queen, empire, country, and Old Saint Nick! The food was excellent and muted the crowd temporarily as they feasted. Both Nephew and Cavendish ate two complete portions. They were in food heaven. As the feast ended, the after-dinner speeches began honoring Queen Victoria and her long and successful reign in generating England into an extremely prosperous world empire.

Lady Jennifer Farnsworth reached over and grasped Ambrose's hand under the table. As he looked, she winked and smiled. Her beauty overwhelmed Cavendish as he compared her to another beauty in his life, other life. After the gracious speeches by the selected speakers, Viceroy Blackwood, Supreme commander of India, approached the podium at the center and gave his closing remarks regarding the conflict in India. In a summary, he honored all the soldiers and sailors who ensured the dominance of the global Pax Britannica. He concluded with his remarks of the bravery and sacrifices made by the "Queen's Own" in the recent conflict in northern India in defeating the huge rebellion of over two-hundred thousand Islamic Pashtun tribesmen.

The Viceroy made a special point of honoring the supreme sacrifice the twenty-one Sikh soldiers of the 36th Regiment who were killed defending the Saragarti Post against an attack by an estimated twelve thousand Pashtun tribesmen under a two-day siege which began on twelve September. He concluded that "In their brave sacrifice, they killed hundreds of the enemy and prevented further destruction of the other two forts in the area by allowing reinforcements to arrive in time to prevent it. The Queen has just honored these heroes by awarding each of these brave soldiers the Order of India medal! Then we had the attacks on our outposts of Malakand and Chakadara in late July! Against incredible odds like at Saragarti! The iron courage and cold steel of British arms held firm against the savage tidal waves bent on our complete destruction! Ladies, lords, and gentlemen, this is the incredible caliber of our soldiers!

It is my great honor to speak of the commander and victor who led our brave army in what will conclude as absolute triumph of arms in the recent military campaigns against the enemies of our empire in India." He gave a short kind speech about General Blood and other commanders in the field serving under him. He then introduced General Bindon Blood stating that he had just arrived from India this day. After a resounding applause, the general spent a few moments praising the bravery and sacrifice of his army in summing up the recent military successes in 1897 against the Muslims beginning with the brave defense of Malakand, then Chakadara, Saragarti and the huge campaign against the Pashtun hordes by his Malakand field force. He continued after the applause died down. Blood concluded. "The war at the Khyber Pass in now reaching a victorious conclusion and a treaty is soon to be confirmed.

Our steadfast determination, professionalism of arms, and cold British steel were the straws that broke the back of enemy resistance and allowed us to claim a resounding victory for Queen, Crown, Country and Empire! May all our sacred fallen rest safely in the arms of Father God! The Sun will continue never to set on the British Empire with Queen Victoria at the helm and soldiers such as these" The applause was deafening, as General Blood smiled across from the podium at Nephew and Cavendish whose table was near the front and gave them an obvious wink, as he then waved at the crowd and backed away from the podium. "Enough said, I would think!" Retorted Colonel Nephew. Both Nephew and Cavendish now had two huge horned flagons of cold ale delivered to them.

Cavendish looked at Jenny. She smiled at him. "Well", she said, "Both of you were talking about wishing you had cold flagons of ale, so I took the liberty of finding you some in a small pub tap room tucked away nearby." She then looked at Cavendish with a large smile across her lips and grabbed his hand. "Captain Cavendish, this is where we left off at Malakand with bullets and bombs about!" She was radiating such beauty from her smile and gleaming eyes. His wish to be with her had come true at such a great moment and dangerous journey. He gave her a deep smile. Colonel Nephew thanked her for the ale as he took a long sip on it but found himself inundated by some very lovely female admirers; he had been flirting with from the table behind him as the guests began to mingle. It was going to be a very long night indeed he mentally speculated.

The music began, and the crowd soon moved into a huge ballroom dancing to the tunes and steps of the day. It seemed like a new fairytale event as the band played and many danced. After Ambrose and Jenny danced a few, she ushered Ambrose into a large side room that appeared to be the mansion pub called "ale room" by Jenny. Nephew closely followed them with two very pretty women arm-in-arm. He introduced them as Anastasia and Beatrice. They were exquisite, beautiful, and sexy as their cleavage pounded against the tops of their tight low-cut satin gowns. One was a raven-haired buxom beauty and the other a petite blonde with immaculately chiseled features! They all sat near the small bar in this castle pub. More ale flowed into their flagons, as tried a variety of cordials; with more laughs and silly banter following over the next hour.

Drunkenness seemed to be widespread at their table as they continued laughing at the many jokes. Nephew looked at Cavendish and floated his eyes at the two women. "Do you think?" "Think what Tiberius?" "Do you think I can love two women at once and how can I explain this to my parents?"

James laughed as he reviewed his reality. "I approve old buddy so go for it; we can handle anything right?" Tiberius winked and sat back down between his new luscious female acquaintances. He took a pull on a fresh flagon of ale with the smile of a predator as his eyes roamed across the very attractive bodacious two women.

Then a gruff voice came from the end of the room from a table near the brightly burning fireplace. "Tell me of the bravery and courage of Colonel Hillary Wadsworth in his fight against the green devils?" Without missing a beat, Lieutenant Colonel Nephew retorted half drunken and brazenly, "He died of syphilis in a whorehouse dear stranger; from what I heard!" The ladies grew silent after a short laugh. The man stood up and walked with a limp on a cane over to them. He had the look of a sullen ball-headed old bastard, with "bad mood" etched on his face. He answered. "Well, I figure Cavendish and Nephew can tell me since his last letters to me included your activities in them!"

"Let's discuss this in private and not for long!" Nephew coldly replied. The three men walked back to the table where the old man had been sitting near the fireplace at the cozy dim lit area at end of the long room and sat down. "Nephew began. "So, who wants to know about "our dear friend "Colonel Hillary Wadsworth, non-hero of the empire and very deceased?" The older gentleman, whose red face was accented in long gray lamb chops spoke. His head seemed to resemble a pumpkin sitting on top of a black tuxedo wall. A pumpkin face that bore a strange resemblance to the person he had mentioned.

"My name is Sir Elroy Wadsworth, and I am inquiring about my son, Colonel Hillary Wadsworth since the official reports on his real fate seem incorrect from my perspective!" Both Cavendish and Nephew looked blankly at each other, then stared at the stranger. Sir Elroy Wadsworth began. "I am very aware of your dislike of my son from your previous testimony at his trial Nephew!" Nephew coldly replied. "He got good people killed in that fiasco and you know this sir Elroy! Your dear son should have been stripped of his rank and privilege then sir! But you and your noble clan buddies saved his ass! If he had been drummed out of the army then, this would have saved many from his next unforgivable disaster! And his bullshit went on to kill…" Tiberius, clearly agitated shut up. He almost said it all but froze. Sir Elroy went on.

"It seems that there has been some sort of blackout on the whole affair regarding my son's actions and his death against this Kali and his legions of green devils that seem to be missing from the tabloids and all the military records thus far. Hillary sent me very detailed letters regarding the destruction and massacre at Chital, his successful military defense of it against an attack by these devils once his relief force deployed there! He cursed both of you for treasonous interfering in his efforts. His last letter I received detailed his crossing into some jungle across a river in pursuit of this foe named Kali and his vile army of green savages not to forget saving all the hostages captured by these cannibals he mentioned.

Then there was no more. I was told in my inquiry to my government sources that he died of the plague along with many residents at Chital, along with some of the soldiers in his command sent there. It is maintained officially that Chital was never destroyed and no massacre or counter defensive efforts by my son occurred. My feelers I sent to investigate say it happened and corroborates with his letters! His letters reflect proof of a quite different story! This different story that the public will soon know when I send them to the tabloids next week!" The eccentric old man gave a deathly stare in silence then finished. "He was also very detailed in both your cowardly and traitorous acts under combat conditions!"

Colonel Nephew looked at Cavendish then at the old man and spoke to Elroy Wadsworth icily. "Sir, "His defense of Chital when it came under attack?" Nephew laughed at him as he looked at Cavendish. "We both are not at liberty to discuss anything related to your son or to anything out of the official channels regarding any of this fantasy mail you have received. I will try and respect your bereavement over the loss of your son, but don't push it…SIR! Whatever you were told by the government is the official story forever and then forever after that forever SIR!! As far as I am concerned, this conversation is over!"

"This conversation is not over!" erupted the old buzzard's broken voice. "You were traitors according to my son!" Old Wadsworth oozed his contemptuous stare. Colonel Nephew was red faced and had murder in his eyes as he looked deep into the old man's eyes. "Traitors? Traitors my ass! I scoff at your pretentious jabber! I would say your son was the fucking traitor to the British high command and to over hundreds of good soldiers he led into a horrible slaughter! Your bastard son's illegal usurpation of command and irresponsible military campaign was responsible for this! One more thing! I personally hold you and your band of worthless nobles responsible for aiding in his ill-fated access to bogus orders!" Sir Elroy tried to talk but Tiberius was on a roll now. He sharply interjected.

"Did his ghost ever tell you this? Did he tell you he forged a phony order from an obscure friendly noble source not even in the proper chain of command to arrange this slaughter sir! Oh yes, there was a huge slaughter in the so named "valley of death! This obscure source had a recent fatal accident so I am told! Hillary died the death of a drunken stupid arrogant coward! For your record!" Elroy's face was a mask of red now. He pointed his finger at them. "I think he was murdered by the likes of you and your gang of cohorts!" Blabbered Elroy. Cavendish steadied Nephew by grabbing his arm and looked at the old man, frothing at the mouth now.

"Your accusations are insane babblings and as stupid as your son! So, fuck him and fuck you mister!" Both the soldiers stood up together and returned to their party without further words. They had said enough. Blood would need to know about these Wadsworth letters and Sir Elroy immediately. As they moved away, they heard the elder Wadsworth threaten. "We shall see who has the last word on this!" Nephew sharply turned. "You do not have any idea of who will get the last word on this yet! Pursue it as you will, but you will be the one who pays, so drop it, your miserable son is dead! He is very dead! That is all you need to know!"

Elroy Wadsworth yelled "Treason in combat is punishable by death!" and as both men turned around, they saw Sir Wadsworth again pointing his finger of accusation at them in an outline to a fire burning behind him in the fireplace. Cavendish added. "Be very careful Wadsworth with your poisonous language!" He countered by pointing his finger back at the old man. They turned and headed back for the table. Old Wadsworth now seemed to filter out of the room. Both men, ruffled at this exposure, this memory, returned to the table. They were comforted by the fact that nobody except their little party was in this small pub within the castle. At least nobody they could see.

With great false smiles, they picked up their large flagons of ale, toasted to the brave fallen, and emptied them. Colonel Nephew wrote a simple message on a piece of paper and hailed one of the man servants outside. Blood would be informed in minutes. Jenny watched as the old stranger scurried out of the room and sensed it was much more than just some casual argument. The name Wadsworth resonated in her mind. She learned over and kissed Ambrose. "So, Ambrose darling, Are you okay? What was that about?" She put her hand in his and squeezed it. Cavendish smiled at Nephew and answered. "We refused to deal with this old bastard father of "never to be Sir Hillary Wadsworth of Chital!" Jenny smiled as she saw the humor in the eyes of both men light up. "What is it Ambrose?" Nephew sensed it and laughed as Cavendish tried to look serious.

He added. "Candidly speaking Jenny, Wadsworth's son gave his last full measure dying terribly by the ancient ritual "death blowjob" of the…the Raktabija!" He then burst out laughing as Cavendish chimed in with a hearty belly laugh and said. "Yes, Jen, it just sucked the complete life out of him…

left him a shriveled husk!" Jenny smiled and retorted. "So how did he fall for this "death blowjob" Ambrose?" Both men were laughing very hard when Cavendish stammered. "On the floor!" The contact laughing made all the ladies laugh with them. My how humor can hide the reality Nephew thought. They all toasted with glasses held high to the justice meted out by the ancient "Death Blowjob" of Raktabija.

Ambrose smiled the smile of a person who had crossed again into that jungle. He was now torn between two worlds. Sweat appeared on his brow, denoting internal turbulence in his soul. He was now observing the slaughter of Wadsworth's command, then in the castle fighting for his life again. The memories of killing the Kali resonated through him as his hands began to shake. He was unconsciously grabbing for the Zulu spear but squeezed Jenny's hand as she held his. She felt him tense up as sweat poured from his brow. He finished the next near full flagon of ale and ordered another one from the bartender who was the only other witness to the verbal exchange between them and Elroy.

Then he looked at Jenny with a sincere but weak smile. "Miss Jenny, someday I will tell you the story, the truths of this series of events; if we, say get closer? Things got very crazy after the Malakand battle; quite unbelievable things happened which were completely off the charts of normalcy. However, it is very classified at this point, and rumors and myths will abound probably forever or until the real truth is revealed or shall I say regurgitated." She smiled. "Darling, do you mean the stories of the green devils, the cannibals, the massacre of hundreds of civilians at Chital and soldiers in some mysterious jungle north of Chital under an idiot named Wadsworth my father discussed with mum and me? Then the retribution of General Blood and some strange allies?"

At this point both Nephew and Cavendish laughed out loud, my had the Ale and cognac done its kind work this night. What else could they do? Cavendish knew if he showed any emotion or spent foolish words, he would verify the inquiry launched by his beautiful companion. "So?", he smiled "Yes Jenny, and there were flying monsters, banshees, giant prehistoric Dogs, dinosaurs, and evil tyrants who loved to dine on sweet ladies! How can this all be true Jen Jen? Why me and Nephew lived it!" The fairly drunken colonel added. "And we flew on the backs of purple unicorns to a city over a million years old after we destroyed the evil lair of that fifty-foot red devil demon!"

Then Nephew added as he cozied up to his two ladies. "I need love and extreme comfort to forget this hell we were in! Ladies, please help me to remove this nightmare!" Anastacia and Beatrice where now rubbing their hands across Nephew and giving each other approving looks. Then Jenny and the girls laughed. Ambrose looked mischievously at Jenny enjoying his buzz. Again. He then took both her hands tickling her stomach as she laughed. Their faces came close and then they stared at each other. Then they kissed a gentle kiss.

She seemed more beautiful than ever to Cavendish, as he gave a secret lament to Pyra. "What a life" he thought. However, he so wanted Jenny, she was there for him in his real life. This was the real world he surmised and liked what he saw. It was a fact of raw nature to him, "Two wonderful loves from two distinctly different worlds chimed through his mind again like it had every day! He knew in his heart that Jenny was his now and forever!

As they were leaving the small castle pub Cavendish pulled the colonel to the side with a happy smile. We need to verify that General Blood got your message about Sir Elroy and his son's letters!" Colonel Nephew smiled back from his extreme buzz, "Why shouldn't we Ambrose?" Cavendish then said with a kind half serious smile "We were not the only ones observing Sir Elroy in the pub during his outburst!" Nephew quizzed "The old bartender?" Then he remembered the powers inherited by his friend from the lifesaving surgery at Hima as Cavendish answered. "Shall I say friends from afar?"

The merriment and dancing continued at the viceroy's castle until late as many elegant ladies and gentlemen danced well into the night to an excellent band. Merriment, mirth, fun, and excessive drinking became the late agenda. The elder Farnsworth and wife joined them after their departure from the castle pub, but were tired and bid farewell. Jenny looked into James's eyes. "I want our date at the hotel to start tonight!" It was very late when the party of five inebriated souls embarked back to the luxurious Majestic hotel in a cold thick snowstorm. The weather had changed to a cold windless falling snow as the horse drawn carriage pulled up in front of the hotel.

The group walked to their rooms continuing their gay chatter in the dimly lit hallway. With a series of hugs and salutes, Nephew with his two luscious girlfriends, and Cavendish and Jenny departed to their rooms. The colonel and his two lovelies soon were in tight clustered embrace under mounds of covers, with carefully played jokes and laughs, and other expected events exploding. Before he climbed into bed with his lovelies, the colonel had quietly barricaded his door with a large oak chair as was his rule and had put a dagger and pistol close by. He had learned to be ready for the unknown, as he had taken the obscure threat of Sir Wadsworth seriously. He wanted to play it safe. Old Elroy was a wealthy and powerful noble and could be dangerous, especially with his threats. This old fart power as a noble with his son's letters definitely represented a serious intelligence breech if they were turned over to the press.

In the other room adjacent to Nephew's, Jenny and Ambrose had settled down on the bed in a more proper way. "Ambrose, is this our first date? The one you promised me at Malakand? And I have something of yours." Jenny then opened her nice purse and produced his service revolver he gave her at the battle of Malakand to defend herself. He gave a loud laugh. "Ha, the gift that kept on giving my sweet!" "This saved my life Ambrose; you saved my life along with the others. I had it engraved!" The inscription read "To my shining knight Ambrose from Jenny, 1897 India!" She then kissed him gently as she handed it to him. Ambrose leaned back and smiled as he checked the pistol which was clean and loaded. "I greatly appreciate your kind gift with a government issue revolver; but it is your memento now and for any future bodyguard work I may employ you on."

He put it back in her hand. She smiled and put it back in her purse. She kissed him again. "So, Captain, what other mementos do you have for me to keep this night?" Ambrose gave a warm smile, "Well Jen, we can look around." She then laughed and put her arms around him, forcing him back on the bed. "I am so cold darling!" He added, "Well, we had better get under the covers before we get frostbite!" She slipped off her dress and its accruements, clad in a corset, garters and thigh high nylons. Ambrose was completely aroused as she slipped under the covers to join her. They took short sips of cognac from his flask, and they joined in a sweet passionate embrace under a pile of blankets bathed in fine silk sheets. Their lovemaking was intimate and intense. They fell asleep peacefully in each other's arms.

As dawn was soon approaching, the snowstorm was again in full gale and the temperatures had plummeted. Winter was now hitting the British Isles in full force. The cold winds, piercing the buildings, were pushing into the hallways and rooms at the Majestic Hotel. Something itched in the back of Cavendish's mind as he lay with Jenny. It was his very active sixth sense working again now, as it had seen the observer in the pub who was invisible to the others.

He looked into the darkness and swore he saw some form, but for just an instant. He awoke sensing something was amiss. He crept out of bed and quickly put on his long woolen bathrobe. He quietly cracked open his hall door and stuck his head out to notice three men standing in the hall attempting to gain access to Colonel Nephew's room. They had a key, but the door was jammed for some reason. They were trying to quietly shove it open, but noise they generating was increasing.

As Ambrose stuck his head out of the door, from nowhere he was caught in the left side of his face near his eye with a strong glancing punch, which knocked him sideways out of his doorway into the hall wall then to the floor. His door loudly slammed shut as he hit the ground. A voice sounded from where he was attacked. "Sir Wadsworth wants a final accounting to you stinking traitors!" As the three men now bashed at Nephew's door, Cavendish grabbed a small table by the leg he had knocked over when he fell. He came up flailing the small table in the direction of the voice, catching the assailant squarely in the face with it. The rather large individual groaned loudly after impact and staggered back against the adjacent wall.

Nephew's door suddenly opened and two of the three men pushing on his door fell into his room. There were shouts, yells and screams from Nephew's room. Cavendish then grabbed a heavy-weighted oil lamp from another hall table and cleaved the skull of the third assailant now standing in front of Nephew's door. He fell like a sack of potatoes as the kerosene pouring from the broken lamp ignited on his clothes. A gunshot rang from the colonel's room just before three shots rang out behind the captain. He ducked back to the floor. One man staggered into the hall falling over his immolated companion, then literally rolled down the stairs.

Ambrose then turned to see Jenny, holding his service revolver, with the barrel smoking in the dim hall light. The body of the rather large man lay at her feet close behind him. Next to the assailant's now dormant hand laid a meat cleaver stuck in the floor. Nephew, completely naked stepped out of his room and kicked the body of the burning thug down the stairs. "You all right Ambrose?" Asked the naked colonel. "Yes, Sir only took one punch to the face!" Nephew smiled and went back inside his room to find some clothes. Within what seemed moments, four men from Scotland Yard and two high ranking intelligence officers were in the hall. Soon, other elements of the police and Scotland Yard were dealing with the smoking body at the bottom of the stairs and combing the hotel. It seemed that there were four bodies. Nephew, who shot the second invader, had stabbed the first one to death after he opened the door forcing them to stumble in. The body of the attacker who Nephew shot, was found outside the hotel covered in fresh snow. The one Jenny had killed lay in the hall. It had all happened within what seemed seconds.

"They were sent by Sir Wadsworth" remarked Cavendish, as he explained the comment by his now deceased assailant to the investigators. The ranking officer said, "We received a warning on this via General Blood late last night and did have people here. However, these assassins had slipped in and were waiting before we arrived. They were in a room down the hall." He pointed to a room at the far end of the dimly lighted hall.

"What is next?" asked Cavendish. The head investigator, smiling through his quit huge moustache replied. "The bodies will be removed, and except for your nice black eye Mr. Cavendish, nothing happened here tonight of any official consequence. These were just a bunch of hooligans we were tracking, trying to rob guests at this hotel. This will be our story if needed. "He smiled and tipped his derby. He then shook hands with both Cavendish and Nephew and they left.

Old Lord Elroy Wadsworth sat alone facing a huge fire in his great fireplace, at his drab cold empty estate. He was wrapped in a blanket waiting for word that his son's antagonists had been executed by his well-paid assassins. The burning fire was the only light in the whole large drawing room area, which reflected of many elegant antiques covered in the dust of neglect. He was drinking shots of expensive fifty-year-old scotch. He knew of the treachery of both Nephew and Cavendish as spelled out by the last letter his son had written. Those two were responsible for his son's failure and death. He seethed as he drank his next shot of scotch from a glass in hand. These two Murderous traitors would die tonight for the insult and treachery against his noble son Colonel Hillary Wadsworth!

He kept pondering his son as the time ticked by in the cold snow ridden night. It went on and on as he continued pouring shots of scotch whiskey down his ancient gullet. It was now early dawn and he continued waiting for word from his hired assassins of the success of their deadly endeavor of vengeance. Something strange began to happen as he stared into the large flames produced by fresh load of logs he dumped in his fireplace. Elroy was now locked into a trance of sorts. He first saw the complete Battle of Malakand and the efforts of Cavendish and Nephew in the combat. Then, the panorama changed as he saw his son and all his exploits running in front of him like some yet to be invented movie.

He witnessed it all in grave detail beginning with the bogus orders he had manufactured by his noble buddy to march his army to Chital. He then saw how his son had tried to execute Colonel Nephew and his escape to General Blood's command. Then he saw the truth in the real massacre at Chital and Cavendish's excellent defense against the green devils in the remains of Chital which his son had no part. He saw in shock the complete massacre of so many ill lead soldiers in the jungle valley; the savagery of the green devils and the grimace of the monster entity Kali now smiling at him! Old Elroy winced at the monster's gaze!

Then he saw in detail how Lieutenant Cavendish and his scouts tried to warn his son's force by bravely attacking the castle lair of the Kali. But it was way too late. He saw Colonel Hillary Wadsworth as he really was; a piece of irresponsible shit and a drunken coward! He saw the reality; in his now broken spirit it was the truth. He had sent two honorable officers to their deaths this night? Then he saw in the fireplace flames the shape-changers and the horror they wreaked upon his son and his corrupt staff who broke the law of the village…his terrifying death, the long post death terror that gripped his soul, and the husk that remained of his son…with his fucking pants down around his boots! Then he heard the mockery of his son's death; "death by the blowjob of Raktabija!"

Elroy bellowed an inaudible scream and litany of words in shock and shame. He picked up his double-barreled shotgun resting on the long divan next to him, finished the bottle of single malt scotch. As some of the scotch ran down his jaw unto his tux Sir Elroy placed the barrel of the shotgun below his jaw. He then pulled both triggers together that gave a coughing loud explosion against the walls of the room. The dual blasts blew his head into bloody shards, scattered across the room creating macabre decorations on the ceiling, walls, and dusty unattended ornate furniture.

The tall thin green form standing in the corner of the shadowed room collected all the letters of Sir Hillary to his father spread out on the table in front of dead headless Elroy. They were tossed into the blazing fireplace; then it left. The picture show and the life of Sir Elroy were both over. This was how Scotland Yard would find him in the morning. The case was closed as a suicide; a grieving father who lost his son to disease in India. The unknighted Hillary Wadsworth whose exploits were never to be mentioned in the official British military history of India.

After Scotland Yard and the special military officers had cleaned up the mess at the Majestic Hotel and left, Nephew had the nervous hotel staff bring up some ice for Cavendish's black eye and two fresh bottles of cold champagne. The group of five sat on Cavendish and Jenny's bed passing around the bottles like pirates. In half drunken graveyard humor, Colonel Nephew finally returned to bed with his insatiable ladies; crawling back under the covers as they cuddled together for the morning frolic. Jenny continued applying ice to Cavendish's left eye after their guests left. She was quiet for the first moments as James Ambrose finally broke his silence. "I am sorry Jenny that I involved you in this mess." She looked at him with worry. "I am not upset for killing that man, just upset that he nearly killed you in front of me with that damn meat cleaver!"

She was silent for a few moments then continued. "Ambrose, if you haven't noticed I am in love with you. I fell in love with you in Malakand, all dirty and bloody! I love you more than ever and you are stuck with me forever like a new hoof on a horse!!" Ambrose looked her deep in the eyes, his love for her was sincere and it was real. Pyra had only sidelined this feeling in his other world, but he now felt what was hidden within him. He kissed her with his eyes misting. "Jenny, I love you as well, very much, and thanks for saving my life!" They both climbed back into bed for a while in a tight passionate embrace as the sun fought to shed light through the cloud cover of the massive snowstorm engulfing London still. After breakfast Jenny and the other two ladies left by carriage. Nephew and Cavendish had a date with the Queen, and Bindon Blood would be there to fetch them at eleven!

After their guests had left, Cavendish was beat and his head hurt from the punch and creeping hangover. He crawled under the large bed cover back in his hotel room like a bear in hibernation and was sound asleep in seconds. He finally awoke to the knocking sound of the maid at his door. "Please come in ma'am!" as Cavendish pulled the covers over his head. Soon he heard the tub being filled with water and finally the tugging of the maid at his feet. "Captain Cavendish! Your water is dawn for your bath, and you have hot tea by your bedside. General Blood will be here at eleven am and it is 8:45 now! Please get up!" The maid's voice was commanding and held a strong foreign accent.

"All right All right…thanks!" Cavendish peered from his covers and looked around his room. It was immaculately clean, as was his dress uniform hanging by the dresser. He then looked at the maid who was looking at him as she left. "An Indian" he thought! The tea, large glass of juice, and bath helped him completely overcome his hangover, but his black eye ached. Evidently the punch had glanced him and knocked him off-balance, so the swelling was slight and the blackness ringed his eye in a growing circle. He drank hot tea, ate some toasted muffins and jam, and forced a shot of cognac down from his refilled flask at the viceroy's stock at the castle the night before. It was a hangover killer, but the glass of juice seemed to dissipate his headache completely. He noticed an eye patch next to his kit, to cover his eye. How nice he thought, what great hotel service!

Donning his bath robe, he knocked on Colonel Nephew's door. He banged several times and finally the door opened. It was a very worn out shabby image Cavendish saw. On further inspection, he saw the room a complete shamble. "You looked better at breakfast my lord!" What the hell' he thought, "Where is the maid?" Tiberius groaned as Ambrose offered him a shot of cognac. After getting Colonel Nephew in the road to recovery by drawing a hot bath, and another sumptuous shot of cognac, room service delivered hot tea and took his uniform to be cleaned and pressed for the lunch with Queen Victoria. It was pure comedy watching Nephew stagger and bump around in his confused efforts to get ready.

Ambrose then helped him get into his pressed uniform and boots. "You seemed like you were coming around well at breakfast Tiberius. Looks like those lasses gave you a real workout!" Nephew looked at him with a weary beaten smile as Cavendish gave him another plug of cognac to help with his hangover event. "Damn champagne! I had a few and if I had only drunk ale!" mumbled Nephew. Then he asked. "Could it be love at first sight with double vision my captain?" "Yes, my fair colonel it was the damn champagne!" Cavendish then returned to his room very amused. As he was finished dressing, he heard a knock on his door.

He opened it and a maid was standing there, an older British blonde buxom woman slightly rotund. "Sir, are you ready for me to clean your room now?" Cavendish looked confused. "I appreciate this, but my room was cleaned sometime early this morning, my bath was drawn, and your wonderful Indian maid even gave me an eye patch!" The china-faced buxom maid smiled but seemed confused at his comment. "Sir, we do not employ any Indians or any other non- English people on our staff at this hotel. It is policy sir!" This now perplexed Cavendish. Then he said. "Better go see how my buddy is doing next door, he needs a lot of help. "The maid smiled in complete confusion and moved down the hall to the colonel's door.

Cavendish closed the door and sat on the bed trying to understand this fathom maid, the Indian one who had visited him so early. It rapidly dawned on him that Pyra must have visited him, warned him last night, and had protected him from execution by Wadsworth's assassins. His weary eyes misted as he contemplated his eternal love for her, and then pondered his obvious love for Jenny. Then he gave out a loud 'dammit!" He would love them both! Love them forever! Enough said! Two great loves surrounded him now and probably forever. He feared that he was going to hurt someone. His divided love between a fantasy and real world was bothering him deeply.

Pyra later smiled deeply into Ravi's eyes. He loved his little girl and admired her. She spoke. "Ambrose is safe from danger now and I saw his human love Jenny. She is so pretty and good for him! But Ravi, I will always be in love with him and told him that honestly from my heart. Is that wrong?" Ravi smiled, "Never is it wrong to love, for love is eternal and forever my little one. We call love the true lifeblood of our Creator. If more humans loved unselfishly as you do, the problems of this world would be nil." Pyra was looking down. "He does love me from one perspective and is in love with Jenny Farnsworth from another!" Ravi laughed. "Prya, two loves from two different worlds? Those were the thoughts I picked up from him before he left Hima.

Mr. Ambrose greatly understands the position he is willfully in, this I am certain, and does fear hurting you as his human life with Jennifer grows." Pyra looked worried and added. "Ravi, he could never hurt me! My love for his soul is eternal and forever!" She had tears in her eyes as Ravi kissed his daughter on the head. "We shall discuss this more my sweet girl, time will serve you and him darling." "Time father?" "Yes child, the passage of time cures all the pains of the heart and clarifies existence! I think it was Lord Buddha that told me that once." Ravi gave a sincere smile as she ran off to play with the other little girls in the beautiful stream that ran near the farming village. Ravi smiled to himself. The passage of time meant something quite different in his world from that of humans. He was also pleased that Ronjin had cleaned up the Sir Elroy Wadsworth dilemma.

By some miracle, Captain Cavendish and Colonel Nephew where all "spit and polish" as the royal coach pulled up to fetch them at eleven on the dime! A miracle by all standards based on all their events the night before. It would be a capital offense to be late for Queen Victoria, the patron mother of all her English children! General Bindon Blood climbed out of the carriage to welcome them. The snowstorm had settled down a little, but drifts of fallen snow completely blanketed the ground in white heaps. They all climbed into the carriage as the horse-drawn carriage moved toward the palace cutting deep rivulets in the drifts as it bumped along.

The general smiled at his two weary charges as he commented. "They found Sir Elroy Wadsworth early this morning. He seems to have blown his head off with a double-barreled shotgun last night. The letters from Hillary was evidently burned in the fireplace. It seems that this case, like that whole bundle of terrible events surrounding the cursed name Wadsworth are now secure again and behind us gentlemen!" He looked at Cavendish. "By the way captain, that eye patch looks great! Distinguished by all counts!"

"Why thank you kind general; my confidence has been restored!" The captain pulled up the patch and showed him his darkened black eye. "That assassin paid dearly for this insult!" Bindon Blood was beaming. "I heard he met his fate from an unlikely source!" They laughed. The carriage was soon in front of the very regal front of Buckingham Palace. Royal Guards, adorned in Bearskin helms and greatcoats served as the honor guard as the trio climbed the steps into the palace. Snow began falling hard again. They were soon walking down a long hall lined with an incredible panorama of tapestries, accruements of pure royal splendor, statues, and paintings of famous British heroes, kings, and queens. The silent tour offered an amazing historical view, although brief.

They were ushered into a private meeting room in the remote part of the palace. It seemed to Blood, Cavendish, and Nephew, that this meeting was to be held in secret. They entered a very comfortable room, complete with a huge fire burning in a very ancient fireplace. The elegance of this place was remarkable. The walls were decorated with more medieval accruements, with suites of armor adorning every corner. Tapestries hung on the walls. The table was huge and made of the wood of some long dead oak tree. The table, chairs, and furniture were the best in hand carved craft. The room had a very relaxed atmosphere, comfortable and warm. They stood facing a small dais with a large ornate chair.

Queen Victoria emerged from a doorway and stood quietly and unsmiling on the small dais. The three soldiers bowed and came to attention. The Queen was dressed in a black gown, with a white shawl around her shoulders, with a very nice smaller crown with jewels on her head of long hair. She was moving slowly and gave the air of a serious and stately leader. She was short and was characterized as dowdy by some critics. Yet her reputation of being stout, strict and a very tough leader preceded her. Yet, she displayed great love for all her subjects. She saw them all as her children. She stood quietly for a few moments observing the three as her face beamed with a warm smile.

At her side was her treasured aide Abdul Karim, a Muslim, seen as her teacher or "munshi". The Queen had born a lot of public criticism when she chose him as her confident. Ambrose had to smile at Karim as he smiled back at the captain. Karim knew that Ambrose saw his real identity. He was more than a simple munshi and Ambrose now had a good feel of how the queen knew of events in India! He was kin to the village. The Queen had been given the title "Empress of India" this year of her Diamond Jubilee celebration. She spoke in a soft but strong voice.

"Good afternoon gentlemen, it is a great pleasure to have you all here, safe and sound." She gave out a new warm smile. Karim, bearded and dressed in his ethnic attire, smiled from his well-groomed beard and bowed. General Blood answered for the three. "It is also a great pleasure and honor for us to have audience with you my Queen!" Queen Victoria smiled back. "Before we sit, I would like to give a well-deserved honor to you General Bindon Blood!" With that, he was asked to kneel in front of the Queen. She tapped her sword on his shoulder and ceremoniously knighted him as Sir Bindon Blood, Lord of The Khyber Pass of India. Both Colonel Nephew and Captain Cavendish gave in to a salute and short round of applause.

The general was handed his certificate of knighthood and handed a beautiful engraved sword in honor. "With great respect, I humbly accept this honor my Queen!" "It is my pleasure Sir Blood! I am sorry that this honor was in secret for now, and we will repeat it when things settle down regarding all the rumors surrounding the debacle in India. Now may we all be seated." The queen was going to sit at the table with them and not on her dais? A large beautiful teapot made of china, brimming with hot tea was poured into their equally ornate teacups. Lunch was served and the party engaged in small talk. It was the best hot stew they had ever tasted. After lunch came a tray of sweets and more hot tea. The only people present were the Queen, Karim, and the three guests.

The Queen seemed very relaxed and in friendly spirits. They answered questions posed by the Queen about their lives, pastimes, and soon moved into the subject of India. Cavendish could not believe he was talking so informally to what history would christen as the most powerful and successful monarch in British history. Karim was very respectful as he shuffled a sheaf of papers beside her. She began her dialogue with an apology as she looked at Nephew and Cavendish. Lunch was over and the more serious part of the meeting began. "I am very sorry for the incident at your hotel last night. It seems that the elder Wadsworth had his moment and like his idiot son, has now joined him. She sipped her tea and looked at Captain Cavendish.

"It is a sad moment in our great military tradition that the whole affair surrounding the green devils and this Kali must never be recorded in our history. There are several reasons for this secrecy. We never want the Russians to know how close they came to fulfilling their plan in conjunction with the Kali's forces and the Mad fakir. We never want the public to know of the disgrace of Colonel Wadsworth and how his unlawful actions led to the massacre of hundreds of British empire soldiers and auxiliaries. We never want our subjects to know of the horror that befell Chital, worse than 1857 by all respect's gentlemen, as you know. Words can never describe how terrible I feel about all those soldiers and their grieving families." Tears began to run down her cheeks. "They were all my children and as Queen mother, I feel that in some way I let them down."

She paused. "Hillary Wadsworth gave the whole command a slip and It was just too late for anybody to stop his ill-fated blunder. Queen Victoria cleared her eyes and smiled. "The official history has been amended to speak of our victories in India, not defeats." She continued. "In Reading these many personal accounts by you and your men was extraordinary to say the least, but I want to hear you tell me of these exploits so I may feel the direct emotional side of this whole affair. Captain Cavendish, please begin, since you seemed to be stuck in the middle of this from the beginning. Also, I do not want you to shield events but level with me on all accounts."

"Yes, my Queen, I will give you my best account!" The Queen relaxed back in her chair and took occasional sips of tea as Cavendish began his tale just before the circumstances leading up to the battle of Malakand. She listened as the captain told his tale, concluding at the terrible end of the Kali by his hands. To save time, and add depth to the account, Colonel Nephew interjected his story as the timeframe of Cavendish's coincided with his story. Over the course of two hours they wove a fascinating firsthand account of the whole campaign. Sir Bindon Blood followed with his professional account of his campaign with deep praise for the warriors from the village.

Queen Victoria was completely mesmerized and only interjected questions to clarify points. Then she seemed to cut from the story with a direct question. "So how would you describe this Kali son?" The captain thought for a moment then spoke. "The Kali, as I saw him was powerful and extremely hypnotic…. dangerous…um…. a soul killer! I wish I could…he trailed off then ended with "I could see how he could easily sway lesser people into his designs. There is more to this story." A fresh pot of tea served in the finest china, and the Queen asked a question that concerned them.

"Tell me the story of Ravi and the village." She gave a smile to Karim as Nephew and Cavendish stared at each other. Cavendish spoke first. "My Queen, how do you know of Ravi?" She gave a sincere smile. He paid me a personal visit after the destruction of Chital by the green devils and just before the destruction of Wadsworth's relief in the jungle! Ravi the sage first visited me in his traditional form in a dream over a year ago. He needed our help for a very serious reason. You might say we became fast friend's boys. He was asking me for help against this civilization killer. He explained Kali and his threat to the world order if Kali was successful in India. I would love to hear your impressions of his people, Hima, and civilization. This is why we discuss this in secret. Outside of being the Queen, I am also a very curious old lady and given to the pains of my age. He knows I love history. You may be free to tell me; it is all right!"

He enlightened the Queen from his perspective. All were amazed at the heart surgery that saved his life. He also enthralled Sir Blood and Tiberius Nephew with his exquisite insight into the race that lived in the village over the next hour. He discussed the genetic bond between the Kali and those of the village, and why the he had to be destroyed. The Kali was one of the powerful fallen angels from an old line as the captain reviewed his terrible litany of evil personages through time. Cavendish told of how Colonel Wadsworth's life really ended in hours of telepathic terror filled pain that drained his soul and turned his body to a dried husk. He then was silent. Queen Victoria patted him on the shoulder and gave a deep affectionate smile.

"After all captain, Ravi had to sell me his horse, which seemed like a unicorn in the beginning. Once I learned the truth and saw the visual of the threat; I gave him my horse, a warhorse in the form of Sir Bindon Blood. We British were the only hope Ravi had in clearing the path in defeating Kali! The dear foolish Wadsworth was an anomaly to our plans." Cavendish nodded his head and cracked a smile at the Queen for the first time in nearly three hours. "You mean that old sage got to you my Lady?" The Queen laughed out loud. "Yes, since a union between my armies and his people was the only way to destroy the evil of Kali.

General Blood had to be brought into this plot by direct interface with Ravi. By complete accident due to Wadsworth, you and your scouts were the chosen interface between the British and the village. I will add that Ravi and I have become quite good friends during this whole process. He is such a graceful gentleman and I love his stories of the past!" She held his hand and squeezed it. He thought of what a grand lady she really was. General Blood now understood how simple it was for him to have a free reign in deploying his forces from throughout northern India to defeat Kali. He had been shocked at the complete absence of the military staff bureaucracy that always stymied and slowed smooth running military responses. Queen Victoria had completely greased the rails per Ravi and this is how secrecy was maintained throughout the whole campaign!

The Queen continued. "Ravi told me other things in our conversations. He told me that although the Kali was the most dangerous one, they knew about, the distinct possibly was that more of these fallen angels of yore, were possibly out there roaming the earth waiting for opportunity to knock! He told me that historical circumstances of revolutions, war, and severe social and economic circumstances are the fuel that energizes them. Meaning that they can grow from a docile state into a dangerous problem!"

"Evil loves basking in chaos according to Ravi." Interjected Cavendish. The Queen took a sip of tea and continued. "Yes, an evil force that radically tears at the very fabric of mankind when it materializes, the Devil of sorts and to ageless match between good and evil personified. Ravi told me he senses another evil coming in the near term, and much worse than Kali. He speculated on his vision of a huge conflict arising from the emerging social, economic, and diplomatic conditions evolving in Europe now. He told me that the conditions for this clash are directly related to the old unresolved tribal conflicts going back to the end of the Roman Empire! The massive chaos generated in this growing disparity among European nations would be a good playing field for a new Kali to rise up! He maintains that if sounder minds prevail this conflict can be averted!"

"When and Where my Queen?" was the simple question of Colonel Nephew? She looked sternly at Nephew. "It seems to point to Germany because of their pure never wavering arrogant militaristic attitudes! This attitude was personified in the wake of their resounding victory over France in the Franco-Prussian War of 1870. Russia is another possibility, but the probabilities keep this vague in future time and space. The terrible war of European nations will be fought he said. Not because the gods ordain it, but solely by the conflicting social and economic conditions that the leaders of mankind create!" She paused as they sipped their tea before she continued.

"Ravi and his council believe that the advent of this new "Kali" may rise out of the aftermath of this next possible war he fears and not the conflict itself. He feared four things emerging now in

European circles at the turn of this century. Ravi called them the Biblical "Four Horsemen of the Apocalypse." They are alliance systems, militarism, nationalism, and the plague of imperialism touching off this calamity." LT-Colonel Nephew shook his head.

"My Queen, from my conversations with Ravi he is also extremely concerned about "causes" that lead to the chaos, that unleash the maniacal egos ruling Europe! These "Horsemen" that Ravi rightfully speaks of have been imbedded in events throughout Europe since the fall of the Roman Empire! This is a fantastic assumption. What else of importance did he say since we have not been privy to his conversation on this subject?" She picked up her bone china teacup and took a slow sip as she adjusted herself. "He also finally answered my direct question of when I would pass on, so I could prepare this country in my demise…. He told me, after much bickering that it would be June 27, 1901!" She again gave a serene resolute smile as she continued speaking.

"Now, my boys, we both have great secrets we must hide!" She rang a small bell and an attendant entered. She ordered him to fetch the best bottle of French champagne, for it was time for a well-deserved drink and to honor the knighted "Sir Bindon Blood of the Khyber Pass." As they sipped their drink, Queen Victoria was transformed into a simple fun lady, with caring and humor to match. She got a rise from the story of both escapes from the clutches of Wadsworth. They talked more of their personal lives and the sort. In the end, they all stood and saluted the Queen and gave a respectful bow. In her turn, she hugged each man and kissed him on the cheek. They parted ways, not as Queen and subject, but as friends. A strong bond had formed between them.

General "Sir" Bindon Blood was silent as they strode out of the palace, contemplating with amazement at all that was said. Both the lieutenant -colonel and captain were amazed that the Queen had been part of the plan with Ravi from the beginning! Colonel Tiberius Nephew was internally focused on a new "Kali" in Germany or Russia, and Captain Ambrose Cavendish was thinking of his date with Lady Jenny Farnsworth in two hours. Queen Victoria watched from a window as the three dear soldiers descended the wind-swept stairs and walked to their carriage in a heavy snowstorm which had been falling for hours. She shivered and asked for a blanket as she returned to the warmth of the huge fire in her private fireplace. She ordered a nice shot of American whiskey and settled in her favorite repose in front of her warm fireplace.

She sat a long while gazing into the flames remembering her youth, her family, marriages, and her life as Queen Victoria of England. She smiled to herself as she sipped the whiskey which warmed her body. What a life she had lived. She smiled at the good times and lamented at the sad; especially the loss of so many soldiers in a strange jungle valley at the base of the mysterious Himalayas. Life seemed so short she thought. She smiled at the ancient old man in robes standing next to her. It was her friend Ravi and he too needed a cup of strong hot tea with milk. However, there was work to be done and Ravi was on time. On June 27, 1901, thirty-two years before the new German "Kali" would come to power, Queen Victoria passed away in her sleep after illness.

The official report recorded for posterity in British Military History recorded the following victorious accounts of the war in the north of India: The Battles of Malakand, Chakadara, Saragarti, and the huge campaigns of the Malakand Field Force were well documented. Sir Bindon Blood's outstanding leadership would later become well known by the writings of second lieutenant named Winston Churchill in his "The Story of Malakand Field Force: Episode in the Frontier War." These battles continued well into 1898, finally ending in a loose treaty regarding control of the Khyber Pass. The only mention Chital had in the annals was that its supply lines were threatened during this 1897 conflict and the outpost town had endured minor attacks. The disaster and victory in the jungle valley was left in the rumor mills.

Most of the British officers and NCOs that led their Indian forces in the jungle valley conflict in the Himalayan Mountains in the south remained on duty in India and other colonies; many until retirement or the outbreak of World War I. World War I battlefields would claim the bulk of these veteran combatants who fought against the Kali's devils in the valley. True to their respect for the Queen, these survivors never spoke publicly of it. However, the stories and tales of it did spread out more as myth than reality…. just the tales of green monsters who devoured children as fuel for scary ghost stories late at night.

Both soldiers pondered it at length over a few ales at the "Owl's Breath or Bite "Pub across from the hotel before Cavendish left for dinner with Jenny and family. Ambrose had cabled his parents just after he returned to England. John and Mary or Miriam, as she liked to be called knew he was home. They were a very close family, and had kept routine contact while in India, with a series of letters, when he was able. They lived in small farming town fifteen miles east of the city of Kingston Upon Hull on an old family estate farm about one-hundred miles northeast of London. Kingston Upon Hull was founded in the 12th Century and was known for early wool production. It was a popular market town with a bustling fishing and whaling hub. This area was the scene of the early battles in the English Civil War. The Cavendish's large farm raised sheep for wool and food and planted potato crops.

Father also was a merchant, who had a nice haberdashery on the eastern edge of the city a few miles from his estate. It was a popular meeting place, and doubled as a nice well-furnished pub. Mother lorded over the farm estate, in which part of it overlooked the River Hull only several miles from the North Sea. She kindly supervised the hired help, as father worked the business. They were both very earthly people, who were generous, and had become more as friends and parents to Ambrose as he grew up. He loved them very much for they were not just parents, but the best of friends.

Cavendish had two sisters and an older brother. His oldest brother and sister had moved away. His brother John was a barrister somewhere in London, who seldom communicated with the family. He was very into his life and his achievements. His oldest sister Rayne was married to a Frenchman, who owned wineries in Western France. She was a real sweetheart, and Jacques; her husband was of the best caliber. Ambrose had loved his lengthy visit with them and their children before he deployed to India.

His youngest sister Elisabeth was a wildcat, what one could construe as the "problem" child. As the youngest, and extremely pretty, had mastered the art of manipulation with sweet smiles when in trouble. She had become spoiled in the wake of her older siblings and developed an air of rebellion as a teenager. She was three years younger than Cavendish and was full of energy. She was classified as a student but seemed confused as she bounced back and forth from school to home routinely. Her father candidly remarked that her activities exhibited an untamed high intellect.

Ambrose loved his baby sister referring to her as a super brat and was the only one who stood up to her shenanigans; as he was the only one baby sister could not manipulate. They fought and often argued when it was time for little pretty Elizabeth to be squashed back into place. Elizabeth loved him and had even learned the art of confiding with him. Elizabeth was now at home probably for the rest of the year. Cavendish could only smile at the possibility of seeing his wild pretty baby sister with the mountains of tussled blonde curls about her head accented by her bouncing oversized buxom breasts.

It was after eight when Cavendish's coach pulled up in front of the stately Farnsworth Estate just west of London. The record snowstorm had been picking up again for the last several hours and the weather had been very hard on his ride. It seemed to be the storm of the century. Soon after the carriage had dropped him off, he was in front of a huge set of double doors. He thanked his stars that long walls on either side of this entrance shielded this doorway, because the cold generated by the wind was teasing his very bones.

The door creaked open as Ridley, the family manservant ushered him in and relieved him of his large military overcoat and hat. Cavendish admired the pristine Victorian demur of this room and downstairs. Jenny waved to him at the top of a rather nice cascading staircase. She was radiant, dressed in a green dress. Soon she cascaded down the huge spiral staircase she was in front of him and they kissed. "Come on my love, let's meet with my father and mother and have some dinner!"

"Sounds good, sorry I was late, but this weather..." "Not to worry, this is one of the worst ones in years, according to my father." As Ambrose entered a huge well-decorated study, he noticed it lined with volumes of books, with an assortment of animal heads and various weapons on the walls. The room smelled of aged wood and pipe smoke. This great study was blessed with a large fireplace and the warm fire crackling within. So, he edged up close to it to draw warmth into his body.

He turned to greet Jenny's parents as they entered the room. They had only briefly met at the Viceroy's ball. "I would like for you to again formally meet my father and my mother!" Sir Roger Farnsworth was a retired admiral and quite an entrepreneur. He had traveled throughout the globe in both military and economic capacities for the government. He was, by all respects, quite a force in British interests in many colonies including India. He was well respected and had become extremely prosperous. "The pleasure is mine once again." Retorted Cavendish, as he shook hands with Sir Farnsworth and his wife. If you were to judge these two by their looks, they both looked very normal, and could, without the expensive trimmings, easily fit into the merchant class like his parents.

Jenny and mother went into the other room to oversee the dinner soon to be served. Ambrose thanked the stars that they were not the stuffed shirt arrogant righteous noble class mindset! "Would you care for a drink and cigar before dinner captain?" "Yes sir, cognac will do for me. It is so cold outside; I think my bones are still frozen!" "One of the worst ones in a long time, so I am told!" Replied Lord Farnsworth as he poured a large shot into a snifter for Ambrose. With drinks in hand, and two Cuban Maduros fired up, the men strode around the room as Sir Farnsworth talked of the animals he had hunted in Africa, or the big fish he had caught. He talked about his service in the Navy, and a little about his work in the economic sector.

He seemed very easy going and the conversation was pleasant. His military career actions were many and had focused on the interdiction and destruction of the many pirate bands roaming the Mediterranean Sea. He had a dry humor that Cavendish liked. Dinner was served. The fare was excellent as expected. Cavendish was famished and the many courses of food were consumed without hesitation. But he had to properly eat the food and not gobble it down, for he was an officer and gentleman! The dinner, headlined by roast prime rib and was very pleasant in flavor quality and size. Sir Farnsworth now spoke as dinner was ending and cordials and dessert was forthcoming. He offered Ambrose another Cubano Maduro and they fired them up.

"So, tell me about your experience in India. I heard all sorts of stories son about what really had occurred there. In perfect lie, Cavendish went on to spin this great story of the Malakand and Chakadara battles. Jenny helped with her account of her moments of terror in the Malakand battle. Cavendish had made her swear to secrecy regarding old man Wadsworth's assassination attempt at the hotel. Her promise to keep quiet was kept. Her smile beamed at him as he continued with the story which was slowly evolving into a tall tale. "So how did you win your VC son?" All he could remember from his certificate were the words "gallant holding action against large enemy forces east of the Khyber Pass."

Using this as fuel for the story, and keeping his mind focused on the real outcome, he spun a good one near the Khyber Pass, honestly lending credit to the others who had stood with him in battle. He was smiling and embarrassed at his valiant story of heroism in the wrong place. "Very good son, did you encounter any of the green devils I have heard about? My intelligence sources told me they seemed to be everywhere in support of the Pashtuns, especially in the north. I heard that Chital was completely destroyed and the population murdered by them and has been a well-kept government secret. I heard all about the terrible plight of Wadsworth's disaster!" Cavendish surmised that his goose of a phony story was cooked and leveled with is host. "I was never to speak to anyone about this by direct orders of Queen Victoria!"

Sir Farnsworth smiled, "Son, my agents are well connected for many economic and security issues within our empire. We had a fair understanding of the real story now hidden from the public. Also, that old bastard Elroy Wadsworth? I know about his attempt on your life as well son." Cavendish realized where this was going. He could or would not tell this story as truth so he gave the most serious stare he could at Sir Farnsworth. "Sir, what you and many others are hearing are myths and the stuff nightmares are made of…they are hideous in nature, scary to say the least! I will tell you a story now beginning with "Once upon a time in India!" He then gave a brief unofficial account of what had really happened as if he was making it up.

Then he said in closing, "I personally killed Kali with a Zulu spear carried by one of my men who was a veteran of the Battle at Rorke's Drift! Now, shall I repeat the official story again, the one approved by the Queen and government?" The Captain then winked and smiled broadly from his gaze. Sir Farnsworth got the message clearly in Cavendish's smile and replied. "Truth without telling the truth lad? Excellent! You have spilled no beans either. I got the official picture of it." He then smiled at Ambrose. His account had coincided exactly with what his agents had told him. He commented to the young captain.

"Just myth I will assume here? Ghost stories my dear Cavendish?" The elder Farnsworth gave out a hearty laugh. "You bet!" replied the captain with a big smile. "I look for those little green monsters with filed teeth and tattoos under my bed every night!" Sir Farnsworth gave a smile. "Mum is the word on all of this since I was briefed by Viceroy Blackwater personally!" Out of respect, the topic was removed from the discussion as Jenny spoke. "Father, how are brother Horace and Annabel doing with the rum business in Jamaica?

Over the next thirty minutes over after dinner cordials Ambrose learned the complete story of Horace Farnsworth and his wife Annabel as owners and proprietors of the huge family rum business with a huge sugar cane estate plantation in Jamaica. They made and exported what was considered as the emergence of the finest white, gold, and dark rums labeled "Jamaican Prime Estate Rum." Cavendish laughed to himself as he had realized this was the brand that Hooky had absconded from the wrecked officers club at Malakand and they all drank while fighting in north India. He related this story to the broad smile of Sir Roger.

The story on this family rum endeavor was one of great initial success, of expansion, and family prosperity. Ambrose mused as he wondered how Old Hooky "RIP" was doing now. He loved this brand of rum! Lady Farnsworth invited Cavendish to stay the night, for the storm seemed raging out of control now. The family coach horses were tendered in warm stables for the night. With final salutations, both elder Farnsworth's retired to bed, leaving Ambrose and Jenny alone on the large couch in front of the fireplace.

They kissed and gave a long mutual hug. After pouring another couple of shots of cognac, they sat watching the fire. Jenny was first to speak. "The story you told about what happened at Chital,

Wadsworth, and General Blood's victory are hard to believe." "Jenny, there will come a day when I will tell you the complete details to this story that even your father does not know. It is not the time now darling." "Okay, tell me later, but tell me one thing. Is there any real truth to these rumors of monsters and cannibals?" Cavendish was silent, gathering his words.

He then looked at her with an intense glare, which startled her momentarily. "Jenny, the absolute truth would make your worst nightmare seem as nothing! Monsters? Yes, darling, there were monsters! Extremely diabolical dangerous monsters that loved the taste of human flesh! I hope I never ever see their ilk again!" He concluded. "I will share one event with you and am very honest on this. I was not joking about killing Kali. In the violent turn of events in the battle, I was the one who finally slew the beast Kali on the ramparts of that evil castle. It will always be a terrible memory darling! The absolute darkness this creature projected as I killed it!" … He went quiet for a few moments then smiled at her. "If you tell anybody this, then I will sexually torture you until you forget all I said!" She hugged and kissed him deeply. "Can you do that anyhow if I threaten to talk?"

It was going on two in the morning. She led him to his bedroom, quite remote at the end of the third floor. She kissed him and told him not to fall asleep too fast, then left. Ambrose knew something was brewing; the night was not over yet! He pulled off his uniform and put one a clean nightshirt by his bed stand then washed his face and brushed his teeth. He climbed into bed and only waited in what seemed minutes, when he saw an image of a woman in a long white gown approach him. For some brief instant, he saw Pyra, then as the form approached his bed, he saw his beautiful Jenny, and began to smell her perfume, deep and good, like a field of flowers.

The lovemaking was intense, hot, and pleasurably rough as both were covered in sweat in the end. They lay together holding each other in sweet embrace. "I love you with all of my heart!' came her sweet voice. I fell for you the moment I first saw you at that polo game in Khar. Cavendish turned to her. "Jenny, I love you and will never feel right if you are not by my side permanently… and I will make it very clear, that I am going to ask for your hand in marriage!" Her mouth opened wide with the announcement. "Oh, When Ambrose, when are you going to ask me?" She gasped. He pretended to look at his pocket watch and then looked back at her wild naked beauty. "How about now! Will you marry me Jenny!" She said, "yes" and "yes" many more times, before, during, and after the next several orgasms in the night.

It was late afternoon the next day when Captain Cavendish was able to gain a return to the Majestic Hotel. The snowstorm had abated somewhat, leaving over three feet of snow throughout the London region. More snow was predicted with the next storm blowing across the English Channel. The attendant behind the counter handed him a note. It was from Nephew. "Meet me across the street for a flagon of cold ale at the Winking Owl? Screeching Owl? Drunken Owl? Fucking Owl? or whatever owl pub but not the Dragon's bite pub!" Ambrose smiled as he ducked back across the street to find his friend. They both would never get the name of this pub right. Tiberius Nephew was taking a long pull on his tankard of ale at the bar as Ambrose shook off the snow from his greatcoat and hung it up next to him.

He then sat down with a fresh tankard of ale landing in front of him. The colonel smiled at his friend. "Well my fine Captain; looks like you were kidnapped last night!" Cavendish smiled back. "Yes, I was drugged and locked up in the keep…then I was subjected to a night of torture and interrogation!" He was smiling…. "Well Ambrose old boyo, she seems like a keeper to me!" "Indeed, my fine colonel, she will be kept! And how are your girlfriends?" Nephew smiled long and happy nodding his head. "Ambrose, Ambrose, Ambrose! They fought for my bones last night and when my bones were left bare, they went after each other's bones! Quite a spectacle to watch and rekindled my fires immensely. I am in love with both of them!"

They laughed and toasted the brews, then drank. Then they ordered another round. Nephew then added. "It seems there has been a lot of steam fired up over this future threat to peace in Europe by the Queen and special confidents. She has formed this organization, a study group at the war college to examine all the prospects of a future conflict in Europe, which in my estimate will cover most of the globe! I hear that many very influential minds are going to be in on it." "So, we are not returning to India in the future as planned?" "Those days are over Ambrose as we have been ordered to serve in this study group…so we will be moving from our dear home at the Majestic Hotel to billets near the war college.

This is a done deal!" He then produced an official document forming this group duly signed by the chief of the general staff and endorsed by Queen Victoria. "It seems that our meeting with the Queen and her friendship with Ravi aroused the need to investigate the roots of any possible threats to peace in the world in the near future." Nephew took a sip form his brew. "Whether we have a new Kali or not, the evolution of these "Four Horsemen" throughout Europe and internationally could have dire ramifications if they all clash at one point. Oh yes, I intercepted a telegram for you from the hotel desk.

Newly promoted Lieutenant Hoskins will be arriving in a couple of weeks to attend Sand Hurst, and to get married to dear Andrea! I do not know of the plans yet, but you will probably know before me." Ambrose looked at his friend after taking a long hit on his ale. "I may soon be in the same situation dear friend!" Nephew gave a laugh

"Rightly ho! So, Dear Cavendish, I also thought of a double marriage after that round with my two maidens last night…decisions, decisions! Life is rough! I will flip the coin twice. They will both win! I can't wait to meet their parents!" More laughs and new rounds of ale were ordered. Tiberius Nephew lowered his voice and looked Cavendish in the eye. "I think our friend and mentor Ravi has either been ill or he is up to something. The war against Kali took a lot out of him.

I picked up a sublime message last night …when I was in peaceful sleep. I do not know the nature or seriousness it is as of yet!" Ambrose was silent, his mind drifted to the village, to his dear friend Ravi, to Hooky, to his many village friends there, and then his emotions rested on Pyra. He knew he was in love with two women and could not help it. The love was the same, yet different in all the ramifications. Tiberius spoke. "Please let me know, if we can do anything for him. He saved my life, was instrumental in our kicking the Kali's ass, and became one of our great friends to boot." "I will keep you posted for sure as the mysterious Ravi allows!"

The ale was going down smoothly. But both men were becoming very hungry, and soon feasted on excellent beef stew at the pub. It was snowing hard again when they left the pub. It was now confirmed as a storm of the century according to the British weather service. Lieutenant Hoskins arrived in London fifteen days later in the wake of the next winter storm to land on the British Isles. The wedding plans were set before Hoskins was due to start the officer's academy at Sand Hurst in mid-January. Nephew and Cavendish reported to the war college on the assigned date for orientation. The study group was just forming, nothing was really coming together yet and would not pick up steam until after the New Year.

It was at this time Captain Cavendish took leave to go visit his parents up north. He had brought several presents for his parents, and sister. He still could not locate or communicate with his brother and just gave up. His oldest sister and family were to spend Christmas at home in France. The weather across France and the channel was just too much. He wanted to make the trip home before Christmas

Day, since he wanted to spend it with Jenny. She had to stay home. Her profession was in helping her father manage the large family business, and it was brisk this time of year.

The train ride from London to the Kingston upon Hull, near where his parents lived seemed to take a long time. The snow was deep and the forecast called for more of it. The train seemed to barely chug along as drifts formed on the tracks. He fell into a slumber and dreamed he was in the jungle near a beautiful stream. It was very sunny, but not too hot. Then he saw Pyra emerge from the water naked, so beautiful, such a smile. She beckoned him to enter the water where she sat. They both embraced and kissed. They just held each other, and then they sat down together in the water.

Ambrose laughed as he saw the horses, they had left behind during the conflict running around playing with the children downstream. He also saw Hooky, wearing the traditional village garb, sporting his weathered pith helmet and using a long walking stick. Bow Dogs seemed to be everywhere near him, never letting him slide from their sight. They looked terribly ferocious but acted like love starved Bulldogs. Then he turned and looked into her deep beautiful violet eyes and kissed her. He just stared as she spoke.

"Ambrose, I will love you all my life, and you can never hurt me or destroy my love for you even after you marry Jenny and have family. I know your heart is troubled over your two love interests, so I want to put your soul at ease! My love is not human, but is deeper, and more elevated in scope. I know you love me so I ask you to enjoy our love in peace. You can never hurt me Ambrose, and I will always have an eye out for you!' Ambrose gave her a gentle kiss. This message was sweet medicine to his troubled vexed spirit. "Pyra, I will love you for my whole life as well and please never forget this.

We are special in many ways. I realize that I live in two worlds, yours and then my earthly one. Your kind comments mean the world to me sweetheart, and my respect and love for you has grown immensely." Pyra smiled, her eyes were wet as she continued. "We exist in a timeless arena dear Ambrose; we exist above your other world of time and space. Love at this level is free from the toils of earth emotions and is pure. Jealousy and possessiveness are not part of our love, love is love with its many varied paths as God teaches. In our belief system, love is the lifeblood and glue of the whole universe. Love is the breath of Great Father God! Without His love, all would be unbalanced chaos!"

She smiled and took his hand…soon they were embraced in her huge bed in the palace. They made great love, free of worry or guilt, surrounded by many burning candles and incense to accent. Afterwards, she kissed him gently on his nose…. He knew, in light of Jenny and their plans, that this lovemaking with Pyra was one last sendoff; one he would never forget!

He saw Pyra as a best friend and true love which was the best of combinations. He also harbored the same for Jenny. Then Ambrose began to jerk, to be pulled, then he heard someone yell the name "Next stop is Kingston Upon Hull!" James Ambrose awoke to the screeching of the train braking on very icy tracks. He lay under a wool blanket in his secluded seat for a few moments and consciously remembered every moment of his visit with Pyra. He felt relief as he felt such great love. But like Pyra said, their love was different than Jenny, for it was so different. He felt elation and not guilt in his farewell "jump" with sweet Pyra. She was a wonderful companion forever.

He then grabbed his bags and made it off the train into the very comfortable station, quaint, warm, crowded, and friendly. He ambled over to a small pub and ordered ale and a shot of dark Farnsworth rum. Mom and dad seemed to be running late because of the storm. He was able to relax and give complete reflection on his dream and kind discourse with Pyra, and his upcoming life with Jenny. "My life is so strange, but strange is good!" was his final reflection on this subject.

As he ordered his third round of dark rum and ale, he felt a tap on his back then turned around. They he saw the round porcelain face adorned with a multitude of blonde curls trapped in a large red woolen cap. It was very bad baby sister Elizabeth, bundled like an artic Penguin, who displayed her usual twisted smile and fiery energetic being. On recognition, they hugged on impact. "My big brother war hero is finally home!" came her first response as Ambrose squeezed her back. "My sweet baby sister…my oh my how blessed I am!" "Now, now Brother your sarcasm can rest!" She was laughing. "Okay my baby super brat! Where is mom and dad?"

"They are at home waiting for you. The weather is very bad, so they sent me with the small two horse sled to fetch you!" Cavendish smiled…the small horse sled meant a wild ride home. So, they polished off two more rounds and ventured outside into the snow. The winds from the North Sea cast frigid blows across the region. Ambrose put his luggage in the rear of the sled as sister opened the huge doors of the livery stable. The two set out in the sled powered by two large workhorses that seemed impervious to the cold and snow. Off they went, trotting through the city, finally into the countryside swerving side to side in good speed as the large horses crushed through the high drifts forming on the road.

They were now just a couple of kids again enjoying a moment from their past when mom and dad used to take them for similar winter sleigh rides. Soon they pulled up in front of what could be described as a rustic county estate home completely adorned in white from the immense snow storms. It was a large long structure in its simple beauty and was being pounded in snow-laden winds. They unloaded the baggage and put the horses safely in the hands of the attendant who cared for the beasts of the farm and unhitched them and led them into a well-heated barn nearby.

John and Miriam Cavendish were waiting in the foyer as they entered the house. Hugs and laughs filled the hallway. The farm cats were allowed to inhabit the huge farmhouse in winter if they decided not to live in the barns or stables, flocked around the captain; searching out new smells along with three old buddy sheep dogs. Cavendish was so happy to be home, to see his parents, as they were to see him. Like John and Miriam, their house was the warmest of places, in fire and in spirit.

After the normal salutations, they all sat in the large living room over a round of hot toddies. The conversation was pleasant and was related to family and farm. Rayne was expecting her next child; older brother John was still the incommunicado barrister in London whom Ambrose could never seem to get in touch with as well. Elizabeth was able to tell her own story with friendly chiding from all present.

Soon, all eyes were on Ambrose. He then told his story in the best light and stayed on course with the official account for now. He excused himself for a moment and pulled something from his baggage. He then approached his father. "Dad, remember the Zulu Spear Sergeant Hook carried with him?" "Yes son, I remember it well! The one that saved his life at Rorke's Drift?" "Well, before he passed on, he gave it to me with his Victoria Cross from that battle as testament to our treasured friendship. "The Zulu Spear from Rorke's Drift!" Exclaimed his father.

Ambrose put both items in his dad's hands. Well, I want you have these as a special gift from me and Hooky! His last words were mount them with his story on a bronze plaque and put it in a place of honor on the wall behind a pub bar. Looks like you have been selected by the Color-Sergeant father!" "John was taken aback for a moment then retorted. "Son, I will proudly hang this spear and VC with a bronze plaque of its owner and his great exploits for Queen, Empire and Country!" Cavendish smiled. Father would learn the truth about Hooky and his RIP later tonight!

"That's the. …Or ARRRRR Mister John Cavendish, that's' the spirit to honor me, by hanging me spear and VC in a pub near thar grog and ale!" The low drawl in imitation by Ambrose of Hook drew a good laugh. They sat to a great dinner of rack-of-lamb, potatoes, and fixings and carried on a long conversation. Miriam and Elizabeth finally cleaned up dinner and left for bed.

Ambrose's father sat smoking his pipe across from Ambrose who wielded a nice Havana Maduro cigar. John had sensed a mystery in his son's voice as he jumped around his account of the India story. "Son," he began in his uncommitted voice, "Tell me what is on your mind. It will never travel beyond this table. "As his story of the real events unfolded, Ambrose finally told his father the real fate of one Sergeant Major Alfred Hook to his great and happy surprise. It was near dawn and both men would sleep late into the morning.

The remainder of the stay was a great event in spite of the predominant winter weather. Father and son spent a good time at the family Pub and store, where plans for both spear and medal and copper plate honoring the famous Hook would be duly installed in the center of the bar back front. The final words on the copper inscription dedicated to the exploits of Sergeant Hook would read. *"May this great hero and warrior of Rorke's Drift and "far" north India always rest in peace in the Village!"* James had even included a nice portrait of a younger Hook when he had received his first VC from the drift battle.

A nice Christmas party was held on the eve before Captain Cavendish was to depart. It was at this time that Ambrose announced his intention to marry Jenny Farnsworth to mother. She was thrilled as could be and was excited to meet her and this meant new grandchildren in the near future. He left in a new snow storm the next day filled with great happiness. His time at home with his parents and baby sister had calmed his soul. The sleigh ride back to the train station seemed wilder than before, and over several departing drinks Elizabeth promised to visit him in London and the New Year's Party he had spoken about. Ambrose boarded the train and returned home in peace. He was in the loving arms of Jenny late that night. They awoke together on Christmas Day. To her joy he placed a nice engagement ring on her finger.

Cavendish was finally able to spend some time with newly promoted 2nd Lieutenant Winston Hoskins who was to be married on December 30th. They met in a small pub near the military district where both were billeted. After the salutations, they sat down for lunch and ale. Hoskins spoke first. "Sir, you would not believe all the debriefings I had to endure regarding our big adventure in India before I was able to come home. Colonel Nephew was able to keep many of the dogs away." Ambrose smiled at the young new officer. "Yes, we all have been debriefed including all those poor buggers that were transferred to duty all over the empire to quell any organized inquiry by the tabloids, since "mum" is the forever golden word."

They spent the remainder of the time actually rehashing the whole campaign in great detail, as well as a few stories of those expert trackers from the village. Hoskins was still amazed at his adventure in Hima at the huge celebration and wild night with those village darlings he later construed as his bachelor party as Cavendish mused. "Look at that event as your bachelor party my friend! I had mine!" They both talked about their women and plans for the future. Hoskins planned on making a career out of the military since he would come up for retirement in 1914 if he chose it.

Cavendish was unsure of his plans. Colonel Nephew had been hinting of the creation of some secret intelligence agency and the name Winston Churchill had popped up. Then there was the offer from Lord Farnsworth to help run the rum company as a partner. The Christmas season prevailed into the small nice wedding of Hoskins and Andrea. It was another wonderful experience where friends and family gathered to celebrate. The season seemed to be moving very fast. They made a formal announcement to her parents of their intentions to marry. The news was warmly received and Cavendish summed his return to England as the best time in his life. The wedding was planned for June 20, 1898.

CHAPTER EIGHT
AN UNEXPECTED JOURNEY

It was on the 28th of January 1898 that most of the recently chosen members of the 'Royal Studies Group' finally met for the first time. The winter weather had hampered much travel. Colonel Nephew and Captain Cavendish knew of a few of the personages present in name only, and many they had never heard before. They had the pleasant company of Sir Farnsworth who wound some interesting stories of his life and experience. The first meeting took place in the wing of a local college in a huge boardroom lined with oak and infested with many shelves of antique books. The room was completely inundated with the smoke from several cigars and pipes today.

The tables were set in a huge oblong circle of sorts, where everyone was in close earshot of each other. There were prominent scientists, economists, historians, philosophers, business executives, and members of all branches of the military. This collection of people came from all over Europe, the United States, Japan, and China. The list of topics on the program was interesting. The hot tea poured like a waterfall into the many china cups as the many conversations added a low din to the large room. All present were handed a program. Both soldiers reviewed this sheet and looked at each other. Nephew smiled, "Ambrose, we may retire here! Look at this?" Farnsworth was smiling at them. "I am retired, so I may have to run and hide!" He was smiling in jest.

INDEPENDENT ROYAL STUDIES GROUP
Established in January 1898
MEMO
TOPICS AND TRENDS FOR RESEARCH, DEVELOPMENT, & DISCUSSION:
GENERAL GLOBAL TRENDS BY IDENTIFIED COUNTRIES (See Reverse)
1898 to 1928
Social Trends (Nationalistic trends) (Internal)
Political Trends (Internal)
Economics (All facets)
Military developments of:
Strategies and Tactics
Force structures and technologies
Alliance systems: Old and projected
Nationalism: Prospects
Imperialism/Protectorates: Current and projected
Future Colonization concerns: Trends and problems
Leadership: Present and future

The members and their areas of research gave brief introductions, as Sir Farnsworth was introduced as the head of the economics section. It seemed as if this studies group was a "who's who" of many expert minds. After a short thirty-minute break, all settled back down to hear the chairman of this studies group give his address. His name was Professor Ferdinand Strosser who was billed as some great obscure mind from Austria. The aging professor, complete with a shabby gray Van Dyke, ruffled gray hair and a monocle slowly moved to the front of the room with the aid of a craggy old cane. He wore a nice old double-breasted suit, which seemed to match his hair color. He seemed very fragile, yet his deep powerful accented voice filled the room as he spoke.

"Greetings to all of you, and it is with great pleasure to have been selected to chair of this esteemed Royal Studies Group. Our mission is not so much in just collecting relevant data in our areas, but to cobble it together into a picture of the root causes that may drive what may come in the future. We need to build accurate models, or possible scenarios of what may come as the world evolves politically, technologically, and economically in the next twenty or so years. This may be critical in the future survival of this planet and future generations. It seems the world order, with its mass industrialization and dubious leadership can and will polarize and possibly lose established control of peace. This could lead to conflict and the folly of war; a war more destructive than all others."

He turned around and signaled an attendant to pull back a huge curtain behind him. It was huge black chalkboard some thirty feet long and twenty feet high. It seemed to span the whole wall. It had many countries listed across the top with arrows pointing down to factors to be researched of each. "In front of us we have an outline on an empty board, except for one box below with the words "Possible world conflict scenarios" in it, otherwise a blank puzzle.

It will be your mission to find all the pieces to fill this blank puzzle board! This picture very well may be what lies ahead of this planet in the next twenty years. Will we enjoy peace or destructive war?" He looked at the German representatives, "We cannot show any bias in this study, but truth in facts presented. Work hard gentlemen and produce for this study a perfect Mona Lisa!" Strosser gave a small half-smile as he tapped his cane on the huge blank chalkboard. "In the next room is a board with all your assignments on it, so you will know who you will be working with. Good Luck and happy hunting!" The group was adjourned and wandered into the next room to view the organization of tasks.

It was also quite obvious that this group would be doing a lot of traveling and research in many European countries. Some of it would be clandestine in nature. Colonel Nephew and Captain Cavendish were assigned to the weapons development part of the military studies committee under the nose of an old war-bird named General B. Marmaduke. He was so old that the joke surrounding his military service was he stood with Wellington at Waterloo. He possessed a wealth of intelligence and would be working on tactics and battle strategies employed with the advent of new weapons.

He made his first indelible comment to them with an old serious smile as his hawk eyes pierced them. "Penetrating the Prussians will be paramount gentlemen! It seems Krupp has been on a roll since 1870! The Napoleonic war of annihilation of total war seems to demand "totally" destructive weapons that could annihilate whole armies, cities, and possibly civilizations. Professor Strosser and General Marmaduke sat with Nephew and Cavendish late in the afternoon as other members were leaving. Over a late cup of tea Strosser laid out his plan for them.

"Gentlemen, it is imperative that we have an idea of what is being prototyped and considered for production in the following countries in Europe, with emphasis on Germany. The Germans are here not to contribute but to spy on our motives and purpose for their government. I am not concerned with other countries such as the United States yet since they are still reacting to the losses in their Civil War, and their isolationist temperament to date. They will only roll around when and if they are faced with a global conflict."

The general read off the following countries to be visited. Marmaduke added emphasis to their visit to Germany. "You boys will go there posing as buyers and sellers of the various British metals considered good in building German weapons. We will send both of you in as agents and brokers for several steel manufacturers in England." Marmaduke added as he looked across to Cavendish and Nephew. "We want you to visit France then Germany on your first trip soon. After trading handshakes, the men departed into a cold January night.

Colonel Nephew commented on the way out. "Ambrose, do you feel anything strange about Strosser?" Cavendish gave a laugh as they climbed into their coach since his senses had betrayed the true identity of Professor Strosser. "It was Ravi!" Nephew had found an exquisite pub named "The Boar's Tusk" near where they were billeted, so they set their sights on well-deserved dinner and drinks. Once in the pub they discarded their warm military overcoats and hats and stood warming themselves by a glowing fireplace. The ale was cold and good, a compliment to the cognac they had sipped on the way. The bill of fare was excellent as they both devoured double portions of Irish Lamb Stew.

It was after ten when they walked the short distance to their apartments, which were only four doors apart. The "goodnights and salutes" were traded and Ambrose unlocked his door and stepped inside. He immediately smelled perfume and then heard the voice of his beloved Jenny. Soon they were snuggled up together, playing, kissing, and fondling each other over a fresh bottle of champagne.

Monday morning came in a rush, as Nephew and Cavendish found themselves back with the Studies group after a decent breakfast in the nearby mess hall at the college. It seemed warmer today with the sun's brightness radiating and shining off the melting snow. The coach ride seemed a lot faster than Friday night. General Marmaduke intercepted them as they walked through the hallway on the way into the great hall. "Good morning, lads, please join me in this side room." They entered a cozy little study and the two soldiers sat down as the old general closed the study door. After pouring some hot tea located nearby, the old general looked at them with his ancient dark eyes and smiled.

"Looks like you both will be going on your trip sooner than expected. You will be leaving next week still posing as sellers of weapons grade steel. Perhaps you can get an advance clear picture of what is being developed. Strosser deems all imputes from you as critical even at this point in time. The type of weapons developed determines much in their strategic use in war my boys! Your passports, cover and itinerary are here. You will be billed as brokers for weapons technologies development and raw materials working for a subsidiary of one of our big companies here in England." He then handed them each their dossiers. The first thing Nephew saw was that he was to keep his real name, as was Cavendish. Marmaduke interjected.

"You kept your names because you will obviously need your military experience in this position and our German friends will thoroughly check both of you out." As brokers you will also bill yourselves a quasi-associate of the British government. This will free you to…." Captain Cavendish finished using an old American phrase used by his uncle; "wheel and deal Sir?" "Yes, wheel and deal? I was thinking of freedom of movement Captain…wheel and deal? I will have to remember that one."

Nephew was looking at his itinerary. "Looks like we began in a couple of weeks or so with our first potential client in Paris!" "Yes, we included a list of all the companies we contacted for your visits already. They are placed in order of who to visit first! Send what you have found via diplomatic pouch if necessary or deliver it in person upon your return. I must leave you now. No need to be in our meeting today, most of the other members are traveling early as well. "The old general left the room as Nephew and Cavendish looked at each other.

"Thank God for the date of June 20th!" reflected Cavendish. "June 20th? What is on June 20th Cavendish?" Inquired Tiberius. "The loss of my bachelorhood mon colonel!" Ambrose smiled.

Nephew retorted. "Really now old chap…. such great decisions!" He smiled back. Cavendish smiled broadly as he put his teacup back on the desk. "I have one more decision I must reveal to you brother Colonel Nephew… I have honestly chosen you to be none other than my best man! This is no joke SIR!" Nephew gave a laugh from under his well-trimmed black moustache. "I humbly accept with great honor!"

That afternoon they went over all the information contained in their briefcases and corroborated on several points. They were to visit France first and Germany with careful emphasis on Krupp and its subsidiaries. If there was any time, they would visit sunny Italy since the Italians were novel in their approach to making weapons. The wish list they were to use was a list that sounded like a science fiction novel. It seemed Ravi was hard at work!

> _Areas of Interest_:

1. _Rapid firing weapons_
2. _Long range and large artillery to include mortars_
3. _Armored type fighting vehicles: mobility of all weapons_
4. _Air machines_
5. _Ships and underwater vessels (omit this, Navy personnel are working on it)_
6. _Use of mustard and chlorine (large purchases) possible gas_
7. _Flame weapons_
8. _Super explosives_
9. _How these weapons fit into modern battlefield strategies_
10. _Anything else regarding possible employment of tactics with these weapons_

The channel seemed much calmer the second-time Cavendish and Nephew crossed this body of water in the third week of February. The bad winter weather had dissipated as the temperatures were rising with increased days of sun. It seemed as if early spring was banging at the door of a still peaceful Europe! They still wore their greatcoats now unbuttoned and fur hats. They sipped from a bottle of Jamaican Prime rum given to them by Sir Farnsworth for their crossing as they stood at the bow of the passenger ship. They watched as it cut a neat furrow into the rather calm seas. It was still cool but the winds had ceased. As the ship made its way south along the French coast, the climate grew warmer and drier. The beauty of the French coastline was always breathtaking.

They first would meet with a few French arms makers near Paris to begin in about four days' time. Then it was off to Germany to meet with a lineup of five arms manufacturers, with the important one being Krupp Industries. Meanwhile Ambrose's beloved sister had invited them to visit their estate in South Western France on their way to do business. The area was called the Sud Quest and they were going to their estate twenty miles west of the city of Bergerac. The sun finally came out full as their ship headed down the Gironde Estuary with its pleasant azure light blue waters. They stripped off their hats and greatcoats, as they enjoyed the wonderful ambiance and warm breeze of the magnificent estuary. The warm breeze was a Godsend!

They had agreed to meet Cavendish's sister at Bordeaux, then travel across the Dordogne River to Bergerac and out to the wine estate Balbain, whose name was camouflaged under the name of a larger more popular wine consortium. He was a well-respected purveyor of the best wines and brandy in this region. His family had been making wine for over two centuries. Colonel Nephew daydreamed as he viewed the lush estate chateaus that faced the river. They were ancient, stately, Romanesque and magnificent in their beautiful architecture. The green foliage on the river did little to mask the beautiful lines of grape vineyards, with the grape vines standing at least eight to ten feet high.

There seemed to be hundreds of vintners about the fields this day already at work at creating the grapes for the best wines on the planet. The scenery was quiet, pastoral, and pleasant in the warm sunlight. They were headed to the heart of where the famous Merlot and Cabernet Sauvignon grapes were grown, not to forget the rare white Ondene grape. Gascony seemed like a blooming paradise to both men.

Cavendish loved his big sister, her family and the children, not to forget the great rich red wines that the estate produced. Jacque Balbain, Rayne's husband was quite a well-known winemaker and had such great wit. The ship docked at Boudreaux at noon in warm breezes. Amid the hustle and bustle of passengers and crews, Captain Cavendish saw his sister, her husband and children on the dock waving at him. They looked like a postcard snapshot in their stature; fine dress and early spring beauty surrounding this port. It was a snapshot right out of the gay 1890s.

Soon they were all together hugging and shaking hands. It was a warm reunion as Colonel Nephew was introduced to his family. They enjoyed a pleasant ride in the warming air from Boudreaux by open carriage to their estate, as Jacques proffered a bottle of his fine 1885 Merlot to his guests. The mood was happy and fun. They seemed to laugh at both Jacques and Tiberius's humor as they played off of each other for the many miles through a greening landscape. Nephew's command of French was impeccable as was Ambrose's, so they all conversed in it.

Spring was around the corner and the estate Balaban was magnificent to behold. The travelers were impressed at the hundreds of rows of grape vines, standing like soldiers at attention in some former Napoleonic Army ready for battle. As they came down a long lane towards the estate, the neatly manicured bushes and landscape were praiseworthy. Once beyond the huge stone wall and iron gates, Colonel Nephew was amazed at the size and beauty of a huge white stone chateau, that seemed to rival most manors he had seen in England. The group entered the chateau from a wide staircase in front. The inside of this grand chateau was adorned with classic French provincial furniture in the hall and main room.

The walls were adorned with many paintings, some of depicting medieval battles, and others of pastoral settings. Cavendish was once told that one of Jacques ancestors was in the fatal French Calvary charge at the Battle of Agincourt where he was captured, spared execution, and kept a prisoner of the English until a hefty ransom was paid for his life. He related this story to Nephew as they viewed a huge wall painting depicting the heavy armored cavalry of French Nobles charging at the English positions. Colonel Nephew smiled and commented that the only thing missing were all the English longbow arrows hitting them! Jacques, always in wit, proclaimed that this painting was made just before the arrows were unleashed!

Laughs came from everybody. However, the French lost the flower of their nobility against the English Longbow that day, with an estimated six-thousand to ten-thousand killed, wounded or captured. The Long bow, was the new deadly technology of that day; which changed the nature of warfare and history. This was a serious silent reminder to Cavendish and Nephew in their quest to try and uncover "new war technology" in the new era of 20th Century! The ramifications would be much worse!

Rayne was a typical English beauty, converted to a beautiful French beauty by her style, dress, and taste. The children seemed like a blur, as they ran about, hugging Uncle Ambrose, and then disappearing to play. He loved them dearly and my how they were growing, especially the new addition that was a baby boy named Ambrose after him. The temperature in this region was a cool sixty degrees at night, very unlike London. Jacques took them on a fun tour of the estate on horseback, from the vines to the many wine cellars, to taste more excellent wines. They were eventually all "wined up" by the end of the tour as they let the horses run hard in the grape fields.

It seemed that every time Ambrose came to see his sister, it was always accented with positive times. He truly loved this very pleasant experience. Jacques had offered him a partnership on a new wine estate he was developing when he retired. This was a huge kind lure to a person who had seen so many negatives of life so far. The very proper servants served up an excellent seven-course dinner the last evening of their visit in the great dining room. The main course was pheasant under glass. The place settings alone were of the finest bone china and the silverware was actually gold ware. Jacques told the story of how one of his late uncles, an American colonial of French extraction, in the American Revolution, had served with Paul Revere later in the war.

As a token of friendship and service, Paul had given him this fine set. Sure enough, Revere's name was embossed on each piece. The dinner was finished and the three men went into a large study to sip some very old and excellent French Cognac. Cavendish passed out some Cuban Maduro's given to him by Sir Farnsworth and they lit them up. In the course of the conversation Cavendish explained their trip to France and to Germany. He told Jacque of his meetings with arms merchants in Paris and dropped M. Lefebvre's name in the conversation. Jacque let out a laugh. "Lefebvre?" he stammered.

"Montesquieu Lefebvre is an old friend of mine from college. He wanted to be a winemaker like me but ended up in ordnance procurement for the French government. I will give you a case of my fine Merlot for him. This should open a few doors! France is such a small world" He then called in a servant and gave him instructions to include a case with their baggage in the morning. He then wrote a short note to be included with the wine. Cavendish and Nephew thanked him with a toast of fresh cognac. The conversation was light and happy until Jacques grew silent.

Then he spoke. "France has been in a state of peace since the Bosch invaded Alsace Lorraine and captured Paris in the Franco-Prussian War of 1870. "I do not trust the German dogs and never will! France wants this region back and the Greater German Empire wants to expand so I hear! I smell a new clash of arms in the future! The thing that bothers me is the unwritten alliances developing across Europe I hear in my wine circles. It seems that Europe will never ever settle these social differences and war will always be waiting in the wings forever it seems." Colonel Nephew smiled and continued the conversation.

"I agree with you mon ami. This is why we are mainly focused on our visit to Germany because of their massive armaments industry! They seem to sell their weapons anybody with cash it seems! However, I do not think we would be welcome in Russia because of our problems with them and their Afghan allies in India. I am certain the Tsar is reeling from the damage we did to their plans!" James Ambrose gave Jacques a short "heads up" on the purpose of the Royal Studies Group and what they were researching for it. He looked across at Nephew who gave a silent broad smile.

"Yes," Jacques replied, it all seems so stupid to me…the world should be drinking wine, not killing over possession of the wine fields! I just have this gut feeling about the future and most Frenchmen feel as I do! It is like a dark nightmare, a winged one, just looking for a place to land. I pray that your group can somehow intervene in this old curse which keeps hanging over Europe; a curse that began in the ancient war between the early tribes in the wake of the Roman Empire!" Both Cavendish and Nephew rested their minds on Jacques reflections as they puffed on their cigars and took a slow long sip of rare cognac. Ambrose reflected.

"In time of peace prepare for war and in time of war prepare for peace! What an accurate reflection of this planet. War is the bottom feeder of politics, a grand extension of political discourse as Nicole Machiavelli once said if I remember. Queen Victoria is as concerned as you are about the future of England and the European continent. The wrong power in the wrong hands with the wrong weapons spells' disaster for all of us. The committee that we work with, as I said is in business to divine possible root scenarios and advanced technologies that could lead us down the road into a war of unfathomable dimensions.

We are not just looking at the next possible European conflict, but the conditions left in the wake of this possible next one that will lead to an even bigger one!" Colonel Nephew concluded. "Beware of the Four Horsemen of the Apocalypse; Alliance systems, militarism, nationalism, and imperialism shielded as colonialism or protectorates! Properly lined up they could spell doom for peace in Europe and the world. The name I love to mask imperialism is called the "protectorate" meaning that we will invade you to protect you from any invasion except ours!" Jacques intervened in a moment of passion. "Curses of egos and arrogance…and slimy politicians invigorated by power and greed! National one-up-man ship for everybody in the realm! Screw them all!"

The next morning, at dawn and after a good breakfast, the two soldiers bid a warm farewell to the wonderful Balbain family. It was during this excellent meal that Ambrose announced his forthcoming marriage to Jenny Farnsworth on June 20th; that Tiberius Nephew was his best man. Rayne was in tears of joy. Jacques was excited and laughed, as he always seemed to do. They would all be there to give James away. He gave each of them each two excellent parting bottles of his private stock of Brandy "Armagnac."

The beautiful experience with his family had cast very positive moods on both men as their train "huffed and puffed" into Paris, France. The winter air seemed to hang over the ancient cultural center of Europe as they arrived from the south. The train station was packed with what seemed hundreds of commuters, all eager to find their destinations. Both men invested in a cup of strong cappuccino as they waited for their cab to their hotel. Paris was Paris surmised Cavendish. He loved the ambiance, the architecture, the winding streets, and the Parisians. He also remembered his attraction to those fine perfumed sultry sexy French women of his younger adventures here. AAAH, and the fine way they smelled and touched he thought.

They had arranged a meeting with M. Lefebvre at his office near the armament's factory in an industrial area east of the city at four in the afternoon. They marveled at the Eiffel Tower as they passed it as they appreciated many other architectural delights. Once in their hotel they rehearsed and revised their story around the case of Balbain's Merlot before they taxied to meet Balbain's old college chum. M. Lefebvre met them at the door of the office building.

He was a medium built man, with a monocle perched above his large dark moustache. Lefebvre gave off the air of a police detective than a director of French armaments. He was dressed immaculately in a fine dark suite and had a short smile on his face. His eyes were sharp and penetrating. After the introductions, they moved into his office. M. Lefebvre lit up a cigarette and offered his guests some as they sat down. The office was drab and seemed gray and lifeless except for all the obvious activity on and around Lefebvre's large desk. He offered them a customary glass of wine.

Colonel Nephew gave the spiel on their purpose for contacting him. They represented a firm that sold raw materials, especially iron ore refined into fine weapons grade steel. M. Was quiet and reserved as Nephew introduced their wares. Then, in an attempt to deliver the left hook, Cavendish put the case of Merlot on his desk and handed Lefebvre the note. He studied it and smiled as he looked up at his two guests. "Jacques Balbain is your brother in law!!!!! This is quite unbelievable and a great surprise! Such a dear friend he is! I wanted to make wine once, and dear Jacque beat me to that profession, but instead of grapes I wanted to grow, I grow armaments!"

He opened one of the bottles from the case and poured a round. As they relished the fine dark red wine Lefebvre spoke. "Gentlemen, I will be glad to help you with any questions regarding what armaments we are developing, and we can do this today since this is the end of the week. Let us savor this wine before we begin?" He laughed as both of his guests nodded in approval and a fresh glass were filled with the dark red tasty wine. He told of the formation of his grand friendship with Jacques in college and would indeed honor this invitation to visit him soon!

A jovial mood prevailed after a couple of bottles had been drained in what could be construed as a "happy hour." M. Lefebvre ushered them into one of the many large doors in a discreet side of the rooms in the huge factory. Most of the workers had left for the weekend. He unlocked the large green door and in they walked. Green trim on red bricks had always had some pastoral appeal to Cavendish. Both soldiers were immediate impressed at the prototypes of huge artillery pieces near the front. The size of the mortars created much interest. They saw several modern and prototype howitzers lined up, complete with their horse drawn caissons.

They continued walking through a maze of strange contraptions of war until they stopped in front of what looked like an armored tractor. "Ah yes, "M. Lefebvre began, "We have been looking at the development of what we can only describe as armored cavalry of the future and a good place to employ the new rapid firing machineguns. We want to protect our infantry and this may be the trick! Engineers at the firm of Renault designed this chassis and we have been experimenting with different weapons on it. We recently tested a heavy artillery piece on this tractor, but the impact of it firing knocked the tank on its side. The lighter artillery seems to be better and machineguns are perfect. This project is a mere infant now. Our Hun friends have not done anything with this concept so we have learned."

Lefebvre tapped the wheel of a huge artillery piece and went on to explain how the big guns would destroy the ever-popular tradition of Napoleonic inspired massed infantry battalions and cavalry in front of their offensives. If they got close then the machineguns would finish them! We will attack to Berlin! We have developed a new rifle from the Chassepot of 1870, which claimed many Prussian lives. He showed them a new Lebel infantry rifle that could now shoot accurately up to twelve-hundred yards. They even took a break from the tour to shoot several rounds from it into a target at the wall in the end of the large warehouse accompanied with a third bottle of Merlot. This new eleven-pound rifle was impressive.

Lefebvre was mostly playing these weapons in the offensive role and was not much concerned with defense during his speech. It seemed that the French strategists wanted to copy the "quick attack" ideal of the Prussians, which, in part, defeated France in 1870. Nephew made good note of this. They drank another bottle of Balbain's finest Merlot and happily fired hundreds of rounds from another prototype machinegun. It had an extremely high rate of fire as it destroyed a line of targets at the end of the warehouse. They were all laughing as they took turns on the gun. To illustrate the offensive strategy and tactics of he perceived French offensive plan he ushered them over to a huge diorama!

According to the ethos portrayed in the detailed diorama, they designed their army for a massive Napoleonic war of offense. Massed artillery barrages, followed by massed infantry with machinegun companies in the mix, armored cavalry leading the infantry grinding the Hun into the ground. The Frenchman talked about airplanes. Nephew studied the diorama at length but had two vexing questions. What if the Huns were so well entrenched in their forward bunkers that many of their machineguns survived? Could direct fire heavy artillery destroy these armored vehicles? He answered his own question with dismay. The massive slaughter of advancing troops on open ground would be terrible!

The grand tour ended back in the Frenchman's office over another fresh bottle of merlot. As they sipped the merlot Lefebvre summed it up. "We want Alsace- Lorraine back and want to get even for this national disgrace of old. Our leaders are extremely adamant about this and general staff wants to bite the Huns hard in the ass!" He laughed. "We do fear the warlike nature of the Hun. We will be ready!" They all toasted M. Lefebvre's words with a couple of wine fueled "Viva La France" cheers. Nephew cut in. "What do you hear of any technological developments or tactics from your Russian counterparts?" The Frenchman replied.

"Russia is a very corrupt monarchy, a throwback from medieval times ruled by powerful wealthy nobles over the vast society of poor peasants. Our agents in Russia tell of a dismal world for the people and suspect they will tire of this corrupt Tsarist yoke soon! So, the Russian "peasant" army will be under trained, poorly armed, and simply said, "poor!", Any advanced weapons will probably be mostly imported from what I learned. Peasant soldiers will be cannon fodder for their feudal masters in a war; especially against these automatic weapons and heavy Krupp artillery we hear being developed! Over all, the Russian army will be poorly equipped to fight a large war.

Cavendish was quietly amazed at how much of the new weaponry had been dumped on Kali! The Frenchman continued. "Like the feudal society of Russia, their military tactics are as antiquated as their weapons. Russian tactics will rely on massed unsupported frontal assaults to bludgeon their enemy. These new automatic weapons will change this aspect of war only after great slaughter is realized. Russia has a surplus of manpower and shortage of weapons I am told." The Frenchman took a sip of wine and smiled as he continued speaking.

I also predict that if social reforms are not instituted in Russia soon and this overbearing corrupt feudal system continues, they will have their own French Revolution! The French revolution came from the wake of the American Revolution. The U.S. Constitution was a perfect document that included the prime parts of Enlightenment Philosophy which had its origins in France. To add insult to injury for King Louis, he had sent thousands of soldiers and sailors to help the Americans defeat the hated British and win independence! M. Lefebvre laughed out loud. "Mon Amis! Man did that backfire here by 1789!"

Then came Napoleon, the dictator that spread the concept of nationalism to the countries that he defeated, who came back to defeat him with their grand national spirit!" Now we have a czar and the rule of his nobility in Russia that refuse to change while the whole world around them has! Just like the power of the Enlightenment and nationalism, Czarist Russia will be destroyed from within in the midst of all the democratic social changes around it! The peasants will angrily wake up tired of this monarchal curse over them and destroy it violently, and sooner than later! All the people need is a good leader!

Both Brits were surprised at what happened next. Lefebvre was interested in the price of the steel they had to sell. Cavendish haphazardly pulled out his notes and gave him the pricing in tons. Lefebvre pulled out his file on steel contractors and reviewed his prices. Then he looked up and smiled, "I think we will be able to do business at your prices. The price of steel has grown higher since the Germans began buying up large quantities of it last year!" Both Nephew and Cavendish looked at each other in askance. Cavendish was nearly laughing when he handed him the information of the British firm selling all the steel products. After all, if they sold steel, they got commissions.

"It is funny what a case of merlot from an old friend can do in business my friends!" Quipped the jovial Frenchman. With all said and done, they parted ways in the most jubilant of moods. He was also going to keep them posted on the evolving weapons and production and promised to visit to his old and dear college mate Jacques Balbain soon. The next day they were heading to Germany to meet with several large armaments' makers over the next couple of weeks. The other French companies were a bust. It seemed these weapons companies throughout the Fatherland were like German breweries, there seemed to be one in every town.

The Germans were the most prolific arms manufacturers of the best weapons and it was a big business. The militaristic Prussian "Greater Germany" common excuse for developing massive inventories of weapons was for self-defense which was seen as comedy by serious observers! But the budding size of these arms enterprises demonstrated "other" dark future intentions. The rising cost of steel due to a massive German procurement program was an unsettling factor to both of them. The reason for their massive steel procurement? Germany was now building a huge deep-water navy to extend their global economic power and naval punch. It took millions of tons of steel to create these new armored ships nicknamed 'Dreadnaughts" by the British builders.

The huge economic boom in Germany had unmasked its designs to disrupt the order of things and challenge the global supremacy of Great Britain in eventual confrontation. Then this conflict on the high seas would no doubt explode in Europe! The rise of a new power in confrontation with an existing power was the basis for the extremely well studied destructive Peloponnesian War between Sparta and Athens. This power struggle between rising and existing powers was eloquently called "Thucydides Trap." By this famous philosopher and general who witnessed it.

However, the boys were not interested in the future shape of global politics but were looking for a German armaments' maker and dealer like Lefebvre to get a firsthand feel for what the Germans were developing. Their handlers had contacted over a dozen German armaments companies throughout Germany and had positive responses from eleven of them regarding steel prices. Nephew had learned that Krupp Industries had their tentacles in many of these smaller companies as they were actually subcontracted by them. Colonel Nephew had dispatched this detailed report via diplomatic pouch from the British embassy in Paris. Professor "Ravi" Strosser was not surprised at this octopus Krupp.

Cavendish, smiling as ever, as Tiberius had also wired the information on the sale of steel to Lefebvre to the British steel manufacturer he represented. They were still laughing over that sale at dinner. They could actually split a twenty-thousand-pound commission if Lefebvre brought all the stuff he ordered. "Viva La Estate Balbain!" cried Tiberius as they laughed over a couple of beers. Their mission was now entering its third week visiting German armaments companies on their list. They had gotten nowhere close to their experience with the Frenchman. Their train trip revealed the exquisite beauty of southern Germany as they crossed the manicured farm fields, the huge foreboding forests, and crossed the pristine wide flowing rivers. They admired the tall German houses in both the farms and villages with their traditional white paint and brown wooden external beams. Everything seemed so clean, neat, and organized.

At the end of two weeks they were ready again for their meeting with Krupp Industries who had put them off twice thus far. Their persistence finally paid off. Both Nephew and Cavendish felt Krupp was the "octopus" behind every armaments company they had visited thus far. There was one other interested manufacturer in the south of Germany which they planned to visit on the way to Italy after Krupp. There would be time to visit Italy sunny, warm, and fun. The next day they traveled to Krupp Industries, which was the center of the German military industrial revolution. It was located in the northwestern part of Germany at the huge manufacturing complex in the Ruhr Valley.

The Germans at Krupp were cordial but crisp, as they were ushered them into a huge meticulous meeting room. After waiting some minutes, a younger man entered who was introduced by an associate only as Mr. Krupp Junior. His impression was not the best. His eyes betrayed the likeness of a hawk or some cold wanton bird of prey neatly dressed in a black business suit. He seemed arrogant and unfriendly as he stared over the rims of his wire glasses, as if he was in some sort of hurry. After a very cold introduction, his associate asked for the prices as Krupp Junior made some comments in German to his associate.

Tiberius Nephew was also fluent in German and picked up the comment, which was something to the effect of "Why would I buy steel and add wealth from my prospective enemies in the next war? It would be little help to our navy would it when they rid the seas of this curse and rule the seas and colonies for the good of the Fatherland? These fools! Tell them their prices are too high and we are done here!" In a very accented English monotone Krupp's point man explained that these prices were too high and that his suppliers were cheaper. He coldly thanked them for their visit, stood, and left the room. They were crisply ushered out of the building and off the property of the vast manufacturing complex complete with the noise and smells of mechanical production.

Nephew smiled at his friend. "I would love to see what is on the assembly line mien Cavendish!" Who smiled back and nodded "yes?" It now seemed that their trip to Germany was becoming a big flop. However, this big flop and Krupp's comments revealed to both men that the Germans had an obvious imperialist eye down the road! The pseudo steel salesman had plans to meet their last contact in two days in southern Bavaria. It was a smaller newer factory complex probably supported by Krupp Junior as well. The other contacted company, located in the city of Hechinger, in Baden-Württemberg, had not responded as Cavendish noted.

It seemed that this factory bore the name Krupp, but probably had some general affiliation with the "little prick" Krupp Junior they had just left. Both men were tired and ventured into a gasthaus that night to enjoy good hearty German music, traditional dinners and to drink some good "kalt bier!" During the dinner and beer, they both knew that they were being watched. They recognized one of the men as being present at the meeting with Krupp. With one eyeball perched on them, the two continued to relish their food, beer, and the music. They pretended that they did not see their observers and continued with their enjoyment.

After dinner, Nephew and Cavendish continued with the fun musical environment in the smoke-filled German pub. The German girls, many of them were very beautiful with bountiful breasts and braided blonde curls. They were also friendly and Colonel Nephew had to restrain his desires to fondling only, since they sensed a potential problem across the room. They soon left the very lively party and walked back to the hotel in the stillness of a cool cloudy night. Like hot and cold, they went from lighted noise to dark cold rained filled silence as they walked.

Once back at the hotel Colonel Nephew spoke. "I bet the German government via Krupp had their foot on the throats of all those companies we visited and now the goons follow us! All the people we talked with over the last two weeks seemed nervous and aloof to any of our questions. However, Heer Krupp Junior seemed very in control. It makes sense to me now, after we discovered we were being tailed tonight. Krupp is the Octopus! It seems that the German government does not want anybody inquiring about their weapons, tactics, or plans, and especially any "we bastard British!"

The "octopus" knew we were coming to those companies well in advance and know we are going to the one tomorrow. I say we evade these guys and drop in on the one that did not respond to our requests. They are located in the same region." Cavendish yawned and nodded in agreement and added. "So how do we evade the tentacles of Das Octopus mien Obrest-leutan?" Nephew laughed, "Ever play hide and seek?"

The next morning, they boarded a train for the last arms manufacturing company on their list. It was located in a town only fifty-five miles east of the one they now intended visiting and not listed on their itinerary. Nephew had carefully studied the train schedule between these towns going to the town of Hechinger where they were going to drop in on the obscure armaments company, which also bore the name Krupp. It was actually simple since the Germans kept their train schedules immaculately accurate to all destinations religiously. Tiberius already saw at what town where they were going to jump from train to train.

If this unintended last stop was another flop, then they would take the train towards sunny Italy over the Alps for a few days. The train station in the early morning was packed with many travelers. A cold mist seemed to hang throughout the area. The rail Bahn was, like the rest of Germany, very tidy from yellow brick wall to yellow brick wall. The smell of coffee and rich morning foods enticed both men into a small café for some espresso and some excellent cooked sausages. They also did this to confirm they were still being followed. It was easy to identify these men since they still wore the long black overcoats and slouch hats as worn in the Gasthaus. They sat apart in another café directly across from them. Two others seemed to have joined them now. The train bound for their next visit pulled out sharply at eight. It was due to stop at their switching point at nine-thirty.

At that time the train west, they wanted, would be stopped as well in the same town aimed west. Once on the train, they settled in a room next to the end of the train car facing the tracks. The "tail" settled into a room down the hall. The train ride ventured into the mountains and offered excellent picturesque sights on the way. At nine-twenty their train chugged into the town where they were going to begin the game of "hide and seek." As the train stopped Cavendish used the bathroom to scout. On his return, he saw one of the goons standing in the hall smoking a cigarette. He returned to the room and reported it to Nephew.

Oberst-Leuten Nephew had already opened one of the sliding windows on the train and was smiling. "We jump when the trains move old boy!" After the Captain, had closed the sliding door Nephew went to work jamming the door mechanism with a piece of steel rod he had mysteriously produced from his briefcase. They carefully pulled the blinds and waited. As both trains began to move, they deftly dropped their bags and slid out the window to the ground. Keeping hidden from any goon eyes, they ran in the opposite direction with the train they had exited and to the end of the train heading west. They quickly chambered into the doorway of a train car several cars down and ducked out of sight.

Meanwhile, Nephew and Cavendish settled in for a wonderful ride west. After over a couple of hours of travel, the picturesque Castle of Hohenzollern, which sat on a huge mountaintop, could be seen from a distance. It was a classic example of castle architecture, with high spires reaching into the sky. It appeared like some giant monument, cut atop the huge dark green forests that surrounded it. This beautiful castle was the ancient seat of the Swabians, and the area it controlled had been viewed as a backwater area, and extremely remote in many areas. The inhabitants in this realm lived hard frugal lives for centuries. According to their economic brief, this area had recently seen the development of textile factories and was to be the new home of the Daimler-Benz motorcar factory.

This area was also full of mysterious myth and lore, the home of werewolf's and witches. Both soldiers did not want to encounter any of them since they had already had their fill of monsters in the living lore in India. Nephew and Cavendish stepped off the train around two-thirty in the afternoon in a dismal gray day and intermittent rain. They waited for forty-five minutes and observed two more trains disgorging their passengers from a small café across from the train station. No one had tailed them at this point and it seemed that they had won their game of "hide and seek!" They now focused on their unexpected visit to the Johannes Krupp Works about four miles outside the quaint Bavarian village they stood in.

They hired a carriage for the journey to the Krupp Works. It seemed like a half hour had passed as they travelled down the narrow muddy road between huge foreboding forests on both sides. The coach halted in front to what resembled some early Industrial Age factory complex surrounded by old beaten and ivy covered stonewalls. It could have been a 17th Century factory from the wear and tear on the outside of this ancient tree infested structure. They paid the driver and disgorged inside the weathered huge wooden main gate. They faced an old stone building that resembled the weathered exterior stone walls of a mediaeval fort that seemed to be the office.

As they looked around the area, they saw many very old newer buildings, made of wood with huge bay doors back as far as the eye could see in the rising mist. Although solid, these old structures bore the dilapidated effects of neglect and harsh climate for decades. The complex reached back into the forest for a good way. The rain continued to pour as the temperature began to slightly drop. It was the type of weather that chilled one to the bone. They walked towards a large set of wooden doors with hypothermia on both their minds. They had no idea if they were to even be admitted to this place. They approached the ancient stone building as both noticed that the outside of the building was unkempt and seemed abandoned. There was no bustle of workers about leaving for the day, and a gloom seemed to prevail.

They walked into the vestibule that resembled more of a musty hunting lodge than an armaments manufacturing plant. A very proper older woman sat at the desk behind an old wooden counter working on some files. Her hair was in a huge bun and her glasses made her look more of a schoolteacher than a secretary. She was the only person present and there were no guards or other people around. This seemed completely out of place as compared to the guard presence at the other German factories, especially at Krupp. Cavendish presented himself and Nephew under their cover as suppliers of raw materials and requested to see the president. The older frau gave them a serene smile as she stood up and approached them. She spoke in very heavy accented English.

"Good day gentlemen, is Mr. Krupp expecting you today?" "Well not exactly mum, we had a request from our company "Shilling and Sons" a dealer of raw steel materials to meet with him, but I think the reply was lost. We were in this area today and came to pay our respects to Mr. Krupp." Nephew rolled his eyes in reaction to the excellent fabricated tale of Cavendish. "Let me see what he is doing." She walked through a beautiful oak door at the end of the long hunting lodge decor. In a few minutes, she returned followed by a rather small man, dressed in a tweed suit, bespectacled, and adorned with a rather long white Van Dyke beard and bushy unkempt white hair.

He looked like some mad scientist except for his very reserved gentle nature. He was very old to the standards of the day. He looked in his eighties. He slowly edged over to the two Brits and looked up from his signature crouched back. In good command of English, he spoke with a very deep strong accented voice, not in place with his image. "Welcome to Krupp Industries, it is nice to have guests from time to time. Please come with me to my office for some hot coffee. It is cold today!" They followed the old man, who also used a cane and made a slow venture into a huge office adorned with ancient bronze statues, and very old paintings.

Some of them looked like the "Masters" created them as they later found to be true. He slowly turned and, in an afterthought, introduced himself as Alois Krupp Senior. The two Brits returned the compliment. He kindly smiled and asked them to sit down as the older frau delivered each an excellent cup of hot coffee and some great chocolates. Krupp spoke as he comfortably leaned back in his large dark leather chair from behind his huge polished desk. "If I remember you were the ones who were selling weapons grade steel products from Great Britain?"

He gave a rather cryptic smile and continued. "I sent your request to visit here off to my nephew Gustav in his main complex in the Ruhr, where the vast new generation of armaments plants are being built. Their designs are new and many; which I developed! This place is too small for what they have planned to build for the Greater German Empire! Besides, I have always been the silent brother, the faceless designer of weapons, where my brother Johannes received all the credit and attention. Ha! That was fine with me and the way I wanted it anyhow." He adjusted his wire-rimmed spectacles. "I suppose they never contacted you one way of the other? such is the way of my nephew... I am sorry for your coming here without his invitation, or mine. It seems this new generation thinks differently.

Since the death of my brother, my nephew now runs Krupp Industries and is consolidating it in one huge new series of factories up north with subsidiaries throughout Germany. He is very close to the government. Everyone who used to be here is gone now except my secretary and me, and my beloved rabbits." He smiled and added, "It seems that I have finally been put out to pasture! This factory per se has been slowly dismantled and shipped away over the last couple of years. I, the great creator am all that remains, minus little if any of my old bargaining power.

My nephew retains me as his designer and consultant. He leaves me alone for the most part, except for his corporate goons who check on me and visits from some of his weapons designers on occasion.

Otherwise, I am very alone for now except for when my dear nephew sends his engineers to pick my aging brain for weapons improvements. Even a few old retired German general friends from the 1870 war visit me occasionally, but that is all." Cavendish was picking up some negative sentiments this Alois Krupp had for his upstart nephew and let him continue. Colonel Nephew had felt the same way, when they had their rude meeting with the little beady-eyed prick! So, when the old man stopped talking the colonel chimed in. He decided to let that meeting with old man Krupp's nephew slide off the radar for now.

"Mr. Krupp, it is a great pleasure accidentally meeting you sir! Krupp is one of the greatest weapons designers in European history. We will not try to sell you anything today sir; just enjoy your company!" Krupp smiled and took a sip of coffee and continued. "Do you know how new weapons change not just battle tactics, but history? The Prussians changed history in this capacity in 1870 when we defeated the French. We destroyed the reign of Napoleon III and turned Germany into the real nation-state, an empire proud of its new nationalism! How did my weapons design change this? It was the huge rifled Breech loading siege artillery and my mobile artillery that beat those French Infantry and their excellent Chassepot rifles!"

Nephew could not help adding, "Like the longbow at Agincourt sir!" Alois Krupp laughed at the comment. "Very true in all respects! Do you know I have spent my whole life studying the historical development of weapons and how they changed history? My favorite weapons designer was Leonardo di Vinci of the Renaissance. He was developing modern weapons designs nearly five hundred years ago. Five hundred years! He had designed airplanes, mobile armored type infantry and fighting platforms, as well as heavy artillery." He then pointed over to a large wall to the left. It was adorned with all sorts of drawings under glass. Nephew got up and looked closely at them. The pictures bore the sketches of Di Vinci's war weapons.

Nephew was mesmerized! He retorted. "They are all originals, signed by the Master himself?" It seemed Krupp came to life after his statement with a resounding proud "YES!" Now Cavendish was up examining them as well. They felt like little kids in a candy shop. They looked at priceless artifacts of Di Vinci as well as others. They finally sat down as both now admired the huge bronze statue of Napoleon on a horse, rearing up. All the while Mr. Krupp spoke like a true tour guide. Krupp told them many things about how he had developed prototypes based on his Renaissance hero. The old man was in his element now and was warming up to his new "boys" in his classroom. Krupp continued.

"If you look on the wall you will see a sketch of a huge device that fired large arrows to punch holes in the walls of forts and the catapult. Alois walked over and tapped his cane on the painting of a Muslim Sultan. "Here is my mentor, Ottoman Sultan Mehmed II who employed the services of a cannon maker named Orban to conquer Constantinople in 1453 by May 29th if my mind serves me. Mehmed enlisted the services of Orban when the Byzantines in this great city could not pay him. They did not have the money. This was the nail in the coffin for the Eastern Holy Roman Empire!

What was the new technology that changed history? It was gunpowder developed by the Chinese crammed into barrels of hollow reinforced tubes to fire all sorts of things like rockets or objects in a direct and indirect fire modes. It was so named the "bombard." Mehmed allowed Orban to create this monster bombard; this prehistoric cannon to join his massed grouping of other lesser caliber bombards facing the Theodosian wall complex of Constantinople, which sat on firm dry ground. Orban's giant child; the super bombard was named the "Basilica." This invention of Orban was a twenty-seven-foot cannon made of brass that could fire a six-hundred-pound stone cannonball, which could hit targets a mile away! The city walls were surrounded by water, which made countless attempts to invade by water impossible, with one exception! This ancient extremely effective super gun destroyed the walls facing the land.

His smaller sized massed artillery fired into the inside of the city walls with further destruction. The physical destruction was measured more by the psychological terror this first concentrated artillery barrage in history produced. My oh my, did the bombard change history that day! After suffering huge losses in infantry and ships during this bloody siege, Mehmed's Janissaries gained access to the city through the huge holes left by the super bombard. The ensuing pillage and slaughter of the population was so terrible it actually saddened this twenty-one-year-old Sultan victor who stopped it. In his capture of Constantinople, he unconsciously made medieval castle design and traditional siege methods obsolete. Mehmet II ushered in the modern use of high caliber artillery along with its use in massed artillery concentrations.

The tactic used with this weapon was my guide in the creation of the "guns of Krupp." This monster bombard did have logistical problems. It took a team of sixty oxen to deliver it and over four-hundred men to man it. Loading and firing it took three hours. This particular first bombard exploded during the final siege since the brass used to create it was flawed and had cracked under the impact of firing seven rounds per day. Most of the gun crew was blown up with it." Old Krupp was on a roll as his eyes seemed to light up as did his expression.

He concluded. "Leonardo di Vinci developed the concept and Mehmed allowed it to be combined with Orban's new age technology to develop the largest cannon in the world." Alois moved to the center of the office and patted the large bronze stature of Napoleon with a smile. "It was this true master of war who truly developed the modern tactical applications of massed artillery in his expert design of battlefield deception tactics to confuse and off-balance enemy armies. What was Master Napoleon's strategy in the employment of massed artillery? It was to annihilate rather than to just defeat the enemy armies that faced him in battle. The old rule of victory in previous wars was defeating a foe by out maneuvering them; not in their annihilation." Alois smiled as his enlightenment resumed.

"In the 1860s, I developed a prototype siege gun that could fire a one-hundred-centimeter round and blow a hole in anything and destroy enemy battle formations at a great distance! But I needed something to counter the very effective Chassepot self-loading French rifle used by the massed formations French infantry and their infant Reffye fifty- barrel volley guns. I then developed rifled breech loading mobile artillery to follow the cavalry which was accurate, faster to the punch, and killed thousands of those Frenchie's as they clutched their new Chassepot rifles to muddy graves." He pulled a Chassepot Rifle complete with its brass handled bayonet attached to it out from behind his desk and handed it to Colonel Nephew. He mused at his guests as Nephew inspected it.

"I have this stuff sitting everywhere!" He then handed Cavendish an 1893 Borchardt automatic pistol that was the first to use a magazine. He showed the officer how to load it. He gave a wizened smile to both men. "You ought to see what Mauser is creating!" Alois was feeling his oats and was revitalized with this great conversation. He poured everyone a large glass of fine German Schnapps. He held his glass up and smiled "To weapons that change history and to the Chassepot!" They were all laughing after the third shot! The ancient little man humorously continued as he pointed again to the magnificent large bronze statue of Napoleon Bonaparte. He spoke "Weapons that destroy need a mother, a mother to guide them into a useful existence of destruction! Napoleon was the mother! Ha Ha Ha." The old man laughed as he downed another shot! His lecture went on. "Napoleon brought the strategy of annihilation of enemy armies into tactical reality! Bonaparte's philosophy? Do not let the enemy lose by maneuver, but by complete annihilation! Thus, was my original plan to develop weapons not just to defeat an army with marginal losses, but design them based on the concepts of Leonardo, Orban, and on the "Mother of Destruction" Napoleon! Weapons designed to annihilate whole armies and cities!"

Both Cavendish and Nephew, feeling the effects of the schnapps gave the ancient old man a hearty round of applause. Mr. Krupp gave a polite bow in return. It was late, and Frau Bergdorf popped in the office door and signaled that she was leaving for the day. All present wished her a good night! Cavendish felt that he was at the only "mom and pop" arms factory in the world now. When they were thinking about leaving, the now cheerful old man, revitalized, ushered them into a grand old room complete with a nice pub demeanor with a hand-carved bar, and all sorts of portraits, weapons and carved animals found inhabiting this small comfortable place.

Alois poured out three glasses of Bavarian brew in tall drinking horns from behind the bar and slid them to his guests. The cold glasses of excellent Bavarian beer hit the spot as Krupp commented. "I so love beer that I had this small gasthaus built for my employees and for my convenience! "Prost!" Yelled Krupp and they all finished the first beer, only to have it replaced with a new one from a tap in the wall. It was here that Alois Krupp, the sacred and secret weapons designer for Krupp Industries disclosed that he was in the Franco-Prussian War and had been on the front lines ensuring his war works of art were being used correctly.

More toasts followed. He insisted that the French had good stuff in 1870, he loved their rifle designs. But good weapons were useless because their generalship was weak in comparison to Von Moltke, who was a personal friend, and master of the quick decisive offense. He even produced the huge German Iron Knight's cross with a large white and black ribbon from the wall behind the bar and put it around his neck. "I keep my Knight's Cross close to the beer! They seem to go good together!" He smiled and told them Moltke had given him the rank of colonel and had awarded this medal for his service in combat, especially seeing that all his weapons were being used with maximum effectiveness on the battlefield!

Everyone toasted his award! Old Krupp was now full of life and everyone seemed loaded. He raised his glass and gave the next toast, which surprised the two Brits. "May we toast the memory of all those fine French soldiers and their horses slaughtered by the great artillery of Krupp in 1870!" Colonel Nephew, feeling the mirth of the drinking had poured out half of his beer in the sink when away using the restroom. He was exploding on his mental notes. Meanwhile, Cavendish and old Alois were having a genuine ball. Feeling hunger strike, Krupp introduced a bevy of sausages and cheese, complete with mounds of crackers…they ate and continued to drink, and the stories of the war in India seemed to enthrall old Krupp.

Finally, thinking it was all over by nine, the men prepared to leave. However, old Krupp looked at them in a serious note. He stared deeply at them and spoke. "Perhaps if I help you understand war technology, you can help me tonight with some very important mission I have to finish before my life is over? I will need your help before it is too late! I cannot trust anybody except Frau Bergdorf, and she is too feeble for what I need." Over the next beer, he outlined his life as a weapons designer and on his great regret to what he produced with chilling horrendous effects in 1870. He hinted of his even greater fear of future destruction and death by his designs! What was being produced was the handmaiden of this terrible reality.

Mr. Krupp smiled, and then invited them to see his special "toyshop." Mr. Krupp had seemed to adopt the two soldiers who had seemed to turn one day in the life of an old genius –warrior into a banner holiday from the drabness of his reclining life. But now there seemed to exist some obscure motive. Old Krupp, who had seemed completely revitalized by all the beer, and schnapps led the two at a faster pace hobbling on his cane into an old warehouse building directly to the far left behind his small office building. The fog was getting thick as the cold rain continued to fall, but the clean air of the Bavarian night felt good to the lungs. He unlocked a huge door and they walked into and lighted the room in the warehouse. He closed the door behind him and locked it.

The huge multi-ton door was built on huge greased rollers by which a child could push shut. The room was empty. Krupp laughed…" You see all of my works are invisible!" He then led them over to a wall across the huge room and pulled down on some hidden lever. The whole wall seemed to drop into the floor. A solid brick wall just dropping slowly into the floor. Alois looked at them in a semi-drunken leer. Krupp's Toy Shop awaits! Please come in and enjoy the fruits of my labors over the last sixty years. Do you know my nephew never saw this room? Nobody has ever seen this but, except you!" Alois put his finger to his lips in the symbol of silence. "Please don't tell him!"

Both Cavendish and Nephew laughed and swore on the Pope that they would never speak or reveal this secret to that little asshole. Krupp made them toast a shot of schnapps to "that little asshole!" "That wall?" stammered Cavendish. "It was a brick wall that just went into the floor!" Alois smiled. "Did you know that as a child I wanted to make watches and just loved the inner workings of them? Building and repairing watches was my hobby!" He paused to light his pipe. "Yes, my sons, when one has money to burn, and the creative genius transcribed from the mind of Leonardo as I the watchmaker; one can create wonders like this to obscure my secret creations as I did years ago.

I may have much wealth left, but no money to burn anymore, to build things such as this special warehouse and other architectural delights you shall soon see to hide my toys! You now stand in a brilliantly constructed timepiece." Old Krupp edged over to a wall and pulled a lever. Then the sound of a multitude of pulleys and other pieces of his clock began a mechanical humming noise. The huge room was bathed in light after he hit a switch that automatically lit many kerosene lamps down the walls. The jaws on both British officers dropped to the floor. A. Krupp then laughed out loud and he nipped again from a bottle of good German schnapps and offered it. Both men easily obliged him.

Colonel Nephew wondered if he was in a museum in some time capsule. Captain Cavendish saw it in the same breath. "Ready for the tour my sons?" The "works" as described by A. Krupp were lined in rows beginning with a basic composite of the master's ancient Renaissance machines. A. Krupp began with the row of flying machines beginning with the flying bird of Leonardo and slowing moving down the line. As they moved down the line Krupp carefully explained how the genius of

Leonardo, applied the study of birds to his creativity applied to his modifications. The models were well detailed with notebooks resting on the individual tables where they were displayed.

There were rows dedicated to every aspect of weaponry. He told them that he fed his nephew, whom he now called "Shithead" technology relevant to what other countries were creating in this point in time. Just basic prototypes! He had to give more recently as part of the bargain for him keeping his little factory as his property for research and development. Then he stopped and turned to the two Brits with a cryptic smile." I also put design flaws in all of it!" "What I am going to show you was not part of the bargain!' Both men looked in amazement as they moved down the lines. They next saw large prototypes of airplanes that would rule the skies in 1939. These were planes with skin on them, some a hard material and others made of metal, complete fuselages with machineguns configured in the wings and in some cases of the larger "bombers" as he called them, everywhere! The composite smaller models seemed to fill the room suspended from the large high ceiling.

Cavendish patted the one prototype plane on the wing and commented. "Have you flown this plane Heer Krupp?" The old man looked at Nephew and smiled; "Yes, one time! And I was responsible for all the UFO sightings last spring! The machineguns really scared the hell out of them." They looked at the wing mounted machineguns and nodded their heads. The old man laughed and continued after showing them how the guns were fired inside the timing rotation of the propeller. Then he explained to them a better design model on these guns installed in the wings as better distributed firepower. He continued. "I envision massed fleets of these airplanes that can deliver death and destruction to cities and troop concentrations!

After all the "Mother of Annihilation" demands weapons to perform this grisly deed, right? The tools to expedite the slaughter of any and all opposing armies, doesn't he?" The next rows of models were tanks. Beginning with Leonardo's "turtle tank" design, which was used to house and protect soldiers and their battering ram from oil and missiles from above, while busting down fortress gates, they began working down the line of models. "Genius Krupp" spoke. "Massed tank armies", as he touched his pointer to what looked like a huge box on crude tractor treads. "I hear the French at the Renault company are doing well on this research" He showed them the next model.

It was a large foreboding beast, much bigger than the Renaults Lefebvre showed them. Maltese Crosses were emblazoned on it. He continued. "Can you imagine what the infantry would think if a thousand of these monsters came up over the hill, kind of adds punch to a cavalry charge?" He laughed a deep penetrating laugh. Cavendish remarked, "How about "scared shitless" Mein alt Oberst!" The old German looked at him with sparkling eyes. Old Krupp was one-hundred and twenty percent in his element now. Then the newer prototypes came into view. They were more refined, lighter, they possessed large barrels and the guns were mounted on what Krupp described as turrets that could move independently of the chassis as these machines moved forward in mass pinpointing and destroying enemy targets with ease.

He showed them how the turret on the large model moved by pointing to a hand crank inside of a small model of it on a table next to it. The schnapps was passed around again. The old German explained how he came up with the aerodynamics of what he called a "main battle chariot" "If the artillery men can adjust their guns to different angles with a crank moving the gun into a new position, then the same type rotating device in this tank would solve this problem. He then showed them the blueprint. Now look at the armor on this one. I have sloped it as to deflect a straight shot into the metal and it works." He pointed back at the lumbering behemoths with the giant crude threads.

"I have passed the models of these slow lumbering creatures and useless flawed technology back to my nephew; but never this new stuff. If only he had been nicer to me and nicer and more civil in general!" Alois winked with a leer. "Basically, "shithead" is an ego maniac prick with huge dollar signs for eyes and very attached to the German "Prussian" general staff! He likes his collection of pussy and opium. I personally believe that he is a dangerous man. Gentlemen I will be coldly honest with you. In all this evolving creation of these war weapons, I saw the light of the future of war in my prototypes.

If this technology is developed, I see incredible destruction by massed armor, artillery, and even mobile infantry formations. I envision extremely fast-moving attacks by these formations ripping up the enemy in quick lightning strikes with hardly a man escaping. I even see flying machines so big that they can dispatch troops on floating umbrellas behind enemy lines!" They did a new round of schnapps as Krupp continued. "The destructive power that could and would be unleashed by the marriage of these weapons and the massed attack tactics would make the Franco-Prussian War of 1870 look obscure by comparison.

The mother of destruction would be proud of this indeed as mother earth would be drowned in blood!" Then he stopped to puff on his pipe and pass around the schnapps again. Both Nephew and Cavendish lit up cigars. Krupp then concluded. "I just do not want to be a party to it now and anymore ever! When I toasted to all the French killed by the huge Krupp guns, I was sincere. I saw many of their young dead faces, covered in shock, blood, dirt, and terror with their bodies in pieces! I bear personal responsibility now and forever for this." He tapped his finger on his Knight's Cross still around his neck. "When I wear my Knight's Cross, I wear it for my victims, never for the victors!"

The tour now covered machineguns, huge heavy artillery and mortars. His row of artillery began with Orban's huge bombast and moved up to more recognizable field pieces used by Napoleon and in the American Civil War. Then came his new creations in artillery. He had a couple of his guns from the War of 1870 next to several modern British light artillery pieces used against the green devils! They were both amazed at a long-barreled prototype gun he developed to shoot down airplane armadas. It was a huge bore caliber and sat on a wheeled chassis. Krupp remarked that this particular gun was so accurate it could be effective against enemy armor and positions nearly a mile away as well.

"Nephew laughed "Tell me you shot this gun Alois?" The old gentleman gave a "bad boy" look. "Yes son, I did and it was behind this factory. I hit both targets perfectly but the third shot went high and completely destroyed an old stone bridge over a mile away. The authorities believed it to be a lightning strike!" he smiled. "this is how I learned this gun could shoot a mile and probably a longer range. Can you imagine a regiment of these guns deployed against an advancing tank army?" Both British officers were floundering in amazement and tank armies and weapons to counter them?

The last artillery prototype model was huge in design and Krupp had it mounted on a railway car. It was a well-detailed six-foot long model that sat on a table. Krupp really loved that one. Watching Krupp mingle within this realm was like watching an expert watchmaker inside one of his watches. Alois commented on the rail gun. "If Mehmet II had rails, he would have put his bombard in it like here. This rail gun is my modern bombard I call Saint Orban! He laughed out loud. The design concepts have been around since rails were invented my boys! This gun is designed to shoot a two-thousand-pound shell and then the rail car it is mounted on rolls down the tracks to absorb the impact of the shot. I estimate this particular model could shoot between fifty to one-hundred miles!

The images had become part of Nephew's brain by now and it was overloaded. Krupp walked them through his development of the machinegun. He began with the basic Gatling gun models and moved up to large crew served ones, which were being developed in other countries now. He showed them how he had applied the swivel-technology to them so they could be repositioned without moving the base. Then to the surprise of both Nephew and Cavendish the old man introduced them to what he termed "individual automatic hand –held weapons." They fired many shots out of his working model down the line to a bunch of mannequins dressed in old uniforms. The weapons firing amused their spirits.

This hand-held automatic prototype was fed by a long ammo holder attached to the bottom of this weapon he called a magazine, like the internal clip of many rounds that resembled the internal clips used in the emerging automatic handguns such as the popular Broom handle Mauser pistol. This new clip or magazine was on the outside. It was very accurate and emptied very fast into the mannequins at the end of the shooting range. Empty brass cartridges dotted the floor as each man fired it in short and long bursts. They soon began firing all sorts of weapons now as thousands of rounds were expended. Both Cavendish and Nephew fell in love with the short machine pistol.

A new bottle of schnapps was produced by the old genius who was having the time of his life now. Old Krupp came to a large table. On it appeared what looked like some ugly ghoul mask and various canisters on it. Old Krupp looked drawn and sad. He took a long pull form the schnapps and was silent, a sad silence. Then he uttered one word, "Gas!" "What kind of gas Heer Krupp?" Krupp looked at Nephew with an old wizened half-smile. I am afraid my nephew is developing a form of chorine and mustard gas that kills people horribly, that if properly developed can kill thousands in a single artillery attack. Now the kind of artillery that kills by explosion, but spreads death by poison gas!

He then walked them over to the biggest artillery mortar they had ever seen. Krupp continued. "This is my one-hundred-and-fifty-centimeter siege mortar gentlemen and can shoot a huge shell larger than a wagon. One of the shells could be a gas shell that could cover thousands of yards as a deadly screen killing infantry or mounted cavalry on contact. All artillery and mortars can be used for this purpose. This gas weapon is only in their planning stage, but they have never seen my designs and after tonight, never will!" He then went back to the table and picked up this ugly mask with the hose hanging from it.

He handed it to Cavendish and told him to put it on. Cavendish complied and found he could breathe air from the canister at the end of the tube. He took it off and handed it to Nephew who tried it. Alois continued. "This is what I term a prototype gas mask to protect our troops from this weapon. So far, this one has worked well. Our potential enemies have nothing yet so I am told, but only time and thousands of deaths from gas will change this. We were having problems with the mask sealing around the face. Several people died at my nephew's factory testing them. "Who were these people? volunteers? "Asked Cavendish.

Krupp looked disturbed" These people were convicts sentenced to death from what I was told. But I later found them to be all Jewish convicts. It seems that Germans have an age-old negative attitude about Jews. They borrowed money from them. I checked out the list of unfortunates and found that these Jews were all common petty criminals, not convicted of dangerous crimes at all as I was told. Gassing Jews now instead of burning them like at Strasbourg during the Black Death! The Jews were blamed for poisoning the wells and creating the plague." The princes burned over two-thousand Jews alive on a huge pyre as punishment for this lie! The reality was killing the Jews whom these unsulpurous princes owned huge usury debts too!"

Krupp's face betrayed grave sadness. "My wife was Jewish, and I so loved her to the day she died and now. I had to hide her true identity from the elite noble class all her life. She was the most beautiful blue-eyed blonde lady whose looks masked her true identity as Jewess. The one hope I have is to be with her again when I die if a forgiving God permits my request." "But you were so lucky to have found such true love" replied Cavendish as his mind trailed off to the "never never land" of Pyra", then to Jenny! Old Krupp smiled and patted him on the shoulder.

He motioned for them to sit down in some chairs around a small table in the middle of the war technology wonderland. The schnapps bottle was empty and Krupp produced a new one. The effects of the German liquor on Krupp and Cavendish were amusingly very telling now as Nephew had skillfully dumped most of his out to keep his mind clear for all the images. The old man looked at them and continued. He put what looked like a hose with a large cylinder with back straps attached to it. "This my friends are another prototype of mine never to be seen by "shithead!" If you remember Greek fire used to burn enemy ships and cities of old delivered by ballista or catapult? Here is compressed Greek fire in a can."

He lit a small flame near the nozzle, aimed it at the bullet-ridden mannequins in the firing range and depressed a lever. A huge ball of flame erupted from the nozzle and reduced the military dressed mannequins to flames as smoke dissipated out hidden vents in the ceiling. All eyes and ears were back on this unique professor of war as he put down the flamethrower and faced them as he spoke. "There are even worse war monsters on my drawing boards my friends?

I have not told you about enriched gunpowder, compressed to make explosions at hundred times worse. Then there are theories of a new type of weapon, and not really new at all if you can decipher the Bible and other ancient works. There were planes that could fly much faster at unimaginable speeds, and then there are weapons that were so powerful that they could reduce cities to barren landscapes in one explosion. I think that is what happened to a city of Sodom and Gomorrah in the Old Testament, and other cities revealed in lost manuscripts like the Vedas, which are thousands of years old. My research of these old manuscripts is extensive! I just wish I had more of them." Cavendish was extremely impressed with Krupp now, for he had seen a glimpse of past super weapons described by Ravi!

Nothing new under the sun my students! We now sit here in the end of the technological stone age innocence of the 19th Century. Although mankind has never evolved socially, his weapons of death have and will…along with his cold reality to use them for reasons of power and greed. This new emerging generation is arrogant, cold and greedy!" Schnapps was passed around as Krupp went on.

"Kids, I saw the carnage firsthand in the Franco –Prussian War of 1870. I was forced to view the carnage generated on the battlefield with my new weapons in the aftermath! This was when I was sickened when I saw firsthand of what the "new" Krupp rifled artillery barrels did to the French infantry, cavalry, and troop concentrations! I woke up! He kissed his large Iron Cross hanging from the black and white throat ribbon. "For all of them! Boys, after the war in 1870 I realized that I was no better than those I despise.

Since mankind has never evolved out of the mindset of tribal rivalries, hell will unleash on this planet again. I have regular nightmares! Those in charge, these people who call themselves leaders will no doubt start one. I believe all the greed involved in imperialist colonization policies by European countries will lead Europe into this next war." "So why do you build these weapons Heer Krupp?" Asked Cavendish. "I designed many weapons in the old days as an apt student of my father, and along with my brother I saw it as a way to get rich in the high demand environment of new weapons. My brother and I remained in the world of greed and extreme luxury.

Extreme wealth had many great benefits if you know what I mean boys.

When I came home from the war, I had seen the realization of exactly how I was making my millions. I was getting rich in providing the tools to kill people; good young men mostly! Power begets riches, and riches beget power in this world! My family made millions by our designs. Then I, driven nearly insane by all of this money lust, went it alone after he died. But the images I saw as I walked on the devastation of the battlefields in the Franco-Prussian War enraged my soul. Body parts, pieces of humans entangled in the wreckage of war, and kind innocent faces who never sought war, torn from their bodies provided my extreme distaste for the reality I was involved in creating." He schnapps was passed as Alois continued.

"They use me to evaluate and develop designs for them now. I am of value from this standpoint. But I will tell you something; I intentionally left out many key components in all my designs I submitted to my nephew's engineers. They were excellent flaws, as excellent as my prototypes here!" Old Krupp gave out a laugh, "Fuck them all and that little shithead jerk nephew! This is not my world any more gentlemen, and I do not want to pioneer new technology that kills millions and will eventually end mankind. All this technology has to do is to fall into evil hands…. cold devilish hands! Then millions of innocent young men will march to their colors in the name of some stupid cause under some new asshole and be annihilated, destroyed… to kill and be killed!

And usually the ones who started war make millions of dollars in war profits invest in the world of blaming others or cheap excuses for the aftermath!" Colonel Nephew spoke. "We have become very aware that there is grave potential for this huge conflict in Europe that will go global, perhaps in the next ten to twenty years. The one you so fear Heer Krupp. I will be completely honest with you since you have been so unselfishly honest with us. We are not steel merchants selling our wares at all but are agents on a fact-finding committee made up of members from several nations commissioned by Queen Victoria to try and find the root; smoldering ember that could ignite this terrible war!

We are looking at all aspects of this from every possible point. We are both sorry if this offends you sir, you have been so generous." He waited for the reaction from Alois. Ancient Krupp smiled through his large ruffled Van Dyke and pulled three cigars out of his small leather cigar case. Each man lit up. There was complete silence as they took healthy puffs. More schnapps was passed out. Old Krupp smiled at his guests as he adjusted his wire spectacles. They fired the next a few shots with the new 7MM Mauser rifle Then they settled back down to finish their cigars over more schnapps.

Krupp began. "I appreciate your honesty, and we have been completely honest with each other tonight. If you help me tonight this toy land of death will not fall into anybody's evil hands forever." Both British officers looked at the old man with smiles as he continued. "Perhaps you can help me with a project after we finish our cigars. I have long feared what you said. I have, as I previously told you, had vivid nightmares of future war. I have heard my beloved wife Ruth calling to me in my dreams to stop it! A terrible war can only be possible with terrible destructive weapons in the hands of terrible monsters!

Alois Krupp then got up and collected all his notebooks of his inventions and carried them over to the two men at the table. He dropped them in front of Nephew. "Better for you British to have a heads up on the Hun my boys! We Germans have absconded with many of your allied weapons designs in their ongoing effort of technological dominance. Once perfected, these weapons are and will continue to be sold to anybody who can afford to buy them, like in the case of Oban selling his bombard to Mehmed II which clearly illustrates that nothing changes my boys except who gives the cash and who takes the goods. Krupp weapons will be sold then shipped all over the planet to their allies!" Then he laughed. "Or to even their enemies to punish bad allies!"

He slammed his hand hard on the wooden table making both Nephew and Cavendish jump in surprise. "Armageddon! The match to the growing powder-keg of Europe and this planet will be ignited! These weapons of destruction will do the rest!" He slammed his fist down on the table again exposing a cruel smile across his bearded face in the dim light. Nephew laughed out loud. Krupp, you scared the hell out of me again old boy!" He smiled back with his wizened half-smile from his well-trimmed white Van Dyke beard. "That was my intention! Europe sits not on an emerging golden age, but on a huge explosive!" They all laughed over Krupp's heavy hand on the table.

As they finished their cigars, as Old Krupp asked a question. "Did anybody know you were coming here? Are you staying at a hotel nearby? "Colonel Nephew carefully told the story of how they dodged the tail by jumping trains and simply coming here as a hunch, not any formal itinerary. "Very good" retorted Old Krupp. "Dearest shithead and the government are the puppet masters for all of these plants anyhow. I also know for a fact that the powers that be at Krupp have heard rumor of this room full of wonders, and not the rooms of stuff I feed to them in my other buildings in this factory. One of my old general friends let this slip once about "my special room". I am always on the watch for the company goons and their companion state police. In this cold foggy rainy night tonight... is perfect to finish my plan.

I am sure they will soon be on your trail by now. Are you armed?" "No, we are not!' toned in Captain Cavendish. The old man moved over to where all his model pistol prototypes rested and hailed for his guests to join him. He opened a hand-carved wooden case and in it were two beautiful long barreled Luger pistol prototypes. "These were a present to me from the old man last year and you may take them with you. He then produced two thirty-two round snail drum magazines that both men had never seen. Cavendish asked, "What in creation is this?"

Krupp continued as if he were teaching a class. "You pull out the standard magazine and insert the snail drum magazine. You fire all thirty-two rounds of nine mm ammo manually until you are done." He then handed them two types of ammo. "Load your snail drum with the standard nine-millimeter ammo and then use the extra magazine to load these rounds. They are my prototype grenade rounds and work well. Better you have these in case you both find yourself in trouble. Make sure you shoot these grenade rounds twenty-five yards away or you may get hit. They are my personal gifts to you lads." He showed them how to load the automatics and they test fired them to get their feel.

Both men were in awe at the accuracy and hitting power generated from these weapons. Old Krupp then produced a couple of attachable shoulder stocks that fit these weapons and their accuracy was flawless. They then test fired the other explosive rounds at another target of a soldier wearing prototype equipment. The round hit the target and blew it into pieces shaking the room. They reloaded the Luger magazines in a new awe and put them in convenient hard-shell holsters attached to their belts including a bag that that held two thirty-two-round snail drums.

Old Krupp then blessed them with four hundred extra rounds of standard ammunition and a box of one-hundred explosive rounds. Feeling no pain from the schnapps, they fired another hundred rounds from the prototype hand held machine pistol designed by the old creator. The rounds just poured out of it to their continued amazement. Old man Krupp reloaded it and slung it around his torso. He then filled a large bag with various items, magazines, ammo, and a few trinkets. He then grabbed the 7MM Mauser rifle and looked at the two amazed guests. "This is a great hunting rifle as well." And smiled. He looked both men closely and continued. "I do not want to be part of this future and now we must complete my last duty to ever have my technology fall into the evil hands of my shithead nephew!"

The little old man looked at them with gratitude. "I somehow feel you were angels sent to help me complete my final plan for my toy shop. I have tried to figure out who would help me turn this wondrous hall of war machines into a lost mausoleum." Alois Krupp paused to clear his throat and took a belt of schnapps. He passed the bottle to a giddy Ambrose and Tiberius. On he went. "Nobody knows about this specially constructed room except myself and now you. I supervised the building of it using different work crews at each stage. This way, no one ever understood what I was constructing.

I got away with it before all the visits and inspections by the state security police with my nephew and his agents after he took control.

He gave a broad smile as he added. "Now let's see how the inner workings of my fine clock work. Now we will wind up my timepiece we stand in one last time." He then leaned back and pulled open a drawer in the old desk and removed a fake bottom. Inside this fake bottom, he pulled out nine large brass keys. Old Krupp then smiled. "It is time to wind my final timepiece gentlemen!" He then explained that this whole hall was actually a large room within the structure of another large room. When the keys were set correctly in the four walls, and a wheel turned, this whole place would descend as a giant coffin into the ground.

He further explained that they were sitting on a floor that had forty feet of hollow ground below it. He then escorted them to each of the keyholes and had them insert all eight keys in the correct position. They were hard to turn and an oil can was fetched. This released the brakes on the lift. The keys all were to be turned straight up, thus releasing the huge pulley weights that kept this secret building within a building above the ground. When all the keys released these pulleys, then a huge wheel had to be turned from above to set the completely free room in the middle of a narrow crosswalk.

This would set the room to descend and this was where Cavendish and Nephew came into the picture. Once that was done then the final key would begin the movement. Krupp described this whole movement like the figures on a German clock. He needed strong backs to turn the huge wheel above. When this main room descended into the ground, the roof of this room, built under the real building roof, was actually created to look like any floor in a warehouse complete with stains in the concrete. After this moved down into the ground, then all that would be left was an empty warehouse building.

The stately old man handed the last key to Colonel Nephew. "To ensure you I am sincere I give you the last key, the one, once inserted will send this whole room into its final resting place and turn my timepiece off forever! Nothing will happen until you perform this last task sir!" Colonel nephew smiled as he put it in his pocket. Both men climbed up a very secluded narrow staircase directly attached to the room, and soon encountered a large wheel laying on its side, like a grain mill, with two large metal poles set in it for pushing the mechanism into place. Wasting no time, they strained on the poles until they heard a creaking noise. They emptied the contents of the oil can sitting next to it. The oil drizzled into the gears.

The wheel had been locked due to a lack of grease in its gears. They then pushed it again and the former resistance gave away as it began to turn and then locked into place as the wheel dropped a foot into position. They heard all sorts of noises revert abating through the whole area. Then there was only one more key to turn to seal this room, and they hurried in suspense to find A. Krupp below. Nothing had happened yet according to Krupp. Both men were nervous and sweating.

They then returned to where the old man in his neat suit stood. He clasped the Seven MM German Mauser rifle in his hand, with a couple of large bags hanging from straps off his body. He looked like he was ready to go hunting in the woods. Both men smiled at the old gentleman as Cavendish relieved him of the two heavy bags he had slung on his shoulders with his bags. He stood by the outer door to the huge room filled with his creations. Old Krupp looked at them then intoned: "Behold the beauty of pulleys and weights my boys! And may all this work of the devil be lost forever." Nephew handed him the ninth key.

Alois Krupp positioned the key in the last hole and turned it three-hundred-and sixty degrees and they watched in amazement as the whole room slowly and quietly slid into the ground, then the narrow crosswalk and the huge wheel, then a three-foot slab of concrete roof positioned above the wheel the men had turned, formed the new floor where the huge old room, with all its dangerous wonders had been but now encased in a huge concrete coffin below them. Instead of viewing a hall of wonders, they all stood looking into a very empty warehouse with a rather unused dusty and multi-stained floor. Krupp then pulled the large brass key from the hole just before the wall descended and gave it to Colonel Nephew. "A memento for you both to remember!" Krupp smiled at them. "Now, I can raise my rabbits and fish without any fear that "they" will find my secrets anymore! I and the world thank you for this help tonight!"

Cavendish and Nephew remained motionless by this event. It was half past five when they re-entered his antique filled office, which seemed as old as him. They rekindled their wits over bottles of fresh milk, water, and coffee. Ancient Krupp seemed happy as a clam and in great spirits. They noticed that the prototype weapon called a sub machinegun was still strapped around his shoulder as his collection of large strapped bags were placed down on the floor behind his desk. Krupp looked at the submachinegun as he laid it next to his chair. He laughed at it as he stood the Mauser against the wall. "HA HA, I have something to keep the foxes away from my rabbits!" Nobody seemed tired, for the adrenalin rush was still in effect for all three men in spite of all the schnapps. Krupp then added with a smile.

"I have the usual driver standing by to take me home but will use him for your hasty exit west to catch a more distant train rather than sending to the local station. Your new destination will be the Baden Mainline at another station several miles from here at Rottweil. This change is in my concern that this station here will be watched now I greatly suspect. The secret police are true bloodhounds and will be searching for your trail and here soon after your ducking out on them yesterday. Anyway, from there you will hopefully extricate yourselves out of our new Greater German empire circa 1871 from Rottweil to Basel France."

At six sharp, Krupp's coachman pulled his coach through the old faded open gates of the factory, barely visible in the morning fog and rain. Cavendish and Nephew had stowed their briefcases in their huge duffle bags to ease in their movement. They loaded their bags directly into the coach and turned to see old Krupp standing in a dignified manner. Colonel Nephew saluted the Old Prussian Colonel, still bedecked with the Knight's Cross, and shook his hand. "Sir, we can never repay you for your generosity or kindness." Captain Cavendish followed suit. Alois Krupp made his final remark. "Gentlemen, perhaps together we saved millions of lives by our actions a few hours ago. Now, I can be left alone in peace until I see Ruth again. Goodbye and farewell my special friends; my kids, my angels of deliverance!"

The horse-drawn carriage made a wide arc in the wet overgrown grassy area next to the office building and headed out of the factory gate at a brisk trot. They were to travel by an old dirt road out of Hechinger, through Balingian across the Black Forest to Rottweil. They moved at a trot down the narrow country road that ran next to some rather large ominous mountains lost in fog after they passed the next city as they moved towards their station of departure.

The sun, obscured by the huge forest trees in the thick fog, was just beginning to climb in the eastern sky as they traveled through the mist and darkness of the country road. Both men were on guard and were looking very hard to see if they were being watched. But the view was so obscured that they, nor any pursuers, could see anything at this point. Tiberius had already loaded one snail drum in the Luger pistol and attached the wooden stock.

Old Colonel Alois Krupp, the unknown master of so many new prototype deadly weapons, ventured to the area where dawn slowly uncovered his special cottage, a well-built shack where his collection of beloved rabbits lived, and began feeding them as he talked to them as if they were his human children. He felt his peace of mind fade as a gruff voice came out of the darkness from outside. "Alois Krupp! Would you please accompany us to your office?" Without a word, and a side-glance at the tall security officer he despised. He replaced his favorite rabbit "Adolph" back in his cage and was escorted to his office by three men. He saw what seemed like dozens of secret police and Krupp goons combing towards every building shadowed in the fog, beginning to break locks and searching with torches. Once in his office the familiar face of the hardened chief of the secret police confronted him.

The other face he hated was the presence of Mr. Schmidt, the chief goon who worked for his nephew and was continuously present with parties of scientists and engineers that came to visit him on rare occasions now. Beside two armed guards were another plain-clothes gentleman who merely introduced himself as one of the agents searching for a couple of British agents who had been seen in the town. He wanted to know if they had been with Krupp and he mildly said "no!" The rotund "new fat-faced" agent continued.

"We know they had to be here Mr. Krupp, since they jumped trains and came in this direction. Your arms factory, although shut down now for production is still very important!" Krupp gave an indifferent look at the fat faced goon. "So, what nameless agent, I did not see anybody! I was feeding my rabbits and dreaming up new weapons!" Replied Alois Krupp sternly. The nameless agent's fat face reddened as he stepped up and slapped Krupp hard in the face knocking him back into his desk chair.

"You are a liar and a traitor! Old bastard!" The fat baby faced agent was now puffed up like some spiny Blowfish. The head corporate goon present chimed in. "You know; I think it is time you swam with the fishes in the stream old man! I think your nephew will agree that you have a bad accident today, maybe fatal?" Old Krupp, sitting in his desk chair where he had been knocked, wiped the blood from his mouth and adjusted his glasses as the nameless large agent with a clean shaved face added a very sarcastic note.

His voice was a shrill falsetto when he blurted. "Oh yes, I forgot to add, that your secretary Frau Bergdorf confirmed the presence of the British here early this morning, just an hour before our arrival here! The poor lady seemed to have a bad fall from her beautiful balcony into that beautiful gorge in front of her house, and well, like you will soon, she died!' The cruel smartass continued. "Why I thought she was so angelic that she could fly down the mountain Krupp!" All the goons and police laughed on this cruel announcement.

Alois hid his shock at this revelation with an old half-smile. Then the company goon Schmidt stood quiet now as another of the corporate goons entered and spoke in low tones to him. Then he turned and made an announcement to Alois. "What was in your now empty warehouse where a huge wall once stood Heer Krupp? It seems that we have discovered a new part of one of your warehouses directly behind this building Krupp and it is empty and the wall is gone! What was in it?" The goon was closest now and had his hands locked on his waist.

Alois did not show the grief that struck him at the murder of his friend, companion, and helper for so many years; or the pronouncement from chief goon Schmidt on the warehouse space newly located. He knew what was to happen next! Old Krupp slowly looked to the chair next to him and there was the prototype Sub machinegun fully loaded with a fresh thirty-two round magazine in it. He then stood and smiled at his tormentors and toasted them with a rather large farewell shot of schnapps.

"It has been a wonderful visit gentleman and I want to make one final toast to Greater Germany before I have my fatal accident! I want to introduce you to one of my special wonders!" As they watched him down the shot, old man Krupp leaned over and deftly flipped off the safety very quickly as he leaned up to his desk. He spoke. "Do you know something, all I want to do is raise my rabbits, to play in the forest and dream up weapons like this! Now you murder my best friend like you murder Jews!"

He pulled the prototype bolt back on the weapon and laughed out loud. There was sarcastic laughter from all present since they had no idea of what old Krupp was aiming at them.

The goon in chief sneered back with a wide smile, "Krupp, I think that your wishes are impossible now! I am certain you will be in the forest soon as food for the wolves! Poor old Alois Krupp was killed by wolves! Then, we are going to have all your rabbits over for a nice feast!" Prussian Colonel Alois Krupp smiled, now aiming what looked like a tube in his hands braced to his right hip and was smiling as he pulled the trigger. The barrel of the weapon caught the goon Schmidt several times in the chest and face as the fire now vectored from left to right as the stunned onlookers jerked back as they were caught chest high by the continuous volley of bullets.

Alois had divined the arc as the best way to shift fire. The uninvited guests stumbled and fell in every which way to the floor. Alois reloaded a fresh magazine and pumped a more bullets into their heads, as a couple of them were still moving and groaning. He then stood over the nameless fat-faced smart ass who had killed his lady. The fat jerk was clutching his stomach, split open from three rounds. "Please Krupp! Please don't kill me for I have a family!" Alois stared blankly at the fat clown squirming and bleeding on the floor. "Do you know that frau Bergdorf had a family of three sons, a daughter and seven grandchildren? You laughed at her as you saw her fly off her balcony down the mountain mein fat bastard!"

Krupp put the barrel in the yelping now gagging mouth of the fat agent and put three rounds in the mouth of fat face. The old man moved over to his desk and sat. These assholes were all dead, the bastards that murdered his life friend Frau Bergdorf! Now for the rest of his visitors! He took another long shot of schnapps from the bottle relishing the moment. Then he reached under his desk and felt for a button. He then pressed the hidden button very hard three times. In an instant every building began blowing sky high in quick succession. The explosions ripped every building in the factory to flaming shreds. The explosions were incredibly powerful and loud as all the windows of his office facing them were shattered in the blasts.

He estimated correctly that most of the secret police and corporate goons died in the blasts. There was one small building besides his office that was saved from the blasts. It was his rabbit house, built and painted to resemble a fairytale cottage. It had originally served as a large playhouse for the many children that used to play on the grounds while their parents worked in the factory. As the years rolled by and there were no children around anymore, Alois turned it into his rabbit house. It was safe and away from his prefabricated explosive devices rigged into every factory building several months before.

This was to be the last act in his attempt to cover up his secret war technology. He addressed the dead lying about his office. "You amateurs should never have threatened me or killed my special frau, for you just loosed the real "Dogs of War" you stupid bastards! Napoleon would be proud of my deceptive annihilation of superior enemy with a new technology!" He patted the warm barrel of his submachinegun, toasted the large bronze statue of Bonaparte and smiled. He then threw his glass at the statue where it shattered.

Alois slung his prototype SMG over his shoulder put a half empty bottle of schnapps in his coat pocket and slowly ventured to the see the wreckage that had once been his prized factory complex. He stood and watched the fires from the destroyed buildings illuminate a smoky pall that hung over the area mixed with the now fading fog of the night. Krupp could feel the heat from fifty yards away. Several wounded and dazed officials stumbled out of the flaming debris and smoke towards old Krupp. "Are you all that survived this terrible explosion?" Yelled Krupp. "Yes!" replied the goon standing in front minus his left arm and bloody from the explosions. Krupp raised his sub machinegun prototype and killed all of them where they stood.

The smoldering remains of every building were strewn everywhere, becoming visible with the rising sunlight illuminating the overcast clouds. Old Krupp searched for any other possible survivors. He found only a couple more secret policemen alive, spared their lives, and sent them back to the office. He told him that he witnessed an attack by unknown terrorists and only survived because he was feeding his rabbits! He had slung the weapon and walked with cane over to where his rabbits were and calmed them by humming a few German tunes out loud. He then went over to a clear spring fed stream and began to toss his prototype SMG into the deep blue part of the spring where he loved to catch fish but changed his mind. Instead, he took it into the rather disheveled rabbit cottage house.

He hung his weapon on a rack of garden and other tools under an old apron, minus the loaded magazine. Even if they found it, they would not understand what purpose it served. He unloaded the magazine and with the other empty ones and a few boxes of ammunition, hid them in a secluded bottom drawer designed for the purpose of hiding things. The interior of his rabbit cottage was a mess anyhow. Besides, there were foxes and wolves about and the 7MM Mauser rifle would not be enough, especially in winter at close quarters, as he guessed.

He pondered the events back in his office then gave first aid to the two survivors. They, like many of the dead were not from this region, but outsiders, government invaders in his estimate. He felt little remorse at what he had done as he sipped a large draft of beer. These invaders were killed interrupting his final plan of removing all trace of his deadly toy factory. Such is life he thought! Wrong place and the wrong time could get one killed. Just like all the French Infantry that found themselves on the battlefield as the huge Krupp artillery began to land among them in 1870!

The tiny fire department and local police were slow in arriving and all they found alive were two shaken and injured state police officers and old man Krupp babbling about some attack on his factory as he was feeding the rabbits in the dawn. This explosion and fire were to be reported as an industrial disaster at one of the Krupp factories. The nephew Krupp paid off the families of the deceased handsomely and life went on. Alois was left alone by his nephew Krupp Junior after a later review of events at the old factory. After all, dead people made bad witnesses as did all the dead goons and state police, especially the ones in Krupp's office!

However, the crafty old man put on a good show of dementia and memory loss gleaned from this destruction of his ancient factory complex and the death of Frau Bergdorf. His rabbits prospered. The authorities concluded that it was some attack of sabotage by many unverified British agents who they had later engaged in a strange deadly firefight at a bridge in the forest road headed for the village of Rottweil.

After a succession of distant explosions that echoed down the valley from behind them, both agents observed a huge glow in the sky, accenting the mist with a distant reddish glow. Nephew and Cavendish knew it had come from the factory! They ordered the driver to stop the carriage. They climbed out on the secluded road in the forest and could see the light emitting vaguely from the explosions in the distance above the trees and lighting the low clouds. Something had gone terribly wrong and this meant something terribly wrong was in store for them if they didn't act fast. The first thing they did was tie up the driver and put him in the carriage.

Captain Cavendish assumed the position of the driver. He had replaced his snail drum magazine with the one loaded with the grenade rounds. They continued the journey as the dawn sky seemed dreary, cloud covered with a good mist fighting against the rays of sunlight. The carriage moved through the shaded gloom of the forest at a steady pace now. As they turned a bend in the narrow road several miles from their destination, Cavendish became immediately aware that a cart blocked the small bridge and several uniformed police, donning their black leather shakos were waiting to intercept them. He noticed more plainclothes people in the mix.

"Hey Colonel! We have company, what are your orders yelled Captain Cavendish in his business voice!" "Ambrose, we can't be captured at any cost so I suggest you clear that bridge with those grenade rounds! I will cover your flanks!" Nephew checked his weapon and attached the wooden stock. He was ready. Captain Cavendish did not have to wait long to make up his mind. As the fast-moving carriage headed for the small bridge, the police on the bridge began shooting at them. As bullets zinged around him on the carriage and within seventy yards, he shot his first grenade round. It landed about ten yards in front of the police and the sudden explosion forced them to dodge for cover on the ground.

Their firing then intensified as Cavendish unleashed a second round, which squarely hit the center of the wagon blocking the entrance to the bridge. The explosion sent the overturned cart up into the air in flaming pieces, blowing it in half scattering debris to the entrance to the bridge. Several police were hit by fragments in the explosion were blown into the air. "Holy shit Nephew!' Yelled the Captain Cavendish, "Did you see that?!" "Yes!" yelled Nephew. "Shoot a few more rounds into the bridge area! Clear it out!" Colonel Nephew began returning fire shooting to the right and left of the bridge as he moved back and forth in the carriage cab. The poor driver was on the floor being trampled by Nephew.

He fired several more volleys from his Luger as he braced it against the window jam. His accuracy made direct hits on several exposed security police. Some fell by the side of the road and a couple fell backwards from the bridge wounded into the cold steep bubbly stream that flowed under the bridge; to be washed over a waterfall below. As this was occurring, Cavendish unloaded three more rounds to the left, front, and right on the bridge. This effect blew the side railings of the bridge to pieces along with the remaining police seeking shelter behind the destroyed wagon. More police officers and pieces of the wagon fell into the white foaming rapids of the mountain stream rushing below the wrecked bridge.

The carriage came to a screeching halt twenty yards away from the bridge as the two lead horses had been shot dead in the last salvo from the security police. Both Brits jumped from the carriage to clean out any more of their attackers. As Captain Cavendish jumped from the cab one of the surviving security policemen shot him twice. As Cavendish stumbled and fell on the damp dirt packed road. Colonel Nephew unloaded five rounds into the rather large cop, who staggered and fell. His black shako bounced on the muddy road. The opposition against them was done. Within seconds Nephew was assessing Cavendish's gunshot wounds. He had been grazed in the left side and had a rather deep wound in his left shoulder.

Nephew stopped the bleeding in a few moments. "Old boy, we must get the hell out of here fast!' As a stunned Cavendish nodded, Nephew was across the bridge searching for a means to escape. In short order, he was back. "We have a nice buggy the police must have used to get here. It has one mean looking horse!" Colonel Nephew made a quick search of the area to check for any more antagonists. They were either dead or had retreated. He untied and freed the very shaken driver of their coach begin to replace his dead horses with two police horses.

Within minutes, Cavendish and their gear were loaded in the buggy they had borrowed from the police and off they went down the road, past the scene of violence and carnage. When they finally arrived in the town of Rottweil some miles away, it seemed that nobody walking the streets seemed out of the ordinary. There was no large police presence at all. In short order, they abandoned the carriage on a side street put a feed bag on the horse, purchased train tickets, and waited in a coffee house next to the station.

Nephew had reloaded his Luger with a standard clip and was ready to fight it out. Cavendish was alert but was beginning to feel great pain in his left shoulder. "Wait until we get on the train Captain! I can help you there, just can't do anything here!" Nephew went silent and they waited. The train pulled into the station and they entered the last car on the train and both immediately entered a coach and closed the door, with the colonel throwing the bags down to the floor. With the curtains closed, the colonel removed Cavendish's coat and shirt to reveal a severe bullet wound to his shoulder. The bullet had lodged in it! Nephew stopped the bleeding then pulled out his aid kit he always carried from habit and gave Ambrose a shot of morphine.

Next, he pulled out a bottle of water and some rather smelly ointment and cleaned the wound. The train pulled out as he was doing this. He then dressed the wound and Cavendish leaned back closing his eyes. The colonel was lost in his thoughts. He surmised that the ambush operation to capture them was not a local concern and that the police they had fought were a combination of state security police and corporate goons. This idea was reinforced by the lack of any police presence in the Bavarian town they had entered to take this train. He pulled out several wallets he had quickly taken off the dead at the bridge and read the identifications.

This evidence confirmed his suspicions. Three of those wallets contained the identities of German state security police, including a full colonel. The last two identities bore the credentials of a senior employees at the Krupp Industries. Then he thought of Old Krupp and wondered of his fate. He removed a load of German and American cash from the wallets of the deceased Krupp Officials and then pilfered the cash from the other wallets. This money may come in handy he thought and he felt that he had earned it this day. Then he laughed; wedding presents of course since the groom would live!

Nephew then opened the window and tossed all the wallets out of the fast-moving passenger train. He knew that they were not far from the French border and if this was an inside state job, it would take precious time to find the site of the ambush, and the bodies. This confirmed his thoughts at the next two and final stop in Alsace –Loraine. Nobody seemed to be looking for them. During the whole trip, Colonel Nephew then pulled out the stack of notebooks Krupp had given him in the toyshop. He was amazed at the clarity in writing and sketches. He was overwhelmed at the content on these future weapons! Cavendish slept as they headed for the coast.

Ambrose awoke in the temple of healing. Pyra had her arms around him as he floated in the shallow healing waters. As he awoke, she kissed him on his forehead and lips. She softly spoke in her sweet harmonious voice. "Sweetheart, you will live and mostly recover from your wounds. However, I fear that your left shoulder may hold a permanent injury. Be not saddened by this, for it is part of your change in this life. I love you forever my Ambrose!" He looked into her beautiful captivating smile, her chiseled Indian face; large purple colored almond eyes, I feel the same my Pyra! Thanks for being here for me!" She smiled and held him very close as he drifted off to sleep. I will always be here for you darling!" Tears rolled down her cheeks.

When Ambrose awoke, he found himself in a very elegant French hospital on the coast of France. In his room sat a plain-clothes man who turned out to be a member of Scotland Yard He was reading a paper and smoking his pipe. Ambrose noticed that all his bandages were fresh and felt acute pain in his left shoulder. The events leading up to this moment were confusing and foggy. He sat up and questioned the well-dressed gentleman sitting near the door.

"Where is Colonel Nephew? Is he all right?" "Yes son" came a low heavily accented English voice. "Your buddy is quite safe as are you this fine day!" "Am I in trouble?" questioned Cavendish. "Quite the contrary lad, you have been under our protection for the last three days in this hospital, under the protection of Scotland yard as requested by the British government, and even the Queen so I am told! I believe your friend had to return a couple of days ago, to England for some urgent business and you should be following him home in a couple more days with me."

Cavendish sighed one of great relief, since the last conscious moment had been Nephew patching up his shoulder on the train after the ambush. A nurse entered the room later to give him some morphine for the pain that was welling up in his shoulder. She also rubbed some dark brown ointment on the entry wounds from the bullets then put fresh bandages on his wounds. The scent smelled vaguely familiar. Ambrose was amazed at the clean pristine whiteness of the walls and floors in the room. With the sun shining in through a large window with large cloth shades blowing in the wind, it seemed he was bathed in pure light. It was a very warm spring day and Ambrose could see the waters of what he thought was the English Channel.

The Nurse smiled at him and turned him on his side to give him a shot of Morphine in his ass. She slapped him on his butt to detract from the painful needle, and then administered the shot. She rolled him back and smiled at him. In perfect French, she asked him if he was all right and that dinner would be served soon. He smiled back as he began to drift. He suddenly thought of his strange foreign maid at the Majestic Hotel after the night they were attacked by Farnsworth's goons. Pyra? it was Pyra! Those eyes, her voice, and the smell of that ointment and from her. Then Ambrose drifted off into a peaceful slumber wondering what else was in store for him in 1898!

CHAPTER NINE
STRAWMAN COMETH

It was a sunny cloudless day today on January 20, 1758. A steady hot breeze filtered in from the bay just beyond the city of Port au Prince. It gave some relief to the crowd waiting for the main event. Before this crowd Mackandal stood unphased as he was tied to the stake that would soon be lit to end his life! It would end his part in the triumphal insurrection of violence against the evil French slave overlords who infested Haiti. These parasites had brought such pain and suffering to lives of his beloved people of Haiti. It was January 20, 1758 and was his last day to live. He sneered at the white French masters who stood by mocking him. He silently wished he had just one more night of freedom to kill and burn more plantations! This one-armed liberator was greatly feared among the French. Mackandal was more than a dangerous leader.

Besides the leader of the resistance, he was also a respected Houngan and master of poisons who had worked his deadly profession on many unsuspecting French victims. He had been captured in a trap as he tried to place his poisons in the water supplies for a whole system of plantations. This plan could have killed hundreds of evil French masters! He smoldered with a hateful smile as the crimes against him were read. He looked across the way at a little boy sitting on a wall. He gave a grim smile and winked. The boy smiled back at him with a reciprocal wink and half smile. The wood under his stake was now lit and Mackandal gave a huge laugh.

"Little" Ayiti Deschamps as the boy was called had been named after the first French governor of Haiti in the 1660s by the one-armed man who found him as an orphan wandering in the jungle. The name "Ayiti" was the old name of this island he had lived since he remembered. Time had completely slipped away from him as he had lived for so long in the jungles before he was found by Mackandal who comically gave him his name since he did not have one. Ayiti had no concept of time even as he saw the civilization in Haiti change and grow. He was a silent observer of the routine death and terror imposed by the White French colonial overlords who ruled over the multitudes of slaves that toiled to death on their huge sugar and coffee plantations. He hated them!

Today, he well understood why the man believed to be his father was to die by the French authorities. His alleged father, Mackandal the one-armed slave had led a continuous bloody slave rebellion against the hated French slave masters who were famous for their incredible brutality against the massive slave population that inhabited this island called Haiti. Mackandal's terrible rebellion was responsible for the murder of some six-thousand French colonists and the pillaging and burning of an unknown number of plantations. Ayiti had once been told one-third of all African slaves shipped to the New World were sent here to work these terrible but profitable plantations.

Little Ayiti sat on the top of a wall with his arms wrapped around his bent legs to watch the public execution of his adopted father. Mackandal had always been good to him. He was a big handsome and very humorous mentor. The authorities were still looking for Ayiti after the French thugs had horribly murdered the other members of his alleged family in a previous home invasion. They were looking for Mackandal when they burst in to the shack where his family lived. He was rightfully accused as the high priest of the massive voodoo cult which was believed by the French to be at the center of the bloody revolt. Hundreds of these cult members had already been murdered by the French masters, as hundreds more waited their turn in dank filthy prisons by eager tormentors and executioners!

Ayiti knew that his small size and ability to hide had literally saved him from the authorities that had attacked his family during the search for his father. He had innocently opened the door of his home after a gentle knock on the door. It was the French authorities, evil, contemptuous, and violent as usual! The slash from the Frenchman's sword cut a deep wound from the right side of his forehead, across the nape of his nose and deeply into his left cheek. He remembered screaming and falling away as if killed. The French killers brutally rounded up the members of his adopted family in their ramshackle three-roomed hut. Temporarily unnoticed, Ayiti was able to slide under the floor near where he had fallen and scamper far into a nearby jungle. He soon resumed his old life in the jungle living among the animals and avoiding the French.

His father had not been there that day, and occasionally visited. Mackandal was always on the run from the authorities and usually dropped by to have sex with two of the prettier women in the house. The French had been frantically searching and even a vague association to the one-armed champion of the oppressed meant a death sentence. Little Ayiti knew Mackandel well and loved his crazy tales and humor. Ayiti also knew of the deep hideous dark side to this champion of the slaves. It was obvious to many that Mackandel especially loved little Ayiti as he was also the loving protector of many little ones orphaned by the despicable killings of the French masters.

Today was to be the end of the one-armed hero. Little Ayiti reflected with feelings of genuine sadness for him. He remembered how he became involved in a few of the raids on plantations firsthand. He was drawn along with a group of other children who were his buddies to view the attack on a nearby plantation and help in the looting. During these escapades, he witnessed the gruesome aftermath of these hate filled violent slave forays. He quickly learned the power of terror channeled by terrible acts he witnessed in the ghastly ends experienced by many French who fell victim. He thought about his third raid on a very prominent plantation that sat next to the ocean.

It seemed that after the French plantation guards had shot several attacking slaves and were captured by the mob. They were burned alive with a few being hacked to death by machetes on the spot. It was the first time he ever saw a white woman gang raped to death on the porch veranda of the great house. All of the other women were savagely raped then most, save a few pretty ones, were bound and thrown alive into the fires of the burning great house of the plantation. Others were tossed into the holding pens of the pigs as what were described as "sweet treats!" The plantation great houses were not burned until everything of value was seized and removed.

He touched his side and felt the long stiletto beautifully inlaid with silver and solid gold crests secretly secured under his long shirt. The Damascus blade, which he would never understand, was sharp and extremely strong. He had retrieved it along with a bag of gold coins, and a beautiful gold ring with diamonds inlaid in some family crest, from some headless plantation owner, sprawled in the hall of his great house, whose personal belongings were bypassed in the killing frenzy of the moment.

Ayiti was intrigued and excited at witnessing the carnage. He became affixed on the concept of terror. He followed a few more attacks with keen interest. He scored his first kill of some French kid hiding in the bushes towards the end of an attack. Ayiti, only a hair taller than the little Frenchie grabbed him by his long locks of hair and pressed the blade of his jeweled stiletto into his back. "Please! Please do not kill me for I am alone and scared!" he whimpered.

But little Ayiti clearly remembered the words of the adult hate-filled slaves who spoke of how evil and dangerous were the French children to slaves. French children were called "little demons" because they had the power, in many cases to have slaves put to a painful death or personally kill slaves for sport, for games, and enjoyment. Having absolute power over slaves, it seemed their love of cruelty had no limits, or end.

It was time to play a game with the little Frenchie who came from this very evil and brutal plantation family! He tied his hands behind his back and then walked him until he found a large remote anthill in the jungle after the sun had risen. He tied the boy to a tree and returned later with some things. He had learned this little game from observing some French thugs perform this rite on two runaway slaves. He then forced the boy down and tied his legs. Then he dragged him to the opening of the huge anthill and tethered him to it on a rope around his neck tied to a long stake he hammered into the ground. The Frenchie was bound tight and began to scream.

Ayiti then forced a crude pouring spout in his mouth and literally forced him to drink a half-gallon of molasses gagging him many times. He then poured the remains of the molasses on the child's face, and body. He watched in the morning light as thousands of large red ants began to pour over this struggling body in waves. The Frenchie, whose head was only inches from the ground screamed long after the red fire ants completely covered him, filling his nose, mouth, and his eyes. The screams of the victim turned to guttural shrieks as the ants poured into every orifice in his body continuously stripping little Frenchie of his flesh!

The consumption and removal of the Frenchie's "sweetmeat' continued as the hoard of large red fire ants harvested a bounty of food and molasses for their nest. He watched in interested cruel vengeful fascination. He relished the complete out of control terror of his victim! It excited Little Ayiti! It was fun! After several hours the ant feasting was over as little Ayiti viewed thousands of red ants picking over a small skeleton in soiled little Frenchie clothes, still tethered to the wooden stake. There would be more victims for this was enjoyable revenge. Their suffering in this torture was wonderful combined with the element of extreme terror! This was just the beginning for little Ayiti's appetite for this form of play.

Ayiti respectfully stared as the fires engulfed Mackandal. He stood resolute, never screaming, as if in some deep trance. All of a sudden there was a flash in the raging fire and all witnessed the shape of some black shadow eject over it. The slaves present began to chant "Our savior of revenge has risen!" The French plantation masters and authorities shuddered at the ominous dark cloud and the chanting. Ayiti mused since the apparition that rose above the fire drew ominous screams from the onlookers. The generated apparition was his parting gift to Mackandal to instill terror in those monsters who had killed him! The dark apparition was created by his thoughts!

Mackandal and his Aunt Sarah, recognizing his unusual powers had been teaching him for several years as a neophyte in their cult of black voodoo. The fire consumed the savior of slaves, turning his once robust black frame into blackened ash statue supported by glistening white skeletal bones. Ayiti watched unemotionally as the now protruding skull of the burning slave leader fell off the smoldering body and bounced off the pyre into the crowd in some act of post death defiance. Someone picked it up and the skull disappeared. It was over for brave Mackandal, but many more in his cult were to be executed next. He walked down a road lost in thought.

Little Ayiti swore that this was not over, NEVER! It was just the beginning, his beginning! Revenge on a huge scale to kill all French colonist invaders would take some time which Ayiti had plenty. He refused to cry and deftly slithered off into the jungle to return to the hidden jungle shack where he now lived with his beloved aunt Sarah who was also on the wanted list. She had been smart enough to stay very clear of anybody connected to her brother Mackandal and live in the jungle. Aunt

Sarah had discovered many special things about her often-strange adopted nephew. He had a powerful mind and could always see clearly in the dark from his illuminated red eyes.

He had the vision of a hawk and seemed to be able to read people's thoughts. He loved the many monkeys that lived in the forest and imitated them at great length when he played with them. He had told Sarah that they had been his friends for so many years when he lived in the jungle. His favorite aunts Sarah and Abigale, the green-eyed twins, had told him he was a special gift of the Loa gods to their voodoo cult. He loved them She and Abigale were the only family he had left now. The rest had met terrible painful ends by the tormentors of the French.

Today was the day when any kindness he had learned turned to abject hate for all things except his aunts and people. The cruelness of his dark nature had now become an insensitive weapon fueled by total hate! Little Ayiti loved to bushwhack many types of people after his first ant hill murder. He chose usually helpless and slow movers with his natural predator skills learned in the jungle. He stabbed them with his stiletto, threw them off high places, clubbed them, and drowned a few older ones, looting their corpses. He was able to lure a few more children away and one older lady he hit with a club who was riding a horse, repeating more anthill amusements.

The French lady was a tough one and took longer for the ants to consume. However, her terrified ravings and suffering were the best right down to her eyeless gurgling as the ants had completely stripped her facial tissue away leaving a mawing skull! He loved the anthill but the swamp was even better. Little Ayiti never hurt animals, for they taught him how to hide and escape. They were his friends. Humans for the most part were not! However, Ayiti had already learned to love the power over helpless victims! It had become a sexual gratification. Today his random cruelness towards Frenchie's had a new profound purpose! The times were changing as of today!

He then remembered in one case the rebellious slaves who had attacked a large well-fortified plantation. There were many slaves killed by security as the slave mob laid siege to it. In the chaos, the mob had caught and had cut the feet off of one very evil plantation owner dubbed "La Monster!" They tied him to a huge rope over a gate then lowered him slowly, down into a pit of starving pigs, which ate him, slowly tearing him to shreds as he wailed in constant torment. Then, they let go of the rope and let the pigs savagely devour what was left! The screaming "La Monster" was finally silenced by a large hog crushing his skull in the muck.

Ayiti marveled at the power and control of the moment! He had learned that terror could be prolonged and ordered. He thought how many of his child buddies had been captured and burnt or fed to the anthills or insects in the swamps by the evil French killers who loved children for many reasons. The pack of buddies he had run with were all missing to date.

Mackandal had told him that the thirst for slaves as free labor began with the Arabs buying the unfortunate Africans captured in tribal wars. When one African tribe defeated another one, they defeated members of the tribe were sold to the Arabs who in turn sold them to the white slavers. Then came the insane cruelty against what they saw as dark subhuman creatures! Most of them were sold in Asia, but many were sold in the Americas. Parts of western Africa became unpopulated because of the demand! The French killers were refined experts at inflicting pain, death, rape, and deep terror on millions of these helpless innocent people trapped here. He hated them!

Sarah and Abigale, like their brother Mackandal, were both very powerful Voodoo priestesses who had both been forewarned by the Loa gods by Ayiti every time the French were about to seize them. If Ayiti knew what love was, he had it for Sarah, who was very dark-skinned beauty and had huge captivating green eyes like her twin sister Abigale. In great sadness, Abigale had disappeared and as rumor had it, she had been kidnapped by British slavers and shipped off to Jamaica and sold. In his silence Ayiti knew this to be true. Both women were extremely beautiful and would be desirable as concubines for some wealthy slave owner. Someone would pay a handsome price for her.

Little Ayiti spent much time with his Aunt Sarah and her twin sister Abigale in their secluded hovel in the jungle. He helped them with chores as they both instructed him in the tenants of the religion of voodoo. Sarah and her twin were both considered by many to be real voodoo queens. She, like her twin sister were both respected and feared. Through the exercise of her powers many people, especially the French, had suffered many macabre and terrible deaths from the effects of their powerful spells.

Aunt Sarah had a very deep intuitive mind and saw incredible gifts and powers that seemed to swirl around her little man's huge aura when she focused on him. She had begun his voodoo training several years before and taught many things of their particular sect of ancient black voodoo religion to Ayiti. What intrigued her was that Ayiti had seemed not to grow up like a normal child. He was just little Ayiti until she encouraged him to look like a teenager once. Ayiti had made the change overnight! He completely embraced the voodoo religion and soon understood all of it.

Sarah believed him to be an actual incarnation of one of the Loa gods because of his special abilities. She had admired and even feared his abilities and was teaching him the power and control of his own "demon posture" to combat those trying to kill him or her. Through much ritual, she had helped little Ayiti grow and change into his new devil form as well as master the complete playbook of Voodoo rites and power.

Sarah had never ever seen anybody make such transformation as him. She always said "Ayiti, you can assume any posture you want to get what you want! Think how many years you have been a small child my dear Ayiti? You can grow into a man any time you desire!" Sarah laughed and played with him. With this memory in his mind, he cracked a smile as he came upon Aunt Sarah's shack in the jungle. He immediately sensed something was very amiss. His thoughts had distracted his focus!

He peered in the door to find that the place had been ransacked and there was blood on the floor! His senses told him Sarah had been captured by the French. He then saw the ugly face of the chief captor of his aunt in his impression of the vibrations in the shack. Someone had turned her in. The leader of this evil party of official government inquisitors and murderers caught her this same day as the death of Mackandal! Ayiti was in panic now. This French savage went by the name of Roichange "The Hook" since he loved to skewer his victims for sport with a meat hook he always had in his belt.

Riochange was rather tall, lanky fellow with long ape-like arms, and bore an extremely ugly freakish face like some hook-nosed troll. Riochange not only worked for the French authorities as a bounty hunter, but also lived on and provided security for one of the largest plantations in Haiti. Slaves on this estate lived in abject terror when his freak-faced, slovenly and unclean smelly personage was present wandering the master's plantation. The slaves could smell him before they saw him approach. They well knew that at any moment this monster would fancy one of them, smack his meat hook into their backs or ass and drag the unfortunate away for possible rape with a painful end in store. Sexual partners did not matter to this French monster although he preferred children the most!

"The Hook" loved to cut the faces off his victims and let them dry in the sun. He made slaves wear them or face the same fate. Ayiti knew that Aunt Sarah was a special case and intensely sought by and feared by the authorities. She was Mackandal's sister for openers! Her capture was a paramount event for this and many reasons. Besides being the sister of Mackandal, she was implicated after the governor's wife ended up with a stomach full of live eels at an elegant state dinner! She died in a horrible way flopping around in her finest gown on the dinner table filled with guests; with the slippery creatures exiting from her mouth, nose, vagina and her asshole. This was her retaliation five months earlier after the capture and murder of her family; the one in which Ayiti had escaped.

Sarah was rightfully accused of this heinous deed and many others. She was accused of plotting revolution with her brother. Sarah was to be burned in public as a witch, but Riochange intervened to have his personal pleasure on her. In the days that passed Ayiti could do nothing to save her from her fate. She was brutally tortured and raped for days by "The Hook" and his crew of savage perverts. Her fingers were chopped off, her toes gone, all cauterized with hot pokers. Her tongue was cut out and her teeth pulled so the sick tormentors could plunge their manhood deep into her gagging throat as she was tied down. She was incessantly raped and abused by this evil pack until her last day.

They somehow kept her alive. Ayiti wanted to help her but she had been specific. He was to give her no help ever if she were captured no matter what befell her! Ayiti was to save himself for future revenge and the salvation of all slaves from these evil white devils. He would be the tool of her revenge! Finally, her tormentors dragged her to a top of a large steep hill and put her inside a barrel. They then nailed long sharp spikes throughout it so the sharp tips lined the inside of this barrel. In one last air of arrogance and hate, Roichange kicked the barrel off the huge tall hill.

It rolled and bounced hundreds of yards down the steep mountainside finally crashing into a bank of rocks at the bottom. It shattered and revealed the remains of aunt Sarah, whose body had been ripped to shreds by the many long sharp nail tips hammered into the barrel. Ayiti saw the terrible end of his beloved aunt Sarah from the nearby jungle and wept in a terrible grief for days after he returned to their hiding place. He remembered that she had left a package for him carefully tucked away in a hidden wooden chest. He opened it up and since she had taught him to read French, he read her message.

His priestess aunt said. "Dear little Ayiti, if you are reading this then my fate has been sealed and I am now gone from the earth. I have conjured up the Loa and they tell me you are a powerful Houngan, a Loa god incarnate! A master Voodoo "king to be!" and are to be instrumental in freeing the slaves from the yoke of the evil white overlords. I know you will be afraid but you are protected and my soul is with you. Be brave my little son! When you are ready to do battle against those oppressors you will assume this form in the ritual, I taught you. The Loa have shown me this image of you. Little Ayiti wiped the tears away and studied the sketch. Her last sentence struck him. "It is time to shed your mantel of boyhood and become the man you are within!"

Inside the chest was an exact doll-like replica of the sketch. Sarah's words continued. "Never let your familiar doll fall into enemy hands for you can be destroyed if it is harmed. Always hide and protect it wherever you go! I have left you some gold I saved as a prostitute for the estate master where I once worked. I lost my place after the master soon found great pleasure in raping young males. I saved you from this fate many times. This money is to help you even if you want passage to find Abigale in Jamaica or when fortunes change on this cursed island." He then stopped reading and opened up a roll of gold coins wrapped in newspaper. He tossed them into a crude wooden chest with the pile of other gold and silver coins he had accumulated.

He continued reading. "You are my Ayiti and I have always loved you as if you were mine and will look after you from the other world wherever you may go. Revenge and retribution touched by extreme terror in your devil form are your weapons; use them wisely! These savages must all pay! LOVE YOU FOREVER! SARAH" Ayiti, sitting in the squalor of the small-bedecked wooden shelter in the jungle wept. He wept for days as his grief turned to even more concentrated hatred. His hate slowly worked his mind into a plan of revenge.

Days, weeks, and months flashed by him as he remained alone in the jungle. He felt strange things in his body, visions, flashes of light, as he brought his inert abilities into practice! Then his soul seemed to explode as he gave a loud chilling wail into the night that made all the animals nearby scamper away in a dark terror. He looked into the broken mirror and saw he had made a complete transformation into the likeness of his familiar doll. He studied his body and soon mused at his very elongated head. and now had twelve sets of eyes in two rows above a large hook nose. Ayiti's mouth that expanded across his face ear to ear was filled with a twisted gaggle of sharp long teeth like some prehistoric deep-sea fish.

His body was long and sealed in a rough brown skin that covered his body. He laughed at the fronds of straw that seemed to protrude from where Sarah had sewn the parts of his doll together. It stuck out around his neck, rear of his head, around his waist, wrists and feet. Even the thread used to sew him together was now evident where it was used. He then noticed that his hands and feet that protruded from his brown skin were strange dark razor-sharp claws. He wore a crown of crooked horns on his head and loved the long-pointed tail he began whipping around.

He was now a giant duplicate of the Loa god familiar Sarah had created. He looked like a huge very ugly monster straw doll. Ayiti's transformation to the shape of his familiar doll brought out an incredible reinforcement evil thoughts and dark intense hate. He felt powerful, free, and indestructible now. His hunger to destroy and consume his enemies overwhelmed him! The words of dear departed Sarah now spoke to him: "You can assume any posture you want to get what you want! Be like the handsome goat poised on a hill before you strike like a dark serpent Ayiti!" He studied the word for posture and concluded she meant shape! He also knew without any voodoo rituals he had assumed this vengeful shape of the straw doll; complete with all the dark vengeful mindset.

Ayiti needed to vent his extreme rage, to satiate it like an opium desired by an addict! As he now transformed from his vengeful form, Ayiti now noticed that he was no longer "little Ayiti!" He had transformed from the straw doll into a vibrant extremely handsome tall light skinned young African man with straight white teeth. Sarah's words had rung true now. Ayiti could be both the handsome goat on the hill and the dark serpent! Several days later he left the jungle hut to hunt those who savagely murdered his beloved Aunt Sarah. Retribution for Sarah and Mackandal were now his first targets, as all the French overlord infesting parasites were next!

Ayiti knew he had to deal with very powerful and dangerous French masters in his quest! The period between 1711 and 1789 was considered the golden age for the French in their kingdom of Haiti. By 1760, Haiti was reaching sound foundations to this golden age. It would be in full zenith by the next century. The prosperity, wealth, and power of the French plantation owners and government was absolute; as were their rule over the life and death of the slaves! The wealth of this French island colony, bolstered by the terrible suffering of thousands of slaves, was titled the "Pearl of the Anilities." The seeds of revolt against this hated curse, deeply manifested by the great hero Mackandal had grown into size and intensity! They were well masked under the pristine ordered surface of this ideal "Pearl" of imperialistic usurpation!

Ayiti knew the layout of cobbled streets and main town of Port Au Prince like the back of his hand. The manicured terraces and clean neat European style architecture of this city bore nothing less than high-end colonial elegance. The lamp-lighted streets seemed filled with all sorts of people. Sailors from the multitude ships docked in the harbor wandered the streets in groups usually drunk. Local plantation owners, all manner of local French colonists and lovely plantation women mingled with the merchant class and visitors.

Ayiti, in his life, had developed quite a fondness for these elegant white French female untouchables. He had enjoyed watching them gang raped and burned in his observations of the attacks on plantations. He was also amused at the other cast of women. The saloons in this mostly white stucco and red clay bricked roof city were full and prostitutes plied their trade anywhere where shadows were plentiful. The drunkenness, laughter, and banter in this city filled the full moonlit night. Then Ayiti sadly compared this panorama to the horrible plight of the other two-thirds of the island population! His brother and sister slaves; seen as sub humans living in horrific conditions!

They all lived in constant fear of being abused, raped and murdered daily and treated worse than the animals that worked the plantations. This island "Hell on earth" was some evil rotten maggot infested cake and all this luxury around him this night was sweet icing which covered it nicely! The sweet icing, at the expense of thousands of slaves would become very thick and tasty over the next fifty years. Ayiti knew this dichotomy of life in Haiti was a time bomb and like an active volcano would explode someday. It would explode in Haiti into a savage unstoppable slave rebellion. He planned to be right in the middle of it; guiding it! Nurturing it like the teat of a mother nursing its baby!

Then there was the monster Riochange! Tonight, he was to pay a warm visit to Riochange "The Hook" and his thugs that had horribly slain his beloved aunt Sarah. This pack of savage murderers lived in a large house near the main gate of a huge plantation many miles away. Ayiti had observed it many times in his quest to keep tabs on his aunt after her capture. She had told him to stay clear and not save her. He had to painfully endure her screams many times from inside this bungalow before she died. They would be safe until he visited them and made them scream in pain and terror!

Like many of these thug murderers under government hire and protection as needed, Messer Riochange was employed on a rather large twenty-thousand-acre sugar cane and coffee plantation some fifty miles to the north. It had over ten-thousand slaves. These French thugs were hired as protection for the masters and security for the plantation in general. Riochange was the French monster incarnate over the poor slaves, often torturing, raping, and killing a few in his daily travels throughout this massive plantation. His meat hook was always dripping blood when he returned to his bungalow shared by his men.

Many times, he would hang the carved up remains of his work on a big hook outside his bungalow to remind everybody of their fate if they defied his rule! The owners, no better than his black heart turned a deaf ear and blindness to all of this terror induced suffering. This was because Riochange's terror was a great inspiration! There was not even a hint of a slave rebellion! It greatly induced the slaves to work hard long hours to death for many, fearing sudden retribution from the monster Roichange and his gang of filthy drunken devil thugs! The masters admired this work ethic and Riochange's guidance was excellent! His model was used by many other plantation owners. There were many other monsters like Riochange plying their evil trade and they would all be dealt with in turn by Ayiti. Riochgange was special and was to be the first!

Ayiti soon left the lights and gaiety of Port Au Prince and began to walk towards this massive plantation in a crushed sea shell covered road surrounded by large trees. He had a lengthy fifty-mile road march if he chose it. However, Ayiti had developed a more expedient method of travel in his time experimenting with his powers in his jungle hut. He began to run down the road constantly increasing his speed. He ran so fast that he felt himself effortlessly lift off the ground and, in some capacity was flying over the trees to his great enjoyment. He had never flown this high before! He had once jumped thirty or forty feet airborne along jungle paths and into trees with the guidance of Sarah; but flying free above the jungle trees was pure delight to him tonight!

He was surprised at the huge dark wings that had sprung out of his back in his impulse to fly high. He appreciated this new ability and laughed! His confidence in what his mind could produce was growing by the minute thanks to his favorite aunt. The moon seemed to illuminate his ominous form as he surveyed the extreme darkness of the land below. But he loved the darkness but begin to see lights in the distance. He soon saw the huge elaborate well-lighted main plantation house on a distant hill and gently sailed down and landed on his feet inside the huge wrought iron gates of the plantation.

Dogs barked in the distance and he scampered quickly into the shadows towards a large white stucco house inside the gates. He knew exactly where he would find his quarry this night. It was late as he had planned. He then noticed the last victim of this monster hanging on the large hook at the front of this place. The poor woman had been flayed alive then burned!

He could hear laughter and tormented screams of pain as he crept up to the huge bungalow that housed Roichange and his plantation guards. The place had walls of white stucco, large verandas with large French windows and a red tiled roof.

A fat white man, an older, sloppy looking Frenchie scumbag walked from the main door to a rail. He threw up and was trying to relieve himself. Ayiti could smell him from his position some thirty feet away. However, as he crept up on him, he had to smile. The drunken idiot had failed to untie his pants and was holding his belt end like it was his cock, and was pissing inside his pants down his leg all the time mumbling inaudible drunken curses.

Ayiti's first stiletto slash took out both the man's Achilles' tendons and in a sudden fit of helpless pain flopped against the rail and fell backwards on the ground. He saw Ayiti's face and tried to scream but the beautiful golden handled long sharp stiletto stopped this as it was plunged deep into the mouth and throat through the back of the head of the old smelly bugger. He squirmed and flopped about like a bug with a needle stuck into it. The stiletto tip was embedded in the deck and pinned this jerk's head to the porch deck.

Ayiti cut the man's throat then wiped off his blade on the dead man's shirt, and re-sheathed it. He deftly moved over to the large window and looked in. He observed a woman being raped on the table by one of the drunken thugs, with another holding her arms at the other end of the table forcing his cock into her mouth. The lighted lamps flickered on this scene and there seemed to be broken glass on the floor. The rather pretty young slave girl being spit-roasted on the table was bleeding from her mouth as she still tried to resist. He also saw the dead mutilated bodies of a couple of slaves on the floor. Ayiti now shape changed into his familiar; the spawn of the Loa gods!

"A busy night in hell," Ayiti thought! Roichange was not in the room. Ayiti could hear more noises from the rear bedrooms in the house. He moved in fast. Both men were very drunk, and the one raping the girl knew something was amiss when he looked up and saw that his buddy's head was gone by the whiplash of Ayiti's tail. The headless standing man still gripped the arms of the girl as blood spewed from the stump of his neck. Then the girl was pulled from the table as the rapist then saw a long red rope or whip come crashing down and slapping hard on the table in front of him. Then he noticed this whip completely chopped his semi-erect manhood from his body. He saw it on the table in front of him as shock begin to set in.

This emasculated French thug stared at the monstrous specter next to him and terror rose in his drunken pained eyes. Before he could move the sword had cut across his face. Blood ran down the front of his dirty white shirt as he tried to scream. Ayiti grabbed the man from the back by his filthy mane of hair and ass then bum rushed him into a large open-hearth fireplace. Ayiti plunged his head face first into the embers as they filled his open mouth. The last thing the thug remembered as he tried to scream was how painful the fire was in the fireplace as his face was burned to a dark crisp!

Ayiti was joyfully holding the man's face down in the embers. He pressed the man's body into the coals with his large clawed foot at the shoulder blades. He relished the agony and the fruitless struggle of the man whose face and upper body were being burned into ashes in rising wisps of steam. Ayiti thought the smell of his burning flesh reminded him of roast pig. He then looked up from his sport at the girl. She stood by the table, frozen with bulging eyes, and transfixed at the evil looking giant doll like monster staring at her with twelve sets of blazing red eyes.

Ayiti thought she had an unnatural beauty about her. He smiled at her with a gaping fanged smile that crossed his whole face. In a low metallic voice, he spoke to her. "Please do not fear me, I am here for them and will never hurt you, just them!" She stayed glued in her place as the candles flickered from a sea breeze that further cooled off the large living room with the smoking body stuck halfway into the bed of coals. The next victim entered the room looking for a bottle of rum. He too was staggering. Ayiti grabbed a long white-hot iron fire poker resting in the coals and like a spear hurled it with amazing power at the drunk slob. The long spear-shaped iron poker caught the French slave driver directly in the right eye and plunged out the back of his head pinning him up against the wall where the end of the red-hot poker embedded into the wall.

His impaled head forced his body to dance in funny spasms against the wall. His sizzling blood was running from his nose and mouth emitting steam as the poker hole smoldered. The death spasms ended as the corpse shit in its pants. The large strange straw doll entered the next room and beheaded three more plantation guards who were passed out on the bodies of another dead slave girl. He chased the slave women still able to run in the bedrooms out the rear door with high pitched screams jumping on the beds and knocking down furniture. They fled in terror at his demonic image. Then Roichange, the star of this hunt, as if part of this ghastly script appeared in the wide hall near the end of the house.

He had been knocked aside by the terrifying fleeing slave girls. He had his meat hook in his right hand and a pistol in the other. Seeing a strange large image in front of him in the shadows in the hall, the French thug fired the pistol point blank at Ayiti. The ball from the pistol hit Ayiti's chest with a thud. He was momentarily stunned by the impact of the bullet but smiled. He was unharmed by the shot. In the dark, with perfect night vision and quickness he relieved Riochange the monster of both his meat hook and empty pistol, as well as both of his hands with one slash of his long-pointed tail. Before the evil Frenchman could move, Ayiti had driven him physically into a wall. The impact knocked him out.

Ayiti then dragged Riochange into the next room by his meat hook slapped deep into his shoulder. The tormentor of slaves was tied to a chair facing the fireplace. Ayiti looked at the girl, still by the table. He looked at her and blinked all his eyes at once as his huge gaping fanged mouth opened. "I command you to find everything of value in this house and put it in this bag!" He tossed her a large bulky bag with carrying handles he found in one of the bedrooms. She stood frozen; petrified in terror. The monster then spoke. "You are protected by me so have no fear unless you refuse to follow my orders then I will eat you!" He smiled with a large massively fanged grimace. She grabbed the bag from the floor. Finally, she came to her senses and began looting the house of gold and silver coins, trinkets, jewelry, pistols, edged weapons, pocket watches, and other things of value. She knew where to look since she was one of the slaves assigned to clean this place.

Tonight, had been her unlucky night since she had worked late and become the fancy of these bloodthirsty killers! To prevent Riochange from bleeding out Ayiti cauterized both raw gaping stumps where his hands used to be. Riochange screamed in delirium muffled by a large gag in his mouth as this was done. He stared in horror at the smoldering and still burning semi-ashes remains of one of his men still in the fireplace and shrieked at what he saw standing before him. His mind could not put into words what he saw. He screamed in uncontrolled agony as the thing wiggled and twisted the meat hook still deeply stuck in his shoulder.

His tormentor was like some animated large doll, a devil doll made of straw, which had many sets of blazing evil eyes set in an oblong head. This was not a costume! It had to be some drunken opium illusion thought Riochange in his agony. It just grimaced at him from its large frame, never talking, just smiling from a broad smile which revealed spiny sharp fangs. Suddenly, another one of Riochange's savages ran into the room with a sword headed for Ayiti.

In one deft move, his tail cut from the man's right shoulder down to his groin. The man stopped and fell to the floor. Strawman grabbed the wounded cutthroat by his hair and flung him into the fireplace to join his buddy. The thug landed on his back and Ayiti held him in the fire with his clawed foot. The coals burned him like the bites of a thousand red ants before the fire consumed him into black skeletal ash. Without missing a beat, Ayiti tortured the evil Frenchie Riochange with his red-hot meat hook for a while, placing it between his toes, his balls, cheeks, arm pits, and burning his hair off his head.

In great relish he sizzled one of his eyeballs down his cheek. As this monster gasped in agony Ayiti stuck the red-hot poker in his open mouth roasting the inside of his mouth and gums; but always keeping Riochange alive. The yelps and wails of Riochange was magnificent music to Ayiti's ears! However, he had plans for his special victim. Sarah needed to be revenged to the exact vision in his heart! Ayiti had previously planned for the terrible end of Riochange. He knew where the nearby swamp was, a small boat, and molasses, plenty of it. It was not far away either. Perfect! The slave girl returned and stood in awe and great fear of the specter Ayiti. She held strapped bag loaded with spoils.

She watched as this thing bundle Riochange out to the large veranda at the front of the house and tirelessly cast him into a small handcart next to it. "Come with me girl!' She nodded and followed Ayiti, dragging a bag full of loot following him as he pulled the handcart a half-mile down a bumpy path to a very secluded part of the swamp. The noise of the night creatures was immense and flying insects buzzed about in the semi darkness created by the large trees masking the light of a beautiful full moon. Ayiti had learned from experience that the swamp was more fun than the anthill. One could never know what just might show up to feast!

In short order, the Frenchman was stripped naked, tied into the bottom of the small boat securely. He could not move. Then his antagonist poured as much molasses as possible down his throat nearly choking him to death. The insects were already landing on the spilled molasses. He then poured a large remainder of the syrupy liquid all over Riochange's burns, his face, and rest of his body. "Sweet meat" Riochange was ready to dine with the swamp! The insects, in the thousands, were now feasting on Riochange's molasses coated body with particular interest in his cauterized stumps and burn wounds. This grand abuser could still hear. Up to this point Ayiti had said nothing. Now he spoke in his low dark voice. "While you die in complete agony, I want you to remember the name Sarah, the beautiful Sarah you gang raped, tortured, and murdered in the barrel roll down the mountain! Please remember my father Mackandal who you burned at the stake!

You are my sacrifice to them and the example of what I will ensure happens to all you scum French parasites who have abused and killed my people since you invaded my island! I am your doom. Look into my eyes doomed one, for I am her revenge tonight!" Riochange stammered from his severely burned mouth in a terror-laden voice with his good eye bulging. "What aunt, what family?" "The pretty one with the green eyes and dark skin!" The evil Frenchie whimpered. "I, I had orders, I, I..." stammered Riochange in painful terror now! Ayiti cut in. "Now I have orders from my gods to rid this island of all of you white devils and you are first!"

The insects were now circling by the thousands over the doomed Riochange; perhaps millions because of his large size, "sweetmeat" Frenchie was soon completely covered by a frenzy of hungry insects that covered his body like a living cake icing. He continued to wail in agony and terror as the gurgled molasses again was poured in his choking throat by a long spout jammed into it. "You, what are you!" screamed to dying Frenchie!

"I am death! I am revenge of the much-feared voodoo masters mon Frenchie!" Then Ayiti pulled the meat hook from his shoulder and ripped a huge hole in Riochange's stomach. Molasses and blood now poured out as a frenzy of insects dived into the pool. The gasping Frenchman squealed in pain and dying terror filled anger, "You are a devil of straw and we will get you bastard!" The little girl who had been mute replied in a transfixed monotone to the evil Riochange. "He is the Strawman of Loa! "The **Straw Man Cometh** to cleanse this island of white French masters, tormentors and parasites! He cometh to visit you tonight and them tomorrow!" She broke into a nervous laugh for she hated this monster and was enjoying his plight.

Then, unceremoniously, without any fanfare of words, the so-named Straw Man demon kicked the boat and it floated out into the swamp waters. Riochange was covered by millions of insects all feasting on his bountiful sweetmeat as the pair on the shore enjoyed his screams of agony as the noise of the insects and other night swamp creatures masked much of the perpetual screams and rant of the specially prepared feast for the swamp! It would take several hours for the millions of insects to find their way up his anus and, into his eyes, ears, brains, and down his throat to the sweet prize of molasses lodged in his intestines.

He would scream until all his vocal cords were eaten. The only thing the insects could not devour was Riochange's skeleton and the unbridled terror born insanity of the condemned man's soul. The small cart was pushed into the swamp. The plantation authorities would find the cleaned skeleton of Riochange tied in the boat later. The Strawman carried the well-filled bag as the two walked back to the bungalow. Once on the veranda, Ayiti effortlessly pitched the body of the slain killer on the porch into the front room.

He then sloshed lantern oil throughout the house with the help of the pretty slave girl and lit it as they stood in front. The bungalow crackled as the flames quickly engulfed it. Ayiti took a large drink from a bottle of dark rum he had taken from the place and put it, along with a couple more bottles into the large floppy bag filled with the treasures liberated from the French monsters. Taking the nameless beautiful slave girl by the hand, and bag of loot in his right, they left as the approaching noise of many was sensed.

As they got to the road Ayiti ran faster holding the girl and the loot effortlessly by his side, then as he securely put his arm around her waist, they left the ground and were in the air. His powerful dark wings easily carried them far into the air and home. The raging flames of the house drew a sharp-lighted contrast on the jungle darkness around it in the distance now. Many from the plantation saw the winged specter crossing the sky in the light of the full moon. Great fear spread as many French now believed it was the vengeful spirit of Mackandal.

Finally, they were both safe in Little Ayiti's jungle hiding place. He learned that the little slave girl was named Eve. She had been naked throughout the ordeal and Ayiti now dressed her in one of Aunt Sarah's nice dresses. They ate some bananas and drank rum. Eve now noticed by the crude candlelight, that she was in the company not of a horrid demon she had named "Strawman", but of a very handsome young light-skinned black man now. Her fear and his hate now subsided as they laughed about the night's events. They would bond much closer before dawn this night.

The French Revolution of 1789 had dire ramifications not just in France, but affected life in the French colony of Haiti. Many bloody slave revolts against the overlords arose in 1791. Under the great leadership of Toussaint L' Ouveture, a new order of landowning free slaves emerged to help quell this problem. This champion also prevented a British invasion in 1798. It was now December in 1803 and Ayiti knew that the moment of liberation and destruction of the French was at hand; in his hands!

General Jean Jacque Dessalines sat with his pretty wife facing the rather youthful Voodoo priest, in what looked like a Catholic Church setting. This priest was renowned as a great healer and beloved patron of the slaves. Dessalines was intelligent, brave but crudely arrogant, who had been a very effective general under L' Ouverture in crushing the French military. He looked like a black stuffed doll in his Napoleonic uniform as he fingered his saber at his side. His head looked too large for his body. He stared quietly at the handsome man wearing the collar of a priest standing in front of him. The room was well-lit and smelled of fresh flowers.

This priest had become very popular over the years by his charismatic sermons and especially his abilities to heal a variety of diseases by this year of 1803. The young priest-healer spoke. "Now that you have attained your power from my power, it is time to purge this island of all whites, all French colonist invaders must die or be enslaved just like they did to us! You are now my tool mon general! I entrust you with this sacred mission to avenge the people who have suffered terribly for generations under these savage parasites! This is now my moment of great revenge for the pain, suffering and death of all slaves incarcerated on this cursed island by these evil savage white devils! This is for Mackandal!" In silence he added Sarah.

The general stammered out arrogantly, "I hate them all as well, but to slaughter them all?" He then looked at his eloquent aging wife who remained silent and staring as if in a trance. She was a very beautiful woman, even at her age, a mulatto given the best genes from her French father and African slave mother. She smiled at him and her eyes flickered. Her real name was Eve. She was the little girl he had saved from Riochange over forty-five years earlier. Her affections and friendship had grown on Ayiti and he had performed special voodoo rituals to keep her young. He had placed her into the general's life for reason.

The general looked at his wife who nodded and said "yes dear, you must do what he says!" then Dessalines looked back and saw a terrifying sight! He now saw a devil demon beast large doll of straw leering at him with a dozen flashing eyes in its oblong head and speaking in some lower form of mechanical voice as it swayed around with its devil tail whipping back and forth. A stream of drool dripped from the many protruding fangs forced out of its mouth by the long grimace. It spoke as it nearly touched the generals face with it!

"Who helped you to capture Toussaint in 1803?" it yelled! "He is now dead from imprisonment in France! Do you think you came to power by yourself you fool! Who gave you the key intelligence of the French army and navy that enabled you to soundly defeat them at the recent Battle of Vertieres on November 18th of this year???" The general wet his pants in fear as Strawman continued. "You will comply with my demands completely, town for town, atrocity for atrocity, never stopping until all men killed, with women and children enslaved or also killed! If you fail, I will find you and take pleasure in preparing your slow painful end in my special swamp! My insects would have a fitful meal in your fat carcass! Now get to work!!!!!! And LEAVE!"

The general was shaking at the multi-eyed specter hovering over him as he stumbled back, tripped and fell over his sword to the floor. He got up then edged his way out of the small white walled church front with the huge cross on it. He was shaking as he left in his carriage never taking his fearful stare at the specter in the shadows of the doorway. Strawman then looked at the general's wife who smiled at the him as she walked over and kissed him hard on his demon face and groped its crotch. She loved it when Ayiti was sexual with her in his Loa demon form. The Strawman could literally do anything with his penis; any size, shape, or create a double.

He had learned to shape change all his body parts, whenever he had in mind. Aunt Sarah had taught him to her pleasure long ago. He had literally blown Eve's mind into incredible new levels of erotic insanity; so many countless times in that jungle hut and later over the span of years after in secret fun together. It seemed the lust of today had been too long in the wings for them both. Today was no different as Ayiti pulled up her long dress and gave it to her with a set of mentally fabricated double erections in both her holes which she loved.

She soon went into a frenzy of organisms as Strawman laughed and finished his pleasure twice. After a violent hard sexual conclusion, Strawman was once again transformed into Ayiti the priest-healer of Haiti. Jean Jacque Dessalines had been Ayiti's chosen target, the one capable to succeed in his plan. He had given Eve to him to be his wife after she had assumed the name of "Beth" to hide her past as "Eve" the slave girl. She had lived with him for several years before he weaved her into the fabric of the rising revolutionary society in Haiti.

Soon after his meeting with Ayiti, General, now Emperor Dessalines began to commit terrible violent genocide against all French residents of the island. He began his executions by overseeing the drowning of over eight hundred French soldiers who were badly wounded in the recent conflict against the rebels and were unable to leave. Next, and against many objections of the locals, he personally visited every town and at his bequest all men and many children were slaughtered. The women and girls were raped and forced to marry the former slaves who had reached prominence. However, many of these unfortunates were horribly abused and many murdered.

In one final tribute, the general later granted amnesty to any Frenchman who had avoided and hid from the original slaughter. When these unfortunates surfaced, they were slain. Even the British sailors on the ships in Port Au Prince observed the wanton murder of several hundred French men, women, and children as they ran for safety in their ships. By April 1804, the island had been cleansed upwards to five thousand white devil French parasites. The massacre had been complete. In his official proclamation to the world Dessalines; "We have given these cannibals war for war, crime for crime, outrage for outrage; I have saved my country and avenged America!" Ayiti sent him a message with one sentence. It read:

"The swamp insects will miss you this night my Emperor! Job well done." Ayiti

The night of the great celebration the young well-known priest was a special guest at the grand palace where the general was enjoying the zenith of his power. It was an elegant affair, large and rowdy. "Doc" Ayiti Deschamps, so named for his healing abilities, drunk on his favorite French champagne went home not to a hovel, but to a recently acquired plantation outside of Port Au Prince in the dawn hours. His carriage stopped at the huge wrought iron gate. The commander of his guards, one Jean Zombi, greeted him. Jean Zombi appeared as a rather tall muscular light skinned mulatto, always with a smile on his face with a very mild-mannered look in his face. This persona completely masked his real character. He was one of the most hateful brutal tormentors and murderers of the French; he was the black Riochange.

Ayiti had recently commanded him to strip a white ex-plantation owner on the steps of the presidential palace and in full view of the new Emperor and onlookers, chopped him painfully to pieces. Emperor Dessalines was terrified and got the picture! The instrument of terror was well applied. Zombi had become a favorite of Ayiti before the uprisings and revolution. Zombi was known for his sadistic brutality on the streets of Port Au Prince and had caught the attention of Ayiti. He was a natural assistant for Ayiti who saw him as his lost brother of sorts. He had a captivating personality and sense of humor Ayiti adored. Fate would later decree that Jean Zombi's namesake would forever herald him as "Father of Zombies!"

The carriage stopped at the huge tall wrought iron gates as drunk Ayiti waved at his beloved comrade Zombi. "He greeted master Ayiti with a wide toothy smile, a salute, and sharp "hello!" His men swung open the elaborate wrought iron gates to his mansion. "Everything is safe mon, welcome home!" yelled Zombi. Ayiti smiled at him and shared an open bottle of champagne with him. Zombi had such charm and humor as he soon had his boss laughing out loud. Finally, the master's coach moved into a huge circular driveway with a fountain centered in the circle. "Doc" Ayiti got out of his coach and walked gingerly up the staircase to the door. The night was warm and the breeze felt good. He had other things on his twisted mind.

Besides the systematic murdering, looting of estates, and robbing banks, Jean Zombi and crew had kidnapped many elegant and attractive white French women for Doctor Ayiti's secret stable as requested in their travels. The powerful priest and healing doctor had acquired a taste for these beautiful refined ladies. He had them imprisoned in the bowels of his estate which was an unfathomable dark filthy bloodstained chamber of horrors.

His Frenchie's had been kidnapped with their wardrobes since Ayiti loved to view them in this elegance. His explicit desire for their flesh had been constantly savored since they had become plentiful from the purges, He relished his power over these elegant victims in the terror, pain, and finally the exquisite sexual pleasure he loved to evoke. Then, when finished with them over time, he would go the final step after sex; he would slaughter and feast on them. Then he would have his basement staff of controlled minions dress up their violated remains in colorful elaborate evening gowns and suspend and mount them in various positions to the walls of his long hallway in his basement lair on the way to his ritual chamber.

He called them his "Beautiful French Butterfly" collection. "Take a beautiful statue, a regal one, and defile it to unimaginable levels!" He laughed as he staggered up the long stairway to the torch lit veranda. He loved the power he felt within him! Life was good as was the fine French champagne magnum he had tucked under his arm! Besides, as his beloved Aunt Sarah taught and demonstrated; Cannibalism was an accepted and enjoyable part of her particular sect of voodoo. Now it was his tasty keepsake!

The three men sat around a hardwood table at the British War College near London England. It was late May of 1898. Professor Ravi Strosser paged through Alois Krupp's notebooks briefly, but to the unknown eye, had read every word and had studied every sketch to detail in milliseconds. Across from his small reclusive study sat Colonel Nephew smoking a nice Cuban cigar. The ancient professor was amazed at the content in these notebooks. "Ravi" Strosser saw the same future vision of huge modern air, artillery, and tank armies destroying everything in their wake in minutes. Total war was no longer a simple theory, but an evolving reality! Ravi saw the savage destructive brutality. Ravi knew this type of warfare had occurred eons ago.

As modern technology erased the old, larger armies were needed to handle it and absorb the losses from it! There was nothing new under the sun as he knew! He fearfully imagined the final level of war… total destruction; annihilation in minutes with a technology not discovered yet in this emerging modern version of civilization. He was astonished at Krupp's models of rockets, crude copies mentally advanced by Krupp from the 3rd century Chinese weapons makers. The world of weapons was now progressing to that final point of extinction as before.

He compared Krupp's inventions to other displayed models, buried deep in a massive time capsule in the Himalayas. It was a time capsule locked in time before the first orange mushroom clouds obliterated civilization so long before! My how mankind is so arrogantly naïve about the true past on this planet. He was now looking down the road maybe fifty years; yes, fifty years at best and Armageddon will come to pass when the next stupid war erupts.! He spoke from his silence. "I am amazed at this information Colonel, Krupp is a genius like Leonardo, as both were conceiving future technologies in weapons long before their time!"

Ravi paused then asked. "What has become of Krupp? Have you heard anything from him since the fight?" Both brits had not heard anything and assumed the worst for old Krupp! Over the next hour Cavendish and Nephew reviewed their verbal report about Krupp and his toyshop. Nephew then produced the Luger pistol, with the attachable stock and snail drum clip from his leather briefcase. Strosser looked at these items with cool amazement. Nephew then handed Ravi one of the 9MM grenade rounds from his vest pocket, who then ran his hands around the projectile and handed it back as he commented. "It is a highly-concentrated powder in a gelatin of some sort!

Damnit! Looks like the concept of highly charged concentrated explosives is upon the world finally!" Ravi smiled at his friend. "Secrecy is the best aid in these times my son, and the Queen decided that I should carry this disguise and position while all this research is going on. Besides, it has been fun being Professor Strosser, rubbing elbows with all the academia's and teatime and culling all the information being passed to me! It has also been fun dining with Her Majesty regularly son. She is such a great soul and the food is always excellent! We are quite good friends now and she has been amazed at all the information and intelligence coming in.

"The Queen and I have come to agreement that this next conflict may be as a result of the global expansion and colonialism of Germany as the new economic "bully" in the school yard to diminish the power of Great Britain and other powers with very broad imperialist ambitions. The Huns are building a huge navy exactly for this purpose and will be a possible flashpoint that will flash back to conflict on the mainland I am afraid! The obvious quest for economic superiority leads to military growth to protect it! And this first terrible conflict may be only years away!" He paused to sip his tea then continued.

"Here is what else we see besides the economic reasons I mentioned. I think that because of this heightened threat posed by Germany, anything perceived as imperialism from one side could set off war! Possible studies of ethnic groups in countries possibly affected like this could be (1) Tribal breakup of the Austro-Hungarian Empire with civil war and powers moving in to grab; (2) Serbia's Slavic union with Russia, protector of all Slavs, (3) Clash on the high seas between Great Britain against expanding German economic and global military naval power and influence.

The German colonies in Africa could be the flashpoint if they expand to grab other European colonies in this region. The status of world economics and war have been closely entwined forever it seems! We must watch these developments with great scrutiny." Ravi paused to sip more tea and refill his cup. "The outcome of this projected Great War is that Germans do not accept defeat. Their militaristic arrogance buoyed in their global economic aims is the key in my estimate, even if they lose the war. You kick them hard and later; they will come back and kick you harder! Now Russia is a great question. Because of the terrible state of its people under a very lopsided monarchy, the risk of a vengeful revolution could be in the offing in the near term. The Tsar has not figured out that the medieval era is dead! We do not see any hard catalyst as of yet, but they exist." The old sage looked at colonel Nephew.

"What would you say colonel?" Nephew was lost in thought, and then spoke as they smiled briefly at each other. "A possible catalyst would come from two sources. I feel the first one is how deadly all these new weapons will be when used against attacking armies. Even Old Krupp called Napoleon the "Mother of Destructive weapons, and annihilation for obvious reasons. Krupp knew how bad these weapons would fare against attacking armies. He fatefully observed the carnage first hand in 1870. Lastly, I see the French as so pissed off, that their national resolve would never allow the Germans to do this twice. So, I feel that the destructive success of these new weapons will fuel resolve and play a major part in this huge clash.

Cavendish concluded. "The Hun and French armies will run at each other like the hunted wild Boar running into the spear! The foes will crash into each other thinking they are gaining ground but all the while dying as the spear deepens and new weapons destroy them! After more associated conversations, Colonel Nephew discussed the injury Cavendish had received in their battle in the bridge, and a lot more on Old Man Krupp, his epiphany moment in 1870 as he watched the destructive power of his guns; on hating his life in making money in dealing death.

He concluded. "You know something, old man Krupp had such a crush on not just present-day history, but on the ancient lore surrounding very ancient past wars on the planet as it seemed he was tuned in. He quoted many sources but only wished he had more of them to study. Ravi was silent as Nephew finished. So, Mr. Alois Krupp is a student of extremely ancient theories of nuclear wars and" "Nuclear wars?" intoned Nephew. "Yes, big giant bombs that split atoms to destroy whole cities and armies in seconds. They destroyed this planet's civilization's and ecosystem more than once long, long ago!

I remember once when my father told me all of what is now the North African Desert was a beautiful paradise, a wonderful civilization. Then, it was destroyed by these "atomic" bombs in minutes by vengeful Atlanteans that I will discuss with you at a later time. The only remains that can be found are huge areas of glass, the heat impact the bombs made on the sandy soil. This happened so long ago. All that is left is a huge wasteland with blowing sand that continues to bury any remains to this once magnificent civilization today! You would be amazed at what treasures lie under all the sand dunes across North Africa and beneath the waters of the Med!"

Ravi then went silent as he thought of old Krupp, the designer of deadly weapons that went straight. They talked a bit longer about the permanent wound that ended Cavendish's military service; then parted with a firm handshake and traditional hug. Lieutenant Colonel Nephew tried to grasp the future bombs described by Ravi with a confused awe; but he well understood it. What in hell was an "atom" he wondered. Ravi quietly surmised that a nuclear age was either a gateway to the stars or the supreme show stopper if used for destructive purposes! It seemed that the show had been stopped more than once over the last billion years!

The weather in the Town of Hechinger near the Black Forest by the end of May 1898 was quite the contrast to the time Nephew and Cavendish were there. It was a warm dry sunny climate now in the low valley dotted with millions of pretty flowers. Old man Krupp, sipping a hot cup of coffee on the wall near his rabbit cottage pondered that it had seemed like years since he had destroyed his factory in his deadly explosions that leveled every building in his plant save a couple. He also could not forget the deadly effectiveness of his submachinegun prototype on all his tormentors. Alois knew it was only a little over three months ago. The authorities who investigated the dead in his office reported that it must had been several British agents that killed them with pistols.

He laughed at their ignorance! Pistols my ass! If killing all these people a second time would have prevented them from finding his toyshop, he would do it again! He saw their blind evil, driven by the bidding of their leader's lust for power and as usual, rabid greed. He was thankful that his "asshole" nephew and the government had rested on the story of a terrorist attack by British agents. This story was confirmed by the battle down the way on the bridge outside Rottweil where the few survivors reported "many" enemy agents had attacked them. He smiled at the surprise the goons and secret police must have had when all those explosive rounds tore into them. His adopted boys had escaped! His eyes teared for the loss of his dear friend and secretary!

Old man Krupp sat in the warm spring morning sunlight patting and talking as he did daily, to his rabbits. Several of them hopped around the area as he smoked his pipe and sipped on a shot of brandy with his coffee. It was a beautiful sunny day in Hechinger and the dry warmth was appreciated. He then noticed that all his loose rabbits hopped away and were hanging around and climbing the legs of a silent stranger standing about twenty feet away. He had appeared from nowhere as Krupp squinted at him.

The stranger was dressed in black, with a rather large fedora on his head. "I see my rabbits seem to like you dear stranger, they tell me you must be a good man." Ravi walked over to where Alois sat, with the bustle of rabbits still hanging around his feet. Krupp was amused at his rabbit's grand show of affection to this stranger. The thin-faced man with a slight greenish complexion smiled then spoke in a perfect southern German dialect. My name is Professor Strosser and my friends call me Ravi. You were very helpful with a couple of friends of mine who stopped by a few months ago."

"Oh Yes, the two British boys Tiberius and Ambrose!" Replied Alois smiling. "Yes, of course, I adopted them for what became a very long night! What a night that was!" Both men panned their view at the destroyed burnt remains of his factory buildings beyond where they sat. "Are they safe Ravi? "Yes, kind sir, thanks to you they were able to, shall I say, escape in good order." Krupp looked relieved. "I am very happy to hear that, for I was worried for them, such nice lads and they helped me close the door on a very important part of my work! Did they tell you anything about my research?" Ravi replied.

"They only told me a few things because they swore to you, they would not let out what they saw. I did not come to ply you for any information unless you authorize me." Krupp then thought deeply. "I think with the help of your boys we prevented my collection of advanced works from falling into the evil hands of my nephew the shithead! May God forgive me for what I have already created kind sir!" Krupp paused and took a shot of brandy and then resumed with a smile on his wily ancient face. Ravi accepted a shot of brandy as they sat together on the wall.

Ravi asked. "Are you going to be all right after all of this Heer Krupp?" "Oh yes," He pointed at the destroyed buildings and rubble piles on his factory lands, "My nephew thinks it was sabotaged by those dangerous British agents, who killed all the police and corporate goons in my office and blew up my factory to halt production. They still can't figure out how they wired all my buildings so fast with explosives. I suggested that it must have been a previous team of these saboteurs! and me? I was feeding my rabbits when the British attacked and somehow survived!"

He then laughed. "What idiots they are thankfully! The authorities played this attack off as botched target because nothing was being produced at this facility. It seems that there was a rather large fight on a bridge on the road outside Rotweil between these British agents and German police. The police lost. I heard that the survivors told of some very powerful, accurate and deadly weapons used against them." Ravi smiled. "You mean the concentrated powder gelatin charges in the Luger rounds?" Krupp looked surprised with a smile and replied. "You bet!"

Ravi studied the little ancient old German with his bushy white hair and large Van Dyke. A couple of rabbits jumped into his lap and he petted them. Ravi looked at Krupp. "They told me you have an interest in ancient times, long dead civilizations destroyed in terrible wars using super weapons and the like?" "Oh, yes Heer Ravi, it has always been my companion group of studies and another reason why I stopped wanting to build weapons. I am afraid mankind will invent powerful weapons mentioned in long lost manuscripts and destroy life, sooner or later. I just wish I had a clearer picture of this history.

Anyway, at this juncture in life, I am completely finished with war. I only hope God forgives me for my greed and enabling others to kill so many with my weapons! I know that there is nothing new under the sun except a new bunch of warmongers willing to use anything to attain power! War technology evolves and mankind doesn't!" Ravi handed the old German a thick valise wrapped with a huge ribbon he had laid on the wall. "As a gift to your curiosity and for your helping my boys out. Thank you for your good heart Mr. Krupp!

I give you a collection of ancient manuscripts and writings I have collected for you regarding ancient civilizations, the impute of extraterrestrial life on this planet, and the fatal wars of destruction which ended many large epochs on this planet. Please enjoy these, and keep up your dedication to your little friends, your rabbits seem so happy as well." Alois responded. "Will you share some fine cheese and salami with me over a cold beer in my little gasthouse next to my office?" Ravi agreed as he sent a message to all the rabbits and they playfully went directly back into their cages in the cottage. Krupp was flabbergasted.

Soon after both ancient gentlemen were seated at the bar eating great sausages and cheese with crackers and sipping beer, which Ravi enjoyed. Old Krupp said. "My loyal rabbit children who care less about weapons and war is all I have left. Honestly Ravi, this is all I want in life now. I would love to show you what I showed the boys before we sealed the crypt, but it is too late for the room is a sealed coffin under wreckage of one of my warehouses forever I pray!" Ravi's smiled back and his warm eyes touched the soul of Krupp. "Since you don't mind, I have already spent several hours down in your crypt of deadly weapons Heer Krupp and must add, that you are a real genius. Leonardo Da Vinci would be proud of you I might add!"

He paused and sipped his beer. "I am the head of a special studies group to divine the possible causes of next major conflict that is brewing between European powers now. I also have my eye on what outcome will exist afterwards. The resulting chaos created after this next terrible conflict will set the stage anew for those of evil intentions sir. Also, you can trust me since I promise that my lips are sealed about your crypt and any whereabouts of it!" Krupp looked confused. "How did you get into it? I sealed it forever from all humans!"

Ravi looked him in the eye. "You are correct Heer Krupp, your crypt is expertly impassible to humans, and I admire your obstacles! I am not what you could call exactly human either!" Krupp gave out a hearty laugh! "Are you from outer space?" Ravi laughed, for his natural body was a very pleasant green now. Krupp stared with a smile then had a new question. "You say you are tracking evil?" Can you explain that?

Over a few more brews, Ravi slowly explained the source of evil he was concerned about. Heer Krupp was now the student. Ravi concluded. "It would be hard to explain to you exactly what I really am, but remember that today as tomorrow, I am your friend Mr. Krupp. Read and enjoy the manuscripts. I put them together personally with my side notes. Perhaps from the reading you will understand more of who I am.

Ravi then shook hands with Krupp, who was still seated, bowed, tipped his hat, and in the blinking of an eye disappeared. Krupp nodded his head and felt it was time for another cold beer. He opened the huge valise and began reading the manuscripts and histories neatly organized in manila folders. He sat there for hours switching to strong coffee, reading and skimming the collection. Ancient manuscripts from throughout the planet, with great side-notes from Ravi.

After lengthy reading he put the manuscripts back in the valise and hid them. He wanted to reflect on these exquisite readings after pouring a shot of Schnapps to kill the effects of the coffee. How little mankind knows what is in their very backyard he surmised…or what really lies beyond the stars; beneath the planet, how little they know! If they did, perhaps the future hell on earth could be stopped. Once earth learned the real truth about its place in the cosmos all the powerful institutions on the planet would have the wind knocked from their sails forever! The curse of greed, and the irresponsible cold-hearted leaders in the current world order would be nil.

In this present world order, when one group of despots were wiped out, more of the same kind would rise to power under any political ideology or religion that was popular. Then it would happen all over again with more dangerous weapons! This was the history of the world! Mankind will annihilate itself again. In a future time, the survivors of this failed world would start throwing rocks at members of other tribes and the same cycle would regenerate again to machineguns, to nukes! He smiled as he reviewed what he had read so far. Ravi's summaries were excellent and allowed him to understand and pinpoint more. He read about the original colonization of earth by extraterrestrials, over one billion years ago, as they colonized thousands of other inhabitable planets.

He learned about their countless epochs of unions and interactions with humans, in peace and war. One epoch after another in symmetrical cycles of birth, life, and death! It seemed that "hate" was the cancer that destroyed the body of civilization! Krupp was amazed when he read of the big event millions of years ago, when a small planet hit earth and completely destroyed a super civilization of floating cities and incredible wonders. That planet became the moon according to the notes. A billion years of earth civilizations, a billion years of earth management by a huge intergalactic council representing thousands of worlds, probably millions. Yet here on earth it seems mankind could not even learn and mutually agree on the correct way to tie a fucking shoe!

If change cannot come from within earth, then it would come from the outside, someday he thought. He began to understood who Ravi was and his ancient race that came from the stars' eons ago; who intermingled with mankind from accident rather than design. He smiled as he finished his last schnapps. Mr. Ravi Strosser looked pretty damn good for being over five-thousand years old he thought! Old Krupp? He surmised that he would never make it to one-hundred? Then he thought about independent floating cities of yore and how he could create a real floating city, one that drew its energy off the earth and sun, or powered by some form of harmless nuclear fission created in that new element called the atom. He laughed. The many secrets that old people possessed! But in this age of young Lions their venerable voices would be impossible to be heard.

June 20, of 1898 was coming soon. Lieutenant Colonel Tiberius Nephew, dressed in his full uniform sat across from Captain James Ambrose Cavendish on the large wooden veranda at the front of the Queen's Military hospital barracks where he was a patient. His wounded comrade was sporting a military bathrobe over some pajamas complete with his billed service hat. It was a sunny warm Spring day and both men were in good spirits. They sipped their customary noon tea and shot of cognac from Nephew's flask. Cavendish summed it up. "Looks like my left shoulder is literally all shot up for good. I will be relegated to the reserve army, which is at least something in case we go to general war again. For now, I am concentrating on my new life as a married man on June 20th and a father as well!"

"A father?" smiled Nephew. "Yes, replied a smiling Ambrose, I am afraid that Miss Jenny Farnsworth went and got herself pregnant on me!" "Was it on you, or under you dear boy?" Both men laughed on Nephew's joke. "Well," continued Ambrose, "At least she will not be showing her new status at the wedding, so the secret will be kept!" "Yes, the things we do for King and Country Cavendish! So, what are your plans after the wedding!"

"I am retiring from the studies group and will head to the Caribbean into the rum business it seems. Germany will play a major part in future hostilities whether they initiate war or follow one of their allies like Austria-Hungary into the mix." Nephew added. "These speculations seem profound Ambrose. I think, from what is being assembled, that the flashpoint may happen in the Balkans! The Austrian- Hungarian Empire is so loaded with various tribal groups, and Serbia is becoming part of the empire's growing problem. Russia does not like the growing power and influence of this adjacent Austrian Empire and is very protective of its little Slavic children in those Balkans."

Colonel Nephew passed a large envelope to Cavendish and he opened it. He pulled out a sheaf of papers. He began to read the official letter on the top. He read it again, and then laughed as he kept reading. Tiberius savored the rest of his tea. Cavendish finally looked up as Nephew added. "Congratulations my comrade in arms! You have been promoted to Major in the reserve home army my boy. If we are called up for the "big one" you shall serve as my adjutant wherever you reside."

Cavendish smiled. "The eloquent old Strosser visited me a couple of days ago, to check in on me. I do not think he is well Tiberius he looks a bit frazzled. Ravi told me to let you know that Alois Krupp survived the mayhem at his old factory and took out a whole bunch of goons and state secret police in his destruction of his many factory buildings." Tiberius nodded his head. "That crafty old man was completely underestimated for sure!"

Cavendish told his friend the nature of his injury after Pyra had told him. Nephew thought for a moment. "Do you love her Ambrose?" "As a matter of fact, I love her very much; like my love for Jenny. However, I mentally had to separate them, as Pyra is my dream love and Jenny, is my real love. It is hard to explain my emotions on this, but my relationship with Pyra seems very intact and she understands and even supports my love for Jenny. We actually talked about it. True love is true love dear Nephew!" "True loves dear Cavendish? It seems as I lose when I am in love and win when I am in lust! But true love for me tis my dream illusion at this point, and carnal lust is my reality my boy!"

Colonel Nephew eyed his gold pocket watch and it was time to go. He opened his leather briefcase and let Cavendish look inside. Inside was the gift old Krupp had bestowed on Cavendish to aid in their escape. "I thought that was lost." "No, I made sure it came home for you. Such a nice weapon this Luger. It is all there, for your war room! I am going to take it to your apartment! I will be back to gather you up after your release in two days and off we will go for that celebration drink for your promotion dear chap!" Nephew stood up and saluted his sitting friend who saluted him back. With a smile on his face, the colonel turned and strode down the long wooden steps to the walkway humming some forgotten tune.

Both men were invited to have tea with the queen a week later. Ravi was present and they reviewed the incident in Germany and especially Krupp's impressive inventions. Nephew was very impressed as he reread the notes on "early warning devices." He had forgotten these radio wave towers completely! Krupp had even considered a counter measure to detect approaching enemy aircraft; like his anti-tank prototype artillery! Then she changed the topic and looked at Cavendish.

"I understand that you are getting married soon Major?" "Yes, my Queen, I am to wed Miss Jenny Farnsworth on June 20 [the] and you are certainly invited!" The Queen made a notation of this. The rest of the time was spent talking about more common subjects and with a lot of humor. Queen Victoria had a great sense of it. It was time to depart since the Queen had a whole list of dignitaries to give audience to this day. She stood to watch them as they left. She looked at her dear friend Ravi. "I think this will be my best audience today and will treasure my sons."

The fanfare leading up to the wedding on June 20, 1898 had been quite a busy affair in the week following the wedding. The wedding was to take place at the big Anglican Church in London, and then the reception and party were to take place at the Farnsworth estate. It was a time of happiness and great excitement. The weather on this day was perfect, bright and sunny with cooling breezes. Jenny had spent a couple of days earlier in the week with Ambrose, but according to custom, she was cloistered away by both girlfriends and family.

Cavendish's family, including the Balbain's were already in London, staying at the elegant Crown Hotel by the Thames River just a block from the tower of London. Major Cavendish had been visiting with his family and friends, walking with them amid the constant bustle of this great city, in the stoic drabness of London, mixed with its very regal beauty now blessed with a cleansing sunlight. However, Ambrose first had to survive his grand surprise bachelor party! He had also been spirited away by his group of military buddies to a bachelor party arranged by Colonel Nephew. The commission money from the sale of steel to Lefebvre in Paris had rented the "Dragon's Breath" Pub from dusk to dawn.

Both post steel salesmen still laughed at the huge commissions they had received. The French had even ordered more than the original order! This celebration eventually evolved into all the trappings of some primal pirate party as it continued. The entrance of Rashid, Hoskins, Holmes, Collins, Griggs, Cornwallis, and King George added greatly to the mirth. The event went until the next morning, until all present, including the rented floozies were worn out. As the front of the pub was alive with singing and tales, the back room had turned into an ad hoc brothel with many affectionate hookers compensated by the steel commission made possible by one case of Merlot given between old friends.

Cavendish, Jacques, Hoskins, and Rashid seemed the only ones who ignored the drunken perfumed and silk covered advances of some quite attractive floozies who offered their wares. Their expertise was greatly appreciated in the back room which was a hopping den of iniquity all night. In the end, both bride and groom were already worn out from all the pre-wedding celebrations. The Dragon's Breath Pub returned to a normal life the next night.

The wedding day of June 20, 1898 was suddenly here. In the professional world of noble weddings in the church, many important royal personages flocked into the huge church bedecked in their finest attire. Soon, all present were silent as they viewed the handsome groom and his groomsmen silently waiting next to the alter, as many peered to the back of the church aisle and waited for Jenny Farnsworth to be delivered to the sacred alter and given away. All who waited silently carefully noted the huge leaded windows and their religious colored beauty that accented the exquisite detail of the great medieval church. The world was at peace. The purity and love of God had blessed this place today.

The warm predawn light in the east on October 17, 1806 hinted to another windless blistering hot day in Haiti. Zombi waited in the secluded grove with his band of henchmen. The bloody reign of Emperor Dessalines was about to come to a sudden violent end before the sun came up. The mosquitoes seemed to exact painful revenge on the assassins as they sat waiting for their quarry in the trees by the side of the road gulping plugs of rum. Since Dessalines rise to absolute power, he had been slowly encroaching on the underlying power of the good Doc Ayiti Deschamps and his network. With the agreed murder of thousands of terrified French colonists, this dictator had become reckless in his respect to Ayiti! Several of the emperor's cohorts had already accosted and killed several of the voodoo masters and close aficionados to Ayiti.

Zombi had survived three assassination attempts to date. One attempt had been made on Deschamps with rumors of more to come! Since Ayiti would be condemned for any attempt on the Emperor, he could not be present tonight. Faithful renegade brother Zombi was chosen to lead this attack while the popular religious leader Deschamps was to appear a large gathering at the Emperor's palace. He would sit at the main table of honor with the Emperor's wife Beth since her husband was gone. This would provide his innocence via public visibility. Strawman would relax later this night with Eve.

Emperor Dessalines had been experiencing growing problems with his anti-government rivals who had been stirring up violence in the countryside attacking his government forces. Although Doc Ayiti had been implicated in this movement. Although Ayiti had no direct contact with the anti-government forces, he did have the ear of the main conspirator against the dictator named Henri Christophe. He was a top aide to Emperor Dessalines. Ayiti had influenced Christophe and had joined forces with him in this gamble. The plan this night was to assassinate Dessalines after he was returning from his surprise attack and destruction of a key rebel stronghold in the north near Pont Larnage.

In a testament of his loyalty, Ayiti had given the location of the rebel hideout to the emperor who was overjoyed at this information. Doctor Ayiti had his own plan! "One ambush leads to another" he had said with a laugh as he told Jean Zombi. Why not allow the "soon to die" bastard emperor his last victory over the anti-government rebels? This faction had to be destroyed anyhow since the rebels hated and feared Deschamps. Zombi laughed as he whispered Ayiti's mantra, "kill two birds with one stone!" As the old saying went? The setup for tonight, had gone perfectly according to plans.

Nearly all of anti-government leaders and their men were meeting in this village hideout to plan the overthrow of Dessalines based on new information. This new vital information was planted by Ayiti to encourage this large rebel gathering at their base camp. Government spies had been dispatched into this area and verified it before the emperor marched. "Two birds would be killed with one stone!" Emperor kills anti-government leaders and Zombi kills the emperor! Future dictator Christophe would be left completely in the dark about Ayiti's grand plan this night! Christophe, was his next puppet and was seated next to him at the celebration this night! Ayiti laughed at the plan just before he gave his after dinner speech. He really loved this shit!

As Zombi and his group of killers set their ambush, government forces completely encircled the rebel stronghold in the night before. They began their assault using light artillery, followed by a cacophony of direct well-aimed rifle fire into the rebel base camp depressed down in a short valley. Every time the rebels tried to break out of the encirclement they were met with deadly direct fire. The muzzle flashes from the artillery could be seen through the dense jungle foliage by Zombi and his henchmen. The rum was passed amid their laughter. On his queue, the assassins, led by Zombi then moved into place along the high road from this stronghold. From this position, they got a bird's eye view of the battle down below viewing it over the forest from their high position. The explosions in the rather well fortified base camp resembled a small village.

The artillery exploded in the huts causing them to burn brightly in the darkness of the jungle. The streets seemed covered with bodies and debris from the constant assault. Amid the glow of burning buildings Zombi watched the futile attempts of the rebels to defend this place. Many of the emperor's troops died as they rushed the burning town to finish off the last defenders. The fighting was savage as the rebels were overwhelmed. All the rebel leaders were killed. The gunfire now became sporadic as dawn approached. The rebels had been destroyed as the next act in this bloody play was soon to begin.

Zombi had placed spies inside Dessalines command to follow his personal movements. They would be waiting by the steep side of a large hill on the only road that went into the depressed hideout. The pompous clown of an emperor would have to come this way. Zombi's man with the fuse was positioned further down the road with his huge set of charges they had planted along a steep tree covered hill covered with masses of moss-covered boulders next to the road. I large deep jungle ravine fell off sharply on the other side of the narrow road. One of his spies returned to confirm that the battle was finished. He reported that all of the foes of Dessalines had been slaughtered in brutal combat along with many of the emperor's men.

He reported that the Emperor and his group were about ten minutes behind him with his small army some hundred yards behind them. Zombi looked at the gold pocket watch given to him by Ayiti and noted it. He then joined his man with the dynamite fuse down the rocky road to oversee lighting the charge after the Emperor's group had passed and his motley army was in front of the explosives. If all went well, the Emperor would be minus dead army and a clean hit. Ayiti would be proud! He laughed "Two birds with one stone!" sang Zombi. Ayiti, miles away at this gala event with the wife of the emperor smiled. He had heard Zombi's voice in his mind.

Within a few minutes Zombi heard a lot of noise, yelling and laughter coming up the road along with the constant jingling of equipment and sabers attached to the horses. The shapes of several horsemen appeared in the road, and the Emperor was clearly seen by the silhouette of his his customary large Napoleonic hat. He was in the middle of the riders. A small caravan of horsemen and wagons followed some distance behind the emperor's group of riders. Zombi ordered his man to light the fuse.

He then jumped on his horse and galloped along the ridge hidden by the trees back to his men in front. Suddenly there was a huge flash followed by a series of explosions smashing the peaceful predawn darkness! The side of the hill exploded upon all those unfortunates in the caravan behind the emperor. The massive explosive cacophony, unleashed the complete hillside above the small road. The avalanche of trees, boulders, and dirt slammed into the crowded column of troops mixed with the wagons pulling the artillery and carrying loot pillaged from the camp.

Celebration now turned to chaos, and death, as all in the impacting blasts from several charges blew debris, men, horses, and wagons pulling light artillery sideways and down a steep tree infested hill in a huge tumbling jumble of wreckage. The impact threw the emperor and the dozen mounted men with him off their panicked horses to the ground. They had just passed the kill zone when it exploded. Their horses, scared by the blast galloped away leaving those in the road crawling in shock with bleeding ears. Zombi and his gang of cohorts were upon the stunned men in the smoke and debris filled dirt road in moments.

In an instant, all of these survivors with one exception were shot, macheted, looted of their valuables, and beheaded. Their severed heads would soon be posted on spikes elsewhere, gratis from the anti-government forces that had ambushed the poor emperor after his victory! Zombi watched the about-to-be deposed dictator grovel around on the ground in fear begging for his miserable life. Blood flowed down the side of his head from his ears from the blast impact with fear betrayed from his wide eyes.

Zombi picked up the emperor's large Napoleonic hat from the road and put it on his head. Zombi then laughed like a Hyena as he reminded the Emperor that doctor Ayiti was very unhappy with him! He grabbed Dessalines by the hair and carved his head off with a sharp knife as he sang a slave song. The dying emperor gasped amid shrieks of pain as he finally died. His head was the prize for his boss. During the painful execution of Emperor Dessalines, swarms of local destitute jungle dwellers had emerged from the jungle and had begun looting the dead and dying troops in the steep wooded deep ravine below. Once mounted on their horses they begin to move from the area.

As fate, would have it, Zombi's group ran directly into the middle of a relief force of anti-government rebels. The huge Napoleonic hat worn by Zombi added to the confusion in the swift collision between rebels and the perceived emperor in their midst. Then everyone began shooting wildly in the morning darkness at point-blank range as swords began slashing on the mark! The combatants screamed as they were hit by bullets or slashed, with many unfortunates falling off their horses and trampled by the melee by terrified horses and riders.

Several of Zombi's men were shot dead after firing point blank into the throng of rebel assailants. This deadly brawl on horseback continued as combatants from both parties fell from their mounts mortally wounded. As the clash climaxed, only four of Zombi's men remained in their saddles. Zombi had been hit in the chest and shoulder but managed to stay on his horse still wearing the emperor's Napoleonic hat pulled down on his head. As the gravely wounded Zombi clung to his saddle, one of his surviving men grabbed the reigns and guided him away into the jungle, back to the estate Deschamps.

Jean Zombi still had the head of the emperor tried to his saddle in a bag, but the heads of the emperor's favorites were lost in the fight. Word of the emperor's death made a small consolation to what Ayiti had lost. In the huge charnel house cellar at the mansion, Ayiti stared at the body of his favorite henchman brother Zombi. Tears of hate ran down Ayiti's face as he looked on. He had not felt this way since his dear Aunt Sarah was murdered by the French savages. Zombi died as he held his hand, but in silent rage "Doc' Ayiti told one of the survivors to fetch Marta, the powerful resident voodoo priestess who served him well in these matters.

They both worked long hours by ritual, by certain medicines, and by the power produced by the Strawman. At dawn the next day Ayiti visited the crypt like room where Zombi's body lay. There was Zombi, sitting up silent, as his eyes, all white, bugged out in a distant lost stare. Ayiti musingly put Dessalines's Napoleonic hat on his numbed head. "Do you know who I am" asked Deschamps. Momentary silence followed as if Zombi was searching mentally across millions of miles.

Then he spoke in a monotone devoid of humor and human passion. "Yes, Doc Ayiti, I know you! I am brother Zombi." Ayiti smiled for two reasons. He had a semblance of his favorite henchman back and it seemed that the voodoo magic of raising the dead had worked twice now. Zombi was alive and Ayiti's method had previously worked on a favorite French lady captive he had incredible amorous fun with and had grown attached to. However, she had managed to hang herself to his great dismay. She was an experiment since his usual methods of controlling his minions did not work on a truly dead person.

But she was restored to life but was different. He soon lost interest in his walking corpse now reeking of filth and bumping around in the dark cellar in a once elegant evening gown completely soiled by her plight. She stumbled listlessly in the damp dark chamber of horrors with a severely crooked neck earned from her meeting with the rope. Besides, Strawman had other fresher French dames cloistered away in cages anyhow. But this lady had been special.

He had his slaves clean up Zombi and feed him raw meat and bananas. He later patted Zombi on the head and poured some dark rum down his throat. He looked into the dead eyes of his favorite adopted brother. "You know something my dear brother Jean? As a tribute to you I will name all those walking dead like you as "Zombies." It had been earlier that year, in a fit of anger that he thrust his right index finger into a captive government official to torture him, but instead, zombified him on the spot into one of his living dead minions. "Experiment, and learn new things" became his motto after this. But at least he had a new dictator to train!

The wedding date of June 20, 1898 for James and Jenny was now at hand! The Farnsworth Estate was crowded with several hundred guests dressed in their finest! The chiseled elegance and beauty of Jenny Farnsworth, in the white finery of her wedding dress, was admired by all who saw her as she walked down the long aisle in the church with her father. Major Ambrose Cavendish beamed a great smile from his place by the alter steps, dressed in his immaculate dress uniform of the 11th Bengal Lancers.

He stood at attention along with his best man Colonel Tiberius Nephew and four other groomsmen, which included Lieutenant Horatio Griggs, immaculate in the dress uniforms of their respective regiments. In contrast, the maid of honor and all bridesmaids were dressed in long flowing bright yellow gowns in the top fashion design popular in the 1890s. As Jenny and Ambrose's eyes met, the stoic gaze changed to all smiles, and even some low laughs.

As Jenny and her father reached the platform the murmuring ceased, for it was show time! After the rituals, the vows were exchanged. The white-haired Priest gave a beautiful speech on the importance and beauty of a good marriage, then finally addressed the couple. "Jennifer Marie Farnsworth, do you take Ambrose James Cavendish to be your lawful wedded husband, in sickness and in health until death due you part?" She smiled and put his wedding band in his finger as it was produced on a small pillow offered by one of his sister's small beautiful daughters and squeezed his hand. "Yes, I DO!" was her answer.

The priest continued. "Ambrose James Cavendish, do you take Jenny Marie Farnsworth to be your lawful wedded wife, in sickness and in health until death do you part?" Ambrose, in a lost moment yelled "YES SIR!" with a moment's lapse continued. "I DO SIR!" The silence was broken by a lot of laughter. He took her wedding band and carefully put it on her hand. The Priest cracked his only smile of the day as he said. "You may kiss the bride Major James Ambrose Cavendish!" They embraced and he gave Jenny a long sweet kiss. The smiling priest finished. There then came a booming round of applause from the packed cathedral.

"By the power invested in me by God, and the Anglican Church of England, and the Queen, I now pronounce you husband and wife!" The applause was enormous. As the new Mr. And Mrs. Ambrose Cavendish walked down the aisle, they waved to the standing crowd as the sound of Scottish Bagpipes could be heard past the sun-drenched open doors outside. Once in the coach they were smiling and kissing and laughing as they took sips from an ice-cold magnum of Champagne. It was part of a wedding present shipment of fifty cases from the famous estate Balbain in Gascony, France.

He looked Jenny in the face. "I will love you forever darling." He kissed her gently on her lips and forehead. Tears welled in her eyes as she smiled back. "Ambrose, I fell in love with you the first time I saw you, and as then, now, and tomorrow, I shall love you forever as well!" She kissed him for a long time, as the carriage ride seemed to bump their kisses about. By the time, they pulled up to the Farnsworth estate, they were working on the end of the second bottle of fine French champagne. The party had begun and would well into the night.

The sit-down dinner for all the guests was a seven-course dinner with the main entrée being Thick Juicy Prime rib. It began at six, which allowed for several hours of games, mirth, and endless cocktails before it was served. A strange looking bird, akin to a delicate Egret, had been watching as the wedding carriage left the church from its perch high up cathedral spire. It had tears in its eyes as it watched. They were not ones of sadness, but tears of great love and joy. Pyra wanted to be here today, for Ambrose and Jenny.

Multitudes of well-dressed young children ran and played against the backdrop of huge white party tents, around many outdoor adult games, and the endless greenery of the fields, touched by immaculately trimmed copses of trees. The Farnsworth estate where this party was held, had twenty-five acres of fields and forests behind the main estate house. The wedding party was a time of happiness, innocence, and love for all attending. The speeches from the main table where eloquent and very humorous, keeping the party spirits high. After the dinner was over, out came the band to play a whole variety of music for the hours of dancing that would ensue. The smell of perfume became mixed with the burning tobacco of both pipes and cigars.

Jenny and Ambrose both left each other's company often to mingle and socialize with the many guests. Ambrose drank and smoked cigars with his military comrades, as Jenny ran with a pack of quite randy acting girlfriends. It seemed to both Jenny and Ambrose that their parents had bonded well, sitting together at their table enjoying the evening of conversation and music. His sister Elizabeth was completely in her element and flirting with many handsome men who crowded around her. Cavendish swore to Nephew that her copious nearly exposed breasts either had grown or her head had shrunk! The colonel stared at her with studied interest!

The dancing finally brought the very separated groups of males and females together in frivolous banter and more drinking. It was long after the children and the old folks had left when the mutual attractions developed between the available and some non-available men and women present. They had taken over the place, with young and old gone, the hair was let down and in several cases; dresses were let down or pulled up in more secluded places. The party was endless fun and many braved it until the next morning. Those who remained were served a nice buffet breakfast with gallons of coffee and hot tea.

Ambrose and Jenny had managed to sneak off before sunrise to consummate the marriage, which had already been consummated many times before, and with child! Early the next morning they appeared at the huge party site. They greeted all those survivors who remained behind to indulge as they both rounded them up for breakfast. Many of the survivors were asleep on tables, under them, and everywhere. Those caught up in mutual passion were found slumbering in very intriguing places and positions in bushes, the manicured copses of trees, and hidden parts of the huge event tent, not to forget the nearby farm buildings.

The hearty souls left on their feet smoked cigars and were still drunkenly nourishing fine American whiskey, cognac, rum, gin, beer, or anything else that was available. Elizabeth was in this group smoking a cigar and sipping a glass of whiskey. Colonel Nephew had been hard to locate but was found snuggled in the back of a carriage in front of the estate with the finest looking bridesmaid, both naked but covered in a couple of blankets.

The sun rose early on May 7, 1842 at the San Souci Palace, near Cape Haitian Haiti. It had been built under the despotic control by Henri Christophe. In the words of the most foreign guests, this magnificent place was the "pure gem" in the West Indies. This exquisite palace was created by Christophe to show the world that the black man could also produce unimaginable wonders like the white man.

San Souci Palace exhibited every modern enmity, with a huge façade in the front filled with immaculately manicured gardens, courtyards, pools, and beautiful architecture spread throughout it. This wonder had put Cape Haitien on the international map of places to see and to visit. However, this marvel built to show the ingenuity and ability of the black race was created at a terrible invisible expense. This marvel generated incredible suffering and death among the thousands of blacks who were conscripted by force to build this testament of black ingenuity. Even the black-hearted Ayiti was angered at the suffering forced on many of his followers who were enslaved by this dictators' thugs to help build it!

This palace was created in a world of pure hell, amid terrible savage transgressions against the population he controlled! Christophe would take his place in history not as a great leader, but another cruel murdering tyrant! Today the San Souci Palace was a paradise for many visitors but a terrible prison for one. It was not the beautiful majestic place for the very popular spiritual healer Doctor Ayiti Deschamps. He had been imprisoned in a special lead-lined sealed room on the second floor awaiting his execution by the hands of Jean Boyer, the iron fisted bloody dictator who had replaced Christophe. He had come to supreme power in Haiti garnering enough of the popular, and influential support.

Things had been shaky since Boyer came to power in Haiti in 1820. The period of chaos following the murder of the emperor had been a sort of golden age for "Doc' Ayiti and his enterprises. His empire greatly flourished under the dictatorship of Christophe. At one point, he even considered being the dictator of the island. However, he felt that times were better for his interests if he stayed out of the limelight and in the sublime darkness he treasured. He could do more and get more results this way for he was the real power then. Today his real power had become useless!

He sarcastically laughed to himself at his current predicament! He now wished he had become the next dictator instead of Boyer; his jailor. He had tried every manner of escape from this lead lined room he could imagine but was crippled because of Boyer's voodoo experts. They had kept him sedated with their powerful voodoo drugs and had severely weakened his powers in this lead room! Ayiti was condemned to their whims, fancies, and grueling torture! He was just another forlorn prisoner, void of hope now and doomed to die. Doomed to die if they could only find something! They had tried to kill him several times but he always came around; back to life. The voodoo adepts and Boyer were terrified of him!

Once upon a time, the good doctor Ayiti was the honored guest under Christophe, basking in the opulent glory of his demonic authoritarian rule in the north of Haiti, while his co-conspirator, one Alexander Petion, created a republic in the south. Authoritarian rule always favored Ayiti, especially when he had decent control over it. But Ayiti had quickly tired of Christophe, who in turn, despised and feared "Little Ayiti," as he often mockingly called him. Ayiti was sensing a clash with this dangerous tyrant and planned for Christophe's exit from power. He began to manipulate the dictator with all sorts of magic potions created by his very effective voodoo priestess Marta.

The voodoo potent was secretly put in his food and drink routinely by Ayiti's people in the palace. This finally produced an incapacitating stroke that kept him bedridden or in a wheelchair to be seen by day. By night, the potent literally turned Henri into what could be seen as a slavering fanged insane devil dog of sorts roaming in the night. One day the dictator was fine, then at night he would turn into a monster half human and half dog, feeding on the flesh and fears of so many locals who dubbed this creature "Wolfman." It was strongly rumored now that Christophe was the "monster from the palace!"

But Ayiti, who had power over his devil dog "wolfman," lost control of Christophe, when he was distracted one night. "Wolfman," now aware of who had done him this way, entered Ayiti's villa one night to kill him. Devil dog Christophe killed a couple of guards then murdered and feasted on poor Marta. Ayiti was not present as poor Henri was captured and returned to his palace. Later, in 1811 it was recorded that Henri Christophe killed himself with a silver bullet, committing suicide over his disability condition and the rumor he wanted to end the curse of the devil wolfman.

Why did it take a silver bullet kill this wolf like creature of the night was the question of the day? What did Christophe know? He knew nothing at all except insanity as he watched the good doctor standing in front of him in his final moments! It was a silver bullet fired into his head by Doc Ayiti disguised as a medical assistant on his staff. Ayiti created a new rumor in his cruel jest. The silver bullet was the only thing that could kill slavering devil dogs or man-wolves by night. In his usual sick humor Ayiti laughed as he then added the full moon as stimulus to transform human into wolf monster; the new shape changer of future legends! "The stuff legends are made of," surmised the new dictator's special prisoner as he smiled from his cracked broken lips. After all, even black-hearted evil has a sense of humor!

He continued reviewing his life and events that brought him to his current predicament. After the death of Christophe, confusion, and chaos reigned in the north. This was the time "Doc" Deschamps came to his zenith and underlying power controlling the rich plantation owners and weak government leaders who replaced "night creature" Christophe. But all eyes on Ayiti did more than fear him; they despised his evil personage to the core and sought to destroy him! The voodoo sects who opposed Ayiti, secretly lined up with Boyer. They were, like the new dictator, driven by extreme terror of his powers.

Ayiti's soon to be main antagonist by 1820, had taken over Haiti in a bloodless coup surrounding himself with the anti-Ayiti voodoo sects. He then initiated his "iron fist" control over the people, becoming the most ruthless of ex-slave leaders to curse the people of Haiti since those enslaved by Christophe forced to build Sans Souci Palace. Boyer's cruelty was even compared to the French overlords! Boyer left Ayiti alone in his world of mystery, but in 1838 Deschamps was implicated in a plot to rid Haiti of this strong-arm dictator.

Hector, the son of one of his female victims, betrayed Ayiti as the main conspirator to Boyer out of revenge. It was revenge for what Ayiti had done to his mother. Jeanette was one of the most beautiful women of Cap-Haitien. She was an elegant mulatto who was at first infatuated by the smooth innocent youthful looks and charm of Doctor Ayiti Deschamps; a man who never seemed to age a day. Later, she disappeared into the recesses of Ayiti's villa for months. It was then rumored that Jeanette was a prisoner and concubine in the mysterious basement complex at Deschamps mansion.

The rumors surrounding Villa Deschamps were nothing less than unfathomable horror! They spoke of unspeakable voodoo rituals, dead smelly walking corpses, human sacrifice, kidnappings, and cannibalism. No sane words would ever be able to describe what Hector and his group found their incursion into this hell before the fateful raid by Dictator Boyer's police. One night, when Ayiti was gone from his mansion, Hector and a few well-armed friends broke into Ayiti's Villa searching for his mother Jeanette. She was found in a state referred to by emerging island lore as "zombie."

She was disheveled, messed up, and filthy, just sitting alone under a flickering oil lamp in a basement room with only the whites of her eyeballs showing. Attempts to revive her and get her out proved fruitless because she became violent and had to be restrained. The group was appalled as they witnessed terrible unspeakable horrors in this basement complex. The sights of rotting women, many skeletons by now, adorning the walls in once elegant filthy soiled dresses alone made all the rescuers physically sick.

In a fit of rage over the terrible condition of his mother, Hector chopped off her head with his machete to end this nightmare. Then, this group killed several zombie guards and a couple of voodoo priestesses trying to block their escape in angry frenzy. Jean Zombi, the king of the zombies appeared in this scuffle at the basement entrance smiling and bellowing something in his inaudible low evil monotone. As the rescuers were ready to kill him, something else appeared in an interior door beside the man Zombi and his bulging eyes with spastic quick movements.

It was a pack of small filthy savage like dwarfs? Children? Ferocious, dangerous and growling. These little monster urchins were the zombified products of offspring from several of Strawman's lovely ladies in the cages! Ayiti saw them as his own special breed and conditioned them to be ferocious guards of his estate. They were fast, vicious, and powerful! In abject terror Hector and his friends fought them killing several with their machetes as they broke free of the basement running in terror from the villa. All of them escaped suffering nasty bite wounds and deep cuts from the razor nail slashes from the little pack of filthy killer midgets. Ayiti sensed this incursion as his child monsters were slain, but it was too late.

Two of the son's friends that accompanied him into this hellhole were members of Boyer's secret police. The secret police under the orders of Boyer surrounded the villa and closed in the next night waiting for Ayiti to return home. Boyer was present during the raid as he had been preparing for this event already. The dangerous master voodoo King! "Doc" Ayiti had no choice but to surrender at the top of the main stairs at the front of his house. Ayiti wanted to negotiate rather than wage a fight. He did not quite understand the gravity of his predicament until he was seized by Boyer's voodoo adepts and given several shots into his neck and body.

Ayiti, now fading into paralysis from the drugs did utter a loud sharp shriek, which warned the others in his villa. Ayiti was put into chains as the attack on his villa commenced. His zombie guards put up a good fight but were all slain by the swords and pistols of Boyer's police. What the authorities encountered upon entering the recesses of the villa was pure revolting horror. The pack of little filthy wild savages, the spawns of Ayiti, emerged from everywhere in the dank cellar, ferociously attacking the invaders who suffered several losses. They were all killed as the police moved through the great house. The villa was cleared as Boyer and his voodoo adepts entered.

The huge dungeon cellar revealed a massive voodoo alter with all its eerie trappings of burning candles, symbols, statues, and the atrocious smell of rotten flesh from both humans and animals. It seemed that cannibalism was the main nourishment of the zombies and killer midgets. This dank evil lair from hell was located in the lower level where several of Ayiti's voodoo adepts and many grislier zombie-like people appeared. They were all killed. The mummified remains of many once elegant French women hung on the walls were now seen by the horrified police and Boyer. This "Butterfly collection" decorated the hallways in their once beautiful but now tattered gowns; like the trophies of some big game hunter.

The smell was horrendous! The mutilated mostly devoured body of Hector's once beautiful mother was found tossed on the blood-stained stinking alter. Several lucky French women were found alive in cages and were released. The pretty ones would be forced against their will into marriage to some of Boyer's confidents. The rest would be gang raped and murdered as was the way Boyer dealt with the evil French savages. The dictator, heeding the advice of his voodoo priests, kept Ayiti constantly drugged and locked in this large leaded metal box for his trip to a specially designed room in the former elegant Sans Souci Palace of Christophe. They wanted to learn his secrets before they killed him!

Like the French plantation raids by the slaves of old, Ayiti's villa was plundered of every valuable, then, with all the dead bodies thrown into it, burnt to the ground. The secret police surrounded it to insure nobody escaped. The Deschamps house of horrors was turned into a flaming inferno. All record of Ayiti's chamber of horrors was destroyed, except in the lips of those who saw its horrors like Dictator Boyer. Unknown to Ayiti, there was one lone survivor from the villa. Jean Zombi was in the carriage house behind the villa finishing his feast on a tasty beggar who had wandered on the property. He heard the high-pitched warning scream from Ayiti and moved into the trees. He watched the complete spectacle some distance away, mumbling, with unchecked tears running down his face from his ever-bulging eyeballs. Zombi had remote feelings for his master. He was the only one to escape alive, if Zombi's condition was considered "alive" in the first place.

The voodoo Loa god sat lost in his thoughts in the corner in this windowless room on the second floor of the palace. Ayiti's mind, cluttered buy powerful voodoo drugs still felt hungry for extreme revenge and to escape. He had several million in currency, jewels, and gold coin deposited in two banks over in Santo Domingo. He also had his very important item there as well. Santo Domingo had become an independent country in 1809, so his wealth was safe from Boyer under a different name. He knew Boyer had wanted to execute him immediately. Ayiti laughed to himself, for unless something was destroyed first? He could not be killed! However, he had endured the horrendous physical pain they inflicted on him.

The other reason he had been kept alive from Boyer's attempts to kill him was because of the demands of Boyer's personal voodoo Kings. They insisted he be kept alive until they could learn and use his powers. They had been picking him apart mentally and physically in awe and fear of his unique powers. A couple of voodoo adepts had seen him transform into Strawman and were terrified of him. He was very dangerous as all rumors taught. They even chopped off his foot and watched it grow back! Rumor in the voodoo community was that Ayiti Deschamps was an incarnated Loa god. He was living up to this image with his tormentors!

So, his life since capture had been a terrible existence locked in an inescapable room lined from top to bottom with lead. They had kept him sedated on drugs as a continuous prevention of him regaining his composure and powers as Strawman. He was so high on the voodoo drugs that he could not transform. His attempts at transforming like a part human and part clumsy doll drew laughs from his tormentors. His drugged powers made him weak and useless but never dead. He was beaten, tortured and deprived of food during his captivity. Yet Ayiti seemed to survive all of it! He would not die; could not die!

The voodoo priests knew that "Little Ayiti" as they called him, had been alive for at least one-hundred years as they traced his whereabouts to the one-armed terrorist Mackandal, his alleged father to 1748. It was now 1842 and this very dangerous voodoo master still looked youthful, say in his mid-twenties? He only had a scar running across his face. But what could he do now? He had been told that he was to be burnt at the stake in two days and his burnt remains chopped into pieces. Ayiti could not imagine the pain because he would regenerate back. Maybe then he could escape? This terrible event was to occur in a private execution tomorrow observed by none other than Jean Boyer!

Jean Boyer! If Ayiti got his claws on him! His painful death would be legendary! Ayiti seethed in hate and wailed aloud in torment lost in his drugged thoughts. Then he heard and felt a rumbling. He was thankful that his familiar doll had never been put in his mansion and removed from his old jungle hideout to Santo Domingo. The voodoo adepts sensed that he had to have a familiar, and in their belief system; Ayiti would have suffered the same fate as his familiar if it burned up in the mansion fire. But a "familiar doll" was only accepted in certain dark cults so Ayiti's doll status was questionable only to them; never to Ayiti!

The low rumbling now turned into a wild shaking. The Sans Souci Palace began to fall apart around Ayiti as his ears picked up the noise outside his cell. He could hear many screams, as parts of the elaborate massive structure begin to disintegrate and crumble. The collapsing palace walls and floors began trapping and instantly killing many people inside the monolithic structure. Ayiti clung to the reinforced door as the whole bottom of his room disappeared down to the next floor. The shaking intensified as he hung now by the door in a floorless room hanging precipitously low as if to collapse. The dust cloud developing from the broken plaster debris filled the air, choking the doctor as he let go and dropped some thirty feet to a rubble strewn second floor. The rumbling was non-stop now.

He rolled weakly on the floor as the broken lead lined room fell behind him. More debris crashed down everywhere. Ayiti Deschamps was laughing out loud but muffled by the huge noise around him. The noise was deafening as the roar from the earthquake grew in intensity. He tried to walk but the shaking and strong drug sedation caused him to flounder and fall, so he began to crawl slowly around broken furniture, masonry, and squirming bodies, as more walls and ceilings crumbled around him. He finally reached a huge staircase that led to the ornate foyer below and impulsively rolled down its length crashing hard at the bottom, strewn with debris and bodies. The shaking greatly intensified. It seemed ages as he crawled to the huge front doors of the dying palace; or bloody "Pearl of Haiti", built on the suffering and deaths of so many!

It seemed a just reward to Ayiti that this San Souci Palace be destroyed this way! Destroyed by the violence that enslaved many souls to build it! Terrified Haitians were running everywhere ignoring him, some even tripping and falling over his dust covered body. He then realized that many of these people were not trying to escape but were looting the palace and ignoring wounded and trapped people who staffed this massive palace. He lay there watching the spectacle of local natives fighting over riches they never dreamed existed in the clouds of rising dust. This scene reminded him briefly of the looting and destruction of so many French plantation great houses.

He watched as more of the palace structure fell into the large open foyer he was lying near. People screamed and as a new round of rumbling commenced. A sea of falling debris now crushed the swarm of looters and helpless staff alike. Ayiti crawled out the huge open palace doors and sat up at the front of the building inside the huge entrance. As he viewed the area, he noticed that many people had been crushed by the stone façade that was the front of the palace. Many people had been terribly squashed to death with mangled limbs sticking out from under the fallen stone blocks. Ayiti became amused at this spectacle and laughed out loud again. He was freed in the same chaos that had protected him for many years.

The destruction of this former San Souci "death camp" of thousands of innocent enslaved souls elevated as the jewel of the Caribbean was just! Ayiti realized that he was still the huge prize to Boyer if this iron dictator survived today! Ayiti had to leave quickly. After more stone blocks fell from the exterior walls he staggered, rolled, and crawled down a part of the front terraced garden which had seemed to be devoid of the many falling stones and other materials. On he crawled and rolled until he reached the wall above the immaculate cobbled circular drive. He found a small carriage with a scared horse still tethered to its post below the palace inside the very elaborate columned driveway. He untied the horse calming it with his deep stare.

By hanging onto the horse, he worked his way to the carriage and barely had enough strength to climb in it. This coach was one used by the local police to patrol San Souci Palace grounds. It seemed the Loa gods themselves had to pick Deschamps up and get him into the small carriage. He leaned back into the seat and let the horse take him where it wanted as he loosely held on to the reins. The horse guided Ayiti down the winding tree lined road near the coastline at a fast trot towards the town of Cap Haitian. The damage and fires caused by the quake were catastrophic and obvious as he saw the smoke as he worked his way into the town. The huge mob filled the streets.

It seemed that nearly every building was damaged or destroyed in the town as fires were burning from many structures. The aftershocks intensified as the smoke had become fog like in the main street. He noticed hundreds of local natives, hardened by forced labor and squalid conditions looting shops everywhere. He passed one huge mob headed for San Souci Palace and gave them a weak wave of his hand. The crowds became denser as he entered the main part of the freshly destroyed town. His carriage was at a crawl due to the mob packing the street. Some people were trying to take this small carriage from him. He was too weak as he kept them at bay with his buggy whip. He looked into the seat and found the hat of a policeman and then found a double-barreled shotgun on the floor of the seat. He was still bleary-eyed but managed to cock it and put on the policeman's hat. A shirtless man jumped up on the horse pulling his carriage facing him.

He was drunk and waving a bottle of rum. "Give me your carriage or I will kill you constable!" He yelled, pointing to the machete in his belt with the hand that held the bottle of rum. Ayiti yelled back. "I will give you this buggy for a sip of your rum!" The rather tall skinny looter nodded and leaned towards him handing him the bottle. Doc took a swig from the bottle, smiled, and pointed the shotgun directly at the man who gave a last astonished look. The shotgun blast hit him in the face and upper torso blowing him off the horse disappearing to the ground. At this sudden loud noise, the horse bolted, and trampled several looters before it cleared the main part of the devastated town street beset in total mob chaos.

Ayiti laughed out loud because this was fun! Finally, there was fun again! The rum had shaken up his spirits and was reducing the heavy effects of the drugs. He took another long swig from the near full bottle of rum. He was alive, free and he planned on keeping it this way! Once he left the town the horse, controlling the drive now slowed down and ambled over to a small white painted circular fountain on the street that ran in front of the huge beach area. The fountain was now broken from the quake, but still full of water. The startled horse began to drink. While the horse was refreshing itself, Ayiti looked around. He loved the beaches and the blue seas, but he then observed that the blue waters seemed to have greatly receded out into the ocean revealing sand beaches as far as he could see.

Then he noticed dogs and other animals running from the area, running fast into the jungle hills off to his left. What was wrong? The buggy horse's ears soon perked and pointed up into the air. Suddenly it began to pull the carriage away from the area where they had stopped. Taking hold of the reins Ayiti permitted the horse to lead. It was trying to pull the coach off the road into the steep jungle hills. Ayiti sensed that something very bad was about to happen. He forced the horse to stay on the beach road until he found a wide dirt path leading away from it and turned the buggy on it quickly. At this point the horse took off pulling the light small two-wheeled buggy faster than it had when they had left the shaking destroyed palace.

It climbed up the steep inclining path more fit for cattle at a very fast pace. Ayiti was bounced all over the driver's seat and fell back into the buggy as the horse recklessly fought up the long steep hill. Ayiti leaned up and looked from the side of the buggy. He saw the interesting sight of many animals of all sorts were running up into the hills. Wild and domestic animals ran together, both predator and prey moved in mass without incident. After what seemed like long minutes, they reached the summit of a large hill that overlooked the town and coastline. He watched the ensuing chaos from a huge hill that dominated the area as he let the tethered horse drink from a small stream.

He witnessed large clouds of dark smoke rising into the blue skies and huge fires burning throughout Cape Haitian below. He could see multitudes of people choking the roads. They reminded him of an army of black ants swarming everywhere over one of his screaming victims of old! But his ants were red. These "ants" seemed completely oblivious to the strange event happening in the ocean. Then an unusual spectacle caught his attention. He had glanced from the melee in the town to the ocean. He was fearfully amazed if he ever feared anything in his life. He saw a huge giant wave rolling across the barren bottom of the bay, and it was coming extremely fast. He instinctively looked down the path to ascertain if he had climbed high enough and then became transfixed as a two or three-hundred-foot series of waves crashed into the shoreline and into the city of Cap Haitian with more huge waves following in rapid succession.

The first wave smashed into the city completely inundated it. This was followed in rapid succession with the waves of the tsunami literally crashing over the buildings. He watched, as the city disappeared in the force of the waves. The army of ants, the fires, and massive wreckage completely disappeared in the massive froth generated by the huge killer waves. Then Ayiti observed the water crashing up the bottom of the hill he stood on. It continued to rise and rise up higher and a multitude of animals shrieked as they fought to climb higher. He took a long plug from the rum and watched, hypnotized by the unfolding disaster.

He would never know or care how many people were killed in this tsunami later recorded as an eight-point one surface quake. Estimates put the number somewhere between five-thousand to over ten-thousand people perished. Observers would say many more disappeared since there was no such thing as a census in Haiti in 1842. The death toll was in the thousands! The tsunami waves stopped some fifty feet below where he, his buggy, and hundreds of animals crouched and watched the destruction. The rising waters bubbling up on the high hills facing the ocean ebbed. He watched as the foamy waters now receded in great haste. Massive amounts of debris along with thousands of bodies were sucked into the ocean.

The thousands of drowned ants sucked into the ocean would offer great feast for the sharks. It would be fun to watch as Ayiti smiled at the thought! The rum and fresh air had seemed to clear his head somewhat of the drugs forced into his system by the voodoo adepts of Boyer. After another sip, he fell asleep in the buggy as the horse guided it to a small road leading from this area of destruction. Ayiti did not know how long he slept as the horse pulled him safety a long way from this area of death, destruction, and Boyer's henchmen!

The wedding a James and Jenny had been wonderful in every way. The group all sat beneath an open stone deck that comprised the rear of the large Farnsworth manor. The July 1898 day was warm and sunny, and a light breeze had kept the heat and humidity away. Those present were the Farnsworth's, their son and wife Horace and Annabelle, and James and Jenny. Lunch was over and it was time for serious discussion. Roger Farnsworth began. "Ambrose, I have been talking to Horace and we both agree that it would be a great opportunity for you and Jenny to help run our rum business in Jamaica.

Demand for our rums has been growing rapidly and you would be invaluable to the operations. We understand that your wound has cashiered any further active career in the military and that you have been relegated to permanent reserves. We could use a good leader like you to help run Jamaican Prime! Think of the great weather son." Ambrose Cavendish took a deep breath and looked down. He remembered well his status and his injury. He looked at Jenny and gave an attempted smile. She clutched his hand and gave her cameo beautiful smile. They were deeply in love. He then looked straight at the Duke. "Tell me more about this venture?"

The successful international entrepreneur gave a smile and spoke. "Years ago, I purchased several sugar plantations for the purpose of shipping sugarcane and molasses to the United States and other countries for many uses. Part of this was to be used to make a wide variety of rum in the West Indies markets. One day, I learned of some very old rum recipes from an old Jamaican rum maker who had retired from the business. As a matter of fact, I came into contact with him over the purchase of his own sugarcane fields that were next to a good plantation I had just purchased.

He made it very clear to me that if he had had proper financial backing that he could have made a great success in the rum market. He was an older gentleman and a widower. I tried some of his rum with Horace he had saved and it was marvelous! I hired him on the spot and he became my manager over the production of the fine rums I am beginning to sell worldwide. Even the British Navy uses it in their grog! However, this increased demand has increased production demands and company growth. This is where you come in son" My old Jamaican needs help!

Cavendish smiled as he remembered the bottles of rum Hook absconded from the destroyed officer's tent at Malakand. "Yes, I have had the pleasure of drinking it, and especially love the Jamaican dark brand!" Farnsworth continued. "You would be given the job of overseeing the production operations for our huge company and plantation in Jamaica, which would give Horace the chance to run the other affairs of the business. I think you both would make a wonderful team and Jamaica is such a beautiful place all year around. You will love it!"

Ambrose looked at Jenny and she replied. I think it would be a wonderful experience for us, to get away from the drabness here and to raise a family as well!" She gave Ambrose that "We are already doing this smile." Ambrose looked back at Horace. "Well old chap, I think you have a new partner!" Horace poured each person a shot of Jamaican rum and then gave a toast! "May we take the globe not by storm, but by our rum!" They all laughed as they drank the extremely smooth tasty rum. Ambrose learned back and reflected as he savored another shot.

He had studied the likes of Horace and Annabelle before with a humorous twist. Horace appeared as a gruff medium built man and strong personage behind a head which seemed larger than his body size. His well-trimmed lamb chops, a popular beard added to his manhood element. His beard surrounded a rather small mouth and delicate lips, as his delicate hands. He bore the air of a man who knew his job, his place in life, but possibly easily intimidated. He just seemed so well groomed and proper, like some storefront manikin. But he seemed very likable gentleman which was a good start.

Annabelle was a completely different animal all together! He did not use the word animal lightly. He chuckled to himself. She was a beautiful brunette with a long mane, extremely buxom, very talkative and bore the demeanor of a high-priced call girl. She had an unusual attraction to her beauty! These two were light years apart in looks, character, and appearance. Such voluptuous lips accented Annabelle's large dark eyes. Her female libido seemed to ooze out of every part of her tight summer dress as her huge nipples indented the front. Ambrose seemed captivated by her as many other men had. He loved his Jenny and never had any thoughts beyond a normal male admiration of sweet Annabelle.

Then he smiled when he thought of Horace and her together and wondered who controlled who? Cavendish had to admit she was a sight to behold. Her exquisite and fun character was not ignored. Ambrose was relieved to know she had a degree in business and worked hard as the office manager and accountant for Horace. Jenny wanted to work in the public relations and sales department, which was an excellent place for her. Horace and Annabelle were to return to Jamaica within two weeks as much had to be learned before Ambrose and Jenny were to follow in three months. Jamaica for Christmas of 1898 seemed interesting. The absence of damp cold weather and snow seemed a dream.

The 1842 quake and tsunami had had very dire effects on Haiti. It had destroyed so much of the already teetering infrastructure in the areas impacted by the quake and tsunami. Ayiti had returned to his secret hiding place after this disaster which had destroyed his wondrous prison at San Souci Palace. This disaster included so many villages and thousands of inhabitants had been killed and missing. As Ayiti had viewed, many were sucked forever into the ocean by the receding waves of the tsunami; food for sharks and orcas drawn to the scene.

Ayiti had taken advantage of the chaos to escape. This horse had warned and saved him from certain death. He ensured it was cared for by giving it to a trusted member of his voodoo church to keep safe and never to work again. He sat in the jungle hideout in an old rocking chair he had made long ago for Aunt Sarah. She had loved it. He missed her terribly now. His revenge and hate for Riochange was now replaced with his dark feelings for Boyer! Hate seemed to give Ayiti some sort of strength and purpose in his existence. Contrary to his respect for animals, he despised humans, especially the ones who got in his way. To him, they were puppets to be toyed with and bent to whatever will he desired, since he had the power to do so! In spite of his powers, this assumed Loa god needed to escape from this island of the damned now! He was severely outnumbered and his powerbase was gone.

It seemed the jungle was growing thick over this little hut, shelved from the world in a dense swath of virgin jungle. Like him, this place would soon disappear. He rocked back and forth in the chair remembering it's creaking sounds when Sarah used to sit in it. She would tell him great stories of the Loa gods and the exploits of the Voodoo masters of old. On his lap sat an old wooden box. He wiped off some wet residue and opened it. Inside was the detailed sketch of his doll; the familiar Sarah had conjured up and created for him under the guidance of the Loa gods. It was safe in Santo Domingo in a bank. If he had kept it in his mansion, he would have burned in the fire that consumed it.

The doll that must always be kept safe from all others according to Aunt Sarah! If it was hurt, so would little Ayiti. He rocked in silence holding the drawing of what his aunt had called his true "Achilles heel" if he ever understood Greek Mythology. He stared at the drawing of it for a long time musing at this little devil doll of straw with claws for hands and feet, of large horns, many eyes, and that gaping fanged mouth that seemed to smile forever. This was the exact likeness of what he transformed into; "Strawman!" as he was called by those few who had seen him. He then pulled out other keepsakes. He held the beautiful gold and silver inlaid stiletto he had killed many with!

He then pulled out the large gold signet ring with a family crest that matched the one on the dagger, adorned with many types of diamonds, rubies, sapphires, and emeralds. How this was missed on the headless body of the dead plantation owner he could not understand, but it was not missed by Ayiti! It was his! His wealth of jewelry, gold and silver had all been looted from his mansion before it was put to the torch! At this point, all he had was one ring left. He put it on his finger and admired its beauty. He then checked the two rolls of gold coins and sack of precious stones he kept in the chest. In case his accounts in Santa Domingo had been compromised, something was left to help him escape. Besides, there was more wealth in this world just waiting for him!

He soon fell into a long sleep since his near fatal ordeal had worn him completely out. The days passed quickly, as Doc Ayiti Deschamps finally awoke. He knew his days in Haiti were numbered. The reports from his followers confirmed that Boyer had survived the quakes. Many miles away, and for over two weeks, the secret police under the direct control of the thug Boyer had been combing the ruins of the San Souci Palace and the area looking for his body. It had obviously yet to be found so their search had expanded south.

The possibility that he was washed out to sea with thousands of others was ignored. Ayiti had escaped in Boyer's eyes and his circle of voodoo adepts confirmed this. These voodoo adepts were driven by abject terror of the Strawman being alive and free. They knew it would soon come for them and had to keep the story of Ayiti the Strawman alive so Boyer would relentlessly hunt for him! So, the intense hunt for Ayiti the voodoo king grew. Boyer shared in their collective terror for the revenge of Ayiti was as legendary as his abilities.

Good doctor Ayiti wondered of a new destination after he collected his wealth in Santo Domingo. He could go to Cuba, Jamaica, or any other place he thought would provide him safe haven. He needed to escape this cursed island. Cuba was controlled by the Spanish which reminded him of the French in Haiti! Cuba was out. Jamaica was actually close and seemed the right choice for now. His other stash of gold coins and precious stones had been secretly deposited in the main bank in this new country by none other than Jean Zombi before his zombie days and was assumed dead now. His bank safe deposit also included several new identities as well. All this was safe there for now. He needed to be far away from here and soon. He then pulled out two rolls of gold coins and small bag of precious stones his aunt Sarah had left him and put them along with the drawing of his familiar and other things into an old shoulder bag hanging on the shed wall.

He rested until late at night. Ayiti then walked through the darkness of a familiar jungle path to the top of a large tall hill. His night vision made it seem like day. He peered out into the dark jungle to the east as he then assumed the form of Strawman. He then shook out his wings as they flapped from his shoulders. It was so nice to be free from the voodoo drugs. Ayiti ran down the steep hill and was soon dancing in great joy on the tops of trees, a few roads and towns above the jungle. He ventured out of Haiti flying far above in the moonlight.

In the morning, after a good bath in a public beach area, he appeared at an expensive clothier in Santo Domingo where he began to transform himself into a respected medical doctor dressed in his finest tropical suite, with trimmed beard and a pair of sunglasses. He emptied his two deposit boxes of his recused fortune, his familiar, and papers. Ayiti then visited a top restaurant having lunch under his new identity of Doctor Emile A. St. Denis. Next to him was a large new suitcase loaded with over a million dollars in gold, jewels, and cash. He smiled to himself as he drank several tropical punches with added shots of rum.

He was now headed to a new island he had chosen; one he had heard good things about and a good distance from Haiti. It was alleged to be the island where his other Aunt Abigail was if alive. His new home would be a British crown colony called Jamaica. He finished his rum, for it was time to leave. He had never been on a ship before and the cruise would be a delightful experience to say the least! For the first time in years he felt like little Ayiti again, the little free spirit moving into a new adventure. An adventure whose ethos would have future terrible ramifications for many!

CHAPTER TEN
WELCOME TO JAMACIA

It seemed that the fanfare of the Cavendish-Farnsworth wedding refused to die down as several parties erupted in the months following the June wedding before their departure to Jamaica. The weather in England was exquisite into the fall. In light of the planned movement of the Cavendish's to their new life in Jamaica, both had accepted the gracious invitation of Duke and Mrs. Farnsworth to live at their estate until they left. It had been a great choice for many reasons. The first was that Ambrose had a direct pipeline of learning the organization and management of the Jamaica Prime Rum Company from Roger Farnsworth, and Jennifer had constant help with her rather obvious pregnancy. Jennifer was bearing a set of twins. It was now November 1898 and time to sail away to their new destiny of Jamaica was upon them!

Ambrose had taken to the game of golf with the elder Farnsworth and introduced him to the fun of skeet and trap. However, Cavendish refused any invitations to go on foxhunts and the like. Somewhere in his soul he had had enough of killing; killing anything. It was part of his soul now, cleansed by the village. He had managed to get Colonel Nephew interested in the game of golf, which offered this professional soldier an endless challenge. This game also served as a common ground with which to meet, play, drink, and converse on things.

The talk of the day was the war between Spain and the Americans. Duke Farnsworth was very interested in Admiral Dewey sinking the whole Spanish fleet ay Manila Bay in the Philippines in April and destroying the remaining Spanish fleet near Cuba nearly three months later. Just like the Indians wanted to rid the British from India, the Cubans and Filipinos demanded the same with US Support and success! Further interest was also discussed regarding the battle for San Juan Hill which occurred on July 1st. Of particular interest to Nephew and Cavendish was how the Americans tactically and offensively masked their Gatling gun fire on San Juan Hill to support infantry attacks on their main objectives.

It was rumored that the Spanish and their German advisors had used German Maxim 1895 machineguns against the "rough riders." However, there had been no hint of it in the battle reports. Nephew had accurately surmised that if machineguns had been used, the Americans would have definitely known it! The U.S. wheel mounted Gatling guns below the hills used to cover infantry attacks up San Juan Hill, was the first known tactical use of machinegun type weapons used in offensive operations. Colonel Nephew seemed impressed and cryptically saw this use as a grave foreshadowing to any future war in Europe!

Before his departure from England, Cavendish spent quality time with his parents in their farm estate up north. Jenny came the first time but was down with morning sickness and unable to return the next time. Tiberius then joined him on this next trip to the Cavendish farm estate. Ambrose noticed a friendly spark developing between his younger sister and Nephew. As the weather began to show signs of the approaching winter, 1898 was fast coming to a close. The farewell dinner and party were held on the 8th of November, with passage to Jamaica to commence on the 9th. Horace and Annabel were extremely excited for their arrival on this beautiful island.

The party at the ever-popular Farnsworth Estate was to begin with cocktails at five. True to the event all invited guests arrived on time. The days had been sunny and warm, but the emerging cold moving across the island nation was evident with the sunset. All fireplaces in the Farnsworth estate were burning bright warmth into the rooms as the guests arrived. Colonel Nephew, as usual, arrived alone dressed in a nice wool pinstriped double-breasted suite, cashiering his usual military dress for the evening. As Cavendish opened the front door, they shook hands. "Good to see you again, old comrade!" Nephew began. "Always a great pleasure my friend, looking like a good steel salesman once again?" Replied a very happy Cavendish, "Drinks colonel?"

"Only if we do a large shot of that poison you will be making somewhere in the tropics!" "Deal!" Cavendish slapped his friend on the back. As they finished their shots, and were sipping ale, Elizabeth Cavendish bounced up with her long blonde curls, blue eyes, and an extra tight corset that made her boobs press out exacerbating their unusual large size barely hiding her dark brown nipples, ready to pop out at any moment. "Hello My brother!" She smiled, kissed Ambrose, and hugged him. Then she locked her arm with his and smiled at Colonel Nephew. "Long time no see my dear colonel!" Ambrose got the silent cue. "Elizabeth, my sister, I give you Colonel Tiberius Nephew again, my comrade, brother in arms and fellow adventurer!"

Sister Elizabeth winked and gave a half-curtsy and rather large smile at the colonel. "It was nice seeing at your farm visit! I am sorry I was busy helping father in town for most of it." Tiberius gave a slight bow of the head and spoke to Ambrose. "So, you were hiding this very beautiful sister from me Cavendish?" Cavendish smiled and retorted. "I have been hiding her from you, secretly in a barn north of here for so many months now!" Elizabeth cut in. "Yes, it was terrible, I was shackled to the barn and forced to milk cows all alone!' She imitated squeezing cow teats with her fingers. Both Cavendish and Nephew laughed. Nephew had to comment.

"Such strong hands and technique you have developed my dear. I bet you are amazing to watch in action!" Elizabeth beamed a smile and continued. "Yes, dear friend of my brother, what talent I have developed!" She squeezed her hand into a fist, giving an alluring smile as she rolled her mirthful blue eyes. Ambrose added with a laugh. "It was hell trying to get her away from the bull! Such fun but no milk!" Elizabeth slapped him on the shoulder. "I see!" added Tiberius, "So we have a "bull milker in our midst" with us this night? How special!" She then squeezed his finger in her fist. "Do you want to know why that bull is in love with sweet Elizabeth dear colonel!" At this point, Ambrose surmised that these two had a continuing mutual interest and excused himself to check on Jenny, who was sitting on a large yellow divan across the room talking with other friends. He walked into the next room and sat next to his beautiful wife, who was showing a rather large stomach at this point. Jenny seemed like she was doing all right and was sipping a little champagne.

She smiled and kissed him as he sat down as he spoke. "Looks like Tiberius and Elizabeth seem to be hitting it off well. How do you feel?" Jenny smiled. "I hurt a lot earlier but am feeling better now, guess it must be the couple of glasses of champagne that helped. I feel so strange being pregnant with twins." Ambrose added, "Christmas and New Year's Eve in the tropics in 1898-99 will also be strange my dear. We embark on the good ship "City of Rome" from the Thames at ten in the morning sharp! Are you ready for the plunge into the colonies darling?" She gave her cameo smile. "Yes, oh yes I am! I am very excited as a matter of fact. I have never been there before and look forward to our new life, together and with a family on the way!"

Jenny had a tear run down her face as she looked into Ambrose's eyes. "I love you so very much!" He stared into her deep blue eyes. "I love you the same Jenny, we are a match made in Heaven rather than Malakand for sure!" The party was very cordial, fun, and actually reserved if one knew the wild bunch of friends that were on hand. It was a mere shadow of the previous grand wedding bash. Jenny turned in after dinner, and the party slowed down to cigars, pipes, scotch and cordials.

It seemed that the relationship between Colonel Nephew and his sister had grown sharply. It was the meeting of two very good comedians to say the least. They were continuously laughing about things and Cavendish even caught them kissing and holding hands. Like many of the other robust partiers, they were slightly intoxicated. Ambrose told his friend to spend the night. Elizabeth put his arm in hers and smiled at her brother. "Why how nice of you to offer this to Tiberius. I shall escort him to his room." The Farnsworth Estate Manor, was a huge multi-story ancient structure with so many bedrooms, even with all the out-of-town guests present, many rooms remained empty. As the night grew late, many went home, while a few others stayed up late to crash in the empty bedrooms. The maids and butlers would be busy cleaning up after the guests in the morning.

Ambrose climbed into bed and snuggled next to his wife who was awake. He held her until they were both asleep. Tomorrow would be the beginning of a new life. Somewhere in a spare bedroom, on the top floor, Colonel Nephew was walking from his bathroom to this bed when the closet opened suddenly and a ghost jumped out and grabbed him. It scared the hell out of him, as he jumped the "Boo Hooing" of the clinging sheet-covered ghost gave way to laughter as the voice under the sheet said "I am the ghost of the haunted bull milker!" Tiberius laughed as a slightly bombed beautiful girl with long blonde curls now appeared from the sheet. Nephew joined her under her long white bed sheet for a kiss and noticed that her bathrobe was open. It revealed the sweetest and most voluptuous gift of warmth he could ever imagine. He wanted in!

All the farewells had been delivered at the party and the Cavendish steamer trunks had previously been stowed on the City of Rome for the journey. Jenny and Ambrose bid an early farewell to their parents over a nice hot breakfast. Not even a mouse stirred as they left the Farnsworth Estate. It was a cold morning and the whisper of a rather good winter was approaching. The coach let them off after their arrival at a nice coffee shop adjacent to the dock area near their huge ship. The ship "City of Rome" sported three huge black stacks and was colored two-tones, with a black hull and white top. It was a huge well-built and sturdy ocean liner. It had been constructed as the fastest passenger ship of the day. Their journey was to take them to Santo Domingo and Cuba before their final destination at the port of Kingston Jamaica. Then this great ship was headed to New York.

They both looked forward to this as an adventure of their lifetimes. This was to be a grand fresh start, a completely new life! In the middle of the Atlantic a short but strong storm came up in the middle of the night, tossing loose furniture and things around in their dark cabin. Jenny awoke and was frightened, as Ambrose seemed to roll around as if in a nightmare trance. Then he began shouting things in his sleep as if he was re-living some bad moments, which seemed to be from India. He had never really talked in any great depth about his experiences in what he called "the jungle" with Jenny. She had only heard the general story of it at dinner that night with her parents, and short unemotional parts of it due to the bustle in their lives and the wedding.

He grasped his chest in pain and rolled on his side. She felt his head and it was covered in sweat. On he talked and mumbled until he was jarred awake by a huge wave that hit the bow of the ship. She held him in her arms and rocked him the best she could in her condition in the dark storm night lit by flashes of lighting. Then as the harsh waves seemed to clear, they settled back into sleep. The next morning, over tea Jenny looked him square in the eyes. "Darling, I think you had a dreadful nightmare last night and you were talking in your sleep a lot as if you were mired in a fierce struggle. You yelled out names like Ravi, Kali, Prya, Fucking Wadsworth, Hook, Griggs and others. You talked of a city you called Hima, and ancient one, where people you identified as shape-changers saved your life in some healing pool. Can you tell me anything about this?"

Ambrose looked at her with very strained eyes, like he was remembering another place, an event. He smiled a fatigued smile and opened his nightshirt. He placed her hand on his heart and looked at her. "Now Jenny, take your hand away and tell me what you see?" She did and looked close to his heart. At first, she could not tell anything, but then in a closer view saw a neat circular scar right on his heart and his chest hair was gone there. She looked at him in a fear and askance. "Is it a bullet wound to your heart? "He nodded in the affirmative. "I was shot through the heart and died." "But Ambrose, how did you ever survive this? Who shot you!"

"Colonel Wadsworth killed me with a bullet to my heart as I was trying to protect some natives in that jungle village, I briefly told you about. However, I never told you about this incident because I did not want to explain the real part of the village, an ancient secluded city where very ancient beings live, who saved my life." "Oh, my God!" stammered Jenny. She put her index finger back on the neat circular scar at his heart which she had never really noticed before now. Ambrose took her by her hands and spoke. "We have been very busy with things since my return Jenny. This was one of the reasons we never had a conversation about what really happened in India after Malakand.

Perhaps this is the best time to tell you everything that really happened beginning with the massacre at Chital and beyond. When I told you, I killed this monster Kali and I was telling the truth!" The general story I told your father was true. But there is much I have not told you or anybody for that matter my dear! "A massacre at Chital?" She queried. Ambrose put his fingers to her lips for silence. After a fresh pot of room service hot tea, poached eggs, sausage and rolls with butter, Major Ambrose Cavendish and Jenny dressed casually and ventured out to the side deck of the ship.

The seas were now calm and the air was warming. He told his story beginning with his killing of the Kali and then jumped back to Chital where this tale began. He did omit one piece of the story, which was about Pyra and his romance. He felt this to be just omission since Pyra was very special in his life and Jenny would never understand. It held deep love for Pyra, a woman who dwelt in his dreams lost in a fantasy world. He smiled as he thought of her now and was certain she had felt it. Jenny took the entire story in and asked many questions to clarify his statements. She was both awed and shocked at the truth surrounding what had happened in Chital and beyond, especially the actions and terrible death of Colonel Wadsworth.

She obviously found many parts of the story hard to imagine. Flying shape-changers who resembled giant cats, killing evil things in the air! She loved the stories of the city of Hima in the jungle and of Ravi. She even laughed out loud when he told her about the real fate of Color-sergeant Hook, keeper of the Bow Dogs. But the explanation of pure evil in the Kali completely mesmerized her. Although she promised never to speak of this, she insisted that her questions, in private, would continue. She said this with a smile. She again placed her finger on the bullet wound on his heart. This validated in her mind, all that her husband had told her.

They were now three days out of port and a nice walk on the deck spelled much warmer breezes to the point of some fine dining on the deck. The sunsets were magnificent and the dining proved both elegant and wonderful, when Jenny was not bed-ridden in pain. She was too sick to tour the port and city of Santo Domingo with Ambrose, but was full steam when they landed at Havana Cuba. They rented a two-horse carriage to tour and to shop. Cuban cigars were a paramount item on the list. They also looked at all the rum and other liquor products being sold and how they were displayed. Jenny already had ideas for this. Jamaican Prime products were evident in many stores and Ambrose tested several shots; some being mixed with juices. They were good and seemed an excellent refresher in the sunny warm climate of Cuba.

The beautiful greenery of Cuba reminded Ambrose of parts of that jungle north of that strange river in India. He shivered somewhat as his memory bank kicked up both good and bad memories. The rum seemed to settle his soul as they enjoyed the sun cast white beaches as they traveled on the road that separated them from the beach and jungle. Their liner docked for the night and they both enjoyed an excellent dinner of fresh grilled lobster and the wonderful strange new music offered by a very vibrant band. The next morning, the City of Rome signaled its departure from Havana harbor with huge blasts from its horns.

They would be landing in Kingston in the next few hours. They were both excited as they drank their morning tea on the foredeck. The warmth, the sun, the climate of the Caribbean had greatly lifted their spirits, and Jenny was feeling better. Their passenger ship docked at Kingston Harbor just after noon to view a throng of people waiting by the pier side against the backdrop of huge palm trees in the outskirts of the port area. The energy was very positive in the sunny warm day. The waters were crystal blue and the ship slowly edged up to the huge dock. Ambrose and Jenny allowed the initial throng of excited passengers to disembark and mingle before they attempted to leave the ship.

They had already made visual contact by waving at Horace and Annabelle from the tall deck of the ship, so when they left, they were easy to locate. "Welcome to Jamaica!" yelled Annabelle as they approached strutting her magnificent voluptuousness about with every curve in her body outlined in a tight long yellow summer dress. There were hugs and kisses all around, as they then moved up the pier side to a beautiful veranda overlooking the harbor. The huge palm trees and ambiance of the scene was breath taking to Jenny, who had never been in this part of the world before. In light of this, Horace ordered rum, pineapple and coconut juice for everybody. Jenny deferred to just the juice with a taste of rum since she was now very pregnant.

Soon, after, the steamer trunks with all their personal effects was unloaded, accounted for, and reloaded onto a couple of Jamaica Prime wagons by servants, the group ventured away towards the new home of Jenny and Ambrose. They all sat in an open carriage, leading the little caravan of two wagons up a steep hill away from the port and up a long winding dirt road mixed with shells for the twenty-mile trip east to their new home on the bluffs above Korset Bay, just south of the town of Whitehall, where Horace and Annabelle Farnsworth had their very excellent estate home. The plantation lands of Jamaican Prime were spread north throughout the Cedar Valley below the Blue Mountain Range. The climate and rainfall near this mountain range made the growth of sugarcane and coffee crops an excellent choice. Jenny and Ambrose would soon love such a beautiful view from their new home that overlooked a beautiful quaint bay with the combination of forest, beach and powder blue ocean making a beautiful contrast of green, white, and blue.

While Horace's workers unloaded their steamer trunks and other luggage into their new home, Jenny and Ambrose followed Horace to see this exquisite view. Horace and Annabelle took them to a nice quaint little restaurant down the road in a small coastal town nearby, on the bluffs overlooking the crystal blue ocean to dine. By late afternoon, the Farnsworth's dropped them off at their new place. Their house servants were a nice young Jamaican couple who had been employed by the Farnsworth's and now were there for the Cavendish's.

They were a very handsome couple and seemed to both have the mixed bloods of Africa, Asia, and native Indian in their genes. They were the Gaylords, both lighter skinned and extremely nice. Her name was Daphne and his name Tully. They lived in a comfortable bungalow with a barn and small farm right down the road close to this fine home. While Daphne continued working on helping Jenny put things away, Tully took Ambrose on a guided tour of his new home.

The structure was a long one-story ranch type house with a small cellar for emergencies. This new home had an incredible array of large picture windows facing the bay. The house had been completely furnished with very beautiful old antique English furniture including a complete silver tea service compliment of the Farnsworths. The interior of this home was built with a combination of bamboo, mahogany, with flair of English craftsmanship. The house sported huge doors that could be opened to allow the nice ocean breezes to inundate the structure. In the middle of the huge living room was a huge sunken circular fireplace with a large stone chimney through the roof.

This long house was huge, with much living space. The area facing the bay was a large wooden deck ending at a manmade rail at the ledge facing sheer bluffs that reached over a hundred feet to the tree line and beaches below. Ambrose loved this place at once, and had a nice weekend to relax in it with his beautiful Jenny. Tully was great and they got along very well. That night, Ambrose sat outside alone as Jenny slept, pondering his new life. As he sipped on his glass of dark rum and pineapple juice on the deck, he watched the sun set in beautiful orange and yellow designs over the ocean falling into night. So far so good he surmised. He would not miss the cold winter encroaching on his home island.

In the next few days, Jenny, with the help of Daphne and Tully shaped up their new home. In honor of this event, Tully cooked some incredible chicken and fish with a local spiced sauce. The four of them sat together enjoying the feast and drinks. Cavendish's gave kind words. "I would like to tell you both how special this dinner is and how you both have welcomed us not as employers, but as family." Tully replied with his cameo broad smile. "It will be an honor serving you, both Daphne and I humbly thank you!" "Tully, Daphne?" began Ambrose. "It is my great honor to have such great people in my service, and yes, you are now part of our family and if you ever need anything please let us know." He smiled as Jenny spoke. "Our home is your home and never forget this!" "Besides" added Cavendish, "you promised to teach me the art of deep-sea fishing Tully!" Tully laughed. "Yes Mr. Cavendish, they wait for us out there, so let me know when you want to start learning and practicing the art!" Ambrose patted him on the back, "As soon as possible!"

The sunset of the second night was another beautiful display. Ambrose sat again watching it from the deck with a Cuban Maduro in one hand and large rum punch drink in the other. Cavendish rested his thoughts on the humble honor of his friends in the ancient village. They had brought out something deep in him; a lesson. The lesson was never look down on anybody; treat them as equals and with respect, and never underestimate. Judge a person by the nature of their character alone and many from all walks of life will respect and befriend you! So many other walks of life in this universe have so many different shapes! He could almost hear Ravi verbalizing it while he was healing in the pool at Hima. How he had come to revere and love that ancient who called him his son!

Horace had given Ambrose more time to settle in before he was introduced to the world of Jamaican Prime Rum. Ambrose reported to the Farnsworth's beautiful mansion estate via a buggy driven by Tully the following Tuesday. It was named "White Hall" since it was near the rural town of Whitehall some ten miles north of his new home on a beautiful winding jungle road. He arrived at seven to a nice working breakfast with Horace and Annabelle. Whitehall Manor was a stately all white mansion, complete with elegant furnishings as if it had been plucked from the English countryside. After reviewing the planned first day events, they departed on a couple of well-bred horses for the short journey to the gates of the Jamaican Prime Estate.

The ride was a beautiful trot through more winding dirt roads amid beautiful jungle forests on both sides. Then, they came to a huge clearing and looked across a slow rise. Across a field saw the gates to the company property, which occupied the Cedar Valley against the backdrop of the beautiful Blue Mountain Range. As they approached the main entrance Ambrose could not help to admire the expertly manicured lawns and trees. The main office building was custom yellow brick and two stories tall with what looked like a crow's nest for observation on top. The out buildings were all tan in color, seemingly built with brick, rattan, and bamboo. It was right out of British colonial construction.

After Horace did some preliminary paper shuffling in his stately oak lined office, he took Ambrose on a mounted tour of the estate. He had explained that he purchased a huge parcel of land of his sugarcane from what used to be independent associates, who had always grown excellent crops. Horace brought their lands to add to his eleven thousand acres of cane. He had begun to include creating recent healthy crops of coffee beans. Coffee was his only diversification. Sugarcane production for rum was his game and life. After purchasing the lands, Horace had smartly hired most of the independent farmers because of their expertise in crop production. Horace had genuine respect of these farmers and they worked well together. Ambrose would soon enjoy this union.

Horace had told him that riding horses was the best way to get around and to view what was going on. He had already told Tully to pick out a couple good horses from his stable at White Hall for Ambrose's personal use. They were to be housed at Tully's barn at his little farm down the lane from Ambrose's new home. They rode lengthy circles around some of the cane fields admiring them. The cane was tall and they observed workers harvesting it by cutting it with large sharp machetes. It was then loaded in bulk on large carts pulled by oxen and a few old horses to be processed. They passed some rather ramshackle houses where the workers lived with their families. Little children ran and played with many very happy dogs. It was a sunny hot day when they finished the tour in the distilling and processing plant.

It was a grouping of large warehouses behind and to the left of the main building. Like the buildings in the front, the architecture of these distillery buildings was identical. Cavendish was impressed at the basic simplicity of the processing steps. The day passed swiftly. The next day Ambrose was introduced to the foremen that ran the distillery and overall plantation operations. He looked forward to this, like meeting with a new non-commissioned officer. A very well dressed stately old Jamaican stepped out of a one-horse carriage and approached them in the afternoon. He was "all smiles," as Cavendish noticed genuine smiles coming from Horace. They shook hands and Horace turned to introduce the elder. "Ambrose, may I introduce Joshua Marley, the great creator of the Jamaican Prime recipes, a former associate, and the gentleman who is my close friend and partner!"

Mr. Marley oversees the complete production operation and the inventory records, as you will. He was an inspiration to my father a few years ago and now is a key part of our operation. Ambrose extended his hand and shook hands with a very stately elder gentleman with a rich local accent. Horace continued. "Joshua was the gentleman who sold us most of this property to the west a few years ago, after he met and befriended my father. Then came his secret family recipes and the union was thus created!" Mr. Marley laughed out loud. "Yes, Mr. Cavendish, they got my property and secret formulas! All I got was a wonderful job I had dreamed of having and a bank full of cash!"

Horace slapped Marley on the back in kind jest. Ambrose smiled and spoke. "Horace has told me great things about you and I look forward to working with you in running operations!" Marley smiled showing his pure white teeth. "This will be great, for the company is expanding rapidly and your help is very needed and well received sir!" Horace finished and looked at his pocket watch. It was getting late. When Ambrose returned home, he found Jenny in bed. Daphne and her nanny named Betsy both sat next to her bedside. Daphne told him that she was having a very bad day with her pregnancy and that nanny Betsy had made a special tea to help her.

Jenny was asleep. Ambrose looked at his wife in the sprawl of a very large comfortable bed of white linen as he looked at Daphne. "What shall we do Daphne?" She smiled in the innocence of her very beautiful oriental accented face. "Perhaps Mr. Ambrose, we should have a doctor look after her. Tully and I know of a great young doctor not too far from here. He has a great reputation in helping many and could possibly help her." Ambrose thought for a minute; anything was better than seeing his wife suffer in this manner. She was some seven months into this pregnancy, and it seemed that her bouts were getting worse. "OK Daphne, get on it. I want to meet this doctor before he sees my wife!" "Yes sir, I will get him here, say tomorrow?" "That will be fine... and thanks."

Daphne smiled back as Cavendish left the room to fetch a nice cool drink. The day was over and he prepared for the third day on his new job as operations manager of Jamaican Prime Rum. He studied the business records and procedures of the rum business well into the night. The next day Tully gave him a ride by buggy to the Farnsworth villa for breakfast in the early morning which would be the new custom before the work day. He told Cavendish that he would have two fine horses stabled for him with by tomorrow. Tully also informed him that the doctor, named Emile Toussaint, would be at his home by early evening. Ambrose smiled and spoke. "Tully, make sure we have food and refreshments ready.

What is his expertise if I might inquire? Tully smiled back and continued. Doctor Emile Toussaint is a very sharp physician for his age, and hails from Santo Domingo originally. He is a great family doctor and seems an expert with children and childbirths. He brought my second child into this world. I think he will be able to help your wife." Realizing that he had little information on Tully and family he asked. "You have children Tully?" Yes sir Mr. Ambrose, I have two small children a couple of years apart.

I have a son who is five, and a daughter who is three. They are, respectfully named Jason and Clara. Ambrose smiled. "You never mentioned this, and I have not seen them yet." Tully laughed. "They are both very shy, and in time they will come out of their hiding to meet you! I have heard rumor that Daphne may be harboring another baby." Cavendish gave a good laugh at Tully's comment. No further words were needed, as they then discussed the art and science of deep-sea fishing.

Ambrose meeting with Horace for a short breakfast was to become a welcome daily pattern in preparation for the workday. It was welcomed companionship with cups of hot tea or coffee and a variety of foods. He had taken to love the poached eggs and bacon masterly served by Annabelle's housemaid. Annabel sometimes would join them for breakfast in a variety of revealing silk nightgowns that disturbed even the most protected desires! She was always at the rum estate by nine; ready to put in a good day's work. Their morning ride now on horseback to the company was exhilarating and cleared Ambrose's head as they rode up the winding dirt road shadowed by the immense trees of the forest.

When they arrived, Joshua met them at the front door of the office building. Horace spoke with his usual low accented jovial business monotone and crisp half-smile. "Good morning my friend. I once again give you Major Ambrose Cavendish of "Her Majesties Bengal lancers" to be broken on the wheel into this business. Be kind now and don't scare him away!" Joshua gave out a laugh. "Yes sir Mr. Farnsworth, I will be very gentle to this new man!" Horace continued. "I have a lot of work to do today, so why don't you two get acquainted on how the operations at Jamaica Prime Rum Company works." As the horses were led away, Horace entered the main office building as Joshua led Ambrose into the first large warehouse building.

Once inside, Ambrose remembered that this building was where the rum was actually bottled from the casks, corked up, and packaged for exit into the world of rum wholesalers, merchants, and the general public. After a few minutes in observing this, "Josh" as he was usually called, led him into a well-ventilated office. It was a large room. The smell of wafting cooking sugar constantly filled the air. It was pleasant. Cavendish saw where Josh had his desk and all his files laid neatly on a large table. He looked at Ambrose with an old smile and pointed to a place off to the left.

"We brought a large desk in here for you yesterday. We will furnish anything that you require. Where do you want to start Mr. Cavendish?" Ambrose thought for a minute then replied. "Operations Mr. Marley! Why not? Teach me how this entire place works from the cane fields to coffee fields, from harvesting, processing, packaging, and to market. The elder Farnsworth previewed the operation with me, but first hand is the best way to truly understand it. I am interested in the manpower as well. In this way, I may be able to help you tailor this operation to run better!" Josh Marley looked at him. "Mr. Ambrose, you are in charge now, and I am only to be an assistant to you. You need to make the decisions now sir."

Cavendish looked Marley squarely in the eyes and replied. "My dear Mr. Joshua Marley, I appreciate your kind consolidation of power to me, but this is not the way I want us to be. You are a far better expert on this production and trade than I ever dreamed of; respectfully. For me to take control over you today, is like giving you control over a regiment of Her Majesty's hardened veteran scouts with no experience in battle!" We shall work hand-in-hand every day, and we will carefully discuss any and all changes to this operation together sir. We will share all power and responsibilities together Mr. Marley! In sharing power, I mean that we individually use our respective powers to get the best results. How do you like them apples?"

Mr. Marley, the well-dressed honed gentleman in his seventies had not expected this reply ever from a white expatriate. He looked at his "new partner" and gave a warm smile before he spoke. "Mr. Ambrose, I never expected this and I humbly thank you. It seems that we of Jamaica have been so used to taking orders from our owners, employers, and former slave masters before the Emancipation Act of 1834, that it is a hard nut to break! Slavery officially ended here in 1838, but the framework still exists in effect for so many years after it seems. The only exception to this was the apprentices who survived and prospered out of reach of the corrupt plantation owners. Horace treated me in the manner as you are treating me. It is a welcome surprise indeed! Horace was not cut from this expatriate mold and respected and appreciated me as a professional. We shall do great things here!" Ambrose slapped his new partner on the shoulder and they shook hands firmly. "Josh, you call me Ambrose as I will call you Josh!" Major Cavendish was well aware of the negative and often terrible imperialist influences had in one country in particular claimed for "king and country! It had nearly killed him!

Both men sat across from each other at a long wooden table as a pot of steaming tea was brought in by one of the Asian workers. Ambrose remarked. "I see many Asians and a lot of Asian blood in the Jamaicans." Josh smiled. The Chinese began immigrating to Jamaica to replace the Jamaican labor force that moved into the apprenticeship programs between 1854 and 1870. Many apprenticeship programs failed. The lines separating the Chinese and Jamaicans soon became blurred. Someday, the bloodlines of China, Africa, Europe, and the natives will blend to create one race in my estimate!" Ambrose appreciated the information. "Imagine that Josh! The true death of racism at hand!" Josh gave a smile and a thumbs up as Ambrose remembered what Ravi had once said.

The future race of "Tan" was presented by Ravi while he was in the healing pool. He said, "In the future mankind will intermarry and blend into one race that will be tan in color; thus, the race of Tan! This blending of all races into one has happened before in past eons!" Cavendish now understood the tan Asian look in Daphne and Tully. Over the tea, they laid out plans to view how all operations worked. Mr. Marley first explained how the manpower organization was set up as Cavendish explained its organization in the military. Where Horace and his people were staff, Marley was the "field marshal" directly responsible for managing the operations and personal.

Josh and Ambrose began their tour at the processing plant and worked back to the cane and coffee harvesting operations. They later reviewed the compiled lists of all rum bottled or put in bulk casks for shipment back in the office. This accounting also included regular inventory of all rum filled oak barrels that were aging the rum. Under them came all the supervisors or overseers who managed the various parts of the rum process. Ambrose designed all the players in a chain of command diagram. Josh Marley had been doing an excellent job! They both reviewed the processing steps from field to the bottle, as Ambrose gave some helpful comments to change some of them.

Then came a visit with the workers a couple of days later. Josh gave Cavendish valuable information. "Before slavery ended, the overseers would routinely whip, torture, and even kill slaves for stupid reasons and even for sport. Today we use no whips or the like. We work as family Ambrose. All our supervisors or overseers have been promoted from the ranks of workers to these posts which I personally set in motion. They know, that only if they fail, a new overseer will replace them. It seems that they all respectfully have worked together with few problems."

On their second leg of the inspection, both rode horses into the cane fields. It was after eleven. Cavendish was still amazed at the large size of the sugar cane and the immensity of the fields. Josh pointed out how they employed the ancient European system of growing three fourths of the land while one fourth lay fallow and rested. By this, the soil was allowed to recharge from the elements. The size of the Blue Mountain range to the north greatly impressed Ambrose. The massive size and greenery of this topography reminded him again of another time and place in India. The hundreds of tall coconut trees and Palms seemed to stand guard around the massive flowing green fields of ripening sugarcane.

The terrain jarred Cavendish's memory of that jungle in the south of the Himalaya, that massif, and the horrors he would never quite be able to forget popped into his mind briefly. He gave a cruel smile of pride as he remembered he had killed that evil monster Kali; gone forever! These were better times now and life was good. Besides, this was Jamaica and not India! He pondered this as they walked out of the long rows of cane being harvested and piled on the large ox-driven carts for the crushers. They walked their horses into a worker's village. The children were running around playing and several dogs were hopping among them barking and playing. He looked in dismay at the dilapidated conditions of the huts and lean-tos.

He studied them for a few minutes then looked at Josh. It seemed that most of the workers went barefoot, as did all these little kids which was normal according to Josh. He looked at his new partner. "These folks need better than this Josh." "Yes sir, but nothing has been done to help them as they seem to accept these conditions. There are no complaints. It seems that life just goes on here without worry. Out of sight and out of mind Ambrose!" Cavendish nodded and asked. "Do any of these children go to schools?" Josh replied. "Some do at a small catholic school down the main road and many others just start working in keeping the mill areas in good order by cleaning up refuse created in the rum process. Others work in the fields when they are able."

Ambrose was lost in thought. He was revisiting the words of Ravi in ancient India again. He looked over to Josh and replied. "These people are employees of this company, and as a first operation, I want new dwellings, good ones built for these workers. Secondly, it will be mandatory that all children attend a school to learn the basics. If we do not have a school, then we shall build one. I had noticed a shed full of lumber and building materials in our initial tour of the processing warehouses. Rather than let it rot, we shall use it. How many of these little worker's communes are there on this property Josh?"

"There are ten spread all around this estate." Ambrose added. "We need to get on this soon. How about medical checkups? Healthy soldiers fight better than sick ones!" "Sounds good Ambrose, but what do you think Horace will say?" "Never you mind my friend, this is where I use the part of my power bargaining. I will get this approved one way or the other." We are a team together Josh, an army of rum makers under the banner of Jamaican Prime!" Josh gave a laugh as Ambrose then promoted him to "field marshal of rum."

Just then a few playful children came up to them laughing. They took the men by the hand and guided them over to a shed next to one of the lean-tos. Under it rested a mother dog and a couple of newborn blonde-haired puppies who had survived birth. They asked Josh if he wanted them. Josh nodded his head negatively and then looked at Ambrose. "Let's see Josh, if I am going to have children, then I had better have some puppies. Tell them I will get them when they are ready." The kids were then all excited. Ambrose looked at the mother and puppies, amid the squalor. They were two little yellow fur balls with closed eyes. Ambrose patted them on their heads. His family was beginning to grow at a rapid pace today.

They finished reviewing the operations and reported to Horace at half past four in the afternoon on Friday. Cavendish took the floor and explained his plans for the worker's houses, schools and medical help. He used the example that well housed, healthy, and educated soldiers made any military operations go much smoother. He talked about all the lumber he had found earlier. Horace seemed oblivious to these conditions, even though he was aware of them. He understood the point Ambrose had made but became insistent. "So, who is going to build these dwellings even if we have the materials?" Ambrose replied. "We can teach them to build sir, haven't they already cobbled together these shacks with frugal supplies? We can pace it out as we supply the materials.

I will direct them on my spare time sir. I also want a small schoolhouse and perhaps an adjacent medical clinic in the premises to educate these kids as well. No need to waste minds!" Horace then speculated. "So, we are going to build a community of sorts, with a school and medical facility?" "Basically! Horace, this company is not going to get smaller, but from what Josh sees, this company is going to greatly expand. We must prepare for the eventually of many more workers and families in our future sir. We take care of our people; they will take care of us. Believe me, I learned this first hand while in India from the best. It is an ownership thing from the ground up!"

Joshua added. "This would be a great plan sir, and perhaps this model will spread to other plantations across Jamaica someday and erase the squalid shadows of slavery induced structures that exist today!" Horace well understood his words and so hated slavery and the framework of this institution that still existed in Jamaica. Horace cracked a smile. "Slavery died here as an institution in 1838, and the life of it just goes on until something happens to change it down the road. This would be a positive plan I feel for not just the future of our company, but for Jamaica and its people in the long run!" Old Joshua gave a wide smile and loudly proclaimed "That is what I am talking about my brothers!"

Horace smiled at his old friend and Cavendish. "As long as this project does not interfere with our production operations; I am completely behind this. Start this project slow and keep it in a sound management level." They all smiled in mutual agreement. "By the way," interjected Horace, "I think this is an excellent plan, why I never even considered this upgrade in workers quarters! I was shortsighted to say the least! Good show!" The meeting concluded with shots of dark rum. It had been a good day of progress and with puppies in the mix! Ambrose and Horace rode back to his estate in very high spirits. Horace had told him that the demand for their rum was growing off the charts. It seemed that Lord Farnsworth had worked the rum into official label as grog with the Royal Navy as hundreds of barrels were headed to her majesty's navy!

He was now working at contracting more local cane farmers and especially looking at buying out more land. The Jamaican Prime rum Estate was growing into a global enterprise. They returned to White Hall manor in the late afternoon. The White Hall mansion was a huge white colonial structure complete with columns reminiscent of the antebellum south in America. Annabelle met them at the door when they arrived. She was her usual happy and extremely ravishing. It seemed to Ambrose that the entire libido in Jamaica had landed on her. She was a real looker, magnified in her very sexy revealing outfits. A lesser man would have lusted on her at the drop of a hat or more likely his pants!

Ambrose enjoyed the view of "sweet Anabelle" who seemed to flash lustful looks his way from time to time and loved to hug him tight at times in her form of hello! He had no interest in her because he was in love with Jenny. Also, it seemed that with a woman of this beauty, there was always a sign hanging on her which read "TROUBLE!" Mrs. "Trouble" invited them to a veranda on the side of the mansion to enjoy the view of well-manicured gardens that stretched to the jungle which led to the ocean. Drinks were served. White Hall Manor sat high on a hill overlooking the whole valley with the ocean accenting the backdrop. She sat across from Ambrose and Horace and began with a question.

"Well Ambrose, how was your day at the office? Has Horace driven you crazy yet?" Ambrose smiled. "Actually, he has not yet, and maybe you can protect me in case he goes wild on me after orientation." Horace added. "Yes Annabelle, once I have him completely trained, I will then put the shackles on him. Probably next week I would guess! Josh is administering the official beat down now!" He smiled at his wife as she continued. "Not your favorite bondage episode on your new foreman?" Ambrose rolled his eyes at the thought of a restrained Annabelle! They all laughed at her comment. She continued. "I hear that Jenny is having serious problems with her pregnancy. I plan on taking the day off of work and going over tomorrow and spending some time helping her and Daphne."

"Greatly appreciated Annabel." Replied James Ambrose. "I am supposed to meet a doctor Toussaint today, who was recommended by both Tully and Daphne as the best person to help Jenny." "Oh, yes he is!" Added Mrs. Annabelle Farnsworth. "I have heard that he has an excellent reputation and has a clinic in Kingston. I have never personally met him." Ambrose was happy to hear this. He looked at his watch and realized that time was slipping away. The doctor would be at his home in less than an hour. He excused himself and was soon on the road in a slow trot home. He was about twenty minutes away by a brisk ride. When he arrived back home after he had dropped off his horse with Tully.

He found Jenny sitting outside in the warm fading light of another beautiful warm day. She was in pleasant spirits as Daphne and Nanny Betsy were there having taken good care of her. "Hello darling Jenny!" She turned around and smiled as he kissed her. Soon, he was seated next to her saying hello to the others and enjoying the wonderful ambiance of the bay below. The doctor arrived at six. Ambrose met him at the door. He was a tall lean and very handsome light-skinned gentleman. Ambrose ushered them in and after introductions were made, they all sat for a nice dinner in the main dining room.

Doctor Emile Toussaint was an impressive man who seemed to be in his early thirties. His smooth mulatto skin betrayed no wrinkles. He spoke with a British accent and was a well-dressed gentleman by all marks. His large smile revealed a complete set of straight white teeth. He had been originally from Haiti, and as fortunes changed in Haiti, he ended up in Santo Domingo where he received a grant to attend medical college. He excelled in school and became a general medical doctor at the top of his class. Emile moved to Jamaica to be with his sister after his mother had passed on. Emile had been in practice for a few years now. Ambrose gave his personal biographical rundown to the doctor after hearing his. The doctor listened with great interest.

It seemed that he was interested in India as others were. Jenny told Emile how they met in the midst of the Battle of Malakand, and how they had planned their first date. Doc Emile laughed as she concluded. "And Emile, you are here today because of what happened on our first date! I just could not control myself with him, and you know the rest!" Emile smiled broadly revealing his white teeth. "Now, now Jennifer, do not be so harsh, look at all the good things about to come into your life!" Ambrose saw just how congenial Dr. Toussaint was, and concluded that he was the right man to help his wife. Once dinner was over, they sat in the huge living room.

Emile did not drink much and settled for a cup of hot tea. He loved the British tea custom. Ambrose had told him of what he had planned to do for the workers at Jamaica Prime and the proposed medical clinic. Emile was very impressed and added that he could assign one of his older nurses to staff it and more when needed. He would, handle the more serious cases if they occurred. Ambrose kindly accepted his offer. It was getting late and Dr. Emile Toussaint added. "I will be back tomorrow to give your wife a complete checkup and make recommendations. Daphne will assist me in this." "Sounds good and we look forward to your help and service!" With all farewells in place, the good doctor stepped out into the dark night and left.

Over the next two weeks Josh and Ambrose gave a complete bottom-up review and assessment of the operations at Jamaica Prime Company, "Purveyors of Jamaica's Best Rum!" Ambrose marveled at the very professionally simple but exacting method of how rum was produced. The sugarcane was cut at its roots in the field, then hauled to the mill where it was methodically crushed several times to glean all of the sugar juice from it. The crushed dry cane trash was used along with wood as cheap fuel heating the boilers, which produced steam to distill the rum. This heating process would be employed later to generate electricity which was becoming a standard utility on the island and planet at this time. The mass was then boiled, thus creating desired crystals and molasses, which were then separated. Sugar is created as a sellable product and the final molasses is pumped into the distillery to create rum.

Once the "dead wash" was ready through fermentation, the distillation process would be next. Jamaican Prime Rums used the ""continuous Still method." The steam applied to the huge kettles essentially created the vapor to make the rum. Finally, the rum, in its varying grades is stored in huge oak barrels for maturity. The barrels of rum, depending on the brand are aged for many years to produce the excellent taste. Ambrose was amazed at the size of the warehouses that housed the hundreds of rums filled in oak barrels. He was very impressed. Ambrose also learned how Marley added his own recipe to some of the barrels to make his special rum. He would add them before the barrels where closed with a large cork tapped by a mallet.

During this period, the first of the new dwellings were built in the little village under the supervision and help of both Josh, Ambrose, and even Horace who had fun. This project, inspired by Ambrose, seemed to create a close bond with them and the workers. The three men taught many workers the trade of carpentry which helped in the building. The workers appreciated this upgrade as a new village replaced the old one next to it. The puppies now had their eyes open and were trying to walk. Both Marley and Ambrose had bonded and grown very close in their work together. All final changes in operations were now noted and were to be presented to CEO Horace Farnsworth for his approval.

A new rum processing plant was being constructed to handle all the new sugarcane being shipped in for rum and sugar production from the distant plantations recently purchased. They were delivered in bulk by boat to the company docks on the coastline of the property. Meanwhile, Horace had just purchased another five thousand acres of cane fields adjacent to his properties and had contracted three other former associates to grow coffee bean crops on the other side of the property. The total land holdings, plus contracted lands now had grown to over thirty thousand acres beneath the majestic Blue Mountains. Christmas was only a week away, and everybody was in a great holiday spirit.

The main changes in operations based on the new growth in the company were easy to understand. It was of great importance to expand the building of new roads from the separate rum and coffee processing centers to intersect at a new main road in front of the company.

Josh and Ambrose had surveyed the path of this new main road, which would link the company to a better accessible road; some five miles straight from the main gate. In this manner, bypassing the usual winding road would save nearly two hours in travel time into Kingston Port and all markets. The other plantation owners affected by this new road concept liked this idea as well. Plans and funding would soon be in motion on these projects, as the other plantations would split the costs to build the main road.

Dr. Emile Toussaint had returned as promised the day after meeting Cavendish. He determined from his medical checkup that Jenny had nothing wrong with her except a hard pregnancy. He had found out from her, that "bad pregnancies" were common in her family history. He had given her some medication to quell the bad moments. He had returned twice to check up on her and had told her that her children would be born in the house unless she traveled to the hospital in Kingston. Jenny declined that offer. The dark tea brought by Nanny Betsy was a godsend for Jenny. It greatly helped relieve her terrible cramps and morning sickness. Jenny had asked Daphne about it. She replied that Nanny Betsy was a very gifted lady of the old religion and this concoction was her favorite medicine for morning sickness.

The estate operations were closed for the Christmas Holiday so the many workers and families could enjoy the holiday together with many in new dwellings. Prior to Christmas Eve day, Horace, Josh, and Ambrose, brought enough chickens for all the families on the plantation estate. He wanted them to have a great feast on Christmas. The chickens were cooked over open fires in spits and smelled heavenly to Ambrose. Horace had made a significant contribution in rum and other sundries for his people. The workers were all dressed in their best clothes and the festive activity was true enjoyment throughout the Jamaican Prime Estate. The dancing, singing and loud drumbeats were obvious throughout the greenery of the estate.

While Ambrose inspected the new dwellings at his first village, the head villager, and overseer surrounded by many children approached him. "Mr. Ambrose" began the headman and a plant supervisor using the name Cavendish liked to be called; "We want to thank you for the great things you are bringing to us. Out of this gratitude, we give you our Christmas presents!' Two little smiling children stepped forward and each carried a golden-haired puppy. Ambrose beamed a great smile. The head man said "Thank you from me, my family, and our village!" James smiled. "Now each of my children will have a puppy to begin life here!" The headman bowed in respect and they shook hands.

Before Ambrose left, he handed out a bunch of hard candy to all the children. As they walked away each holding a happy puppy, Josh spoke. "Ambrose, it looks like you have made a lot of friends in your time here, and I can visibly see how hard they work now; because they work for you, me, and Horace. They know someone cares for them." Ambrose smiled back at his friend. "My treatment of these fine people is based on the advice and conduct of a better man than myself!" He smiled in remembrance of his mentor Ravi and others of the mysterious village.

Christmas in Jamaica was a great time and everybody received an abundance of gifts. The two puppies took center stage. The Farnsworth's held a grand Christmas party at White Hall for friends, as was their tradition on Christmas Eve. The mansion was crowded with friends, local politicians, and members of his company staff for a great party. Even Dr. Toussaint was present. Jenny, because of his and Nanny Betsy's help, was able to be at the great celebration. What a different Christmas than England she surmised. Instead of freezing in snow storms and damp weather, she sat outside on a veranda admiring the beautiful landscape of the enormous gardens behind the estate, kissed by a setting sun which illuminated the sky and ocean waters in exploding orange and golden hues.

Ambrose clasped her hand and kissed her on the cheek. "This weather is pure frozen hell! We need to go back to London!" She squeezed his hand and smiled. The torches were being lit throughout the huge garden and on the steps of the four staircases leading to the beautiful estate gardens and walkways into the forest. Dinner was served as a huge smorgasbord of nearly every kind of native seafood, chicken, pork, and beef. The food was excellent in all respects. Unlike the late partying of old, the Cavendish's bid farewell to Horace, Annabel, Josh, Dr. Toussaint, and others as they left for a nice open carriage ride home around ten. Tully and Daphne had come with them and now returned for the nice evening ride home. They were greeted by nanny Betsy upon their return.

Tully and Daphne had become so special to them, and to show it, Ambrose and Jenny were giving Tully a brand-new fishing boat complete with all new rods, reels, nets and the rest of it. Josh had been instrumental in helping Ambrose select the boat and all the gear. He made Ambrose promise to take him fishing! As they enjoyed a nightcap Ambrose smiled at his friend and laughed at the note, he handed him. It read. "This is your boat Tully and such a fine choice by you; Merry Christmas! It is you that now must promise to take me, Horace, and Josh fishing!" Tully was floored and speechless after he read it. Daphne then emerged carrying the two puppies wiggling their tails and soon licking everybody.

Jenny, as the rest had fallen in love with these two little creatures that seemed to look more like Golden Retrievers every day. Once out of their formal clothes and into relaxing ones after the gaylords left. Ambrose and Jenny loaded them up with many gifts for them, their kids, and for Nanny Betsy. They sat outside watching the bay below and the half-moon reflecting off it. The millions of stars and mild sea breeze accented this wonderful night. They saw a few fires on the beach far below the bluff amid the faint echoes of the distant drum beats. Cavendish had asked Tully earlier what they were. Tully added that "Jamaicans celebrate Christmas with a blend of both Christian and African beliefs. You are witnessing these rituals that will last well into the night." A flash of the green devil's fires in the huge valley and their silent standing in long rows crossed the Major's mind. He quickly returned to the present.

Ambrose fetched some refreshments and returned to where Jenny was sitting outside. The puppies were fast asleep, piled together on a large comfortable rattan couch in the main room. She had a pineapple juice with a hint of dark rum, and he had one with added juices to make a punch and shots of white and dark Jamaican Prime Rums. She looked at him and kissed Ambrose on the lips as they sat in a Rattan love seat. "Ambrose, this is our first Christmas as man and wife and the best Christmas I have ever had, and I love you!" "I love you as well darling!" She laughed. "I wonder how warm it is in London?" Ambrose, looking at the torchlight activity far below on the beach laughed back. "I hear that London is in the storm of the century now!"

They ended the night peacefully climbing together into bed. Tully returned the next morning and invited Ambrose to go on their first deep-sea fishing expedition the next day. After all, the note Ambrose gave to Tully on Christmas Eve further stated; "If you like your gift located at # 7 boat dock, then you must take me, Josh and Horace fishing as soon as possible!" Besides, the estate is closed for the next three days." They had taken his new fishing vessel out the day after Christmas to break it in. Josh had joined the group. They had caught several good fish including a Marlin, two Grouper, and swordfish. Captain Tully was at the helm as Ambrose had christened him Captain by giving him one of his extra billed military hats. Another fishing trip was already planned.

After a long and painful labor, Jenny gave birth to a beautiful pair of twins at dawn on February 16, 1899. John and Beatrice Cavendish were extremely healthy babies and came into the world under the professional care of Dr. Emile Toussaint. The sun came up to find Jenny sleeping with sedative, and an extremely exhausted little party of helpers. The warm sunny morning was beautiful, as Ambrose prepared a nice breakfast for Emile, Tully, Annabel, and Daphne, who had borne the brunt of the nearly ten hours of labor. Nanny Betsy watched the children.

Horace had given Ambrose the week off to ensure all things went well. Josh could easily run the show. After breakfast, he let the doctor bed down in a spare bedroom as Daphne, revived with a good breakfast of poached eggs returned to her watch. Annabel soon recovered and sat with Daphne to help attend to Jenny and the newborns. The puppies played with a newly discovered litter of kittens in the shed. The Cavendish family was now a crowd!

Cavendish was too exhausted to even talk to anybody after the birth of the twins. He was lost in his new world of children, puppies, kittens, and Jamaica Prime operations. He sat out in his favorite rattan love seat on the deck enjoying the warm breezes and waiting to help his wife. He was awakened three hours later by the gentle licking and pawing of his golden colored puppies and three kitten tagalongs. The puppies were a male and female aptly named "Alois" and "Victoria." They would soon follow him everywhere when they weren't intrigued with kittens at play. He fetched a fresh cup of tea, as the house was now completely quiet. He was feeling a little better now that he had slumbered with his wonderful puppies and three kittens piled in his lap. The six kittens would soon bear the names of his scouts.

Since Christmas many things had happened in this new year of 1899. The organizational projects were going ahead of schedule. Josh and his personal leadership with the workers and born very positive results and many positive changes. The roads around the production facilities and main road had been widened and were now being covered with crushed seashells. Most of the worker's dwellings had been built. Many of the workers had learned basic carpentry from Ambrose and Horace and had given remarkable help in the construction of these new dwellings. The coffee and rum processing centers were becoming completely separate production centers, and business was booming. Life was great for all!

Everything seemed perfect in this magnificent paradise as James Ambrose reviewed his life one day while walking in the jungle. It seemed as if a decade had passed since 1897, yet it was only Spring of 1899. Ambrose could not believe all the events that had transpired for him since that opening salvo at the Battle of Malakand July of 1897. He was amazed at all the events that had occurred. He felt he had been aptly blessed in this world now. His mind, on occasion drifted back to the horrible events in that jungle valley but rested positively on wonders of the Village and to Pyra. He told her he loved her with a smile on his face. Later, he felt hers and soon saw Ravi's. His bond with the shape changers was complete and forever.

It was September of 1843. Ayiti the refugee; now Doctor Emile A. St. Denis under his new identity, was enjoying his travel by ship from Santa Domingo to his new life in Jamaica. He had been landlocked on that hated island Haiti for centuries it seemed! So long he could not remember! The calm peaceful boat trip from Santo Domingo, to Jamaica via Cuba seemed a very peaceful way to settle into his new life of chaotic schemes in a new land.

Doctor Emile St. Denis was greatly enjoying the cruise until he noticed there were some strangers observing him after his ship left Cuba. They carelessly followed him as he moved from the decks to the dining room and to his room. He had left Santo Domingo with two large suitcases. In one he had meticulously hidden all his important information in the linings of his suits and suitcase. He had hidden a small fortune in the other suitcase. This trove included rolls of gold coins, and bags of precious diamonds, rubies, and emeralds looted from the unfortunates in Haiti over the years.

He had been accustomed to escaping quickly from danger and had unconsciously done it this time. He had used the names of St. Denis and another as his cover and to protect his bank accounts in Santa Domingo. He had also used this second alias of John Phillip Thierry with complete documents to rent the room next to his and also had it on his bank accounts. He had placed his suitcase full of his wealth in the spare cabin. He sensed who these people were working for but would find out personally and soon before port in Jamaica!

He carried all his new identity papers and passport on him at all times. His name of St. Denis was on the ship's passenger manifest. When he returned to his cabin, someone had carefully gone through his suitcase. A fine string, he had attached across the opening was broken. He smiled the first evil grimace of his trip. He checked the other cabin and his things had remained untouched. He would find out tonight who these people were and figured that sooner or later they would come for him or at least question him. So, he played the part of the leisure casual tourist, oblivious to his trackers, wandering the ship's salons, eating dinner, and walking the decks.

Three men finally approached him on the aft deck. One of them was brandishing a pistol. "Mr. Deschamps, I presume!" Uttered the lead stranger in the group, illuminated from the shadows by the light of a full moon. Ayiti smiled at them noticing all wore very ill-fitting suits. "I am afraid that you are mistaken, for I am Doctor Emile St. Dennis, a doctor from Santo Domingo on a vacation to Jamaica to visit some friends!" "Move along peacefully with us!" spoke the man with the pistol aimed at him. "Why of course, I want to clarify to you who I am so we can dispense with this investigation!" Ayiti already had recognized the face of the first man. They were Boyer's people!

They led him downstairs into a secluded part of the ship, into a room adjacent to the ship's engines. The only window in this empty room was one circular window with a large latch. When he walked into the room, he saw two other shapes sitting in some chairs. "Please sit down here!" Said a man pointing a chair separated from the other ones. Ayiti sat down quietly and waited. He counted five men and mused at them. "I guess you must be Boyer's goons coming to fetch poor Ayiti?" No one answered him but a kerosene lamp now exposed these others.

He immediately saw the head voodoo adept, Boyer's voodoo king and his chief tormentor! The other was another powerful voodoo adept who spoke! "We do not want you to miss you private burning and complete dismemberment with Dictator Boyer!" He then cackled a grunting evil laugh and holding up a syringe of potent voodoo drugs. The first man he had recognized on the deck was the cruel unsmiling and murderous head of the dictator's secret police.

This professional killer showed no emotion as the voodoo man again cackled at him. "Little Ayiti Deschamps, you are very missed by President Boyer. Why he was so afraid that you may have been hurt in the earthquake! We meet again, one last time Ayiti! Since we who survived the quake never found your body, had to put our special powers into effect to find you. Here we are to end your evil demonic reign of terror!" The chief voodoo adept added.

"Now you have become the refined Doctor Emile St. Denis? Did the tsunami change you? We could not find you Little Ayiti anywhere! We were so sad you had died? Boyer cried! But alas! We discovered your whereabouts after your surprised entry into Santo Domingo! Here we are together again in great reunion! Let me introduce Officer Ian Peacock who joined us in Cuba, the liaison for the Jamaican government." The young clean-cut uniformed officer stepped from the shadows and tipped his hat. The voodoo priest continued. "Boyer personally wired this consulate to tell them he wanted you back for murderous crimes and execution. So, this is your fate now my "Little Ayiti Boy!"

They all laughed as two henchmen bound him to the chair with rope as a pistol was aimed at his face. "When we land in Jamaica you will be held for immediate return to Haiti for trial and execution by public burning only after we give you a special long and painful sendoff party!" Ayiti then looked at the young Jamaican officer. "Mr. Peacock, did it ever occur to you that it is Boyer who is the murderer, and I am but a simple person who opposed his terrible suppression and murder of many innocent Haitians and escaped his evil?" Peacock retorted.

"We Jamaicans are well aware of the transgressions and reputation of Dictator Boyer, but this is out of my hands sir! It seems that a huge reward has already been paid to certain Jamaican officials for your return. I am sorry." Then Ayiti's gaze shifted over to the Doctor Franz, another voodoo tormentor who had something in his hands. It was Ayiti's sacred familiar voodoo doll, taken from his bag. He cursed at his carelessness for he had somehow missed its disappearance from his suitcase! He should have hidden it better; in the next room he had rented. The voodoo man laughed as he pulled out a long sharp needle.

"Ayiti, little Ayiti? I have your life in my hands now!" He then stuck a needle into the side of the doll's head and in sudden great pain, Ayiti fell tied to the chair to the ground squirming and yelling in pain. For the next twenty minutes the voodoo man pierced the doll with the needle driving him crazy with pain. Peacock ordered the voodoo man to stop it! He finally did after a couple more jabs. An angry disgusted Peacock helped Ayiti off the floor as he was moved in the chair to the dim lighted corner. Blood flowed from multiple places on his face, head, body, and groin where the doll had been pricked with the needle.

Ayiti was smiling however. These idiots had been used to torturing him in a very sedated state and had forgotten his powers which were fully restored. Only that syringe of voodoo poison could stop him and this would not happen! He prayed that these voodoo amateurs were stupid and did not inject his familiar with the poison! His tormentors were fearful and no one in the room wanted to really touch him or search him. The "Boyer" voodoo chief ordered his two henchmen to put a sack over his head. The voodoo man continued sporadic needle poking the doll making Ayiti winch in pain. Boyer's chief of the secret police began punching Ayiti in the face cloaked under the cloth sack on his head.

Ian Peacock knocked the thug chief out cold with a hard-right hook to his head and turned to the voodoo leader in front of Ayiti. "If you do not stop this violence on this helpless man, I will personally protect him without any of you until we get to Jamaica!" The henchmen drew pistols on the constable as the leader talked. "You have no clue how evil and dangerous this creature is constable Peacock! If you only know what he did! We promise we will leave him alone for Boyer! But you go!" Constable Peacock left in disgust, but he did not like the vibes in this room. He went to the bar to calm his nerves with some drink. Meanwhile Ayiti now sat motionless as if in a death trance under the sack which covered his head.

Boyer's henchmen stood with their pistols trained on him as the chief voodoo priest approached him and deftly plunged the poison filled syringe into his neck emptying it with a cackling laugh! He stabbed the needle into the seated Ayiti as he yelled each time it was pierced! Tiring of this sport, the voodoo king stuck the syringe into the neck of Ayiti! When he plunged the needle into the neck of Ayiti, his body felt very light. The voodoo king pulled the burlap bag from Ayiti's head and viewed a perfect wooden dummy head like a puppet!

The jaw of the puppet moved said "Ouch! Ouch!" The voodoo master never realized in the shadows of the hold that he just injected a large puppet with his valuable poison! Ayiti had created a likeness of himself in the chair with the sack over his head as the Jamaican constable had accidently run interference for him. He had removed himself into another corner of the room behind his tormentors throwing painful noises from his doll to keep the tormentors occupied. There, all his hate, venom, and anger manifested into his demon form.

Strawman needed to rescue his familiar from harm's way first! He edged towards the voodoo master that held his doll. He was to die first, but carefully first. After all, He held Ayiti's life in his hands according to Sarah his beloved aunt; something about his "Achilles Heel." His quick approach to Boyer's voodoo chief went unnoticed until he was within inches. Strawman came into view as the tormentor shrieked in terror after seeing the exact image of the doll he was tormenting! Boyer's voodoo master now stabbed at the doll with a sharp dagger. In his haste, he missed the kill shot and plunged the dagger deep into its right ankle.

Before Boyer's voodoo adept could correct this mistake, Strawman ripped his head from his body and tossed it against the wall as his life blood squirted from the stump of his neck into the air. Strawman grabbed his familiar and the knife from the now dead Voodoo adept. In one neat throw, he stuck its tip deep into the throat of the henchman standing at the door. Strawman was staggering in a terrible pain from his ankle as he attacked the three other men turned in his direction and began emptying their revolvers into Strawman with little effect.

Within seconds, the Strawman slashed the next goon across his neck with his tail decapitating him in one swift motion. It now blocked the door trapping his two favorites. Next came the chief voodoo adept and his main tormentor. He grabbed him by the shoulders and completely chewed his face off down to his skull. He tossed him shrieking into the wall. The chief of the secret police had reloaded his pistol and again emptied it into Strawman with no effect. The Straw monster grabbed his face with its talons and deftly tore his face off leaving him screaming in agony. The police chief screamed as Strawman punched his talon through his stomach ripping out his intestines! In seconds it had the faceless man by the hair and seat of his pants. The man was screaming in terror as his guts dragged on the floor. Ayiti grimaced a fanged smile as he saw the small circular window.

The small circular window was open and was a decent fit for one's head and part of their torso as wide as the collar bones! With superhuman power the Strawman rammed the police chief forcefully through the window punching his body out and into the ocean tearing his shoulders and arms off as part of his entrails draped from the bloody window. He picked up the lifeless face of the police chief he had cut from his head and smacked it on the wall spattering blood from it. He grabbed the severely injured head voodoo master yelping in terror and sent him into the ocean in the same manner he had dispatched the chief.

Strawman stuffed the remaining body parts of his former tormentors of Boyer into the Caribbean in glee. The sharks would have a nice surprise feast tonight thanks to Boyer! He was covered in blood as he reanimated back into Ayiti. He was in great pain from the stab wound to his ankle and from the pin pricks from Boyer's very dead Voodoo king of Haiti! he limped over to claim his familiar which he had put in a corner. To stop the oozing holes in his body from the needle pricks he figured that he would need to mend his doll. He would try to fix the partially severed ankle as well.

He had to get off this ship, in Jamaica but not at his original point of disembarkation at Kingston. The Jamaican authorities would be on his trail for sure since there was a Jamaican constable on board to escort him. He calmed from rage after he changed back to his handsome form of Doctor Emile St. Denis! He had to think calmly now! As he changed his form and reconstituted his body his calm returned. When he was Strawman? He was a wild demon! His injured leg bled as did the injury inflicted on his doll familiar.

The ship was due to dock first in the small port of Montego Bay with its final destination at Kingston. He had a fresh plan for Peacock. In his search of the remaining three bodies in the hold, He had found another syringe filled with the same powerful drug on the headless other voodoo adept. It was like the one injected by the head voodoo king on his dummy form. Their arrogant underestimation of him was their end! Ignoring the rest of the carnage in the room, he left after putting his doll in his coat pocket.

Returning to his cabin Ayiti cleaned himself off in the sink in this room and put on fresh clean clothes. Thanks to Sarah who taught him sewing, he carefully patched up the holes in his familiar stifling the blood flow from these small wounds. His ankle was another story so he wrapped it but had to limp from the pain. He then began to search the ship for the Jamaican constable. He finally saw Inspector Peacock standing at the bar drinking. The bar was very crowded, so he slouched his Panama hat over his face and asked the bartender what Peacock was drinking.

He ordered the same drink. When the bartender turned away, he slipped some of the voodoo potent from the syringe into the cocktail. He stirred it until it mixed with the contents of the drink. Then, pretending to have an afterthought, told the bartender to give it to the constable compliments of Dictator Boyer telling him all was calm below. It was delivered and the grateful Peacock consumed it as he looked for his benefactor. Ayiti ordered himself a whole bottle of dark rum and left. Rum always seemed to relax him.

A very clumsy drunken stupor soon invaded the Jamaican police inspector after drinking only half of his cocktail. He collapsed and would be out for a while; long enough for this ship to dock in Montego Bay and for Ayiti to escape. After he left the bar, Ayiti, or doctor Emile St. Denis for a little longer, went to his room and secured his suitcase. He then moved to the empty room next to his and waited. He had taken and reloaded two pistols he confiscated from the deceased police henchmen. He spent more time mending his doll with thread from a sewing kit in the cabin. Each time he pierced the doll with the needle he winced in pain. The damaged ankle was reinforced but only partially fixed. He still had a limp; but the oozing black blood had stopped. The ship was to dock in an hour now.

Meanwhile, Inspector Peacock had been completely disabled by the strong narcotic and had been returned to his cabin. Peacock would be found in a comatose state lying unmoved in his cabin bed by the Jamaican constables upon the ship docking in the port of Kingston a day later. He would recover consciousness until three more days passed in the hospital. Meanwhile, police officials would be shocked and confused by the gruesome evidence left in the hold room below deck on the ocean liner. The bodies of three gruesomely murdered Haitian officials and massive blood trails covered the floor of the hold room. Two others were missing and somehow had been stuffed out a small circular window into the ocean.

Doctor St. Denis, the man apprehended by the Haitians for extradition, was missing. It was noted that a terrible super human force had squashed the bodies through the small circular cabin window like a meat grinder. Then, in the blood splattered on the walls shockingly, the remains of a man's face mixed in the blood was found stuck to the wall over the window. It was like a mask; the face of the Haitian secret police chief! Inspector Peacock would not be privy to any of this information until he had fully recovered.

Ship records revealed this Doctor Emile St. Denis from Santo Domingo had a destination to the port in Kingston. This terrible incident was over two weeks old when Officer Peacock fully regained his senses. He then was able to review the evidence in the grisly aftermath. He knew that this fugitive was Ayiti Deschamps and was responsible for the horrible murders of five men. The trail for this strange and dangerous man had grown stone cold! Since Montego Bay was the second to last stop, it was the only possible landing place for this fugitive. Peacock was amused since he, like the other Jamaican officials involved kept the reward money given to him. In spite of the objections raised from Boyer's people. His problem was obvious; Ayiti Deschamps was missing in Jamaica!

It was the start of another beautiful day in December of 1844 at the two-hundred and ninety-acre plantation of Rose Hall Manor. The ageless dark-haired beauty Annie Patterson Palmer sipped her tea on the large open veranda at the rear of her huge home overlooking the ripe green cane fields as ocean waves which pummeled the white beaches beyond. She loved to watch her slaves work, and play. She immensely enjoyed it when they were beaten and sometimes tortured by her hand selected overseers. She always kept her face partially covered to confuse her identity to the public for reason. Her interaction with the public was very limited, but her unfortunate workers dubbed "slaves" knew her well!

Many "slaves "as her lovers had endured and succumbed to her evil designs. Today she calmly searched for a new lover in the bright sunlight. She was hungry for a young woman this time. It was a common myth throughout the region that Rose Hall was rife with ghosts, evil monsters, and the undead. The workers and overseers lived in abject terror when she was present. If she showed a fancy in any of them, then their days were numbered. They disappeared once in Annie's grip. She was known to all as "The White Witch of Rose Hall." The Emancipation of Slaves in 1834 may have ended slavery as an institution, but in practice, it still existed in certain places. Rose Hall was the worst example. Annie Palmer had a special persuasive dark talent for keeping her people in her fold.

Her three husbands had experienced mysteriously deaths attributed to sickness, insanity, and extreme drunkenness. Her last husband, the late John Palmer died in in 1827. But the tales of their deaths seemed otherwise. The stories of her few surviving house servants that had escaped Rose Hall bespoke of an evil terror which dominated Rose Hall's great house. The appearance of apparitions in the fields of the three-legged demon horse and the "Rolling Calf;" a demon bull that seemed to always spell death, were common place. By all tales and stories, Annie Palmer was a powerful evil witch, a dangerous master of the "black arts" which she had learned from a close bonding and love affair with a high voodoo queen priestess from a very obscure and evil sect while growing up in Haiti.

Annie Palmer left the chaos in Haiti seeking fame and fortune in the British colony of Jamaica. Haiti had become slim pickings for Annie. Rather than finding a rich British expatriate, she had taken a common lover first. He was huge slave leader named Takoo. Annie later attacked one of his family members over a love triangle with fatal consequences. This proved to be a huge mistake for Annie. In revenge, this huge powerful slave killed her in 1831 during the violent slave rebellions throughout Jamaica. Takoo was also known to be a powerful local obeah man or African voodoo master. His Haitian mother Abigale had been kidnapped by slavers from Haiti to Jamaica and sold to a wealthy British expatriate. It was alleged that she was a powerful voodoo queen by her own right.

Annie's grand mistake occurred later when Takoo's granddaughter Millicent became the unfortunate target of this "White Witch" because of her passion for a new bookkeeper at Rose Hall named Robert Rutherford. Robert was actually a polished gentleman who came into this level of business to learn the rum trade. Annie Palmer had fallen in love with him at first sight. Millicent, who was Rutherford's housekeeper, had also fallen for him. This love triangle came to a grievous end after an ugly fight between the two women. Millicent was struck down by the powerful black magic witchcraft of Annie Palmer. According to legend, an "Old Hige" or vampire demon sent by Annie, attacked and killed the beautiful mulatto woman. It sucked out her life each night until she was a lifeless husk.

Takoo sought ultimate revenge on Annie for this horrible death. During the slave revolts Takoo, with other slaves invaded Rose Hall in the dead of night to avenge his beloved granddaughter. Takoo strangled Annie to death in the great house, but before her death she was able to temporarily leave her body in a voodoo trance. Takoo killed her but her spirit returned to reanimate her body soon after. Although Annie Palmer's body was immediately buried in the aftermath of her murder, the locals later saw her alive, riding her horse through the fields of Rose Hall at night with her head bent to the side because of her broken neck.

However, unknown to the many who saw this apparition, it was just a projected apparition rather than the real Annie; for her spirit had been trapped in the bounds of the great house of Rose Hall by a powerful spell from Takoo and his mother Abigale! This specter of the resurrection of Annie Palmer fueled the endless horror stories surrounding the White Witch of Rose Hall. Takoo, like many other slaves in the rebellion, was hunted down by the authorities and reportedly killed. His body was never found. Since those days, Annie had remained aloof and alone, and a great mystery to the local residents on nearby plantations.

However, from her prison at Rose Hall, Annie continued to satisfy her needs by choosing and trapping lovers from her crop of ex-slaves. It didn't matter if they were young men or women to her; she had acquired tastes for both long ago. She had a new suitor come into her world in 1843; a wealthy plantation owner, who like the former husbands and lovers, was enamored with her exquisite crème-skinned beauty set in her small girlish frame of four foot eleven inches. Beneath this elegant beauty and charm rested an evil coiled spirit; one that longed to escape!

Her dark eyes were virtual magnets, which could captivate in extreme lust, or send flashes of terror to whomever she desired. This is how she projected herself to her workers from her prison. Yet, the beautiful smile from her well-chiseled lips seemed to disarm even the strongest. Annie Palmer played her new suitor hard and sucked his very spirit dry. The poor bloke got drunk one night and fell from the top to bottom of the huge staircase in the great house. His neck was broken. His body was dead but like her other husbands, his spirit was trapped in her dark web. Some people collected insects; Annie collected souls! Life continued at Rose Hall.

Ayiti had never expected any problems on his journey to Jamaica. He thought he had made a clean escape from Boyer the clown! But in his gay abandon in Santo Domingo had underestimated the powers and reach of the voodoo adepts working for Boyer. They had found him! Ayiti had jumped ship as planned at Montego Bay and was hunted for several weeks after. Out of his constant precaution, he had brought with him two completely different identities that he used now. It was now December of 1844 and hopefully he had been forgotten as many months had passed since his escape. Since he had an ample supply of cash and gold coin with him, he did not need to draw anything from the banks under his discarded name of Emile St. Denis, or, his other name of Thierry. He had rented a small beachside cottage on the coast of Montego Bay.

It sat near the beach this day, next to a forest of huge Mangrove trees, whose huge coiled roots encroached throughout the dark muddy swamp off to his right. Ayiti was bored and seemed to have a permanent ankle injury from his ordeal with Boyer's voodoo master in the ship. The knife wound to his "familiar" doll had delivered a deep wound to his right ankle that would not fully heal. It was permanent and oozed black blood occasionally; a crusty hole that never healed. Aunt Sarah had never told him how to fix an injury to his familiar doll. The use of sewing up the holes was his idea and had worked. He used a cane at times now, but always walked with an obvious limp. The only time he could walk normally was when he transformed into his familiar; the Strawman.

Handsome Ayiti had little problem seducing local prostitutes for his personal enjoyment of sex, torture, and feasting! They were seldom missed and he was very discreet in hiring them. He had consumed only six to date. He routinely dumped their remains deep in the Mangrove jungle when done abusing them as food for wild animals. Like most people who lived in Montego Bay and the surrounding area, the tale of Annie Palmer seemed to be a common piece of lore. He had paid little interest in this until he shared a meal with an older doctor who had actually treated Mrs. Palmer.

Ayiti showed a bare interest in his stories, since they seemed to be the same type tales as others; but he did pay attention to the doctor's demeanor as he told his tales. Ayiti heard a rambling fear in his voice, and a passive terror in his eyes. This was the first time he felt that there was perhaps some real truth in this Annie Palmer myth. He needed to pay a visit first in spirit then second in the flesh. In consulting a map of the area, he learned that Rose Hall and all its sprawling plantations was only a scant eight miles from his cottage as the "crow flies." As the 'Crow's fly' was what he was interested in since like the crow, he was going to fly! Tonight, he was going to run on the tops of the tall strong coconut trees in the light of the moon. The winged Strawman was back.

Ayiti felt great as his focus animated him into his Strawman form. It had been a long time since he had transformed other than tormenting his hookers. The Strawman was soon leaping over the forests and cane fields as it finally saw the elegant three-story great house of Rose Hall. The moonlight cast a huge shadow on what Ayiti saw as a house of pure beauty and foreboding. He began to sense a strong dark presence as he crept into a set of open doors on the first floor. He placed himself in a corner to observe. He did not have to wait very long. At three in the morning the house was alive. Formless creatures of darkness slithered past him, darker than darkness were these visitors from other realms that harkened to the evil of Rose Hall. He then moved to the second floor as the physical banging of doors, rattling of windows, and constant wailing and screams filled the air.

The Strawman was impressed and it felt good being surrounded by such darkness. In the first bed room, he saw the shape of a white man sitting on the bed. It watched as he saw the man rushing the closed door in a ghost-like spirit banging against it then bouncing back onto the floor. This man's face bore terrible insanity and madness, like a caged animal that was dying. It was definitely trapped in this room. He found that two more rooms contained two more forlorn desperate spirits of men, trapped in the same way. The best prisoned soul one was the fourth man trapped in a closet who was raving and wailing at his dire predicament! This Mrs. Palmer loved to keep her collection of men in cages, created by her energy; dark energy. The same type of powerful dark energy that had trapped her!

Noises in the hall propelled him from the room into the hall where he bumped into several curious dark red midgets' that could be classified as "imps" of some infernal region. After a brief scuffle the Strawman playfully overpowered them and chased them into the walls. He laughed, if he knew what "cute" meant, it was they who were "cute" to his macabre tastes! They hopped and squeaked, had huge bug eyes, floppy ears, gaping fanged mouths, short tails all wrapped in fat crimson red bodies. Then he heard a voice behind him calling him. He turned around to see the image of a petite short woman, beautiful and surrounded in a colorful ethylic glow. Her light illuminated the end of the hall. The Strawman silently moved in her direction.

Her image of beauty did not fool him and she sensed it. Her clear etheric glow was a façade since it was completely surrounded by the Stygian darkness of evil energy. The pretty woman in the long dress asked. "What brings you into my domain this night straw demon? Do you come to feast on my flesh, or to destroy me?" Strawman felt her power and abject evil burst on him in a sudden rush. He was un-phased by it and even smiled from his wide fanged grimace. Strawman, in his deep evil monotone replied.

"I seek neither, I came to seek the truth in all the tale's I have heard about the "White Witch" for I request a personal tour!" Then the beautiful image faded and was replaced by an evil dark female specter, a dark evil banshee soul gaping over him as it levitated from the floor. Its eyes were huge and bulging the size of oranges, and its mouth seemed to resemble the maw of some hideous sea creature. As a wealth of long black hair hung past its feet. Ayiti beheld a powerful and dangerous nightmare creature before him.

He smiled from his wide fanged mouth at a specter that would paralyze a mortal in immediate terror. Strawman gave a laugh. "Do you believe in love at first sight dearest Annie Palmer? Your beauty is captivating me by all standards, and you are very alive!" Strawman held his ground as the hideous specter reduced itself back into a sultrier evil looking Annie Palmer. She gave a very eerie but unmistakable laugh. "Do you love my beauty strange demon?" Strawman grimaced a wide smile showing all his fangs. "Yes, your beauty weakens me and I find your personality as great as your looks dear Annie! I am smitten by you!"

She began to show great sexual allure at this point, imitating the image of his favorite long dead French lady she caught swirling in his thoughts; which excited him. "Will you visit me in the flesh straw demon?" "It will be my pleasure to have tea with you late this afternoon!" Ayiti answered. "I will see you then oh illustrious mistress of this house of Rose Hall whose beauty has stolen my dark heart!" She curtsied in her form and was gone. He watched as the glow from her very darkened etheric force soon disappeared down the hall into her master bedroom. Strawman then smacked an annoying slimy dark demon in the face that leered at him. It ran to the ceiling and scampered away screeching. He could hear the terrifying female whimpering from the bedroom as he left. Annie had reentered her flesh to consume another lover. But Ayiti also sensed a very powerful dark entity or force around her.

Sarah had taught him about the powerful dark realms. He understood the channeling of spirits from other realms but he had little use for it since Strawman the Loa god was enough. "You ask for help from the other side, then you owe them," as Aunt Sarah had told him. Now that he knew the truth about this witch, and far more powerful than a common one! He danced back above the trees in the waning moonlight along the coast. Strawman danced across the waves crashing on the sand beach for he was happy this night. Did Strawman have his first crush? At least Ayiti had a new friend and perhaps a better place to hide from the authorities. Sooner or later the police would be tipped off to the missing hookers in this small town of Montego Bay Jamaica!

The next day he rode his rented horse down a rough road from Montego Bay to Rose Hall. It seemed that Jamaican public works was non-existent from the shape of the road he traveled. The dirt and shell covered road had deep holes in it, and in places, fallen trees littered the path. At times, Ayiti had to walk his horse for fear of it turning an ankle and then limping like he did.

The trees were a mixture of many different varieties, whose names were unknown to him. He loved the coconut trees and enjoyed their fruit and juice mixed with rum. They lined the road as thick as a wall in parts. He finally came to the front gate of Rose Hall and rode in. The many workers briefly stared at him but silently went back to their labors. Overseers walked among them brandishing long whips. He ignored them as he made his way to the great house. It seemed that they were expecting him as he dismounted and handed the reigns of this mount to a large silent attendant.

He was ushered into the house by well-dressed female servants. He noticed that all of these servants and the attendants outside seemed to be in some type of trance. This reminded him of his minions in Haiti that he had transformed. He was ushered into a main room where Annie Palmer stood dressed in her finest. She smiled as she spoke. "Little Ayiti Deschamps is alive and well today!" He was shocked at her name-calling. I am Doctor Emile A. St. Denis, and…" She cut in with a fond smile again. "Let us have tea my big liar, guest, and voodoo monster!" "It would be a great honor he answered." He followed her to a room overlooking the veranda and the huge spread beyond the Great House. Once seated, Annie spoke. "In many, many different circles you have become famous and very hunted Ayiti. My have you had such a run on the dictators until you met your match with Boyer!

I knew of you and your activities through my contacts in Haiti awhile back and know of your unusual powers of darkness. They say you are an incarnate Loa god? Remember that I too grew up in Haiti, the favorite of the powerful "Queen" of voodoo in the south of Haiti. She, along with many, including my parents died in a plague. I came here, as a girl in her teens, to seek my fortune!" Ayiti reminisced about Annie's voodoo queen mentor. He had known her as a smart pretty young girl long ago who did have the power. He did not tell Annie that he finally seduced, raped, and made her a tasty meal! Very tasty indeed!

"Yes, voodoo masters seem to grow on trees!" Ayiti nodded and began, "Your queen was against me and business was business then! I had powerful enemies out to destroy me constantly, and this is why I sit before you now. It was time I left cursed Haiti. Yet, Boyer sent his assassins to capture and return me to that monster on the ship that was bringing me here to live. I would like to get my hands on him! So, you know me and that the authorities seek me?"

She smiled back gracefully as she sipped her tea, her crooked neck covered by a shawl made her head tilt to the right thanks to her former lover Takoo! Annie's image of beauty and sensuality was without question. She continued. "Boyer does not matter to me...what matters is that you have surfaced and I can use you here. I can employ you to help me manage my estate and be my companion if you wish. I need someone out there with my slaves to better control them! Also, poor Annie gets very lonely. My last suitor wore out, expired down my staircase! He now lives in one of my closets.!" Annie gave a sad playful frown and continued.

"I need someone to oversee my overseers as well. I have withdrawn from direct control due to my, say "injury," and rumor of failing health. My workers and even overseers have been getting lazy and stealing from me. It seems that they have created a system of graft and theft over the last few years. Not just here at Rose Hall but at Palmyra, my other huge land holding adjacent to this property. I need to continue keeping a low profile now and my terror tactics are not as effective as they used to be. Are you with me Mr. Deschamps or is it St. Denis, or is it...?" Ayiti smiled showing his perfect white teeth that reflected on his tan-skinned very handsome face. "The honor is mine Annie Palmer.

Call me what you want. My new identity is that of a man named John Phillip Thierry, an engineer from France I am told! When do you want me to start?" Annie gave a loud laugh "Thierry? St. Denis? Deschamps, or that monster asshole Strawman doll who came to me sincerely last night? HA! Who gives a shit? She got up and approached him. She found "Little Ayiti" to be a robust handsome mulatto and thus called him thus. He felt her wild passion and it aroused him as he stared at her full breasts with rose red nipples nearly completely protruding from her low-cut long dress, revealed as her shawl opened.

He also saw the damage to her neck. It was bent to the side as if she was a broken doll; carelessly dropped. But she was of legendary beauty as he felt her hands caress his head and pull his face into her perfumed breasts. "You may start in my employ now if you like my "Little Ayiti" whose black heart was stolen by me last night!" Ayiti smiled. "But of course, Miss "White Witch" Palmer, my pleasure." He laughed. What size and shape he was going to create in his pants for her today? He would make it memorable since first impressions were important!

CHAPTER ELEVEN
PARADISE TO HELL!

The idyllic world that Jenny and Ambrose had created in their new existence since December of 1898 in Jamaica seemed to go on without end. The beautiful sunny warmth of the island continued to be the atmosphere surrounding the good tidings. The twins were now, along with the puppies, were past two years of age. Tully and Daphne's three children were regulars at the Cavendish's as was Nanny Betsy, the centerpiece of child rearing in her kind but stern ways of disciplining five little ones. There were six playful dogs from both homes with a bunch of friendly cats in the mix as well. Jennifer was pregnant again and hopefully this pregnancy would go better. The year 1890 seemed to be passing fast.

Jamaica Prime had grown into a booming business empire over the past two years. The changes made by the recommendations set forth by Josh and Ambrose were helpful in streamlining the rum and coffee production to their timely export to many important clients worldwide. The size of the estate had tripled in size. Ambrose and Josh easily put in ten-hour days most of the time, as Jenny had worked in the export marketing sales in the grand building. She worked only on certain days, so she could spend time with her children. Horace had been very busy traveling the region looking for more estates to buy, as well as traveling to other islands and other potential markets.

The growing popularity of these rum products kept Horace extremely busy as Annabelle worked regularly to help manage the overflowing office traffic. Otherwise, she was left to her own whims and fancies as the very attractive wealthy wife of the owner of one of the largest rums and coffee producing estates in Jamaica. Ambrose had kept his close contact with his friend Colonel Tiberius Nephew, especially since he and his sister Elizabeth had become an item of great significance in the last year. Rumor had it that they were going to be married. Ambrose always smiled at this possibility since Tiberius would soon be his brother-in-law!

Plans were still obscure for these two comedians. The good side of this was that they were coming to Jamaica for a month, so Christmas of 1900 was to be a memorable one. Duke and Lady Farnsworth would be present along with Jake and Miriam Meyers from St. Louis, Missouri. Christmas vacation at the turn of the century would prove to be more than memorable for many reasons. Horace was now in Montego Bay for the possible purchase of the plantation at Palmyra, outside of the growing port city, which sat adjacent to an estate called Rose Hall. He also had interest in purchasing it as well. It seemed like a great economic investment with the booming port of Montego Bay right down the street! The possibilities were endless and the price for these properties was fair.

Horace Farnsworth found Montego Bay quite changed since his last visit some years before. The streets and roads were paved, and the town bore a tropical elegance that emanated business, tourist, and population growth. Montego Bay had become a great harbor for the booming import and export activity throughout this region. This would serve Horace's future enterprise well. Besides his lawyer, Horace Farnsworth had brought Annabelle, who insisted she travel with him on this trip. They met after a nice lunch with the local magistrate in Montego Bay to discuss plans for the purchase of Palmyra and possibly Rose Hall. Both estates where in some private holding.

The small party rode their horses down the road towards the estates of Palmyra and Rose Hall in the early afternoon, which had long since been cleared of debris and paved with tons of crushed sea shells. The canopy of huge trees lined the road for a few miles after they passed the large Mangrove swamp forest that grew as an ominous shaded domain. The local magistrate who joined them on their excursion was a very talkative. He resembled an accountant in his wire-rimmed glasses and white tropical suit. He poured stories of Rose Hall and the "White Witch" Annie Palmer into their ears as they rode towards the estates.

They were well received and very fascinating to Annabelle. Soon, they sat on their mounts at the gates of Palmyra, and soon rode in the warm sunlight to the great house. An elderly white man named Bart Rogers, met them and introduced himself as the legal advisor to the estate. The group followed him to a large veranda that overlooked cane fields and a great view of the ocean and beaches. Horace did find it strange that no workers were present in the fields of exquisitely manicured sugarcane on this fine day during the work week.

Over a pot of tea, they discussed the sale of the estate. The price seemed reasonable and the lawyers and magistrate begin to lay out the terms of sale for Palmyra. He would have to check with the Rose Hall property owner however. As they were working Horace asked if he could look around the property. Annabelle declined since she was happy sitting on the veranda drinking a very refreshing gin and tonic with fresh limes. The long ride had worn her down somewhat.

Mr. Rogers told him to have a look. The great house was a very clean and well-kept property, but carried an air of emptiness, of a sort of loneness. Soon he came to a large painting of a woman, breathlessly beautiful in her features and long black curls. Even the painting exerted an aura of extreme sensuality. He surmised that this was the late Annie Palmer. "You are correct sir!" Startled, he turned to find a housekeeper standing in the doorway who had just divined his thoughts. He studied her young pretty face and her clean well ironed white housemaid uniform.

Unlike the usual friendliness of Jamaicans, she seemed droll and reserved as she spoke. "Do you like her sir?" Horace smiled at her listless tone as his mind skipped over the fact that she had read his exact thoughts. "Why I find her extremely beautiful indeed!" He retorted. "Annie Palmer is the mistress of these lands." Continued the maid. Farnsworth sought to clarify. "I thought that Mrs. Palmer was deceased?" The maid gave him a deep distant stare. "She may have been dead to the world of the living in 1846 sir, but her presence always seems to be among us, especially at night.

We must always do our jobs properly, or she has been known to visit those who slack on their jobs or steal." She suddenly went silent as if she had broken a rule. Being very aware of how superstitious many Jamaicans were, he let it rest. As she followed him silently, Horace visited other parts of the house and even took a short walk in the expertly manicured gardens. He finally returned to the veranda where a pitcher of pink rum punch was being served. Annabel was becoming tipsy and very friendly.

At the conclusion of the meeting, over cigars, the magistrate invited them to return to Montego Bay with a ride through the Rose Hall estate. It was near dusk. By cutting across the Rose Hall property it would cut the return trip by at least thirty minutes. The path from Palmyra to the Great House at Rose Hall was very defined and paved with crushed seashells. It seemed to Horace that a lot of work had been done to maintain Rose Hall as well as they rode through it. They were immaculate! What a motivated work force he would inherit!

As the small group bounded along the path, Horace noticed workers in the distance in the fields. As they approached several near the path, they scattered. This activity seemed very strange. The magistrate stopped the group in front of the Great House of Rose Hall. It was immaculate and very beautiful to behold to Horace and Annabelle. As a matter of fact, it was breathtaking. The magistrate invited them to take a tour but since the sun was low in the western sky and dusk was at hand, Horace declined. The horses seemed restless and nervous as they sat in their saddles viewing the great house.

Horace, like their horses, sensed some sort of malevolence about. Something was out of balance. He felt as if something was staring into him. It was unnerving as he sensed it. Finally, and gladfully, they moved on and out of the main gates of Rose Hall back to Montego Bay. Horace seemed to laugh to himself as they trotted back down the road growing in the shadows of dusk. The sensuousness of Annie Palmer's portrait had aroused him and would satiate his lust as he always did on a wife that never tired of sexual arousal.

He had panned the group of riders below after they had stopped in front. Then he saw her, and became completely transfixed! He watched intently as they sat on their mounts viewing the great house. The handsome well-dressed man called "Doc" by his minions and slaves at these estates, peered from the second story window as the party rode away down the lane. More buyers he thought as the woman with these men captivated his eye and disturbed his crotch. He stared intently as his thoughts danced around and through her imagining every detail of her body. She was more than just a beautiful woman, dressed in a white dress with long beautiful hair cloaked in a Beaver type hat.

She was a very sensuous lady whose presence had now completely mesmerized his soul. He was moved by her, feeling the old hunger and began to feel a bevy of genuine urges he had not felt in what seemed as decades! He thought of the French woman of this same strain in Haiti long dead. Then there was Annie, oh yes, sweet insane sexual Annie! He moved downstairs with his limp into the veranda on the rear part of the great house. He ordered his slave housekeepers to fetch him a bottle of rum and a glass of coconut juice. The mere presence of this woman had moved him and now galvanized his spirit!

He sat next to the estate lawyer who was working on a pile of paperwork at the table where he sat. The presence of Messer Thierry always unnerved the estate lawyer. There was a deep malevolence emanating from this gentleman! Ayiti had to know about this woman but camouflaged this design in discussing these possible new buyers. The potential buyer was Horace Farnsworth, owner of Jamaican Prime Rum Estates and the pretty lady with him was his wife Annabelle. Ayiti smiled like a Cheshire cat as he said her name silently on his lips! In a silent victory of information, he finished his second drink. He had learned to savor a shot of rum with a shot of the coconut juice as a favorite drink and offered one to the evasive companion at the table. He began to think of "Annabelle "as he consumed his third concoction. He relaxed back in his chair with his mind reviewing every feature of the beauty on that horse. Her image consumed his thoughts.

The Haitian voodoo master of many names and questionable age felt his boredom and strange loneness completely stymied by the appearance of this lady Annabelle! What did he have to lose? Yet what could he gain in his evolving plan to steal her! Dear Annie, in the flesh was long gone by now. The authorities were informed of her death in 1846, but in reality, she lived in seclusion until 1865. She chose to die in 1846 in the public eye because the authorities were closing in on her for the disappearance and possible murder of three husbands and another idiot suitor. He mused as he thought of "Sweet Annie who by now, as the years passed, had come completely unhinged for reason!" She was forever trapped in the great house of Rose Hall!

He reminded himself of how Annie's dark soul became chained to Rose Hall by powerful dark conjuring voodoo spells concocted by Takoo's mother Abigale out of revenge for what she did to his family. All the powers Ayiti possessed could weaken, but not break the spell that kept Annie's soul trapped in the great house. Ayiti would not invite the dark forces to do this! Once you use them, they own you! All Annie could do is project her image outside in a variety of forms, but her dark soul could never exit! Takoo, the great master of the art of African voodoo and his powerful mother Abigale had closed the trap forever with the help of dark forces from beyond! However, there was one flaw in it that Annie had figured out if she could use it.

Ayiti had entertained the thought that Takoo's mother was his aunt Sarah's twin sister Abigale, who became one of the most powerful voodoo sorceresses to ever come to Jamaica. However, these players were dead and it mattered little to Ayiti. Abigale hated Annie Palmer for what she had done to her son and family. The entrapping curse had been sealed by human sacrifice and ritual cannibalism. It was rumored that Abigale herself alone had set this ethereal trap for Annie. This powerful barrier trap was set when Takoo confronted Annie that terrible night at Rose Hall.

When Annie went into her trance to escape her body as Takoo choked her to death, she soon found herself trapped in the solitary confines of her house. Her body was useless to escape since the vibrations of this curse rested on her vibrations. She was blocked from animating the bodies of her servants. There was a simple reason for this problem, as the very intelligent White Witch soon figured out! It had to do with the different vibration patterns between the races of blacks and whites. Every species had its own vibrations as does all the races of mankind and all animal life.

Her attempts to escape for many years in her body, then in spirit after 1865 were never ending! Annie was being driven into creeping slow madness, the same madness she had endeared upon her collection of souls of her imprisoned husbands also within the confines of Rose Hall. Annie's dark soul was buried alive in a coffin which was her great house! Two things had to happen according to her findings: The host had to be Caucasian, a female of her race and secondly, they would have to invite her into their body freely and under no duress!

Therefore, the intended host could invite her into their body by invitation or through intimate sexual contact where their vibrations would mix! This realization had not dawned on her twisted mind until very recently in the last few years! Ayiti had been of little help citing this revelation as more of "Annie's Madness!" A Caucasian female of British extraction was a perfect match! But where in hell could one be found with lesbian tendencies to invite her escape? Annie's physical remains had been entombed in a nearby bird sanctuary, but her restless desperate evil spirit constantly roamed the great house babbling and terrorizing visitors sensitive to her. After watching insane Annie's antics grow, Ayiti had become greatly humored by it! It was downright hilarious to watch as she assumed all manner of hideous shapes to torment visitors who possessed even a shred of clairvoyance!

The many plantation workers that Ayiti had systematically zombified and controlled since he came here in 1844 were completely immune to her spasmodic hauntings. The house staff was given into a hypnosis to deal with Annie. Ayiti well remembered how they had hit it off from the first moment they met. Like most men, he was completely captivated by her beauty and perverse sexual appetite. They enjoyed nearly twenty-two years of great evil pleasure; a friendship of demons from hell to earth. Many unfortunate victims had vanished from the estate and Montego Bay over these years, dying terrible deaths in their evil nighttime romps. Rumors of the terrible fates on these missing people added to the mystique of the Rose Hall lore.

He missed those wild days with Annie, but her imprisoned soul, like those of the three husbands and suitor in the closet, had been driven to complete madness. She was insane, with her twisted dark soul changing into many shapes as she roamed the house at night. Her insanity had detached her from him nearly all the time now. He avoided her by staying at the great house at Palmyra. The good side was that before Annie had gone crazy, she had made him the silent owner of Rose Hall.

Doctor Emile St. Denis had been missing for over fifty years now. Ayiti, under the persona of John Phillip Thierry knew he had fallen completely off the radar with the police authorities decades ago. Besides, Boyer was long dead anyhow! The caretakers and lawyers who managed the affairs of Rose Hall and Palmyra never questioned him even as the decades passed. He had moved throughout the island without problems for the last several years. He surmised that Inspector Ian Peacock was very old or deceased by now. The books on him had to be closed. If time was anybody's companion, it was Ayitis! He was now reenergized completely by the sight of that beautiful woman on the horse, and yes, "time was on his side!".

Her image had knocked him completely out of the humdrum world he had succumbed to for so many years at Rose Hall after Annie lost her body. In 1845, Ayiti was told by his followers in Haiti that Jean Zombi had not been destroyed in the attack on his mansion. He had wandered in the forests and jungles until accidently found by Ayiti's people. In 1846 he had his old favorite brother Jean Zombi the "zombie" shipped out of Haiti in a crate to Montego Bay and brought to Rose Hall. Zombi, in his new role, was used as an effective instrument of terror to keep the multitude of un-zombified plantation workers in line; slaves by intimidation and not freed by emancipation.

He would order his star zombie out of his lair in the basement only at night to do his bidding. Although Zombi still walked the earth and understood Ayiti, his physical makeup was terrible. Most of his face had deteriorated away, leaving a skull protruding across his nose less skinless face and exposed pate. Ayiti designed a demon mask of his likeness of Strawman for him to cover his face made of pure silver. Previously, Zombi had literally been a big hit in Haiti before he was found alive by and spirited by Ayiti's followers into a hiding place for shipment and reunion to a joyous Ayiti.

Before Zombi was rescued and delivered to Jamaica he continued obeying Ayiti's original orders in wreaking havoc and death on the authorities controlled by Boyer. He nearly killed the rotten dictator the night he got into his well-fortified residence. Zombi did climb into the dictator's bed and raped his wife before feasting on her. Boyer had not been there that fateful night! Zombi walked out of the palace in a hail of bullets fired into him. They could not kill the walking dead. The image of Zombi was a slow walking night monster, but in fact, he was extremely fast in his pursuit and lethally quick in killing. Few saw his movements as none of his victims ever survived to recount his speed. The sightings of the horrific specter of Mr. Zombi stalking in the moonlight illuminating invoked fear and terror among Haitians. This walking dead monster feasted upon the living to satiate his hunger. The name "Zombi" became the fearful reference to the undead by what Haitians and later the world mind would call "Zombies!"

Jean Zombi had been a welcome joy back in Ayiti's life! He became extremely effective in his new role of terrifying the plantation workers into submission. If they broke the rules? Zombi ate them and left the remains for others to see. Ayiti had become listless, uncaring, and very isolated in recent years. The thrills he had enjoyed in his crazy days in Haiti and with Annie Palmer were gone. He had been condemned as it seemed to live now on a desert island uninhabited and devoid of any real desires or challenges. It had been dangerous to grab people from Montego Bay in the last few years since authorities had become strong and ever vigilant. The authorities seemed to have their eyes fixed on Rose Hall.

Today out of the blue, he had just found his saving grace sitting on a horse in front of Rose Hall of all things! The Loa gods had answered his wishes! This beautiful woman named Annabelle, would free him from his doldrums and idle torment. He was completely enthralled by her beauty and feeling her libido! Ayiti felt an erection as he thought of his possibilities with this woman, one he would have soon! In his life of unchallenged boredom this was a chance he was ready to take! She would be his! He soon satisfied his erupting passion for Annabelle on one of the pretty house servants at Palmyra.

Ambrose Cavendish sat in a large open-air restaurant on a small hill overlooking Kingston harbor surrounded by a group of large palm trees. The Christmas spirit in this season of 1900 had now taken complete hold in the island. He was enjoying another perfect warm day sitting in the shade of huge palm trees thinking of the great reunion now in store. He sat with Horace enjoying tall gin and tonics, smoking Maduros as they waited for the ship to arrive from England. Uncle Jake and Miriam had arrived three days earlier and were touring somewhere today. On board the arriving ship were the Farnsworth's, Colonel Nephew, and his wonderful lady, who was Ambrose's pretty sister Elizabeth.

The tall ocean steamship appeared in the horizon and soon hailed with horn blasts from its bridge as it slowly edged into port. The parties were joined on the huge dock amidst its alabaster colored buildings. After hugs and handshakes, the group moved to the open restaurant relaxing before the trip back to the Farnsworth's estate and Cavendish's house. The drinks were poured from a large pitcher filled with ice, from iceboxes lined with steel that insulated the blocks of ice from melting. The first commercial electric powered refrigerators would not be produced until J.M Larsen created them in 1913. The advent of electricity was changing the pastoral scope of this island nation daily. Its uses seemed to be creating generator powered systems in everything now. Massive technological changes via electricity had ushered in a new age.

Ambrose could not help but smile at Tiberius and Elizabeth. He had introduced them after all. But what amused him was their aura of maturity and properness that seemed to abound from them as they approached him. After handshakes and hugs, it took a couple of rum punches and a cigar for Nephew and sister each to bring them out of this façade of "properness." It seemed that they were both happy together as they held hands and were all smiles. He noticed a large diamond engagement ring on her left hand. Duke and Lady Farnsworth seemed extremely jovial and very glad to be off the ship. The sea travel had been hard on the elder Lady Farnsworth who was showing weakness in her age now. They leisurely basked in the warm air with great enjoyment now being off the ship. England, according to Tiberius, as well as Europe, were beset with another extremely cold and snowy winter again.

The open horse driven coach trip from Kingston into the hills overlooking the bay was breathtaking to all newcomers and enlightened their spirits. The warm sunlight kissed the huge palms and other greenery outlined by the many white sand beaches and mystic hills. Where the Farnsworth's and Nephew had been accustomed to this type of tropical wonderland, it was a brand-new world for Elizabeth. She loved it! Since the parties rode in two coaches, Horace continued on with his parents to his estate in White Hall as Ambrose's coach continued on to their sprawling large bungalow overlooking the bay.

Tully and some helpers were present and unloaded suitcases and took them to the room where Tiberius and Elizabeth were going to reside for their time. It was down the hall from where the Meyers were roomed. Jenny was overjoyed to see them arrive and introduced her twin children and dogs to them as they played in and outside of the house. Towards dusk, the Farnsworth clan from White Hall arrived outside to join in the delightful family gathering. As the evening began to close in and appetites grew, Daphne and nanny Betsy prepared a large dinner for them consisting of rack of lamb, Grouper, and lobster as the main dishes of choice.

The dinner was excellent. The conversation was cheerful with the usual humorous banter. Elizabeth and Annabelle helped Daphne and Betsy clean up after dinner as they continued drinking a good red wine in this process. The senior Farnsworth's and Meyers took a long stroll down the path behind the house to the bluff above the ocean. Cavendish and Nephew sat on the long deck overlooking the bay under a star-studded sky as they smoked some fine Maduro cigars with a companion bottle of cognac. Nephew looked at his old friend with a smile. "Cavendish, my dear fellow, do you know I will become part of the family in the near future?"

Ambrose laughed. "My brother in arms is now to be my blood brother?" Nephew laughed and they toasted. He continued. "So, you got my sister pregnant?" Tiberius caught with the joke laughed out loud. No, not that I know of…and you know we are saving that blissful passionate moment for the wedding night!" "Right! So, noble, but hadn't you practice before the wedding night?" Tiberius laughed. "Yes, we have performed several dry runs my dear future brother-in-law. I think we have the basic positions in place." Tiberius took a plug of cognac and a pull from his cigar. Ambrose toasted. "To those blessed positions! They all worked on Jenny"

Ambrose left for a minute and returned with some Christmas presents for his friend. Nephew opened the packages and found that he was the new owner of a huge Panama hat, a nice shirt, three boxes of Cuban Cigars, and a case of Jamaican Prime Special rum. "Thanks, my friend, I could not ask for more, and they will be all put to good use!" Now, I have one for you, a sentimental one. He left and returned with a large wooden box with rope handles on it. He placed it on the ottoman in front of Cavendish who opened it. He pulled out the packaging material and looked at it with a smile.

He pulled out a letter and read it. It was a letter from old Krupp to Colonel Nephew and another one from Nephew to him. He smiled and laughed as he read it. Nodding his head, he picked up the large long metal object and pulling the folding stock out he aimed it. He saw "KRUPPMP1895" stamped on it. He inquired to his friend about it. "Ambrose, "MP1895" means machine pistol model 1895." "Great Caesar's Ghost, I thought this piece went into the crypt or was destroyed! Unbelievable Tiberius! You are giving me this prototype hand held machinegun to hunt boars with?" He was laughing out loud as he inserted an empty long metal magazine in it. "Yes, my dear friend, I heard you were going and did not want to hear of your ass stuck on a boar's tusks!"

Inside the wooden crate were several hundred rounds of 9MM ammo and another four thirty-two shot magazines to add to the one already attached to the weapon. He then pulled out one of two very expensive bottles of Schnapps included in the wooden box. He looked at Nephew with a smile. "We owe our mentor and friend Krupp a toast." He examined a weapon which in the future would be called the "MP38 Schmeisser." Ambrose grabbed a couple of crystal flute glasses from the rattan tiki bar on the deck. Tiberius commenced to fill them with sturdy shots of Heer Krupp's schnapps.

Not only was Krupp toasted several times, but Napoleon; the "Mother of Annihilation" was toasted, Krupp's weapons designs were toasted, the crypt was toasted, Krupp's 1870 Knight's Cross was toasted, his rabbits were toasted three times, Ravi was toasted with the village (and Pyra) Then came the "fuck you" toasts to that asshole nephew of Krupp, Wadsworth twice, to their victory at the bridge in Germany, memory of all the dead henchmen, those Luger pistols, To the death of Kali and thousands of green devils; and a solemn final toast to Queen Victoria! The first bottle was polished off! Both men were drunk and laughing from their toasts and consumption of a bottle of a-hundred and twelve-proof schnapps! While Tiberius went to relieve himself, Ambrose read the letter from Alois.

July, 1899

My Dear Boys!

I had the strangest visitor recently. He turned out to be a wonderful person and a close friend of yours whose name is Ravi Strosser. He told me the good news that both of you escaped Germany. From what I learned in the aftermath of your encounter with the police and goons, those grenade rounds must have done the trick! I have been amazed at the incredible information he bequeathed me. As for me and my rabbits? We survived to onslaught of the goons. This gift really worked well! I bagged all my tormentors in seconds in my office!

Anyway, I found my Mauser rifle more suited at keeping the wolves away from my rabbits than my sub machine gun (MP1895). But I loved shooting it, especially at the vermin who came to kill me. I have decided to bequeath this prototype to you boys as a gift for your help and for the friendship you generated from Ravi. Enjoy it and boys? Don't fight over it after you drink my schnapps!

My Best to you Both
Alois Krupp Senior (and my rabbits)

Later, after some strong coffee and comical banter with the girls who were feeling little pain now either, both men sat again outside under a beautiful panorama of brilliant stars dotting the dark sky. They sat smoking cigars and enjoying the breeze still feeling the silly effects of the schnapps. "Anything new in the world of intelligence!" Asked Ambrose. "Let's see" began Tiberius; "We are convinced the German leadership has become a bunch of strong-armed warmongers under the love and guidance of the Prussian General Staff.

The growth of standing armies is on the rise in many countries fired up by that good old nationalistic spirit taught to them by Napoleon's conquests of old. France seems to be building up its armies predictably to offensively corner the threat from Greater Germany and launch the grand offensive that will reclaim Alsace Lorraine into French dominion when the opportunity knocks. The Huns continue to build up their navy and the ire of we British! Our agents have seen evidence of those new Krupp Guns, the huge ones being test fired routinely. I actually witnessed them in action in a covert visit to Germany. They are battlefield nightmares Ambrose!" Uncle Jake joined them on the deck with a cool bottle of beer. He was amazed at the MP1895 and listened as the conversation continued. He commented on Russia since he was an expert on its history.

"Russia completely supports a unified Balkan Empire! They are very concerned about all the factionalism in the Balkans, since the Austria-Hungarian Empire is known as the collector of tribes! As long as the tribal factions are separated in the Balkans, it will be easier for them to grab them like many others into their fold! I feel that sooner than later they will make a play to add it into its fold under the imperialistic "protectorate." Russia is watching developments in the Balkans, and as the "Mother of all Slavs," this could spell a flashpoint if the Austria-Hungarian Empire takes a hard plunge south. Also, the unrest among the Russian peasant population has been quietly growing for many years. The Tsar had better remedy his corrupt feudal model before a few million peasants do!"

The three men sat reflecting their knowledge of current events as they sipped their cognac and smoked fresh cigars. They overlooked the stars over the bay. Ambrose changed the subject. "How is Ravi? Any word from him?" Interjected Cavendish as he was more focused on Pyra than his question. Nephew added. "That campaign against the Kali seemed to weaken him greatly. I do not think he has fairly recovered from it but not completely. Ravi is very old and was injured a lot more than he had told us in the fight." He smiled as he picked up Ambrose's thoughts. "Pyra is beautiful as ever and said hello! Ronjin told me the last time we spoke that Sergeant Major Hook (RIP) and his swarm of Bow Dogs also say hello and give their love! Do you know Hooky has a girlfriend?"

Ambrose looked over to Nephew with a laugh. "Tell Hooky the same from me and my father; that his Zulu spear and his VC are safely mounted behind the bar at my father's pub complete with a brass plate of the famous exploits of our dearly departed hero of Rorke's Drift!" Nephew looked over to Ambrose. "Elizabeth took me to your father's pub more than once and I have personally seen it and that great picture of him. Will do!" Tiberius held up his glass in toast. Cavendish joined in the toast. He missed his Color Sergeant a lot!

The two comrades discussed the war and all the things that occurred as sort of a reality check, a balm for chilling memories. Uncle Jake was all ears and added that he would love to write the real account in the jungle someday. Jake had been informed of a general idea of the war in the jungle. Both British officers gave him a thumb up gesture with smiles. Finally, Nephew gave a serious look as they now toasted Queen Victoria. "Our friend Queen Victoria has been very ill as of late. It seems that the date of her passing is on schedule. Hip Hooray for our friend and queen mother!" Horace now joined them along with Duke Farnsworth for more interesting banter. After an hour Annabelle approached them. 'Darling it is time to go. Mother is very tired and we have a big week planned!" When they had all retired from the deck Tiberius looked at Ambrose. "That Annabelle is quite the work of art my future brother in law!"

Earlier that day, Horace's carriage was returning to their mansion after they parted ways with the Cavendishs from the port. The elder Farnsworth had spotted a man standing by the side of the road nearly hit by the carriage as it passed. 'Damnit!" he yelled, "What's wrong with these people, didn't he see us coming?" Horace looked back as they passed the point where the man had been standing and saw nobody at the side of the road. After another turn, they pulled up in the large circular driveway of their white columned mansion. The sight of this man in the road had disturbed Sir Farnsworth since he had seemed very out of place. He expected to see a simple poor native, but this simple native he saw was well dressed!

Once inside White Hall, they all relaxed with cold gin and tonics as they begin to unwind. They would be leaving in a couple of hours for a great dinner party at the Cavendish's tonight. They soon moved to comfortable chairs in the manicured garden enjoying the beautiful orange sunset and fading light. The men smoked cigars together as the ladies engaged in the important small talk from England and Jamaica. Lord Farnsworth looked at Horace. "So how is my son-in-law handling the rigors of Jamaican Prime?" Horace laughed. He and Mr. Marley have been doing a splendid job in re-organizing several of the functions and the road projects I told you about via my letters. Honestly, I couldn't ask for a better team!

Our production has more than tripled and we barely are keeping up with the demand. The Americans are really beginning to buy our brands these days. Jenny has also come up with the idea of longer aged spiced rum designed and sold as our Special Estate Rum in limited quantities. She got the idea from the distillers of their rare scotch brands! She and Josh have been experimenting with new flavors after he taught her how he flavored rums. Seems this concept has been working very well.

You will be greatly impressed when you tour the estate. It has really expanded father. I am purchasing the complete estate of Palmyra to the west of Montego Bay and will also buy the haunted estate of Rose Hall when I find out if the owner will sell it. Palmyra is an excellent place by the ocean and well kept." Time was running now so it was time to leave for the dinner party over the bay. After a great night and after the farewells, The Farnsworth's returned to White Hall on the road darkened by the night. It had been a long fun day for all, and everybody soon bedded down for the night. Horace stayed up working as usual in his small office.

Annabelle was soon asleep in the large master bed upstairs. She began to have strange unusual erotic dreams and woke up a couple of times very aroused and sensing a presence in her room. She returned to slumber. Ayiti sat in one of her bedroom chairs in the shadow of the open veranda doors in the bedroom admiring her incredible beauty. He was entertaining her and touching her private parts with his nasty erotic thoughts pressed into her mind. She was very wet and finally had an orgasm in her slumber! He was awestruck by her! The dogs began barking below in the backyard; fearful barking. Ayiti quieted them by his silent command.

Ayiti had left Annabelle's bedroom since her husband was now walking up the stairs to bed. Soon after, he sat quietly in one of the chairs by the huge garden, patting the silent dogs sitting next to him and thinking. If he was to claim his prize, he had to be careful, but how careful? He had to snatch her from somewhere other than this place. He decided to follow her and learn of her habits and places she went. Annabelle was the most captivating woman he could remember; even more than the French woman! How to meet her was his question? But his real question was how to successfully kidnap her and hide her forever from her powerful family and the authorities?

Christmas Day was in two days and all sorts of plans had been made for the classical English holiday dinner party planned at the Farnsworth's. It was to be a bash fit for the queen by all indications. All presents would be exchanged on Christmas Eve both at Cavendish's and the Farnsworth's to clear the path for the dinner party the next day. Horace, Ambrose, and Josh had made great plans for a huge annual Christmas party for all the workers at the rum estate on Friday the day before Christmas Eve. Horace pulled no strings now in spending good money for presents and food for his workers. This event for the workers and families was a celebration that would run from Friday into Saturday night. The effects Ambrose had made in upgrading the workers lives had reigned in such a positive galvanizing effect on their ranks. Mutual loyalty was their bond!

"What a great day to be alive!' Spouted Colonel Nephew, as he had just landed his first swordfish. Tully had helped him get it in the boat and was smiling broadly as he always did. They caught several game fish over the next few hours with Josh Marley being the champion. This Thursday before the holiday had been a banner fishing day as all present had consumed a decent quantity of beer, made cold by a couple of large blocks of ice stowed in one of the compartments in the boat stern. The fishing crew consisted of Captain Tully, Ambrose, Tiberius, Sir Farnsworth, Horace, Josh Marley, and Elizabeth who caught the second largest grouper. Spirits were very high as beer and shots of rum continued to flow back at the dock. The day was perfect with clear blue skies and great breeze off the beautiful waters.

"Fresh fish for everybody tonight" exclaimed Ambrose in a happy beer and rum buzz. "We shall grill Swordfish steaks for dinner tonight smothered in lemons, garlic and roasted almonds. We shall have it at my house! Are you in Mr. Josh Marley?" The old rum master, who had his permanent residence at the estate smiled back. Since it was Thursday and the company were closed for the holidays. It would be nice to see everybody together, especially Duke Farnsworth, his great friend who had been his ticket to success here. "Yes, Mr. Ambrose, you can count me in!" smiled Josh Marley.

The bounty of caught fish not chosen for dinner would be delivered as part of the huge company party meal to be added to roast pigs, and chickens on the spit. Horace would have his servants deliver the fish. The seafood dinner party at Cavendish's was set for seven that evening and all the Farnsworth's were present for a great seafood fare of swordfish steaks and other delicacies created by Daphne and Jenny, who had learned to be a great cook under the tutelage of Daphne and Nanny Betsy. The cocktail hour began at five thirty.

Colonel Nephew was impressed at the relaxed carefree attitudes that had been adopted by Cavendish, his wife, Horace and that remarkable Annabelle. "Oh, Annabelle" he thought; in my day! He admired her beauty and sexy ambiance. He also appreciated the spirit of respectful friendship between they the expatriates with their native servants. It reminded Tiberius of how he and Ambrose melded with their native noncoms and enlisted men in India. It was exactly like their interaction with Ravi and the village! Ambrose had brought that spirit here to Jamaican Prime Rum!

Freedom from stress made people happy surmised the colonel who seemed to have too much of it in his life. Nephew's world in England, aside from his wonderful relationship with Elizabeth, was extremely demanding and stressful. The need for especially good intelligence in these times never ended. After a great day fishing, excellent dinner fare, several rum punch drinks and a cigar, he relaxed into the mood completely with the rest of his companions. Tiberius felt he could do this for the rest of his life and with his Elizabeth! The excellent dinner was served on the outside torch-lit deck and was an excellent fare from appetizers to dinner, and on to dessert.

The gathering continued well into the night where stories abounded from all sides. Even Ambrose asked Tiberius to move to Jamaica after marrying his sister and be a junior member of Jamaican Prime, an invitation he did not take lightly. But Colonel Nephew was on a serious quest for "Queen and Country" that he could never ignore. Besides, there was a new person involved in the queen's secret intelligence operations whom he greatly liked and often shared cigars with.

In his heart, like his very concerned wonderful Queen; Hell was a cruel vision on the not too distant horizon. The stupid inevitable clash of civilizations was mankind's cardinal blunder; one to rear its ugly face across Europe and perhaps the globe! Evil intentions seemed coiled deep in the minds of all men! The weakness in human nature seemed the flaw to prescribe this madness into the light! He had listened well to the words of Ravi. But what constantly intrigued him was Ravi's focus on the aftermath of this next terrible future war, as if he was fishing for another fallen child lost in the chaos and destruction of Atlantis. Ravi's future focus in the wake of a war in Europe that had not even began had completely awed the colonel. But then, Ravi alone had awed the hell out of him!

He remembered Ravi's remarks well as if they were tattooed to his soul. "Evil loves and grows in the chaos created in the failure of human civilizations! Son, this next terrible clash will set the stage for a much worse one as this has happened long before! One must study the science of "cause and effect" in all interactions! So much truth can be revealed by this and the real nature of the conflict can be found! But the span of human life is short, as are man's aspirations and goals! Mankind is shortsighted and hamstrung by this!" Tiberius took a pull on his Cubano and toasted Ravi once more with a fresh shot of Krupp schnapps.

The next day was Christmas Eve and it seemed that this holiday spirit came alive at breakfast. The party and exchange of Christmas presents later that evening was full of excitement. As the Christmas party at the Cavendish's grew late and the adults entered their social hour. Nanny Betsy took control of all the children and this merry group of children and dogs followed Aunt Betsy down the road to Tully and Daphne's house. Once home, they had played games with nanny, as the dogs romped around their fun. They were all getting tired. She finally shooed all their tired bodies into a large bed and put them all to sleep with a kiss for each and a pretty African lullaby. They all loved Nanny Betsy.

All five dogs soon climbed into the bed with the kids. It was a real pile in the bed as Betsy gave an approving smile and blessing. Nanny Betsy then settled into her favorite rocking chair with a nice cold drink to relax. It had been such a wonderful day for her and it was very late in the night now. She would not go to her room until Tully and Daphne relieved her. In a short time, the old woman sensed something strange outside the front of the house. Her conditioned Instinct sent a cold chill down her spine! She became very aware of something very out of place; something of terrible malfeasance lurked nearby for a strange reason.

Her many years as a respected voodoo priestess of old had conditioned her for vibrations to all spirits who came into her presence. She sensed abject dark evil now. She questioned her feelings. Feeling things beyond one's normal senses was part of her early training in the art and they were manifest in her. She cautiously stepped outside on the front porch where she had first sensed this aberration and peered across and up the road. Then she saw it! By the moonlight, she saw an imposing man whose shadow crossed the road from where he was standing in the faint moonlight. He was some hundred yards up the road from their house, standing still as a statue and staring up the road at the Cavendish house.

What was strange was that the dogs, which usually barked at anything, were quiet. They were asleep. Sensing her presence, the tall man turned and stared in her direction. She was suddenly filled with a great fear as his sinister gaze penetrated her. Panic set over her, for the eyes of this man were red beacons, red like the fires of hell. Then he was gone in a flash, as if he just disappeared into thin air. But it was not the actions that had jarred her spirit; it was that gaze, one of pure evil. She moved back into the house wondering why it was here? She locked the door and sat down into her rocking chair in the darkened room lit by one kerosene lamp. As she rocked in the chair, she began to rhythmically chant an old chant to her gods, to protect her from evil spirits! Her former instinct compelled her now.

In the darkness of the room she chanted and rocked. This creature of darkness was getting closer as she sensed it with the hair on the nape of her neck standing straight up. Then she felt a cold claw rest on her right shoulder as she bravely turned to see who it was touching her. She saw it had twelve rows of eyes glowing red beacons in the shadows, shadows blacker than the night! Its fanged wide smiling grimace shocked and froze the poor old soul where she sat by the flickering light. All the fires of its mental hell rolled into her mind in an instant from its many eyes! She saw it for what it was in her last breath! ….and why it had come?

When Tully and Daphne returned an hour later, they found her sitting in her rocking chair, very dead. It would later be found that the old woman had died of a massive heart attack. However, the question of what gave her death-wielding heart attack remained. Both Tully and Daphne could not ever get Nanny Betsy's facial expression to leave them. The old woman's face was a death grimace of pure terror. Her mouth was wide open and her eyes had bulged to white orbs from her eye sockets. She had been terrified into death by something! One check on the children found them and the dogs piled together in bed sound asleep and unmolested.

Tully ran back to the Cavendish's to report this terrible event to the festive group. Josh, Tiberius, and Ambrose returned with him in great haste. Upon arrival it was evident to Cavendish's special senses that she had died of shock generated by something powerful, of great malfeasance. Josh felt the same with something deeper in detail. Unknown to anybody present, Joshua Marley was a very powerful Obeah man from long ago, a student of Takoo's ancient sect and secretly still guided major voodoo activities in this region of Jamaica. He was a master and seen as sort of a father figure to the many younger voodoo priests and priestesses.

Marley was confused now at the vibrations he picked up. He instinctively sensed as Ambrose had, that some very malevolent force had entered this house. The hair on the nape of his neck had stood straight up when he first entered it. Powerful evil had crossed this threshold! He touched the body of Nanny Betsy and felt a shockwave as he sensed the monster face of this malevolent entity. He walked outside to get some fresh air. The dogs had not been aroused, since all five of them were still sleeping with the children. His question was why it came here this night? Had Aunt Betsy provoked this visit from something she had done in the old days?

He felt that it was doubtful since as he was aware of all serious voodoo activities in this region, and besides, he had been a faithful friend of Nanny Betsy for many years! He would put his telepathic feelers out tonight! For now, he would stay at this place, as Ambrose walked all the sleepy little ones and their dogs up the road and safely home under a brilliant peaceful star-studded night. Josh Marley was joined by Tiberius who was armed with a double-barreled shotgun. Joshua was sure of one thing aside from the power of this thing; its vibrations were foreign.

Once again, Ayiti quietly sat on the balcony adjacent to Horace and Annabelle's large bedroom. He had watched her undress and prepare for sleep alone. He was mesmerized with a revived crazy lust as he watched her asleep. Her body was perfect. Her wasp-like waist complemented her large breasts and well-rounded ass. Her milky white skin seemed to ooze a wild sexual libido. His urges for this woman were almost uncontrollable now. He then thought of his killing of the old servant woman chanting in the chair. Just one face-to-face from Strawman did the trick on the old crone's heart. He had only touched her shoulder, but his hideous gaze had smashed her soul. Yet killing her as a possible witness would be part of his losing control before his game began.

Ayiti had checked out the house overlooking the bay only to get a feel for the connection between them and Annabelle since he watched her and her assumed husband ride to this abode by the bay in a buggy. He instinctively knew that if that old woman had lived, then rumors of an evil presence would filter out and security would be informed. Better a rumor of evil than a witness to it! He needed to be invisible until … until this Annabelle was his. He was amazed at how his powers were so focused on his lustful weakness of the flesh for this woman. It had been an age ago that Ayiti had felt this incredible urge.

It was as strong as his hell-bent revenge had been to those who had murdered Sarah as well as those Haitian fools that wronged him, or more appropriately "fucked him!". Ayiti spent the next day eavesdropping on her conversations by use of his keen sense of hearing at great distances. He now began concocting a good plan based on this learning of her usual shopping excursions she often made to Kingston. He laughed to himself as he flew high across the island back to his lair at Rose Hall. He would be back shortly to make Annabelle his!

The local constables came early the next morning to record the death and have the body of dear Nanny Betsy removed. Josh Marley spent the next day meeting with several voodoo leaders and friends who oversaw the region. It took him all day and into the evening to ask the fundamental question; was there any sign or rumor of any malfeasant presence?" The gut reaction was "No, none had been detected or heard of in this region at all." Josh then instructed his priests to check with the other voodoo priests across the island to determine anything strange occurring. This seemingly fruitless search began. Josh had previously instructed Tully, Daphne, and the Cavendish's to treat this unfortunate death as a simple heart attack. He told them in serious words that there was more involved. They both understood this.

Ambrose well understood this since his enhanced senses had also kicked in to the strange evil vibrations surrounding Nanny Betsy. Plans for a nice funeral had been arranged for Tuesday of the following week. All costs were covered by James and Jenny. It would be a funeral in the tradition of Jamaican religious beliefs. Josh knew that paying a normal significance to this unfortunate death would prevent a public panic. It was a key in unraveling exactly what or who had killed her. Nanny Betsy was an old friend and had no current connection with anything that would terrify her to death like this. Josh knew that something new was in the mix, but what could it be?

On Monday, as planned, Colonel Nephew and Elizabeth, under the guidance of Ambrose and Josh, made a lengthy tour of the Jamaican Prime estate by horseback. It was fun and took the immediate edge off the death of Nanny Betsy. At the conclusion of the tour, from the cane fields, to the new small villages, and to the processing plants, Elizabeth left the three men to visit Jenny and Annabelle in the main office building. The three men sat together in Josh and Ambrose's large office adjacent to the warehouse. Each sipped a glass of the new Jamaican Prime "Special" Rum and puffed on cigarettes donated by Nephew.

There was a momentary silence as Ambrose began the conversation. He looked squarely at Josh. "I sensed that the tragic death of Nanny Betsy was far from natural. I sensed the evil Josh!" I saw her face that was a death mask of pure terror reminiscent of poor "Old Wad!". The kind of terrorized death mask I saw in India, during the war against Kali and the green devils. Josh looked back. Cavendish had never spoken about any green devils he fought in India. He had heard the stories of the war in northern India, official ones from the newspapers of the day.

But this was a different spin on the subject and Ambrose's tone was remote and cold. Josh answered as he gave him and Tiberius a concerned fatherly gaze. "Mr. Ambrose, you are very correct. I felt the presence of something powerful and very evil had been in that house; I saw its terrible face when I touched the body of dear Betsy. Something literally scared her to death, yet any motive to this killing remains very obscure and senseless to me. She was a great woman, honest, and well loved by everybody."

Then Tiberius pulled up a large piece of paper with some sketches on it. Josh and Ambrose took a pull on the excellent rum and watched in silence as he spread the piece of white paper out on the table where they sat. Nephew then slid the paper over in front of the two men. Three sets of prints were numbered. "Gentlemen, when I left Tully's house in the morning after nanny had died, I investigated any evidence of footprints. I checked the road and then backtracked to the house." He showed them the area sketch of the road and to the house. I found a pair of footprints about seventy yards up next to the road facing Cavendish's house. They were regular large barefoot prints.

Then this person turned around facing Tully and Daphne's home. I backtracked towards the house where I saw strange prints in the sand right in front of the porch where they stopped. I checked the doors and windows and found no forced entry." "But Tully told me that Nanny Betsy always locked the door at night!" "If so" continued Tiberius, "something was able to open that door and enter at will. If Nanny had opened the door, then we would have found her on the floor would be my estimate, but that is a moot point to the other evidence." He pointed to the second sketch over to reveal what resembled strange large claw/hoof prints of some sort. "These were the different foot prints of something and it was found in the sand in front of the porch facing the house.

I found this set of them indented deep in the sand as if it had jumped from the air to create them. Now the compelling evidence I see, was that whatever it was, according to the barefoot prints seemed to be looking up the road away from Tully's house first." "How do you figure that?" came Cavendish's reply. Nephew smiled back after sipping some more rum and puffing on his cigarette. "Because the same foot prints were found on the other side of the road and were good imprints. The position of the prints showed that whoever it was, was looking up the road, then moving to get a good view of us on the deck!" He paused then finished. James, your house is the only house up the road so it was looking at you! Nanny Betsy must have interrupted it and so she was killed for it to cover its tracks so to speak!"

Ambrose was silent before speaking. "But why would this be happening? According to Ravi and Ronjin, we completely destroyed every one of the Kali's so-called staff members, so none of them could be looking for us now?" Josh added. "So far, according to my close contacts, nothing unusual has been going on anywhere on the island." More questions now seemed to surface in their minds now. The group then rounded up their horses for a ride through the shade covered road from the rum estate back towards Tully's house. Elizabeth would ride home with Jenny later.

When they arrived at Tully's place, they met a sullen Daphne and her children. She had taken off a couple days of her duties at Jenny's request to tend to the loss of nanny Betsy and console her kids. Both Nephew and Cavendish watched in amazement as Josh carefully performed some ritual over the foot prints and then the deep claw like prints next to the porch. He spent thirty minutes carefully analyzing the second set of prints. At one point, he rested the side of his face on the prints. Then, as if struck by lightning, he reeled back suddenly and moved away from them. Both men saw the look of extreme fear in his face. He was shaking as they helped him to his feet. Finally, he nervously stammered. "Pure evil came here in the night! Powerful entity was here; foreign to Jamaica I know!

A demon! One that changed shapes and jumped from the road to visit nanny Betsy! I get the same feeling, but much stronger here as I did with touching her body the night of her death! Since there were no prints between the foot imprints next to the road and the deep large claw prints next to the porch in the sand, it must have jumped some fifty feet from the road to the porch area." Josh scratched his head then continued. "I rechecked all of this. But why here? Why?" The words "shape Changer" caught the immediate attention of both soldiers. They instinctively knew more than they said. Marley continued speaking nervously. "Bad things to come to all of us with the power I sense from this dark creature!"

He looked imploringly at his two companions "We need to find it, divine what it came here for, find its lair and destroy it!" "Use voodoo Josh?" "Yes Mr. Ambrose, we must fight fire with fire, but yet, we do not have any clue on it!" Cavendish smiled at this unusual man. "Can you tell me about voodoo, teach it to me?" Joshua Marley gave a wide smile. "I am in a position to teach you as much as you want to know. I will gladly do this if you tell me about this Kali and the green devil cult?" Ambrose gave a reassuring look. "You have a deal!" after Tiberius and Ambrose left Marley pulled out a pencil. He then sketched the image of the evil face he had seen in his vision after touching the body of Nanny Betsy. He stared at it and his fear exacerbated again.

Ayiti's impatience was obvious as he sat in the tree line across from the White Hall mansion behind the large white picket fence that lined this part of the road. It was late afternoon and five days had passed since he had killed the old black lady. He then saw a couple of women, very pretty ones, ride up to the front of the mansion. Once dismounted, they ventured into the large white columned home. It reminded him of those European French estates of old, the ones plundered and burned during the slave rebellions of yore in Haiti. He slipped around behind the house and hid within earshot of the three women now sitting together on the veranda.

He listened the idle women chatter as they enjoyed a few drinks. Then, his ears perked up as he heard Annabelle invite them to go on a shopping trip in Kingston the next day. She named off several stores and ended the list with a name and "our last stop for the day." He felt that his chance to kidnap her was a good possibility. He was excited and slipped away. He had a plan formulating in his mind. The thought of his hands and mouth on her body was driving him into an erotic frenzy! Ayiti realized that he had never ever felt this intense "lightening" attraction to a woman like this ever!

Nanny Betsy was buried in a small service Tuesday according to custom. Many voodoo priests and priestesses were present as Marley helped preside over the painful solemn funeral. Both James and Jenny Cavendish were present along with Tully and Daphne to pay their heartfelt respects. After it was over James joined the group in the production office as they talked about the possibility of what it was that attacked Nanny Betsy. He learned of Josh's great prominence in the voodoo community and was impressed. He mused at the phrase "Never judge a book by its cover!"

This was here where he first heard of the famous sect of Voodoo hunters; Warriors of the old school who killed with arrows, spears, clubs, machetes, and knives. Cavendish was impressed at how they were organized to find this night demon. James well remembered what Ravi had told him. "The Kali feared a spear over a pistol shot and therefore he was vulnerable to a primitive weapon before he knew how to defend against weapons. The learned mindset of these powerful entities in this kind of belief system can be their death warrant!" When in reality the Kali died from the fear of the Ironwood Zulu spear rather than the strike! Then there was the ancient specially made dagger that was designed to kill any of these beings.

Ambrose knew that Marley and his hunters would get to the bottom of this. The terrible image of this night demon was very alive in both men's minds. Thursday morning came fast. Joshua and Ambrose had returned to work on Wednesday to oversee the operations. Today Colonel Nephew, Uncle Jake, and Major Cavendish went to hunt wild Boar in the Blue Mountains that lined the north part of the Jamaican Prime estate. It was also the day that Jenny, Elizabeth, and Annabelle went on a shopping trip to Kingston. Lord Farnsworth went deep sea fishing with Tully as his wife and Aunt Miriam joined the old admiral in the boat.

Josh had supplied a couple of worthy guides to help the boys hunt wild Boar, which commenced early after sunrise. The men each carried high-powered Colt .45 automatic pistols and long fifteen-foot sharp flexible metal spears. Uncle Jake, a gun enthusiast, had given him a pair of them as a Christmas present and had brought his own. These were official US Army Colt prototypes; sturdy and well-made weapons. His uncle had also added one case of ammunition. Uncle Jake had connections! They had test fired them a couple of days earlier into the ocean from the rear stone viewing area. They were powerful and very effective show stoppers at close quarters. They punched like the .45-wheel gun Ambrose had used to kill green devils with in the jungle war.

Cavendish had also strung Krupp's sub-machine gun on his shoulder as a precaution, in case they really screwed up on the hunt and needed some backup firepower besides the automatic pistols and spears. Uncle Jake had a ball shooting Krupp's invention. The guides each carried shotguns as well. Ambrose had never hunted wild Boar in these mountains before because of the obvious demands of his job and family. He had been taught how to hunt them by his worker buddies at the rum estate. Horace had told him to take the day off and if he returned without a boar, then Ambrose owed him a one hundred-pounds in gold coin. Horace would pay one hundred pounds in gold coins each for the first three Boars killed if they were so lucky.

It was a fair bet since the guides furnished by Josh were the best. The traditional Boar kill would begin with impaling a charging boar on a long flexible wire spear, then killing it as it plunged forward as the grounded spear pierced it deep, with a couple of pistol shots to the head. Tiberius laughed at the pronouncement of this method; "just like killing the undead old top but we now have spears instead of sabers!" It was a true all man kind of hunt which Elizabeth would have loved. They group dismounted their horses at the base of the mountain with an attendant. the five men arduously trekked up through the heavy forested hills to a good ambush site often used by the workers.

The guides led them up to the small field loaded with tubular plants the wild boars loved. It was a favorite hunting site. The guides had told them that the Boars would suddenly attack with or without provocation. If they had children with them, they would always attack! When they found this small open area, the guides located fresh tracks of some rather large Boars. They followed the tracks into a small field of overgrown vegetation as rays of sunlight broke through the tall forest trees. "Dis is a good place mon!" explained one of the smiling young guides named Benjamin Jobo. "We got many here before! Now make sure that your spear is stuck deep into the ground to hold when the boar attacks! If the spear is not rooted, it will eat your face off with its sharp tusks." Jobo was smiling.

Nephew looked at Cavendish as they were placed about thirty yards apart out of sight of each other in the foliage. Uncle Jake was placed father off the left. The guides stepped back into the brush behind them, armed with shotguns. They pointed out to the trio their trees as emergency backup in case the boars got loose! Time went by as the sunrise gave off a hot temperature amid the humidity of the leafy jungle floor. The morning mists were gone. They sweated and waited quietly as their military training snapped in. They had all been told that tubular growth was ideal; honey to the boars.

Colonel Nephew had figured out that he would see a charging boar no farther than twenty feet to his front if he were lucky. Then, after an hour of waiting in the hot greenery of the forest jungle, they all heard the snorting of a group of boars as they entered the area and the yapping squeals of little ones bumping into their mothers. It was a large group. Then, as expected a couple of large boars sensed their presence. Instantly, with ears up, they broke from the herd and charged.

It reminded Cavendish of a land shark of sorts with the brush being its water. They came at a high rate of speed snorting and whining as its large brown furry body smashed the brush towards him. As one went for Ambrose, two adults charged at Nephew. The first one ran perfectly onto his long flexible spear as he held and aimed it firmly. This first boar was grounded trying to go through the spear as it thrashed for the colonel. Then the second one busted from the foliage and charged at him. My gosh he thought, they were big, pissed off and ugly!

Rather than play with both, he turned to the one stuck on the spear and fired three shots from his Colt .45 into its large contorted face. He did not look to see if it was dead because he had to jump off his position and was barely missed by the tusks of the second boar missing him by a mere couple of feet! It squealed into the brush. They could now hear Uncle Jake firing from his adjacent position to the right of Cavendish. The second one that passed Nephew kept going and disappeared into the green forest floor.

Suddenly a huge boar sprang from the brush at Cavendish who had been distracted by Nephews pistol shots. Cavendish quickly aimed his spear with the behemoth yards away and his spear caught it in a shoulder missing the kill shot! It was only grazed and forced the spear out of the ground as it moved to the right. Cursing, Cavendish then fell backwards and was trying to get distance from the enraged beast when he heard the guides, in the trees yelling and motioning at him. He fired several shots from his .45 into the speared boar to his right now and backed up and leaned on a tree. The guides were frantically yelling at him and pointing off to his left.

Holstering his automatic pistol, turned to the left and quickly brought the Krupp Model 1895SMG up and took off the safety. The guides continued screaming and pointing in the direction directly in front of him, but the thick undergrowth prevented him from seeing anything. Suddenly another boar busted from the thick brush only yards away. He was now trapped between two dangerous boars. Facing the enraged boar, he fired out a long burst of 9MM bullets from his hip emptying half of the magazine of thirty-two rounds at it. He swung around behind the tree to avoid its charge as it hit the tree with a loud thud.

Then he heard the loud snorting of the first boar that had pierced his spear. The machinegun fire had momentarily stopped it, but now it was moving at him. This time Ambrose aimed the SMG and carefully emptied the remaining dozen rounds into its head. Everything was suddenly quiet. He saw that both boars he had machinegunned were dead. Uncle Jake's pistol fire had been completely obscured by the loud fire from the SMG. But Jake had bagged one as well. All three men were drawn by the sudden boar attack. Both guides jumped out of their tree.

Nephew was beaming as his old khaki uniform was soaked with sweat. Nephew yelled. "Ambrose? Jake? Are you all right???" Ambrose!" "Yes Nephew, one of these buggers nearly got me but I finished it!" The guides left their protective trees and ventured over to where Cavendish had killed his wild hogs by automatic fire. The weapon's rapid discharge had amazed them. They next went over to where the colonel had speared the first boar and found him standing over it. He delivered a "coup de grace" shot to finish it. They all walked over to where Uncle Jake was now standing.

Nephew stood in the small clearing with one foot on the large hairy beast and a flask in one hand and his trusty .45 in the other. He took a grand sip of special rum. "Looks like I got a picture-perfect kill old boy!" He was laughing. "Ambrose, did you get the one I sent to you? I was very busy with this one." "Yes Nephew, I was very thankful for your kind gift, it almost ran up my ass but Krupp saved me again!" They looked at Uncle Jake who was also smiling. "We heard you firing at something so what happened?"

Jake was laughing. "The boar coming after me startled and scared the shit out of me so I grabbed my spear and ran back a few feet behind a tree and emptied a magazine into it as it charged me! The monster tried to knock the tree down! My rounds wounded it, then I speared the bastard!" "So, you killed the monster backwards?" added Nephew. Jake laughed, "Why not?" Ambrose took a large plug from the rum offered by Nephew and passed it around the group.

"Colonel" began Ambrose, "Since you gave me the Krupp weapon that saved my ass, in honor of your perfect kill, I now bequeath you that .45 you so gallantly used in direct combat against the boar!" Tiberius tipped the flask. "I am humbled by your generosity and hunting spirit Major! I gracefully accept this gift!" More rum was passed around with water. Four Boars had been killed. Both the guides were impressed and joined in the rum salute. It was a very quick kill they said. Ambrose let them both fire the sub machinegun in great fun; a weapon, that would not be created for another thirty-four years and used by a belligerent attack on September 3, 1939 in a yet to be created country named Poland.

The four deceased wild boars were hoisted by the group into sturdy tree limbs by their feet and gutted. The throats were cut first to drain out the blood, and then all the entrails went next. The guide named Jobo completed this task with long razor-sharp knife on the first boar as the boys watched. Then they pitched in a helped gut the other three since the other guide had left to fetch the horses. Ben Jobo, a mere lad estimated each boar had to weigh between one-hundred and fifty and two-hundred pounds each. The other guide soon returned with the horses and donkeys to carry out the prizes.

There was enough meat on these boars to feed all the workers and then some! It was midafternoon when the jovial group returned to Jamaican Prime. They quenched their thirst on gin and tonics over crushed ice. Horace and Josh joined them for these celebration drinks. They were impressed at the fruitful bounty from the hunt! Horace flipped three-hundred shiny gold crowns to both Ambrose, Tiberius and Jake. He then tossed fifty crowns each to the guides as a gift from the bet. The great stories of the hunt enthralled and humored Horace and Joshua over the next hour!

Then Horace had one of his men take several pictures of the armed group standing in front of the boars that were now suspended on huge ropes behind them. "Thanks for your gift boys!" He said. Looks like everybody gets fresh wild boar tonight for dinner. The girls are all gone to Kingston and we shall enjoy the magic cooking of our Jamaican chefs and joyous company of our workers. "Colonel Nephew looked with studied interest as the boars were put on large spits, prepared and hoisted onto pre-prepared cooking fires build in the ground in pits.

Word of the boars killed spread throughout the estate. As the cooking progressed, he watched as the master cooks applied some local marinade to the now cooking beasts. They were constantly basted and turned slowly on the hand-cranked spits. The body cavities of the boars were stuffed with Mangos and Apples then sown up. Dinner would be a late affair. Many workers showed up with their families with extra side foods to compliment the feast. Horace donated many cases of rum to the village women who created the most divine rum punch as they did for the Christmas Party days earlier.

Fun and excellent food were had by all this night. Nephew was having a riot with the villagers, as he, Jake, and Ambrose frolicked and danced to the primitive music and drumbeats. Horace even joined them for a while. It was very obvious to Colonel Nephew that these workers adored Horace and would follow him anywhere. The rum consumption seemed to take center after the wonderful Christmas Boar was served under the beaming lights produced by many torches spread on tall poles in the area. The great Boar hunters, now greatly bombed, sat around one of the many bonfires enjoying the wonderful Christmas celebration with the workers and families. One great and memorable hunt was now ended; as another hunt had already begun!

Just before noon as the boys were fighting boars in the Blue Mountain Range, three lovely ladies, dressed in their finest light tropical dresses arrived by open coach in the downtown Kingston shopping district. Their spirits were high, as Annabelle had described the great stores they were to visit. There were so many new styles of clothes and other nice things to find this day. As one hunt was in progress, another planned sinister hunt was about to bear fruit as well!

As the ladies purchased items, they handed them to Annabelle's two servants Vincent and Nickolas. These two had driven them in a two-horse coach into town. They had been part of the estate staff at White Hall for a long time and were used to the antics and routine of Miss Annabelle. Vincent was an older gentleman and Nickolas was younger. He did most of the carrying of purchased goods and Vincent guarded the contents stored in the rear of the coach from theft as it waited on the cobblestone streets in the elegant shopping area in downtown Kingston.

By late afternoon the girls had done most of their shopping with only a couple of stores left to visit. They had taken a lot of time in each store and Nicholas had been very busy hauling their wares to the coach. He got to rest as the ladies had a late lunch at a posh restaurant inside one of the best hotels in Kingston. The food was excellent as they enjoyed a nice buzz from several drinks. Afterward, in happy half-drunk moods, they ventured to the next to last shop. The late sunlight accented the beauty of Kingston as the girls merrily laughed and played like children into their next place.

They were on their way to the last one on Annabelle's list. It was a dress shop specializing in the latest French tropical fashions on a side street secluded off the main avenue. Annabelle had yet to visit it since it was a relatively new addition. Excited and in great moods, the three ladies entered it. The owner, a very well-dressed handsome mulatto gentleman named Masseur Roftus, met them at the door. He was quick with wit and humor and soon had the ladies laughing.

He began showing the wares of his shop and they all were having a great time trying the new dresses on and parading around the shop. Roftus joined in the fun. After a while he looked at the three very pretty ladies and smiled showing his perfect white teeth. "May I offer you some rum punch ladies, to keep you merry?" They all agreed and Masseur poured them glasses of tasty punch. He already had one in his hand. The drinks soon had a special effect on the women. They became boisterous and very drunk.

Nicholas was on hand to take the purchased items to the carriage and store them with the other merchandise. He looked at Vincent upon his return with a laugh. "Des women having a ball in there Vincent, like a party of sorts. We may be here all-night mon! What should we do?" Vincent smiled at the younger man. "We do what we always do with Lady Annabelle and wait! I will check on her as usual in a while and you can guard the coach. The horses had already been fed and watered." He shared a small pint of rum with Vincent as they milled around the coach which was sitting up the street on the main road.

Two hours passed and Vincent decided to venture into the posh dress shop to see what was going on with Annabelle and the two other women. It was dusk now. The sun was now nearly gone and it was getting late. The kerosene lamps were being lit on the streets as he walked down the side street to the door of the shop. He tried to open the door but it was locked. This was strange, so he knocked, and knocked on the door for ten minutes until he wondered where they had gone? This was not like Annabelle!

There were no lights in the shop, so he went around to the back of the store. He knocked on the door but there was again; no answer. "Where had his ladies gone?" He found the rear door to be unlocked and entered the store in the dark. He called out Annabel's name several times and then stopped. He lit a small kerosene lamp hanging near the rear door and began moving into the store front. The store was now dark and he was nervous for some reason. His better instincts told him to get a constable, but fearing for Mrs. Annabelle, he continued on. As he left the rear room, he tripped over something on the floor.

He shined the lamp close and saw an arm protruding from a pile of boxes. He removed the boxes and found the body of what would later be identified as Masseur Roftus on the floor. He saw that this man's s head had somehow been crushed flat like a pancake! He noticed that the pool of blood surrounded this dead man had coagulated. He had been dead for a while was his estimate. A foreboding fear struck Vincent as he pulled out his knife and ventured into the main room of the shop. He discovered Jenny and Elizabeth fast asleep with their heads resting on a table. They were alive but passed out cold. Annabelle was nowhere to be seen but he heard noises from the office. He then moved into a very small office.

His lamplight exposed two people, one was Annabelle and the other was some very strange looking man. He was sexually engaging her dog style over the desk. When Vincent looked at the man's glare, he shouted at them more from the fear of what he saw in the man's face as it turned to him. He was looking at the face of a monster! Before he could move, he saw some object, shiny by the lamplight coming at him. He felt a sharp pain in his forehead as a sharp dagger stuck ten inches through his skull into his brain. He was dead before he hit the ground.

Ayiti had been guided by his frantic lust for Annabelle and realized how careless he had been to have tasted Annabel's wares here. She was completely out of sorts since he had laced the lady's drinks with his special medicine. He put her near lifeless body on his shoulder and headed deftly to a small carriage parked the rear ally where a motionless Jean Zombi waited for his master. The carriage left completely unnoticed by anybody. They went directly to Kingston harbor in a hurried pace for a boat he had rented under an alias. The coach was left at the secluded dock and the horse was freed. This mini coastal steamer was headed to Montego Bay.

Nicholas waited for nearly two more hours before he grew apprehensive and was now worried. Something was very wrong! It was nearly half past ten. Vincent would have been back long before now. This made little sense for these women to be literally partying in a clothes shop and this late? He approached this shop and like Vincent, found the front door locked and lights out! He entered the rear door now left ajar and to his horror, he found the dead body of the shop owner inside the door by tripping over it. He found a second kerosene lamp and began calling out for Vincent and Annabelle.

He ignored the two women at the table as he soon found Vincent lying in the office doorway, with a dagger stuck deep into his forehead. In a panic, he went to the table where the two women were passed out. They were now groggy and were beginning to wake up still under the effects of the loaded drinks. Annabel was nowhere to be found. He unlocked the front door and soon found a couple of constables walking down the street.

The shop was eventually filled with police. This was now a huge crime scene of a double murder. The very young Chief Inspector named Oscar Peacock had arrived and took charge of the crime scene as evidence was surveyed. It was nearly two in the morning when a very inebriated foursome returned down the moonlit road, stopping in front of White Hall on their horses. Horace dismounted in clumsy fashion and bid a good night to his companions. They had been singing and laughing all the way. They bid Horace a good evening and leisurely moved down the road towards the Cavendish house overlooking the bay. In thirty minutes, after enjoying a slow starlit ride were home. Daphne, Tully, and Miriam Meyers were up waiting for them.

They were very concerned since the girls had yet to return from Kingston! Something was wrong, very wrong! About five minutes later Horace arrived on his horse in a gallop. He ran in the house excited. "Are the girls here he stammered?" Ambrose looked at him squarely. "No, they are not here." Horace blurted. "We must ride to Kingston; it will take about forty minutes with a fast trot." Tiberius, feeling the effects of the rum from the workers party spoke. "We are still a bit tipsy boys. Let's get some coffee in our bodies and get a little straight first!" added Cavendish. "Showing up drunk or falling off a horse in the dark would be foolish now."

A pot of coffee was brewed and as they sipped it, they all heard horses, voices, and sounds of a carriage arrive outside. They watched as the chief inspector of the Kingston Constabulary walked through the door with both Jenny and Elizabeth behind him. They looked disheveled and very worn out. Other police officials came in bringing a very shaken Nicholas. Cavendish and Nephew instinctually latched on to their ladies and hugged them. Jenny was wiped out and took rest on a nearby couch. Coffee was served as Horace asked the whereabouts of his Annabelle. The chief inspector was a very young gentleman who kindly introduced himself as Oscar Peacock. He seemed very intelligent and astute officer as he confronted the men with the details.

They listened carefully to the evidence presented. What had happened to Annabelle Farnsworth? The chief inspector told that it seemed that someone had used the shop as a trap to kidnap her for reasons unknown. Evidently the owner had been murdered and someone had taken his place. This same person later killed poor Vincent as he must have surprised whoever was doing the mischief. Both Jenny and Elizabeth seemed more drugged than drunk and confusingly talked of the so-called owner who was a handsome tall mulatto man who seemed a very smart and very funny. He was refined and polished.

The drinks offered by the phony Masseur Rolfus had obviously drugged them. Nicholas then verified what Peacock's information. The real Rolfus had his head crushed nearly flat, and poor Vincent had a dagger stuck deep into his head. Joshua Marley and his young understudy Ben Jobo soon arrived. They listened to the information supplied by Peacock, Nicholas, and the ladies in fearful silence. "What is being done now to find my wife?" stammered a stricken Horace. "We have sent patrols down every road leaving Kingston and are searching the harbor and any small docks in the area. Whoever kidnapped Mrs. Farnsworth has a good head start sir." Replied Inspector Peacock.

Our search for your wife is ongoing now Mr. Farnsworth!" Horace was silent as the police bid a "good night" and left. It was late and slowly, all of the party at Cavendish's home found places to sleep. Horace sat up for the rest of the night frozen in worry. Something was bothering him, perhaps dreams? Why did he seem to feel or somehow sense this obscure kidnapper? Josh and Ben returned to Cavendish's home just after the sun came up as everybody was awake. Josh went into the kitchen and brewed a large pot of coffee and helped Daphne fix some breakfast.

Tully arrived the next hour with all the kids and dogs in tow. Jenny was ill from her ordeal and was in bed. The drug slipped on her had made her very sick. Dr. Toussaint had been dispatched. The rest of them sat quietly assessing what had happened and possible motives. Soon, five men were riding towards Kingston. They were heading to the clothier's shop where this fateful incident had occurred. All of them were lost to their thoughts as they rode. Josh needed to see it, and feel the vibrations as did Ambrose. The astute investigative eye of Colonel Nephew would also help.

The five horsemen reached the shop and dismounted within the hour. The front door was open as inspector Peacock met them at the door. Several constables were still inside. "Good morning gentlemen" began Peacock. He looked very proper dressed professionally in his police uniform. He ushered them into the shop where he bid them to be seated. A pot of fresh tea appeared and all settled into a cup. The chief continued. "We did not find Annabelle last night. We did, however, find a carriage near the east dock abandoned and the horse wandering loose nearby. We suspect that Annabelle's kidnappers must have taken her away by boat. Nothing else seems to have surfaced yet.

I have already telegrammed all the other constabularies on the island to be on the lookout for this man and your wife Mr. Farnsworth. No unusual boat has been located and the dock ship manifests are being reviewed." Meanwhile, Josh was up and moving through the shop to the small office. He already sensed the same malignant force around poor Betsy. Traces of its aura were still evident to one who was trained to sense them. Ben Jobo, his chief understudy in voodoo sensed the same things. No policeman could ever divine this type of evidence. He nervously continued his search as Ben Jobo followed him. Cavendish was also vectoring in on the same evil vibrations as he followed them.

Josh entered the office the auric presence of this thing was so strong, he had to step back. Even his young understudy felt it and stopped. Joshua saw the ornate bloody dagger, actually a stiletto lying upon a red stained white cloth on the desk. He smelled the evil hand that had held it as he looked closely. It was here and sensed what had occurred. Then he reached over and picked up the stiletto, covered in gold and silver with a coat of arms inlaid in it with jewels. As he picked it up, he shuddered and dropped it back on the desk. He backed fearfully from the room harboring great inner fear. He felt a mortal chill race up his spine as he stumbled into the front of the shop where the others were. He saw this thing and also knew what it had been doing to Annabelle on that desk!

Ben Jobo touched the dagger and pulled his hand away as if he had been burned. He had been shocked by the evil auric presence. When Ambrose picked it up, he momentarily saw a tall evil specter which seemed to have a head filled with red eyes. Then he remembered the red eyes from another time; Kai! Something terrible now manifested in their lives, something dark and evil. Josh spoke nervously. "It was here, this creature from the pit! It was the same thing that murdered Aunt Betsy! Perhaps the legend of it is true now. What I sensed; was the intense evil power it does possess!" "What creature from the pit Josh?' Asked a frantic Horace Farnsworth. Josh looked at his friend painfully.

"legends, very old ones spoke of a powerful Haitian voodoo king said to be a Loa god, with incredible powers and cunning and a very evil force; a monster to all who survived meeting it. It was alleged that this dark creature of many shapes manipulated the dictators and was responsible for many gruesome deaths in Haiti where it came from. This was the one, according to lore, that came to these shores long ago escaping the wrath of Dictator Boyer of Haiti." Then he went quiet as he assembled more thoughts.

"It was on a ship headed for Kingston in 1842 and was captured on board by several of Boyer's henchmen. This voodoo king was to be returned to Haiti for execution! However, all of Boyer's men were horribly slain after they captured it on the ship. Afterwards, this monster of the dark realms disappeared, never to be found. It just became part of one myth of many on this island!" Inspector Oscar Peacock looked very serious and had a distant look on his face as he spoke as if hypnotized.

"This incident on the ship was no myth! I think we need to talk to the person who had the firsthand experience on this ship in 1842. My Great Uncle Ian Peacock was the constable that met up with Boyer's men in Cuba and was on the boat when this evil man headed to Jamaica was captured." He then rolled up the stiletto in paper to take to visit the old retired constable. By early afternoon, the group was seated on the rustic veranda of a nice old bungalow that overlooked a beach south of Spanish Town.

Officer Peacock introduced his Uncle Ian Peacock to the gentlemen as they sat around a large table. The old constable was pushing into his late eighties. Hot tea was served as a bottle of rum was put on the table. Everybody opted for the tea, as Cavendish and Nephew took a couple of shots of rum. They were still feeling the effects of the previous night's gala party wild boar feast at the estate. They needed to bite the snake that had bitten them. Old Uncle Ian Peacock was a delightful old man with long lines in his face topped with a full head of bushy white hair. The pleasant formalities lasted for a while as they spent time trading stories around the table.

Then young Oscar Peacock spoke. "Grand Uncle, something terrible has happened to Horace Farnsworth's wife Annabelle. She was kidnapped under terrible circumstances yesterday in Kingston. We fear who may have kidnapped her uncle and this is why we visit." Old Ian sensed something different than a routine kidnapping and asked. What has kidnapped her son?" A confused Oscar took a breath. "Joshua seems to believe it was a powerful entity, the mythological voodoo king who escaped custody on that ship from you in 1842." Young Peacock looked at his uncle who was becoming lost in his past thoughts now. "Uncle, can you tell your story to them, about the man escaping the wrath of Dictator Boyer?" The group watched as the old man's mood changed as he took a large plug from the rum bottle. He solemnly looked at each guest as they saw obvious ancient fear in his eyes. He was silent after taking a second shot of the rum, then began his story.

"I remember seeing him clearly in that room in the hold of the ship after they brought him in. He was an extremely handsome mulatto man with a broad smile and perfect white teeth. Boyer's men began torturing this man they called "Little Ayiti" and I refused to be part of it and left." Old Ian then laughed. "Ha, after he slaughtered Boyer's men, "Little Ayiti" was kind enough to buy me a drink where I was at the crowded bar on the ship. Ayiti had drugged the drink! The bartender told me this drink was from president Boyer as a thank you for helping catch this man named to me earlier as Dr. Emile…a…Emile St. Denis." Ian laughed in remembering this event. "How considerate Ayiti was in buying me a drink! I did not recover completely for nearly three weeks from the opiated zombie like effects of the potent.

After I awoke in the hospital days later, I was informed as to the grisly fate of Boyer's people holding this rascal below deck." Ian Peacock then gave the details of the savagely murdered henchmen. He retorted that "I will never forget the photo of that bloody face, smacked on the wall above the window in that hold!" The description given by the old retired police chief ran through Joshua's mind like a lightning bolt! He then remembered how Messier Roftus's head had been smashed flat as if two sledge hammers had hit the sides of his head at the same time. Oscar, who bore a much younger image of his great uncle asked. "So, the ship docked in Kingston without this Ayiti?" The old man thought.

"Exactly, this ship docked in Montego Bay first and then Kingston was the final stop here before it departed for the next island stop. There was no evidence to show where he got off the boat, only that his port for disembarkation was Kingston. I feel that he jumped ship somewhere near the port of Montego Bay or hopefully stowed on the ship and perhaps continued on to another island! After many months and no evidence of him being sighted; he was filed away." Old Peacock took another shot of rum, joined this time by Ambrose, Horace, and Tiberius. Old Peacock continued.

"We had scourged the whole area at Montego Bay for several weeks trying to find this mystery man but to no avail. The authorities searched throughout the island for over a year for him. The trail of this "Little Ayiti" literally ended on the boat. This is why we came to believe he actually sailed as a stowaway to another island. I remember well before his death when the leader and voodoo master of Boyer's henchmen told me this "Little Ayiti!" was a powerful dangerous monster with many great evil powers! He was facing execution by Boyer personally, but the huge Cape Haiten earthquake and tsunami of 1842 destroyed San Souci Palace and "Ayiti" managed to escape. Sans Souci Palace was destroyed and the great tsunami further destroyed Cape Haiten and much of the coastline killing thousands."

He sipped some rum and continued his story. "All I can tell you is that I saw his red-eyed gaze as he looked at me in the hold of that ship; he looked into my soul with terrifying effect. The thought of him still runs shivers up my old spine!" Josh pulled the jeweled stiletto with the elaborate coat of arms from the wrapping and laid it before the old man. "Can you tell me who the coat of arms belongs too?" Ian studied it and looked up. This is the original coat of arms for the first ruler/governor of Haiti named Deschamps! Where did you get this?" Josh replied. "It was stuck through the skull of one of Farnsworth's servants who must have interrupted him in the shop where Annabelle was kidnapped sir." "Looks like this is evidence that this kidnapper has a definite connection to Haiti!" added Tiberius. Josh then wrapped up the knife and put it in his side pocket.

Ian added. "I now remember Joshua; The name of this monster spoken by Boyer's head security man was "Ayiti Deschamps" masked in the identity of Doctor Emile St. Denis when he was in route here to Jamaica! I bet he had several identities." The group, enjoying the sun and company of the venerable old Mr. Peacock telling stories for a little longer then they all left. The name "Ayiti Deschamps" was on all their lips. Who was this man, this handsome youngish looking man who fled Haiti on this ship long ago in 1842? The group bid Ian Peacock farewell and Horace gave him a stack of pounds and a case of fine Jamaican Prime Rum as a gift. When they returned to the police station there was some information waiting for them.

The expensive dagger pulled from Vincent's skull had belonged to a cousin of the first governor of Hispaniola named Deschamps. He was savagely murdered along with his entire family and plantation staff when his plantation was burned in a slave revolt in the late 17th century. His initials were on it. Also, it was confirmed that the ship that brought this mysterious Dr. St. Denis to Jamaica sailed from Santo Domingo in 1842. It would later be discovered that this Ayiti has a dark violent history in Haiti. But the odd piece of this disturbing puzzle was that this Ayiti Deschamps was traced back as far as the 1750s; alleged to have been the son of the one-armed revolutionary Mackandal! Mackandal was burned at the stake in 1758.

The police sergeant reading the report handed it over to constable Peacock. Cavendish looked at Nephew. "This guy would be well over one-hundred and fifty years old now and he was seen as a handsome young mulatto man described by both Jenny and Elizabeth; then by old constable Peacock who saw him the same way in 1842!" Both Ambrose and Tiberius did not like hearing this detail one bit. This reminded them of another place, time among people where age was a strange factor.

According to Ravi, the Kali, in a former guise had led some of the bloody conquests of the conquistadors, which recorded him over four hundred years old when he met his fate at the end of Hook's Zulu spear in the jungle battle compliments of Captain James Cavendish. Then there was also the Kali's interlude after he escaped from his life as Cortes as a master entrepreneur of slaves from Africa to the New World. His business operation, according to Ravi, was located on an island in the Caribbean!

It then dawned on both men as they remembered how Ravi had been concerned if Kali had created any offspring in his travels in the New World! it was still a possibility. Having sex with a human was one thing, but a child by hybrid/hybrid parents with their joint gene pool would present a powerful offspring! Ravi had feared this combination in constant concern about Bad apple offspring. In Colonel Nephew's estimate the pieces were now fitting too well regarding this Ayiti character. Was Ayiti an offspring of the fallen Kali? A double hybrid monster perhaps?

"Little Ayiti" possibility being this son of Kali was only conjecture at this point with no real proof. Other than rumor, no special talents had been observed in this person of interest in this kidnapping! It was a kidnapping thus far except for one flattened head of the shop owner done with great force. But if this Ayiti was that double hybrid offspring of Kali, then the words of Ravi cut deep. Cavendish fearfully remembered Kali's final gaze well. Its powerful magnetic eyes ripped his very soul hard after he had plunged the Zulu spear in it to the hilt under its throat!

Constable Oscar Peacock was working on the many possible whereabouts of Annabelle, since she could be anywhere or even taken from Jamaica completely! As he continued with his police investigative action, Joshua Marley obviously took the voodoo route. At this point, all Horace, Ambrose, and Tiberius could do was wait for marching orders if anything came up. All of this seemed surrealistic at this point. Upon their return to the Cavendish house they found everyone in better spirits in spite of the events. Ambrose and Tiberius were completely washed out and both went to bed upon their return. Ambrose, in a dream state, found himself in the jungle and walked upon a clearing to find Pyra; as beautiful as ever.

He approached her and held her hands. Then she stepped back and warned! "Beware Ambrose, Beware!" Then suddenly an evil green-faced Kali rushed from the bushes and grabbed her. When Ambrose saw this, Pyra had changed into the likeness of Annabelle! It licked her face fondling her then gave a cruel evil laugh. Then holding her fast, it carried her up a large tree and flew away. Cavendish had tried to grab her from it but became mired in quicksand. Ambrose woke up with a start as Jenny hugged him. He was shaking as if he had Malaria and yelling for Pyra. Jenny held him and kissed him. He stared at Jenny. "Pyra just told me the fate of Annabelle!" He knew the truth clearly.

Pyra was symbolizing the kidnapping of Annabelle and there was great danger here! It was an ancient creature of the night that had kidnapped Annabelle! "Little Ayiti" was gaining prominence in this now! When he woke up Jenny asked who Pyra was from his dreams. He told her, as before, that she was Ravi's wonderful daughter and his special friend since he had saved her and Ravi's life. Telling her the truth of his love for her would only confuse and anger Jenny. Eternal love was very different than temporal! He told her what Pyra had revealed in the dream. He needed to see Joshua immediately.

The next day all seemed to be a normal one at the Jamaican Prime Estate since the workers were largely unaware of the fate of Annabelle at this point. The cycle of growing, harvesting, and production of coffee and rum continued. This machine was well greased by the constant efforts of Ambrose, Josh, and the excellent managers they had employed from the workers. Horace had been alone in his office all day. Ambrose and Tiberius entered the rustic office in the production building he shared with

Josh Marley at ten. Josh was sitting at his desk sipping some tea quietly. He smiled at Ambrose as he entered. The early heat of the day forced him to take off his white summer double-breasted suit jacket. He grabbed a cup of hot tea and sat across from Marley, as was their custom before they began the day.

There was no usual breakfast served this day at White Hall for understandable reasons of the kidnapping and the late arrival of Ambrose with his friend to work this day. Ambrose had to tell Joshua about his dream. After exchanging their "good mornings" Josh asked "is Jenny all right?" as Ambrose replied "Yes, the doctor is with her now and she seems to be coming around." "That is good my friend. Horace is in his office and not seeing anybody today. He seems to be in a world of despair now because of the disappearance of his wife and murder of Vincent." Ambrose sipped his tea and looked serious at Marley.

"I can only imagine Josh and I need to tell you about a dream I had last night! Before this, I need to tell you more detail of my exploits in India; what I have not completely told yet. I want you to divine your own thoughts on this." He had to smile as he began. "Once upon a time in the wilds of India!" He drew a comical smile from both Tiberius and Josh. Over a few cups of hot tea and for over an hour with prompts from the colonel, Ambrose gave a complete rundown of his events in India. He was factual and concise in his details regarding the village, of Ravi, Pyra, the shape changers and the history of the evil Kali. Josh listened with great interest often asking for clarification. Then finally, once Ambrose had told his story, he then told Marley of the dream he had last night.

Josh was quiet for a moment as Nephew looked him squarely in the eye. "What Ambrose told you is the truth since I was next to him throughout that terrible ordeal. It sounds to me we may have "The Son of Kali" running about?" Ambrose was thinking about the special ring and of informing Ravi. Josh was obviously awed in what Ambrose told him. After all, how many outsiders really took the powers of voodoo seriously anyhow? He then stabbed the jeweled stiletto into the table. The sunlight through the windows made the jewels in the handle sparkle.

He gave his usual smile as said. "I carefully divined the vibrations from this dagger last night with the help of one of my most powerful old priestesses and know that a terrible evil has come to this island long ago! It has lived among us dormant for years but now has awakened." Marley sipped his tea then continued. "I have my sources scouring for information on this person named "Ayiti" or "Emile St. Denis" in Haiti now. I also wired my sources high in government last night and will check later. Your dream and your information, in my way, verify what I read from this dagger long in the possession of this monster! We may be fighting for our lives to get Annabelle back, if she is alive." He paused and sipped his tea then went on.

"I have also wired my special friend and student of the art for information I feel is necessary in locating Annabelle! If I am correct, this could mean a very deadly struggle from the voodoo to the real world for us all. Now that you have told me the truth, I shall tell you my story." He gave his usual wide friendly smile as Nephew poured each a nice round of rum to compliment the fresh cups of hot tea. He began "Once upon a time in Jamaica …" His audience of two laughed. The old venerable man told Ambrose exactly who he was in the voodoo community. He was identified as a powerful priest as a small baby. He was favored by the gods of Loa as a child and blessed by Abigale the famous priestess kidnapped from Haiti.

Her son was the famous voodoo master named Takoo who he knew as a small child. He loved the great Takoo! Joshua laughed. "The relationship did not end well for the slave owner who did not know his slave Abigale was a most powerful voodoo queen! His balls and penis fell off one night and he was driven to madness and vile end along with those who had kidnapped her! Abigale then became a rich mistress turning this slave owner's beautiful wife into her special sex slave and servant." They all laughed. Ambrose nodded approval to his revelations. They were now on the same page.

The stories continued with Tiberius adding the humorous tale of Wadsworth's death by a fatal demon blowjob. The mirth to the morning teatime had been achieved under the dire circumstances. All they could do was carry on and wait for a wealth of information that was building from many requested sources. The rumors of Annabelle's unfortunate kidnapping permeated the community at the rum estate. Regardless of this, the estate workers worked as hard as usual. By the end of the day Josh sat down with Ambrose and Tiberius in their office and reviewed a pile of some very interesting telegrams left on his desk. It seemed that the rumor mill was beginning to focus on the legends and myths of Rose Hall near Montego Bay from Marley's sources.

These rumors were based on old myths and ghost stories as Josh saw it. But even the worst rumor can produce a lead, like an answer to a long dead question. Josh had also received a telegram from an old voodoo adept and aficionado from Haiti. He was a very young adept that was under the tutelage of one of the voodoo masters who confined Ayiti for execution by Boyer in 1841-42. He had seen Ayiti in his prison in the blood drenched monument to black slaves called San Souci Palace. It was in this exquisite place was where this very dangerous Ayiti, possessor of the actual powers of the Loa gods was brought to end his days.

He described with great revulsion, the horrors of Ayiti's estate, of his zombies and killer midgets, and lair from the dark side quickly burnt to the ground with all the occupants inside by Boyer's people. He further described the sealed lead room at the palace where Ayiti was held and all the specific drugs that were administered to weaken his abilities. Then came the huge earthquake and destruction of the palace and local towns soon swallowed by the huge tsunami that killed thousands. He further told of the massive national manhunt to capture and kill this monster at the fiery stake. Boyer was deathly afraid of him. This source also concluded that all the voodoo community was terrified of this voodoo king from Hell and glad when he disappeared.

The gruesome murders of Boyer's men on the ship was also reviewed. The source concluded that If you weren't working for Ayiti, then you were targeted for death or the life as one of his undead slaves. The information was revealing and startling. Ayiti was described in all counts as a very handsome tall young mulatto man with perfect white teeth. It was the face Joshua had seen in the office of the shop owner. This was the same description given by both Jenny and Elizabeth! Then Josh read another telegram that made his heart skip a beat as he sat up in his chair. It was from a man he was waiting to hear from regarding Rose Hall from across the island who stated in his brief telegram; "I know where she is, but I need to see you on this.

The person said he would be there in the morning." Josh Marley handed the telegram to Ambrose with a forlorn look on his face as Cavendish and Nephew read it over. He then looked at Marley. So where do you think she is Josh?" The old man paused then looked at Ambrose. "The telegram was sent from Montego Bay!" Josh added. "Annabelle is at Rose Hall Estate I will bet!" "What is Rose Hall Estate?" Inquired Nephew. Old Marley smiled. "If rumors are true, she is at a place which has been rumored to be the hotbed of demonic activity ever since one Annie Palmer came to it in the early 19th century as a girl from Haiti seeking fame and fortune." Then Josh thought deeper and replied. "She was considered a powerful Haitian witch by all surviving accounts! This Annie was trained by the best adepts to harness her unusual powers."

Colonel Nephew added. 'What is all this voodoo shit from Haiti anyhow?" Old Marley laughed at the colonel. "It seems that so many Africans were brought to that island as slaves and they brought along their grand religion which is voodoo. In its purist form, it is the religion of willpower, of forcing one's powers of suggestion upon another. But it goes deeper than that my friends" He continued after a sip of tea. "Rose Hall could have been a perfect place for this monster Ayiti to somehow hide, to grow invisible from the world if, if he had a positive relationship with the White Witch!" But the tales of the ghost of the White Witch were told as ghost stories and old wives' tales; untested rumors without answers perhaps?

Tiberius added an investigative thought. "I remember Horace telling me he had been looking for new properties to buy from around the island to increase his production of sugarcane. Horace heard a knock on his large office door. He had been shocked into deep depression and was taking it out on a bottle of malt scotch. "Come in please!" He mumbled from his half-drunk stupor. The three men entered his very immaculate office which reminded Cavendish of a cleaner version of Old man Krupp's heavily wood paneled office. It was also minus the Da Vinci signed sketches and the large bronze statue of Napoleon on his horse defiantly pointing to his Old Guard! All three men sat down and now joined Horace at a long oak table with chairs. There was a silence as they saw their boss raked by depression and anxiety.

Tiberius Nephew questioned Horace after they settled down. "Can you tell me where you have been looking for properties as of late?" "What difference does this make colonel!" Colonel Nephew gave his best stare above his neatly manicured black moustache. "It could mean a lot possibly in finding Annabelle's' whereabouts sir!" Horace perked up and stared at the men from his haggard unshaven face as he took another plug of scotch, this time directly from the bottle. He began to rattle off several names of estates as the party listened. So far, they were just names to the men. Colonel Nephew then asked a very strange question as his analytical mind buzzed. "Horace, did your wife ever join you on any of these visits?" Horace looked perplexed as he thought then answered.

"Well yes she did one overnight trip last month where we were negotiating a deal with the trustees of Palmyra estate outside of Montego Bay. She wanted to shop and see Montego Bay." "What estate was nearby? Can you remember?" They wanted him to say it and watched as Horace remembered, as his face turned into a mask of fear. "It was the estate next to Palmyra, the adjoining property of Rose Hall. Why we took Annabelle by it to see it as we left after the meeting with the estate lawyer! Oh, my god!" he yelled as he remembered how spooked all their horses were in that sunny pleasant breezy Jamaican afternoon. He now remembered the strange bad feelings that he felt sitting in front of this place for only a few minutes, the nervous fear in the horses, and how strange the workers acted! How he felt something or somebody staring into his very soul! "Odd Zogs!" he murmured.

He learned back in his cushioned brown leathered chair and stared at his guests in a foreboding shock. Horace then explained his reflections there to them. Later that night Tiberius, Ambrose, Marley, Horace, and Young Oscar Peacock sat on the large open deck at the Cavendish house. They had enjoyed a wonderful dinner and Elizabeth joined them as it was getting late under the stars. They talked over the details of the probability that this Ayiti had seen Annabelle at Rose Hall and kidnapping her for whatever purpose he had. Nanny Betsy was a victim of this plot. This creature was caught spying on the Cavendish house the night Horace and Annabelle where there. It was stalking her obviously and poor nanny Betsy was a witness to Ayiti's snooping. She had died because of this.

Out of the sky-blue Ambrose asked Oscar an offbeat question. "Oscar, can you tell me the place in the Caribbean where the huge slave empire was conducted back in the early colonies?" The very young inspector thought for a minute then replied. "Do you mean the place where the slaves were delivered and then processed for sale in the western Hemisphere?" Catching on to the drift Tiberius answered. 'Yes Oscar, the place where all these operations took place; an island with a huge crab claw geography at one end?" Before Oscar Peacock could reply, Marley answered. "That place was on the island of Hispaniola, or Haiti when slavery was in high demand in the 1500s." James Ambrose slowly stared at Tiberius Nephew. "I think we may have found a son of the Kali?" The tale of Ravi had just hit them both like a mental five-hundred-foot tsunami!

The man behind the telegram speaking of Annabelle's whereabouts arrived the next morning at the production office. The group waiting there was impressed by the size of this black man. He was very dark skinned and carried an extremely strong build. He could have been one of those muscular giant African slaves of old. He exhibited a rather hard-dangerous look on his face at first. They bid him to enter and have some tea as the introductions were made. Afterwards his face bloomed into a kind friendly almost childlike smile. His age was masked in his very youthful looks. All present felt he was a man of resolute purpose.

He was silent at first harnessing his extreme mental power. Josh had not seen him in many years and knew that he was more than a messenger. At his age he was respected a powerful voodoo priest, descendent of the famous Takoo and his incredible mother Abigale. Joshua knew Young Takoo well from many past years of bonding from teaching him as a lad. The voodoo community was truly a small world! All present would soon know of Takoo. Young Takoo gave a bow and hug to Marley first, then shook hands very pleasantly with the others and sat down.

He wasted little time. "My name is Winthrop Takoo, great grandson of the late Takoo, who killed the "White Witch" at Rose Hall in the slave rebellion of 1831. My great grandmother Abigale and he trapped her soul at Rose Hall where she still wanders her great house prison today." Winthrop gave a great smile then continued. "Takoo was later allegedly killed by the authorities later in a big manhunt and his body was never found. He survived his terrible wounds and lived for several years after in seclusion.

I grew up in a small village with my family all under an assumed name since my parents feared the curse and wrath of Annie Palmer who was an extremely powerful adept in many forms of witchcraft and African sorcery. She was also a product of Haiti. My family feared her since many had seen her alive on her estate for years after her death riding her horse at night around her estates. I knew this was a projection for her soul was trapped in the house in her broken neck body! My family worried about her escape! Things changed at Rose Hall.

Rumors told my family that a powerful evil accomplice came on the Rose Hall scene in 1844. I was born that year and my great grandfather, who was partially paralyzed by a bullet used to sit with me while my parents worked in the cane fields. It was this regular daily companionship with Old Takoo that saved my life. Every day that I went to stay with my grandfather I was always brought out in a large basket that resembled one to put goods from the market. The person who took me was not a family member but an acolyte of my grandfather. She would go to market to keep this cover in place. Remember that Takoo was wanted by the authorities and he also feared revenge from the white witch if she ever could somehow escape the entrapment blocking spell.

This all went well until I was two years old. Annie Palmer got her revenge with the help of this demon. One night in late 1846 the demonic evil monster cohort of Annie Palmer found my family. I was not present that terrible night. I had stayed with my great grandfather for that week. It was a sad day when Old Takoo heard the news. His family had been terribly slain. This stranger committed a savage ritualistic murder on my parents and sisters. My father, son of Takoo, was crucified upside down and burned by dark forces. Annie Palmer was responsible! My mother was recovering from what Takoo suspected was the "Old Hige" before that terrible night. He had stopped this curse and had redirected it to one of Annie's servants and favorite lovers.

"What is an "Old Hige" Winthrop? Asked Cavendish. "It is a terrible vampire sent from the pit to drink the blood of living people and suck out their life energy as it terrorizes them. My great aunt Millicent was murdered by the white witch in this manner; thus, spawning Abigale and Takoo's revenge." "What about my wife Annabelle?" Inquired a nervous Horace. Winthrop Takoo looked grim as he looked his way. "My sources that monitor Rose Hall informed me that there was a new Annie Palmer present in residence a few days ago.

This "New Annie" has also been seen at the great house in Palmyra. The Rose Hall plantations all have eyes and ears! When I was informed of the kidnapping of Mrs. Farnsworth, I knew right away this woman was her! This is why I am here! The monster who killed my family still lurks there and now I have purpose to destroy this demon of straw!" Tiberius pushed his sketch of this demon over to young Takoo that he and drawn from the imputes of both Ambrose and Josh.

He briefly stared at it and looked up. "This is the Strawman!" Then he composed himself and continued. "I inherited the powerful traits of my grandfather who passed away in grief a couple of years after the murders. In seclusion, Takoo trained me to master his arts for the day I could finally extract revenge for my family over this monster! He smiled a Joshua and then looked at the others. "Uncle Joshua guided and helped me to hone these skills for years after!"

Horace fearfully asked; "How do we get her back Takoo?" He looked at Josh with a long stare. "We are dealing with both dangerous physical and non-physical enemies as you need to understand." Exclaimed Josh. Young Takoo added with a very serious air. "We need to know exactly where Annabelle is located when we attack to rescue her! This demon and Annie are very powerful and our haste in this rescue will help protect us from their evil forces!" For the next couple of hours, the group covered every physical aspect of rescuing Annabelle out of the clutches of Ayiti and his clan of undead minions who guarded these estates at all times.

Winthrop Takoo concluded. "I am completely at your service because I want to save your wife Horace, but also I want to destroy this monster you named Ayiti once and for all. My quest is personal, revenge for what this demon did to my family in honor of my great grandfather whose name legacy I bear." Horace patted Takoo on the back with a thankful look. Ambrose thought of informing Ravi for his possible help. He still wasn't sure if Strawman was one of the lost children yet! In the next fortnight, he would be. W. Takoo noted that many forces would be guarding Ayiti and Annabelle and many of the workers acted like zombies and would do the bidding of their master. He also added that workers not affected by Ayiti's special treatment feared another entity on the properties.

It was one who he called the "Night Specter!" It was one of a different nature of zombie with a silver mask that covered its face and head that roamed the property only at night terrorizing them into submission. His sources said "it liked to feast on the living flesh of those workers who did not do their work well!" Nephew laughed. "Sounds like Wadsworth!" Winthrop paused then continued. "However, I have a weapon special for this Strawman! I have developed something from an old master who taught my great grandfather which may give us the break we need to rescue Annabelle safely. I think this may destroy this demon as well if used correctly!

This master of voodoo had studied the development of power to enhance spells based on what he called the "ancient way!" He taught grandfather Takoo the use of large ancient cut crystals to amplify the many effects of our rituals and spells, and in rare cases obliterate enemy voodoo kings in old wars. Old Takoo had introduced this art to me at the secret cave where large crystals grew to me as a child. The last two years of my studies with Takoo were on the use of crystals in ritual! He told me this power method of crystals was part of the actual power that bound Annie Palmer to Rose Hall.

I learned that Abigale was adept in this secret art. I have worked with these for many years now and have perfected their use!" Young Takoo gave a large childish smile now.

"I will prepare a destructive ruse for Mr. Ayiti using my crystal method that draws him out to find it. The large crystal I employ will be cut in two pieces. The vibrations of what I put into the one I use in powerful ritual will transfer completely to where the other half of crystal has been placed. My ritual will send the lure of ominous mystery and fear into Ayiti that will force him to react like a bee to honey! When he is out, trying to find the source of all the vibrations I have sent? We will rescue your wife Horace!" Ambrose added; "So what you are doing is like sending a real bad phone message to this monster?" Young Takoo smiled. "Precisely Mr. Cavendish!"

Horace questioned, "Can't we just tell Inspector Peacock to raid rose Hall and get her that way?" Takoo looked at Oscar Peacock who had sat quietly listening to the conversation and interjected. "No Mr. Farnsworth, for you do not know the ominous depth of what we are dealing with here. The police will be used after our plan has borne positive fruit." Nephew, always thinking on the move replied. "But, why not use the police as a ruse to get a jump on the great house and secure Annabelle? We have the crystal and police ruse together! Inspector Peacock, what do you think?" He smiled. "I am completely at your service and this sounds like a capitol idea!"

Takoo then added. "According to the old voodoo master that taught my grandfather, the ancients used crystals to send communication messages in one of many uses! We shall send a big message to Mister Ayiti and blow him out of his socks! If we only had something of his to use in the drawing ritual." Joshua smiled as he pulled the bejeweled stiletto from his desk, and stabbed it the rough table. He smiled at his old student. "your wish is my command! A keepsake from monster Ayiti!" YoungTakoo held it and immediately picked up the sinister vibrations on it.

He spoke. "What I plan to do is to transfer our ritual, which will be a safe distance from the threat of Ayiti, via the crystals right to a location in Rose Hall before the rescue attempt. The full voodoo ceremony I perform will be magnified into the crystal we place at Rose Hall." He smiled a broad grin. "This knife has Ayiti's deep vibrations all over it! Trust me that he will be drawn into my trap and hopefully be destroyed in it! I will be employing my best adepts. Depending on how powerful this Ayiti is will determine how our explosive ritual affects him. This is why we must know the exact location of Mrs. Farnsworth and be fast in snatching her."

Young Takoo confirmed the details already possessed by the group. This demon Ayiti came from Haiti and his actual age is a question mark. He was first recorded as a fugitive by the French authorities in 1756. He was identified as a small boy called "Little Ayiti Deschamps by the surviving French records. Ayiti could be in a broad area of at least two-hundred years old, but probably longer! Very old tales told of some huge conflict between very powerful beings when Haiti was a slave empire several hundred years ago! He added that "Voodoo can do strange things to those who practice it! One benefit is that used correctly can keep the practioner alive much longer than normal people."

Nephew looked squarely at Ambrose who had a very serious look on his face. The nonverbal question between them was that "Do we need to summon Ravi?" Both men quietly pondered the possible reality that they had stumbled on to a feared offspring of the Kali. Time and action could only tell this, since so much of this story was shrouded in rumor and rumors of rumors at this point. They would feel out the situation first in this rescue mission. They would not summon Ravi until they knew for sure the true nature of this Ayiti. He could just be one of voodoo's strange powerful bedfellows after all. It was hard to ponder the curse of Kali before them again.

The plans were now set for this rescue of Annabelle! Cavendish asked Takoo a question. "So how are you going to kill Ayiti? I heard that the only way to kill him was to destroy some doll?" The man, coal black in color smiled from his strong resolute face. "What you say is true in most respects, but when I have this monster close to the crystal, I will explode it in his face vaporizing him with its huge power! Hopefully sir." Colonel Nephew was extremely impressed how all the elements involved in this rescue attempt had were quickly organized with a good plan into one resolute force. General Bindon Blood would have been impressed!

Annabelle finally awoke in a very strange bedroom with many thoughts running though her confused brain feeling the effects of drugs continually slipped to her. She had no idea that she was the new guest at Rose Hall and Palmyra depending on the night. It seemed that her kidnapping had happened months ago, but it had only been a few days now. She lay in a huge bed of white linen and large canopy above her head. Her whole body seemed to ache, as she saw temporary flashes of what gave her painful erotic aches.

She was caught between terrifying blurred memories in the dress shop and extreme carnal satisfaction; a satisfaction she had never imagined possible. The sun cast indirect light upon her from the shuttered windows. Annabelle almost didn't care at this point, for she yearned for more sexual opium from that tall handsome mulatto man with the pure white straight teeth. She then heard the noise of a door being unlocked and saw a shadow move inside silhouetted by the light in the hall. The shadow put a tray down next to her bed and soon she felt a hand stroking her head.

The shadow spoke in a low soft monotone. "I have brought you some juice and fresh fruit to enjoy my dear." Before she could speak the shadow sat her up in the bed and put a glass of liquid to her mouth, forcing her to drink it down. She rolled her eyes up to gaze at the shadow. It was him, that handsome shop owner. His eyes stared into hers and she started to feel some wild malfeasance grow in her mind and groin. Her well-proportioned ivory skinned partially clad body ached, but it was a different ache of wild steamy expectations to come. The flashbacks emerged, demonic, wanton, raw, and forbidden! She was completely overwhelmed and loved it!

Her body had become the clay this man had played with for days. The flashback had now become reality as she succumbed into what was a sheer fantasy as compared to her former life. Horace was good, but this strange man was so far beyond that now! What she had experienced so far was like a dream, as she had been broken from her haughty arrogant mindset to become his sex slave; the tool of his extreme carnal designs. Annabelle thought her beauty and exquisite body was now just a doll, a plaything bent to the will of the new owner, her slave master. Madness was just around the corner as he began working on the orifices and every inch of her sweet body. Later that night, Annabelle's limp body was moved from Palmyra over to the great house at Rose Hall. She later awoke in another large bed with white linen sheets, and huge silken covered canopy.

She was weak from the unknown narcotics in her drinks, but also as if every ounce of energy had been driven from her in the wild unbridled sexual frenzy imposed upon her by this stranger. She wanted more of it and need it badly! She smiled as she lamented for more now; she was totally addicted to it. A door had been opened in her mind, one that was wide open to the first hard sexual assaults first forced upon her. She felt that she was being slowly devoured. Annabelle had given herself to this strange nameless man, had even, in her passion told him she loved him. Then he would work her over, stuffing her every orifice with unimaginable delights.

She became automatically wet now, as she heard him returning? Then she saw a woman from her drugged lazy weak gaze, a dark-haired woman of great beauty at the end of the room. This woman approached her in a long white shimmering gown and was smiling. She sat on the edge of the bed and began rubbing her face gently as she began to speak. "So, master Ayiti has brought you into my bedroom for a nice rest? My, are you a pretty one, like me." This lady began licking her on the back as she rolled her on her face. Perhaps we both will have a surprise for our friend when he returns. But first, I want to taste your sweet wares! May I taste them my dear?" Annabelle was so weak she gave a weak "yes."

Annie perched her buttocks up under her bent knees and began licking down her back to her beautiful rounded ass, engulfing her abused parts with her tongue and mouth for a long time. Once again, Annabelle now succumbed to the otherworldly fetishes of another dark being. She had never been with a woman before and Annie Palmer now opened another forbidden door of lesbian pleasure in her. Besides, Ayiti was in Montego Bay now looking to find a ship to leave Jamaica with his new woman.

Annie Palmer was enjoying immense pleasure with her new slave using the expert touch of a woman well experienced in the art of lesbianism! At least she could materialize into her physical body in her prison. All taught to her by Ayiti! Because of this, the new guest Annabelle was great sport for several hours who tasted delightful. Besides this fun on this submissive beautiful lady, Annie had a more important plan to unfold. She made this beautiful lady of perfect English extraction beg her to enter her numerous times during her intimate inexhaustive play in her sweating writhing body. Annie was going to escape with dear Annabelle; but inside her! Ayiti had never know that this weak link was real! He had scoffed it off as part of her insanity! The weak link in the old entrapment spell was about to be broken!

According to the information provided by a few of Takoo's people on the estate, Annabelle would be kept at the Palmyra location for two nights. On the third night, she would be returned to Rose Hall to the second-floor master bedroom in the front of the house for one night only. Then returned to the other house. The rescue attempt was tonight as Mrs. Farnsworth was definitely at Rose Hall. The plans for her rescue had been set in motion and were ready! Winthrop Takoo had already set the ritual up and had the second half of the inert large crystal secretly placed on the grounds of Rose Hall.

It was located a good mile from the great house at Rose Hall across a long sugarcane field on a high hill by a small forest of trees. The ritual itself was set on a secluded beach nearly ten miles away on the coast, ample distance for the plan to work and a quick safe exit from the area by boat as planned. The physical rescue force included another fifty of Winthrop's men armed with machetes, long spears, and a few crossbows to run interference against any opposition at the estate during the raid. Cavendish and his small group were assigned the task to breech the great house and seize Annabelle from Rose Hall.

Cavendish, Nephew, and Horace Farnsworth, dressed in police uniforms with Constable Peacock were to lead the assault. The boys were backed by a dozen armed constables and several of Takoo's voodoo adepts. They would help in the attack by fighting the dark spirits guarding Annabelle. More of Young Takoo's voodoo hunters were joined by another dozen police that would help secure the area in front of the house and secure the escape route to the beach at Palmyra. Once Annabelle's freedom had been confirmed, then a huge police raid would follow soon afterwards. Several voodoo adepts would go for Ayiti at the crystal.

Oscar Peacock surmised correctly, that the very action of Ayiti moving Annabelle between the two estates often, related his fear of someone figuring out who he was and where he lived. Peacock wondered about all the terrible rumors and myths of evil of Rose Hall that could become a real problem for this rescue operation if true. Oscar Peacock reminded himself of all the childhood ghost stories he had heard around the campfires as a child regarding Rose Hall. If they were true? He knew one thing, that the truth would soon be known! The chickens were soon coming home to roost at Rose Hall! Ayiti and his minions would be waiting for them.

Winthrop Takoo assembled his huge and powerful voodoo ritual at midnight on the beach on the night of the rescue attempt. Joshua assisted him in this ritual. Fifty of his best handpicked adepts throughout Jamaica were assembled on the beach in a circle around a huge fire. They were ready to send their dark exorcising hell as the first step in saving a lady and in destroying Strawman! This was all business now as they received word that this Ayiti had returned to Rose Hall where Annabelle was also. The effects of this powerful ritual would be transferred in its full effect to the crystal at Rose Hall by three in the morning. Voodoo spotters near the crystal would telepathically transmit its effects on the monster to Young Takoo who would pass it on to his adepts at Rose Hall. The rescue attempt would then commence.

By two in the morning, an hour before the ritual released its power at Rose Hall, the assault group waited in a secluded place outside the front gate at Rose Hall. The attack and crystal attack, would be the signal which would be an unmistakable lightshow for some, and a jarring metaphysical hell for others. Once Ayiti had been spotted going towards the crystal, they would launch a rescue mission. The three Brits were armed with pistols, shotguns and knives. Colonel Nephew sported Old Krupp's prototype later to be called the MP38 Schmeisser. Josh's three men in the front, though armed with machetes, were well armed with what an outsider would term as "magic potents" and spells to cast as weapons against whatever else existed in the house besides humans.

The information given by Winthrop's informers gave the location of Annabelle upstairs in the main bedroom; Annie Palmer's bedroom! She had been brought to Rose Hall early this evening. Next to this crystal on the beach alter was Ayiti's once treasured ornate Deschamps dagger as a ground to draw him in. Whoever had touched this dagger or ever had been near it could be brought up in images from the crystal's power. Takoo had already reviewed many images from this dagger and planned exactly which image to conjure up to draw in this Haitian monster of old.

The rum estate, White Hall, and the Cavendish were under constant guard by well-armed voodoo hunters this night. No one really knew what to expect except Josh and Winthrop Takoo. Security had been placed as a precaution. Tiberius and Ambrose were only slightly vexed that they had not summoned Ravi. So far, they believed that this was a localized matter, and that rumors may have made a bigger monster out of this Ayiti than imagined. This seemed to be the hard evidence thus far which still rested on a bed of old rumors and tales to them. They felt that the firepower rendered by the army of voodoo masters would bring down this "Ayiti" monster. In spite of the best plans and support, they both felt an inner fear, that they may have been wrong and underestimated this Strawman! This anxiety was in the backs of their minds. They were going into the breech again; into a dark dangerous uncharted realm as in India! As fate would have it; Ravi got a pass this night. Ambrose had seen Pyra's beautiful face flash into his mind with "caution" etched across it!

Ayiti had entered the darkened bedroom to find Annabelle lying on her back with pillows behind her head smiling at him. This was the first time he had seen anything of this sort from her. He had massively dominated her since she came into his world. Until this moment she had been his complete submissive slave, twisted firmly and violently to his every whim and fancy. Annabelle was smiling at him. "Are you feeling better my dear?" He quizzed. "Oh yes master, I feel so much better now, come to me!" Blankly, Doc Ayiti approached her and sat next to her. He noticed that she was wearing a nice clean gown and that all her makeup was perfect.

"I wanted to look perfect for you my master!" She crooned. He smiled a disarming smile and liked this woman coming to him freely. She looked so arousing to him that he popped an erection. In the darkened room her beauty was breathtaking. She pulled him down on the bed and kissed him deeply, if not savagely. "Do you want me Ayiti? Want me now! I am in love with you and forever!" He kissed her a long kiss, then sat up and looked at her. Something seemed strangely amiss and he could not place it. Then Annabelle spoke in her weak beaten voice. "You have forced me into a world that I have now chosen and this is why I made myself beautiful for you. I do not want to go back to where I came from but want to be in your embrace for your pleasure my master!" She then, forced his head down to her ripe large soft breasts.

She held him there and grabbed his erection. Ayiti, loaded with a bottle of rum and coconut juice was amused and caught in wonderment. Annabelle pulled down his pants and took him deep down her throat. He gave in to her advances and Annabelle was driven wild by his rough dominating pleasure. She was screaming in pure delight as he finished in her. In the midst of his demonic orgasm with wonderful acting Annabel, he felt something strange enter his mind. It was like a force driven towards his soul by some distant wind approaching fast.

Several miles down the coast fifty-two master voodoo adepts stood in a huge circle around the crystal focusing all of their mental energies at the large polished crystal ball that sat in an elevated platform in front of a huge bonfire; one crystal here and the other planted at Rose Hall. Both crystals had been cut from the same huge chunk of crystal in the secret cave. The ritual bonfire illuminated the tops of the gentle waves of the ocean lapping in low sounds to the rear of the crowd. Millions of stars dotted the dark night sky.

Winthrop Takoo and Joshua Marley both stood in the middle beside an old large handmade crude wooden chair. All present were dressed in the ancient costumes of their voodoo society. Winthrop "Young" Takoo gave the call for the Loa gods, then called on the spirit of his grandfather Takoo. The group began chanting to draw in this great spirit. All minds focused on Ancient Takoo as his apparition soon appeared sitting in the old chair. Then Takoo the Younger began to recite an incantation in a lost tongue as the group recited the words and focused their minds on the crystal. Soon, it was glowing brightly. There was total focus from all the silent adepts into the crystal.

Now fully powered, the crystal magnification began working its effects on the distant Ayiti who was mesmerized and by the emanations of it from Annie's bedroom at Rose Hall. Then, as if on cue, as if the apparition of Old Takoo knew the approximate position of Strawman next to the other crystal. The form of Old Takoo stood and spread out his arms then gave a loud howling scream; shrill and otherworldly in the dark night. All the adepts then gave the same high-pitched shrill! The crystal to his front flashed in a huge bright illumination as the other crystal exploded in Strawman's face miles away at Rose Hall. The transfer of the deadly spell was complete!

Young Takoo and Marley both smiled, for in their mutual deep trance, they as the others had witnessed the other crystal exploding in the monster's face. All the adepts sang a beautiful goodbye lament to Old Takoo as his image dissipated. Farewell incantations and blessing were given to the Loa gods and to old Takoo. Then there was a brief silence among the group then they all cheered. "Perhaps Strawman is dead we pray?" remarked Josh. "We can only hope my teacher!" commented Young Takoo. The group cleaned up the site, buried the fire and removed the crystal still giving off a glow. They all moved to the beach, since the rescue boat would be arriving soon. The Strawman had been sacrificed this night.

It grew stronger in his mind and was both unsettling but captivating. Ayiti climbed off Annabelle where she lay spread-eagled face down on the bed and went to the large open window. He looked out into the fields of darkness adjusting his night vision feeling something but saw nothing in the moonlight kissed cane fields. Then he saw it! At a distance off to the left a strange blue light began to appear in a copse of trees on a distant small hill from where he stood in the window. This wind was coming from the light. It became stronger and soon emitted a white flash, like a ball of fire going in all directions. The unsettling effect was luring him but now turned into a gnawing sharp pain, not for his body, but in his dark soul.

It was driving him and drawing his confused mind out. It knocked him to the ground in some invisible internal agony as he left the bedroom and ran out the main door downstairs. He was knocked down a second time then got up agonizing, but now in rising evil fury. Annabelle was also rolling around in great discomfort moaning. He let out a loud screeching noise to alert his minions and charged out into the driveway in a demonic rage. He had been attacked, and it was powerful. He ran towards the light, changing into the Strawman as he loped to the flashing light beyond. He would deal with this intrusion on his own terms now. Several of his zombified workers, in obvious confusion, saw their master and systematically followed Strawman into the long cane fields as it loped towards the disruption beyond the trees.

The group led by Colonel Nephew watched from behind some large bushes at the main gate as the unsettling spectacle of the man, running from the great house shape-change into some elongated headed form of demon as it ran across the cane fields with long arms flailing wildly. Everybody was awed at this terrifying sight. Inspector Oscar Peacock saw this apparition as well as his system was now shocked into the reality he feared! Nephew signaled to the rest of the group to mount as the monster disappeared in the trees before the hill. The voodoo adepts received the message from Young Takoo to attack Rose Hall! In a quick pace the rescue party galloped up to the front of the great house and jumped from their mounts. Dressed in police uniforms they quickly bullied their way past several mute servants into the large foyer followed by the adepts. Fear ran through every member of this party from what they had seen running across the cane field.

Now they all sensed something above the foyer, something lurking in the dark hallway on the second floor! Cavendish and Horace ran for the steps leading to the second floor. Two of the voodoo men ran in front up the stairs. Young adept Ben Jobo stayed close behind Cavendish as they climbed the long winding staircase. Nephew guarded the bottom at the staircase with the others. An aura of complete dark evil aura engulfed the men as they climbed to the top of the stairs. It was like climbing in quicksand to all of them. The two voodoo priests ritually cast verbal incantations and tossed small bottles of voodoo spells that flashed when they were smashed on the walls and floor. They reached the top of the stairs. They were now terrified at the immense black force which seemed to surround them.

Suddenly something lurched from the darkness beyond darkness and tore into the voodoo adept in the lead. He was flung screaming from the balcony as blood splattered from his face on the others behind him. The second adept doused the black imp like thing with some liquid, he tossed on it. It wailed and caught fire running backwards on several bent legs. Jobo saw this as the voodoo adept crashed past him to the entrance floor and was able to accurately throw a couple of bottles of the voodoo potent across the walkway that adjoined the staircase to the left.

The contents of the bottles flashed and burned several things masked in the darkness. But he saw more things emerging from the other side of the second-floor hall. Jobo then used his crossbow effectively delivering several ampules of his voodoo magic into other dark entities above from the right. The darkness exploded again into fire as the slimy minions of the dark realms wailed as they burned. The path to Annie Palmer's bedroom had been cleared of dark forces. As the dark supernatural forces were destroyed by the voodoo adepts, the physical battle began.

Ambrose saw two silent zombies guarding the bedroom door and they charged him. At ten feet he blew them apart with twelve-gauge shotgun blasts! Horace ran past him and kicked the bedroom door open. They both rushed in to find Annabelle lying unconscious on a large white-canopied bed. Horace quickly went to his wife's side. "Annabelle! Annabelle! It is Horace, I am taking you home now!" She mumbled. "Oh Horace, I thought you forgot me, please save me from this horrible place!" She began to weep as she put her arms around his neck. With that, Horace picked her up in his arms and followed Cavendish to the stairs.

Another zombie appeared on the walkway attempting to block their escape. Ambrose fired his stagecoach style double barreled shotgun blowing its head to pieces. He had learned in India that to kill the walking dead, the head needed to be destroyed. He reloaded it and quickly emptied both barrels into another zombie as it had also attempted to cut off their escape. He reloaded. The noise of the shots he fired was deafening and the flashes from the shotgun blasts blinded his open right eye. However, experience had taught him to keep one eye shut when firing in the dark.

His left eye was fine and as they were moving quickly down the stairs. Just before this happened, Colonel Nephew faced several jerkier walking minions who had entered from the rear of the house. They had machetes. He could hear the police out front firing behind him now. The seemingly normal servants had disappeared. He released the safety on his "Krupp" masterpiece and fired a steady burst of 9MM bullets into them left to right and high across their faces. The attackers fell back into the wall to the ground. He replaced his empty magazine with a fresh one and delivered headshots to those who stood back up.

As they went outside, many zombies were running towards the constables and voodoo hunters at the front of the great house. It now became a shooting range of sorts as everybody shot down these undead that seemed to move much faster at them. Coup D' Grace headshots finished many of them after they we were shot down. As the battle ended in the front, yells and screams were heard a fair distance behind the Rose Hall great house. Takoo's boys were delivering a surprise blow to the small camp identified as where the zombie like worker/guards lived. They had, in the plan launched this attack from the rear oceanside of the estate. This attack was intended to interdict the Strawman if he attempted to escape with Annabelle! However, a strange creature had been aroused in that melee of spears, machetes and crossbows!

This thing seemed impossible to kill. He took a quick toll on a couple of Winthrop's followers as they were slashing zombie workers to death. This undead creature had a silver mask of some demon about its face and head. Its silver mask was ripped off in the fight exposing a bare skull face! It had been stabbed, slashed, and had several crossbow bolts stuck in it; but was still offering a fight. The voodoo hunters gave it wide berth and moved away. Several ran in terror back to the beach at Palmyra where the escape boat waited to take the rescuers back to the other side of the island. Jean Zombi was too late to stop Annabelle's rescue and watched silently in front of the great house as a group of riders headed down the path towards Palmyra.

Meanwhile, just before the attack on the great house commenced, Strawman, in a mindless rage had run through the trees directly into the area where the crystal sat flashing out powerful luminous lights and vibrations. Then Ayiti saw the image of his beloved Aunt Sarah standing in front of the powerful flashing light. He sensed that everything was out of place but could not control himself. He was being drawn in by this luminous tractor beam of light! Ignoring the strange situation, he ran towards his beloved Sarah yelling her name. The image spoke to him. "Oh Ayiti, it is Sarah who has come to visit you this night! How I love and miss you my little son!" Ayiti had become completely disorientated induced on him by the extreme vibrations.

But now his dark heart had been transfixed by this moment! "Sarah! Sarah!" He screamed from his fanged grimace as he cocked his head to the side! Then suddenly the white cleansing light of the ritual now sent huge shockwaves into the black soul of Ayiti drawing him painfully closer to touch the clear image of his Aunt. Then Sarah's image disappeared and Ayiti now faced a large crystal emitting a brilliant and painful light in large pulses. He stumbled in complete disorientation and crawled to the source for the light where he found a large glowing rock. He was drawn to it like a rat to a ball of cheese. Then it exploded as he grabbed for it. The mortal pain inflicted upon him touched every cell in his body and soul!

The explosion sent a huge ball of light in every direction witnessed by the rescue party as they began their attack. Soon, the rescue was over and Annabelle was safe! The party made it to the beach at Palmyra in a near gallop and splashed man and horse into the surf. They rode their horse neck high to the medium sized steamboat whose steam engines were on full. In a short time, the horses were abandoned and set free to romp and play in the night surf later rounded up by the constables after the morning raid. Both Cavendish and Nephew saluted Oscar Peacock as the boat chugged away.

The large boat had moved out into deeper waters to make its way down the coast to pick up the party of Voodoo priests and acolytes who had performed the successful voodoo ritual. The small steamship chugged along the coastline and would travel back to the huge docks below the bluffs at The Jamaican Prime rum estate. The dangerous chaos that rent the night was now replaced by soft sea breezes and mild night air under a starry night. Three voodoo hunters had died and several others including constables had been wounded. The voyage calmed the combatants who survived this ordeal. Annabelle was going home safe!

Ayiti, lay on the ground gazing into the dawn's light. His strength was wholly depleted as he felt paralyzing pain from the explosion. The glowing rock had exploded in his face. That is all he remembered. He was blown far into the air and found himself hanging from a large limb of a tree. Then his painful crazed mind sensed people searching the grounds below him around the hill. He knew they were looking for him and did not move. After a short while they left. Finally, he dropped from the large tree to the ground. He lay there in great paralyzing pain for hours after the sun came up.

He was suffering from both wounds of his soul and body. Shards of crystal protruded from his face down the front of his body. He had no clue what had happened or how that shiny rock had been placed on his property? His body was covered in a black ash since he had been burned all over his body. Then he watched a huge police raid on Rose Hall as they finally left later in the day. He barely stumbled across the long cane field towards the great house after sunset that day. His brain was lost in a deep fog as he walked to the front of the great house. He then fell into a chair.

The first person he then saw was Zombi standing silent guard in torn clothes covered in blood. His undead buddy had six crossbow bolts sticking in his body. His servants entered scared to high heavens. These non-zombified mind-controlled panic-stricken servants gave him details of the police raid at dawn and abduction of the beautiful white woman from the upstairs bedroom in the night. They told him of the violent deaths of many of his special workers as he viewed their bodies lined up next to the house. Ayiti was infuriated to the point of insanity but too weak to do anything. Ayiti ordered Zombi taken to his special voodoo doctor for repair.

He had never been attacked like this in all his years. He ordered his servants to take him upstairs and laid in Annie's bed. He laid there for hours and wondered why Annie's restless spirit had not shown up, Ayiti finally drifted into a coma. It would take much time to heal from this attack! Ayiti awoke and knew immediately in essence, who had spawned this outrage! It was Annabelle's husband who had enlisted voodoo forces against him! How stupid had he been regarding this possibility! He drifted back to sleep and no Annie had visited him!

Ayiti knew that had he not been in the form of his familiar Strawman that he probably would have died; doll or no doll! He had been attacked by an incredible power! But he was alive! During his slumber his resident voodoo priestess and her acolytes had cleaned all the crystal shards from his face and body. He was covered in bloody bandages now. His physical pain was slowly subsiding now, but the pain in his dark soul was still excruciating. He was still very weak. Hell, was coming to White Hall, to all of them! Annabelle was his forever and she loved him! Ayiti had never felt this way about any woman in his life and would not be denied his fine prize. Annabelle was his now and forever!

After a week of bedrest Ayiti reviewed the carnage in this great house and viewing the bullet holes and sensing the remnants of the voodoo magic evident on the white walls of the stairs and upstairs hall. He sensed the violent well-coordinated assault here as all his guards had been killed on this second floor with many dead below. He was surprised that all the dark imps surrounding Annie had disappeared. Ayiti sensed they had been killed and suspected Annie was perhaps gone as well! The powerful voodoo that nearly killed him must have destroyed her!

He painfully sat on the bed nearly two weeks later, reminiscing only a short time ago he had the fresh embraces of Annabelle Farnsworth. He felt the urge to fuck just thinking about her. He summoned Annie Palmer to ask what she had seen in this invasion. No Annie appeared after calling her name several times. Annie had disappeared before in her complete insanity but he sensed her spirit had been destroyed.

Then a strange afterthought came to him in a flash! Had Annabelle picked up a traveling buddy? Annie Palmer? The way Annabelle had accosted him into a sort of combat sex? The fact that Annabelle was cleanly dressed with an array of Annie's fresh makeup? Before, Annabelle had been defiled and broken into his personal slave whore! Ayiti barely believed the weak link in the curse once told him by Annie once in her insane ravings. She had said that she could never escape in any bodies of servants or other natives because of the difference in their vibrations. Besides, she had to be invited by the host to enter it!

Who in blazes would allow another spirit to take over their body? Nonsense! Snapped Ayiti. There was something else? Another way to enter a body but his usual sharp mind could not remember it! Then Ayiti remembered another part of this from insane Annie's blathering. It exposed a possible grim reality. Annie could not escape in the bodies of any natives, but could escape in a body of one akin to her racial incarnation? This would be another Caucasian of like vibrations. Vibrations? Vibrations of the native race was incompatible to her! Vibrations were the weakness in this masterful entrapment block of Old Takoo and his mother Abigale and were a way out as well?

According to his memory there was no ritual Annie could do to enter anybody's body other than the consent of an idiot! But was there some ritual Annie performed on Annabelle to enter her body? Something had to occur between them physically? He laughed, knowing Annie, she probably would have raped Annabelle silly! Ayiti had blindly answered his question in twisted mirth. He yelled. She had made Annabelle desire her sexual advances which was akin to inviting her into her body! Was that right? "That bitch!" He had to laugh his evil laugh at this thought! So, when he rescued Annabelle, he would then have to get Annie out of Annabelle's body?

He screamed and gave off his sickening high pitched wail then laughed aloud taking a huge plug of rum! It did not matter to him at this point. He would fuck them both until he pulled Annie out... maybe not! He drank more rum. At the end of his thoughtful inner conversation he felt that it was probably a certainty that his favorite Annie Palmer; scourge of the tourists was dead! It seemed to him that this powerful light would have also destroyed her as well! He held up his bottle of rum. "Rest finally in peace... I mean finally oh beautiful queen of the infernal regions!"

Revenge was his lifeblood! Strawman and his minions would soon be on their merry undead way across the island! Violent revenge on all those who took Annabelle and did this to him! They would all die in terrible ways! Annabelle would soon be back in his arms! Ayiti smiled an evil demonic grimace, for he well knew how to bring Hell into the picture! He summoned Zombi who was now fixed! He would convert all of his workers who had not run away after the attack into zombies. He needed to increase his army for his plan. Just a few of his favorite servants were spared to manage Rose Hall in his absence. He would return briefly with Annabelle after his retribution on so many before he left Jamaica forever! How dare they mess with him and taken his incredible prize love from him; if "love" was ever the correct word for Ayiti.

CHAPTER TWELVE
EVIL AT THE DOOR

Annabelle and the rescue party boarded the ship amid the chugging strain of the medium coastal steamer engine as it backed away from the dark shore. It then turned and began to cruise at a good pace down the coast to recover the voodoo masters some ten miles away; then back safely to home port. Ambrose and Tiberius stood at the front of the bow smoking Cuban Maduros and passing a flask of rum between them. Both men reflected on the night's events in silence. The beauty of the starlit sky and cool night ocean breeze calmed both men from the terror encountered in Rose Hall. Cavendish spoke.

"This mess is far from over Tiberius and we both know that if this voodoo monster survives; it will probably be coming our way with all his friends!" Tiberius exhaled the smoke from his Maduro. "Reminds me of our old buddy Kali and all his friends!" Ambrose added. "No doubt my friend. It seems that Annabelle is terribly worn out and needs rest and a doctor's exam." Tiberius took a plug on the flask and replied. "Hell, has come before my dear friend and we beat it! But I think that we need to call on Ravi now and inform him of the details about our little new evil guest in the mix if it survived this attack."

Cavendish retorted with a hard-serious stare. "My senses tell me that we are dealing with the spawn of one of those very evil beings and all we have will not be enough! When I saw it shape change as it ran across that field? Also, my senses felt that old evil when we got to the second floor in Rose Hall. It felt like Kali had been there kind friend!" Nephew gave a worried look as he had sensed the exact same vibes when the monster transformed as it ran across the field. Cavendish concluded. "When we get back, I will get the ring and summon him. WE need to tell Ravi." Nephew smiled and patted his soon to be brother in law in the shoulder. "I left mine in England. I fear that we will need the cavalry to turn the flank old top! We may have just met the son of Kali!"

Down below in the small steamer Horace sat over Annabelle staring intently into her beautiful face. He noticed several streaks of gray hair in her tousled mane. She was sleeping peacefully and Horace told her how much he loved her and that all would be well several times. He kissed her lips and she stirred slightly. He kissed her on her lips again exhilarated by her being back in his life. She then opened her beautiful brown eyes. "Oh Horace, I love you so much! I want to start a family!" Her words seemed rather strange since she never wanted children. This was a welcome change since he wanted a family.

She kissed him and hugged him tightly, obscuring her pupils which turned jet black as the dark soul hiding within. It was early morning when the steamboat pulled up to the elaborate docks below the bluffs below and behind Jamaican Prime estate. As planned, there were horses and wagons ready to take everybody away. Once back at White Hall, a huge repast was presented for the brave adepts who had saved Annabelle and hopefully destroyed Strawman. It was decided to place many voodoo hunters as security at Jamaica Prime and White Hall. If Strawman had survived?

Marley, Nephew, Cavendish, and Young Takoo left after eating and rode back to the Cavendish house. Jenny and Elizabeth were waiting for them. A round of hot tea was poured for everybody as James fetched the ancient ring. Both Marley and Takoo thought this monster had been destroyed in the blast from the crystal since no remains of it were located at the site. After a round of conversation in the large living room it was decided that everybody would stay at a hotel in Kingston until the status of Strawman was verified. This was a safe move just in case.

Jenny then stood up. "I appreciate your kind concern for me because I am pregnant, but I will stay here and defend my home!" Elizabeth stood up. "And I will join her in this defense as well. We have guns and will also have the protection of constables and Takoo's men soon." James Ambrose returned to the room with a smile. "We shall see ladies, after I have council with my great friend Ravi. At the end of an anxious day Young Takoo, Marley, and Nephew joined James Ambrose in a short walk down the bluff trail in the jungle off to the east of the house. The group soon was in the overlook area viewing the beauty of the western part of the bay.

The four men sat together in the night on the stone lined deck above the bluffs as they watched a grand orange sunset on the horizon. Josh and Takoo filled them in on the results of the ritual and the hopeful demise of the monster called Strawman. It was again an extravagant beautiful night; the ambiance was enchanting. James asked them all to sit down on the lounge furniture in the viewing area near the old stone wall separating them from the steep bluff that offered an excellent seaward view. James pulled out the ancient ornate ruby ring and went through the simple instructions to contact Ravi. Then they all sat talking about a "what if" strategy in the obvious defense of Annabelle, their homes and the rum estate in case it lived.

All the men sensed that there would be dangerous repercussions if Strawman was not dead! It seemed as if thirty minutes passed as they continued talking. Then, an old man in long red robes approached them. "Good evening my friends, greetings from me and the village. I do sense the honor of your call?" Cavendish stood and looked into Ravi's eyes and in an instant Ravi read his mind and saw the entire series of events pass through his consciousness. Telepathy was such a good form of communication.

"My oh my!" he soon retorted; "seems you do have a real problem with this devil?" Introductions were made, and handshakes and bows were given. Ravi then sat among them with his ancient venerable smile. Josh and Young Takoo were mesmerized completely by the presence of Ravi. They figured him to be a Loa god. Ravi listened as they all shared their information as he listened intently. After an hour, Ravi stood up. He smiled at them. "It seems that this creature lives and survives by the complete faith in its…" He was lost for words here. Josh added "the protection of his familiar?" Ravi smiled since he was unused to this lingo. He looked at Ambrose.

"Remember when I told you how the powerful beings can indoctrinate themselves into their own destruction…create their own "Achilles Heel with a notion something frivolous is really dangerous? Then this object becomes dangerous to them?" Ambrose remembered this immediately. Ravi continued. "If this creature is one of the old ones, it will not allow itself to die unless we find his familiar, which makes it immortal to anything we do to it! We must find it's familiar or doll! If not, we will have to incapacitate it until we can locate his doll you speak about?" Ravi thought about it for a moment then continued.

"Ambrose, do you remember when I told you why the Zulu spear killed the Kali when bullets and bombs could not?" Ambrose nodded as Ravi went on. The Kali had a fear of weapons fashioned from Mother Nature and not mankind for whatever reason from its past. This Ayiti, or Strawman firmly thinks that if its familiar doll is destroyed so will it be destroyed in the same way. We find this doll, we kill Strawman! If not? Then Strawman will not die. Ravi smiled at the four men. "I have a plan for this Ayiti! We can trap him, incarcerate him until we can find this doll. We will have to work fast on preparing for his visit!"

Then he looked intently at the men. "Unfortunately, if he believes in the power of his familiar then I sense he was not killed by the crystal. This Strawman will be coming soon. He looked at Marley and patted him on the shoulder and reminded him of his impute. "Your plan borrowed from those who dealt previously with this beast is excellent. We will work our trap around your plan, the one you got from the Haitian voodoo adepts under Boyer. Then, when this monster is contained, we will seek out the doll and destroy him!" Then he reflected for a moment and resumed his conversation. He looked at Nephew and Cavendish. "This monster could very well be the offspring of Kali as you say."

"Why do you think that Ravi?" Inquired Tiberius. The venerable ancient looked at him. "His shape changing abilities you witnessed are one significant clue but there is another one! Haiti was the island where we attacked Kali three hundred odd years ago but failed to kill him. Haiti was an immense stronghold prison rife with terrible misery and suffering for many thousands. It was this island where Kali, the king of slavers had established his empire! Here these poor slaves were parceled out into this hemisphere to be sold! I now remember well the part of this island that is shaped like a huge open crab claw! This previous revelation dawned on me when I passed over it on the way here tonight." He smiled and added. "Sometimes an old person forgets!"

Colonel Nephew enjoying Ravi's humor added. "Being 5,000 years old is no excuse Ravi!" After the laughs subsided Cavendish then spoke. "We need to deal with the double threats of this monster as we will likely deal with his horde of zombies as well!" To weaken our defenses in protecting Annabelle, this Ayiti will more than likely pull diversionary attacks on the rum estate and probably at my house. White Hall sits between them both. We need to prepare our defenses very soon for tomorrow this enemy will be coming at us from many directions!" With the basic plan of action set down, they all returned to the Cavendish home.

Ravi made some requests and was soon he and Josh left for the huge workshop at Jamaican Prime to prepare a special gift for this Ayiti if needed. "Trap and contain it until we locate the doll; then we kill it" resonated Ravi's words in the back of Cavendish's mind. Just before the dawn Ravi sat outside the workshop sipping a glass of hot tea with Joshua. In careful guidance from Josh, he explained how Ayiti had been caged in Haiti at the San Souci Palace. Ravi had created a special rendition this night! Ravi was lost deep in thought as they sipped the hot tea. The Spawn of Kali crossed his mind? An extremely dangerous spawn if Kali had mated with even a hybrid of their race. Marley's historical story on this Ayiti Deschamps concerned him greatly. Ravi sighed and closed his eyes if just for a few minutes. Josh asked him a question. "What is refrigeration sir?" Ravi answered him for there was a new twist to his old trap!

By mid-morning the group minus Horace assembled in Marley and Cavendish's production office at the estate. Horace was absent and it was excusable since he needed to be with Annabelle. After hot tea and idle conversation, Ravi stood up folding his hands in front of his robe giving a serene smile to all present. "Our main goal is to destroy this beast! In case it is too strong and we cannot find his little doll, here is the plan hatched with the guidance of Mr. Marley. I have taken the liberty with the help of Mr. Marley and a couple of estate engineers to fabricate a large lead box, a coffin of sorts with my added technology while you slept.

I used Mr. Marley's guidance on a similar lead container plan with some innovations of my own, so if you will follow me?" As they were finishing up their tea, Young Takoo pulled out Ayiti's very ornate bejeweled stiletto from his belt and thrust it in the table with a grand smile at Marley. "Here is the dagger of Ayiti that was so effective in our crystal trap for him." Marley smiled as he pulled it from the table and put it in his belt. He appreciated the memento. Ravi told how impressed he had been with Takoo's use of crystals used in his attack on this alleged "Son of Kali." He explained that this voodoo master Takoo's teacher had discovered the tip of the ancient iceberg regarding this incredible crystal technology!

It had been mastered to great lengths by the ancients in every manner of energy, communication, and travel over a million years hence. Ravi smiled as he added "There is nothing new under the sun!" It had been a voodoo ritual transmission Ayiti would not soon forget. Ravi knew that this magnified powerful blast experienced by this Strawman should have killed him "if" he was a lesser creature! It was its absolute belief in his ultimate protection by his familiar that could have saved him from complete destruction. Ravi's concern strongly rested on one other possibility; This Ayiti Strawman was another fallen one of great power!

He later shared his observations history of crystals to the group as they wandered down to the workshop to view the new creation. The short walk to the workshop invigorated the tired men as the rays of sunlight cleansed them from their sleepiness. They entered the large room and Ravi pointed to a huge square lead box on in the middle of the room. Marley walked up and touched it with pride. He had fallen asleep before its completion. It was an exact smaller dimensional copy of the square lead room used at San Souci Palace. The huge sliding lid on top and the strong iron bars that would seal it were perfect in every detail. "I liked this containment plan Joshua and forgive me if I had to research your mind to get the exact picture of it." Marley laughed.

Ravi then looked at his companions. "I have also added something else to this lead box gentlemen, which are called refrigeration coils that will turn the water we fill the lead box with into ice!" "Refrigeration? Ice?" Questioned Colonel Nephew. "Yes, son, remember when you were drinking cold drinks at the village that had cubes of ice in them?" Cavendish answered. "I well remember those cubes of ice in the drinks you gave me when I was recovering." Ravi began with his comments. "Well, my comrades, we connect the wires of this box to the kerosene powered generators at Whitehall, and when the time comes pull the lever on the back of this box, we will be making a giant cube of ice!

If we cannot kill this Ayiti Strawman, then after we will drug him with the voodoo cocktails, we then entomb him in ice." He then pointed to a series of copper wires and tubing that nobody had ever seen before. These are what we call "refrigeration coils" and once the power in generated through them; they will turn cold freezing the water within this lead box." Tiberius had to laugh. "Do you mean we are going to trap this monster in a giant ice cube?" Ravi smiled back. "Absolutely my son!" Ambrose asked. "I wonder how we are going to get Strawman into this box? I do not think we can just ask it?" The ancient sage paused and looked at him with his usual smile. "We will deceive it then ambush it! A good deception plan has worked many times for us against these fallen ones in the past!"

Marley thanked both the engineers who had helped Ravi. One of them replied. "Mr. Marley, all we did was show him where the materials were, he requested and he did the rest. I never saw a person move so fast and precisely in building anything in my life." Replied one of the engineers. His companion who also looked bewildered then added. "I swear mon, that he was like green lightening and wonder if he is human?" Ravi laughed at them. "Well, if I was not human last night, I am now." His gaze at them calmed their souls.

Ravi continued. We need to get this loaded and delivered as soon as possible to White Hall; to the basement. I have laid out the plan to lure Strawman into our trap. I am afraid we will have to use Annabelle as the bait but am afraid we have no other choice! Strawman must be completely fooled and enticed into our ambush!" Ravi's next move was to pay a visit to White Hall to meet Annabelle and cue her in on the plan to capture this monster. This item would be delivered carefully to White Hall today. The group settled back into the small office for more hot tea and conversation. Horace was still absent.

The atmosphere at White Hall seemed to achieve some normalcy in the wake of the terrible events the morning after the rescue. Horace entered the master bedroom and had pulled the long white drapes closed after he had opened the French doors to the small balcony patio outside their master bedroom on the second floor. Horace took in a breath of fresh air from the morning sea breeze as he peacefully looked out across the manicured gardens at the rear of the mansion. It was the best new day in his life! Then he turned around to see his wife lying peacefully still in a white long nightgown on their large bed. His maids had given her a nice bath after they returned from the rescue mission.

Annabelle, even in her sleep exuded vivacious libido. Her long curls and full bosomed body crowned it. Then she began to moan. "Horace? Horace?" She called out. He approached the bed and sat over her looked into her beautiful brown eyes as they opened. Then he heard the click in the bedroom door lock as he looked up to see if anybody was there. No one was at the now locked bedroom door. Then he looked back at his wife's face and what he saw shocked him. He was now looking at the twisted dark-eyed face of a she-demon, transformed into an ugly mask. What had happened to his "sweet Annabelle?" He was now looking at the face of a different woman; one that now resembled the demon face in the huge portrait at Palmyra!

It spoke in a deep octave as he realized who now stared into his soul; Annie Palmer! "Oh Horace! Horace my beloved husband, let us consummate our love now! Let's start a family!" It cackled out loud as poor Horace found himself trapped in her viselike super human grips. He struggled and then looked back at the demon face. He clearly saw the face of Annie Palmer, then it changed back to his wife! He screamed as she rolled him over onto his back holding him firm on the bed pushing her large breasts into his face. "Do you love me dear husband like I am going to love you now? We are going to have a wonderful time now and guess what? You get to fuck both of us!"

His possessed wife punched him in the face and began to rip off his clothes. Horace tried to scream but demon Annie-Annabelle shoved a pair of her under garments into his mouth gagging him. She then grabbed him violently by his balls. The medium built non-muscular Horace was powerless in the grasp of Annie Palmer who now wore the body of once sweet Annabelle! Above her head, he saw the form of some dark evil being, an observant dark cloud against the white ceiling. Pure terror entered his mind now!

Annie Palmer controlled the weaker spirit of Annabelle as she took violent sexual delight upon him, which was non-stop. He tried to escape but was dragged back pulling over furniture he had clung too. In more ways than one Horace's mind was being blown completely from any mental balance he had previously enjoyed. In the essence of his mindset he was truly "fucking scared!" Annie Palmer was free from her Rose Hall prison by using Annabelle as her escape vehicle. Once she finished her sexual feast and torture on Horace, she would rob the place blind and be gone forever from this cursed island.

No one would ever find Annie Palmer, dressed in the body of beautiful Annabelle again and eventually driving her poor beaten spirit out completely! Takoo and Abigale be damned! She had defeated them! Annabelle's vibrations had furnished the hole in Takoo's prison box and she would never let this one pass! By using extreme gratifying sexual measures on Annabelle, she had gotten her to "invite" her in. The vibrations were perfect! But for now, she desired to satiate her evil desires on Horace! The servants heard Horace screaming at first, then all the crashing of furniture and banging going on in the room. They found the door to the bedroom locked.

Two of the maids jumped into the carriage in the front of the mansion and drove it at a high rate up the crushed shell-covered road to Jamaican Prime. Another maid rode a horse at a gallop towards the Cavendish house. It was just after noon when two terror-stricken maids barged into the office where the group of men sat. They all looked at them as one spoke. "You must come to White Hall now, for bad things go on in the master bedroom sirs!" Marley looked at Young Takoo as both felt very bad premonitions. Marley helped the scared maids sit at the table as Nephew poured them and he a round of rum. Cavendish joined them. At the same time the other maid had alerted Jenny and Elizabeth at the Cavendish home, so they all fortunately arrived at the same time in the front of White Hall where all the household servants nervously stood outside.

Such a beautiful day thought Marley as he entered, to be spoiled! Young Takoo went outside and climbed the long trellis to the second-floor master bedroom as Nephew, Cavendish, Marley, led by Ravi went up the circular staircase. The door was locked and Colonel Nephew tried to kick it open but to no avail. Ravi then grabbed the doorknob and with one swift turn twisted the handle and opened it as the door swung open. They all walked in to find Annabelle sleeping innocently on the broken bed. However, the room was a shambles and bloodstains were evident throughout the rumpled sheets on the bed. There was no Horace in sight.

Moaning was heard from a huge walk-in closet. Cavendish opened it and, in the shadows, saw poor Horace, completely naked and suspended and impaled by coat hooks in his back at the end of the closet. Ambrose approached to find him covered in blood with carved etchings on his face and body. His hair seemed to be bleached white as his eyes rolled in a mysterious terror that had paralyzed his mind. "Horace? Horace?" yelled Ambrose, but Horace only gave out low whimpers. Marley and Takoo studied the eloquent restive body of Annabelle in apprehension. However, Ravi saw Annabelle for what she was; possessed!

Tiberius and Ambrose lifted Horace off the hooks and wrapped him in a bed sheet. They carried him quickly downstairs and put him on the long counter in the kitchen. Jenny and Elizabeth stared at this human wreck in great shock. Horace was moaning and reaching for something in thin air. James Ambrose looked over to the ladies. "He is still alive and needs immediate medical attention. His back has holes in it and the bleeding must be stopped! We must go upstairs for this problem is not over." Then they all heard a huge crash from upstairs. The two men ran back up the stairs.

After Horace had been removed the three men stood looking at Annabelle. Ravi ordered Young Takoo and Marley to stand back and said. "It seems there is more to this picture than you can see!" Ravi gazed around the room with his mind's eye. Something else was in this room besides the demon that possessed Annabelle which he had immediately seen. The invading spirit of Annie looked like some wigging parasite over poor Annabelle's! Then he saw a huge black cloud going straight for Young Takoo and in lightning speed dove and knocked Takoo away into a piece of bedroom furniture.

Ravi yelled. "There is another one in here be on guard! Seems this entity has a friend from beyond." Annie Palmer sat up in Annabelle's body and leered in her demonic face and wailed. "We will destroy all of you now!" The bedroom door again slammed shut as Annie-Annabelle jumped to her feet and levitated above the bed. Ravi quickly hit her full force with a dose of cleansing white light and knocked her against the wall and back to the bed. "Takoo!" Yelled Ravi. "Annie has been knocked from Annabelle's body, protect it!" Young Takoo then jumped upon her prostrate body and pulled her off the bed to the floor.

However, he hit his head hard against the wall and was knocked unconscious as he held on to Annabelle and covered her body with his. Then came the dark cloud across the room. Ravi pushed Marley against the closet wall and faced it. He quickly shape-changed into a whirling green form as it came. In his mind's eye, he saw a large powerful demon, which had changed into some black octopus like creature with its tentacles extended at him. Ravi let it come in and completely embrace him in its dark cloud. Then he let loose with a powerful blast of white light which illuminated the room in a flash as his whirling form tore into it.

The octopus like demon screamed and wailed in psychic pain and seemed to explode, for its wounds in his realm were real and fatal. This thing was not the first one Ravi had dispatched in his many years. The explosion of light literally blew it away, beyond this dimension back to the evil source that had created it. "Big, arrogant, and stupid!" thought Ravi who was weakened by his explosion of energy that had destroyed it. Marley and Young Takoo had turned in their third eyes and they all saw the specter of Annie Palmer standing on the bed staring down at Annabelle on the floor. She was covered by a semi-conscious Takoo on the floor next to the wall.

Before Ravi could move, Marley, rough looking in his ethylic form, spit something into her face breaking her gaze. She wailed and tossed poor Marley back from the bed where she stood. Nephew and Cavendish could not jar open the door so they went outside to climb up the trellis. Now Ravi faced a super pissed off bitch demon, a concentration of pure evil. Annie sensed that Ravi was not a normal voodoo man after he destroyed her infernal guardian. As she faced him, she composed herself into her human form of petite beautiful Annie Palmer and smiled at Ravi.

"Please help me stranger, for I am the real victim of these evil voodoo men and I do not want to fight you, but want to live in peace!" Ravi stared at her in silence at the dark aura that surrounded her innocent specter. He saw Annabelle moving and freeing herself from under Young Takoo's body. Sensing that Annie was going to reoccupy her Ravi dashed between them. Annie was startled by the specter of a giant green being staring at her with huge golden hypnotic eyes. It spoke. "You may not continue with Annabelle and must go back to where you came demon! You are done here!"

Annie then came right at Ravi with a shrill wail exhibiting the image of some horrible witchlike banshee with its outstretched claws slashing at Ravi. The fight was now on! As they fought Annabelle stood up startled at the disaster commencing around her. She could see some invisible battle going on where huge dents were made in the walls and ceiling and with the bedroom furniture being shattered. Then she had a sudden recollection of what had happened to her after she was kidnapped from the shop. It was like some silent film of her kidnapping, of how Ayiti had sexually abused her in all sorts of shapes and forms, of how she had been held prisoner in her body by some thing before her now!

Then she painfully remembered what she had done to her husband Horace by her hands. She had impaled his body on coat hooks in the closet! She let out a cry believing that she had murdered him! Terrible worthless emotions cascaded into her mind now. She then felt so worthless as her mind drudged up how she was defiled; a sex puppet by some dark hideous creature! then she sensed this terrible creature fighting to get to her with some invisible force. Fearing this specter Annabelle did not want to be dominated again! She loved Horace and could not live knowing Horace was dead by her hands. She ran towards the French doors sensing that Annie was right behind her! Yet she failed to see Ravi holding Annie at bay.

Annabelle Farnsworth, beloved wife of Horace climbed on the balcony rail, looking down at Cavendish and Nephew who were just below on the trellis then dove from it. Both men, from their vantage point saw her impaled through her chest by the metal spears that topped the wrought iron gate that led to the garden two stories below. As Ravi kept Annie Palmer at bay in the shattered bedroom, he saw something else come into view from the etheric. It was the energy forms of a very large man and much older woman. They were both Africans and exhibited very powerful spirits! They wore war paint and colorful voodoo dress.

They stood next to Young Takoo who was now sitting on the edge of the bed holding his bruised head in his hands. Both touched him on his head and he looked up at them. Then they were suddenly with the White Witch embracing Annie Palmer from two sides, holding her tight. The old man with the large fire in his eyes yelled aloud as he pressed his raging face against Annie's. "Oh, Annie! Annie! Annie Palmer, dear "White Witch" of Rose Hall! You think you escape from us; you think we not watch the white bitch! You kill my daughter Millicent, our family and expect to be forgiven?

You think you escape in the body of this woman? No, No, you will dwell in your box we made for you forever for we resealed it!" Then the old woman, behind her, speared the apparition of Annie Palmer through her body with her dark hands as she gave a sinister laugh. Annie was now screaming in terror and obvious pain. The powerful old woman rested her chin on the White Witch's shoulder as she squirmed in obvious fear and terror. "You responsible for killing my son Takoo and all his family except little baby Takoo! And I delight in we returning you to your tomb at Rose Hall!" Annie tried to struggle against them as they both assumed very evil looking specters of voodoo adepts and then they were gone as one.

Marley, helped Young Takoo to his feet and they joined Ravi and Joshua on the balcony. They all stared in sadness as Nephew and Cavendish removed the impaled body of Annabelle from the metal spears of the wrought iron fence below. Young Takoo had tears running down his face as he looked at Marley. "This is so sad to lose her and I feel responsible in part." Marley hugged the large man and looked at him. "Mr. Young Takoo, you did all you could and the responsible one for this was Ayiti and this Annie Palmer witch! Never feel bad son."

Then Takoo gave a sad half-smile. "Did you see my grandfather and great grandma Marley?" Mr. Joshua Marley retorted. "Yes son, from my mind's eye I saw it all and they put Annie back in her box at Rose Hall." Takoo smiled. "My grandfather Takoo and great Mama patted me on my head and told me how much they loved me. I was able to tell them how much I loved them! Then grand Mama Abigail smiled and winked at me and told me something of interest.

She told me that her twin sister Sarah was the keeper of Ayiti in Haiti long ago! That Ayiti was a very old creature of the dark!" Ravi had been listening and asked. "Did Abigale say how old this Ayiti was?" Young Takoo replied with confusion on his face. "She said it was hundreds of years old and ran with the animals in the jungle until found by Mackandal who was alleged to have been his father!" Ravi picked up this information with grave concern. Strawman was a fallen one! Then he commented to Josh and Young Takoo. "When you think about it, it is such a small world!" He smiled and patted Takoo on the shoulder.

This would be a long day for everybody! A real problem now presented itself to Ravi. Annabelle was to have been used as bait to lure the Strawman into the ambush! She was dead and her family devastated! Horace was severely injured and a basket case even he could not help fix at this juncture. Ravi begin to think about the only alternative at hand. He told them not to worry for he had a plan he had already considered before this tragedy. Both Nephew and Cavendish saw extreme fatigue in the ancient sage's eyes. Horace was sent to the Cavendish's to be examined and given first aid by Doctor Tourissant.

Ravi soon returned to the Farnsworth's shattered master bedroom. He began carefully studying all of the pictures and everything Annabelle even to her perfumes. He had also taken the liberty of holding his hands on her forehead and running his hands across her body for a few minutes to pick up a good set of her vibrations to copy. Yes, he had one excellent plan left! If he could hate, it was these monsters like Annie, Strawman and Kali. These damned authors of chaos, misery, and death!

However, Ravi's kind had never hated or ever sought revenge! To hate or seek revenge was as below him and his race. No hate was necessary ever, just cleansing retribution; business!

The only thing his kind could feel was pity for these terrible beings. To hate anything was a sin and blocked any soul's ability to evolve to the light! If his race ever had to use their powers to destroy, it was in protection and self-defense for the innocent or meek as in the case of Kali to name but one. Now it was the case of this Strawman, no doubt the spawn of Kali! Over the ages it was their guidance, leadership, and sound advice in preparing humankind against evil. He mused. Yes, advice was cheap and effective in so many ways only if mankind listened and heeded it! He then thought about what was evolving in Europe!

Back at Rose Hall Annie Palmer awoke from a long sleep. She woke up and walked to the window in a sleepy daze. She opened the shutters and stared out across her estate. She began to walk out on her balcony and bumped into an invisible barrier. She shuddered in remembrance and turned around sensing that she was not alone. Then she was terrifying as she saw Old Takoo and Abigale standing near her beaming smiles. Abigale spoke in the kindest demeanor from a serene face. "Welcome home! Forever dear Annie! We wanted to make sure you got here safely!" Then they were both gone just like that.

Annie then remembered all of it in horrible realization; she was back in her box! She cried, screamed, and wailed as she ran through her house banging against the invisible shields that trapped her at every opening in the house. As she ran by the dining room table below for the third time, a cup and saucer fell and broke on the floor. The estate lawyer, a local chief constable, and an advisor who had been summoned to the estate because of the recent extreme problem and police raid nights watched the cup and saucer fall and break on the floor. The lawyer commented. "Ha, it must be that pesky ghost!" The estate advisor laughed. "Oh, this place is very haunted so I am told!" They laughed again.

The terrible events of this day seemed evident to everybody as they sat together in the beautiful garden behind White Hall Estate. Several days had passed with no counter attacks from Strawman or his zombies. Joshua, Winthrop Takoo, and Ravi had been banged up pretty good in their fight against Annie. Horace was critical and completely out of sorts mentally and physically. Annabel Farnsworth was dead. A sad listless day of sorrow had passed into days of anxiety for all the residents at Jamaican Prime, the Cavendish house, and especially at White Hall.

The preparations to defend the Jamaican Prime Estate, White Hall, and the Cavendish home had been put in place. They faced two different battles that would be waged; zombies on one side and Strawman on the other! The workers at the estate were informed and prepared for the possible attacks. The influx of over a hundred voodoo hunters into this area over the past week, bolstered a positive presence as they prepared for a strange conflict. Over this defense were thirty well-armed constables led by Chief inspector Oscar Peacock. Jenny and Elisabeth, who refused to leave, were fortified by several voodoo men and three constables. Horace had been brought there and was now under the care of Doctor Emile Tourissant. Young Takoo's very young powerful adept and budding adolescent warrior, Benjamin Jobo was charged to watch over the Cavendish abode. The lure and ambush for Strawman was ready at White Hall.

The lead box with strange attachments was moved into White Hall in a secluded end of the huge basement into a storage area. It was attached to the house kerosene powered generators and filled with water. This was the place where Ayiti would be drawn. Ravi had covered the plan in detail with Marley, Young Takoo, Cavendish and Nephew. They all had their parts in this hopeful last act of Strawman. The weakened Ravi would play a key role in capturing this Ayiti demon. No attacks had materialized anywhere on the perceived targets from Jamaica Prime down to the Cavendish home in nearly two weeks now. Maybe Ayiti was destroyed after all?

Ravi sat on the balcony outside the master bedroom on the second floor with his friends Tiberius, Ambrose and Mr. Marley. They had discussed many things besides the possible origins of Ayiti. Marley had been completely impressed when Ravi announced his age and the many things, he had seen over his earth span of some five thousand years. Ravi then turned to his company. "I think it is time for an honest search of the Rose Hall area to possibly determine where our unwelcome guests are hiding. Ayiti is alive and they are out there. The only unusual thing reported so far by Peacock was the disappearance of most of the workers at Rose Hall and Palmyra.

Ravi drifted off into what appeared a nap. He was gone. The ancient sage quietly drifted very high over the Cavendish house and searched the surrounding area carefully around White Hall. Nothing was found high or low. He then performed the same duty throughout the Jamaican Prime estate. All was quiet and no intruders were seen. He was impressed at how the workers and voodoo men had prepared their defenses in conjunction with the constables. He took a break and played with a litter of happy puppies that saw his form near one of the villages. Then he was off, aloft over the island taking in many of the sights and sounds of the Jamaican culture late at night as he passed towards Montego Bay and Rose Hall.

Ravi wondered in deep solitude as he passed these tiny villages which was the beginning of many cultures. Once the city state was established, he had seen them rise into great civilizations. Some flourished for many ages as others disappeared into the dust they once rose from! destroyed from internal corruption, invaded into extinction, or squashed by mother nature's power! Not even this world order would be spared when its day of final reckoning was at hand.

Birth, life, decline, and death were the way of all living things; of all civilizations! The reasons for this cycle seemed to be all the same in his estimate; an estimate he could not shake for he had seen it many times in his life on earth. He smiled as he remembered his early teachings about all living things in this dimension through the eyes of the powerful benevolent ancients referred in these times as angels. He marveled at the friendly insight "THEY" had given him. My how the civilizations of mankind resembled but huge nests of insects from his view. Ants built nests, but weren't mankind's cities nests as well?

But then came the next lesson. It was when he was far above earth viewing earth through the eyes of the angels. He saw millions of lights inundating the planet in the oceans and land. He was instructed to look closer. Then young Ravi saw the essence of all these lights which were the souls of all living things enclosed in what man would call clay!

He witnessed the beauty of God's creation of his light force incarnated into this level of existence! He observed hundreds if not thousands of these lights leaving the planet and disappearing. The voice told him that "These are the souls who have finished their lives and are returning home!" Ravi never forgot this lesson and his great bond with the angels, the gardeners of the worlds! If mankind would only live by that one simple rule; that golden rule of Father God! "Do unto others as you would be done by!" My oh my would life for all be better! This statement was construed as religion! It was not! It was good philosophy to all life; his message.

Good souls built, sustained life, and learned! The bad ones in their greed destroyed it! "They" also told him to view the various colors in the lights that inhabited the clay. They were of many colors and shades. The teacher then said "The colors of these lights determine the various levels of the souls. The teacher smiled and added in jest "One cannot hide their true colors of their actions and thoughts from Father God!"

Ravi had seen the demise of most civilizations began with corrupt leadership usually inherited from good constructive kings or Caesars that had greatly increased the power and wealth of their respective kingdoms. The power and wealth of these powerful kingdoms or civilizations were then passed from good constructive hands to poorly trained, lazy, and morally bankrupt heirs. The creation of the greedy overbearing corruption seemed to wind its way into every facet of the respective empire. They sucked the wealth from the treasury like insatiable parasites!

Ravi mused with a low smile; "Power corrupts! Absolute power absolutely corrupts!" summed up by a master of political science named Machiavelli! Mankind just cannot help itself! Absconded wealth and resources, weaken all facets of a civilization. Soon comes the breakdown of morals, family structures and increasing weakened governments. Then and finally, against underpaid weakened armies come their rebellions and powerful invasions! This also includes massive migrations of so many unwieldy groups that break the treasury and finally steamroll the culture and civilization into oblivion. Then the simple pastoral life of the survivors returns, returns until …? Ravi gave a laugh.

He would ponder this later since Rose Hall was now below him with the illumination of the lights of Montego Bay in the distance casting back the darkness around it. He began a thorough search of it and Palmyra carefully looking for any signs of Ayiti and his cohorts. Ravi knew he was no spring chicken by any measure. He was very tired at this point and glad he had not found Ayiti. Annie Palmer was insidious and dangerous, not to forget her tentacled dark friend from outside this dimension. The spiritual wounds of having dealt with the likes of Annie Palmer and her guardian demon had taken a toll on his old bones. He now wondered about this demon called Ayiti, who now seemed to be the ancient spawn of the Kali.

He stopped in the Great house at Rose Hall with no desire to be seen by the "reboxed" Annie Palmer. But he had to search it. The stench of evil seemed to coat every room like dark syrup as he journeyed through the house. Ravi casually passed a group of small slimy reddish imps who stayed away from his light. Although he sensed the footprint of "reboxed" Annie Palmer about the house, he correctly sensed that Ayiti was not here. The effects of the fight to free Annabelle on the dark second floor were evident in smashed furniture, bullet holes in the walls, and dried blood trails of the dead where they fell in combat.

He then entered a bedroom and saw the etheric form of a man driven beyond insanity and trapped. He sat on the bed weeping. Ravi soon perceived that it was one of Annie's murdered husbands bound here. Boxes for everyone he thought! As the spirit stared at him Ravi put his hand on the man's head. The man looked up and his mortal pain ceased. "Go home son, go to the light you now can see and have sought for so long. I have freed you!" In an instant the forlorn soul was gone, to rightfully return to the other side as all living things eventually go. He freed two others trapped in the same conditions. Finally, he found one more severely distraught soul boxed in a dark closet bearing the same fate in the next room. Annie's collection of tormented murdered husbands was freed. Annie had held them with her harnessing powers just as the powers of Abigale and Old Takoo had snared and boxed her with their immense powers.

My how the power of suggestion could be a real dangerous obstacle if one of great power was led to believe it as fact. Good riddance he thought. Annie sensed his presence! She cut to the chase but he left Rose Hall before she could confront him. Her twisted crazy face, slapped to the large bay window like the underside of a snail! He gingerly moved behind the house not looking back. He walked until he saw a campfire burning around a few tired looking hovels. The few humans sitting around it continued to stoke it mechanically as he approached.

He looked into their eyes and saw that their souls were trapped into blind servitude by super hypnosis rather than zombie dead. He well remembered the minions under the control of the Kali; tranced to follow orders not zombie robots; as the word "zombies" now caught up with his vocabulary. He stood in front of them and in a kind flash of energy released them from their mental prisons. With that, they looked around dazed and confused as if they had awakened from a deep sleep. In short order, they all ran away as if ghosts were chasing them.

They were not the zombies Young Takoo had talked about! He completed his search and his senses told him Ayiti was gone from this area. He and his zombies had to be in route to White Hall! After completing an area search nothing was found! Strawman must be on his way! the tired old sage floated down to the beautiful white beach north of Palmyra. He plucked a couple of large coconuts from a tall tree as he was landing and enjoyed their juice as he sat on the beach.

He spotted several Porpoises' frolicking in the surf and waded out into the surf to enjoy their mirthful friendship and play. Ravi was at peace since he loved these very intelligent mammals as the one surviving species genetically engineered in long dead Lemuria. They were his old friends and he loved them. He eventually returned to the white sand beach and sat facing the east since the sun would be rising in an hour. He felt a deep pain in his chest and knew that his days were numbered now. He had been gravely wounded against Kali, roughed up by Annie, and still had to face this Strawman.

However, Ravi was also an ancient warrior and knew the immortal code in every warrior's fate; death! Ravi gave a smile to the first rays of light of the rising sun as he followed a few points in his life across the centuries he had lived on this planet in his present incarnation. He thought of some of the recent highlights in his existence and his travels throughout civilizations. His mind was drifting to olden times.

His great friendship with King Asoka was always a positive part of his experience. By every standard, Asoka was a great "enlightened" ruler who applied a moralistic approach to his rule incorporating the teachings of Hinduism and his conversion to Buddhism as his rule. From the advent of his empire in 268 B.C. he expanded a great empire that encompassed nearly all of India. He is still revered as the greatest king and leader in all of Indian history. Asoka possessed a huge army, but seldom used it after his conversion to Buddhism, rather infusing the teachings of Buddhism into his governance of India, remarkable diplomacy and shrewd economic plans.

They had become very good friends when Ravi served as an advisor to him while the king came to power and later when Asoka needed them to help destroy the evil rise of another death cult in 245 B.C. After their union finished off this problem Ravi was asked to join Asoka's royal council as an advisor. They became so close, almost like brothers over the years. Ravi marveled at how Asoka peacefully expanded his empire through trade, creating rest stops for all weary travelers crossing though his kingdom.

He created hospitals for humans and special ones for all the animals. He created an excellent civilization in India. "Do as you would be done by!" was his mantra. His passing was a very sad note for Ravi. Those kings who followed Asoka soon wrecked this magnificent peaceful empire and pushed it back into the same type of Dark Age that ended the Western Roman Empire. My how the loss of one great leader can spawn such terrible heirs; such low born parasites!

He had to smile when he thought of Confucius. He was another dear friend who he spent hours traveling with him as he attempted to spread his teachings of "Duty and humanity" throughout China during the violent "Period of the Warring states" which had commenced as an Armageddon since 403 B.C. They loved playing checkers as they philosophized on political and ethical solutions to the problems rather than using spiritual ones. Confucius wanted practical solutions that could be understood and applied by people from all walks of life daily. It was a genius concept!

The wit and consummate humor of this great thinker offered Ravi such a wonderful discourse. He laughed as he remembered how Confucius would read one of his parables to him and then give a comical verbal antidote to it. So many times, they would simply laugh. What a master prankster this great philosopher was with those he disliked. But the genius and works of Confucius was a dynamic and effective tool in bringing eventual order and civility to the violent world of China in those days. The great philosopher was also one hell of a checkers' master as well. Ravi relished the exact phrase Confucius wrote regarding duty:

> "If there is a righteousness in the heart, there will be beauty in the character. If there is beauty in the character, there will be harmony in the home. If there be harmony in the home, there will be order in the nation. If there be order in the nation, there will be peace in the world."

His thoughts wandered to another great leader he had come to know from his wanderings into Europe in the days of Rome. He thought of his friendship with Octavian who became Caesar Augustus, the first emperor of the Roman Empire in 27 B.C. He was impressed by the size and organization of the Roman Empire. Ravi remembered observing the huge bloody land and sea battle of Actium in Greece in 31 B.C between Augustus against the might of Anthony and Cleopatra! Octavian was victorious and became "Imperator" with absolute power. How Ravi loved the life in Rome in those days. The beautiful and exciting life of ancient Rome was an incredible experience.

He had actually fallen in love with a beautiful woman, a young oracle he was council too. Ravi laughed as he remembered. He marveled at his human side and how she had captured his heart! Their "puppy love" endured until she died an old woman in his arms! Pyra often said that "love was eternal" and his love for this oracle truly was eternal. He bonded with Caesar Augustus out of curiosity and they became good friends over the years. What a good intelligent and caring man he had been. Augustus expanded the Roman Empire to greatness. He was a good considerate man but understood the consequences of not enforcing Roman authority and the Law, as conflicts against invading tribes on the periphery of the emerging "Pax Romana" were constant.

Ravi still remembered how Augustus was devastated after three of his Legions were slaughtered in the forests of southern Germany by a well-planned ambush by unified Germanic tribes. They attacked the legions in dense forest trails where they could not assume effective battle formations. "Varus, give me back my legions!" was his sad lament over the slaughter of his vaunted legions in those deep foreboding forests! "Ah Germania!" as he repeated the thoughts of General Bindon Blood in his concern of the impending disaster of Wadsworth's army in the jungle. But, like the post Asoka Mauryan Empire, its growing extravagances, corruption, and neglect of the affairs of state allowed it to collapse into the worst dark age of invasions. These terrible rulers who came to power, in all cases forgot the Confucian "Call to duty!"

Ravi smiled when he thought of Jesus Christ and His sermons by the Sea of Galilee. He was able to attend one and they were wonderful and inspiring to the mark! Jesus of Nazareth was a very busy man in great demand as Ravi never had any opportunity to meet Him. He well remembered the stories of The Christ and his travels to the ancient Occult centers during his time in the wilderness. He rose from the dead to teach mankind that life was eternal and forever. Ravi remembered again the millions of lights in earth his guides showed him; like fireflies of eternal life moving freely to enter into fresh clay born anew or be released from it when life was over!

Then the old sage thought of the opposite end of this spectrum. It was evil; real evil that existed not just in this world, but throughout the universe. The gift of free will to all living things was a calling card for both good and evil. Mankind always had the choice; always! He knew that sooner or later, as throughout all history, another great teacher would come to teach and reinforce the teachings of God. The prophets of the Great Father never stopped visiting to educate billions in this dimension! Ravi surmised that any man induced philosophy or religion that brought goodness and union to humans was a blessing of light. On the backside, if religious movements divided mankind or inspired hate or violence to others? They were nothing more than evil cults no matter how popular they became!

Ravi then had to smile as his thoughts moved to the vexing question put to him by his beloved Color-Sergeant Hook regarding the origin and way of the shape-changers. Poor old Hooky was afraid that he would shape change into something he could not escape from. He sat with Hooky in a beautiful terraced garden surrounded by his tribe of Bow dogs that day and answered him. When one passes on, they return to the dimension they exist in the cosmos. Remember that the Christ said "In my house there are many mansions!" What he was saying was that in my house are many dimensions! Ravi told him that "the only being or souls you will see after death are the ones you are compatible with, never the bad ones." The third dimension is the melting pot for all types of souls; good and bad. Some philosophers call this level of existence hell! However, the dimension of hell is farther down the spectrum of dimensions!

Then he remembered another thing he told the color sergeant. "Those who are adept in the ways of life after death, have command of their energy. The soul is a pure energy source that like an athlete training for the Olympics, can train the soul's energy source to change form as it wishes. When my race was invited to come to earth, it already had a sound grasp of this art of shape changing in the Astral. The massive destruction of the world civilization by the immense cataclysms forced survivors of my race to fight to exist. Over the course of many millennia we learned to adapt Astral shape changing to our clay; into this third dimension. Another words, we could change the shapes of our physical bodies.

In simple terms he told Hooky that we mastered "Mind over matter!" However, the lesser fallen souls lost to the chaos of the day either knew of this special ability or fell into it by what I term as "accidental learning!" The fallen ones learned of this power and wielded it to manipulate mankind. Thus, the war between the good and evil sides of my race continues the fight on this planet." The keeper of the Bow dogs was put to ease with this revelation. Ravi ceased his recollections and took a sip of coconut juice from the hole in a fresh coconut. He stood up on the beach at Palmyra and stretched his body. He smiled as he reviewed the many old faces, he had conjured up this peaceful morning on such a beautiful beach. But he also knew his visit to this island would not end peaceful.

Ravi ventured into the surf to give farewell hugs to a few of his favorite fish the laughed as that bronze statue of Napoleon in Krupp's office pointing at his loyal "Old Guard" popped up in his mind. During Napoleon's bloody empire building in Europe he accidently spread the precepts of nationalism to his defeated nations. These nations, full of their new nationalism mobilized to defeat the grand master of annihilation with it! The Old Guard? They refused to surrender when all was lost at Waterloo. The surviving commander of the Old guard when asked to surrender remarked "The Old guard dies! It never surrenders!" British light artillery accomplished this at point blank range. Ravi remembered Ronjin observing that terrible event disguised as a British cavalryman. Nationalism! One of the four Horsemen of the Apocalypse alive and well in the so-called modern Europe now!!

"He who lives by the sword dies by it! Be it Napoleon or Kali!" He sadly understood that the Europe of today would never learn this. They had never examined the current discord among them to solve the problems. This discord between modern European nation states now were products of a failure to repair vexing tribal problems that began with the fall of the Roman Empire and flourished now! Most of this had to do with boundaries of all things! An impending huge war in the so-called "modern Europe" was inevitable because of the failure to address the lingering problems.

All his kind could ever do was to advise humans, never force them! Such was their original mandate as teachers long ago! The Royal Studies Group was an example of raising the collective consciousness to advise and to persuade mankind to think and to fix the problems before they erupted into war. The "Four Horsemen of the Apocalypse" were now freely roaming all of the European peninsula looking to roost!

Would a massive destructive war in Europe really change anything? The survivors would rekindle the unsolved tribal problems once again! Old drawn out causes create big events, with disastrous effects. Lingering effects born of these old causes became new causes! Humanity seemed to evolve this way and was never ending. Fix the cause, then change the event for the better! Destroy this karmic wheel of death generated by the negative greed of humankind! He thought; if humans lived for at least three-hundred years then they might learn their destructive patterns well and cease them.

But with the life span of the average human between sixty and seventy years of age (if they were not killed sooner), this realization was impossible. Humans were born before, during, or after event catastrophes; never understanding the complete picture of cause-event-effect; just pieces of this picture drowned in rumors and opinions. Ravi knew that once this cycle of humanity developed a nuclear capability in conjunction with this constant turmoil among nations; the end would have wings. What occurred in the past would repeat! The advent of nuclear technology was the test; would mankind use it to grow peacefully into the universe or destroy itself? Pandora's Box was simple to open but very hard to divine its contents!

The advent of the next chaos driven Kali was a given in his mind. Where in hell would this one come from, he wondered? My oh my; was this current world order becoming ripe for it! He mentally shelved these concerns for the future since he had a more vexing situation now. If Strawman and his ilk were not in this region of Jamaica! Ravi watched the orange sun orb grow as it rose in the east. He needed to get back since he knew in his old bones that hell was about to be unleashed on the other side of this island. Ayiti and his zombies were coming for the kill and were surely nearby now!

Ayiti was seething with rage as he stared out into the ocean from his remote jungle-hiding place some twenty miles from Rose Hall Estate. The origin of his rage was how he allowed himself to be ambushed like some novice! This terrible attack had jarred his powerful dark soul into jelly and paralyzed in a state of uncontrolled insanity! Every cell in his body screamed in pain as if the effects of the strange light from the crystal rock were still tearing at his dark soul. He had been drawn to this light that had produced the troubled image of his long dead beloved Aunt Sarah.

Why in hell had he fallen for it like a fool? But then he had never been drawn to such a powerful tool used for the purpose of destroying him! Even in his form of Strawman he had suffered burns that covered the front of his body and left shards of crystal in his face and body even after he transformed back to his human form. Undoubtedly his Strawman transformation had shielded him from possible destruction!

He was slowly regaining his sapped energy and composure, enough to get Annabelle back! His refuge at Rose Hall had been destroyed. The police knew who he was and he could never go back. He smoldered as he correctly surmised that it was an attack generated by the Farnsworth's, voodoo allies combined with the police. This now reminded him of his plight against dictator Boyer and his henchmen in Haiti of old as he grimly smiled. He would with great enjoyment terrorize and painfully slaughter all of them!

Annabelle would be his again and soon! Annie Palmer was missing and he presumed she was killed in the crystal attack. In the days following this attack and raid he rounded up all his surviving zombified minions wandering his estates and summoned anybody unconditioned left at the plantation. His restored favorite Jean Zombi had greatly helped in this roundup. One by one and alone, he transformed each of them into his undead soldiers. He then armed them with all manner of tools, spears, bows, and machetes. In this jungle hideout Ayiti stripped all his bulging eyed zombies naked and painted their faces a milky white. Over a hundred now sat in silence in a long row behind him waiting to be unleashed at his telepathic command.

He had telegraphed the captain of the ship he had reserved in Montego Bay to fetch him this night from a remote dock he could see from the jungle now. Then, as he waited his mind's eye again saw the group of police and a few individuals what he surmised were voodoo men and women, moving in from Montego Bay to invade Rose Hall again. He knew what they were looking for and it had been safely removed and hidden. The image of Annabelle consumed his mind as he thought of the devilry, he had done to her! He was excited and wanted to do it again soon!

Jean Zombi sat next to him, completely still and wearing the silver demon mask mostly recovered after the deadly attack on Rose Hall. He patted his beloved pet monster Zombi on the head as it made little crooning noses like a puppy. "Where was the fucking boat?" He mumbled. It was very late! Ayiti let out a mysterious high-pitched noise like hot steam emitting from a tea pot airing his frustration and extreme anger. This attitude changed him into Strawman in his hate and lust for revenge! He consumed a full bottle of rum with his monster. They would all die horribly! The children he had observed at that house next to the bay? He would eat them alive one by one before he raped and ate their pretty momma!

Nobody was going to keep his Annabelle from him or make a fool of Ayiti! Nobody! She was his love slave and his everything now! He felt an excitement stirring in his dark soul this night, like it did when he was raiding French plantations and murdering and raping the classy French women with glee. He became sexually aroused by these insidious thoughts and of voluptuous Annabelle as they cascaded across his brain. The tramp steamer finally docked by the light of a large moon. Then after the loading of the deadly cargo was completed, it steamed down in the direction of the intended targets of Jamaican Prime, White Hall, and the Cavendish residence.

Ravi had met with his crew and had informed them of the situation. Ayiti and his minions were gone from Rose Hall and probably very close now. Security was tightened and buffed up at this time. Another peaceful night ebbed in behind the sunset of the fading orb of the sun. Preparation at the rum estate was put on high alert again. The children and women of the workers had been ordered to stay indoors as several mounted constables rode through the property in pairs. The workers had also stood down in their huts heavily armed with shotguns, Boar spears, machetes and a few rifles. Everything was silent when one little boy named Joseph wandered outside to check on his dogs that were yelping. He patted them, as they seemed to whine in fear.

He then witnessed a couple of constables watering their horses in the middle of the worker's village. "Little Joe" then watched a scary spectacle as both men began to wince as several crossbow bolts pierced them. As they fell, three naked men with ghost faces descended on them with machetes. There was no noise that came from this attack. In fear, he climbed back into the open window and yelled. "Papa, I think they here!" As distant gunfire now erupted by the estate distillery buildings across the cane fields. The workers now exited from the houses and confronted the three ghost faced zombies. In quick order the three zombies were speared, shot, and hacked to death. The battle had begun!

When the workers and many voodoo hunters emerged from the workers camp, they were soon engaged in a bloody free-for-all fight with many naked white-faced invaders! The distant gunfire just before the battle at the large workers camp came from the large group of constables and voodoo hunters protecting the distillery and production facilities. Peacock had waited for the line of unusual looking zombies to get close before his men opened up with rifle, crossbow, and pistol fire. After depleting the attackers and slowing them, a line of voodoo hunters charged them.

Several constables joined the voodoo hunters in their charge. They chopped the zombies to pieces. Several constables and voodoo hunters were wounded with a few killed. Before all the zombies were found and killed, they set two of the buildings on fire with the melee continuing in shadow forms near the flames. The attackers were outnumbered but their ambush evened the odds. The machetes, knives, crossbows, and long wire boar spears of the voodoo hunters begin to find their marks on the naked white-faced attackers. As the zombies were subdued by any means, the voodoo hunters beheaded all of them where they fell. By dawn, the Jamaican Prime estate was secure.

The attack on the Cavendish house began suddenly with arrows wounding three and killing another constable and voodoo hunter guarding the perimeter of the house. Then a group of zombies came swinging their machetes as they barged into the deck and house in their jerky stumbling but deft movements. Benjamin Jobo and the inspector sergeant named "Dunn" were the only two of five that remained untouched after the initial onslaught. Three other men guarding the other side of the house fired several rounds at the approaching zombies but were forced back into the jungle. The first zombie to enter the house kicked in the glass door from the deck and stepped in.

Jenny had gone to the bedroom to protect Horace as Elizabeth stood in the living room with Jobo and the constable. The opening shots of the constable made little impact on the huge naked man with a white-painted face with the whites of his eyes bulging. At this point, Elizabeth stepped forward and rode the bullets from the Krupp SMG up the zombie's body from his groin into his head. It bumped back against another zombie behind it and fell forward. At this point, Ben Jobo, the constable and Elizabeth unloaded pistol, sub machinegun and shotgun fire into it, cutting it to pieces. More zombies approached. Elizabeth methodically reloaded a fresh magazine.

Jenny stood behind the bed guarding her brother as the glass shattered behind the long drapes on the other side of the room. She aimed her shotgun and blew a hole in the chest of the first zombie to step into the room from the side deck. The blast knocked it back outside to the deck. Then a second one popped its white painted face through the drapes with a machete protruding in front of it. Jenny's second shotgun blast removed its head from its shoulders as blood and brains splashed on the walls and drapes. Jenny grabbed her brother and pulled him to the floor from the bed. She reloaded with two rounds from her pocket as she aimed at the third naked zombie as it jumped like a giant frog into the middle of her room holding a pitchfork as her first shot missed. As it jumped right at her aiming its pitchfork at her midsection, she fired her second shot point blank.

This round caught the zombie directly in the face as it landed in a crouch in the bed in front of her. Jenny screamed as the shotgun blast blew the white painted head to pieces as the body flopped into the middle of the room. The smell of cordite and blood taunted her nostrils as she aimed the shotgun at another attacker. As she reached for more rounds, she suddenly realized that she was out of ammunition. She had forgotten to grab the box of shells from the other room. Jenny Cavendish screamed as she stepped back and tripped over the body of her unconscious brother whom she had pulled from the bed to the floor behind her.

On it came, now jumping on the bed like the other zombie in a muted attack position brandishing a long knife. Two more oddly pained zombies entered through the shattered bay window. At that point, Jenny swung the butt of her shotgun striking the zombie to her front across the head knocking it against the wall. She then fell back grasping the shotgun like a club. Elizabeth stepped into the room and laced the zombie closest to Jenny with several rounds from the Krupp machine pistol forcing it into a jerking dance as it bounced to the floor with three of ten bullet holes in its head.

She then threw Jenny a box of shotgun shells and smiled. "You kill them by shooting them in the head sister!" Jenny swore that her sister-in-law was having a great time. Elizabeth, and a reloaded Jenny, beheaded by double .00 Buck, the two other zombies thrashing towards her covered in torn drapes with swinging machetes. Elizabeth waited until the threat in the bedroom ended, then moved back into the main room to help young Jobo who had impaled two thrashing zombies with his boar spear and was cleaving off their heads with his long sharp machete.

Elizabeth stepped up next to Jobo and emptied the rest of the thirty-two-round magazine into two more zombies crashing through the smashed picture window. Elizabeth killed them a second time. Jenny had just reloaded when a fifth and final zombie crashed into the room knocking down the drapes as it stumbled swinging his machete wildly. In a fit of rage and in near point-blank range, Jenny fired both rounds from the shotgun knocking it back. She reloaded as it came at her again minus a chest cavity.

In a fit a rising anger, she aimed her shotgun only a couple of feet from the zombie and fired both barrels. The white pained face and head of this last assailant completely disintegrated into the ceiling. She tripped back and hit the closet wall from the recoil. There she reloaded the shotgun from her knees and waited for more of these very unwelcome guests!

Meanwhile, with the house cleared of these strange invaders, constable Dunn, Ben Jobo, and Elizabeth went zombie hunting outside the house. Jenny could hear the sound of excited voices intermingled with the rat-tat-tat of the sub machinegun, shotgun blasts, and pistol shots. Then all seemed to go quiet as Jenny heard their footsteps enter the house. Elizabeth was calling her name and finally peeked in her bedroom door. She saw Jenny sitting against the wall, loaded shotgun in hand and with Horace's head resting in her lap. Dead zombies ringed her position in the destroyed bedroom. "Jenny? Jenifer! are you, all right?" "Yes dear, never felt better in my life" As she gave a sarcastic smile at her. "I just want to sit here for a few minutes. Are you safe?"

"We are all right, and killed six in the living room and five more zombies outside! They were so rude coming through the door without knocking first!" She laughed at her joke as she continued. "Jobo has already beheaded them and needs to do the same to your bedroom guests so they will not come back to life. Jenny understood as Jobo came in and performed the grim task of beheading the dead zombies that still had heads that squirmed around on the floor as he decapitated them. He looked at her when he was done. Jobo was an extremely tall lad, with a wiry build like a tree and a full smile illuminated by deep blue eyes. Jenny had heard he was only twelve years old as their bond had now formed. The young voodoo adept commented in his high voice. "Mum, whoever made these zombies is truly a powerful dangerous mon!"

They cared for their wounded men and covered up the two who had been killed by the crossbows. The group sat in the kitchen as Elizabeth poured round after round of rum. Jenny laughed as she listened to their conversation from the other room. These three were talking as if they had just had a successful hunting trip into the wild! She joined them for one huge belt of Jamaican Prime gold rum. Then they began to hear a whole series of distant muffled gunshots several miles up the road.

White Hall was now under attack. Jenny looked at the huge clock in the living room. It was well after midnight now.

As Ravi and company had accurately perceived it; the deflecting attacks began at the two other locations before the main attack at White Hall. They also estimated that the attack would come probably from all four sides at White Hall Manor. The constables and voodoo men had been well concealed around the estate house and avoided the first barrage of crossbow bolts that stuck into the architecture like cactus spines and shattered every window on the first floor. Their return gunfire hit the mark on the first wave of strangely naked white-faced attackers charging at them from the rear of the house.

The few that attempted to gain access from the sides of the place were killed at point blank range by shotgun wielding constables waiting inside next to the shattered windows. Accurate rifle fire from the second-floor balconies soon broke up the attacks killing many. A sea of white-faced naked attackers surged at the front of the mansion! As rifle and pistol fire downed many from the front, it appeared that these ranks swelled with fresh attackers. The guns of these defenders now turned to defend the front of White Hall.

Cavendish, Nephew, Marley, and Young Takoo remained on the first floor of the mansion supporting the constables in this fight. They were firing from the large French style windows as they dodged the sporadic rifle and crossbow fire. Tiberius Nephew was using an elephant gun liberated from the Cavendish house as Ambrose was firing his German Luger. The impact of the elephant gun on several attacking zombies just blew their bodies to pieces. Several of the grenade rounds fired by Cavendish exploded and silenced the rifle fire from behind the white picket fence across the road. Then the pushing throng of zombies charged in mass against the huge double front doors!

However according to plan, they, the constables and voodoo men moved back into the house and to the rear. The action was now taking place in front. Cavendish, Takoo, and Nephew joined Marley in the basement. The front of the mansion was piled with bodies now as the zombies continued bashing at the huge reinforced front door. Suddenly the door was blown from its hinges by some powerful force. In the doorway stood the monster extraordinary: Strawman. The zombies that remained stood silently behind him.

From his grimace of victory Strawman saw Annabelle from across the foyer as she had just descended the spiral staircase. She was radiantly beautiful in her long white dress and looked scared. Ayiti spoke in the low metallic monotone of Strawman. "I have come for you Annabelle, for you to be my bride forever!" As he began to walk, she shuddered and ran to the basement stairs. She looked back as its hypnotic soul bashing flashing red eyes penetrated her deep. She screamed and ran down the basement stairs screaming in terror. Ayiti followed. Strawman now came to the bottom of the stairs looking at her radiant beauty only feet away. The wounds from the crystal and incredible lust for Annabelle obscured his usual sharp senses. He walked towards her as she had moved back into the storage area. She cried in great fear.

The act continued as she lamented to the monster. "I do not want you Ayiti, for I love Horace! Please leave my life and me in peace! Haven't you done enough damage?" The Strawman cackled a loud leering laugh. "I do not care about your life, your husband, or anything except that you are mine now and will come with me…and if not my queen, then my slut slave forever!" Annabelle wailed in grief and turned away as the monster Loa god moved up behind her and grabbed her breasts from behind.

His lust was now epic, much greater than his favorite French lady of old; all of his ancient pets put together! Strawman bellowed. "I will fuck you now into submission for me forever! He had never felt so moved by this woman. She would be his queen! Then beautiful Annabelle turned and faced him as his dozen red flashing eyes then beheld not Annabelle but the most terrible demon face, he could remember. Unused to ever being terrorized, he shuddered impulsively. The claws of this new Annabelle banshee dug deep into Strawman's thick hided chest as it yelped in sudden panic and pain. Black blood from the deep claw wounds now gushed down its front.

"Do you really love me demon! Will you really fuck me into submission oh monster? I give you the love back you gave me!" All of a sudden, this horrible apparition that used to be Annabelle bit deeply into the strange nose of the Strawman sending shockwaves of pain into it. He was feeling pain in his familiar form! The image of banshee Annabelle exploded in an array of blinding white light, followed huge slashing talons and gnashing fangs. Strawman shrieked loudly in fear and pain under this sudden attack as his face was being torn open. It began to fight back. Two zombies now began to walk down the basement stairs. Colonel Nephew wheeled around from a wall divider at the bottom of the stairs and shot both of them in the head with well-trained blasts. Colonel Nephew shot them again as they landed at the bottom of the stairs. He reloaded his pump twelve-gauge shotgun as he then looked up the stairs to see another zombie!

It was a tall one with a silver skull mask reflecting from the electrical basement lights. All hell was breaking loose in the struggle with Strawman now. Ravi had launched a powerful disabling attack on the monster which was still floundering from his powerful blows and delivering dangerous counter blows in the scuffle. Young Takoo attempted grabbing it around its bulbous large body but only managed to hold one of its huge talon arms holding his arms down. This distraction was enough for Marley who hooked his left arm around the neck of the hideous beast and plunged a large needle of a syringe into his neck forcing the strong voodoo cocktail into him.

The effects of the voodoo cocktail were profound as this huge powerful giant devil doll wailed in fear, pain, and hate. It knew in an instant what had been injected into it! Strawman broke loose from Takoo's powerful grip throwing both he and Joshua to the ground. Cavendish then hit Strawman with a huge iron bar across his oblong head. Strawman knocked him to the ground. Ravi was again attacking the Strawman with the facial image of Annabelle's face as his powerful claws ripped new gouges in its head and face which oozed dark blood everywhere. Blood as black as its soul! Ravi felt great weakness as he struggled with this strange demon. This monster was not dying, just weakening. He yelled "this hideous thing needs to be put in the lead box before it kills us all!

Meanwhile, Nephew emptied all seven rounds of .00 Buck into this new skull faced zombie as it walked down the stairs as it jerked from the rounds which blew holes in its large torso, denting the silver mask it wore. Each shot knocked it back, but to little avail as it came on. Zombi then backhanded Nephew just after the colonel had struck him across his head with the butt of the shotgun. The colonel disappeared through a collapsing wall divider into a side room at the bottom of the stairs from the blow. Zombi then began walking and echoing a high-pitched wail as he approached his master who was caught in mortal conflict with a strange assailant.

Just as Zombi was within a dozen feet, Cavendish jumped up and aimed his Luger pistol right at his chest. "Farewell you bastard!" he yelled as he fired a Krupp special grenade round at Zombi's chest. The blast disintegrated the monster Zombi into pieces as the concussion from the blast blew out the lights and knocked all the combatants to the ground. The basement was a smashed wreck from the blast as water from the broken water pipes in the ceiling sprayed the area and quickly began filling the basement. Shrapnel from the grenade round affected everybody as they all bled from wounds and suffered mild concussions.

Strawman stood up first now laughing in spite of his wounds. He now faced the form of a huge bloodied cat as he was beginning to feel the extreme effects of the cocktail Marley had injected into him. Strawman was dizzy and very disorientated but still free and ready to fight. He yelled in his low-pitched wail. "You are all to be my special zombies now!" Cavendish witnessed this doll like monster in full view in the basement shadows. He was mesmerized by its multiple red glaring eyes and horrible fanged and twisted mouth. A crooked set of horns seemed to rest on its oblong head.

Marley attempted stabbing another syringe of voodoo cocktail into the side of Strawman but slipped in the rising water just as the tail of this monster barely missed him. The power of the whipping tail tore through a large wooden "I" beam behind Joshua cutting it in half. The Strawman then launched his whipping tail at Ravi who grabbed it and used it as a lever to throw the monster sideways into a wall. As this occurred Cavendish looked at the water and the light bulb smashed in the explosion. He then remembered a story he had read about people being electrocuted by electrical currents in water. New technology had its dangers!

He then saw the large smashed lamp used to illuminate the basement. He saw that its power cord was still plugged into the wall socket. Using his knife, he pulled the power cord up from the water and cut it from the broken lamp. "Out of the water now everybody! Hurry!" He yelled. He saw them all jump out of it and then looked square at Strawman. Their eyes became locked in a hard stare. Ambrose then jumped on a chair, hung on to a wooden floor beam and plunged the open end of the power cord into the rising water. The invisible electric current flashed through the water and suddenly all witnessed Strawman filled with the pulses of thousands of watts of electricity. It screamed in mortal pain as it stared at Cavendish and his wire in the water.

The Strawman's body was turned into a giant light bulb emanating a huge ball of flashing electric light. Watching Strawman turn into painful toast amused Ambrose as he gave a leering smile at this monster. Cavendish pulled the exposed cord end from the water the party rushed the Strawman. The monster demon was shape changed to half Ayiti and half Strawman; burnt black by the electric current. Young Takoo pulled open the huge lid on the lead box and Nephew, Cavendish, and Marley stuffed severely burned and shocked Strawman into it head first. Marley, who had retrieved his syringe of toxic voodoo cocktail, jammed it into the back of Strawman and injected it. The heavy lid was replaced, the huge iron bars were inserted in their grooves on top. They all stared at each other in unbroken silence.

Ravi limped over to the lead box and pulled the huge lever sending the electrical current through the modern refrigeration coils he had built in the warehouse. The sound of the refrigeration generator kicked on. The group was spent mentally and physically by this titanic struggle against Strawman. They all sat in the dark shadows of a basement dimly illuminated by the sun light coming in the small basement windows. They had all suffered wounds from the grenade round, and injuries from the battle with Strawman.

No one spoke until Nephew broke the silence. He approached from then other end of the rather large basement where he had landed unconscious from Zombi's strike into an adjacent room next to the stairs. Thankfully he had been knocked on a top of a pile of boxes and had escaped the electric currents in the water which formed around the boxes under him. He took a long plug from a bottle of rum and handed it to Ambrose. Tiberius added with a jovial smile "Gentlemen! Nothing like a shot of good rum after fighting a monster!"

As the bottle of Jamaican Prime Rum was passed, everyone could hear a faint banging from inside the large lead box. They listened to a strange muffled wailing echoing from with it. The rum was passed around and even Ravi took a pull on the bottle. The sound of sporadic gunfire could still be heard from above. Then Colonel Nephew, who sported a deep bloody gash on the side of his head spoke. "Folks, we did it!" Then he yelled, "We got this bastard!" The group was just too exhausted to move from the darkened basement for the next few minutes as they listened to the sounds from within Strawman's crypt. Each one of them deeply feared it breaking out.

They sat in the basement pondering what had just occurred. This monster Strawman had been reduced from a holy terror to a faint noise. Hopefully trapped forever in a giant ice cube. Trapped until his familiar doll was found and destroyed! Kill the doll! Kill Strawman! Annabelle was dead and Horace was a serious mental wreck. White Hall was a wreck, and they had no idea if the zombie attacks at the other two places were successful or deadly. There was little clue at this point as Ambrose had great concern for Jenny.

A noise from the flooded floor hidden in the shadows caused them to break their thoughts and look. It was the head of Mr. Zombi, decapitated by the grenade round blast and still wearing his silver mask! It was calling for its master with the water on the basement floor filling his mouth. Nephew then put the barrel of his shotgun against the talking decapitated masked skull of Jean Zombi. He kicked the mask from the undead head. "Your master is in our custody beast…take a long-deserved rest! You are fired!" He pulled the trigger and the loud echoing blast blew the babbling skull to pieces in the water. The colonel retrieved the dented solid silver demon mask that resembled the face of Strawman, and placed it on top of the lead crypt. They all toasted it. Little did Tiberius ever realize that he was the last human hit by Jean Zombi; root of the zombie myth and culture forever!

Ravi was leaning back against a wall. He spoke weakly. "We trapped a very powerful one today, perhaps as powerful as Kali my sons. I hit him with several devastating kill shots and this Strawman seemed to absorb most of them. He was able to strike back very hard!" In a silent agreement all of them left the basement to be haunted by this event for the rest of their lives. Young Takoo summoned two of his men to guard it armed with syringes of voodoo cocktails. This guard duty of Young Takoo's voodoo men would last for many years from this day forth. Colonel Nephew added. "We need to take this box and dump it in the Arctic and keep it frozen forever boys!"

Almost on cue the group looked at the battered and bloody face of Ravi, who concluded. "That Arctic plan will be a good plan if we do not discover Strawman's familiar doll and destroy it! It is his learned belief that gives him such immortal power; that as long as his doll is not hurt, nor will he be hurt. I sense that I was unable to destroy Strawman today because he holds this belief completely. His powerful mind rules over his matter gentlemen. Thus, this monster lives until we locate his doll!" There was silent agreement as the men now ventured upstairs.

The interior and outside area of Whitehall was a shamble. The naked bodies of the zombies sporting white painted faces littered the mansion grounds. Most of the bodies rested in piles to the front of the mansion. The voodoo men beheaded them all as was the precautionary custom in dealing with the undead. Although the mess was slowly cleaned up, White Hall would never be the same to anybody after these events. Tiberius stood at the front of the place as he saw two riders' approach. It was Elizabeth and the young voodoo adept named Jobo. She was smiling as she studied the carnage and bodies in the front. He smiled at her as he noticed the sub machinegun resting across the front of her saddle. She spoke with a cheerful smile patting the weapon. "This weapon really kicked ass and I want one as my wedding present!" Nephew smiled at her. "When it is actually invented and, in the market, I will gladly buy you one!"

Elizabeth continued. "I do hope everybody is safe. Jenny and I survived it, but with losses sadly. Did you get the monster darling?" Nephew smiled at her. "Yes, my cuttlefish, we bagged it and sealed it up for eternity but could not kill it. Ravi and Joshua talked about destroying some doll. So, what in dickens are you two up to?" Asked a smiling Tiberius Nephew. Young Ben Jobo smiled and held up his crossbow. He added. "Miss Elizabeth and me are zombie-hunting sir! We bagged a couple down the road on our way up here.

Elizabeth smiled as she patted the sub machinegun. "I just love this honey! It is great fun firing from a horse." Nephew laughed again. He took them on a tour of the battleground and then to the basement where two nervous voodoo men stood near the huge lead box. Tiberius explained how Strawman's tomb worked as his future wife, sister of Ambrose marveled at the refrigeration coils freezing the water in the box. They became nervous as a beating noise continued from within this crypt. One of the voodoo hunters guarding it looked at her. "Strawmon not happy!"

The voodoo hunters erected two huge cremation pyres in the back of the mansion. Many decapitated bodies of the dead zombies were stacked among the wood as Tiberius had used the same method used to destroy the remains of the Pashtuns at Malakand, Chital, and in the jungle north. The smell of burning flesh was ripe in the air and reminded both Nephew and Cavendish of these other episodes in their lives. Both the officers stood with Young Takoo, and Marley watching the blaze as more bodies were tossed into the white-hot fire.

Marley looked sadly at his companions as they stared from the flames in the once elegant back yard garden of White Hall mansion. "Once a place of great life and joy, but now it is the place of emptiness, sadness, and great death my friends." During all this clean up Ravi found a spare bedroom and rest. James and Tiberius, as were Young Takoo and Marley, were very concerned about his condition. He had refused their offer to get medical help from the village. Something in Ravi was going on and concerned them.

When they returned to the Cavendish abode, they found that Tully and Daphne had returned and were helping Jenny and others clean up the mess. The dead zombies had been loaded on a farm wagon and were now headed to the pyres at White Hall. When Jenny saw her husband, she ran up to him and put her hands around his neck and held him tight. "Thank the Father that you are alive and safe and I love you so much!" "I love you so much too sweetheart!"

She looked at his face and saw where the blood had dried around the shrapnel wounds in his face. As the group sat a round of stiff drinks were served. Doctor Tourissant and his assistant, also present, removed the metal shards from both the faces and bodies of Nephew and Cavendish. They two soldiers downed several cool bottles of beer and rum shots in this process. What a day it had been! Marley and Young Takoo had been lucky since they had been behind Strawman when the grenade blast occurred.

Jenny greeted her parents and the Meyers who showed up an hour later. They were smitten at the death of Annabelle as they were filled in on the terrible events that occurred in the night. Lord Farnsworth looked at Doctor Tourissant and Jenny. "How is my son?" The initial look from the doctor related Horace's condition before he spoke. The sadness in Jenny's face enforced this. "Mr. Farnsworth, Horace seems to be in a deep shock and his mind seems to be shattered from what happened." Jenny added. "I think dear Horace will never be the same!" Lord Farnsworth became deep in thought for a moment then spoke as he looked at his wife. "I think we will take Horace home with us and get him some psychiatric help. It looks like you, Mr. Cavendish are now the CEO of the rum company until we can see how Horace recovers." Ambrose nodded in silence.

Later in the day Tiberius and Ambrose rode to the rum estate and were greeted in the front by many workers, voodoo men, and the constables. Constable Oscar Peacock shook their hands as they approached the group. He was wearing a large bandage around his head and smiled at them. "We held them off and destroyed them. They burned down one building warehouse which was used to cremate over fifty zombies. There was large pile of assorted weapons taken from the dead zombies. It seemed that all the workers and their families were present.

Ambrose ordered several men to fetch a few cases of rum so these victors could celebrate. Ten workers, seven voodoo hunters, and three constables had paid with their lives in this attack. Both James Ambrose and Tiberius joined the crowd in several toasts. It seemed that this victory was no different than the ones in India. It was victory for them and death for another strange enemy. They drank many toasts before returning at dusk to White Hall. The estate was in good hands with the loyal supervisors of Jamaican Prime.

As the two men drew closer to White Hall the special ring on Ambrose's right hand began to vibrate and give off a beautiful red glow from the large ruby. He had been summoned by Ravi. Marley and Young Takoo had stayed at the rum estate to help oversee the cleanup. Both British soldiers, victors in another fight in a strange conflict dismounted in front of White Hall mansion and noticed that the cleanup was going well. The many bullet marks on the stone pillars and frontage of the mansion were obvious in the fading sunlight and the white picket fence across the road had been completely destroyed.

Ravi was gone from the house and Ambrose knew where he was now. The message from Ravi was dire for he was near death. In short order, Nephew and Cavendish went down the narrow jungle trail behind the house to the stonewall viewing platform that overlooked the bay below. They found Ravi resting prostrate on one of the lounge chairs in this viewing area, dressed in his red robes. "Ravi! Ravi! Yelled Ambrose as they went to his side. They looked into his face and as usual, Ravi was smiling. "I am here my sons, waiting to go home. My wounds are mortal I fear."

Tiberius and Ambrose each got on a side of their venerable friend and held his hands. Nephew spoke. "They got to get you to that healing pool, Ambrose, call them!" Ravi looked serenely at them. "They are on their way sons for I have called them. My wounds are beyond the help of the healing pools now. Such is the plight of an over active old man!" The ancient sage was smiling to pass on his humor. In what seemed moments, Ambrose felt a warm hand on his shoulder. He knew it was Pyra. She then kissed him on the head.

Both men looked up to see her, Ronjin, and three others from the village. The two medical doctors from the village looked over Ravi closely for a couple of minutes and looked sadly at Ronjin. The elder medical doctor then looked at them. "Ravi is finished my brothers, say your goodbyes." Each one from the village held Ravi by the hand and kissed him on his head as was the custom of respect and love in the village. Prya was last. She wept as she laid her head-on Ravi's chest. "I love you father and I am so sad!" Ravi looked her in the eyes. "I have always been so blessed to have such a wonderful girl and will always watch over you after I return to the other side my beautiful child." He then kissed her on the cheek, then her head.

Then he looked at Tiberius and Ambrose who had tears running down their faces as they held Ravi's hands. The venerable ancient spoke. "How wonderful it has been to have you in my life at a time when we needed the kinder touch of humans to help us against a great enemy. I see you not just as friends but as my sons, human sons that I can count on my fingers as truly the best friends I made in this world for so many centuries. Go in peace and live good lives for you both will never be forgotten." He then looked at Ronjin and Pyra. "You now know what duties lie forth in your lives from this point. I love you and all the village. Please tell them." With that last sentence, Ravi died. There was silence.

The medical attendants wrapped him in a large ceremonial cloth as Ronjin looked at the two Brits in great sadness and grief. "Take care my brothers and we will not be far from you." As he stepped aside Pyra walked up to the men. She kissed Colonel Nephew on the cheek and turned to Ambrose.

She had tears in her eyes for she had lost her father. Ambrose hugged her tightly and kissed her. "My love for you is deep and eternal my sweet Pyra! This is like yours; forever!"

He then held and kissed her deeply on the lips, not from passion, but from true love. She replied. "Our love is eternal and forever Ambrose and my eye will be watching over you!" There would come that day together perhaps, for time and circumstance would tell she thought as tears ran down her beautiful face. Both men watched as the little party carried the wrapped body of Ravi away for ceremonial cremation at Hima.

They just disappeared as if they walked into thin air. After this sad event, they stood over the bay peering into its darkness brought on by a small sliver of a new moon. They talked of the past, present and possible future events. It was time for a healthy dose of cognac back at White Hall! They celebrated the loss of Ravi as British soldiers did when one of their fellow comrades in arms died. They both got completely toasted.

After what seemed an eternity of downing and struggling in the dark sealed water filled enclosed box Ayiti was now completely under the numbing effects of two voodoo cocktails injected into him. He had contemplated escape but now drifted like some particle completely submerged in the watery crypt. His curse was that he could not die! He just floated lifeless. He moved from a semi-conscious state into uncontrolled unconsciousness; still affected by the powerful effects of the opium laced voodoo cocktail.

His mired reflections within this watery crypt became confusing. He had received terrible painful wounds fighting against that strange powerful cat demon who had fooled him as being that of Annabelle. He resembled a perfect copy of her! His body was burnt black from end to end. Strawman now existed in a clauster phobic world of terror and complete painful mortal agony now. His would heal but the pain of them mending was hell!

The effects of the drugs were making him silly and he was seeing all sorts of things now. His composure was shot! He could not fully regain his form as Strawman because of the powerful effects of this voodoo cocktails. Just like in Haiti! He cursed this for a long time. He knew it was the same cocktail which helped the voodoo men under Boyer keep him sedated and under their control. Strawman and been savagely fried from the strange lightening weapon used by that cursed British man!

Strawman was fading and the water he was submerged in was growing so cold in his darkness! What to do? He swore that he would escape and not just kill all who stole his Annabelle and cast him into this watery pit! He would terrorize and murder them in the most gruesome fashion. He seethed at the last face he saw! It was a white man, clean cut and handsome to the standard. He had seen him at the Cavendish house before while stalking Annabelle. He was Cavendish! He and his family would be the first to pay his grisly price upon his escape! He would eat his children one piece at a time as they screamed in mortal terror and agony! He loved the fresh taste of children!

In his painful madness Ayiti asked a vexing question. What of Annabelle? Where had she gone? And what in blazes was that entity that had so perfectly copied her and lured him to the basement? It was a perfect image of her in every respect! Her vibrations, mannerisms, and even her perfume was correct! Then that entity mocked me when it wore her face in its attack on me! One Ayiti went as his mind faded to near a jumbled coma. He now sensed that the water temperature had grown much colder. Extreme revenge was the only thing that fueled him and kept him squirming like a fish in this dark tank. He would soon escape and have his retribution!

Ice crystals soon formed and he had no clue why this was happening. Chunks of ice began to replace the crystals and curtail his movement. Finally, solid ice trapped his struggling arms and legs as his floundering ceased. He felt a deep fear and yelled from a mouth and lungs long filled with water. He could no longer move at all. In this encroaching frozen imprisonment that had overwhelmed him; he screamed in terror, an emotion he had never imagined or felt before!

Ayiti did not like this feeling! He was the master of fear and terror not its victim! Soon, he was like some fish frozen solid in the ice of winter. All his movement completely stopped. He screamed in terror for the claustrophobia that engulfed him in the dark waters of his tomb. He wailed past insanity! Ayiti, a perceived god of Loa and scourge of both Haiti and Jamaica drifted into a semi-coma, trapped from any form of escape from the lead box and ice which was his tomb! He longed for freedom! He seethed in his encroaching madness; his cup of revenge spilled over!

His mind would not rest or turn off! "Cavendish and his cohorts did this!" It screamed as diminishing and forgotten bubbles of air boiled from his lungs and froze. He cried like a dying animal for Annabelle and for his waning freedom to escape and kill all of his tormentors! "What have you done to Annabelle!" He roared from his crypt prison with his mouth frozen wide open in the ice cube that entombed him now! The powerful Loa god was locked completely in a frozen darkness lost beyond sanity; mindful of one thing: **VILE REVENGE!**

Printed in the United States
By Bookmasters